Size

and

Size 14 is not Fat Either

Meg Cabot is the author of the 'Princess Diaries' series as well as several other novels for teenagers. Her books have sold millions of copies round the world – and two million in the UK alone.

She has lived in various parts of the US and France, but now lives in Key West, Florida, with her husband and one-eyed cat, Henrietta.

Also by Meg Cabot

The Guy Next Door
Boy Meets Girl
Every Boy's Got One
Queen of Babble
Queen of Babble in the Big City

and published by Macmillan Children's Books

All American Girl
Nicola and the Viscount
Victoria and the Rogue
All American Girl: Ready or Not
Avalon High
Teen Idol

The Mediator: Love You to Death
The Mediator: High Stakes
The Mediator: Mean Spirits
The Mediator: Young Blood
The Mediator: Grave Doubts
The Mediator: Heaven Sent

The Princess Diaries Guide to Life
The Princess Diaries
The Princess Diaries: Take Two
The Princess Diaries: Third Time Lucky
The Princess Diaries: Mia Goes Fourth
The Princess Diaries: Give Me Five
The Princess Diaries: Sixsational
The Princess Diaries: Seventh Heaven

Meg Cabot

Size 12 is not Fat and Size 14 is not Fat Either

PAN BOOKS

Size 12 is not Fat first published 2006 by Avon Books,
an imprint of HarperCollins Publishers, USA.
First published in Great Britain in paperback 2006 by Pan Books.
Size 14 is not Fat Either first published 2006 by Avon Books,
an imprint of HarperCollins Publishers, USA.
First published in Great Britain in paperback 2007 by Pan Books.

This omnibus first published 2008 by Pan Books
an imprint of Pan Macmillan Ltd
Pan Macmillan, 20 New Wharf Road, London N1 9RR
Basingstoke and Oxford
Associated companies throughout the world
www.panmacmillan.com

ISBN 978-0-330-45780-4

A US size 12 is a UK size 14/16.

1 3 5 7 9 8 6 4 2

A CIP catalogue record for this book is available from
the British Library.

Printed and bound in Great Britain by
Mackays of Chatham plc, Chatham, Kent

Size 12 is not Fat

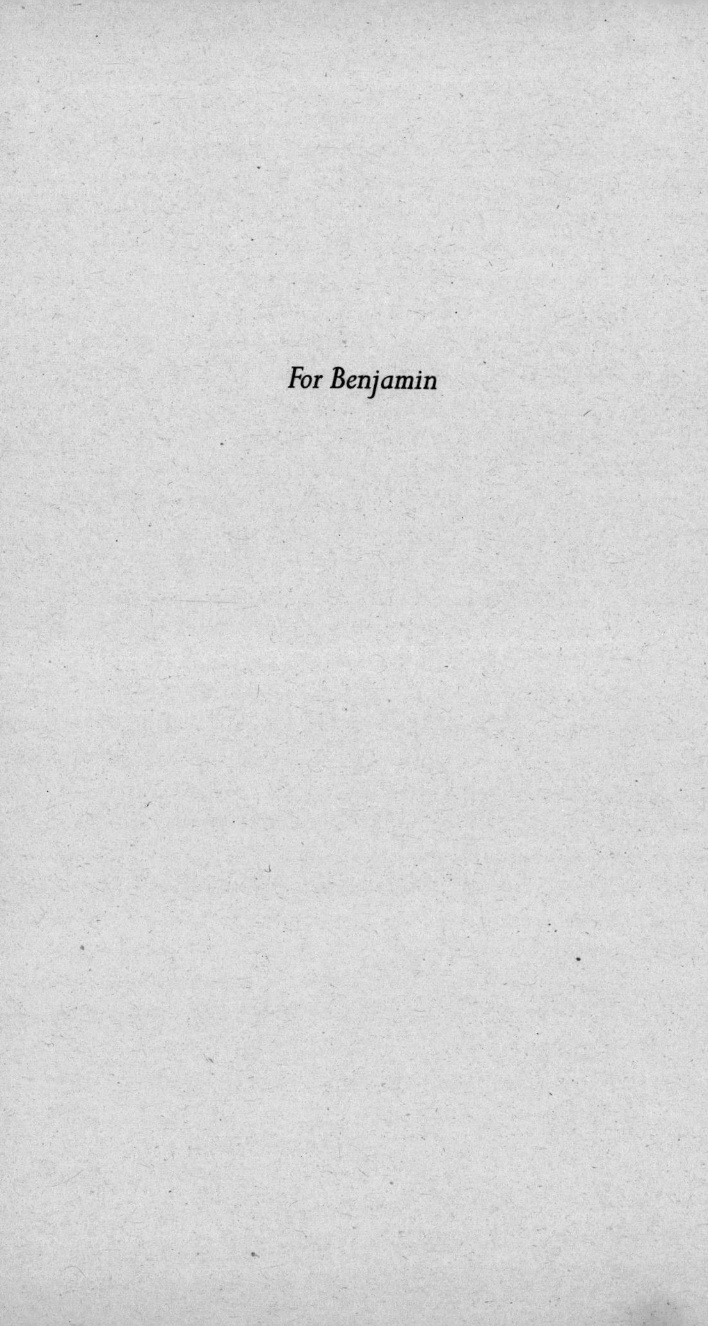

For Benjamin

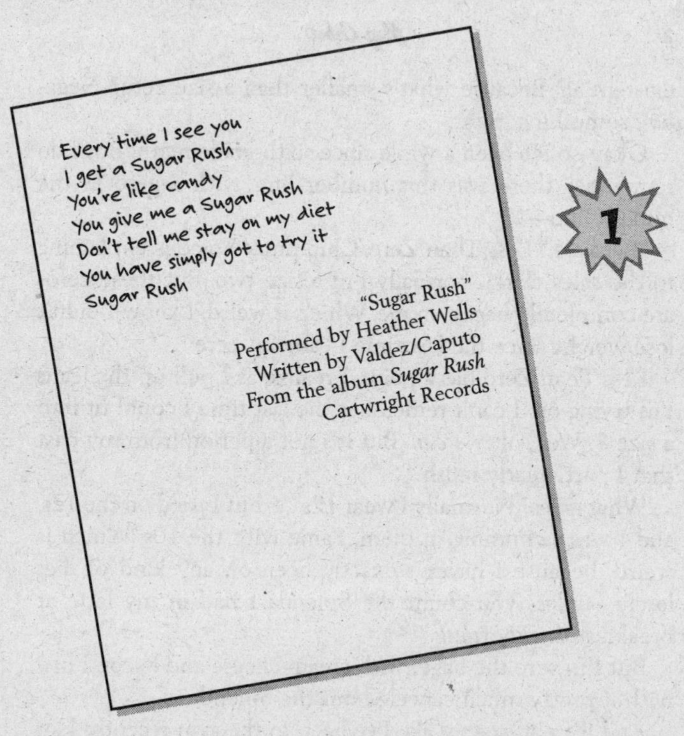
Every time I see you
I get a Sugar Rush
You're like candy
You give me a Sugar Rush
Don't tell me stay on my diet
You have simply got to try it
Sugar Rush
"Sugar Rush"
Performed by Heather Wells
Written by Valdez/Caputo
From the album Sugar Rush
Cartwright Records
1

"Um, hello. Is anyone out there?" The girl in the dressing room next to mine has a voice like a chipmunk. "Hello?"

Exactly like a chipmunk.

I hear a sales clerk come over, his key chain clinking musically. "Yes, ma'am? Can I help you?"

"Yeah." The girl's disembodied—but still chipmunklike—voice floats over the partition between our cubicles. "Do you guys have these jeans in anything smaller than a size zero?"

I pause, one leg in and one leg out of the jeans I am squeezing myself into. Whoa. Is it just me, or was that really existential? Because what's smaller than a size zero? Negative something, right?

Okay, so it's been a while since sixth grade math. But I do remember there was this number line, with a zero in the middle, and—

"Because," Less Than Zero/Chipmunk Voice is explaining to the sales clerk, "normally I'm a size two. But these zeros are completely baggy on me. Which is weird. I know I didn't lose weight since the last time I came in here."

Less Than Zero has a point, I realize as I pull up the jeans I'm trying on. I can't remember the last time I could fit into a size 8. Well, okay, I *can*. But it's not a period from my past that I particularly relish.

What gives? Normally I wear 12s . . . but I tried on the 12s, and I was swimming in them. Same with the 10s. Which is weird, because I haven't exactly been on any kind of diet lately—unless you count the Splenda I had in my latte at breakfast this morning.

But I'm sure the bagel with cream cheese and bacon I had with it pretty much canceled out the Splenda.

And it's not exactly like I've been to the gym recently. Not that I don't exercise, of course. I just don't do it, you know, in the gym. Because you can burn just as many calories walking as you can running. So why run? I figured out a long time ago that a walk to Murray's Cheese Shop on Bleecker to see what kind of sandwich they have on special for lunch takes ten minutes.

And a walk from Murray's over to Betsey Johnson on Wooster to see what's on sale (love her stretch velvet!): another ten minutes.

And a walk from Betsey's over to Dean & Deluca on Broadway for an after-lunch cappuccino and to see if they have those chocolate-covered orange peels I like so much: another ten minutes.

And so on, until before you know it, you've done a full sixty minutes of exercise. Who says it's hard to comply with the government's new fitness recommendations? If *I* can do it, anyone can.

But could all of that walking have caused me to drop *two whole* sizes since the last time I shopped for jeans? I know I've been cutting my daily fat intake by about half since I replaced the Hershey's Kisses in the candy jar on my desk with free condoms from the student health center. But still.

"Well, ma'am," the sales clerk is saying to Less Than Zero. "These jeans are *stretch* fit. That means that you've got to try two sizes lower than your true size."

"What?" Less Than Zero sounds confused.

I don't blame her. I feel the same way. It's like number lines all over again.

"What I mean is," the sales clerk says, patiently, "if you normally wear a size four, in stretch jeans, you would wear a size zero."

"Why don't you just put the real sizes on them, then?" Less Than Zero—quite sensibly, I think—asks. "Like if a zero is a really a four, why don't you just label it a four?"

"It's called vanity sizing," the sales clerk says, dropping his voice.

"*What* sizing?" Less Than Zero asks, dropping her voice, too. At least, as much as a chipmunk *can* drop her voice.

"You know." The sales clerk is whispering to Less Than Zero. But I can still hear him. "The *larger* customers like it when they can fit into an eight. But they're really a twelve, of course. See?"

Wait. *What*?

I fling open the door to my dressing room before I stop to think.

"I'm a size twelve," I hear myself saying to the sales clerk.

Who looks startled. Understandably, I guess. But still. "What's wrong with being a size twelve?"

"Nothing!" cries the sales clerk, looking panicky. "Nothing at all. I just meant—"

"Are you saying size twelve is *fat*?" I ask him.

"No," the sales clerk insists. "You misunderstood me. I meant—"

"Because size twelve is the size of the average American woman," I point out to him. I know this because I just read it in *People* magazine. "Are you saying that instead of being average, we're all fat?"

"No," the sales clerk says. "No, that's not what I meant at all. I—"

The door to the dressing room next to mine opens, and I see the owner of the chipmunk voice for the first time. She's the same age as the kids I work with. She doesn't just *sound* like a chipmunk, I realize. She kind of looks like one, too. You know. Cute. Perky. Small enough to fit in a normal-sized girl's pocket.

"And what's up with not even *making* her size?" I ask the sales clerk, jerking a thumb at Less Than Zero. "I mean, I'd rather be average than not even *exist*."

Less Than Zero looks kind of taken aback. But then she goes, "Um. Yeah!" to the sales clerk.

The sales clerk swallows nervously. And audibly. You can tell he's having a bad day. After work, he'll probably go to some bar and be all "And then these women were just ON me about the vanity sizing . . . . It was awful!"

To us, he just says, "I, um, think I'll just go, um, check and see if we have those jeans you were interested in the, um, back."

Then he scurries away.

I look at Less Than Zero. She looks at me. She is maybe twenty-two, and very blond. I too am blond—with a little help from Lady Clairol—but I left my early twenties several years ago.

Still, it is clear that, age and size differences aside, Less Than Zero and I share a common bond that can never be broken:

We've both been dicked over by vanity sizing.

"Are you going to get those?" Less Than Zero asks, nodding at the jeans I have on.

"I guess," I say. "I mean, I need a new pair. My last pair got barfed on at work."

"God," Less Than Zero says, wrinkling her chipmunk nose. "Where do you work?"

"Oh," I say. "A dorm. I mean, residence hall. I'm the assistant director."

"Rilly?" Less Than Zero looks interested. "At New York College?" When I nod, she cries, "I thought I knew you from somewhere! I graduated from New York College last year. Which dorm?"

"Um," I say, awkwardly. "I just started there this summer."

"Rilly?" Less Than Zero looks confused. "That's weird. 'Cause you look so familiar . . ."

Before I have a chance to explain to her why she thinks she knows me, my cell phone lets out the first few notes of the chorus of the Go-Go's "Vacation" (chosen as a painful reminder that I don't get any—vacation days, that is—until I've passed my six months' probationary period at work, and that's still another three months off). I see from the caller ID that it is my boss. Calling me on a Saturday.

Which means it has to be important. Right?

Except that it probably isn't. I mean, I love my new job and all—working with college students is super fun because they're so enthusiastic about stuff a lot of people don't even think about, like freeing Tibet and getting paid maternity leave for sweatshop workers and all of that.

But a definite drawback about working at Fischer Hall is that I live right around the corner from it. Which makes me just a little more accessible to everyone there than I'm necessarily comfortable with. I mean, it is one thing to get calls at home from work because you are a doctor and one of your patients needs you.

But it is quite another thing to get calls at home from work because the soda machine ate someone's change and no one can find the refund request forms and they want you to come over to help look for them.

Although I do realize to some people, that might sound like a dream come true. You know, living close enough to where you work to be able to drop by if there's a small-change crisis. Especially in New York. Because my commute is two minutes long, and I do it on foot (four more minutes to add to my daily exercise quota).

But people should realize that, as far as dreams coming true, this one's not the greatest, because I only get paid $23,500 a year (about $12,000 after city and state taxes), and in New York City, $12,000 buys you dinner, and maybe a pair of jeans like the ones I'm about to splurge on, vanity sized or not. I wouldn't be able to live in Manhattan on that kind of salary if it weren't for my second job, which pays my rent. I don't get to "live in" because at New York College, only residence hall directors, not assistant directors, get the "benefit" of living in the dorm—I mean, residence hall—they work in.

Still, I live close enough to Fischer Hall that my boss feels like she can call me all the time, and ask me to "pop in" whenever she needs me.

Like on a bright sunny Saturday afternoon in September, when I am shopping for jeans, because the day before, a freshman who'd had a few too many hard lemonades at the

Stoned Crow chose to roll over and barf them on me while I was crouching beside him, feeling for his pulse.

I'm weighing the pros and cons of answering my cell—pro: maybe Rachel's calling to offer me a raise (unlikely); con: maybe Rachel's calling to ask me to take some semicomatose drunk twenty-year-old to the hospital (likely)—when Less Than Zero suddenly shrieks, "Oh my God! I know why you look so familiar! Has anyone ever told you that you look *exactly* like Heather Wells? You know, that singer?"

I decide, under the circumstances, to let my boss go to voice mail. I mean, things are going badly enough, considering the size 12 stuff, and now this. I totally should have just stayed home and bought new jeans online.

"You really think so?" I ask Less Than Zero, not very enthusiastically. Only she doesn't notice my lack of enthusiasm.

"Oh my God!" Less Than Zero shrieks again. "You even *sound* like her. That is so *random*. But," she adds, with a laugh, "what would Heather Wells be doing, working in a dorm, right?"

"Residence hall," I correct her automatically. Because that's what we're supposed to call them, since calling it a residence hall allegedly fosters a feeling of warmth and unity among the residents, who might otherwise find living in something called a dorm too cold and institutional-like.

As if the fact that their refrigerators are bolted to the floor isn't a dead giveaway.

"Oh, hey," Less Than Zero says, sobering suddenly. "Not that there's anything wrong with it. Being assistant director of a dorm. And you're not, like, offended I said that you look like Heather Wells, are you? I mean, I totally had all her albums. And a big poster of her on my wall. When I was eleven."

"I am not," I say, "the least bit offended."

Less Than Zero looks relieved. "Good," she says. "Well, I guess I better go and find a store that actually carries my size."

"Yeah," I say, wanting to suggest Gap Kids, but restraining myself. Because it isn't her fault she's tiny. Any more than it is my fault that I am the size of the average American woman.

It isn't until I'm standing at the register that I check my voice mail to see what my boss, Rachel, wanted. I hear her voice, always so carefully controlled, saying in tones of barely repressed hysteria, "Heather, I'm calling to let you know that there has been a death in the building. When you get this message, please contact me as soon as possible."

I leave the size 8 jeans on the counter and use up another fifteen minutes of my recommended daily exercise by running—yes, *running*—from the store, and toward Fischer Hall.

2

I saw you two
Kissin' and huggin'
You told me
She's just your cousin
You Wish
You Wish
You Wish
If you want me
You gotta be true
So what does that mean
About me and you?
You Wish
You Wish
You Wish
"You Wish"
Performed by Heather Wells
Written by Valdez/Caputo
From the album *Sugar Rush*
Cartwright Records

The first thing I see when I turn the corner onto Washington Square West is a fire engine pulled up on the sidewalk. The fire engine is on the sidewalk instead of in the street because there's this booth selling tiger-print thongs for five dollars each—a bargain, actually, except that when you look closer, you can see that the thongs are trimmed with this black lace that looks as if it might be itchy if it gets, well, you-know-where—blocking the street.

The city hardly ever closes down Washington Square West, the street where Fischer Hall is located. But this particular Saturday, the neighborhood association must have called in a favor with a city councilman or something, since they managed to get that whole side of the park shut down in order to throw a street fair. You know the kind I mean: with the incense guys and the sock man and the cartoon portrait artists and the circus-clown wire-sculpture people?

The first time I went to a Manhattan street fair, I'd been around the same age as the kids I work with. Back then I'd been all "Ooooh, street fair! How fun!" I didn't know then that you can get socks at Macy's for even less than the sock man charges.

But the truth is, it turns out if you've been to one Manhattan street fair, you really have been to them all.

Nothing could have looked more out of place than a booth selling thongs in front of Fischer Hall. It just isn't a thong kind of building. Towering majestically over Washington Square Park, it had been built of red bricks around 1850. I'd learned from some files I'd found in my desk on my first day at my new job that every five years, the city makes the college hire a company to come and drill out all the old mortar and replace it with new, so that Fischer Hall's bricks don't fall out and conk people on the head.

Which is a good idea, I guess. Except that in spite of the city's efforts, things are always falling out of Fischer Hall and conking people on the head anyway. And I'm not talking about bricks. I've had reports of falling bottles, cans, clothing, books, CDs, vegetables, Good & Plentys, and once even a whole roasted chicken.

I'm telling you, when I walk by Fischer Hall, I always look up, just to be on the safe side.

Not today, however. Today my gaze is glued to the front door of the building. I'm trying to figure out how I'm going to get through it, considering the huge crowd—and New

York City cop—in front of it. It looks as if, along with dozens of tourists who are milling around the street fair, about half the student population of the building is standing outside, waiting to be let back into the building. They have no idea what's going on. I can tell from the questions they keep shouting to one another in an attempt to be heard over the pan flute music coming from another booth in front of the building, this one selling, um, cassettes of pan flute music:

"What's going on?"

"I dunno. Is there a fire?"

"Someone prolly let their potpourri boil over again."

"Naw, it was Jeff. He dropped his bhang again."

"Jeff, you suck!"

"It wasn't me this time, I swear!"

They couldn't know there'd been a death in the building. If they'd known, they wouldn't be joking about bhangs. I think.

Okay, I hope.

Then I spy a face I recognize, belonging to someone who DEFINITELY knows what's going on. I can tell by her expression. She isn't merely upset because the fire department won't let her back in the building. She's upset because she KNOWS.

"Heather!" Magda, seeing me in the crowd, flings a heavily manicured hand toward me. "Oh, Heather! Is terrible!"

Magda is standing there in her pink cafeteria smock and leopard-print leggings, shaking her frosted curls and taking long, nervous drags on the Virginia Slim she's got tucked between her two-inch-long nails. Each nail bears a mini replica of the American flag. Because even though Magda goes back to her native Dominican Republic every chance she gets, she is still very patriotic about her adopted country, and expresses her affection for it through nail art.

That's how I met her, actually. Almost four months ago, at the manicurist. That's also how I heard about the job in the dorm (I mean, residence hall) in the first place. The last assistant director before me—Justine—had just gotten fired for embezzling seven thousand dollars from the building's petty cash, a fact which had enraged Magda, the dorm—I mean, residence hall—cafeteria's cashier.

"Can you believe it?" Magda had been complaining to anyone who would listen, as I was having my toes done in Hot Tamale Red—because, you know, even if the rest of your life is going down the toilet, like mine was back then, at least your toes can still look pretty.

Magda, a few tables away, had been having mini Statues of Liberty air-brushed onto her thumbnails, in honor of Memorial Day, and was waxing eloquent about Justine, my predecessor.

"She order twenty-seven ceramic heaters from Office Supply and give them to her friends as wedding presents!"

I still have no idea what a ceramic heater is, or why anyone would want one as a wedding gift. But when I'd heard someone had been fired from Magda's place of work, where one of the job benefits—besides twenty vacation days a year and full health and dental—is free tuition, I'd jumped on the information.

I owe Magda a lot, actually. And not just because she helped me with the job thing, either (or because she lets me eat free in the caf anytime I want—which might be part of the reason why I'm no longer a size 8, except in vanity sizing), but because Magda's become one of my best friends.

"Mag," I say, sidling up to her. "Who is it? Who died?"

Because I can't help worrying it's someone I know, like one of the maintenance workers who are always so sweet about cleaning up spilled bodily fluids, even though it's not in their job description. Or one of the student workers I'm supposed to supervise—*supposed to* being the operative words, since in the three months I've worked at Fischer Hall, only a handful of my student employees have ever actually done what I've told them to (a lot of them remain loyal to the sticky-fingered Justine).

And when any of them actually do what I ask, it's only because it involves something like checking every single room after the previous residents have moved out and cleaning out whatever they've left behind, generally half-full bottles of Jägermeister.

So then when I get to work the next day, I can't get a single one of them to come downstairs and sort the mail, because they're all too hung over.

But there are a couple kids I've genuinely come to love, scholarship students who didn't come to school equipped with a Visa that Mom and Dad are only too happy to pay off every month, and who actually need to work in order to pay for books and fees, and so will take the 4 P.M.–midnight shift at the reception desk on a Saturday night with a minimum of begging on my part.

"Oh, Heather," Magda whispers. Only she pronounces it Haythar. She is whispering because she doesn't want the kids to know what's really going on. Whatever it is. "One of my little movie stars!"

"A student?" I can see people in the crowd eyeing Magda curiously. Not because she's weird-looking—well, she IS kind of weird-looking, since she wears enough makeup to make Christina Aguilera look as if she's going au naturel, and she's got those really long nails and all.

But since it's the Village, Magda's outfits could actually be considered kind of tame.

It's the "movie star" thing people don't get. Every time a student enters the Fischer Hall cafeteria, Magda takes his or her dining card, runs it through the scanner, and sings, "Look at all the byootiful movie stars who come to eat here. We are so lucky to have so many byootiful movie stars in Fischer Hall!"

At first I just thought Magda was trying to flatter the many drama students—and there are tons, way more than pre-med or business majors—that go to New York College.

Then one Fix Your Own Sundae day, Magda dropped the bomb that Fischer Hall is actually quite famous. Not for the reasons you'd think, like because it's on historic Washington Square, where Henry James once lived, or because it's across the street from the famous Hanging Tree, where they used to execute people in the eighteenth century. Not even because the park was once a cemetery for the indigent, so basically all those benches and hot dog stands? Yeah, they're sitting on dead people.

No. According to Magda, Fischer Hall is famous because they shot a scene from the movie *Teenage Mutant Ninja Turtles* there. Donatello or Raphael or one of the turtles—I can't actually remember which one—swung from the Fischer Hall penthouse to the building next door, and the kids in the building all acted as extras, looking up and pointing amazedly at the stunt turtle's feat.

Seriously. Fischer Hall has quite an exciting history.

Except that the kids who acted in the movie as extras have long since graduated and moved from Fischer Hall.

So I guess people think it's weird that Magda is still bringing it up, all these years later.

But really, you can see how the fact that a scene from a major motion picture was shot at her place of work would be, to someone like Magda, just another of the many things that make America great.

But you can also see how, to someone who doesn't know

the story behind it, the whole "my little movie star" thing might seem a little . . . well, wacko.

Which probably explained why so many people were looking curiously our way, having overheard her outburst.

Not wanting the kids to catch on that something was seriously wrong, I take Magda by the arm and steer her toward one of the potted pines that sits outside the building—and which the students unfortunately tend to use as their own personal ashtray—so we can have a little privacy.

"What happened?" I ask her, in a low voice. "Rachel left a message that there'd been a death in the building, but that's all she said. Do you know who? And how?"

"I don't know," Magda whispers, shaking her head. "I am sitting at my register, and I hear screaming, and someone says that a girl is lying at the bottom of the elevator shaft, and that she's dead."

"Oh my God!" I'm shocked. I'd been expecting to hear about a death from a drug overdose or violent crime—there are security guards on duty twenty-four hours a day in the building, but that doesn't mean the occasional unsavory character doesn't manage to slip inside anyway. It *is* New York City, after all.

But death by *elevator*?

Magda, moist-eyed, but trying valiantly not to cry—since that would tip off the students, who are prone to dramatics anyway, that something is REALLY wrong (it also wouldn't do anything much for Magda's many layers of mascara)—adds, "They say she was—what do you call it? Riding on top of the elevator?"

"Surfing?" I am even more shocked now. "Elevator surfing?"

"Yes." Magda carefully inserts the tip of a finely crafted nail at the corner of her eye, and dashes away a tear. "That is why they are not letting anyone inside. The little movie stars need the elevator to get up to their dressing rooms, but they have to move the—"

Magda breaks off with a sob. I put my arm around her and quickly turn her toward me, as much to comfort her as to smother the sound of her crying. Students are glancing curiously our way. I don't want them to catch on that anything is seriously wrong. They'll find out, soon enough.

Only they probably won't have as hard a time believing it as I was.

The thing is, I shouldn't have been so surprised. Elevator surfing is a problem campus-wide—and not just at New York College, but at universities and colleges all over the country. Teenagers with nothing better to do than get high and dare each other to jump onto the roofs of elevator cabs as they glide up and down the dark, dangerous shafts. There'd been account after account of kids getting themselves decapitated in drunken dares.

I guess it was bound to happen at Fischer Hall sometime.

Except.

Except that Magda kept saying "she." That a *girl* had died.

Which is weird, because I've never once heard of a *girl* elevator surfing. At least not in Fischer Hall.

Then Magda lifts her head from my shoulder and says, "Uh-oh."

I turn to see what she's talking about and suck in my breath real fast. Because Mrs. Allington, the wife of Phillip Allington—who last spring was inaugurated as the college's sixteenth president—is coming down the sidewalk toward us.

I know a lot about the Allingtons because another thing I found in Justine's files—right before I threw them all away—was an article clipped from the *New York Times*, making this big deal out of the fact that the newly appointed president had chosen to live in a residence hall rather than in one of the luxury buildings owned by the school.

"Phillip Allington," the article said, "is an academician who does not wish to lose touch with the student population. When he comes home from his office, he rides the same elevator as the undergraduates next to whom he resides—"

What the *Times* totally neglected to mention is that the president and his family live in Fischer Hall's penthouse, which takes up the entire twentieth floor, and that they complained so much about the elevators stopping on every floor on their way up to let the students out that Justine finally issued them override keys.

Aside from complaining about the elevators, President Allington's wife, Eleanor, seems to have very little to do. Whenever I see her, she's always just returning from, or heading off to, Saks Fifth Avenue. She is uncannily committed to shopping—like an Olympic track athlete is dedicated to her training.

Only Mrs. Allington's sport of choice—besides shopping—seems to be consuming vast amounts of vodka. When she and Dr. Allington return from late-night dinners with the trustees, Mrs. Allington inevitably kicks up a ruckus in the lobby, usually concerning her pet cockatoos—or so I've heard from Pete, my favorite university security officer.

"The birds," she'd once told him. "The birds hate your guts, fatty."

Which is kind of mean-spirited, if you think about it. Also inaccurate, since Pete isn't a bit fat. He's just, you know. Average.

Mrs. Allington's drunken verbal assaults are a source of much amusement at the hall's reception desk, which is staffed round the clock by student employees—the ones I'm supposed to supervise. Late at night, if Dr. Allington isn't home, Mrs. Allington sometimes calls down to the desk to report all sorts of startling facts: that someone has eaten all her stuffed artichokes; that there are coyotes on her terrace; that tiny invisible dwarfs are hammering on her headboard.

According to Pete, the students were at first confused by these reports, and would beep the resident assistants, the upperclassmen who, in exchange for free room and board, are expected to act as sort of house mothers, one per floor. The RAs in turn would notify the building director, who would board the elevator for the twentieth floor to investigate.

But when Mrs. Allington answered her door, bleary-eyed and robed in velour—I know! Velour! Almost as good as stretch velvet—she'd just say, "I don't know what you're talking about, fatty."

While behind her (according to various RAs who've repeated this story), the cockatoos whistled maniacally.

Spooky stuff.

But apparently not as spooky to Mrs. Allington as it is to the rest of us, probably because she never seems to remember any of it the next day, and heads off to Saks as if she were a queen—the Queen of Fischer Hall.

Like now, for instance. Loaded down with shopping bags, Mrs. Allington is looking scathingly at the cop who is blocking Fischer Hall's front door, and going, "Excuse me. I live here."

"Sorry, lady," the cop says. "Emergency personnel only. No residents allowed back in the building yet."

"I am not a resident. " Mrs. Allington seems to swell amid her bags. "I'm . . . I'm . . ." Mrs. Allington can't seem to quite figure out what she is. But it's not like the cop cares.

"Sorry, lady," he says. "Go enjoy the street fair for a while, why dontcha? Or there're some nice benches over in the park there. Whyn't you go relax on one till we get the all-clear to start lettin' people in again, okay?"

Mrs. Allington is looking a bit peaked as I come hurrying up to her. I've abandoned Magda because Mrs. Allington looks as if she needs me more. She's just standing there in a pair of too-tight designer jeans, a silk top, and tons of gold jewelry, the shopping bags drooping in her hands, her mouth opening and closing in confusion. She is definitely a little green around the gills.

"Did you hear me, ma'am?" the cop is saying. "No one's allowed in. See all these kids here? They're waiting, too. So either wait with them or move along."

Only Mrs. Allington seems to have lost the ability to move along. She doesn't look too steady on her feet, if you ask me. I step over and take her arm. She doesn't even acknowledge my presence. I doubt she even knows who I am. Though she nods to me every single weekday when she gets off the elevator across from my office door on her way out to her latest binge—I mean, shopping expedition—and says, "Good morning, Justine" (despite my frequently correcting her), I suppose seeing me on a weekend, and out of doors, has thrown her.

"Her husband's the president of the college, Officer," I say, nodding toward Mrs. Allington, who appears to be staring very hard at a nearby student with purple hair and an eyebrow ring. "Phillip Allington? He lives in the penthouse. I don't think she's feeling too well. Can I . . . can I just help her get inside?"

The cop gives me the eye.

"I know you from somewhere?" the cop asks. It's not a come-on. With me, this line never is.

"Probably from the neighborhood," I say, with excessive cheer. "I work in this building." I flash him my college staff

ID card, the one with the photo where I look drunk, even though I wasn't. Until after I saw the photo. "See? I'm the assistant residence hall director."

He doesn't look impressed by the title, but he says, with a shrug, "Whatever. Get 'er inside, if you want. But I don't know how you're gonna get 'er upstairs. Elevators are shut down."

I don't know how I'm going to get Mrs. Allington upstairs, either, considering she's so unsteady on her feet, I'm practically going to have to carry her. I fling a glance over my shoulder at Magda, who, seeing my predicament, rolls her eyes. But she stamps out her cigarette and heads gamely toward us, ready to offer whatever aid she can.

Before she quite gets to us, though, two young women—garbed in what I consider standard New York College attire, low rider jeans with belly rings—come bursting out of the building, breathing hard.

"Oh my God, Jeff," one of them calls to the bhang dropper. "What is up with the elevators? We just had to walk down seventeen flights of stairs."

"I'm going to die," the other girl announces.

"Seriously," the first girl pants, loudly. "For what we're paying in tuition and housing fees, you'd think the PRESIDENT would be able to invest in elevators that don't break down all the time."

I don't miss her hostile glance at Mrs. Allington, who made the mistake of letting her photo be published in the school paper, thus making her a recognizable target around the dorm. I mean, residence hall.

"C'mon, Mrs. Allington," I say quickly, giving her arm a little tug. "Let's go inside."

"About time," Mrs. Allington says, stumbling a little, as Magda moves to take hold of her other arm. The two of us steer her through the front door to cries—from the students—of "Hey! Why do *they* get to go in, but we don't? We live here, too!" and "No fair!" and, "Fascists!"

From the careful way she's putting one kitten heel in front of the other, I'm pretty sure Mrs. Allington is already a little tipsy, even though it's not quite noon. My suspicions are confirmed when the three of us pass into the building and Mrs. Allington suddenly leans over and heaves her breakfast into one of the planters in the front lobby.

It definitely looks as if Mrs. A. had a few Bloody Marys to go with her eggs this morning.

"Santa Maria," Magda says, horrified. And who can blame her?

I don't know about anyone else, but when I throw up (and, I'm sorry to say, it's something I do regularly every single New Year's Eve), I like a little sympathy, even if the whole thing's my own fault.

So I pat Mrs. Allington on her padded shoulder and say, "There. Don't you feel better now?"

Mrs. Allington squints at me as if she's noticing me for the first time.

"Who the hell are you?" she asks.

"Um," I say. "I'm the assistant building director. Heather Wells. Remember? We met a couple of months ago?"

Mrs. Allington looks confused. "What happened to Justine?"

"Justine found another job," I explain, which is a lie, since Justine was fired. But the truth is, I don't know Justine's side of the story. I mean, maybe she really needed the money. Maybe she has relatives who live in Bosnia or somewhere really cold, and they don't have any heat, and those ceramic heaters kept them alive all winter. You never know.

Mrs. Allington just squints some more.

"Heather Wells?" She blinks a few more times. "But aren't

you . . . aren't you that girl? The one who used to sing in all those malls?"

That's when I realize that Mrs. Allington has finally recognized me, all right . . .

. . . but not as the assistant director of the building she lives in.

Wow. I never suspected Mrs. Allington of being a fan of teen pop. She seems more the Barry Manilow type—much older teen pop.

"I was," I say to her, kindly, because I still feel sorry for her, on account of the barf, and all. "But I don't perform anymore."

"Why?" Mrs. Allington wants to know.

Magda and I exchange glances. Magda seems to be getting her sense of humor back, since there is a distinct upward slant to corners of her lip-linered mouth.

"Um," I say. "It's kind of a long story. Basically I lost my recording contract—"

"Because you got fat?" Mrs. Allington asks.

Which is, I have to admit, when I sort of stopped feeling sorry for her.

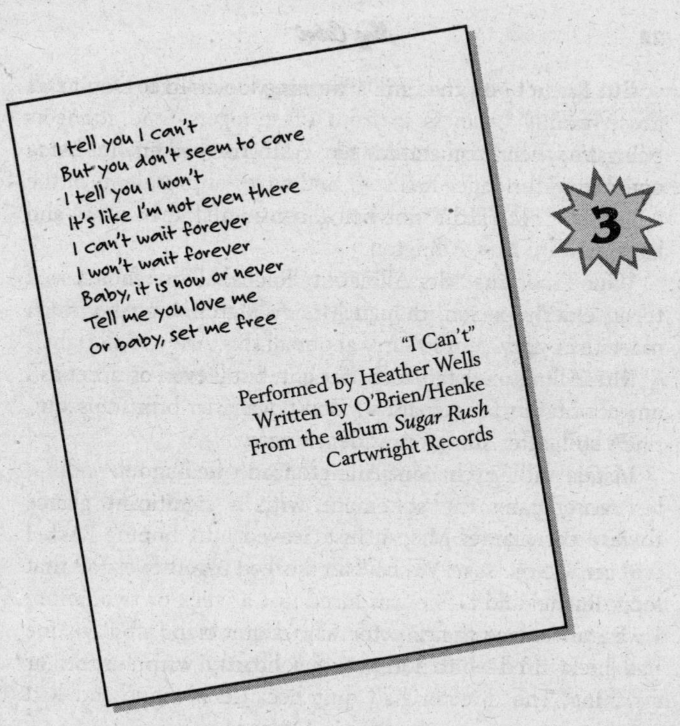
I tell you I can't
But you don't seem to care
I tell you I won't
It's like I'm not even there
I can't wait forever
I won't wait forever
Baby, it is now or never
Tell me you love me
Or baby, set me free
"I Can't"
Performed by Heather Wells
Written by O'Brien/Henke
From the album *Sugar Rush*
Cartwright Records
3

Fortunately I'm spared from having to make any sort of reply to Mrs. Allington's remark about my weight by the fact that my boss, Rachel Walcott, comes hurrying up to us just then, her patent leather slides clacking on the marble floor of the lobby.

"Heather," Rachel says, when she sees me. "Thank you so much for coming." She actually does look sort of relieved that I'm there, which makes me feel good. You know, that I really am needed, if only $23,500-a-year worth.

"Sure," I say. "I'm so sorry. Was it—I mean, is it—someone we know?"

But Rachel just gives me a warning look—like "Don't talk about family business in front of strangers," the strangers being Mrs. Allington and Magda, cafeteria workers not being considered residence hall staff, and wives of presidents of the college DEFINITELY not being considered that way—and turns toward Mrs. Allington.

"Good morning, Mrs. Allington," Rachel all but shouts, as if to an elderly person, though Mrs. Allington can't be much more than sixty. "I'm so sorry about all this. Are you all right?"

Mrs. Allington is far from all right, but—even as upset as I am about the fat remark—I don't want to blurt this out. She's still, after all, the president's wife.

Instead all I say is "Mrs. Allington isn't feeling too well."

I accompany the statement with a significant glance toward the planter Mrs. A. just heaved into, hoping Rachel will get the message. We haven't worked together for all that long, Rachel and I. She was hired just a week or two before I was, to replace the director who'd quit right after Justine had been fired—but not out of solidarity with Justine, or anything. The director had quit because her husband had gotten a job as a forest ranger in Oregon.

I know. Forest ranger husband. Hmmm. I'd have quit to follow him, too.

But while Rachel is new to the live-in position of director of Fischer Hall, she's not new to the field of higher education (which is what they call it when you're involved in the counseling, but not the teaching, part of college life, or at least so I read in one of Justine's files). The last dorm—I mean, residence hall—Rachel, a Yale grad, ran had been at Earlcrest College in Richmond, Indiana.

Rachel told me that it had been a bit of a culture shock, coming to New York City from a place like Richmond, where people don't even have to lock their doors at night. But as far as I can tell, Rachel hasn't exactly suffered any long-term hardships from her stint in the Hoosier heartland. She has a wardrobe any New York career gal would be happy to call her own, heavy on the Armani and the Manolos, which—considering her salary (not much more than mine, since directors get a free apartment in the building thrown in as part of their pay package)—is quite an accomplishment. Faithful weekly attendance of designer sample sales helps keep Rachel on the cutting edge of fashion. And her strict adherence to the Zone and two-hour daily workouts ensure that she stays a size 2, enabling her to fit into all those models' castoffs.

Rachel says that if I stop eating so many carbs and spend a half hour on the StairMaster every day, I could easily get back down to a real size 8. And that this shouldn't be a hardship for me, because you get free membership at the college's gym as part of your benefits package.

Except that I've been to the college gym, and it's scary. There are all these really skinny girls there, flinging their sticklike arms around in aerobics classes and yoga and stuff. Seriously, one of these days, one of them is going to put someone's eye out.

Anyway, if I lose enough weight, Rachel says, I'll definitely get a hot boyfriend, the way she's planning to, just as soon as she finds a guy in the Village who isn't gay, has a full set of hair, and makes at least a hundred thousand a year.

But how on earth could anyone ever give up cold sesame noodles? Even for a guy who makes a hundred thousand dollars a year?

Plus, um, as I frequently remind Rachel, size 12 is not fat. It is the size of the average American woman. Hello. And there are plenty of us (size 12s) who have boyfriends, thank you very much.

Not me, necessarily. But plenty of other girls my size, and even larger.

But though Rachel and I have different priorities—she wants a boyfriend; I'd just take a BA, at this point—and can't seem to agree on what constitutes a meal—her, lettuce, no dressing; me, falafel, extra tahini, with a pita 'n' hummus starter and maybe an ice cream sandwich for dessert—we get along okay, I guess. I mean, Rachel seems to understand the look I shoot her about Mrs. Allington, anyway.

"Mrs. Allington," she says. "Let's get you home, shall we? I'll take you upstairs. Would that be all right, Mrs. Allington?"

Mrs. Allington nods weakly, her interest in my career change forgotten. Rachel takes the president's wife by the arm as Pete, who has been hovering nearby, holds back a wave of firemen to make room for her and Mrs. A. on the elevator they've turned back on especially for her. I can't help glancing nervously at the elevator's interior as the doors open. What if there's blood? I know they said they'd found her at the bottom of the shaft, but what if part of her was still on the elevator?

But there's no blood that I can see. The elevator looks the same as ever, imitation mahogany paneling with brass trim, into which hundreds of undergraduates have scratched their initials or various swear words with the edges of their room keys.

As the elevator doors close, I hear Mrs. Allington say, very softly, "The birds."

"God," Magda says, as we watch the numbers above the elevator doors light up as the car moves toward the penthouse. "I hope she doesn't throw up again in there."

"Seriously," I agree. That would make the ride up twenty flights pretty much suck.

Magda shakes herself, as though she's thought of something unpleasant—most likely Mrs. A.'s vomit—and looks around. "It's so quiet," she says, hugging herself. "It hasn't been this quiet around here since before all my little movie stars checked in."

She's right. For a building that houses so many young people—seven hundred, most still in their teens—the lobby is strangely still just then. No one is grumbling about the length of time it takes the student workers to sort the mail (approximately seven hours. I'd heard that Justine could get them to do it in under two. Sometimes I wonder if maybe Justine had some sort of secret pact with Satan); no one is complaining about the broken change machines down in the game room; no one is Rollerblading on the marble floors; no one is arguing with Pete over the guest sign-in policy.

Not that there isn't anybody around. The lobby is jumping. Cops, firemen, college officials, campus security guards in their baby blue uniforms, and a smattering of students—all resident assistants—are milling around the mahogany and marble lobby, grim-faced . . .

. . . but silent. Absolutely silent.

"Pete," I say, going up to the guard at the security desk. "Do you know who it was?"

The security guards know everything that goes on in the buildings they work in. They can't help it. It's all there, on the monitors in front of them, from the students who smoke in the stairwells, to the deans who pick their noses in the elevators, to the librarians who have sex in the study carrels . . .

Dishy stuff.

"Of course." Pete, as usual, is keeping one eye on the lobby and the other on the many television monitors on his desk, each showing a different part of the dorm (I mean, residence hall), from the entranceway to the Allingtons' penthouse apartment, to the laundry room in the basement.

"Well?" Magda looks anxious. "Who was it?"

Pete, with a cautious glance at the reception desk across the way to make sure the student workers aren't eavesdropping, says, "Kellogg. Elizabeth. Freshman."

I feel a spurt of relief. I have never heard of her.

Then I berate myself for feeling that way. She's still a dead eighteen-year-old, whether she was one of my student workers, or not!

"How did it happen?" I ask.

Pete gives me a sarcastic look. "How do you think?"

"But," I say. I can't help it. Something is really confusing me. "Girls don't do that. Elevator surf, I mean."

"This one did." Pete shrugs.

"Why would she do something like that?" Magda wants to know. "Something so stupid? Was she on drugs?"

"How should I know?" Pete seems annoyed by our barrage of questions, but I know it is only because he is as freaked as we are. Which is weird, because you'd think he's seen it all: He's been working at the college for twenty years. Like me, he'd taken the job for the benefits: A widower, he has four children who are assured of a great—and free—college education, which is the main reason he'd gone to work for an academic institution after a knee injury got him assigned to permanent desk duty in the NYPD. His oldest, Nancy, wants to be a pediatrician.

But that doesn't keep Pete's face from turning beet red every time one of the students, bitter over not being allowed into the building with their state-of-the-art halogen lamps (fire hazard), refers to him as a "rent-a-cop." Which isn't fair, because Pete is really, really good at his job. The only time pizza delivery guys ever make it inside Fischer Hall to stick menus under everyone's door is when Pete's not on duty.

Not that he doesn't have the biggest heart in the world.

When kids come down from their rooms, disgustedly holding glue traps on which live mice are trapped, Pete has been known to take the traps out to the park and pour oil onto them to free their little paws and let them go. He can't stand the idea of anyone—or anything—dying on his watch.

"Coroner'll run tests for alcohol and drugs, I'm sure," he says, trying to sound casual, and failing. "If he ever gets here, that is."

I'm horrified.

"You mean she . . . she's still here? I mean, it—the body?"

Pete nods. "Downstairs. Bottom of the elevator shaft. That's where they found her."

"That's where who found her?" I ask.

"The fire department," Pete says. "When someone reported seeing her."

"Seeing her fall?"

"No. Seeing her lying there. Someone looked down the crack—you know, between the floor and the elevator car—and saw her."

I feel shaken. "You mean nobody reported it when it happened? The people who were with her?"

"What people?" Pete wants to know.

"The people she was elevator surfing with," I say. "She had to be with someone. Nobody plays that stupid game alone. They didn't come down to report it?"

"Nobody said nothing to me," Pete says, "until this morning when a kid saw her through the crack."

I am appalled.

"You mean she could have been lying down there for hours?" I ask, my voice cracking a little.

"Not alive," Pete says, getting my drift right away. "She landed headfirst."

"Santa Maria," Magda says, and crosses herself.

I am only slightly less appalled. "So . . . then how'd they know who it was?"

"Had her school ID in her pocket," Pete explains.

"Well, at least she was thinking ahead," Magda says.

"Magda!" I'm shocked, but Magda just shrugs.

"It's true. If you are going to play such a stupid game, at least keep ID on you, so they can identify your body later, right?"

Before either Pete or I can reply, Gerald, the dining director, comes popping out of the cafeteria, looking for his wayward cashier.

"Magda," he says, when he finally spots her. "Whadduya *doing*? Cops said they're gonna let us open up again any minute and I got no one on the register."

"Oh, I'll be right there, honey," Magda calls to him. Then, as soon as he's stomped out of earshot, she adds, "Dickhead." Then, with an apologetic waggle of her nails at Pete and me, Magda goes back to her seat behind the cash register in the student cafeteria around the corner from the guard's desk.

"Heather?"

I look around, and see one of the student workers at the reception desk gesturing to me desperately. The reception desk is the hub of the building, where the residents' mail is sorted, where visitors can call up to their friends' rooms, and where all building emergencies are supposed to be reported. One of my first duties after being hired had been to type up a long list of phone numbers that the reception desk employees were to refer to in the event of an emergency of any kind (apparently, Justine had been too busy using college funds to buy ceramic heaters for all of her friends ever to get around to this).

Fire? The number for the fire station was listed.

Rape? The number for the campus's rape hotline was listed.

Theft? The number for the Sixth Precinct.

People falling off the top of one of the elevators? There's no number for that.

"Heather." The student worker, Tina, sounds as whiny today as she did the first day I met her, when I told her she couldn't put people on hold while she finished the round of Tetris she was playing on her Game Boy (Justine had never had a problem with this, I was told). "When're they gonna get rid of that girl's body? I'm losing it, knowing she's, like, still DOWN there."

"We saw her roommate." Brad—the guy with the misfortune to be the resident assistant on duty this weekend, meaning he has to stay in the building at all times, in case he's needed . . . like in the event of a student death—drops his voice conspiratorially as he leans across the desk toward me. "She said she didn't even know Beth—that's the dead girl—she said she didn't even know Beth *knew* about surfing. She said she had no idea Beth hung out with that crowd. She said Beth was kinda *preppie*."

"Well," I say, lamely. I can tell the kids are looking for some kind of words of comfort from me. But what do I know about helping kids cope with the death of a classmate? I'm as freaked as either one of them. "I guess it just goes to show you never really quite know someone as well as you think you do, doesn't it?"

"Yeah, but going for a joyride on top of an elevator?" Tina shakes her head. "She musta been crazy."

"Prozac candidate," Brad somberly agrees, exhibiting some of that sensitivity training the housing department has drilled so hard into their RAs' heads.

"Heather?"

I turn to see Rachel's graduate assistant, Sarah, coming toward me, a thick file in her hands. Garbed as always in the height of New York College graduate student chic—overalls and Uggs—she grabs my arm and squeezes.

"Ohmigod," Sarah says, making no attempt whatsoever to lower her voice so that it isn't audible to everyone on the entire first floor. "Can you believe it? The phones are ringing off the hook back in the office. All these parents are calling to make sure it wasn't their kid. But Rachel says we can't confirm the deceased's identity until the coroner arrives. Even though we know who it is. I mean, Rachel had me get her file and told me to give it to Dr. Flynn. And would you look at this file?"

Sarah waves the thickly packed manila file. Elizabeth Kellogg had a record in the hall director's office, which means that she'd either gotten in trouble for something or been ill at some point during the school year . . .

. . . which is odd, because Elizabeth was a freshman, and the fall semester had only just begun.

"Getta loada this." Sarah is eager to share all she knows with me, Brad, and Tina. The latter two are listening to her with wide eyes. Pete, over at the guard's desk, is acting like he's busy watching his monitors. But I know he's listening, too. "Her mother called Rachel, all bent out of shape because we allow residents to have any guests they want, and she didn't want Elizabeth to be able to sign in boys. Apparently Mom expected her daughter to remain a virgin until marriage. She wanted Rachel to make it so that Elizabeth was only to be allowed to sign in girls. Obviously there are issues at home, but whatever—"

It's the job of the GA—or graduate assistant—to assist the director in the day-to-day operations of the residence hall. In return, GAs receive free room and board and practical experience in higher education, which is generally their chosen field.

Sarah's getting a lot more practical experience in the field here in Fischer Hall than she'd bargained on, what with a dead girl and all.

"Clearly there was some major mother-daughter rivalry going on there," Sarah informs us. "I mean, you could tell Mrs. Kellogg was jealous because her looks are fading while her daughter's—"

Sarah's undergrad degree is in sociology. Sarah thinks that I suffer from low esteem. She told me this the day she met me, at check-in two weeks earlier, when she went to shake my hand, then cried, "Oh my God, you're *that* Heather Wells?"

When I admitted that I was, then told her—when she asked what on earth I was doing working in a college residence hall (unlike me, Sarah never messes up and calls it a dorm)—that I was hoping to get a BA one of these days, she said, "You don't need to go to college. What you need to work on are your abandonment issues and the feelings of inadequacy you must feel for being dropped from your label and robbed by your mother."

Which is kind of funny, since what I feel I need to work on most are my feelings of dislike for Sarah.

Fortunately Dr. Flynn, the housing department's on-staff psychologist, comes hurtling toward us just then, his briefcase overflowing with paperwork.

"Is that the deceased's file?" he demands, by way of greeting. "I'd like to see it before I talk to the roommate and call the parents."

Sarah hands him the file. As Dr. Flynn flips through it, he suddenly wrinkles his nose, then asks, "What is that smell?"

"Um," I say. "Mrs. Allington sort of—well, she, um . . ."

"She yorked," Brad says. "In the planter over there."

Dr. Flynn sighs. "Not again." His cell phone chimes, and he says, "Excuse me," and reaches for it.

At the same moment, the reception desk phone rings. Everyone looks down at it. When no one else reaches for it, I do.

"Fischer Hall," I say.

The voice on the other end of the phone isn't one I recognize.

"Yes, is this that dormitory located on Washington Square West?"

"This is a residence hall, yes," I reply, remembering, for once, my training.

"I was wondering if I could speak to someone about the tragedy that occurred there earlier today," says the unfamiliar voice.

Tragedy? I immediately become suspicious.

"Are you a reporter?" I ask. At this point in my life, I can sniff them out a mile away.

"Well, yes, I'm with the *Post*—"

"Then you'll have to get in touch with the Press Relations Department. No one here has any comment. Good-bye." I slam down the receiver.

Brad and Tina are staring at me.

"Wow," Brad says. "You're good."

Sarah gives her glasses a push, since they've started to slide down her nose.

"She ought to be," she says. "Considering what she's had to deal with. The paparazzi wasn't exactly kind, were they, Heather? Especially when you walked in and found Jordan Cartwright receiving fellatio from . . . who was it? Oh yes. Tania Trace."

"Wow," I say, gazing at Sarah with genuine wonder. "You really put that photographic memory of yours to good use, don't you, Sarah?"

Sarah smiles modestly while Tina's jaw drops.

"Heather, you went out with *Jordan Cartwright*?" she cries.

"You caught him getting head from *Tania Trace*?" Brad looks as happy as if someone's just dropped a hundred-dollar bill in his lap.

"Um," I say. It's not like I have much of a choice. They can easily Google it. "Yeah. It was a long time ago."

Then I excuse myself to go search for a soda, hoping a combined jolt of caffeine and artificial sweeteners might make me feel less like causing there to be yet another death among the building's student population.

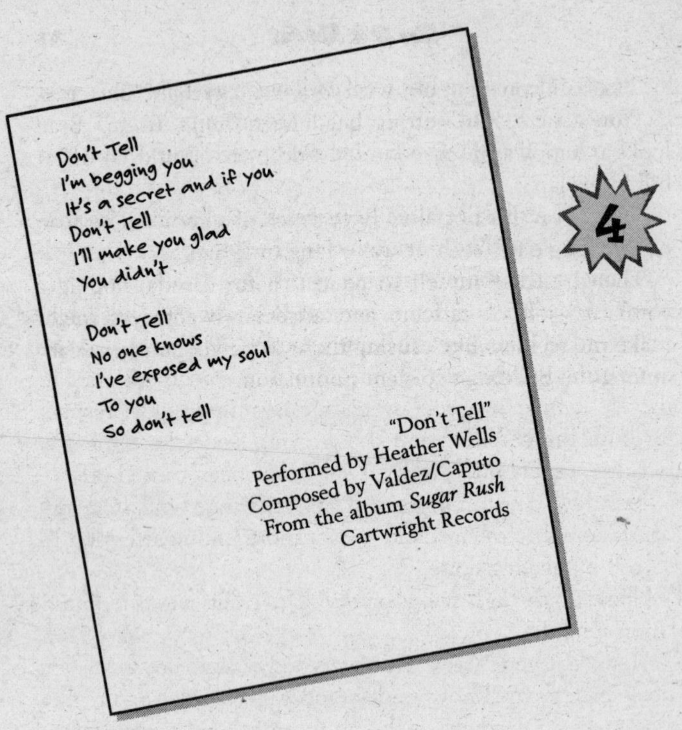
Don't Tell
I'm begging you
It's a secret and if you
Don't Tell
I'll make you glad
You didn't

Don't Tell
No one knows
I've exposed my soul
To you
So don't tell

"Don't Tell"
Performed by Heather Wells
Composed by Valdez/Caputo
From the album *Sugar Rush*
Cartwright Records

4

The closest soda machine is located in the TV lounge, where all of the college's crisis management people are congregated. I don't want to risk asking Magda for a free one from the caf when she's already in trouble with her boss.

I only recognize a few of the many administrators in the lounge, and then only from being interviewed by them when I'd applied for my job. One of them, Dr. Jessup, the head of the housing department, detaches himself from another administrator's side when he notices me, and comes over, looking very different in his weekend wear of Izod shirt and Dockers than he did in his usual charcoal suits.

"Heather," Dr. Jessup says, his deep voice gruff. "How's it going?"

"Okay," I reply. I've already jammed a dollar into the machine, so it's too late to run away—though I'd like to, since everyone in the room is staring at me, like, *Who is that girl? Don't I know her from somewhere? And what's she doing* here?

Instead of running, I make a selection. The sound of the can hitting the slot at the bottom of the machine is loud in the TV lounge, where conversation is muted out of respect for both the deceased and the grieving, and where the TV, which normally blasts MTV 2 24/7, has been turned off.

I retrieve my can from the machine and hold it in my hands, afraid to open it and attract more undue attention to myself by making noise.

"How do the kids seem to you?" Dr. Jessup wants to know. "In general?"

"I just got here," I say. "But everybody seems pretty shaken up. Which is, you know, understandable, considering the fact that there's a dead girl at the bottom of the elevator shaft."

Dr. Jessup widens his eyes and motions for me to keep my voice down, even though I hadn't been speaking above a whisper. I look around, and realize there are some administrative bigwigs in the TV lounge. Dr. Jessup is hypersensitive about his department being perceived as a caring, student-oriented one. He prides himself on his ability to relate to the younger generation. I realized this during my first interview, when he'd narrowed his gray eyes at me and asked the inevitable question, the one that makes me want to throw things, but that I can't seem to escape: "Don't I know you from somewhere?"

Everyone thinks they've seen me somewhere before. They

just can't ever figure out where. I get "Didn't you go to the prom with my brother?" a lot. Also, "Weren't you and I in one of the same classes in college?"

Which is especially weird, because I never attended a single prom, much less college.

"I used to be a singer" was what I'd said to Dr. Jessup, the day of my job interview. "A, um, pop singer. When I was, you know. A teenager."

"Ah, yes," Dr. Jessup had said. " 'Sugar Rush.' That's what I thought, but I wasn't sure. Can I ask you a question?"

I'd twisted uncomfortably in my seat, knowing what was coming. "Sure."

"Why are you applying for a job in a residence hall?"

I'd cleared my throat.

I wish VH1 would do a *Behind the Music* on me. Because then I wouldn't have to. Explain to people, I mean.

But it's not like I'm *Behind the Music* material. I was never famous enough for that. I was never a Britney or a Christina. I was barely even an Avril. I was just a teenager with a healthy set of lungs on her, who was in the right place at the right time.

Dr. Jessup had seemed to understand. At least, he'd tactfully dropped the subject after I mentioned the stuff about my mom fleeing the country with my manager—and oh yeah, my life's savings—my label dropping me, and my boyfriend, too, in that order. When I was offered the position of administrative assistant to Fischer Hall, at a starting salary that equaled what I used to earn in a week on the concert circuit, I accepted without hesitation. I wasn't seeing much of a long-term career in waitressing—which, for a girl who doesn't even like standing up to wash her hair, can be brutal—and getting a college education seemed like a good idea. I have to wait until I pass my six months' probation—just three more to go—but then I can start enrolling in as many courses as I want.

The first class I'm going to take is Psych 101 so I can see if I'm really as filled with neuroses as Rachel and Sarah seem to think.

Now Dr. Jessup is inquiring about Rachel's mental health.

"How's she holding up?" Dr. Jessup wants to know.

"I guess she's okay," I say.

"You should buy her some flowers, or something," Dr. Jessup says. "Something to perk her up. Candy, maybe."

I say, "Oh, that's a good idea," even though I have no clue what he's talking about. Why should I buy flowers or candy for *Rachel*? Does Elizabeth Kellogg's death affect Rachel more than it affects Julio, the head of the maintenance staff, who'll probably be the person hosing Elizabeth's blood out of the elevator shaft later on? Is anybody buying candy for *Julio*?

Maybe I should just buy flowers for both of them.

"Rachel's not used to the city yet," Dr. Jessup is saying, by way of explanation, I suppose. "This is bound to shake her up a little. She's not a jaded New Yorker yet, like some of us. Right, Wells?" He winks.

"Right," I say, even though I still have no idea what he means. Would a Whitman Sampler be enough, or did he want me to go all the way to Dean & Deluca's and buy a bunch of those petits fours? Which would be okay, because then I can get myself some of those chocolate-covered orange peels.

Except . . . Rachel doesn't eat candy. It's not on the Zone. Maybe I should get her some nuts?

But our conversation comes to an abrupt end when President Allington comes striding into the lounge.

I'll tell you the truth. I never recognize Phillip Allington at first glance, even though I've been seeing him get off the elevators every weekday morning since last June, when I started working at Fischer Hall.

The reason I never recognize President Allington is because President Allington doesn't exactly dress like a college president. His ensemble of choice is white trousers—which he continues to wear well after Labor Day, regardless of Miss Manners—gold New York College T-shirt (tank top for really humid days), Adidas, and, in inclement weather, a gold and white New York College letter jacket. According to another article I found in Justine's files, the president feels if he dresses like a student, he'll be more accessible to them.

But I've never seen a New York College student dressed in the school colors. They all wear black, to blend in with the rest of the New Yorkers.

Today President Allington has opted for the T-shirt rather than the tank, even though the temperature outside is over seventy degrees. Well, maybe he had a meeting of the board of trustees to attend, and wanted to dress to impress.

It isn't until all the other administrators immediately rush over to him to make sure the president knows what an integral part he or she is playing in the resolution of what will no doubt be referred to on Monday in the student-run newspaper as "The Tragedy" that I'm like, "Oh, yeah. That's the president."

Ignoring everyone else, Dr. Allington looks directly at Dr. Jessup and says, "You should do something about this, Stan. This is not good. Not good at all."

Dr. Jessup looks as if he wishes *he* were the one at the bottom of the elevator shaft. I don't really blame him, either.

"Phil," he says to the president. "It happens. In a population this big, there are bound to be some deaths. We had three last year alone, and the year before that, there were two—"

"Not in my building," President Allington says. I can't help thinking that he is trying to sound like Harrison Ford in *Air Force One* ("Get off my plane").

But he sounds more like Pauly Shore in *Bio-Dome*.

This seems to me like an appropriate time to go back to my office. I find Sarah there sitting at my desk, talking on the phone. No one else is around, but there's still a disagreeable amount of tension in the room. It seems to be emanating from Sarah, who slams the phone down and glares at me.

"Rachel says we have to cancel the hall dance tonight." She is practically glowering.

"So?" This sounds like a reasonable request to me. "Cancel it."

"You don't understand. We've lined up a real band. We stand to lose about fifteen hundred dollars from this."

I stare at Sarah.

"Sarah," I say. "A girl is dead. *Dead*."

"And by veering from our normal routine because of her selfish act," Sarah says, "we will only cause her death to be romanticized by the student population." Then, coming down off her grad student high horse for a second, she adds, "I guess we can make back the lost revenue in T-shirt sales. Still, I don't see why we should cancel our dance, just because some nutcase took a dive off the top of an elevator."

And people say *show biz* is rough. They've obviously never worked in a dorm.

Excuse me, I mean, residence hall.

5

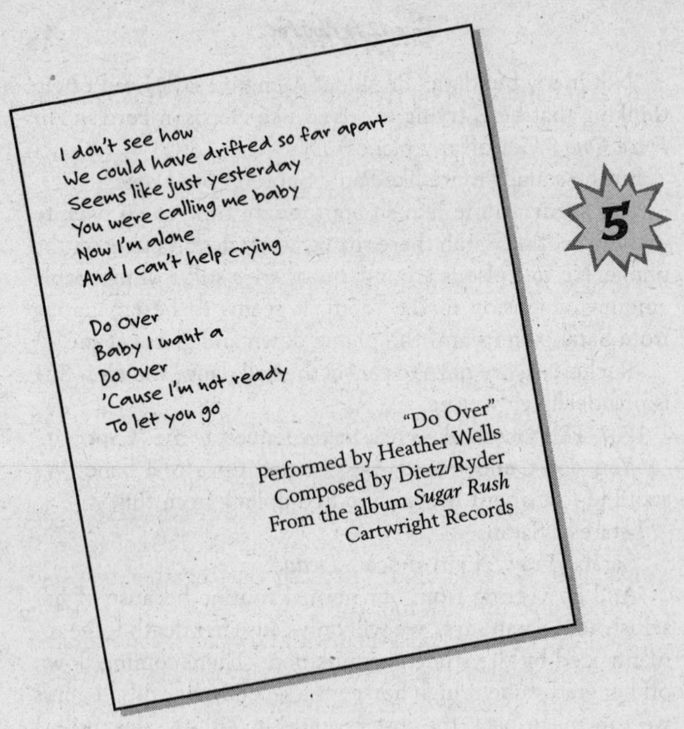
I don't see how
We could have drifted so far apart
Seems like just yesterday
You were calling me baby
Now I'm alone
And I can't help crying
Do Over
Baby I want a
Do over
'Cause I'm not ready
To let you go
"Do Over"
Performed by Heather Wells
Composed by Dietz/Ryder
From the album *Sugar Rush*
Cartwright Records

Being this is New York City, where so many unnatural deaths occur every day, it ends up taking the coroner's office four hours to get to Elizabeth's body.

The coroner arrives at three-thirty, and by three thirty-five, Elizabeth Kellogg is declared dead. Cause of death, pending an investigation and autopsy, is recorded as acute trauma, in the form of a broken neck, back, and pelvic bone, in addition to multiple fractures to the face and extremities.

Call me a dreamer, but I don't think anybody in the student population will be romanticizing her death when they find *this* out.

Worse, the coroner says he thinks Elizabeth has been dead for nearly twelve hours. Which means she's been lying in the bottom of that elevator shaft since the night before.

And okay, he says she died on impact with the cement floor, so death was instantaneous. It's not like she'd lain there, alive, all night.

But still.

There's no hiding the coroner's van, or the body that is eventually trundled out of the building and into it. By four o'clock, the entire student population of Fischer Hall knows there's been a death. They also know, once the elevators are turned back on, and they are finally allowed to take them back to their floors, how she died. I mean, they're college students: They're not stupid. They can put together two and two and come up with four.

But I can't be too concerned with how the seven hundred residents of Fischer Hall are dealing with the news of Elizabeth's death. Because I am too busy being concerned with how Elizabeth's parents are dealing with the news of her death.

That's because it was decided by Dr. Jessup—a decision backed up by Dr. Flynn—that because of Rachel's previous contact with Mrs. Kellogg concerning Elizabeth's guest privileges, she should be the one to make the call to the dead girl's parents.

"It will be less of a shock," Dr. Flynn assures everyone, "for the Kelloggs to hear the news from a familiar voice."

Sarah is unceremoniously banished from the office once the decision is made, but Dr. Jessup asks me to stay.

"It'll be a comfort to Rachel," is what he says.

He clearly hasn't seen Rachel in action in the cafeteria,

cussing out the salad bar attendants for accidentally putting full-fat ranch dressing in the fat-free ranch dispenser, the way I had. Rachel is hardly the type who needs comforting.

But who am I to say anything?

The scene is excruciatingly sad, and by the time Rachel hangs up the phone, I have what feels like an oncoming migraine as well as an upset stomach.

Of course, it could be the eleven Jolly Ranchers and the bag of Fritos I'd had in lieu of lunch. But you never know.

These symptoms are made worse by Dr. Jessup. Chagrined by Dr. Allington's remarks, the assistant vice president has thrown caution and New York City health codes to the wind, and is smoking energetically, his rear end resting against the edge of Rachel's desk. No one offers to open a window. This is because our office windows are on the ground floor, and every time you open them, some wit walks up to them and yells, "Can I have fries with that?" into our office.

It is right then that it occurs to me that Rachel is finished with her phone calls, and that I am no longer needed to be a comfort to her. There is nothing more I can do to help.

So I stand up and say, "I'm going to go home now."

Everyone looks at me. Fortunately Dr. Allington has long since departed, as he and his wife have a house in the Hamptons and they head out there every chance they get.

Except that today Mrs. Allington wouldn't leave through the front door—not with the coroner's van parked out there on the sidewalk, behind the fire engine. I had to turn off the alarm so she could leave by the emergency exit off the side of the cafeteria, the same door through which the security guards usher the Allingtons' more prestigious guests—like the Schwarzeneggers—when they have dinner parties so that they don't have to be bothered by any students.

The Allingtons' only child, Christopher—a very good-looking guy in his late twenties, who wears a lot of Brooks Brothers, and is living in graduate student housing while attending the college's law school—was behind the wheel of their forest green Mercedes when they finally left. Dr. Allington solicitously placed his wife in the backseat, their overnight bags in the trunk, then hopped into the front seat beside his son.

Christopher Allington peeled out so fast that people attending the street fair—oh yes. The street fair went on, in spite of the fire engine and coroner's wagon—jumped up onto the sidewalk, thinking someone was trying to run them down.

I'll tell you something: If the Allingtons were my parents, I'd have tried to run people down, too.

Dr. Flynn recovers from my announcement that I'm leaving before anybody else. He says, "Of course, Heather. You go on home. We don't need Heather anymore, do we, Stan?"

Dr. Jessup exhales a stream of blue-gray smoke.

"Go home," he says to me. "Have a drink. A big one."

"Oh, Heather," Rachel cries. She leaps up from her swivel chair and, to my surprise, throws her arms around me. She has never been physically demonstrative with me before. "Thank you so much for coming over. I don't know what we would have done without you. You keep such a level head in a crisis."

I have no idea what she's talking about. I hadn't done a single thing. I certainly hadn't bought her those flowers Dr. Jessup had recommended. I'd calmed the student workers down, maybe, and talked Sarah out of having her dance, but that's it, really. Not exactly anything life-saving.

I look everywhere but at anyone else's face as Rachel hugs me. Hugging Rachel is a lot like hugging—well, a stick. Because she's so thin. I sort of feel bad for her. Because who wants to hug a stick? I know all those guys who go after models do. But I mean, what kind of normal person wants to hug, or be hugged by, a lot of pointy bones? It would be one thing if she were *naturally* pointy. But I happen to know that Rachel starves herself in order to be that way on *purpose*.

It's just not right.

To my relief, Rachel lets go almost immediately, and as soon as she does, I hurry from the office without another word, mostly because I am afraid I will start crying if I speak. Not because of her boniness, but because it all just seems like such a *waste*. I mean, a girl is dead, her parents devastated. And for *what*? A thrill ride on top of an elevator?

It just doesn't make any sense.

Since the alarm to the fire exit is still turned off, I leave the building through it, relieved that I don't have to pass the reception desk. Because I seriously think I might lose it if anyone says a single word to me. I have to walk all the way down to Sixth Avenue and around the block to avoid running into anyone I know—passing right by Banana Republic, which does carry size 12 clothing, but rarely has any in stock, because, being that it's the most common size, they can never keep enough of it on the racks for everyone—but it's worth it. I am in no shape for small talk with anyone.

Sadly, however, when I get to my front door, I discover that small talk is exactly what I'm in for. Because lounging on my front stoop is my ex-fiancé, Jordan Cartwright.

And I'd truly been convinced my day couldn't get any worse.

He straightens when he sees me, and hangs up the cell phone he'd been jawing into. The late-afternoon sunlight brings out the gold highlights in his blond hair, and I can't help noticing that in spite of the Indian summer heat, the lines pressed into his white shirt and—yes, I'm sorry to have to say it—matching white pants look perfectly crisp.

With the white outfit, and the gold chain around his neck, he looks like he's AWOL from a really bad boy band.

Which, sadly, is exactly what he is.

"Heather," he says, when he sees me.

I can't read his pale blue eyes because they're hidden by the lenses of his Armani sunglasses. But I suppose they are, as always, filled with tender concern for my well-being. Jordan is good at making people think he actually cares about them. It's one of the reasons his first solo effort, "Baby, Be Mine," went double platinum. The video was number one on *Total Request Live* for weeks.

"There you are," he says. "I've been trying to reach you. I guess Coop's not home. Are you all right? I came down as soon as I heard."

I just blink at him. What is he doing here? We broke up. Doesn't he remember?

Maybe not. He'd obviously been working out. Like majorly. There's actual definition to his biceps.

Maybe a dumbbell fell on his head or something.

"She lived in your building, didn't she?" he goes on. "The girl on the radio? The one who died?"

It is totally unfair that someone who looks so hot can be so . . . well, lacking in anything remotely resembling human emotion.

I dig my keys out of the front pocket of my jeans.

"You shouldn't have come down here, Jordan," I say. People are staring—mostly just the drug dealers, though. There are a lot of them in my neighborhood, because the college, in order to clean up Washington Square Park for the students (and, more importantly, their parents), puts all this pressure on the local police precinct to scoot all the drug dealers and homeless people out of the park and onto the surrounding streets . . . like, for instance, the one I live on.

Of course when I'd accepted Jordan's brother's offer to move in with him, I didn't know the neighborhood was so bad. I mean, come on, it's Greenwich Village, which had long ago ceased to be a haven for starving artists, after the yuppies moved in and gentrified the place and the rents shot sky high. I figured it had to be on par with Park Avenue, where I'd been living with Jordan, and where "those kind of people," as Jordan calls them, simply don't hang out.

Which is a good thing, because "those kind of people" apparently can't take their eyes off Jordan—and not just because of the prominently displayed gold chain.

"Hey!" one of them yells. "You that guy? Hey, are you that guy?"

Jordan, used to being harassed by paparazzi, doesn't bat an eye.

"Heather," he says, in his most soothing tone, the one he'd used during his duet with Jessica Simpson on their Get Funky tour last summer. "Come on. Be reasonable. Just because things didn't work out between us romantically is no reason why we can't still be friends. We've been through so much together. Grew up together, even."

This part, anyway, is true. I'd met Jordan back when I'd first been signed by his father's record label, Cartwright Records, when I'd been an impressionable fifteen years of age, and Jordan had been all of eighteen. Back then, I'd truly believed Jordan's whole tortured artist act. I'd believed him when he insisted that he, like me, hated the songs the label was giving him to sing. I'd believed him when he'd said he, like me, was going to quit singing them, and start singing the songs he'd written himself. I'd believed him right up to the point I'd told the label it was my songs or no songs, and the label had chosen no songs . . . and Jordan, instead of telling the label (also known as his dad) the same thing, had said, "Maybe we better talk about this, Heather."

I glance around to make sure his current performance isn't for the benefit of a hidden camera. I totally wouldn't put it past him to have signed up with some reality show. He's one of those people who wouldn't mind watching his own life broadcast on national television.

That's when I notice the silver convertible BMW parked by the hydrant in front of the brownstone.

"That's new," I say. "From your dad? A reward for taking up with Tania Trace?"

"Now, Heather," Jordan says. "I told you. The thing with Tania—it's not what you think."

"Right," I say with a laugh. "I suppose she fell down and just happened to land with her head in your crotch."

Jordan does something surprising then. He whips off his sunglasses and looks down at me very intently. I'm reminded of the first time I ever met him—at the Mall of America. The label—namely Jordan's dad—had arranged for Jordan's band, Easy Street, and me to tour together, in an effort to bring out the maximum number of preteens—and their parents, and their parents' wallets—possible.

Jordan had given me the same intent look then that he was giving me now. His "Baby, you got the bluest eyes" hadn't sounded a bit like a pickup line then.

But what did I know? I'd been yanked out of high school my freshman year and had been on the road ever since, heavily chaperoned and making contact with guys my own age only when they came up to ask for my autograph. How was

I supposed to know "Baby, you got the bluest eyes" was a pickup line?

I didn't realize it until years later, when "Baby, you got the bluest eyes" showed up as a line from one of the singles off Jordan's first solo album. It turns out he'd had a lot of practice saying it. With sincerity, even.

It had certainly worked on me.

"Heather," Jordan says now, as the rays of the sun, filtering through the treetops and apartment buildings to the west, play over the even planes of his handsome, still slightly boyish face. "We had something, you and I. Are you sure you really just want to walk away from that? I mean, I know I'm not exactly blameless in all this. That thing with Tania . . . well, I know how that must have looked to you."

I stare at him incredulously.

"You mean like she was giving you head? Because that's how it looked to me."

Jordan flinches as if I'd hit him.

"See?" He folds his arms across his chest. "See, that's exactly what I mean. When we first met, Heather, you never said crass things like that. You've changed. Don't you see? That's part of the problem. You're not the same girl I knew all those years ago—"

I decide that if he drops his gaze to my waistline, where I've changed the most since ten years ago, I was going to belt him.

But he doesn't.

"You've gotten . . . I don't know. Hard, I guess, is the word," he goes on. "And after what you've been through with your mom and your manager, who can blame you? But Heather, not everyone is out to steal all your money and flee to Argentina with it like they did. You've got to believe me when I say that I never meant to hurt you. We just drifted apart, you and I. We want different things. You want to sing your own songs, and you apparently don't care if doing so destroys your career—what's left of it. While I . . . well, I want—"

"Hey!" yells the drug dealer. "You're JORDAN CARTWRIGHT!"

I can't believe this is happening. First Elizabeth, now this.

What does Jordan want from me, anyway? That's what I can never figure out. The guy is thirty-one years old, six-two, and worth a *lot* of money—way more than the hundred thousand a year Rachel is looking for in her ideal mate. I mean, I know his parents weren't exactly thrilled when the two of us moved in together. It hadn't looked good, two of their most popular teen performers, shacking up . . .

But had our *entire* relationship just been an elaborate attempt to get back at Mr. and Mrs. Grant Cartwright for allowing their youngest son to audition for the Mickey Mouse Club, like he'd begged them to back when he was nine, to his everlasting shame? Because of course *serious* rockers don't have photos of themselves in Mickey Mouse ears being shown in *Teen People* every other week . . .

"Jordan," I say, cutting him off as he is listing the things he wants out of life, most of which have to do with bringing a little sunshine into people's lives, and why is that so wrong? Except that I never said it was. "Could you please just *go away*?"

I jostle past him, my keys in my hand. I guess my plan was to unlock the door and get inside before he could stop me.

With three locks to undo, though, a quick escape is kind of tough.

"I know you don't take me seriously as an artist, Heather," Jordan goes on. And on and on. "But I can assure you that just because I don't write the songs I sing, that doesn't make me any less creative than you are. I do practically all my own choreography now. That move I did on the 'Just Me and You Now' video? You know, this one?" He does a quick step-ball-change, accompanied by a pelvic thrust, on the front stoop of the brownstone. "That's all mine. I know to you that might not be much, but don't you think it's time you took a good look at your own life? I mean, what have *you* been doing that's so artistically fulfilling lately? This stupid dorm thing—"

Two locks down. One to go.

"—and living down here with drug addicts at your doorstep . . . and with *Cooper*! With *Cooper*, of all people! You know how my family feels about *Cooper*, Heather."

I do know how his family feels about Cooper. The same way they feel about Cooper's grandfather, who came out of the closet at the age of sixty-five, bought a bright pink stucco brownstone in the Village, then willed it to his black sheep grandson, who'd moved into the garden apartment, turned the middle floor into a detective agency, and offered the top floor to me, rent-free (in exchange for doing his billing), when he'd found out about my walking in on Jordan and Tania.

"I mean, I know there isn't anything going on between you two," Jordan is saying. "That's not what I'm worried about. You aren't Cooper's type."

He can say that again. Sadly.

"But I wonder if you're aware that Coop has a criminal record. Vandalism. And yeah, he was a juvenile, but still, for God's sake, Heather, he has no respect for public property. That was an Easy Street marquee he defaced, you know. I'm aware that he always resented my talent, but it's not my fault I was born with such a gift—"

The third lock springs open. I'm free!

"Good-bye, Jordan," I say, and slip inside, shutting the door carefully behind me. Because, you know, I don't want to slam it in his face and hurt him, or anything. Not because I still care, but because that would be rude.

Plus his dad might sue me, or something. You never know.

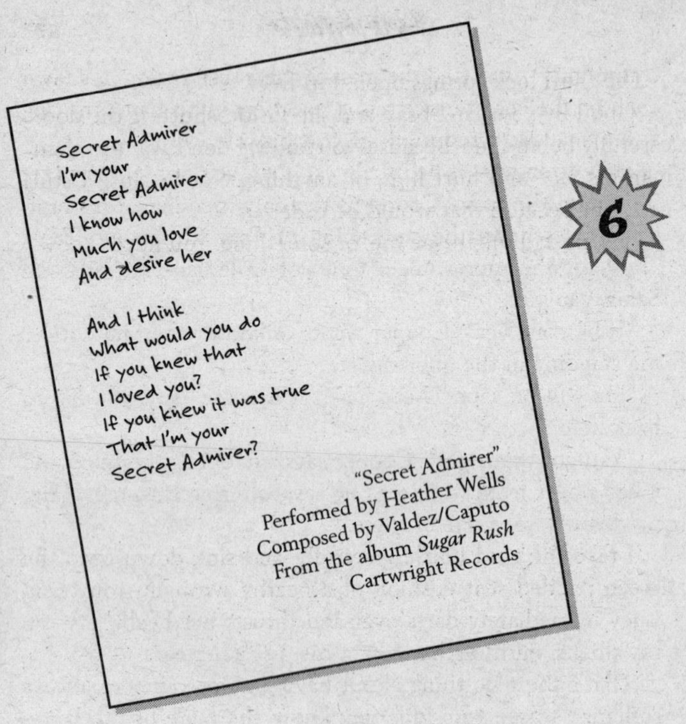

Secret Admirer
I'm your
Secret Admirer
I know how
Much you love
And desire her

And I think
What would you do
If you knew that
I loved you?
If you knew it was true
That I'm your
Secret Admirer?

"Secret Admirer"
Performed by Heather Wells
Composed by Valdez/Caputo
From the album Sugar Rush
Cartwright Records
6

Jordan is pounding on the door, but I'm ignoring him.

It's cool inside the brownstone, and smells vaguely of toner from the photocopier in Coop's office. I start up the stairs to my apartment, thinking Lucy—have I mentioned her? She's my dog—will want to be let out, when I happen to glance down the hall and see that the French doors to the back terrace are open.

Instead of going upstairs, I go down the hallway—Cooper's grandfather had it papered in black and white stripes, which was apparently all the rage in the seventies gay community—and find the man of the house sitting in a lawn chair on the back terrace, a bottle of beer in his hand, my dog at his feet, and a red mini-Igloo at his side.

He's listening—as he usually is, when he's home—to a jazz station on the radio. Cooper is the only member of his family who eschews the screeching of Easy Street and Tania Trace for the more dulcet tones of Coleman-Hawkins and Sarah Vaughn.

"Is he gone yet?" Cooper wants to know, when he notices me standing in the doorway.

"He will be soon," I say. Then it hits me. "Are you *hiding* back here?"

"You got that right," Cooper says. He opens the Igloo and takes a beer from it. "Here," he says, offering it to me. "I figured you'd need one of these."

I take the cold bottle gratefully, and sink down onto the green padded seat cushion of a nearby wrought-iron chair. Lucy immediately darts over and thrusts her head between my thighs, snuffling happily at me. I rub her ears.

That's the nice thing about having a dog. They're always so happy to see you. Plus, you know, there are health benefits. People's blood pressure goes down when they pet a dog. Or even a cat. It's a documented fact. I read it in *People* magazine.

Of course, pets aren't the only thing that can help keep your blood pressure down. Sitting in a really tranquil place can do it, too. Like, for instance, Cooper's grandfather's terrace and the garden below, which are totally two of the best-kept secrets in Manhattan. Leafy and green, surrounded by high, ivy-covered walls, the place is this tiny oasis carved from a former eighteenth-century stable yard. There's even this little fountain in the garden, which Cooper, I see, has turned on. It gurgles comfortingly in the late-afternoon stillness. As I stroke Lucy's ears, I can feel my heart rate returning to normal.

Maybe when I pass my six months' review, and I'm finally able to enroll in school, I'll become a pre-med major. Yeah, it'll be hard to do with a full time job—not to mention Cooper's billing. But I'll find a way to make it work.

And then maybe later I'll get like a scholarship or something to medical school. And then, when I graduate, I can take Lucy with me on rounds, and she can calm down all of my patients. I'll totally eradicate heart disease, just by having my patients pet my dog. I'll be famous! Like Marie Curie!

Only I won't wear uranium around my neck and die of radiation poisoning like I read that Marie Curie did.

I don't mention my new plan to Cooper. Somehow, I don't think he'd fully appreciate its many facets. Although he's a pretty open-minded guy. Arthur Cartwright, Cooper's grandfather, angered by the way the rest of the family had treated him after he'd revealed he was gay, had left the majority of his vast fortune to AIDS research; the entirety of his world-class art collection to Sotheby's to auction, with the provision that all proceeds from the sales go to God's Love We Deliver; and almost all the property he'd owned to his alma mater, New York College . . .

. . . all except his beloved pink brownstone in the Village, which he'd willed to Cooper—along with a cool million bucks—because Cooper had been the only member of the Cartwright family to have said, "Whatever floats your boat, Gramps," when he'd heard the news about his grandfather's new boyfriend, Jorge.

Not that Jordan and the rest of the Cartwrights had been overly worried by Arthur's cutting them off. There'd still been plenty of money left in the Cartwright family bank vault for everyone else.

Still, it hadn't exactly made Cooper, already the family scapegoat for getting himself thrown out of multiple high schools and choosing college over a place in Easy Street—not to mention his tendency to date highly attractive heart surgeons or art gallery owners named Saundra or Yokiko—the most popular member of the Cartwright clan.

Which truthfully doesn't seem to bother him. I've never met anyone who seems more content with his own company than Cooper Cartwright.

He doesn't even *look* like the rest of his family. Dark-haired, whereas the rest of them are blond, Cooper does have the requisite Cartwright good looks and ice blue eyes.

Though his eyes are where any resemblance to his brother Jordan ends. Both are tall, with gangling, athletic builds.

But whereas Jordan's muscles have been honed by a personal trainer several hours a day at his personal home gym, Coop's are from playing aggressive rounds of one-on-one down at the public basketball courts on Sixth and West Third, and from—though he won't admit this—high-speed on-foot pursuits through Grand Central on behalf of whatever client he's currently employed by. I know the truth because, being the one who does his client billing, I see the receipts. There is no way someone can go from a cab—a six-dollar trip ending at 5:01—to a Metro North ticket booth—round-trip ticket to Stamford, departing at 5:07—without running.

Because of all this—the niceness, the eyes, the weekend-hoops thing . . . not to mention the jazz—of course I've fallen madly in love with Cooper.

But I know it's completely futile. He treats me with the kind of friendly nonchalance you'd normally reserve for your kid brother's girlfriend, which is what I am apparently destined to remain to him, since, compared to the women he dates, who are all waiflike, gorgeous, and professors of Renaissance literature or microphysicists, I'm like vanilla pudding, or something.

And who wants vanilla pudding when they can have crème brûlée?

I'm going to fall in love with someone else just as soon as I can. I swear. But in the meantime, is it so wrong that I enjoy his company?

Taking a long sip from his beer, Cooper studies the tops of the buildings around us . . . one of which happens to be Fischer Hall. You can see the twelfth to twentieth floors, including the president's penthouse, from Arthur Cartwright's backyard garden.

You can also see the vents to the elevator shaft.

"So," Cooper says. "Was it bad?"

He doesn't mean my encounter with Jordan. This is obvious by the way he nods his head in the direction of the college campus.

I'm not surprised he knows about the dead girl. He would have heard all the sirens and seen the crowds. For all I know, he could even have a police scanner tucked away somewhere.

"It wasn't pretty," I say, taking a sip of my beer while massaging Lucy's pointed ears with my free hand. Lucy is a mutt I'd picked up from the ASPCA shortly after my mother took off. I'm sure Sarah would say I adopted Lucy as some sort of surrogate family member, since I'd been abandoned by all of mine.

But since I'd been touring all the time, I'd never been able to have a pet, and I just felt like the time had come to get one. Part collie and seemingly part fox, Lucy has a laughing face I'd been unable to resist—even though Jordan had wanted a pure breed, if possible a cocker spaniel. He hadn't been too happy when, instead of Lady, I'd come home with the Tramp.

But that had been all right, because Lucy never liked Jordan anyway, and had promptly shown her disapproval of him by eating a pair of his suede pants.

Strangely, she doesn't seem to have a problem with Cooper, a fact I attribute to Cooper's never having thrown a copy of *Us Weekly* magazine at her for chewing on his Dave Matthews Band CDs. Cooper doesn't even own any Dave Matthews Band CDs. He's a Wynton Marsalis fan.

"Anybody know how it happened?" Cooper wants to know.

"No," I say. "Or, if someone does, they aren't exactly coming forward with the information."

"Well." He takes a swig of beer. "They're just kids. Probably afraid they'll get into trouble."

"I know," I say. "It's just that . . . how could they have just *left* her there? I mean, she had to have been there for hours. And they just left her."

"Who left her?"

"Whoever she was with."

"How do you know she was with anybody?"

"Nobody goes elevator surfing alone. The whole point is that a bunch of kids climb on top of the elevator through the maintenance panel in the ceiling, and dare one another to jump off the roof of their car they're riding on, onto the roof of a second car as it passes by. If there's no one to dare you, there's no point."

It's easy to explain things to Cooper, because he's a very good listener. He never interrupts people, and always seems genuinely interested in what they have to say. This is another character trait that sets him apart from the rest of his family.

It's also one that I suspect aids him in his line of work. You can learn a lot from letting other people talk, and just listening to what they have to say.

At least, it said this once in a magazine I read.

"The whole point is that kids dare each other to make bigger and braver leaps," I say. "You would never elevator surf alone. So she had to be with someone. Unless—"

Cooper eyes me. "Unless what?"

"Well, unless she wasn't elevator surfing at all," I say, finally voicing something that's been nagging at me all day. "I mean, girls don't, generally. Elevator surf. At least, I've never heard of one, not at New York College. It's a drunk-guy thing."

"So." Cooper leans forward in his lawn chair. "If she wasn't elevator surfing, how did she fall to the bottom of the shaft? Do you think the elevator doors opened, but the car didn't come, and she stepped out into the shaft without looking?"

"I don't know. That just doesn't happen, does it? The doors won't open unless the car is there. And even if they did, who would be stupid enough not to look first?"

Which is when Cooper says, "Maybe someone pushed her."

I blink at him. It's quiet in the back of his brownstone—you can't hear the traffic from Sixth Avenue, or the rattling of bottles from Waverly Place as homeless people go through our garbage. Still, I think I might not have heard him correctly.

"Pushed her?" I echo.

"That's what you're thinking, isn't it?" Cooper's blue eyes reveal no emotion whatsoever. This is what makes him such an excellent PI. And why I continue to believe there might be hope for him and me romantically after all—because I've never seen anything in his eyes to lead me to believe otherwise. "Maybe she didn't slip and fall. Maybe she got pushed."

The thing is, that is EXACTLY what I'd been thinking.

But I'd also been thinking that this sounded . . . well, too nuts ever to mention out loud.

"Don't try to deny it," Cooper says. "I know that's what you're thinking. It's written all over your face."

It's a relief to burst out with, "Girls don't elevator surf, Coop. They just don't. I mean, maybe in other cities, but not here, at New York College. And this girl—Elizabeth—she was preppie!"

It's Cooper's turn to blink. "Excuse me?"

"Preppie," I say. "You know. Clean-cut. Preppie girls don't elevator surf. And let's say that they did. I mean, they just LEFT her there. Who would do that, to a friend?"

"Kids," Cooper says, with a shrug.

"They aren't kids," I insist. "They're eighteen years old."

Cooper shrugs. "Eighteen's still a kid in my book," he says. "But let's say you're right, and she was too, um, preppie to be elevator surfing. Can you think of anyone who'd have a reason to want to push her down an elevator shaft . . . providing they could figure out how to do this in the first place?"

"The only thing in her file," I say, "is that her mom called and asked her to restrict her guest sign-in privileges to girls only."

"Why?" Cooper wants to know. "She got an abusive ex-boyfriend the mom wanted PNG'd?"

A PNG, also known as a persona non grata memo, is issued to the dorm security guards whenever a resident—or her parents, or a staff member—requests that a certain individual be denied entry to the building. Since you have to show a student or staff ID, driver's license, or passport to be let into the hall, the guards can easily deny entry to anyone on the PNG list. Once, my first week, the student workers issued a fake PNG against me. As a joke, they said.

I bet they never did that to Justine.

Also, I can't believe Cooper has been paying such close attention to my ramblings about my crazy job at Fischer Hall that he even remembers what a PNG is.

"No," I say, flushing a little. "No boyfriend mentioned."

"Doesn't mean there isn't one. The kids have to sign guests in, right?" Cooper asks. "Did anyone check to see if Elizabeth had a boyfriend—maybe one Mom doesn't know about—over last night?"

I shake my head, not taking my gaze off the back of Fischer Hall, which is glowing red in the rays from the setting sun.

"She had a roommate," I explain. "She's not going to be having some guy spend the night with a roommate right there in the bed across the room."

"Because preppie girls don't do things like that?"

I squirm a little uncomfortably. "Well . . . they don't."

Cooper shrugs. "Roommate could've stayed the night with someone else."

I hadn't thought of this. "I'll check the sign-in logs," I say. "It can't hurt."

"You mean," Cooper says, "you'll tell the police to check the sign-in logs."

"Police?" I am startled. "You think the police are going to get involved?"

"Probably," is Cooper's mild reply. "If they harbor the same 'preppie girls don't do that' suspicions you seem to."

I make a face at him just as the doorbell rings and we hear Jordan bellow, "Heather! Come on, Heather! Open up!"

Cooper doesn't even turn his head in the direction of the front door.

"His devotion to you is touching," Cooper remarks.

"It's got nothing to do with me," I explain. "He's just trying to annoy you. You know, get you to throw me out. He won't be happy until I'm living in a cardboard box on the median of Houston Street."

"Sounds like it's over between you two, all right," Cooper says, wryly.

"It's not *that*. He doesn't still *like* me. He just wants to punish me for leaving him."

"Or," Cooper says, "for having the guts to do your own thing. Which is something he'll never have."

"Good point."

Cooper's a man of few words, but the words he does use are always the exactly right ones. When he heard about my walking in on Jordan and Tania, he called my cell and told me that if I was looking for a new place to live, the top-floor apartment of his brownstone—where his grandfather's houseboy had lived—was available. When I explained how broke I was—thanks to Mom—Cooper said I could earn my keep by doing his client billing and entering the piles of receipts he had lying around into Quicken, so he didn't have to pay his accountant $175 an hour to do it.

Simple as that, I left the Park Avenue penthouse Jordan and I had been sharing, and moved into Cooper's place. After only a single night there, it was as if Lucy and I had never lived anywhere else.

Of course, the work isn't exactly easy. Coop had said he thought it would total maybe ten hours a week, but it's more like twenty. I usually spend all day Sunday and several nights a week trying to make sense out of the piles of scrap paper, notes scribbled on matchbooks, and crumpled receipts in his office.

Still, as rent goes, twenty hours a week of data entry is nothing. We're talking a West Village floor-through that would easily go for three thousand a month on the open market.

And yeah, I know why he did it. And it's not because deep down inside he has a secret penchant for size 12 ex–pop stars. In fact—like Jordan's pounding on the door just now—it's got nothing to do with me at all. Cooper's motivation in letting me move in with him is that, in doing so, he's really bugging the hell out of his family—primarily his little brother. Coop revels in annoying Jordan, and Jordan, in return, hates Cooper. He says it's because Coop is irresponsible and immature.

But I think it's really because Jordan's jealous of the fact that Cooper, when his parents tried to pressure him into joining Easy Street by cutting him off financially, hadn't seemed to mind being poor in the least, and had in fact found his own way in the world without the help of Cartwright Records. I've always suspected that Jordan—much as he loves performing—wishes he'd told his parents where to go, the way Cooper—and eventually me, too—had.

Cooper obviously suspects the same thing.

"Well," he says, as in the background, we hear Jordan shout, "*Come on, I know you guys are in there.*" "Much as I'm enjoying sitting here listening to Jordan have a meltdown on my stoop, I have to get to work."

I can't help staring at him as he puts down his beer bottle and stands up. Cooper really is a choice specimen. In the fading sunlight, he looks particularly tanned. But it isn't, I know, a tan from a can, like his brother's. Coop's tan is from sitting for hours behind some bushes with a telephoto lens pointed at a motel room doorway . . .

Not that Cooper has ever told me what, exactly, he does all day.

"You're working?" I ask, squinting up at him. "On a Saturday night? Doing what?"

He chuckles. It's like a little game between us. I try to trick him into letting slip what kind of case he's working on, and he refuses to take the bait. Cooper takes his clients' rights to privacy seriously.

Also, he thinks his cases are way too kinky for his kid

brother's ex-girlfriend to hear about. To Cooper, I think I'll always be a fifteen-year-old in a halter top and ponytail, proclaiming from a mall stage that I'm suffering from a sugar rush.

"Nice try," Cooper says. "What are *you* going to do?"

I think about it. Magda is pulling a double at the cash register in the caf, and would want to go straight home afterward to wash the smell of Tater Tots out of her hair. I could call my friend Patty—one of my former backup dancers from the Sugar Rush tour, and one of the few friends I have left from back when I'd been in the music business.

But she's married now, with a baby, and doesn't have much time for her single friends anymore.

I realize I'm probably going to spend this night as I spend most other nights—either doing Cooper's data entry or twiddling around with my guitar, a pencil, and some blank sheet music, trying to compose a song that, unlike "Sugar Rush," doesn't make me want to puke every time I hear it.

"Oh," I say casually. "Nothing."

"Well, don't stay up too late doing *nothing*," Cooper says. "If Jordan's still out there when I leave, I'll call the cops and have that Beemer of his towed."

I smile at him, touched. When I *do* get my medical degree, one of the first things I'm going to do is ask Cooper out. He can't seem to resist super-educated women, so who knows? Maybe he'll even say yes.

"Thanks," I say.

"Don't mention it."

Cooper goes inside, taking his radio with him, leaving Lucy and me alone in the slowly creeping shadows. I sit there for a while after he's gone, finishing the rest of my beer, and gazing up at Fischer Hall. The building looks so homey, so tranquil. It's hard to believe it had been the scene of so much sadness a little earlier in the day.

It isn't until it has grown dark enough that lights begin appearing in the windows of Fischer Hall that I finally go inside.

And when I do, it hits me that Cooper's warning when I'd told him I was going to do nothing tonight had been a bit on the wry side. Is it possible that he knows that I hadn't really meant what I said? Is it possible that he *knows* what I do every night . . . and that it isn't nothing? Can he hear my guitar all the way downstairs?

No way.

But then why had he said the word *nothing* like that? So . . . I don't know. *Meaningfully*?

I can't figure it out.

But then, let's face it, guys have always been something of a mystery to me.

Still, when I get out my guitar that night, I play it extra softly, just in case Cooper does come home unexpectedly. I'm not about to let anyone—not even Coop—hear my latest stuff. Not after the way his dad laughed at me the day I played it for him, not too long before Jordan and I broke up.

Angry-girl rocker shit, Grant Cartwright called my songs. *Why don't you leave the songwriting to the pros*, he'd said, *and stick to doing what you do best, which is belting out top forty and power ballads? By the way, have you put on some weight?*

One of these days, I'm going to show Grant Cartwright what an angry-girl rocker *really* looks like.

Later, as I'm washing my face before bed, I look out the window and see Fischer Hall all lit up against the night sky. I can see the tiny forms of students, moving around in their rooms, and can hear, faintly, the sound of music being played from a few of those rooms.

It's true someone in that building died today. But it's also true that, for everyone else, life goes on.

And it's going on now, as girls primp in front of their bathroom mirrors in preparation for going out, and boys chug Rolling Rocks as they wait for the girls.

Meanwhile, through the vents along the side of the building, I see intermittent flashes of light as the elevators glide silently up and down their shafts.

And I can't help wondering what happened. What made her do it?

Or . . .

Who?

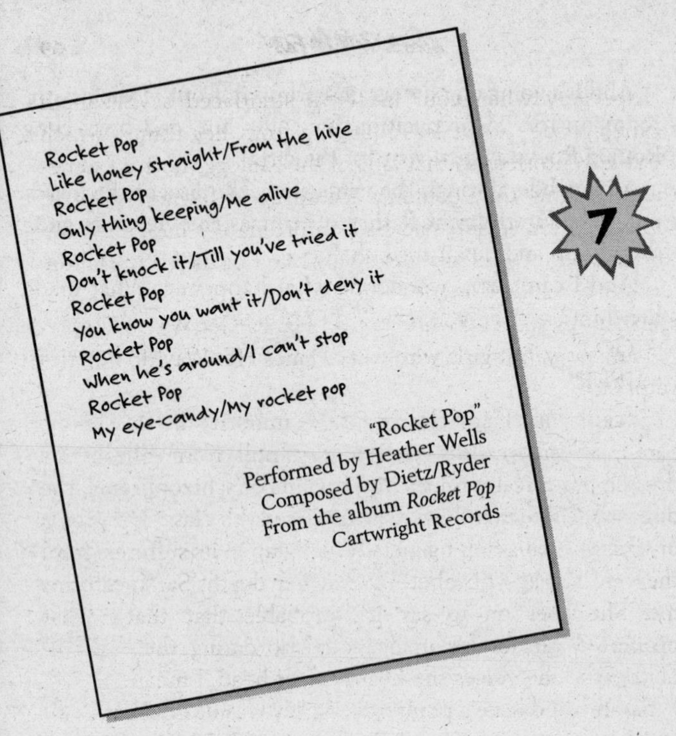

7

Rocket Pop
Like honey straight/From the hive
Rocket Pop
Only thing keeping/Me alive
Rocket Pop
Don't knock it/Till you've tried it
Rocket Pop
You know you want it/Don't deny it
Rocket Pop
When he's around/I can't stop
Rocket Pop
My eye-candy/My rocket pop

"Rocket Pop"
Performed by Heather Wells
Composed by Dietz/Ryder
From the album *Rocket Pop*
Cartwright Records

On Monday, Sarah and I let ourselves into Elizabeth's room to pack up all her belongings.

This is because her parents are too distraught to do it themselves, and ask that the residence hall director's office do it for them.

Which I can totally understand. I mean, the last thing you expect when you send your kid off to college is that three weeks later, you're going to get a call informing you that your daughter is dead, and that you need to come to the city to pick up all her stuff.

Especially when your kid is as straitlaced as Elizabeth seemed to be . . . at least, judging from her things, which Sarah inventoried (so that later, if the Kelloggs noticed something missing, they couldn't accuse us of having stolen it, something Dr. Jessup said had unfortunately happened before in cases of students' deaths), while I packed. I mean, the girl had seven Izods. Seven! She didn't even own a black bra. Her panties were all white cotton Hanes Her Way.

I am sorry, but girls who wear Hanes Her Way do not elevator surf.

Except that I am clearly in the minority in this belief. Sarah, as she records each item I pull from Elizabeth's dresser, pontificates on the finer points of schizophrenia, the disease she's currently studying in her psych class. Symptoms of schizophrenia don't generally show up in its sufferers until they are the age Elizabeth was at her death, Sarah informs me. She goes on to say it's probable that that's what prompted Elizabeth's uncharacteristic daring the night of her death. The voices she heard in her head, I mean.

Sarah could have a point. It certainly wasn't Elizabeth's alleged boyfriend, as Cooper had suggested. I know, because first thing Monday morning—before I even grabbed a bagel and coffee from the caf—I checked the sign-in logs from Friday night.

But there's nothing there. Elizabeth hadn't signed anyone in.

While Sarah and I spend the entire day packing Elizabeth's things—never encountering her roommate, who appears to spend every waking hour in class—Rachel is busy arranging the campus memorial service for the deceased, as well as getting the bursar's office to refund Elizabeth's tuition and housing fees for the year.

Not that the Kelloggs seem to appreciate it. At the memorial service in the student chapel later on that week (which I don't attend, since Rachel says she wants an adult presence in the office while she's out, in case a student needs counseling, or something—the residence hall staff is very concerned about how Elizabeth's death might affect the rest of the building's population, although so far they've shown no sign of being traumatized), Mrs. Kellogg assures all present, in strident tones, that the college isn't going to get away with causing her daughter's death, and that she herself isn't going to rest until the parties responsible are punished (at least according to Pete, who pulled a double and was guarding the chapel doors at the time).

Mrs. Kellogg refuses to believe that any sort of reckless behavior on Elizabeth's part might have brought about her own death, and insists that when her daughter's blood work is returned in two weeks, we'll see that she's right: Elizabeth never drank, and certainly never did drugs, and so was not hanging out with a bunch of trippy elevator surfers the night of her death.

No, according to Mrs. Kellogg, Elizabeth was pushed down that elevator shaft—and no one's going to tell her otherwise.

Mr. and Mrs. Kellogg weren't the only ones going through a hard time in the aftermath of their daughter's death, however. After seeing what Rachel went through that week, I started to understand what Dr. Jessup had meant. About the flowers, I mean. Rachel totally deserved some.

Really, what she deserves is a raise.

But, knowing the college's general stinginess—there's been a hiring freeze since the nineties, which is lifted only for emergency appointments, like my replacing Justine—I doubt a raise is forthcoming.

So on Thursday, the day after the memorial service, I slip out to the deli around the corner, and instead of buying myself a pack of Starburst, an afternoon pick-me-up latte, and a lottery ticket, as is my daily ritual, pick up instead their best bouquet of roses, which I then put in a vase on Rachel's desk.

It's actually scary how excited she gets when she walks in from whatever meeting she's been attending, and finds them.

"For me?" she asks, tears—I'm not kidding—practically springing from her eyes.

"Well," I say. "Yes. I feel bad about all you've been going through—"

The tears dry up pretty quick after that.

"Oh, they're from you," she says, in a different voice.

"Um," I say. "Yeah."

I guess maybe Rachel thought the flowers were from a guy, or something. Maybe she met one recently at the gym. Though if she had, I'm sure Sarah and I would have heard about it. Rachel's way serious about it—finding a guy to settle down with, I mean. She fully stays on top of her weekly manicure and pedicure appointments, and she gets her roots done twice a month (she's a brunette, so she says her gray really shows). And of course she exercises like a demon, either at the college gym, or by running around Washington Square Park. I guess four times around the park is a mile or something. Rachel can go around like twelve times in half an hour.

I have pointed out that she can get the same health benefits from walking around the park that she can from running around it, while avoiding shin splints and knee problems in later life. But every time I mention this, she just looks at me.

"It's been hard on *all* of us, Heather" is what Rachel says now, slipping an arm around my shoulders. "It hasn't been easy for you, either. Don't deny it."

She's right, but not for the reasons she thinks. She thinks it's been hard on me because I've had to do a lot of the grunt work—you know, begging for boxes from Maintenance to put Elizabeth's stuff in, then packing them, then dragging them to Mail Services to ship them, not to mention rescheduling all of Rachel's judicial hearings, dealing with the whiny student workers (who insist they should get bereavement days off from doing the mail, even though none of them actually knew the deceased—Justine would have given them time off, they claim).

But to tell the truth, none of that had been as hard as admitting to myself that Fischer Hall, which I'd come to think of, since I'd starting working there, as one of the safest places in the world, is actually . . . not.

Oh, not that I have any proof that Elizabeth did get pushed, the way Mrs. Kellogg thinks. But the fact that she'd died at all . . . that part has me fully wigging. The students who go to New York College are pretty spoiled, for the most part. They have no idea how good they have it, these kids . . . loving parents, a stable source of income, nothing to worry about except passing midterms and snagging a ride home for Thanksgiving break.

I myself haven't been as carefree as they are since . . . well, since the ninth grade.

And the fact that one of them did something so incredibly stupid as jump on top of an elevator and try to ride it—or worse, jump from the top of one car to another—and that someone else—someone in this building—was there at the time, and witnessed it—saw Elizabeth slip and fall to her death, and yet hadn't come forward . . .

That's what was really freaking me out.

Of course, Cooper is probably right. Probably, whoever was with Elizabeth at the time of her death doesn't want to come forward because he's afraid he'll get in trouble.

And I suppose it's even possible Sarah's right, and Elizabeth could have been suffering from the early stages of schizophrenia, or even a clinical depression, brought out by a hormone imbalance, or something, and that's what made her do it.

But we're never going to know. That's the thing. We're never going to know.

And that just isn't right.

But it doesn't seem to bother anybody but Mrs. Kellogg.

And me.

That Friday—nearly a week after Elizabeth's death—Sarah and I are sitting in the hall director's office, ordering stuff from Office Supply. Not ceramic heaters to give away to our friends, but actual stuff we need, like pens and paper for the copy machine and stuff.

Well, okay, *I'm* doing the ordering. Sarah is lecturing me about how my weight gain probably represents a subconscious urge to make myself unattractive to the opposite sex, so that none of them can hurt me again the way Jordan hurt me.

I am refraining from pointing out to Sarah that I am not, in fact, fat. I have already told her, several times, that size 12 is the size of the average American woman, something Sarah should well know, since she is, in fact, a size 12, too.

But it's pretty clear to me by now that Sarah just likes to talk to hear the sound of her own voice, so I let her go on, since she has no one else to talk to, Rachel being in the cafeteria attending a breakfast reception for the New York College basketball team, the Pansies.

Yes, that's really their name. The Pansies. They used to be called the Cougars or something, but about twenty years ago a bunch of them got caught cheating, so the NCAA dropped them from Division I to Division III, and made them change their name.

As if being called the Pansies isn't embarrassing enough, President Allington is so hot to win the Division III championship this year that he's recruited the tallest players he can find. But since the good ones all went to Division I or II schools, he just got the leftovers, like the ones with the worst academic records in the country. Seriously. Sometimes the players write notes to me about things that are wrong with their rooms, in barely legible handwriting, with many spelling errors. Here's an example:

"Deer Heather. Theirs something wrong with my toilet. It wont flosh and keeps making this sond. Pleaze help."

Here's another:

"To who it conserns: My bed is not long enuf. Can I have new bed. Thanx."

I swear I am not making this stuff up.

Sarah and I don't hear the scream, although later we hear that she apparently screamed the whole way down.

What we do hear are running footsteps in the hallway, and then one of the RAs, Jessica Brandtlinger, skids into the office.

"Heather!" Jessica cries. Her normally pale face has gone white as paper, and she is breathing hard. "It happened again. The elevator shaft. We heard a scream. You can see her legs through the crack between the floor and the car—"

I am up before she's gotten half a sentence out.

"Call nine-one-one," I yell to Sarah, on my way out. "Then find Rachel!"

I follow Jessica down the hall toward the guard desk and the stairs to the basement. Pete, I see, is not at his desk. We find him already in the basement, standing in front of the elevator bank, shouting into his walkie-talkie as Carl, one of the janitors, is trying to pry open the elevator doors with a crowbar.

"Yes, another one," Pete is yelling into his walkie-talkie. "No, I'm not joking. Get an ambulance here fast!" Seeing us, he lowers the walkie-talkie, points at Jessica, and shouts, "You: Go back upstairs and call this car"—he slaps the door to the left-hand cab—"to the first floor and hold it there. Don't let anyone on or off, and whatever you do, don't let the doors close until the fire department gets here and turns it off. Heather, find the key."

I curse myself for not grabbing it on my way downstairs. We keep a set of elevator keys behind the reception desk: an override key, like the ones the Allingtons were issued when they moved in, so they can bypass floors on their way to the penthouse; a key to the motor room for repairs; and a key that opens the doors from the outside.

"Got it!" I yell, and tear back up the stairs, right behind Jessica, who has run back up the stairs to call the elevator to the first floor and hold it there.

When I get to the reception desk, I tear open the door and rush through it, heading straight for the key cabinet, which is supposed to remain locked at all times—only the desk worker on duty is allowed to hold the key.

But with the building maintenance staff, and resident assistants constantly borrowing keys so they can make repairs, clean, or let locked-out students into their rooms, the key cabinet is rarely, if ever, locked, the way it's supposed to be. I find the doors to it yawning wide open as I flash by Tina, the desk worker on duty.

"What's going on?" Tina asks, nervously. "Is it true there's another one? At the bottom of the elevator shaft?"

I ignore her. That's because I'm concentrating. I'm concentrating because I have found the elevator override key, and the key to the motor room.

But the key to the elevator doors is gone.

And when I check the sign-out sheet hanging on the door to the key cabinet, there is no signature for it, or any indication it was ever checked out in the first place.

"Where's the key?" I demand, swinging on Tina. "Who has the elevator door key?"

"I—I d-don't know," Tina stammers. "It wasn't there when I came on duty. You can check my duty sheet!"

Another change to the way Justine had run things that I'd implemented upon being hired—besides the key sign-out sheet—was forcing the desk workers to keep a log of what happened during the shift. If someone borrowed a key—even if they signed it out—the desk worker was still supposed to record the fact on his or her duty sheet. And the first thing a desk worker was supposed to do upon arriving at the desk was jot down which keys were in and which were out.

"Then who has it?" I cry, grabbing the logbook and flipping to the previous desk worker's duty sheet.

But while there are entries for every other key taken during the previous worker's shift, there's nothing about the elevator door key.

"I don't know!" Tina's voice is rising to dangerously hysterical levels. "I swear I didn't give it out to anyone!"

I believe her. But that doesn't help the situation.

I whirl around to run back downstairs and tell Carl to break down the doors, if he has to. But my way is blocked by President Allington who, along with some other administrative types, has come out of the cafeteria to see what all the commotion's about.

"We're trying to have an event in there, you know," is what he snaps to me.

"Yeah?" I hear myself snapping back. "Well, we're trying to save someone's life out here, you know."

I don't stick around to hear what he has to say in reply to

that. I've grabbed the first aid kit from the desk and am racing back down the stairs . . . only to encounter Pete, looking pale, making his way slowly back up them.

"I couldn't find the key," I say. "Someone's got it. He's going to have to force the doors open . . ."

But Pete is shaking his head.

"He already did," Pete says, taking my arm. "Come on back upstairs."

"But I've got the kit," I say, waving the red plastic case. "Is—"

"She's gone," Pete says. Now he's pulling on me. "Come on. And don't look. You don't want to look."

I believe him.

I let him steer me up the stairs. As we enter the lobby, I see that the president is still there, standing around with some basketball players and the same administrators in their gray suits. Beside them, Magda, who has emerged from behind her cash register to see what's going on, makes a bright splash of color in her pink smock and fuchsia hot pants.

Magda takes one look at my expression, and her face crumples. "Oh no! Not another of my movie stars!"

Pete ignores her, goes to the phone by the security desk, and holding up a key chain, on which is attached a student ID card—and a little rubber replica of the cartoon character Ziggy—begins reading the information from the ID card to his superiors at the security office.

"Roberta Pace," he reads tonelessly. "Fischer Hall resident. First year. ID number five five seven, three nine—"

I stand a little ways from both the security and the reception desks, feeling myself begin to shake. I don't know the name. I don't ask to see the photo on the ID. I don't want to know if I knew the face.

It's right then that Rachel rounds the corner from the ladies' room.

"What's going on?" she asks, her gaze going from my face to Pete's to President Allington's.

It's Tina, behind the desk, who speaks.

"Another one fell off the top of the elevator," she says, in a small voice. "She's dead."

Rachel's face drains of all its color beneath her carefully applied MAC foundation.

But when she speaks a few seconds later, there is no tremor in her voice. "I assume the authorities have been notified? Good. Do we have an ID? Oh, thank you, Pete. Tina, beep Maintenance, and have them turn off all the elevators. Heather, can you call Dr. Jessup's office, and let them know what's going on? President Allington, I am so sorry about this. Please, go back to your breakfast . . ."

Aware that I'm shaking and that my heart is beating a million times a minute, I slip back to my office to start making calls.

Only this time, instead of calling Dr. Jessup's office first, I call Cooper.

"Cartwright Investigations," he says, because I've called him on his office line, hoping he'd be there.

"It's me," I say. I keep my voice down, because Sarah is in Rachel's office next door, calling each of the resident assistants on their cell phones and telling them what's happened, then asking them to come back to their floors as soon as possible. "There's been another one."

"Another what?" Cooper asks. "And why are you whispering?"

"Another death by elevator," I whisper.

"Are you serious?"

"Yeah," I say.

"Dead?"

I think about Pete's face.

"Yeah," I say.

"Jesus, Heather. I'm sorry."

"Yeah," I say, for the third and final time. "Listen . . . could you come over?"

"Come over? What for?"

The firemen from Ladder #9 come striding past our office door just then, in their helmets and coats. One of them is carrying an axe. Obviously, no one told New York's bravest what the nature of the emergency was when they called.

"Downstairs," I say to them, pointing to the stairs to the basement. "Another, um, elevator incident."

The captain looks surprised, but nods and leads what has suddenly turned into a very grim procession past the reception desk and down the stairs.

To Cooper, I whisper, "I want to get to the bottom of what is going on over here, and I could use the help of a professional investigator, Cooper."

"Whoa," Cooper says. "Slow down there, slugger. Are the police there? Aren't they professional investigators?"

"The police are just going to say the same thing about this one that they did about the last one," I say. "That she was elevator surfing, and slipped."

"Because that's probably what happened, Heather."

"No," I say. "No, not this time. Definitely not this time."

"Why? Is this latest one preppie too?"

"I don't know," I say. "But that's not funny."

"I didn't mean it to be funny. I just—"

"She liked Ziggy, Coop." My voice cracks a little, but I don't care.

"She liked what?"

"Ziggy. That cartoon character."

"I've never heard of it."

"Because it's like the uncoolest cartoon character ever. No one who likes Ziggy is going to elevator surf, Coop. *No one*."

"Heather—"

"And that's not all," I whisper, as Sarah's voice drifts from Rachel's office, self-importantly intoning, "We need you to come back to the building as soon as possible. There's been another death. I am not at liberty to reveal the details just now, but it's imperative that you—"

"Someone took the key," I tell Cooper.

"What key?" he wants to know.

"The key that opens the elevator doors." I am losing it. I know I am. I am practically crying. But I struggle to keep my voice from shaking. "No one signed it out, Coop. You're supposed to sign it out. But they didn't. Which means whoever has it doesn't want anyone to know. Which means whoever has it can open the elevator doors anytime they want . . . even if there's no car there."

"Heather." Cooper says, in a voice I can't, even in my agitated state, help finding incredibly soothing. And sexy. "This is something you need to tell the police. Right away."

"Okay," I say, in a small voice. In Rachel's office, Sarah is going, "I don't care if it's your grandmother's birthday, Alex. There's been a *death* in the building. Which is more important to you: your grandmother's birthday, or your job?"

"Go tell the police exactly what you told me," Cooper's soothing, sexy voice is saying in my ear. "And then go get a big cup of coffee with lots of milk and sugar in it and drink it all while it's still hot."

This last part surprises me. "Why?" I say.

"Because I have found in my line of work that sweet milky drinks are good for shock when there is no whiskey available. Okay?"

"Okay. Bye."

I hang up, and then I call Dr. Jessup, and explain to his assistant—because she says Dr. Jessup is in a meeting—what's happened. Upon hearing the news, his assistant, Jill, says, in an appropriately panicked voice, "Oh my God. I'll let him know right away."

I thank her and hang up. Then I stare at the phone.

Cooper is right. I need to tell the police about the key.

I tell Sarah I'll be back in a minute, and leave the office. I walk out into the lobby—and find it a sea of confusion. Basketball players mingle with firemen. Administrators are on every available phone, including Pete's and the one at the reception desk, doing damage control. Rachel is nodding her head as the fire chief tells her something.

I glance toward the front door of the building. The same police officer who'd been there the day Elizabeth died is standing there again, not letting any of the kids outside back into the building.

"You'll get back in when I say you'll get back in," the cop is snarling at a skinhead with a lip ring who is going, "But I have to get to my room to get my project! If I don't turn in my project by noon, I'll get an F!"

"Excuse me," I say to the cop. "Can you tell me who is in charge here?"

The cop glances at me, then jerks a thumb in Rachel's direction.

"Near as I can tell, that one over there," he says.

"No," I say. "I mean, is there a detective, or—"

"Oh yeah." The cop nods toward a tall, gray-haired man in a brown corduroy jacket and plaid tie who is leaning against the wall—and, though he probably doesn't know it, getting glitter all down his back, since he's brushing up against a poster urging students to attend an audition for *Pippin* that is heavy on the Elmer's glued glitter. Except for an unlit cigar at the corner of his mouth that he appears to be chewing on, he is doing absolutely nothing at all.

"Detective Canavan," the cop says.

"Thanks," I say to the cop, who is telling another resident, "I don't care if you're bleeding out the eyes. You're not getting back into this building until I say so."

I approach the detective with my heart in my throat. I've never spoken to a detective before. Well, except for when I was pressing grand larceny charges against my mom.

"Detective Canavan?" I ask.

I realize at once that my first impression—that he is doing nothing—was totally wrong. Detective Canavan isn't doing nothing at all. He is staring fixedly at my boss's legs, which look quite shapely beneath her pencil skirt.

He rips his gaze from Rachel's legs and looks at me instead. He has a bristly gray mustache that actually looks quite good on him. Facial hair so rarely flatters.

"Yeah?" he says, in a smoke-roughened voice.

"Hi," I say. "I'm Heather Wells. I'm the assistant director here at Fischer Hall. And, um, I just want to tell someone—the elevator key is missing. It might not mean anything—keys go missing here all the time. But I just thought someone should know. Because it seems really weird to me, these girls dying from elevator surfing. Because, you know, girls just don't. Elevator surf. In my experience."

Detective Canavan, who has listened attentively to my whole speech, waits until my voice peters out before taking the cigar from his mouth and pointing it at me.

" 'Sugar Rush,' right?" he says.

I am so surprised, my jaw becomes unhinged. I finally manage to stammer, "Um, yes."

"Thought so." The cigar goes back between his teeth. "My

kid had a poster of you up on the door to her bedroom. Had to look at you in that damned miniskirt every time I went to tell her to turn down her damned stereo."

Since there is absolutely no reply I can make to this statement, I remain silent.

"What the hell are you doing," Detective Canavan asks, "working here?"

"It's a long story," I say, really hoping he's not going to make me tell it.

He doesn't.

"As my daughter would say," Detective Canavan says, "back when she was your biggest fan, *Whatever*. Now what's this about a missing key?"

I explain it to him again. I also mention, in passing, the part about Elizabeth being a preppie, and Roberta liking Ziggy, and how both of these facts made them highly unlikely candidates for elevator surfing. But mostly I dwell on the missing key.

"Lemme get this straight," Detective Canavan says, when I'm done. "You don't think these girls—who were both, if I understand it, freshmen, new to the city, and full of what my daughter, the French major, calls the *joie de vivre*—were going for joyrides on top of your building's elevator cars at all. You think someone is going around, opening the elevator doors when there's no car there, and pushing these girls down the shaft to their deaths. Have I got that right?"

Hearing it put like that, I realize how stupid my theory sounds. More than stupid. Idiotic, even.

Except . . . except Ziggy!

"Let's just say you're right," Detective Canavan says. "How did whoever is doing this get the elevator key in the first place? You said you guys keep it in a lockbox behind—what is it? That desk there?"

"Yeah," I say.

"And who has access back there? Anybody?"

"No," I say. "Just the student workers and building staff."

"So you think some guy who works for you is going around, killing girls? Which guy, huh?" He points at Pete, standing behind the guard's desk, speaking to one of the firemen. "That one there? Or what about that guy?" He points at Carl, who is still visibly pale, but is nevertheless describing what he'd seen at the bottom of the shaft to a uniformed police officer.

"Okay," I say, starting to feel like I want to die. Because I realize how stupid I was being. In about five seconds, this guy had shot so many holes in my theory, it looked like a big chunk of Swiss cheese.

But still.

"Okay, so, maybe you're right. But maybe—"

"Maybe you better show me where you keep this missing key," Detective Canavan says, and straightens up. I am delighted, as I follow him toward the reception desk, to see that I was right: There is pink glitter all over his shoulders, as if he's been fairy-dusted.

As we approach the reception desk, I see that Tina has disappeared. I throw a questioning look at Pete.

"Packages," Pete interrupts his conversation with the fireman to say to me, meaning that Tina is escorting the mail carrier to the room down the hall where we lock arriving packages until the students can be notified to come down to the desk to claim them.

I nod. Rain or shine, sleet or snow, the mail must get through . . . even if there's a girl lying dead at the bottom of the elevator shaft.

I slip behind the desk, ignoring the phones, which are ringing off the hook, and head straight for the key cabinet.

"This is where we keep the keys," I explain to Detective Canavan, who has followed me through the door to the reception desk and now stands with me behind the counter. The key box is large and metal, mounted to the wall. Inside the box is hanging rack after hanging rack of keys. There are three hundred of them, one spare for every room in the building, plus assorted keys that are for staff use only. They all look basically the same, except for the key to the elevator doors, which is shaped a little like an Allen wrench, and not a typical key at all.

"So to get at them, you have to get back here," Detective Canavan says. I don't miss the fact that his gray eyebrows have raised at the sight of all the mail bags, slumped haphazardly on the floor at our feet. The desk is hardly what you'd call the most secure area in the building. "And to get back here, you have to pass the security desk, which is manned twenty-four hours a day."

"Right," I say. "The security guards know who is allowed behind the desk and who isn't. They're not going to let someone go back here unless they work here. And usually there's a worker behind the counter, anyway, who wouldn't let anybody have access to the keys unless he or she was staff. And even then, we make them sign them out. The keys, I mean. But no one signed the elevator key out. It's just . . . gone."

"Yeah," Detective Canavan says. "You said that. Listen, I got some real crimes—including a triple stabbing in an apartment over a deli on Broadway—that I need to investigate. But plĕase, show me where this elusive key, which could prove that the young lady in question didn't die accidentally, normally hangs."

I flip through the hanging racks, thinking that I'm going to kill Cooper. I mean, I can't believe he talked me into doing this. This guy doesn't believe me. It's bad enough he's seen that poster of me from *Sugar Rush*. If there's anything that can undermine a person's credibility, it's a life-sized poster of her in a pastel tiger print mini screaming into a microphone at the Mall of America.

And okay, my conviction that girls don't elevator surf—particularly preppie, Ziggy-loving girls—may not be what anyone could call rock-solid proof. But what about the missing key? What about THAT?

Except that, as I flip to the rack that normally holds the elevator door key, I see something that makes my blood run cold.

Because there, in the exact place it's supposed to go—the exact place it wasn't, just moments ago—is the elevator door key.

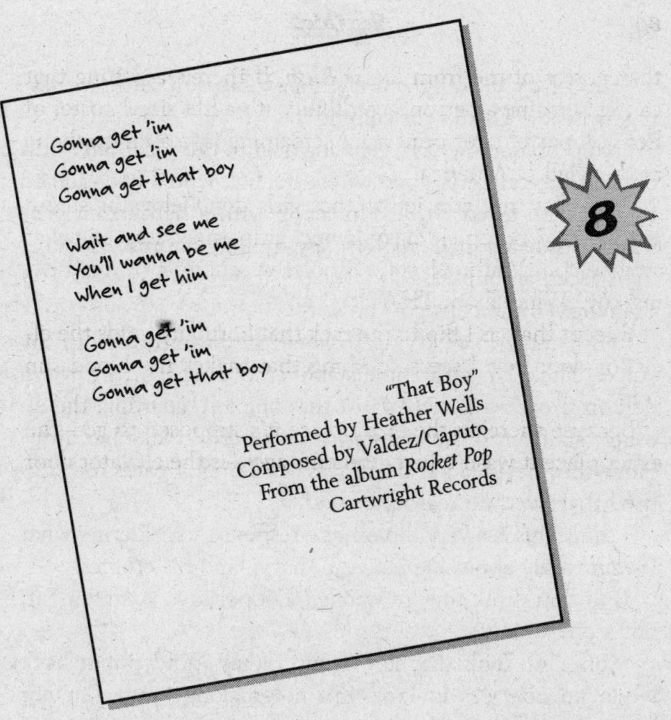
8
Gonna get 'im
Gonna get 'im
Gonna get that boy
Wait and see me
You'll wanna be me
When I get him
Gonna get 'im
Gonna get 'im
Gonna get that boy
"That Boy"
Performed by Heather Wells
Composed by Valdez/Caputo
From the album Rocket Pop
Cartwright Records

He says he'll be here in five minutes, but he's in the lobby in less than three.

He's never been inside the building before, and looks strangely out of place in it . . . maybe because he isn't tattooed or pierced like everyone else who passes by the desk.

Or maybe it's just because he's so much better-looking than everybody else, standing there with his bed-rumpled hair (although I know he's been up for hours—he runs in the morning) and his banged-up leather jacket and jeans.

"Hey," he says when he sees me.

"Hey." I try to smile, but it's impossible, so I settle for saying, instead, "Thanks for coming."

"No problem," he says, glancing over to the TV lounge, just outside the cafeteria door, where Rachel, who'd been joined by an ashen-faced Dr. Jessup, along with a half-dozen panicked residence hall staffers, are milling around, looking tight-faced and upset.

"Where'd the cops go?" he asks.

"They left," I say, trying to keep the bitterness from my voice. "There's been a triple stabbing in an apartment over a deli on Broadway. There's just that one left, guarding the elevator shaft until the coroner can get here to take her away. Since they decided her death was accidental, I guess they figured there was no reason to stay."

I think this is a very diplomatic response, considering what I *want* to say about Detective Canavan and his cronies.

"But you think they're wrong," Cooper says. A statement, not a question.

"Someone took that key, Coop," I say. "And put it back when no one was looking. I'm not making it up. I'm not insane."

Although, the way my voice rises on the word *insane*, that claim may actually be debatable.

But Cooper's not here to debate it.

"I know," he says gently. "I believe you. I'm here, aren't I?"

"I know," I say, regretting my outburst. "And thanks. Well. Let's go."

Cooper looks hesitant. "Wait. Go where?"

"Roberta's room," I say. I hold up the master key I've swiped from the key box. "I think we should check her room first."

"For what?"

"I don't know," I say. "But we have to start somewhere."

Cooper looks at the key, then back at me.

"I want you to know," Cooper says, "that I think this is a bad idea."

"I know," I say. Because I do.

"So why are we doing it?"

I am about five seconds from bursting into tears. I've felt this way since Jessica first burst into my office with the news about another death, and my humiliation in front of Detective Canavan hasn't helped the matter any.

But I struggle to keep the hysteria from my voice.

"Because this is happening in *my* building. It's happening to *my* girls. And I want to be sure it's happening the way these cops and everyone are saying it's happening, and that it's not . . . you know. What I'm thinking."

"Heather," he says. "Remember when 'Sugar Rush' first came out, and all that fan mail started arriving at the Cartwright Records offices, and you insisted on reading it all, and personally answering it?"

I bristle. I can't help it.

"Hello," I say. "I was fifteen."

"It doesn't matter," Cooper says. "Because in fifteen years, you haven't changed. You still feel personally responsible for every person with whom you come in contact—even people you've never met. Like the reason you were put on earth is to look out for everybody else on it."

"That's not true," I say. "And it's only been *thirteen* years."

"Heather," he says, ignoring me. "Sometimes kids do stupid things. And then other kids, because they are, in fact, just kids, imitate them. And they die. It happens. It doesn't mean a crime has been committed."

"Yeah?" I am bristling more than ever. "What about the key? What about *that*?"

He still doesn't look convinced.

"I want you to know," he says, "that I'm only doing this to keep you from making an even bigger mess out of things than they're already in—something, by the way, at which you seem to excel."

"You know, Coop," I say. "I appreciate that vote of confidence. I really do."

"I just don't want you to lose your day job," he says. "I can't afford to give you health benefits on top of room and board."

"Thanks," I say snarkily. "Thanks so much."

But it doesn't matter. Because he comes with me.

It's a long, long walk up to Roberta Pace's room at the sixteenth floor. We can't, of course, take the elevator, because they've been shut down. The only sound I hear, when we finally reach the long, empty hallway, is the sound of our own breathing. Mine, in particular, is heavy.

Other than that, it's quiet. Dead quiet. Then again, it's before noon. Most of the residents—the ones who hadn't been awakened by the ambulance and fire engine sirens—are still sleeping off last night's beer.

I point the way with my set of keys and start toward 1622. Cooper follows me, looking around at the posters on the hallway walls urging students to go to Health Services if they're concerned that they might have contracted a sexually transmitted disease, or informing them of a free movie night over at the student center.

The RA on sixteen has this thing for Snoopy. Cut-out Snoopys are everywhere. There's even this posterboard Snoopy holding a real little cardboard tray with an arrow pointing to it that says, "Free Condoms Courtesy of New York College Health Services: Hey, for $40,000 a year, students should get something free!"

The tray is, of course, empty.

On the door to 1622, there is a yellow memo board, the

erasable kind, with nothing written on it. There's also a Ziggy sticker.

But someone has given Ziggy a pierced nose and someone else has written in a balloon over Ziggy's head, "Where Are My Pants?"

I raise my set of keys and bang on the door, hard, with them.

"Director's Office," I call. "Anybody there?"

There's no response. I call out once more, then slide the key into the lock and open the door.

Inside, an electric fan on top of a chest of drawers hums noisily, in spite of the fact that the room, like all the rooms in Fischer Hall, has central air conditioning. Except for the fan, nothing else moves. There is no sign of Roberta's roommate, who is going to be in for quite a shock when she gets back from wherever she's gone, and finds herself with a single room for the rest of the year.

There's only one window, six feet across and another five feet or so high, with twin cranks to open the panes. In the distance, past the garden rooftops and water towers, I can see the Hudson, flowing serenely along its way, the sun's rays slanting off its mirrored surface.

Cooper's squinting at some family photographs on one of the girls' bedstands. He says, "The dead girl. What's her name?"

"Roberta," I say.

"Then this bed's hers." She's had her name done in rainbow letters on a sheet of scroll paper by a street artist. It is hanging over the messier bed, the one by the window. Both beds have been slept in, and neither roommate appears to have been much concerned with housekeeping. The sheets are tousled and the coverlets—mismatched, as roommates' coverlets so often are—are awry. There is a strong Ziggy motif in the decorating on Roberta's side of the room. There are Ziggy Post-it Notes everywhere, and a Ziggy calendar on the wall, and on one of the desks, a set of Ziggy stationery.

Both girls, I notice, are Jordan Cartwright fans. They have the complete set of Easy Street CDs, plus *Baby, Be Mine*.

Neither of them owns a single CD by yours truly. Which is no real surprise, I guess. I was always way more popular with the tween set.

Cooper gets down onto his knees and starts looking under the dead girl's bed. This is very distracting. I try to concentrate on snooping, but Cooper's butt is a particularly nice one. Seeing it so nicely cupped by his worn Levi's as he leans over, it is kind of hard to pay attention to anything else, even though, you know, this is very serious business, and all.

"Look at this," he says, as he pulls his head and shoulders from beneath Roberta's bed, his dark hair tousled. I quickly readjust my gaze so it doesn't look like I'd been staring below his waist. I hope he doesn't notice.

"What?" I ask intelligently.

"Look."

Dangling from the end of a Ziggy pencil Cooper pulled from the pencil jar on Roberta's desk is a pale, limp thing. Upon closer examination, I realize what it is.

A used condom.

"Um," I say. "Ew."

"It's pretty fresh," Cooper says. "I'd say Roberta had a hot date last night."

With his free hand, he picks up an envelope from the pack of Ziggy stationery sitting on Roberta's desk, then drops the condom into it.

"What are you doing?" I ask in alarm. "Isn't that tampering with evidence?"

"Evidence of what?" Cooper folds the envelope over a couple of times, and sticks it in the pocket of his coat. "The police already determined there hasn't been a crime committed."

"Well, so what are you saving it for?"

Cooper shrugs and tosses away the pencil. "One thing I learned in this line of work: You just never know."

He looks around Roberta's room and shakes his head. "It does seem weird. Who has sex, then goes elevator surfing? I could maybe see it if it were the other way around—you know, all the adrenaline, or whatever, from risking your life, making you randy. But before? Unless it's some kinky sex thing."

I widen my eyes. "You mean like the guy likes to have sex with a girl, then pushes her off the top of the elevator?"

"Something like that." Cooper looks uncomfortable. He doesn't like talking about kinky sex practices with me, and changes the subject. "What about the other girl? The first one. You said you checked, and she hadn't signed anyone in the night she died?"

"No," I say. "But I checked just before you got here, and Roberta didn't sign in anyone last night, either." Then I think of something. "If . . . if there'd been something like that in Elizabeth's room—a condom or something, I mean—the cops would have found it, right?"

"Not if they weren't looking for it. And if they were really convinced her death was accidental, like this last one, they wouldn't have even looked."

I chew my lower lip. "Nobody's moved into Elizabeth's space. Her roommate has the place to herself now. We could go take a look at it."

Cooper looks dubious.

"I will admit it's weird about this kid dying the way she did, Heather," he says. "Especially in light of the condom and the key thing. But what you're implying—"

"You implied it first," I remind him. "Besides, we can *look*, can't we? Who's it going to hurt?"

"Even if we did, it's been a week since she died," he points out. "I doubt we're going to find anything."

"We won't know unless we try," I say, starting for the door. "Come on."

Cooper just looks at me.

"Why is proving that these girls didn't cause their own deaths so important to you?" he demands.

I blink at him. "What?"

"You heard me. Why are you so determined to prove these girls' deaths weren't accidental?"

I can't tell him, of course. Because I don't want to sound like what Sarah would be bound to brand me if she knew—a psychopath. Which is how I know I *would* sound, if I told him what I feel . . . which is that I owe it to the building—to Fischer Hall itself—to figure out what's really going on in it. Because Fischer Hall has—like Cooper—saved my life, in a way.

Well, okay, all they've saved me from is waitressing for the rest of my life at a Senor Swanky's.

But isn't that enough? I know it doesn't make any sense—that Sarah would accuse me of transferring my affection for my parents or my ex onto a pile of bricks built in 1850—but I really do feel that I have a responsibility to prove what's happening isn't Fischer Hall's fault—the staff, for not noticing these girls were on a downward spiral, or whatever—or the girls, who seem too sensible to do something so stupid—or even the building itself, for not being homey enough, or whatever. The school newspaper had already run one "in-depth" report on the dangers of elevator surfing. Who knows what it was going to print tomorrow?

See. I said it's stupid.

Still, it's how I feel.

But I can't explain it to Cooper. I know there's no point in my even trying.

"Because girls don't elevator surf" is all I can come up with.

At first I think he's going to walk out, the way Detective Canavan did, without another word, furious at me for wasting his time.

But instead all he does is sigh and say, "Fine. I guess we've got another room to check."

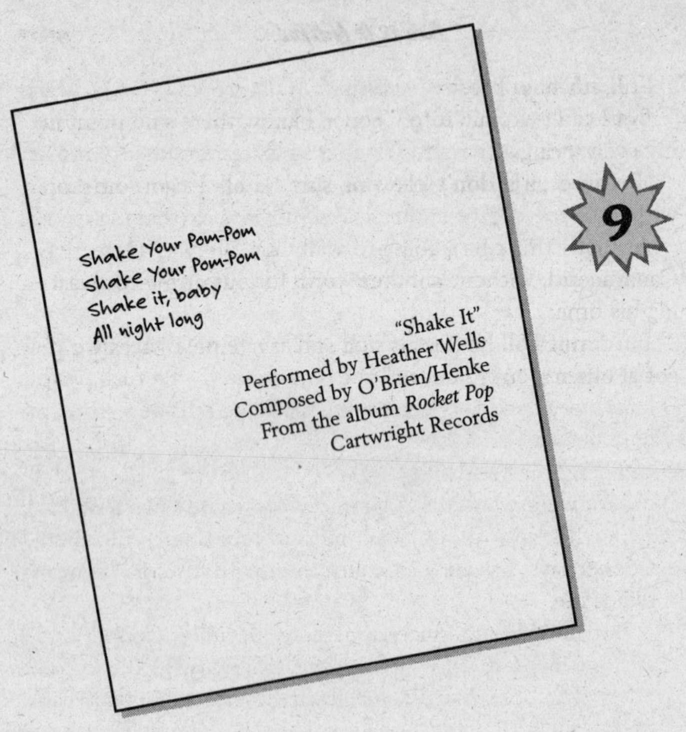
9
Shake Your Pom-Pom
Shake Your Pom-Pom
Shake it, baby
All night long
"Shake It"
Performed by Heather Wells
Composed by O'Brien/Henke
From the album Rocket Pop
Cartwright Records

Elizabeth Kellogg's roommate opens the door to 1412 at my first knock. She's wearing a big white T-shirt and black leggings and she's holding a portable phone in one hand and a burning cigarette in the other.

I plaster a smile on my face and go, "Hi, I'm Heather. This is—"

"Hi," the roommate interrupts me to say, her eyes growing wide as she notices Cooper for the first time.

Well, and why not? She's a healthy red-blooded American girl, after all. And Cooper does bear more than a slight resemblance to one of America's most popular male heartthrobs.

"Cooper Cartwright," Cooper says, flashing the roommate a grin that, if I hadn't known better, I'd have sworn he'd practiced in the mirror and reserved only for extreme cases like this one.

Except Cooper is not a practicing-smiles-in-the-mirror type of guy.

"Marnie Villa Delgado," the roommate says. Marnie's a big girl like me, only larger in the chest than in the tush, with a lot of very dark, very curly long hair. I can tell she's sizing me up, the way some women will, wondering if I'm "with" Cooper, or if he's fair game.

"We were wondering, Marnie, if we could have a word or two with you about your former roommate, Elizabeth," Cooper says, revealing so many teeth with his grin, he nearly blinds me.

But not Marnie, since, apparently deciding Cooper and I are not an item (how could she tell? Really? How come other girls—like Marnie and Rachel and Sarah—know how to do this, but I don't?), she says, into the phone, "I gotta go," and hangs up.

Then, her gaze fastened hypnotically on Cooper, she says, "Come on in."

I slip past her, Cooper following me. Marnie, I see at once, has done a pretty fast job of redecorating after Elizabeth's death. The twin beds have been shoved together to form one king-sized bed, covered by a giant tiger-striped bedspread. The two chests of drawers have been stacked one on top of the other so Marnie now has eight drawers all to herself, instead of four, and Elizabeth's desk is currently being employed as an entertainment unit, with a TV, DVD player, and CD player all within arm's reach of the bed.

"I already talked to the police about her." Marnie flicks ashes onto the tiger-striped throw rug beneath her bare feet and turns her attention momentarily from Cooper to me. "Beth, I mean. Hey. Wait a minute. Don't I know you? Aren't you an actress or something?"

"Me? No," I answer truthfully.

"But you're in the entertainment industry." Marnie's tone is confident. "Hey, are you guys making a movie of Beth's life?"

Before Cooper can utter a sound, I ask, "Why? You think, uh, Beth's life has cinematic potential?"

Marnie's trying to play it cool, but I hear her cough as she takes a drag from her cigarette. She's definitely a for-dramatic-effect-only smoker.

"Oh yeah. I mean, I can see the angle you'd want to work from. Small-town girl comes to the big city, can't take it, gets herself killed on a stupid dare. Can I play myself? I totally have the experience . . ."

Cooper blows our cover, though, by going, "We're not with the entertainment industry. Heather's the assistant director of this building, and I'm a friend of hers."

"But I thought—" Marnie is really staring at me now, trying to remember where she's seen me before. "I thought you were an actress. I've seen you somewhere before—"

"At check-in, I'm sure," I say hastily.

"Your roommate," Cooper says, looking up from a survey he seems to be making of the small kitchen area, in which Marnie has stowed a microwave, hot plate, food processor, coffee maker, and one of those scales people on diets use to measure the weight of their chicken breasts. "Where was she from?"

"Well," Marnie says. "Mystic. You know, Connecticut."

Cooper is opening cupboards now, but Marnie is so confused, she doesn't even protest.

"Hey, I know. You were on *Saved by the Bell*, weren't you?" she asks me.

"No," I say. "You said Eliz—I mean, Beth—hated it here?"

"Well, no, not really," Marnie says. "Beth just didn't fit in, you know? I mean, she wanted to be a *nurse*."

Cooper looks at her. I can tell he doesn't hang around New York College students much, because he asks her, "What's wrong with nurses?"

"Why would anybody come to New York College to study to be a *nurse*?" Marnie's tone is scornful. "Why pay all that money to study here when you can go some place, you know, *cheap* to study to be a nurse?"

"What's *your* major?" Cooper asks.

"Me?" Marnie looks as if she wants to say the word *Duh*, but doesn't want to be rude. To Cooper. Instead, she grounds out her cigarette in an ashtray shaped like a human hand and says, "Acting." Then she sits down on her new king-sized bed and stares at me. "I know I've seen you somewhere before."

I pick up the hand ashtray to distract her—both from trying to place me and from noticing what Cooper is doing, which is some major snoopage.

"Is this yours or Elizabeth's?" I ask her, even though I already know the answer.

"Mine," Marnie says. "Of course. They took all of Beth's stuff away. Besides, Beth didn't smoke. Beth didn't do anything."

"What do you mean, she didn't do anything?"

"What I said. She didn't do anything. She didn't go out. She didn't have friends over. And her mother—what a trip! You hear what she did at the memorial service? The mother?"

Cooper is scouting out the bathroom. His voice, as he calls out from there, is muffled.

"What did she do?" he asks.

Marnie starts fishing around in this black leather backpack on the bed.

"Spent the whole thing saying she was going to sue New York College for not making the elevators more surf proof. And what are you doing in my bathroom?"

"I understand Elizabeth's mother wanted her daughter's guest privileges to extend only to females," I say, ignoring her question about Cooper's presence in her bathroom.

"Beth never said anything to me about that." Marnie finds her cigarette pack. It is, thankfully, empty. She tosses it on the floor and looks annoyed. "But I wouldn't be surprised. That girl was like from another century, practically. I don't think Beth'd ever even *kissed* a guy until a week or two before she died."

Cooper appears in the bathroom doorway. He looks way too big to fit through it, but he manages, somehow.

"Who?" I ask, before he has the chance to butt in. "What guy?"

"I don't know." Marnie shrugs, bereft without her cigarettes. They made nice props, since she was playing the grieving roommate, and all.

"There was this guy she was going on about, right before she . . . you know." Marnie makes a whistling sound and points at the floor. "Anyway, they'd just met. But when she talked about him, her whole face kinda . . . I don't know how to explain it."

"Did you ever see this guy?" I ask. "Do you know his name? Did he go to the memorial service? Was he the one who talked Elizabeth into elevator surfing?"

Marnie balks. "Jesus, you ask a lot of questions!"

Cooper comes to the rescue. As always.

"Marnie, this is really important. Do you have any idea who this guy was?"

For me, she balks. For Cooper, she is more than willing to try.

"Let's see." Marnie screws up her face. She isn't pretty, but she has an interesting face. Maybe good for character roles. The chubby best friend.

Why is the best friend always chubby? Why isn't the heroine ever chubby? Or, you know, not chubby, but a size 12? Or maybe even a 14? Why does the heroine always wear a size 2?

"Yeah, she said his name was like Mark, or something," Marnie says, breaking in on my thoughts on sizeism in the entertainment industry. "But I never saw him. I mean, they started going out just a week or so before she died. He took her to the movies. Some foreign film at the Angelika. That's why I thought it was so strange—"

"What?" I shake my head. "That what was so strange?"

"Well, I mean, that a guy who liked, you know, *foreign* films would be into elevator surfing. That's so . . . juvenile. The *freshmen* guys are into it. You know, the ones with the baggy pants, who look about twelve years old? But this guy was older. You know. Sophisticated. According to Beth. So what was he doing, encouraging her to jump around on top of an elevator?"

I sit down next to Marnie on the enormous bed.

"Did she tell you that?" I ask. "Did she tell you he wanted her to go elevator surfing with him?"

"No," Marnie says. "But he had to have, right? I mean, she'd never have gone alone. I doubt she even knew what it was."

"Maybe she went with some of those freshmen guys you mentioned," Cooper suggests.

Marnie makes a face. "No way," she says. "Those guys'd never have invited her along with them. They're too cool—or think they are—to be interested in someone like her. Besides, if she'd been with them, she wouldn't have fallen. Those guys wouldn't have let her. They're good at it."

"You weren't here, were you, the night she died?" I ask.

"Me? No, I had an audition. We aren't supposed to audition as freshmen, you know"—she looks sly—"but I figured I had a good shot. I mean, come on. It's Broadway. If I got into a Broadway show, I'd quit this place in a New York minute."

"So Elizabeth had the room to herself that night?" I ask.

"Yeah. She was having him over. The guy. She was real excited about it. You know, she was making a romantic dinner for two on the hot plate." Marnie looks suspicious. "Hey—you're not going to tell, are you? That we have a hot plate? I know it's a fire hazard, but—"

"The guy, Mark," I interrupt. "Or whatever his name was. Did he show? That night?"

"Yeah," Marnie says. "At least, I assume he did. They were gone by the time I got home, but they left the dinner plates in the sink. I had to do them, to keep them from attracting bugs. You know, you would think for what we're paying to live here, you guys would have regular exterminators—"

"Did anyone else meet him?" Cooper interrupts. "This Mark guy? Any of your mutual friends?"

"Beth and I didn't have any mutual friends," Marnie says, a bit scathingly. "I told you, she was a loser. I mean, I was her roommate, but I wouldn't have *hung out* with her. I didn't even find out she was dead until, like twenty-four hours after the fact. She never came back to the room that night. I just figured, you know, she was over at the guy's place."

"Did you tell this to the police?" Cooper asks. "About Elizabeth having the guy over the night she died?"

"Yeah," Marnie says, with a shrug. "They didn't seem to care. I mean, it's not like the guy murdered her. She died because of her own stupidity. I mean, I don't care how much wine you've had, you don't jump around on top of an elevator—"

I suck in my breath. "They were drinking? Mark and your roommate?"

"Yeah," Marnie says. "I found the bottles in the trash. Two of them. Pretty expensive, too. Mark must have brought them. They were, like, twenty bucks each. The guy's a big spender, for someone who lives in a hellhole like this."

I catch my breath.

"Wait—he lives in Fischer Hall?"

"Yeah. I mean, he'd have to, wouldn't he? 'Cause she never had to sign him in."

Good grief! I'd never thought of this! That Beth might actually have had a boy in her room, but that there was no record of her having signed one in, because he hadn't *had* to be signed in. He lives in the building! He's a resident of Fischer Hall, too!

I look up at Cooper. I'm not sure where all this was leading, but I have a pretty good idea that it's leading somewhere . . . somewhere important. I can't tell if he feels the same, though.

"Marnie," I say. "Is there anything, anything else at all that you can tell us about this guy your roommate was seeing?"

"All I can tell you," Marnie says, sounding annoyed, "is what I already said—that his name is Mark or something, he likes foreign films, has expensive taste in wine, and that I'm pretty sure he lives here. Oh, and Beth kept saying how cute he was. But how cute could he be? I mean, why would a cute guy be interested in *Beth*? She was a dog."

The student-run newspaper, the *Washington Square Reporter*, had run a photo of Elizabeth the Monday after her death, a photo from the freshmen class yearbook, and Marnie, I'm sorry to say, wasn't exaggerating. Elizabeth hadn't been a pretty girl. No makeup, thick glasses, outdated, Farrah Fawcett–style hair, and a smile that was mostly gums.

Still, photos by school-hired photographers are never all that flattering, and I had assumed that Elizabeth was actually prettier than this photo indicated.

But maybe my assumption was wrong.

Or maybe, just maybe, Marnie's jealous because her roommate had a boyfriend, and she didn't.

Hey, it happens. You don't need a sociology degree—or a private investigator's license—to know that.

Cooper and I thank Marnie and leave—though we couldn't escape without Marnie launching, once again, into a chorus of I-*know*-I-know-you-from-somewhere. By the time we make it out into the hallway, I'm cursing, as I do nearly every day, my decision—or, I should say, my mom's decision—to forgo my secondary education for a career in the music industry.

Trudging back down the stairs in silence, I wonder if Cooper is right. *Am* I crazy? I mean, do I *really* think there's some psycho stalking the freshwomen of Fischer Hall, talking them into elevator surfing with him after having his way with them, then pushing them to their deaths?

When we reach the tenth-floor landing, I say, experimentally, "I once read this article in a magazine about thrill killers. You know, guys who murder for the fun of it."

"Sure," Cooper says dryly. "In the movies. It doesn't happen so often in real life. Most crimes are crimes of passion. People aren't really as sick as we like to imagine."

I look at him out of the corner of my eye. He has no idea how sick my imagination is. Like how at that very moment I was imagining knocking him down and ripping off all his clothes with my teeth.

I wasn't. Well, not really. But I could have been.

"Somebody should probably speak to the other girl's roommate," I say, resolutely pushing away my fantasy about Cooper's clothes and my teeth. "You know, the one who died today. Ask her about the condom. Maybe she knows who it belonged to."

Cooper looks down at me, those ultra-blue eyes boring into me.

"Let me guess," he says. "You think it might belong to a guy named Mark who likes foreign films and has expensive taste in Bordeaux."

"It won't hurt to ask."

"You got a guy on your staff who fits that description?" Cooper wants to know.

"Well," I say, thinking about it. "No. Not really."

"Then how'd he get the key from behind the reception desk?"

I frown.

"Haven't worked that part out yet, have you?" Cooper asks, before I can reply. "Look, Heather. There's more to this detective stuff than snooping around, asking questions. There's also knowing when there's actually something worth snooping around about. And I'm sorry, but I'm just not seeing it here."

I suck in my breath. "But . . . the condom! The mystery man!"

Cooper shakes his head. "It's sad about those girls. It really is. But think about how you were when you were eighteen, Heather. You did crazy things, too. Maybe not as crazy as climbing onto the roof of an elevator on a dare, but—"

"They didn't," I say, fiercely. "I'm telling you, those girls did not do that."

"Well, they ended up at the bottom of a shaft somehow," Cooper says. "And while I know you'd like to think it's because some evil man pushed them, there are nearly a thousand kids who live in this dorm, Heather. Don't you think one of them might have noticed a guy shoving his girlfriend down an elevator shaft? And don't you think that person would have told someone what they'd seen?"

I blink a few more times. "But . . . but . . ."

But I can't think of anything else to say.

Then he looks at his watch. "Look. I'm late for an appointment. Can we play *Murder, She Wrote* again later? Because I've got to go."

"Yeah," I say, faintly. "I guess."

"Okay. See you," he says. And continues down the stairs at a clip so fast, there's no way I'll catch up with him.

Though on the landing below, he stops, turns, and looks up at me. His eyes are amazingly blue.

"And just so you know," he says.

"Yes?" I lean eagerly over the stair railing. *The reason I'm so against you investigating this on your own,* I am expecting—well, okay, hoping—he'll say, *is because I can't stand the thought of you putting yourself in harm's way. You see, I love you, Heather. I always have.*

"We're out of milk," is what he says instead. "Pick some up on your way home, if you remember, okay?"

"Okay," I say weakly.

And then he's gone.

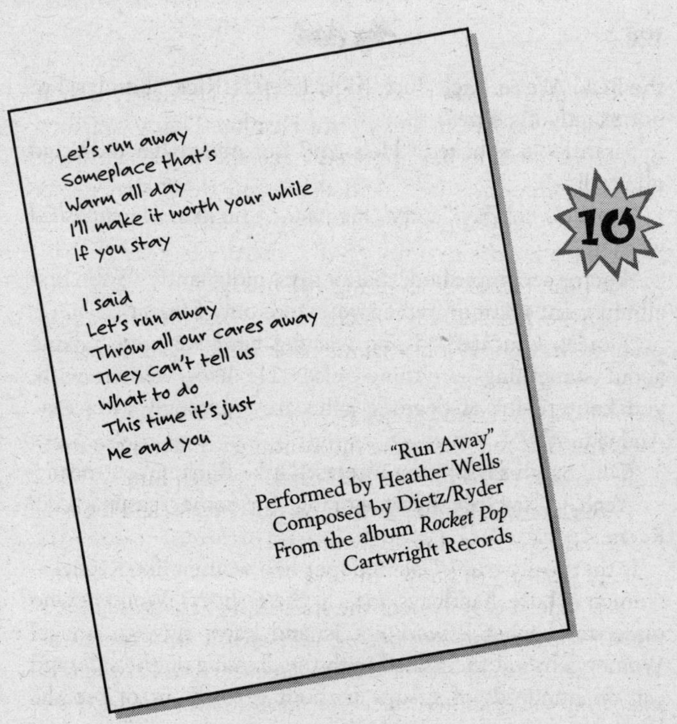
16
Let's run away
Someplace that's
Warm all day
I'll make it worth your while
If you stay
I said
Let's run away
Throw all our cares away
They can't tell us
What to do
This time it's just
Me and you
"Run Away"
Performed by Heather Wells
Composed by Dietz/Ryder
From the album *Rocket Pop*
Cartwright Records

"Who was that?" Sarah wants to know. "That guy who left just now?"

"That?" I slip behind my desk. "That was Cooper."

"Your *roommate*?" I guess Sarah has overheard me on the phone with him or something.

"Housemate," I say. "Well, landlord, really. I live in the top floor of his brownstone."

"So he's cute *and* rich?" Sarah is practically salivating. "Why haven't you jumped his bones?"

"We're just friends," I say, each word feeling like a kick in the head. We're. Kick. Just. Kick. Friends. Kick. "Besides, I'm not exactly his type."

Sarah looks shocked. "He's *gay*? But my gaydar didn't go off at all—"

"No, he's not gay!" I cry. "He just . . . he likes *accomplished* women."

"You're accomplished," Sarah says, indignantly. "Your first album went platinum when you were only fifteen!"

"I mean educated," I say, wishing hard we were talking about something—anything—else. "He likes women with, you know, a lot of degrees. Who are stunningly attractive. And skinny."

"Oh," Sarah says, losing interest. "Like Rachel, you mean."

"Yeah," I say, my heart sinking, for some reason. "Like Rachel."

Is that really true? *Does* Cooper like women like Rachel—women whose handbags match their shoes? Women who understand what PowerPoint is, and know how to use it? Women who eat their salad with the dressing on the side, and can do hundreds of sit-ups without getting out of breath? Women who went to Yale? Women who shower instead of bathe, the way I do, because I'm too lazy to stand up that long?

Before I have a chance to really think about it, Rachel comes running in, her dark hair mussed, but still sexy-looking, and says, "Oh, Heather, there you are. Where have you been?"

"I was upstairs with one of the investigators," I say. It's even true. Sort of. "They needed to get into the dead girl's room—"

"Oh," Rachel says, losing interest. "Well, now that you're back, could you call counseling services and see if they can see someone right away? Roberta's roommate is in a state—"

I perk right up.

"Sure," I say, reaching for my phone, my promise to Cooper that I would quit playing *Murder, She Wrote* promptly forgotten. "No problem. You want someone to walk her over there?"

"Oh, yes." Rachel may have been dealing with a tragedy, but you would never have known it to look at her. Her Diane von Furstenberg wrap dress clings to her lithe figure in all the right places, and none of the wrong ones (the way wrap dresses do on me) and there are bright spots of color in her cheeks. "Do you think you can find someone?"

"I'd be happy to help," I say.

Sure, I feel a twinge of guilt as I say it. I mean, that my willingness to lend a hand has more to do with a desire to question the dead girl's roommate than actually to help her.

But not enough to stop myself.

I call counseling services. Of course they've already heard about "the second tragedy," so they tell me to bring the roommate, Lakeisha Green, right over. One of my job responsibilities is personally to escort students who've been referred to counseling services to the building that houses it, because once a student who was sent over by herself got lost on the way and ended up in Washington Heights wearing her bra on her head and insisting that she was Cleopatra.

Seriously. You can't make this stuff up.

Lakeisha is sitting in a corner of the cafeteria under a kitten poster Magda had hung on the wall to brighten the place up, since, as Magda puts it, antique stained glass windows and mahogany wainscoting are just plain "ugly on the eye." Magda is there, too, trying to coax Lakeisha into eating some Gummi Bears.

"Just a few?" Magda is saying, as she dangles a plastic bag full of them in front of Lakeisha's face. "Please? You can have them for free. I know you like them, last night you bought a bag with your friends."

Lakeisha—just to be polite, you can tell—takes the bag. "Thank you," she murmurs.

Magda beams, then, when she notices me, whispers, "My poor little movie star. She won't eat a thing."

Then, in an even lower voice, Magda asks, "Who was that man Pete and I saw you with today, Heather? The handsome one?"

"That was Cooper," I say, since I've told Magda all about Cooper . . . as one does, naturally, discuss hotties over sloppy joes on one's lunch break.

"*That* was Cooper?" Magda looks aghast. "Oh, honey, no wonder—"

"No wonder what?"

"Oh, never mind." Magda pats me on the arm in a gesture that would have been comforting if I hadn't, you know, been terrified of being poked by one her nails. "It will turn out all right. Maybe."

"Uh, thanks." I'm not at all sure what she was talking about . . . or that I wanted to know. I turn my attention to Roberta Pace's roommate.

Lakeisha looks really, really sad. Her hair is done up in braids all over her head, and at the end of each braid is a brightly colored bead. The beads click together whenever Lakeisha moves her head.

"Lakeisha," I say, gently. "I understand you have an appointment to speak to someone at counseling services. I'm here to walk you there. Are you ready to go?"

Lakeisha nods. But she doesn't stand up. I glance at Magda.

"Maybe she wants a rest," Magda says. "Does my little movie star want a rest?"

Lakeisha hesitates a moment. Then she says, "No, it's okay. Let's go."

"You sure you don't want a DoveBar?" Magda asks. Because DoveBars are, actually, the solution to nearly every problem in the universe.

But Lakeisha just shakes her head, causing her hair beads to rattle musically.

Which is surely how she stays so skinny. Refusing DoveBars when offered, I mean. I can't remember ever turning down an offer of free ice cream. Especially a DoveBar.

Our walk out of the building is slow-paced and somber. They are letting students back into the building a few at a time, with the warning that they'll have to use the stairs to get to their rooms. As one might expect in such a small community, word of another death has spread fast, and when the students see Lakeisha and me leaving the building together, there is a lot of whispering—"That's the roommate," I hear, and someone else responding, "Oh, poor thing." Lakeisha either doesn't hear it or chooses to ignore it. She walks with her head held high, but her gaze lowered.

We're standing on the street corner, waiting for the crossing sign to change, when I finally get the courage to bring up what I want to know.

"Lakeisha," I say. "Do you know if Roberta had a date last night?"

Lakeisha looks over at me like she's seeing me for the first time. She's a tiny little thing, all cheekbones and knees. The little bag of Gummi Bears Magda had pressed on her, and which she still carries, seems to be weighing her down.

She says, "Excuse me?" in a soft voice.

"Your roommate. Did she have a date last night?"

"I think so. I don't really know," Lakeisha replies, in an apologetic whisper that's hard to hear above the sound of all the traffic. "I went out last night—I had dance rehearsal at eight. Bobby was asleep by the time I got back. It was real late, after midnight. And she was still asleep when I went down to breakfast this morning."

Bobby. Had they been close, Lakeisha and her Ziggy-loving roommate? They must have been, if she'd called her Bobby. What am I doing, interrogating the poor girl this way, after she's had such a shock?

Is Jordan right? About what he'd accused me the other day. Had I turned hard?

I guess so, since next thing I knew, I was trying again.

"The reason I ask, Lakeisha—" I feel like a total and complete heel. Maybe it's all right, you know, if you feel like a jerk. Know what I mean? I mean, I've read that crazy people—sorry, I mean mentally disturbed people—never consider themselves mentally disturbed. So maybe real jerks never consider themselves jerks. So the fact that I *feel* like a jerk means that I couldn't possibly *be* one . . .

I'll have to remember to ask Sarah.

"The reason I ask is that the police"—slight lie, but oh well—"the police found a used condom under Roberta's bed this morning. It was, uh, pretty fresh."

This seems to clear a little of the fog out of Lakeisha's head. She looks at me, and this time, I can tell she really sees me.

"Excuse me?" she asks, in a stronger voice.

"A condom. Under Roberta's bed. It had to have been from last night."

"No way," Lakeisha says, firmly. "There is no way. Not Bobby. She's never—" She breaks off and studies her Nikes. "No," she says, again, and shakes her head with such force that the beads on the ends of her braids click like castanets.

"Well, someone had to have left that condom," I say. "If it wasn't Roberta, who—"

"Oh my God" Lakeisha suddenly interrupts, with actual excitement in her voice. "It had to be Todd!"

"Who's Todd?"

"Todd is the man. Bobby's man. The new man. Bobby never had a man before."

"Oh," I say, somewhat taken aback by this information. "She was . . . um—"

"A virgin, yeah," Lakeisha says, distractedly. She's still trying to digest the information I've given her. "They must have—they must have done the deed after I left. He must have come over! She musta been so excited."

Then Lakeisha's excitement dies and she shakes her head again. "Then she had to go and do something so stupid—"

Okay. Now we were getting somewhere.

I slow down my pace, and Lakeisha slows hers as well, unconsciously. We are within two blocks of the counseling center.

"So elevator surfing wasn't something your roommate did regularly?" I ask, even though I already know the answer.

"Bobby?" Lakeisha's voice breaks. "Elevator surf? No! Never. Why would she go and do something so stupid? She's a smart girl—*was* a smart girl," she corrects herself. "Too smart for that, anyway. Besides," she adds. "Bobby was afraid of heights. She never even wanted to look out the window, she thought we were up too high as it was."

I knew it. I *knew* it. Someone had pushed her. It's the only explanation.

"So this Todd guy," I say, trying not to let my eagerness show. Also the fact that my heart had begun slamming a mile a minute inside my chest. "When did Roberta meet him?"

"Oh, last week, at the dance."

"Dance?"

"The dance in the cafeteria."

We'd ended up not canceling the dance that had been planned for the night of Elizabeth's death. Sarah hadn't been the only one to throw a fit at the suggestion—the student government had rebelled as well, and Rachel had caved. The dance ended up being very well attended and there'd only been a single moment of unpleasantness, and that was when some Jordan Cartwright fans got all riled up over the music selection, and nearly came to blows with some residents who preferred Justin Timberlake.

"Todd was there," Lakeisha says. "He and Bobby started hanging out together that night."

"This Todd," I say. "Do you know his last name?"

"No." Lakeisha looks momentarily troubled. Then her face brightens. "He lives in the building, though."

"He does? How do you know?"

" 'Cause Bobby never had to sign him in."

"And this Todd guy—" I'm practically holding my breath. "You met him?"

"Not met him, but Bobby pointed him out to me at the dance. He was kinda of far away, though."

"What'd he look like?"

"Tall."

When Lakeisha doesn't go on, I prompt, "That's it? He was tall?"

Lakeisha shrugs.

"He was white," she says, apologetically. "White guys . . . they all. You know."

Right. Everyone knows all white guys look the same.

"Do you think this Todd guy"—now Lakeisha is calling him "this Todd guy," too—"had something to do with . . . what happened to Bobby?"

"I don't know," I say. And as I say it, I realize we're at the building that houses the campus counseling services. So fast! I'm disappointed. "Oh. Well, Lakeisha, this is it."

Lakeisha looks up at the double doors without seeming

really to see them. Then she says to me, "You don't think—you don't think this Todd guy . . . *pushed* her, or anything, do you?"

My heart slows, then seems to stop altogether.

"I don't know," I say carefully. "Why? Do you? Did Roberta mention that he was . . . abusive?"

"No." Lakeisha shakes her head. The beads click and rattle. "That's just it. She was so happy. Why would she do something so dumb?" Lakeisha's eyes fill with tears. "Why would she do a thing like that, if she'd found the guy of her dreams?"

My feelings, exactly.

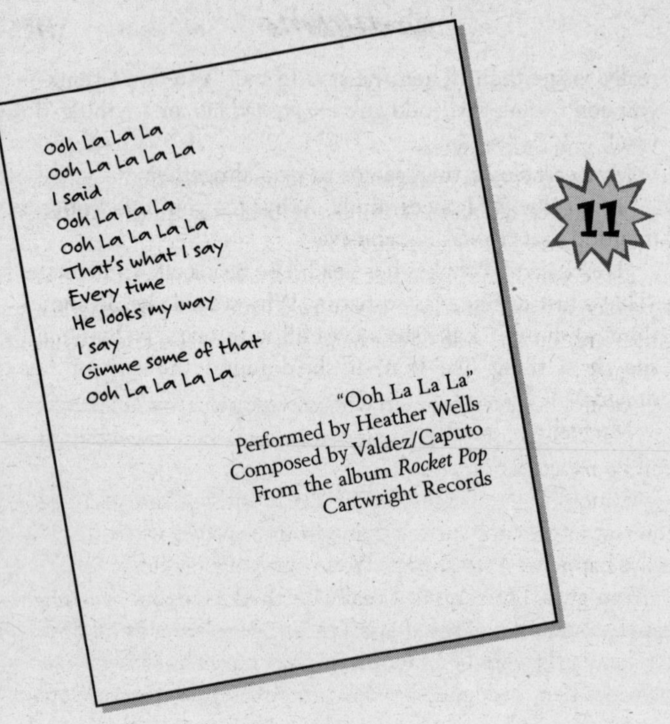
Ooh La La La
Ooh La La La La
I said
Ooh La La La
Ooh La La La La
That's what I say
Every time
He looks my way
I say
Gimme some of that
Ooh La La La La

"Ooh La La La"
Performed by Heather Wells
Composed by Valdez/Caputo
From the album *Rocket Pop*
Cartwright Records

11

I fill Magda and Pete in on the whole thing during our lunch break. I tell them what's going on, including the part about Cooper—

But not that I'm madly in love with him or anything. Which of course makes the story much shorter and far less interesting.

Pete's only response is to scoop up a forkful of chili and eye it dubiously.

"Are there carrots in this? You know I hate carrots."

"Pete, didn't you hear me? I said I think—"

"I heard you," Pete interrupts.

"Oh. Well, don't you think—"

"No."

"But you didn't even—"

"Heather," Pete says, carefully placing the offending carrot on the side of his plate. "I think you been watching way too much *Law and Order: Special Victims Unit.*"

"I love you, honey" is what Magda has to say about it. "But let's face it. Everyone knows you're a little bit"—she twirls a finger around one side of her head—"cuckoo. You know what I mean?"

I cannot believe a woman who would spend *five hours* having the Statue of Liberty air-brushed on her fingernails is calling *me* cuckoo.

"C'mon." I glare at them. "Two girls with no history of an interest in elevator surfing dying from it in two weeks?"

"It happens." Pete shrugs. "You want your pickle?"

"You guys, I'm serious. I really do think someone is pushing these girls down the shafts. I mean, there's a pattern. Both of these girls were late bloomers. They never had boyfriends before. Then, suddenly, a week before they died, they both got boyfriends—"

"Maybe," Magda suggests, "they did it because after saving themselves for the right man for all those years, they found out sex wasn't so great after all."

All conversation ceases after that, because Pete's choking on his Snapple.

The rest of the day is a blur. Because the two deaths occur so close together in the semester, we're bombarded by the press, mostly the *Post* and the *News,* but a *Times* reporter calls as well.

Then there's the memo Rachel insists on sending to all the residents, letting them know that a counselor will be on hand twenty-four hours a day this weekend to help them all through their grief. This means I have to make seven hundred photocopies, then talk the student worker into stuffing the memos into three hundred mailboxes, two for each double room, and three for the triples.

At first Tina, the desk worker, outright refuses. Justine, it seems, had always simply made one copy per floor, then hung them next to each set of elevators.

But Rachel wants each resident to receive his or her *own* copy. I have to tell Tina that I don't care how Justine had done things, that this is how *I* want things done. To which Tina actually replies, dramatically, "Nobody cares about what happened to Justine! She was the best boss in the world, and they fired her for *no good reason*! I saw her crying the day she found out! I *know*! New York College is so *unfair*!"

I want to point out that Justine was probably crying tears of relief that she'd only been fired and not prosecuted for what she'd done.

But I'm not supposed to mention the fact that Justine had been fired for theft in front of the students—kind of for the same reason we're not supposed to call the place we work a dorm. Because it doesn't foster a real feeling of security.

Instead, I promise to pay Tina time and a half to get the memos distributed. This cheers her right up.

By the time I get home—with milk—it's nearly six. There's no sign of Cooper—he's probably on a stakeout, or whatever it is private eyes do all day. Which is fine, because I have plenty to keep myself occupied. I've smuggled home a building roster, and I'm going through it, circling every resident named Mark or Todd. Later, I'm going to call each one, using the building phone book, and ask them if they knew Elizabeth or Roberta.

I'm not really sure what I'm going to say if any of them say yes. I guess I can't come right out and be all "So . . . did you shove her down the elevator shaft?" But I figure I will deal with that when the time comes.

I am just settling down in front of the roster with a glass of wine and some biscotti I found in the cupboard when the doorbell rings.

And I remember, with an almost physical jolt, that I volunteered to babysit for Patty's kid tonight.

Patty takes one look at me after I open the door and knows. She goes, "What happened?"

"Nothing," I assure her, taking Indy from her arms. "Well, I mean, something, but nothing happened to me. Another girl died today. That's all."

"Another one?" Frank, Patty's husband, looks delighted. There's something about violent death that makes some people very excited. Frank is evidently one of them. "How'd she do it? OD?"

"She fell off the top of one of the elevators," I say, as Patty elbows Frank, hard enough to make him go *unngh*. "Or at least, that's as close as we can figure out. And it's okay. Really. I'm all right."

"You be nice to her," Patty says to her husband. "She's had a bad day."

Patty has a tendency to get fussy when she's going out. She isn't comfortable in evening clothes—maybe because she still hasn't lost all of the baby weight yet. For a while, Patty and I tried going power walking through SoHo in the evenings, as part of our efforts to do our government-suggested sixty minutes of exercise per day.

But Patty couldn't seem to pass by a shop window without stopping, then asking, "Do you think those shoes would look good on me?" then going inside and buying them.

And I couldn't pass a bakery without going in and buying a baguette.

So we had to stop walking, because Patty's closets are full enough as it is, and who needs that much bread?

Besides, Patty has nowhere to wear all her new stuff. She's basically a homebody at heart, which, for a rock star's wife, is not a good thing.

And Frank Robillard is a rock star with a capital S. He makes Jordan look like Yanni. Patty met him when they were both doing Letterman—he was singing, she was one of those showgirls who stands around holding the cold cuts party platter—and it was love at first sight. You know, the kind you read about, but that never happens to you. That kind.

"Cut it out, Frank," Patty says to her one true love. "We're going to be late."

But Frank is prowling around the office, looking at Cooper's stuff.

"He shot anybody yet?" he asks, meaning Cooper.

"If he had, he wouldn't tell me," I say.

Since I've moved in with Cooper, my stock has gone way up with Frank. He never liked Jordan, but Cooper is his hero. He'd even gone out and bought a leather jacket just like Cooper's—used, so it's already broken in. Frank doesn't understand that being a private investigator in real life isn't like how it is on TV. I mean, Cooper doesn't even own a gun. All you need to do Cooper's job is a camera and an ability to blend with your environment.

Cooper's surprisingly good, it turns out, at blending.

"So, you two going out yet?" Frank asks, out of the blue. "You and Cooper?"

"Frank!" Patty screams.

"No, Frank," I say, for what has to be the three hundredth time this month alone.

"Frank," Patty says. "Cooper and Heather are roommates. You can't go out with your roommate. You know how that is. I mean, all the romance is gone once you've seen someone in their bathrobe. Right, Heather?"

I blink at her. I have never thought of this. What if Patty is right? Cooper is never going to think of me as date-worthy—even if I win a Nobel Prize in medicine. Because he's seen me too many times in sweat pants! With no makeup!

Patty and Frank say their good-byes, then Indy and I stand and wave to them as they go down my front steps and climb back into their waiting limo. The drug dealers on my street watch from a respectful distance. They all worship Frank's band. I am convinced that the reason Cooper's house is never graffitied or robbed is because everyone in the neighborhood knows that we're friends with the voice of the people, Frank Robillard, and so the place is off-limits.

Or maybe it's because of the alarm and the bars on all the ground and first floor windows. Who knows?

Indy and I spend a pleasant evening watching *Forensic Files* and *The New Detectives* on the TV in my bedroom, where I'm able to keep an eye on both my best friend's child and the back of Fischer Hall. Looking up at the tall brick building, with so many of its lights ablaze, I can't help remembering what Magda had said—her joke about Elizabeth and Roberta ending it all over discovering that sex isn't all it was cracked up to be. Bobby had been a virgin . . . at least according to her roommate. And it seemed likely that Elizabeth Kellogg had been one as well.

Is that it? Is that the link between the two girls? Is someone killing the virgins of Fischer Hall?

Or have I seen one too many episodes of *CSI*?

When Patty and Frank arrive to pick up their progeny just after midnight, I hand him over at the front door. He'd passed out during *Crossing Jordan*.

"How was he?" Patty asks.

"Perfect, as always," I say.

"For you, maybe," she says with a snort as she shifts the sleeping baby in her arms. Frank is waiting in the limo below. "You're so good with him. You should have one of your own someday."

"Twist the knife, why don't you," I say.

"I'm sorry," Patty says. "I love having you sit for us, but you do realize you've never once said you couldn't because you were busy? Heather, you've got to get back out there. Not just with your music, either. You've got to try to meet someone."

"I meet plenty of people," I say defensively.

"I mean someone who isn't a freshman at New York College."

"Yeah," I say. "Well, it's easy for you to criticize. You've got the perfect husband. You don't know what it's like in real life. You think Jordan was an anomaly? Patty, he's the *norm*."

"That isn't true," Patty says. "You'll find someone. You just can't be afraid to take a risk."

What is she talking about? I do nothing but take risks. I'm trying to keep a psychopath from killing again. Isn't that enough? I have to have a ring on my finger, too?

Some people are never satisfied.

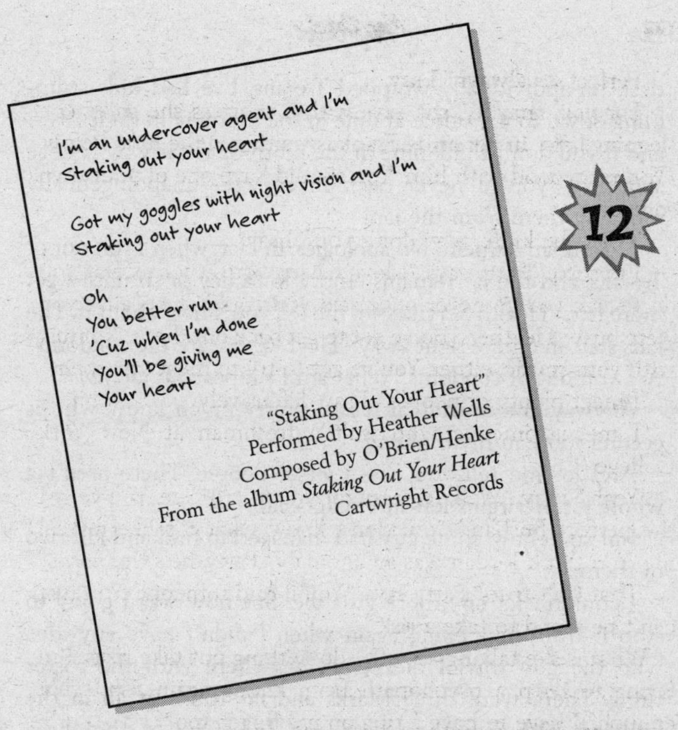

I'm an undercover agent and I'm
Staking out your heart
Got my goggles with night vision and I'm
Staking out your heart
Oh
You better run
'Cuz when I'm done
You'll be giving me
Your heart
"Staking Out Your Heart"
Performed by Heather Wells
Composed by O'Brien/Henke
From the album Staking Out Your Heart
Cartwright Records
12

No matter how much I try to shake it, the thought stays with me all weekend. The Virgins of Fischer Hall.

I know it sounds insane. But I just kept thinking about it.

Maybe Patty's right, and the kids in the dorm—residence hall, I mean—are taking up the space in my heart where love for my own kids would be if, you know, I had any. Because I can't stop worrying about them.

Not that there can be that many more virgins left in the building—which I happen to be in a position to know. Ever since I swapped the Hershey's Kisses in the candy jar on my desk for individually wrapped Trojans, I've had kids stumbling down to my office at nine in the morning in their PJs—and if you don't think nine in the morning is early by college standards, you've never been in college—unapologetically plucking them from the jar.

No embarrassment. No apologies. In fact, when I run out of Trojans, and the jar remains empty for a day or so until I get more from Health Services, let me tell you, I hear about it. The kids start in on me right away: "Hey! Where are the condoms? Are you out of condoms? What am I supposed to do *now*?"

Anyway, the upshot of it is, I pretty much know who is getting some in my building.

And let me tell you, it's a *lot* of people. There aren't a whole lot of virgins left in Fischer Hall.

But somehow, some guy had managed to find and kill two of them.

I couldn't let any more girls die. But how was I going to stop it from happening again when I didn't have any idea who the guy was? I didn't get anywhere with the roster thing. There were three Marks and no Todds at all in the building, although there was one Tad. One of the three Marks in the building was black (he was a resident on Jessica's floor—I called her to ask) and another Korean (I called his RA as well), which ruled them both out, since Lakeisha had been sure the guy was white. Tad was so obviously gay that I just stammered an apology and said I'd gotten the wrong number when he picked up the phone.

The third Mark had gone home for the weekend, according to his roommate, but would be back on Monday. But according to his RA, he was only five foot seven, hardly what you'd call tall.

I guess you could call the investigation—such as it was—stymied.

And with Cooper in absentia all weekend, it wasn't like I could ask for his professional advice on the matter. I'm not sure if he was hiding from me, or busy working, or busy—well, doing something else. Since I moved in, Cooper hadn't had a single overnight guest—which for him, at least if Jordan is to be believed, might be a record dry spell. But given how frequently he was gone from the townhouse for days at a time, I could only assume he was crashing at the home of his current flame—whoever she might be.

Which was typical of him. You know, not to rub it in my face that he's getting some, while I'm most definitely not.

Still, I had a hard time appreciating his courteousness as the weekend wore on, and I was still no closer to figuring out who was killing the Virgins of Fischer Hall. If, um, anyone was.

Which might be why, when Monday morning finally rolls around, I'm the first one in the office, latte and bagel already ingested, deeply engrossed in Roberta Pace's student file.

The file's contents are remarkably similar to Elizabeth's, although the two girls came from different sides of the country—Roberta was from Seattle. But they'd both had interfering mothers. Roberta's mother had called Rachel to complain that Roberta needed a new roommate.

Which startles me. How could anyone not like Lakeisha?

But according to the "incident report"—one of which is filled out whenever a staff member has an interaction with a resident—when Rachel spoke to Roberta, it turned out to be Mrs. Pace, not her daughter, who had the problem with Lakeisha. "It's not that I don't like black people," Mrs. Pace had told Rachel, according to the report. "I just don't want my daughter to have to *live* with one."

This is the kind of stuff, I've discovered, that people in higher ed have to deal with every day. The good thing is, usually it's not the kids with the problem, but their parents. As soon as the parents go back home, everything ends up being okay.

The bad thing is—well, that people like Mrs. Pace exist at all.

I force myself to read on. According to the report, Rachel called Roberta down to the office and asked her if she wanted a room change, the way her mother said she did. Roberta said no, that she liked Lakeisha. Rachel reports that then she let Roberta go and called the mother back, gave her our standard speech in such cases—"Much of a college education takes part outside the classroom, where our students experience new cultures and ways of life. Here at New York College, we do everything we can to encourage cultural diversity awareness. Don't you want your son/daughter to be able to get along with every sort of individual when he/she enters the workforce?"

Then Rachel told Mrs. Pace that her kid wasn't getting a room change and hung up.

And that was it. That was the only thing in Roberta's file. The only sign at all that she'd had any sort of trouble adjusting to college life.

Except, of course, that now Roberta is dead.

I hear the ding of an elevator, and then Rachel's heels clacking on the marble floor outside our office. A second later, she appears in the doorway, a steaming mug of coffee that she's brought down from her apartment in one hand, and the morning's *Times* in the other. She looks startled to see me at my desk so early. Even though I live four minutes away from it, I'm almost always five minutes late to work.

"Oh my goodness," Rachel says, looking pleased to see me. "Aren't you here early! Did you have a nice weekend?"

"Yeah," I say, closing Roberta's file, and kind of sliding it under some other stuff on my desk.

Not that I don't have every right to be reading it. It's just that I feel kind of reluctant to tell Rachel what I suspect—about the girls being pushed, and all. I mean, technically, I probably should have said something about the key, or the condom, at least, or that both girls had recently met a guy . . .

But I can't help wondering—what if Cooper is right? What if Elizabeth and Roberta really did fall, but I make this big stink about how I think they'd been murdered? Would Rachel mark down in my employment file that I suffer from paranoid delusions? Could something like that keep me from passing my six months' probation? Could they fire me for it, the way they had Justine—even though I'd fully kept my hands off the ceramic heaters?

I'm not about to risk it. I decide to keep my suspicions to myself.

"Mostly," I say, in reply to Rachel's question about my weekend. Because, aside from calling about the Marks and Todds, I'd done nothing but walk Lucy, watch TV, and fiddle around with my guitar. Hardly anything worth reporting. "You?"

"Terrible," Rachel says, shaking her head. Although for someone who's had such a bad weekend, she looks really great. She has on a new suit, really well-cut. The black brings out the ivory in her skin, and makes her hair seem an even deeper chestnut. "Roberta's parents came in," Rachel goes on, "to pick up their daughter's things. It was just a nightmare. They plan on suing, of course. Though on what grounds, I can't imagine. Those poor people. I felt so sorry for them."

"Yeah," I say. "That had to suck."

The phone on Rachel's desk starts ringing. "Oh, hello, Stan," she says, when she answers it. "Oh, thank you so much, but I'm fine, really. Yes, it's been just awful—"

Wow. Stan. So Rachel's on a first-name basis with Dr. Jessup now. Well, I guess if a couple of kids in your dorm—oops,

I mean, residence hall—die, you get to know the head of your department pretty well.

I start going through the briefing forms the weekend desk attendants have left me. I can generally get payroll, the budget, any memos that need to be typed, and the desk coverage schedules done by eleven in the morning. Then I have the rest of the day free for cruising the Net, gossiping with Magda or Patty, or trying to figure out who might be killing girls in my place of work, which is how I've already decided I'm going to spend this particular Monday.

I just haven't quite figured out how.

I'm just finishing up the payroll when this pair of Nike-encased feet appear in my line of vision. I lift my head, expecting to see a basketball player—hopefully with a semilegible note I can add to my collection.

Instead, I see Cooper.

"Hey," he says.

Is it my fault my heart flips over in my chest? I mean, I haven't seen him in a while. Like almost seventy-two hours. Plus, you know, I'm totally man-starved. That has to be why I can't take my eyes off the front of the jeans he's wearing, white in all the places where the denim's been stressed, like at his knees and other, more interesting places.

He also has on a blue shirt beneath his rumpled leather jacket—the exact same blue as his crinkly eyes.

"Wh—" is the only sound I can get to come out of my mouth, on account of the jeans . . . and the my-being-a-total-loser-who-is-completely-in-love-with-him part.

I watch as he takes a newspaper out from beneath his arm, unfolds it, and places it in front of me.

"Wh—" I say again. At least, that's how it sounds to my ears.

"I wanted to make sure you knew about this," Cooper says.

"You know, before *Us Weekly* starts calling, and catches you by surprise."

I look down at the paper. It's the *New York Post*. On the front page is a large, blown-up photo of my ex-fiancé and Tania Trace dining at some outdoor café in SoHo. Underneath their images are the words, in eighteen-point type at least:

THEY'RE ENGAGED!

13

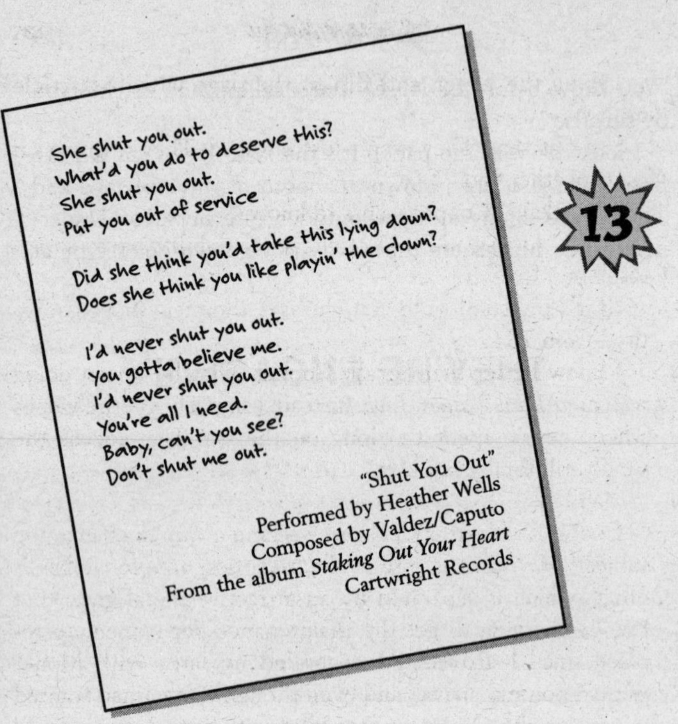

She shut you out.
What'd you do to deserve this?
She shut you out.
Put you out of service

Did she think you'd take this lying down?
Does she think you like playin' the clown?

I'd never shut you out.
You gotta believe me.
I'd never shut you out.
You're all I need.
Baby, can't you see?
Don't shut me out.

"Shut You Out"
Performed by Heather Wells
Composed by Valdez/Caputo
From the album *Staking Out Your Heart*
Cartwright Records

Wow. That didn't take long. I mean, considering we've only been broken up for, what? Four months? Five, maybe?

"Wh—" seems to be the only sound I am capable of making.

"Yeah," Cooper says. "That's what I thought you'd say."

I just sit there, looking down at the photo of Tania's ring. It looks just like MY ring. The one I'd ripped off my finger and thrown at them when I'd caught them going at it in our bedroom.

But it can't be the same ring. Jordan is cheap, but not THAT cheap.

I open the paper, and flip to the page with the article on it.

Look at that. They aren't just engaged. They're going on tour together, too.

"You okay?" Cooper wants to know.

"Yeah," I say, glad I've gotten back the ability to say something besides "wh."

"If it's any comfort to you," he says, "her new single got retired from *TRL*."

I know better than to ask Cooper what he's been doing watching *Total Request Live*. Instead, I say, "They retire videos when they've spent too long on the list. That means the song's still totally popular."

"Oh."

Cooper looks around, clearly seeking a way to change the subject. My office is sort of the reception area for Rachel's office, which is separated by an attractive metal grate that I've been trying to get the maintenance department to replace since I arrived. I'd decorated my area with Monet prints upon my arrival, and even though Rachel had wanted to replace the Giverny water lilies with anti–date rape and community development posters, I had held my ground.

I read in a magazine once that Monet is soothing. That's why you see prints of his work in so many doctors' offices.

"Nice place," Cooper says. Then his gaze falls on the jar of condoms on my desk.

I feel myself turning crimson.

Rachel chooses that moment to hang up the phone and lean out of her office to ask, "May I help you?"

When she sees that the visitor to our office is of the male persuasion, over six feet and under forty—not to mention totally hot—she says, in a completely different voice, "Oh. *Hello*."

"Good morning," Cooper says politely. Cooper is unfailingly polite to everyone but members of his immediate family. "You must be Rachel. I'm Cooper Cartwright."

"Nice to meet you," Rachel says. She shakes the hand he offers and smiles beatifically. "Cooper . . . Cooper . . . Oh yes, Cooper! Heather's friend. I've heard so much about you."

Cooper glances in my direction, his blue eyes crinkling more than ever. "You have?"

I wish the floor would open up and swallow me whole. I try to remember what I've ever said to Rachel about Coop. Besides the fact that he's my landlord, I mean. Because what if I said something really indiscreet, like that Cooper's my idea of a perfect mate and that sometimes I fantasize about ripping his clothes off with my teeth? I've been known to say things like that sometimes, when I've had too many Krispy Kremes combined with too much caffeine.

But all Rachel says is "I suppose you've heard about our troubles here."

Cooper nods.

"I have."

Rachel smiles again, a little less beatifically this time. I can tell she's mentally calculating how much Cooper's watch must cost—he wears one of those gadget-heavy black plastic ones—and deciding he can't possibly be worth a hundred grand a year.

If only she knew.

Then the phone on her desk rings again, and she goes to answer it. "Hello, Fischer Hall. This is Rachel. How may I help you?"

Cooper raises his eyebrows at me, and I remember, in a rush, what Magda had said, about Rachel being Cooper's type.

No! It isn't fair! Rachel is EVERYONE'S type! I mean,

she's attractive and athletic and well put together and successful and went to Yale and is making a difference in the world. What about ME? What about girls like me, who are just . . . well, nice? What about the *nice* girls? How are *we* supposed to compete with all of these competent, athletic, shower-taking girls, with their diplomas and their Palm Pilots and their teeny tiny butts?

Before I have a chance to say anything in defense of my kind, however, one of the maintenance workers comes rushing in.

"Haythar," Julio cries, wringing his hands. He's a little guy, in a brown uniform, who without being asked to, daily cleans the bronze statue of Pan in the lobby with a toothbrush.

"Haythar, that boy is doing it again."

I blink at him. "You mean Gavin?"

"Sí."

I glance over at Rachel. She's gushing into the phone, "Oh, President Allington, please don't worry about me. It's the *students* I feel for—"

I sigh resignedly, push back my chair, and stand up. I'm just going to have to face that fact that where Cooper is concerned, I'm always going to look like the world's biggest spaz.

And there's nothing I can do about it.

"I'll take care of it," I say.

Julio glances at Cooper, and, still wringing his hands, asks nervously, "You want I should come with you, Haythar?"

"What is this?" Cooper looks suspicious. "What's going on?"

"Nothing," I say to him. "Thanks for dropping by. I have to go now."

"Go where?" Cooper wants to know.

"I just have to deal with this one thing. I'll see you later."

Then I hurry out of the office and head for the service elevator, which is reserved for use of the maintenance staff only, and has one of those metal gates inside the doors to keep students out . . .

Only I know which lever to push to throw the gate back. Which I push, then turn to say, "Ready when you are" to Julio—

Only it isn't Julio who's followed me. It's Cooper.

"Heather," he says, looking annoyed. "What's this all about?"

"Where's Julio?" I squeak.

"I don't know," Cooper says. "Back there, I guess. Where are you going?"

From inside the elevator shaft, I can hear whooping. Why me? Why, God, why?

There's nothing I can do about it, though. I mean, it's my job. And it will mean a free medical degree, eventually, if I can stick it out.

"Can you work a service elevator?" I ask Cooper.

He looks even more annoyed. "I think I can figure it out."

More whooping from inside the shaft.

"Okay," I say. "Let's go then."

Cooper, looking curious as well as annoyed now, follows me inside, ducking so as not to hit his head on the low jamb, and I pull the grate shut and yank back the power lever. As the elevator lurches upward with a groan, I put a foot on the siderails and, with a heave, grab the sides of the wide opening in the elevator's roof where a ceiling panel has been removed. Through it, I can see the cables and bare brick walls of the elevator shaft, and high overhead, patches of bright light where the sun peeks in through the fire safety skylights.

Cooper's curiosity quickly fades, so that all that's left is annoyance.

"What," he asks, "do you think you're doing?"

"Don't worry," I say. "I'm okay. I've done this before." My head and shoulders are already through the hole in the elevator's ceiling, and with another heave, I wiggle my hips through it, too.

Then I have to rest. Because that's a lot of upper body lifting for a girl like me.

"*This* is what you do all day?" Cooper, down below me, demands. "Where does it say in your job description that you are responsible for chasing after elevator surfers?"

"It doesn't say it anywhere," I reply, looking down at him in some surprise through the opening between my knees. The dark walls of the elevator shaft slip past me like water as we rise. "But somebody's got to do it." And if I don't, how am I ever going to pass my six months' probation? "What floor are we on?"

Cooper glances through the grate, at the painted numbers going by on the back of each set of elevator doors.

"Nine," he says. "You know, one slip, and you could end up like those dead girls, Heather."

"I know," I say. "That's why I have to stop them. Somebody might get hurt. Somebody else, I mean."

Cooper says something under his breath that sounds like a curse word . . . which is surprising, because he so rarely swears.

One floor later, two walls of the shaft open up, so that I can see into the shafts of the building's other elevators. One of the elevators is waiting at ten, and by craning my neck, I can see the other about five floors overhead.

The whooping is getting louder.

Right then, Elevator 2 starts to descend, and I see, perched on the cab's roof, amid the cables and empty bottles of

Colt .45, Gavin McGoren, junior, film major, diehard *Matrix* fan, and inveterate elevator surfer.

"Gavin!" I yell, as Elevator 2 slides past me. Unlike me, he's standing upright, preparing to leap onto the roof of Elevator 1 as it goes by. "Get down from there right now!"

Gavin throws me a startled glance, then groans when he recognizes me between the cables. I see several flailing arms and legs as the friends he's surfing with dive back down through the maintenance panel and into the elevator car, to save themselves from being ID'd by me.

"Aw, shit," Gavin says, because he hadn't been quick enough to escape, like his friends. "Busted!"

"You are so busted you're gonna be sleeping in the park tonight," I assure him, even though no one's ever gotten thrown out of the hall for elevator surfing . . . at least until now. Who knew, in light of recent events, if the board of trustees would get a backbone? You have to do something really bad—like hurl a meat cleaver at your RA, as a kid had done last year, according to a file I'd found—to be asked to leave the residence halls.

And even then, the kid was allowed back the following fall, after proving he'd spent the summer in counseling.

"Goddammit!" Gavin screams into the shaft, but I don't worry. That's just Gavin.

"Do you think this is funny?" I ask him. "You know two girls died doing this in the past two weeks. But you just woke up this morning and thought you'd go for a joyride anyway?"

"They was amateurs," Gavin says. "You know I got the creds, Heather."

"I know you're a jackass," I reply. "And stop talking like you come from Bed-Stuy, everyone knows you grew up in Nantucket. Now get down. And if you aren't in Rachel's office by the time I'm downstairs, I'm having the locks changed on your door and confiscating all your stuff."

"Shit!" Gavin disappears, slithering through the elevator cab's roof and scraping the ceiling panel back into place behind him.

Elevator 2 begins its long descent to the lobby, and I sit for a minute, enjoying the darkness and the lack of noise. I really like the elevator shafts. They are the most peaceful places in the whole dorm—I mean, residence hall.

When people aren't falling down them, anyway.

When I let myself down—and no judge would give me a ten for my dismount—Cooper is standing in one corner of the car, his arms folded across his broad chest, his features twisted into a scowl.

"What was that?" he asks, as I reach for the control lever and start bringing us back down to the main floor.

"That was just Gavin," I say. "He does that all the time."

"Don't give me that." Cooper sounds genuinely angry. "You did that on purpose. To show me what a *real* elevator surfer is like, and how much the two dead girls don't fit the bill."

I glare at him. "Oh, right," I say. "You think I prearranged that whole thing with Gavin? You think I knew in advance you were going to come over to shove my ex's engagement announcement in my face, and I called Gavin and was like, 'Hey, why don't you take a spin on Elevator Two and I'll come up and bust you to prove to my friend Cooper the difference between real elevator surfers and wannabes'?"

Cooper looks slightly taken aback . . . but not for the reason I think.

"I didn't come over to shove it in your face," he says. "I wanted to make sure you saw it before some reporter from the *Star* sprang it on you."

Realizing I'd maybe been a little harsh, I say, "Oh yeah. You said that."

"Yeah," Cooper says. "I did. So. Do you do that a lot? Climb on top of elevator cars?"

"I wasn't climbing. I was sitting," I say. "And I only do it when someone reports hearing someone in the shafts. Which is another reason it's so weird about Elizabeth and Roberta. No one reported hearing them. Well, until Roberta fell—"

"And you're the one who has to go after them?" Cooper asks. "If someone hears them?"

"Well, we can't ask the RAs to do it. They're students. And it isn't in the maintenance workers' union contract."

"And it's in yours?"

"I'm nonunion," I remind him. I can't help wondering what he's getting at. I mean, is he actually worried about me? And if so, is it just as a friend? Or as something more? Is he going to throw on the brake and stop the elevator and snatch me into his arms and whisper raggedly that he loves me and that the thought of losing me makes his blood run cold?

"Heather, you could seriously injure, if not kill, yourself doing something that stupid," he says, making it pretty obvious that the snatching me into his arms thing isn't going to happen. "How could you—" Then his blue eyes crinkle into slits as he narrows them at me. "Wait a minute. You *like* it."

I blink at him. "What?" Yeah, that's me. Miss Ready with a Comeback.

"You do." He shakes his head, looking stunned. "You actually enjoyed that just now, didn't you?"

I shrug, not sure what he's talking about. "It's more fun than doing payroll," I say.

"You like it," he goes on, as if I hadn't even said anything, "because you miss the thrill of standing up in front of thousands of kids and singing your guts out."

I stare at him for a second or two. Then I burst out laughing.

"Oh my God," I manage to get out, between guffaws. "Are you serious with this?"

Except that I can tell by his expression that he is.

"Laugh all you want," he says. "You hated singing the schlock the label gave you to sing, but you got a kick out of performing. Don't try to deny it. It gave you a thrill." His blue eyes crackle at me. "That's what all this is about, isn't it? Trolling for murderers and chasing elevator surfers. You miss the excitement."

I stop laughing and feel color heating up my face again. I don't know what he's talking about.

Well, okay, maybe I did. It's true I'm not one of those people who get nervous about performing in front of a crowd. Ask me to make small talk with thirty people at a cocktail party, and you might as well ask me to define the Pythagorean theorem. But give me a song set and stick me in front of a microphone? No problem. In fact . . .

Well, I sort of enjoy it. A lot.

But do I miss it? Maybe a little. But not enough to go back. Oh no. I can never go back.

Unless it's on my terms.

"That's not why I went after Gavin," I say. Because really, I don't see the connection. Chasing after elevator surfers is nothing like performing in front of three thousand screaming preteens. Nothing at all. Besides, don't I get enough psychoanalyzing from Sarah every day? Do I really need it from Cooper, too? "He could have killed himself up there—"

"You could have killed *yourself* up there."

"No, I couldn't," I say, in my most reasonable voice. "I'm really careful. And as for—what did you call it? Trolling for murderers?—I told you, I don't believe those girls were—"

"Heather." He shakes his head. "Why don't you just give your agent a call and ask him to schedule a gig for you?"

My jaw drops.

"What? What are you talking about?"

"It's obvious you're aching to get out there again. I respect the fact that you want to get a degree, but college isn't for everyone, you know."

"But—" I can't believe what I'm hearing. My hospital ward! My Nobel Prize! My date with him! Our joint detective agency and three kids—Jack, Emily, and baby Charlotte!

"I . . . I couldn't!" I cry. Then latch on to my one excuse: "I don't have enough songs for a gig."

"Could have fooled me," Cooper says, his gaze on the numbers of the floors we're passing at a dizzying speed, 14, 12, 11. . . .

"What—what do you mean?" I stammer, my blood suddenly running cold. It's true, then. He *can* hear me practicing He can!

It's Cooper's turn to look uncomfortable, though. From his scowl, it's clear he wishes he hadn't said anything.

"Never mind," he says. "Forget about it."

"No. You meant something by it." Why won't he just admit it? Admit that he's heard me?

I know why. I know why, and it makes me want to die.

Because he hates them. My songs. He's heard them, and he thinks they suck.

"Tell me what you meant."

"Never mind," Cooper says. "You're right. You don't have enough songs for a gig. Forget I said anything. Okay?"

The cab hits the main floor. Cooper yanks back the gate and holds it open for me, looking less polite than murderous.

Great. Now he's mad at me.

We're standing in the lobby, and since it's still pretty early in the morning—for eighteen-year-olds, anyway—we're the only ones around, with the exception of Pete and the reception desk attendant, the former engrossed in a copy of the *Daily News*, the latter listening enraptured to a Marilyn Manson CD.

I should just ask him. Just come out and ask him. He's not going to say it sucks. He's not his father. He's not Jordan.

But that's just it. I can take criticism from Cooper's father. I can take it from his brother. But from Cooper?

No. No, because if *he* doesn't like it—

Oh God, stop being such a baby and DO IT. JUST ASK HIM.

"Heather," Cooper says, running a hand through his dark hair. "Look. I just think—"

But before I have a chance to hear what Cooper just thinks, Rachel rounds the corner.

"Oh, there you are," Rachel says when she notices us. "Gavin's in my conference room. I'm going to have a word with him in a minute. Thanks so much for making him come down. In the meantime, Heather, I was wondering if you could have the student worker go around and tape up these fliers."

Rachel hands me a sheaf of papers. I look down at them, and see that they are announcements for a lip-synch contest the student government has decided to throw in the Fischer Hall cafeteria after dinner.

"At first I wasn't going to let them," Rachel seems to feel the need to explain. "I mean, holding something as silly as a lip-synch contest, in light of two such tragic deaths . . . but Stan thinks the kids can use something to take their minds off it. And I couldn't help but agree."

Stan. Wow. Rachel sure is getting chummy with the boss.

"Sounds good to me," I say.

"I was just heading into the cafeteria for a refill before tackling Gavin." Rachel holds up her American Association for Counseling and Development coffee mug. "Anybody care to join me?"

She says it to both of us, but her gaze is on Cooper.

Oh my God. Rachel has just asked Cooper to have coffee with her. *My* Cooper.

Of course, she doesn't know he's *my* Cooper. He's *not* my Cooper. And the way things seem to be going, he'll probably never be . . .

Say no. I try to send my thought waves into his brain, like on *Star Trek. Say no. Say no. Say no. Say—*

"Thanks, but I can't," Cooper says. "I've got work to do."

Success!

Rachel smiles and says, "Maybe some other time, then."

"Sure," Cooper says.

And Rachel click-clacks away.

When she's gone, I say, showing no sign that I had, seconds before, been using Vulcan mind control on him, "Look. I gotta get back to work." I hope he isn't going to bring up what we'd been talking about in the elevator. I don't think I could handle it. Not on top of the announcement of Jordan's engagement. There's only so much a girl can take in one day, you know?

Maybe Cooper senses this. Either that or the fact that I won't meet his gaze tips him off.

In any case, all he says is, "Gotcha. I'll see you later, then. And Heather—"

My heart gives a lurch. No. Please, not now. So close. I'd been so close to escaping—

"The ring," he says.

Wait. What? "Ring?"

"Tania's."

Oh! Tania's engagement ring! The one that looks exactly like the one I threw back in his brother's face!

"Yeah?"

"It's not yours," Cooper says.

Then he leaves.

14

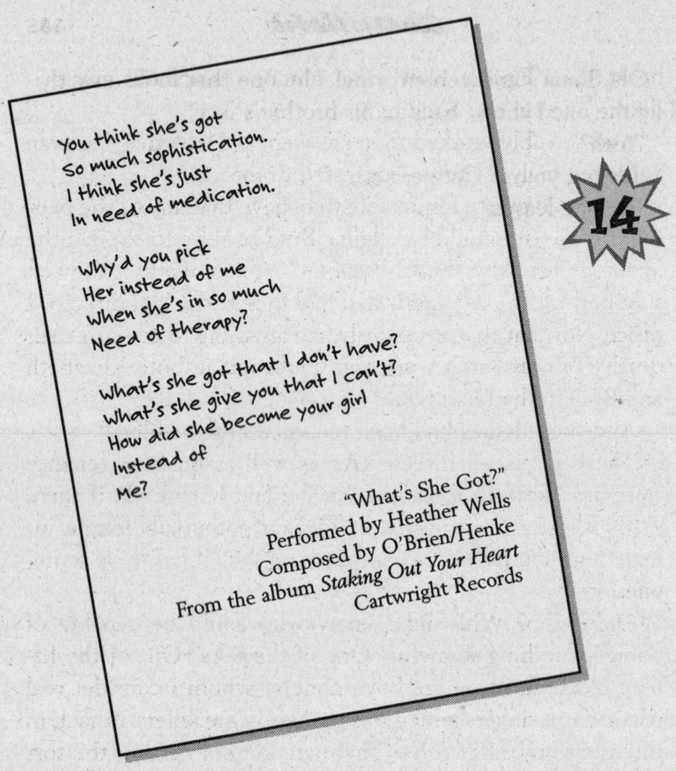

You think she's got
So much sophistication.
I think she's just
In need of medication.

Why'd you pick
Her instead of me
When she's in so much
Need of therapy?

What's she got that I don't have?
What's she give you that I can't?
How did she become your girl
Instead of
Me?

"What's She Got?"
Performed by Heather Wells
Composed by O'Brien/Henke
From the album *Staking Out Your Heart*
Cartwright Records

It's actually kind of appropriate that the student government decides to throw a lip-synch contest at Fischer Hall. Because, let's face it, New York College is primarily filled with kids who, like me, love to perform.

Which is probably why they asked me to be one of the judges, an honor I readily accepted. But not because I needed to—as Cooper had suggested—feel the thrill of performing again, but because I figured if I were ever going to find the mysterious Mark/Todd (if he existed at all), it was going to be at some Fischer Hall social function, since the guy evidently lived in the building.

And possibly worked there, as well, as Detective Canavan had—teasingly, I know—suggested to me.

It seemed pretty impossible to believe that any of the people I work with could be a killer. But how else to explain the apparent access to the key cabinet? Not to mention the fact that both of the dead girls had had files in the hall director's office. Not that that necessarily had anything to do with their deaths. But, as Sarah would no doubt put it, both Elizabeth and Roberta had had issues . . .

And those issues had been recorded in their files.

The thing is, all fifteen RAs, as well as the maintenance staff, have keys to the office Rachel and I share. So if there really is some guy cruising the files for potentially fragile, inexperienced girls he can easily seduce, then it has to be someone I know.

Only who? Who did I know who could be capable of doing something so awful? One of the RAs? Out of the fifteen of them, seven are boys, none of whom I consider real particular swingers, much less psychopathic killers. In fact, in the tradition of RAs, all of them are kind of nerdy—the sort who actually believe their residents when they insist they were smoking clove cigarettes, not pot. They seriously can't tell the difference.

Besides which, everybody in the whole building knows who the RAs are. I mean, the staff performs safer sex skits and stuff at dinnertime. If Mark or Todd had been an RA, Lakeisha would have known him by sight.

As far as the maintenance staff is concerned, forget it. They're all Hispanic and over fifty, and only Julio speaks enough English to be understood by someone not bilingual.

Plus they've all worked in Fischer Hall for years. Why would they suddenly start killing people *now*?

Which, of course, leaves just the women on the staff. I should, in light of diversity awareness, include them on my list of suspects . . .

Only none of them could have left that condom in Roberta's room.

But I guess I'm the only one who considers it odd that two girls—who each had a file in my office, and who each happened to have found a boyfriend within a week of each other—both happened randomly to decide to go elevator surfing, then plunged to their deaths at around the same time the key to the elevator doors went missing, only to reappear shortly after the discovery of at least one of their bodies.

Which is why at seven o'clock that night, I slip from the brownstone—I haven't heard a peep from Cooper since the elevator incident that morning, which is fine with me, because frankly, I don't know what I'm going to say to him when I *do* see him again.

It's also why I consequently walk right into Jordan Cartwright, who is just coming up the front stoop.

"Heather!" he cries. He has on one of those puffy shirts—you know, like the kind they made fun of on *Seinfeld*—and a pair of leather pants.

Yes. I am sorry to have to say it. Leather pants.

What's worse is, he really does look quite good in them.

"I was just coming to see how you are," he says, in a voice that drips with concern for my mental health.

"I'm fine," I say, pulling the door closed and working the locks. Don't ask me why we have so many locks when we also have a burglar alarm and a dog and our own Rastafarian community watch program. But whatever.

"Have a nice evening," one of the drug dealers urges us.

"Thank you," I say to the drug dealer. To Jordan, I say, "I'm sorry, I really don't have time to chat. I've got somewhere to go."

Jordan trots down the steps behind me.

"It's just," he says, "I don't know if you've heard. About Tania and me. I meant to tell you the other day, but you were so adversarial—I didn't want you to find out this way, Heather," Jordan says, keeping pace with me as I tear down the sidewalk. "I swear. I wanted you to hear it from me."

"Don't worry about it, Jordan," I say. *Why* won't he go away? "Really."

"Hey." One of the drug dealers blocks our path on the sidewalk. "Aren't you that guy?"

"No," Jordan says to the drug dealer. To me, he says, "Heather, slow down. We've got to talk."

"There's nothing to talk about," I assure him, in my most cheerful voice. "I'm good. Everything's good."

"Everything's *not* good," Jordan cries. "I can't stand to see you hurting like this! It's tearing me up inside—"

"Oh, hey," I say to the drug dealer who is trailing after us. "This is Jordan Cartwright. You know, from Easy Street."

"The dude from Easy Street!" the drug dealer cries, pointing at Jordan. "I knew it! Hey, look!" he calls to his friends. "It's the dude from Easy Street!"

"Heather!" Jordan is swallowed up in a crowd of autograph seekers. "Heather!"

I keep right on walking.

Well, what exactly was I supposed to do? I mean, he's engaged. ENGAGED. And not to me.

What more is there to say? It's not like I don't have more pressing concerns right now, too.

Rachel seems kind of surprised to see me walk through the

doors of Fischer Hall at night. She's standing in the lobby just as I come in, and her eyes get kind of big.

"Heather," she exclaims. "What are you doing here?"

"They asked me to judge," I say.

For some reason, she looks relieved. I realize why a second later. "Oh good! Another judge for the lip-synch! How great! I was hoping Sarah and I wouldn't have to judge on our own. What if there's a tie?"

"Heather." Jordan comes bursting into the lobby.

And all around us, breaths are sucked in as he is immediately recognized. Then the whispering begins: *"Isn't that—no, it couldn't be. No, it is! Look at him!"*

"Heather," Jordan says, striding up to Rachel and me. His gold necklaces rise and fall beneath the puffy shirt as he pants. "Please. We've got to talk."

I turn to Rachel, who is staring at Jordan with eyes that are even bigger than when I'd walked in.

"Here's another judge for you," I say to her.

Which is how Jordan and I end up sitting in the front row of about three hundred cafeteria chairs, facing the closed-off grill and salad bar, clipboards in our laps. You can imagine how difficult this makes it for Jordan to talk to me about our relationship, as he is so desperately longing to.

But this is just fine by me. I mean, the truth is I'm only here to hunt for the mysterious Mark and/or Todd, and my being a judge isn't exactly helpful in this capacity.

But if it keeps me from having to listen to Jordan as he tries to make excuses for his behavior—though why he should care what I think of him, when he's made it so perfectly obvious he doesn't want to be with me anymore, I can't imagine . . . maybe Sarah can explain it—it's fine.

The kids are all in a dither about Jordan. They hadn't known there was going to be a celebrity judge. (I don't count.

The few kids who'd recognized me at check-in could not have cared less. Tonight, it's all about Jordan . . . even though I'm afraid some of them are making fun of him, on account of the puffy shirt and Easy Street and everything.) Jordan's presence does seem to give the contest an air of legitimacy it lacked before.

It also seems to make the competitors even more nervous.

There's an elaborate sound and light system set up over by the salad bar, and all sorts of students are milling around, chatting and noshing on free soda and chips. I look for couples, trying to single out any boys and girls in close conversation, thinking that if Mark or Todd is going to strike again, there is a bevy of freshwomen here for him to choose from.

But all I see are groups of kids, boys and girls, white, African American, Asian, you name it, in baggy jeans and T-shirts, screaming happily at one another, and tossing back Doritos.

Mmmm. Doritos.

Sarah, seated next to Jordan, can't take her eyes off him. She keeps asking him searching questions about the music industry, the same ones she'd asked me when she'd first met me. Like, had he felt like a sellout when he'd done that Pepsi ad? And hadn't he felt that performing at the Super Bowl halftime show had been degrading to his calling as a musician? And what about that calling? Did it bother him that he knew how to sing, but not how to play a single instrument? Didn't that, in a way, mean that he wasn't a musician at all, but merely a mouthpiece through which Cartwright Records could deliver their message of corporate greed?

By the time the lights go down, and the hall president, Greg, gets up to welcome everyone, I'm feeling a little sorry for Jordan.

Then the first act comes on, a trio of girls lip-synching Christina's latest, with choreography and everything. With the lights down, I'm able to scan the audience without looking too obvious.

There are a *lot* of students there. Nearly every seat is filled, and the cafeteria can hold four hundred. Plus there are people lining the back of the room, hooting and applauding and, in general, acting like eighteen-year-olds away from home for the first time. Beside me, Jordan is staring at the Christina wannabes, his clipboard clutched tightly in his hands. For someone who's been shanghaied into the job, he seems to be taking it way seriously.

Or maybe he's only acting interested in order to keep Sarah from asking him any more questions.

The first act comes to a hip-grinding stop, and a quartet of boys leaps into the spotlight. Heavy bass begins to shake the cafeteria walls—they're performing "Bye Bye Bye" by 'N Sync—and I feel pity for Fischer Hall's neighbors, one of which is an Episcopalian church.

The boys throw themselves into their act. They have the choreography down pat—so much so I practically wet my pants, I'm laughing so hard.

I notice Jordan isn't laughing at all. He doesn't seem to understand that the boys are making *fun* of boy bands. He is carefully scoring them on originality and how well they know the lyrics.

Seriously.

Glancing over my clipboard as I score the boys' act—I give them mostly fives out of ten, since they don't have costumes—I notice a tall man wander into the dining hall, his hands buried deep in the pockets of his khakis.

At first I think it's President Allington. But the president never wears khakis, preferring, as I think I've mentioned before, white Dockers. The newcomer is entirely too well-dressed to be the school's president.

When he moves into a shaft of light that spills from the Coke machine, however, I realize that it's Christopher Allington, the president's son. So my confusion is understandable.

It isn't unusual for Christopher to drop by. I mean, even though he has his own place at the law school dorm, his parents do live upstairs. He'd probably come over to visit them, then stopped in the caf to see what all the noise was about.

But when he moves toward a group of students leaning against a far wall and begins chatting casually to them, I start to wonder. What *is* Christopher doing here, exactly? He's a law student, not an undergrad.

Pete had told me that when the Allingtons first arrived from the college somewhere in Indiana where President Allington had worked before, there'd been a big hush-up over the fact that Christopher hadn't scored high enough on his LSATs to get into New York College. Apparently his father had pulled some major strings, and gotten him in anyway.

But then, with an alcoholic mother and a father who wears tank tops in public, the poor kid probably doesn't have much in the way of gifts from the Allington gene pool anyway, and needed the extra help.

'N Sync pounds to a finish, and then an Elvis impersonator gives it a go. During his rendition of "Viva Las Vegas," for want of anything better to do, I watch Christopher Allington mingle. He works his way through the crowd until he's settled himself in a chair behind a whole row of girls. They're all freshmen—you can tell by their giggly awkwardness. They aren't quite in the New York College groove yet, as their unpierced faces and undyed hair and Gap clothing prove. One of them, a bit more sophisticated than the rest, turns in her seat and begins talking to Christopher, who leans forward to hear her better. The girl sitting next to her resolutely refuses to join in the conversation, keeping her face forward.

But you can tell she's eavesdropping like anything.

Elvis finishes to respectable applause, and then Marnie Villa Delgado—yes, Elizabeth Kellogg's roommate—takes the stage. Everyone gives her an extra hand. I try not to let myself think that the ovation is for having scored herself a single room for the rest of the semester.

Marnie, wearing a long blond wig and a pair of low-ride jeans, bows politely. Then she launches into a song that sounds vaguely familiar. I can't place it, at first. All I know is that it's a song I don't like very much. . .

And then it hits me. "Sugar Rush." Marnie is giving her all to the song that had made mine a household name . . . thirteen years ago. And only if that household contained a pre-adolescent girl.

Jordan, beside me, guffaws. Some of the students who know about my past laugh along with him. Marnie herself even gives me a sly look while she mouths the line, "Don't tell me stay on my diet/You have simply got to try it."

I smile and try not to look as uncomfortable as I feel. It helps to look back at Christopher, instead. He's still chatting up the girls in the row ahead of him. He has finally attracted the attention of the shy girl, who, while not pretty, has a more interesting face than her more vivacious companion. She has turned in her seat and is timidly smiling at Christopher, hugging her knees to her chest and pushing back wayward tendrils of reddish hair.

Up front, Marnie is tossing her blond wig—not to mention her hips—around in a manner that the crowd seems to find hilarious, and which I can only hope is not supposed to be an accurate imitation of me.

And that's when it hits me—out of the blue—that Christopher Allington could be Mark.

Or Todd.

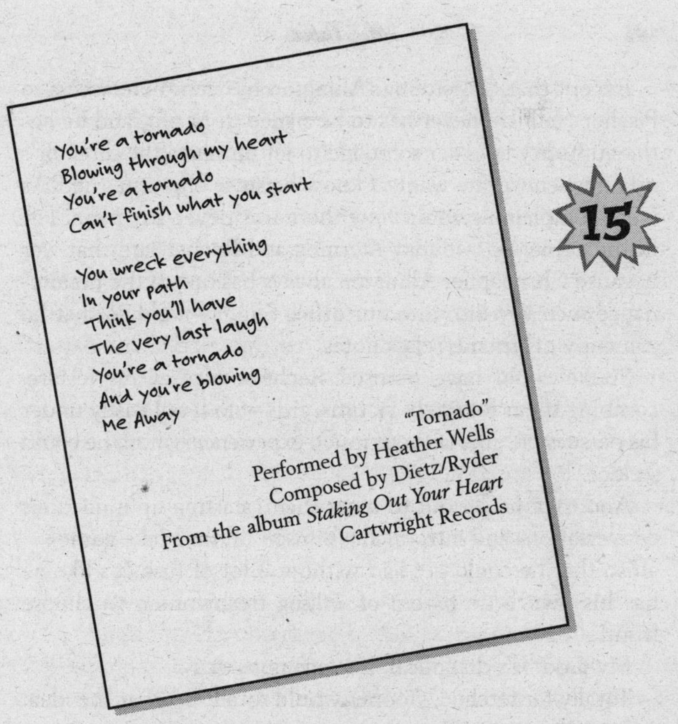

You're a tornado
Blowing through my heart
You're a tornado
Can't finish what you start

You wreck everything
In your path
Think you'll have
The very last laugh
You're a tornado
And you're blowing
Me Away

"Tornado"
Performed by Heather Wells
Composed by Dietz/Ryder
From the album *Staking Out Your Heart*
Cartwright Records

15

I guess you can say my blood went cold.

Okay, it didn't really. But it does feel kind of like someone has spilled some really cold Diet Coke down my back, or something.

All of a sudden, my palms are so sweaty I can hardly hold on to the clipboard. My heart starts hammering unsteadily, the way it had that time I'd sung those songs I'd written myself for Jordan's dad, and he'd laughed at me.

Christopher Allington? Christopher Allington? No way!

Except . . .

Except that Christopher Allington has complete access to Fischer Hall. He never has to be signed in or out, and he has the authority to order someone to let him into the director's office whenever he wants. I know because one time the RAs were complaining about how there was never any paper left in the copier on Monday morning and Rachel said that was because Christopher Allington always has one of the maintenance men key him into our office Sunday night so that he can copy his friends' class notes.

So he could have perused Rachel's files at his leisure, combing them for likely victims, girls who'll fall easily under his persuasion, girls without much experience, whom he could seduce.

And then he set out to meet them, starting up innocuous conversations and introducing himself under a fake name . . . all so that he could get laid without a lot of fuss. It's like he has his own little harem of willing freshwomen to choose from!

My God. It's diabolical. It's ingenious. It's . . .

Totally far-fetched. Cooper would totally scoff at the idea.

But Cooper isn't here . . .

And Christopher Allington *is* way charming. Over six feet tall, with kind of longish blond hair that he wears feathered back, he has the boyish good looks of . . . well, a guy from a boy band. What freshman girl wouldn't be flattered by his attentions . . . so flattered that she'd have sex with him on a comparatively short acquaintance? My God, he's cute, older, sophisticated . . . Any eighteen-year-old girl would go ga-ga over him. Any *twenty-eight*-year-old girl would go ga-ga over him. The guy is fine.

But why did he *kill* them? Scoring babes is one thing, but killing them afterward? Doesn't that kind of defeat the purpose? If they're dead, you can't score with them again.

More importantly, *how* did he kill them? I mean, I know how—if, indeed, they were being killed—but how was he managing to push full-grown women down an elevator shaft when, undoubtedly, they'd be struggling against him? Drugs? But wouldn't the coroner's office have found some evidence of that?

My face feels hot. I fan it with my clipboard, turning my attention back toward Marnie. She's just winding up for her big finish, which involves hip gyrations the likes of which I haven't seen since Shakira's last performance on the MTV Music Video Awards. She *definitely* isn't imitating me. I've always been a rotten dancer, the despair of every choreographer I've ever met. I had difficulties, as they liked to point out, detaching my brain from my body, and just letting go.

Marnie pulls some kind of Carly Patterson back handspring thingie that ends in a set of splits and has the entire cafeteria on their feet, cheering. I rise to my feet as well . . . then start toward her. Lakeisha may have gone home, but Marnie's still here, and might be able to confirm whether or not her roommate had ever hooked up with Christopher Allington.

But Jordan grabs me by the arm before I've gone two steps.

"Where are you going?" he asks worriedly. "You aren't trying to sneak out of here before we've had our talk, are you, Heather?"

Jordan smells of Drakkar Noir, which is distracting. He'd worn Carolina Herrera for Men when he'd been with me, so clearly the Drakkar Noir is courtesy of Tania.

"I'll be back in a minute," I say, patting him reassuringly on the arm—his very buff arm. He's been bulking up for his next tour, and it shows. In a good way. "I promise."

"Heather," Jordan begins, but I won't let him finish.

"I promise," I say. "When this thing is over, we'll have a nice, long chat."

Jordan looks placated.

"All right," he says. "Good."

I see Marnie cross to the side of the dining hall where all the other acts have gathered to await the decision of the judges, and while the next group sets up for their performance, I hurry over to her.

Marnie has pulled off her blond wig and is wiping sweat from beneath her eyes. She smiles when she sees me approach.

"Marnie," I say. "Nice performance."

"Oh, thanks," she simpers. "I was worried you'd be mad. I finally figured out who you were, as you can see."

"Yeah," I say. "Look, I have to ask you something. Could that guy Elizabeth was seeing right before she died . . . could his name have been Chris?"

Marnie, clearly disappointed that the only reason I've sought her out is to talk about her dead roommate some more, shrugs unconcernedly.

"I don't know. It was something like that. Chris or Mark."

"Thanks," I say. She turns to say something slighting about one of the other acts to the trio of Christina wannabes, and I have to reach out and tug on her sleeve. "Uh, Marnie?"

She glances back at me. "Yeah?"

"See that girl over there in the fifth row, about ten seats over, talking to that blond guy?"

Marnie looks. Her eyebrows raise.

"That guy's a babe. Who is he?"

"So you don't know him?"

"Not yet," she says, making it clear she intends to rectify that situation.

I try to hide my disappointment. Maybe if I can get my hands on a photo of Christopher Allington, I could waylay Lakeisha outside one of her classes and get her to make an ID that way . . .

Then I think of something.

"Do you know the girl?" I ask Marnie.

She purses her lips.

"Kinda. She lives on the twelfth floor. I think her name is Amber or something."

Amber. Perfect. I have a name now, and a floor to go with it.

I get back to my seat just as two guys in drag launch into a rendition of "Dude Looks Like a Lady." Jordan leans over and whispers into my ear, "What was that all about?"

I just smile and shrug. There's no point trying to scream above the sound system, and besides, Sarah is eyeing me critically from over her clipboard. I don't think she appreciates me fraternizing with the contestants, since it might render me less than impartial in my judging.

So I sit helplessly in my chair while Christopher Allington is possibly—probably—schmoozing with his next victim. Amber—from what I can tell, given that I'm only able to catch brief glimpses of her, not wanting to look as if I'm staring—seems to be coming to life under Christopher's attentions. She fiddles with her red-brown hair and squirms in her seat, grinning nonstop and generally acting like a girl who has never had a handsome boy pay attention to her in her life. I watch worriedly, chewing my lower lip, wondering if tomorrow morning, we're going to find Amber at the bottom of the elevator shaft.

Except that I can't really see Christopher as the murdering type. The deflowering type, yeah. But a murderer?

Then again, Evita Peron's husband had been a notorious letch, and I read somewhere that he killed a bunch of people in Argentina, which is why Madonna didn't want people to cry for her in that song.

Finally the lip-synch ends. Greg, the hall president, comes out and announces that the judges should begin deliberating. Everyone else gets up and heads for the Doritos (luckies). Rachel scoots her chair around so that she is facing me and Jordan and Sarah.

"Well," she says, smiling at me. "What did you think?"

I think we've got a problem, I want to say. A really big problem. And not with the contest.

But instead I say, "I liked Marnie."

Jordan interjects, "You would! No, those guys who did the 'N Sync song were much better. They really had the choreography down. I gave 'em tens."

Sarah says, "Their ironic take on the boy band *was* deeply amusing."

"Um," I say. "I liked Marnie."

"And she's been through so much," Rachel agrees, earnestly. "It's the least we can do, don't you think?"

Just wanting to get the whole thing over with as soon as possible so I can make up an excuse to go talk to Chris, I say, "Yeah, okay. So let's give Marnie first place, 'N Sync second, and the Christina trio third."

Jordan looks a little peeved by the fact that we've basically ignored his input, but he doesn't argue.

Rachel goes off to tell Greg our decision, and I turn in my seat to spy on Christopher some more . . .

. . . just in time to see him leaving, one arm draped casually over Amber's shoulders.

I'm out of my chair like a shot, without a word to Jordan or anybody. I hear him call after me, but I don't have any time to waste with explanations. Christopher and Amber are already halfway through the TV lounge. If I don't act fast, that girl might end up as a stain on the elevator motor room floor.

But then, to my astonishment, instead of turning toward the elevators, Amber and Christopher actually walk out the front doors of the building.

I follow, darting past the groups of kids congregated in the lobby. Nighttime is when the hall really comes alive. Residents I've never seen before are leaning against the reception desk, chatting with the student worker on duty. The guard—not Pete, who works days—is harassing a clique of kids who claim to know someone on the fifth floor whose name they couldn't remember. Why can't the guard just be a pal and let them in?

I bolt past all of them, throwing open the doors and stumbling out into the warm autumnal evening.

Washington Square Park is crawling with cops at night, cops and tourists and drug dealers and chess players, who sit at the benches in the chess circle until the park closes at midnight, playing by the light of the street lamps. High school kids from Westchester, in their parents' Volvos, tool down the street, playing their radios too loudly and occasionally having their cars impounded for creating a public nuisance. It's a wild scene, and one of the reasons why so many kids request rooms overlooking the Square . . . when there's nothing on TV, there's always the park to watch.

Which is precisely what Christopher and Amber are doing. They're leaning against one of Fischer Hall's outdoor planters, smoking cigarettes, and watching the NYPD make a bust across the street. Christopher has his arms folded across his chest, and is puffing away like Johnny Depp or someone, while Amber twitters like a little bird, holding her cigarette like someone who isn't used to holding one at all.

There isn't a moment to lose, I can see that. I approach them, trying to look casual. I imagine that's how Cooper would have handled the situation, anyway.

"Hey," I say amiably to Christopher. "Can I bum a smoke?"

"Sure," says Christopher. He draws a pack of Camel Lights from his shirt pocket and hands me one.

"Thanks," I say. I put the cigarette between my lips, then lean down so Christopher can light it with the Zippo he's brandished.

I've never been a smoker. For one thing, if you're a singer, it messes up your vocal cords. For another, I just don't get how a cigarette could ever be better than a Butterfinger, so if you're going to indulge, why not go the way of delicious peanut buttery crisp?

But I stand there and pretend to inhale, wondering what I should do next. What would Nancy Drew do? Jessica Fletcher? That other one, what was her name? On *Crossing Jordan*? God, I totally suck as a detective. What's going to happen after Cooper and I get together—you know, after I get my degree and all? How are we going to be all Nick and Nora Charles, when Nora can't hold up her share of the detecting? This is a very distressing thought. I try to push it from my mind.

Across the street, the cops are busting some drunk who thought it would be amusing to expose himself to the people sitting in the chess circle. I don't know why some men feel this compulsion to show off their genitalia. It's invariably the guy with the least interesting appendage, too.

I say as much to Christopher and Amber. You know, to make conversation. She looks startled, though Christopher laughs.

"Yeah," he says. "There should be a law. Only drunks with at least six inches should be allowed to drop trou."

I look at him, my eyebrows raised. Trou. He's kind of funny, Christopher Allington. Did Ted Bundy have a sense of humor? He did when Mark Harmon played him in that movie I saw on Lifetime the other night . . .

Across the street, the drunk is hurling insults at the cops who've cuffed him, and a few people in the chess circle are shouting back at him. Chess players are not anywhere near as mild-mannered as they've been made out to be by the media, you know.

"Oh my," Amber says, when one particularly colorful epithet reaches us. "They sure don't talk like that to the police back home."

"And where's home?" I ask her, nonchalantly flicking my ash on the sidewalk. At least, I hope I look nonchalant.

"Boise, Idaho," Amber says, as if there's more than one Boise.

"Boise," I echo. "Never been there." Total lie. I'd performed at the Boise Civic Center before five thousand screaming preteens during the Sugar Rush tour. "How about you?" I ask Christopher.

"Nope," he says. "Never been to Boise. Hey, don't I know you from somewhere?"

"Me?" I try to look surprised. "I don't think so."

"Yeah," he says. "I do. Hey, you in law school?"

"No," I say, flicking more ash. They may give you cancer and everything, but cigarettes really do make great props if you're trying to look casual. For instance, while catching a possible murderer.

"Really?" Christopher blows pale smoke from his nostrils. No fair! He knows smoke tricks! " 'Cause I swear I've seen you somewhere before."

"Probably right around here. I've seen you lots. You're President Allington's son, Christopher, aren't you?"

You'd have thought I'd smacked him in the face with a sack full of Gummi Bears, he looks so surprised. For a second I think he's going to swallow his cigarette.

But he recovers himself pretty quickly.

"Uh, yeah," he says. His eyes are gray, and at the moment, still friendly. "How'd you know?"

"Someone pointed you out," I say. "Do you live here? With your folks?"

That stings. He says quickly, "Oh no. Well, I mean, I have my own place, but it's in the law school dorm, over there—"

"You're not an undergrad?" Amber asks. She clearly isn't very swift on the uptake. "You're a law student?"

"Yeah," Christopher said. He doesn't look quite as comfortable as he had before I'd mosied over and dropped my little bomb. Poor guy. He doesn't know I have even more ammunition up my (capped) sleeve.

"I didn't know you were President Allington's son," Amber says, with something like reproachfulness in her little Minnie Mouse voice.

"Well, it's not something I like to advertise," Christopher mutters.

"And I thought you said your name was Dave."

"Did I?" Christopher finishes his cigarette, drops the butt on the sidewalk, and stamps it out. "You must not have heard me right. It was kind of loud in there. I'm sure I said my name's Chris."

Across the street, the cops haul the pantless drunk into a squad car. Now they're all standing around, filling out forms attached to clipboards and drinking coffee somebody's bought from the deli around the corner. The drunk bangs on the car window, wanting some coffee, too.

Everyone ignores him.

Okay, this sucks. I'm turning out to be world's worst detective. I'm definitely going to have to take some courses in criminal justice. You know, when I pass my six months' probation and can start taking classes free.

"It's so sad, isn't it?" I ask, in a voice even *I* think sounds way too chipper—sort of like Less Than Zero's voice from the jean store the other day. "All the losers there are in this city, I mean. Like that pants-dropping drunk getting hauled away right across the street. Oh, and those stupid girls here in the buildings. The ones that died—what was it, again? Oh, yeah. Elevator surfing. Can you believe anyone would do anything that dumb?"

I glance at Chris to see how he's taking this direct reference to his victims. But he doesn't look disturbed at all . . .

. . . unless you can call pulling out another cigarette and lighting it disturbed.

Which, uh, I guess it is. In a way. But not in the way I meant.

"Oh," gasps Amber, in a valiant attempt to hold up her end of the conversation. "I know! That was so sad. I knew that last girl, sort of. One time I got stuck in the elevator with her. It was only for about a minute, but she was freaking out, because she hated heights. When I heard how she'd died, I was like, 'What?' 'Cause why would somebody that scared of heights do something so dangerous?"

"Roberta Pace, you mean?" I slide my gaze toward Chris, to see how he reacts to the name.

But he's busy checking his watch—a Rolex. A real one, too, not one of those ones you can buy on the street for forty bucks, either.

"Yeah, that was her name. God, wasn't that sad? She was so nice."

"I know," I nod gravely. "And what's even weirder than her being afraid of heights, but elevator surfing anyway, is that I heard just the day before she died, she'd met some guy—"

I don't get to finish my sentence, though. Because just then iron fingers close around my upper arm, and I suddenly find myself yanked from behind, hard.

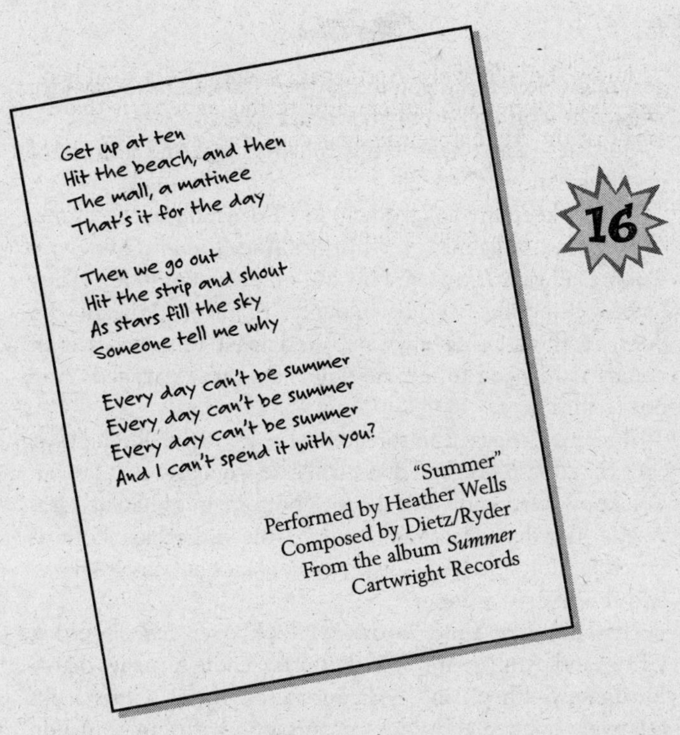

16

Get up at ten
Hit the beach, and then
The mall, a matinee
That's it for the day

Then we go out
Hit the strip and shout
As stars fill the sky
Someone tell me why

Every day can't be summer
Every day can't be summer
Every day can't be summer
And I can't spend it with you?

"Summer"
Performed by Heather Wells
Composed by Dietz/Ryder
From the album *Summer*
Cartwright Records

Stumbling, I put out a hand to steady myself, and feel the unmistakable ripple of rock-hard—and gym-formed—abdominal muscles beneath my fingers.

Is there any part of Jordan Cartwright that isn't hard?

Including, apparently, his head?

He drags me a few feet away from Chris and Amber.

"What do you think you're doing?" Jordan demands, ripping the cigarette from my fingers and stomping on it. "You're *smoking* now? A few months of living with that degenerate Cooper, and you're *smoking*? Do you have any idea what that stuff will do to your vocal cords?"

"Jordan." I can't believe this is happening. And in front of my prime suspect!

I try to keep my voice down, so Chris won't overhear me.

"I wasn't inhaling," I whisper. "And I don't live with Cooper, all right? I mean, I do, but on a separate floor." Then I stop whispering, because suddenly I'm furious. I mean, who does he think he is, anyway? "And what business is it of yours? Do I need to remind you that you're engaged? And not to me?"

"I may be engaged to someone else, Heather," Jordan says, "but that doesn't mean I don't still care—deeply—about you. You know, Dad said you'd hit rock bottom, but I had no idea. A guy like that, Heather? *Really*? I mean, he has about as much fashion sense as"—he throws a glance at Chris's khakis, and shudders—"Cooper!"

"It's not like that, Jordan." I look over my shoulder. Chris and Amber are still there, far enough away that—fortunately—they can't hear our raised voices. Chris looks relatively unaffected by my conversation with him, but I do notice that every now and then, his gray-eyed gaze strays toward us. Is he afraid? Afraid that the jig is up at last?

Or is he just wondering where Jordan bought his puffy shirt?

"Don't look," I say softly to Jordan. "But that guy I was talking to? I think he might be a murderer."

Jordan looks over at Chris. "Who? That guy?"

"I said don't look!"

Jordan tears his gaze from Chris and stares down at me instead. Then he reaches out and crushes me to his chest.

"Oh, you poor, sweet girl," he says. "What's Cooper done to you?"

I struggle to break free of his smothering embrace—or at least to speak without getting chest hair in my mouth.

"This doesn't have anything to do with Cooper," I say, conscious that the student worker at the desk is trying to hide a smirk as she watches us through the window. "Girls are dying in this building, and I think—"

"So this is where you two disappeared to!"

We both spin around and stare wide-eyed at Rachel, who'd slipped outside unnoticed by either of us.

"You missed the awards ceremony," Rachel chastises us, jokingly. "Marnie was so thrilled to win that she cried."

"Wow," I say, without the slightest enthusiasm. "Neat."

"I came looking for you two," Rachel says, "because I thought you might want to join me for a drink in my place . . ."

Jordan and I exchange glances. There is a desperate glint in his. I don't know what he sees in mine. Probably confusion. Rachel had invited me up to her place only once before, for a glass of wine after the first freshmen check-in of the semester, and I'd been totally uncomfortable not only because, well, she's my boss, and I was desperate to do whatever I had to do to make sure I passed my six months' probation, but also because . . .

Well, Rachel's apartment is really clean. Not that I'm messy, or anything, but . . .

Okay, I'm a little messy. I will admit there's a lot of stuff jammed in my closets and under my bed and sort of, well, all over the place.

But at Rachel's, everything had been put neatly away. There were no stray copies of *Us Weekly* next to the toilet, like at my place, or bras hanging off any doorknobs, or wadded-up Ho Ho wrappers on the nightstand. It was like she'd been expecting company.

Either that, or she keeps her place that clean all the time . . .

But no. That can't possibly be true. That just isn't even *human*.

Plus, I'd noticed that the few CDs she *did* have—neatly stacked, in alphabetical order—were by artists such as Phil Collins and Faith Hill.

PHIL COLLINS. AND FAITH HILL.

Not that there's anything wrong them. They're actually very talented artists. I totally loved that "Circle of Life" song the first fifty times I heard it . . .

"Actually, Rachel," I say carefully, "I'm kinda tired."

"Me, too," Jordan chimes in quickly. "It's been a really long day."

"Oh," Rachel says, looking distinctly disappointed. "Maybe another time, then."

"Sure," I say, not looking at Jordan—because really, this whole thing is all his fault. Rachel would never have invited me up for drinks if it hadn't been for Jordan. She had pretended not to recognize him, but I'd overheard one of the RAs tipping her off. Tomorrow she'll probably be all over me with questions about his eligibility.

Because he's worth WAY more than a hundred grand.

"Well," I say. "See you in the morning."

"Right. Good night!" Rachel smiles. To Jordan, she says, "Nice meeting you, Jordan!"

"Likewise," says Jordan, almost as if he means it.

Then, taking Jordan's arm, I steer him back toward Waverly Place, before the conversation can get any more awkward, and he can embarrass me any more in front of the people I work with.

"Oh my God," I say to him, as we walk. "What do you think I should do? About Amber, I mean? What if she turns out to be his next victim? I'll never forgive myself . . . although I totally busted him in front of her, with the whole 'Dave' thing. Don't you think I busted him? Don't you think she'll be a little wary of him now? Oh God. Do you think I should go to the police? I don't have any proof it's him, though. Except . . . except Cooper probably still has the condom! I could use it as some kind of leverage—like, 'Confess or I'll take it to the cops.' Or something."

Jordan, beside me, sounds horrified.

"*Condom?* Heather, what are you—"

"I told you," I say, stomping a foot. "I'm trying to catch a killer. Or at least I think he's a killer. I can't be sure. Your brother thinks I've got an overactive imagination. But you think it's weird, don't you, Jordan? Two girls dead in as many weeks, neither of them with a reputation for elevator surfing, and both of them just having a boyfriend for the first time? I mean, doesn't that sound suspicious to you?"

We turn the corner onto Waverly Place, and one of the Rastafarians approaches, hoping, I guess, that I'd change my mind at last and would take him up on his offer of "Smoke? Smoke?"

Instead of ignoring him and answering my question, Jordan snarls, "Back off!" at the drug dealer, who really isn't a very threatening presence. I mean, I'm way taller and probably twenty pounds heavier than he is. No wonder the poor guy looks so surprised at Jordan's outburst.

Which is when I realize who's really standing in front of me. Not a friend. Not even an acquaintance. But my ex-boyfriend.

"Oh, just forget it," I say, and drop his arm before heading home.

The only problem is, Jordan follows me.

"What'd I do?" he wants to know. "Heather, just tell me. I'm sorry. It's just that I don't know how you expect me to react. Dead girls and condoms and drug dealers. And you *smoke* now. What kind of life is this, Heather? What kind of life?"

I start up the steps to Cooper's brownstone, fumbling for my keys in the light from the street lamp.

"Look," I say. I'm working the locks as fast as I can, conscious that Jordan has come up the stairs behind me, and is blocking all the light from the street lamp with his big, puffy shirt. "It's *my* life, okay? Sorry it's such a mess. But you know, Jordan, you had a hand in making it that way—"

"I know," Jordan cries. "But you wouldn't go to counseling with me, remember? I begged you—"

Both of his heavy hands land on my shoulders, this time not to shake me, but to turn me around to face him. I blink up at him, unable to see his features because the street lamp behind him has made a halo around his head, casting everything within it into dark shadows.

"Heather," Jordan goes on, "every couple has problems. But if they don't work through them together, they won't last."

"Right," I say sarcastically. "Like we did."

"Right," Jordan says, looking down at me. I can't see his eyes, but I can still feel his gaze burning into me. Why's he looking at me like that, anyway? Like he . . . like he . . .

"Oh no," I say, taking a hasty step backward—right into the door. The knob presses hard against my back. "Jordan . . . what are you doing here? I mean, what are you *really* doing here?"

"My parents are throwing an engagement party for me," he says, in a voice that suddenly sounds hoarse. "For Tania and me, I mean. Back home. At the penthouse. Right now."

Mr. and Mrs. Cartwright hadn't thrown an engagement party when Jordan and I had gotten engaged. Instead, Mrs. Cartwright had asked if I was pregnant.

I guess she couldn't think of any other reason her son would bother to get himself engaged to a girl whose career was on the wane and waistline on the rise.

"Well, shouldn't you be there, then?" I ask him.

"I should," Jordan says. And suddenly I realize he doesn't just sound hoarse. He sounds miserable. "I know I should. Only . . . only all I've been able to think of all day is you."

I swallow hard and try to think rationally. After all, I'm a girl detective. That is what girl detectives do. We think rationally.

But there's something about Jordan's proximity—not to mention the misery . . . and raw need . . . in his voice—that's making this really difficult.

And the weight of his hands on my shoulders is very pleasant. And suddenly, I don't even mind the smell of Drakkar Noir so much.

And in the dark, of course, I can see neither the gold necklace nor the ID bracelet he's wearing.

I know! ID bracelet!

"I just," I babble, trying to keep down this wave of hysteria that's threatening to engulf me. "I just think maybe the excitement of it all—the announcement, the reporters—is getting to you. Maybe if you just go home and have an Advil—"

"I don't want an Advil," Jordan murmurs, drawing me close. "All I want is you."

"No," I say, feeling panicky at the touch of puffy shirt to my cheek. "No, you don't. Remember? You keep telling me I've changed. Well, I *have* changed, Jordan. We both have. We've got to move on, and start living our own—separate—lives. That's what you're doing with Tania, and that's what I'm doing with . . . with . . . " With who? I don't have anybody! It isn't fair that he has somebody, and I don't.

"Well, with Lucy," I finish—quite bravely, in my opinion.

"Is that what you want?" Jordan asks me, his lips alarmingly close to mine all of a sudden. "For me to be with Tania?"

I can't believe what I'm hearing.

"*Now* you're asking?"

And the next thing I know, he's stooped down low and is pressing his mouth over mine.

Ordinarily I'm pretty clear-headed in situations like this. I mean, usually when a guy starts kissing me—not that this happens very often—I have the presence of mind to either tell him to stop if I don't like it, or kiss him back if I do.

But in this particular case, I'm so surprised, I just sort of freeze. I mean, I'm still conscious of the doorknob pressing into my back, and the fact that all the lights in the house are out, which means Cooper isn't home yet—thank God!

But beyond that, and some mild embarrassment that the drug dealers, out on the street, are whooping encouragingly, "Go for it, mon!" I don't feel . . . anything.

Anything but good, I mean.

I know as well as the drug dealers that it's been a while since I'd gotten any.

It must have been a while for Jordan, too (either that, or Tania isn't quite pulling her weight in bed . . . which isn't surprising, given that she can only weigh like one-ten, tops), because all I do is slide my arms up around his neck—force of habit, I *swear*—and the next thing I know, he's slammed my body back against the door, the front of his leather pants molded to me so closely that I can feel the individual rivets on his fly . . .

. . . not to mention the thickening, er, muscle beneath those rivets.

Then his tongue is inside my mouth, and his hands in my hair . . .

And all I can think is *OH NO.*

Because he's engaged. And not to me. And I—well, really, I am NOT that type of girl. I'm NOT.

But this little voice inside my head keeps going, *Maybe this is how it's meant to be,* and *Hmmm, I remember how this feels,* and *Well,* he *certainly doesn't seem to mind those added pounds,* which makes it VERY hard to do the right thing, which is push him away.

As a matter of fact, well . . . the little voice is making it *impossible* to push him away.

I guess all those choreographers were wrong. You know, about me having trouble turning off my brain and just letting my body go. Because my body is humming along just fine, without any support from my brain at all . . .

It begins to look as if it would behoove us to get indoors, considering the supportive shouts of the drug dealers, so I twist around and finally get the door open, and we kind of fall into the dark foyer . . .

. . . where I press both my hands against his chest and use my one last moment of sanity to say, "You know, Jordan, I really don't think we should be doing this—"

But it's too late. He's already pulled my shirt from the waistband of my jeans. Next thing I know, his hands are cupping my breasts through the lace of my bra while he kisses me. Deeply. Like he means it, even.

And okay, yeah, I do think—briefly—of reminding him that just that morning, I had been reading all about his engagement—to someone else—in the paper.

But you know, sometimes your body just takes up where your mind leaves off.

And my body seems to be on autopilot, remembering all the good times it had once had with the body that's currently pressed up against it.

And it's pretty much begging for more.

Then it's like I can't think at all for a while. Except . . .

Well, I do have this one thought, toward the end. This thought I really wish I hadn't had.

And that's *Wrong brother*.

That's all. Just that I'm definitely, positively rolling around on the floor with the *wrong brother*.

And I'm not real proud of it.

The worst part of it is, it isn't even that good. I guess the best I can say is that it's quick—thank God, because the hallway runner is beneath me, not the most comfortable carpet in the house. And it's safe—Jordan came prepared, like any good Easy Street member.

Other than that, it doesn't end up being much different than the sex we used to have every Monday, Wednesday, and Saturday . . .

. . . with the obvious exception being that, this time, *I'm* the other woman.

I wonder if Tania ever felt as guilty about it as I do. Somehow, I doubt it. Tania doesn't strike me as someone who ever feels guilty about anything. I once saw her throw a Juicy Fruit wrapper on the ground in Central Park. She doesn't even feel guilty about *littering*.

Another notable difference to our post-breakup sex, as opposed to our pre-breakup sex, is that Jordan gets up almost immediately after we're finished and starts getting dressed. Back when we'd been dating, he'd just roll over and go to sleep.

When I sit up and stare at him, he says, "I'm sorry, but I gotta go," like someone who just remembered a real important dental appointment.

Here's the *really* embarrassing part: I feel kind of sad.

Like there'd been this part of me that had been sure he'd roll over and say he was going to call Tania and break up with her RIGHT NOW because he wants to be with me forever.

Not, you know, that I'd have gone back to him if he had. Probably not.

Okay, definitely not.

But it's . . . well, it's *lonely*, when you don't have anyone. I mean, I don't want to come off sounding like Rachel. I'm not saying that if I had a boyfriend—even Cooper, the man of my dreams—it would cure all my problems.

And I'm not about to start eating salad with no dressing if that's what I have to do to get one—I'm not *that* desperate.

But . . . it would be nice to have *someone* care.

I don't mention any of this to Jordan, though. I mean, I have *some* pride. Instead, when he says he's leaving, I just go, "Okay."

"I mean, I would stay," he says, tugging his shirt over his head, "but I got a real early press junket tomorrow. For the new album, you know."

"Okay," I say.

"But I'll call you tomorrow," he says, fastening the buttons of his fly. "Maybe we can have dinner, or something."

"Okay," I say.

"So, I'll call you," Jordan says, from the foyer.

"Sure," I say. I think we both know he's lying.

After he leaves, and I've locked up behind him, I creep up the stairs to my apartment, where I'm met by an extremely exuberant Lucy, eager for her evening walk. As I look for her leash, I glance through the windows of my kitchen, and see the upper floors of Fischer Hall.

I wonder if Christopher Allington has managed to talk his

way into Amber's pants as easily as Jordan Cartwright talked his way into mine.

Then I remember that said pants are still downstairs, and I hurry down to get them before Cooper comes home and finds the proof of my profound stupidity on the hallway runner.

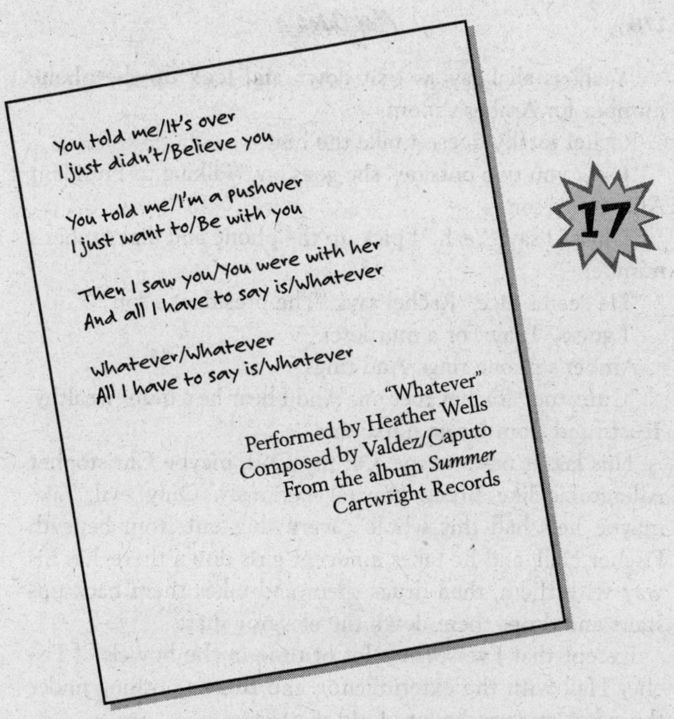

You told me/It's over
I just didn't/Believe you
You told me/I'm a pushover
I just want to/Be with you
Then I saw you/You were with her
And all I have to say is/Whatever
Whatever/Whatever
All I have to say is/Whatever
"Whatever"
Performed by Heather Wells
Composed by Valdez/Caputo
From the album *Summer*
Cartwright Records
17

I'm right about one thing:

Rachel is *totally* curious about Jordan, and the nature of my relationship with him.

The minute I walk into the office the next morning—wet hair, mug of steaming coffee from the caf in my hand, big scarlet letter on my blouse (just kidding about that last part), Rachel is all "So you and your ex-boyfriend seemed to be getting along pretty well last night."

She has *no* idea how true this statement really is.

"Yeah" is all I say, as I sit down and look up the phone number for Amber's room.

Rachel totally doesn't take the hint.

"I saw you two outside," she goes on. "Talking to President Allington's son."

"Chris," I say. "Yeah." I pick up the phone and dial Amber's number.

"He seems nice," Rachel says. "The president's son."

"I guess," I say. For a murderer.

Amber's phone rings. And rings.

"Cute, too," Rachel goes on. "And I hear he's quite wealthy. Trust fund from his grandparents."

This last is news to me. Oh my God, maybe Christopher Allington's like Bruce Wayne! Seriously. Only evil. Like maybe he's had this whole cavern dug out from beneath Fischer Hall, and he takes innocent girls down there, has his way with them, then drugs them and takes them back upstairs and drops them down the elevator shaft . . .

Except that I've spent a lot of time in the bowels of Fischer Hall with the exterminator, and there's nothing under there but mice and a lot of old mattresses.

Someone picks up the phone in Amber's room. A girl's voice says sleepily, "Hello?"

"Hello," I say. "Is this Amber?"

"Uh-huh," the sleepy voice says. "This is Amber. Who's this?"

"No one," I say. Just wanted to make sure you were still alive. "Go back to sleep."

"Okay," Amber says groggily, and hangs up the phone.

Well, Amber's still alive, anyway. For now.

"So are you and Jordan getting back together?" Rachel wants to know. She doesn't seem to think my calling students and waking them up for no apparent reason at all strange.

Which actually says a lot about the weirdness of the place where we work, and our jobs there. "You make the cutest couple."

Fortunately I'm saved from having to reply by my phone, which begins ringing right then. I answer it, wondering if Amber has caller ID and wants to know what the hell I'm doing, waking her up at nine in the morning on a school day.

Only it isn't Amber on the other end. It's Patty, going, "Okay, tell me everything."

"About what?"

I'm not actually feeling very good. All I wanted to do when I woke up this morning was pull the covers back over my head and stay in bed forever and ever.

Jordan. I slept with *Jordan*. Why, God, why?

"Whadduya mean *about what*?" Patty sounds shocked. "Haven't you seen the paper today?"

I feel my blood run cold for the second time in twenty-four hours.

"What paper?"

"The *Post*," Patty says. "There's a photo of you two kissing right on the cover. Well, you can't really see that the woman's you, but it's definitely not Tania Trace. And it's definitely Cooper's front stoop—"

I say a word that sends Rachel skittling out of her office, asking if everything is all right.

"Everything's fine," I say, placing a shaking hand over the receiver. "It's nothing, really."

Meanwhile Patty is busy squawking in my ear.

"The headline says *Sleazy Street*. I guess they mean because Jordan's scamming on his fiancée. But don't worry, they call you the 'unidentified woman.' God, you'd think they'd be able to figure it out. But it's obviously an amateur shot, and your head is in shadows. Still, when Tania sees it—"

"I don't really want to talk about this right now," I interrupt, feeling queasy.

"Don't want to?" Patty sounds surprised. "Or can't?"

"Um. The latter?"

"I gotcha. Lunch?"

"Okay."

"You are such a dope." But Patty is chuckling. "I'll swing by around noon. Haven't seen Magda in a while. Can't wait to hear what SHE has to say about this."

Neither can I.

I hang up. Sarah comes in, full of eager questions about—what else? Jordan. All I want to do is curl up into a ball and cry. Why? WHY? WHY had I been so WEAK?

But since you can't cry at work without seventy people coming up to you and going, "What's wrong? Don't cry. It'll be okay," I pull out a bunch of vending machine refund requests and started processing them instead, bending over my calculator and trying to look super busy and responsible.

It isn't like Rachel doesn't have plenty to do herself. She found out earlier in the week that she'd been nominated for a Pansy. Pansys are these medals, in the shape of a flower, that the college gives out to staff and administrators every semester when they've done something above and beyond the line of duty. For instance, Pete has one for ramming this girl's door down when she barricaded herself behind it and turned on the gas in her oven. He completely saved her life.

Magda has one, too, because—weird as she is, with the movie star thing—the kids, for the most part, just adore her. She makes them feel at home, especially every December, when, in disregard of all campus regulations, Magda decorates her cash register with a stuffed Santa, a miniature crèche, a menorah, and Kwanzaa candles.

I personally think it's nice that Rachel got nominated.

She's dealt with a lot since she started here at Fischer Hall, including two student deaths in two weeks. She's had to notify two sets of parents that their kid is dead, pack up two sets of belongings (well, okay, I did that, both times), and organize two memorial services. The woman deserves a pansy-shaped medal, at the very least.

Anyway, because of her Pansy nomination, Rachel is automatically invited to the Pansy Ball, this black-tie affair held annually on the ground floor of the college library, and she's all aflutter about it, since the ball is tonight and she keeps insisting she has nothing to wear. She says she's going to have to go hit some sample sales at lunch to see if she can find something suitable.

I know what this means, of course. She'll be coming back with the most beautiful gown any of us has ever seen. When you're a size 2, you can just pop into any store and find hundreds of totally stunning options.

When I'm finished with the refund requests, I announce that I'm going to disbursements to get them cashed, and Rachel waves me away, thankfully not commenting on the fact that I hate waiting on line at Banking (which was Justine's favorite place) and usually send a student worker to do it.

Of course, on my way to disbursements, I swing by the caf to see Magda. She takes one look at my face and informs her supervisor, Gerald, that she's taking a ten-minute break, even though Gerald's like, "But you just went on break half an hour ago!"

Magda and I walk out into the park, sit on a bench, and I pour out the whole stupid Jordan story.

When she's done laughing at me, Magda wipes her eyes and said, "Oh, my poor baby. But what did you expect? That he was going to beg you to come back?"

"Well," I say. "Yes."

"But would you have gone with him?"

"Well . . . no. But it would have been nice to be asked."

"Look, baby, you know and I know that you are the best thing that has ever happened to him. But him? He just wants a girl who will do whatever he say. And that is not you. So you let him stay with Miss Bony Butt. And you wait for a *nice* man to come along. You never know. He might be closer than you think."

I know she's talking about Cooper.

"I told you," I say, miserably. "I'm not his type. I'm going to have to get like four degrees just to compete with his last girlfriend, who discovered a dwarf sun, or something, and got it named after her."

Magda just shrugs and says, "What about this Christopher you were telling me about, then?"

"Christopher *Allington*? Magda, I can't date him! He's a possible murderer!"

When I reveal my suspicions concerning Christopher Allington, Magda gets very excited.

"And no one would suspect him," she cries, "because he is the president's son! It's like in a movie! It's perfect!"

"Well, almost perfect," I say. "I mean, why would he go around killing innocent girls? What's his motive?"

Magda thinks about that for a while, and comes up with several theories based on movies she'd seen, like that Chris has to kill people as an initiation rite into some kind of secret law school society, or that possibly he has a split personality or a deranged twin. Which brings her around to the fact that Chris Allington is probably going to be at the Pansy Ball, and if I really want to play detective, I should wrangle myself a ticket and go observe him in his natural element.

"Those tickets cost like two hundred dollars, unless you're nominated for a Pansy," I inform her. "I can't afford one."

"Not even to catch a murderer?" Magda asks.

"He's only a *potential* murderer."

"I bet Cooper could get a pair." I'd forgotten that Cooper's grandfather was a major New York College benefactor, but Magda hasn't. Magda never forgets anything. "Why don't you go with him?"

I haven't had much to smile about lately, but the thought of Cooper putting on a tuxedo does make me kind of laugh. I doubt he's ever even owned one.

Then I stop smiling at the idea of my asking him to go with me to the Pansy Ball. Because he'd never agree to it. He'd want to know why I want to go so badly, then lecture me for sticking my nose where it doesn't belong.

Magda sighs when she hears this.

"Okay," she says, regretfully. "But it could have been just like a movie."

I spend my time at Banking carefully *not* thinking about the night before—which had definitely been nothing like a movie. If it had been like a movie, Jordan would have showed up this morning with a big bouquet of roses and two tickets to Vegas.

Not, you know, that I'd have gone with him. But like I said, it would have been nice to be asked.

I'm walking back across the park, toward Fischer Hall, mentally rehearsing the "I'm sorry, but I just can't marry you" speech I decide I'm going to give to Jordan in case, you know, he *does* turn up with the flowers and the tickets, when I look up, and there he is.

No, seriously. I practically bump into him on the sidewalk in front of the building.

"Oh," I say, clutching an envelope filled with dollar bills to my chest protectively, like it might be able to ward him off. "Hi."

"Heather," Jordan says. He's standing beside a black stretch limo parked—not exactly unobtrusively—in front of the dorm. He's obviously just come from his press junket. He doesn't have any roses with him, but he does have on multiple platinum chains and a very hang-dog look.

Still, I don't feel too sorry for him. After all, *I'm* the one with the rug burns on my ass.

"I've been waiting out here for you," Jordan says. "Your boss said you'd be back within the hour, but—"

Oops. It's eleven-thirty, and I'd left the office at ten. Rachel probably hadn't anticipated my heading out to the park to chat with Magda.

"Well," I say. "I'm back." I look around, but I still don't see any flowers. Which is fine, since I've forgotten my speech anyway. "What's up?"

You are not getting back together with him, I tell myself, firmly. You are *not* getting back together with him. Even if he crawls on his knees . . .

Well, maybe if he crawls on his knees.

No! Not even then! He's the wrong brother, remember? The wrong brother!

Jordan looks around uncomfortably. "Listen. Can we go somewhere and talk?"

"We can talk right here," I say. Because I know if I go off somewhere alone with him, I might do something I'll regret later.

Might? I already *had*.

"I'd feel better," he says, "if we could talk inside the limo."

"*I'd* feel better," I say—stay strong, stay strong—"if you'd just say what you have to say."

Jordan looks surprised at the firmness of my tone. It surprises me, too.

That's when I realize that he probably believes I think we're getting back together or something.

Ahem.

Next thing I know, he's spilling his guts right there on the sidewalk.

"It's just that . . . I'm . . . I'm really confused right now, Heather," he says. "I mean, you're so . . . well, you're just great. But Tania . . . I talked it over with Dad, and I just . . . well, I can't break up with Tania right now. Not with the new album coming out. My dad says—"

"*What?*" I can't believe what I'm hearing. I mean, I believe it. I just can't believe he's actually saying it.

"Seriously, Heather. He's really pissed about that photo in the *Post*—"

"You don't think that *I*—"

"No, no, of course not. But it looks really bad, Heather. Tania's got the best-selling album on the label right now, and my dad says, you know, if I were to leave her, it'd really hurt *my* new album's chances of—"

"Okay," I say. I don't think I can bear to hear any more. This so isn't anything I'd rehearsed a speech for. "It's all right. Really, Jordan. It is."

And the weirdest thing is that, at that moment, it kind of *is* all right. Somehow, hearing Jordan tell me that he can't get back together with me because his dad won't like it completely snuffs out whatever romantic feelings I still have for him.

Not that I had any. Anymore.

Jordan's mouth kind of falls open in astonishment. He'd clearly been expecting tears of some kind. And in a way, I *do* feel like crying. But not because of him.

I don't see any point in telling Jordan that, though. I mean, the guy has enough problems as it is. Sarah would probably have a field day diagnosing all his deep-seated neuroses . . .

Jordan returns my smile with almost childlike relief, and says, "Wow. Okay. That's just . . . that's really sweet of you, Heather."

Strangely enough, all I can think of at that moment is Cooper. Not, you know, how sad it is that I think he's so hot, and he barely knows I'm alive . . . except, you know, for the fact that the pile of receipts on his desk keeps slowly disappearing.

No, I find myself actually praying that Cooper, wherever he is, doesn't happen to pick up a copy of this morning's *Post*. Because the last thing I want is him knowing I'd been making out with—and thank God this was all the *Post* had photographic evidence of—his brother on his front stoop . . .

I don't know if it's because I've been working in Fischer Hall for so long that I've sort of developed a sixth sense about these things or what. But it's right about then that I feel something. A sudden rush of air, a shadow out of the corner of my eye, and I let go of Jordan's hand fast and yell, "Look out!" before I'm even completely aware of what's happening.

Then the next thing I know, there's a sickening thudding sound, then a crash. Then dirt and sharp things are flying through the air.

When I take my arms away from my head and uncover my eyes, I'm horrified to see Jordan sprawled across the sidewalk next to his limo, a huge gash on the side of his head from which blood is pumping steadily, making a soup out of the fine layer of dirt, geraniums, and cement shards that litter the area.

I'm transfixed with shock for a second or two.

Then I'm on my knees at Jordan's side.

"Ohmigod!" A girl who'd been standing a few feet away, trying to hail a taxi, comes running up. "Ohmigod, I saw the whole thing! It was a plant! A potted plant! It came flying down from that penthouse up there!"

"Go inside," I say to her, in a calm voice I don't recognize as my own, "and tell the security guard to call an ambulance and the police. Then ask the desk attendant for the first aid kit."

The girl does as I say, wobbling on her high heels. She's all dressed up for a job interview, but doesn't seem to realize that she's going to be very, very late for it.

What had that instructor said, way back when I'd first trained for this position, about CPR?

Oh, right. Stop. Look. And listen.

I stop and see with relief that Jordan's chest is rising and falling. He's still breathing. A pulse beats in his neck, hard and steady. He's unconscious, but not near death—yet. The planter has struck a glancing blow, sliding down the side of his head, behind his ear, and causing a huge welt on his shoulder. His shirt is torn right through.

Blood is still coursing from the open wound on his head, though, and I'm considering whipping off my own shirt to use as a bandage—that wouldn't make me *too* popular with the guys in the chess circle—when the limo driver comes running around the car, at the same time that Pete comes bursting through the front door of the residence hall.

"Here, Heather." He thrusts the reception desk first aid kit at me, his dark eyes wide. "I got an ambulance on the way, too."

"Is he dead?" the limo driver asks nervously, a cell phone to his ear. Undoubtedly he's on with Jordan's dad.

I hand over my envelope from Banking to Pete, then rummage through the first aid kit, find a rolled up Ace bandage, and shove that into the wound. It turns dark red almost immediately.

"Go get me a towel, or something," I say to Pete, still in this strange, calm voice that sounds so unlike my own. Maybe it's my future voice. You know, the voice I'm going to use in my medical practice, after I get my degree. "There are some linens left over from summer conference housing in the package room. Go get me a couple towels."

Pete is off like a shot. People have started to gather around, Fischer Hall residents as well as people from the chess circle in the park. They all have plenty of medical advice to offer.

"Lift up his head," one of the drug dealers urges me.

"No, lift up his feet," someone else says. "If the face is red, raise the head. If the face is pale, raise the tail."

"His face is red, mon."

"That's just from all the blood."

"Hey, isn't that Jordan Cartwright?"

Pete returns with several clean white towels. The first turns red after only a minute or so. The second seems to do the trick. Blood stops gushing out so alarmingly as I press the towel to Jordan's head.

"How did it happen?" everyone keeps asking.

A man from the chess circle volunteers: "I saw the whole thing. You're lucky you weren't killed, lady. That thing was heading straight for you. If you hadn't jumped outta the way—"

The police arrive before the ambulance, take one look at what I'm doing, and apparently approve, because the next thing I know, they've started shooing people away, telling them the show is over.

I say, urgently, "Take statements from the witnesses! This thing didn't just fall, you know. Somebody pushed it!"

Everyone gathers eagerly around the policemen, wanting to tell their story. It's right around then that Rachel comes running out of the building, her high heels clacking on the pavement.

"Oh, Heather!" she cries, picking her way through the shards of cement and clods of dirt and geranium. "Oh, Heather! I just heard. Is he—is he going to be—"

"He's still breathing," I say. I keep the towel pressed to the wound, which has finally stopped bleeding. "Where's that ambulance?"

But right then it pulls up, and the EMS workers leap out and, thankfully, take over. I'm more than happy to get out of the way. Rachel puts an arm around my shoulders as we watch them take Jordan's vital signs. One of the cops, meanwhile, goes inside, while the other one picks up one of the larger chunks of planter and looks at me.

"Who's in charge here?" he wants to know.

Rachel says, "I guess that'd be me."

"Any idea where this came from?" the cop asks, holding up the slab.

"Well, it looks like one of the cement planters from the Allingtons' terrace," Rachel replies. She turns and points up, toward Fischer Hall's facade. "Up there," she says, craning her neck. "Twentieth floor. The penthouse. There are planters like this lined all around the terrace." She quits pointing and looks at me. "I can't imagine how it could have happened. The wind, maybe?"

I feel really cold, but it isn't from any wind. It's as warm a day in fall as any.

Magda, who has joined us, seems to agree.

"There is no wind today," she says. "On New York One they said it would be mild all day long."

"None of those planters ever blew over before," Pete says. "And I been here twenty years."

"Well, you can't be suggesting someone pushed it," Rachel says, looking horrified. "I mean, the students don't even have access to the terrace—"

"Students?" The cop squints at us. "This some kind of dorm, or something?"

"Residence hall," both Rachel and I correct him automatically.

The EMS workers load Jordan onto a backboard, then onto a stretcher, and then into the back of the ambulance. As they are closing the doors, I glance at Rachel.

"I should go with him," I say to her.

She gives me a little push toward the vehicle. "Of course, you should," she says kindly. "You go. I'll take care of things here. Call me and let me know how he is."

I tell her I will, and hurry after the EMS guys, asking them if I can hitch a ride to the hospital with them. They're totally cool about it, and let me take the passenger seat of the cab.

From the front seat, I can look back through this little door and see what the paramedic who isn't driving is doing to Jordan. What he is doing to Jordan is asking him what day of the week it is. Apparently, Jordan's regaining consciousness. He doesn't know what day of the week it is, though, and only grunts in response, like someone who'd really like to go back to sleep.

I think about suggesting that they ask him who he's engaged to, but then decide this would be too mean.

As we pull away from the hall, I notice that Rachel, Sarah, Pete, and Magda are all huddled on the sidewalk, gazing worriedly after me.

I realize then, with a kind of pang, that yeah, okay, maybe I don't have a boyfriend.

But I do have a family.

A weird one, maybe.

But I've got one.

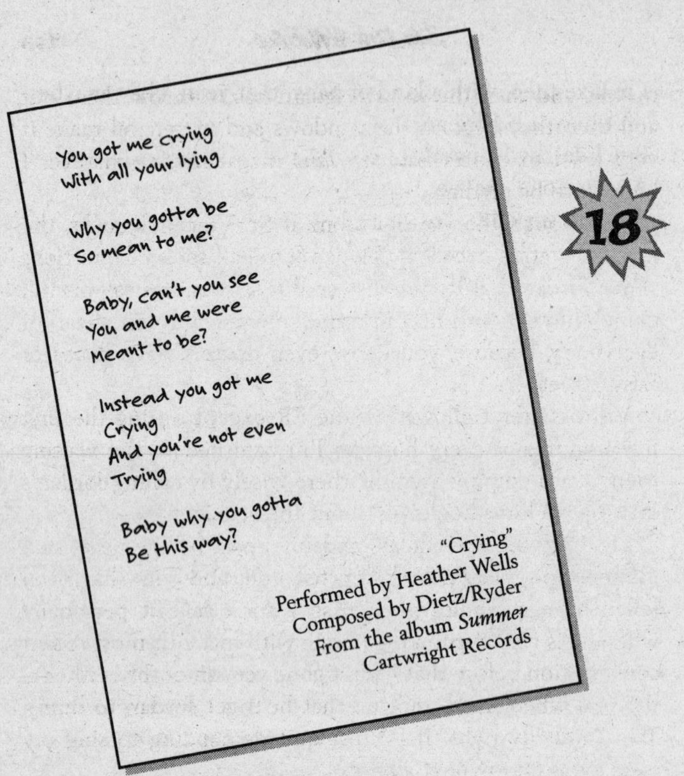
You got me crying
With all your lying

Why you gotta be
So mean to me?

Baby, can't you see
You and me were
Meant to be?

Instead you got me
Crying
And you're not even
Trying

Baby why you gotta
Be this way?

"Crying"
Performed by Heather Wells
Composed by Dietz/Ryder
From the album *Summer*
Cartwright Records
18

In the nearly four months since I started working at New York College, I've been to just about every emergency room in Manhattan with various sick or injured students. St. Vincent's isn't really one of my favorites. There's a TV in the waiting room and everything, but it's always turned to soap operas, and the candy machine is always out of Butterfingers.

Also, a lot of junkies go there to try to convince the triage nurse that they really need some morphine for these mysterious pains in their feet. The junkies are entertaining to watch for a while, but when they start withdrawing they get hostile, and then the security guard has to throw them out and then they beat on the windows and in general make it very hard to concentrate on *Jane* magazine or whatever I happen to be reading.

But though the waiting room at St. Vincent's sucks, the medical staff is excellent. They ask me all sorts of questions about Jordan that I can't answer. But as soon as I say his full name, they whoosh him into the emergency room ahead of everybody, because, you know, even doctors have heard of Easy Street.

Visitors aren't allowed in the ER except during the first five minutes of every hour, so I'm banished to the waiting room. But I employ my time there wisely by calling Jordan's dad to give him the details about the accident.

Mr. Cartwright is understandably upset by the news that his most popular male solo artist—oh, and son—has been felled by a geranium planter, so I don't take it personally when he is very curt on the phone with me. Our most recent conversation before that hadn't gone very smoothly, either—the one where he'd told me that he'd get Jordan to dump Tania and "fly right" if I'd just quit demanding to sing my own songs on my next album.

Mr. Cartwright is kind of a jerk. Which might be why Cooper hasn't spoken to him in almost a year.

After I hang up with Jordan and Cooper's dad, I can't think of anyone else to call. I guess I could let Cooper know his brother's been hurt.

But Cooper is bound to ask what Jordan was doing at Fischer Hall in the first place. And the truth is, I'm not the world's greatest liar. I just have this feeling Cooper will see right through any attempt on my part to pull the wool over his eyes.

So I sink into a plastic chair in one corner of the waiting

room and have fun watching other emergency patients being carted in instead of making any more phone calls. It's just like *Trauma in the ER*, on the Learning Channel, only, you know, live. I see a jovial drunk with a bleeding hand, a frazzled mom with a baby she's spilled her cappuccino on, a kid in a school uniform with a big cut on his chin being steered around by a nun, a construction worker with a broken foot, and a bunch of Spanish women with no visible problems who talk very loudly and get yelled at by the triage nurse.

I sit for twenty more minutes, and then the security guard announces that everyone waiting has five minutes to see their loved ones in the ER. So I herd along with the nun and the nervous mom and the Spanish ladies through the double doors and look around for Jordan.

He is unconscious again, or at least his eyes are closed, the white bandage around his head contrasting startlingly with the deep tan of his skin. (His parents have a really nice summer place in the Hamptons. The pool has a waterfall and everything.) They'd put his gurney in a pretty secluded, quiet section of the ER, and when I ask, the nurse tells me a bed is being prepared for him upstairs. They're still waiting for his X-rays, but it looks as though a concussion is likely.

I guess I must look really worried or something since the nurse smiles at me and puts her hand on my arm and says, "Don't worry. I'm sure he's going to be back to doing dance moves in no time."

In spite of the nurse's assertion, I can't bring myself to leave him there all alone. I can't believe no one from his family has shown up yet! So when my five minutes of standing there and staring at Jordan are up, I go back to my plastic seat in the waiting room. I'll stay, I decide, until he's moved upstairs, or until a member of his family arrives. I'll just hang out till they get here. And then—

And then I don't know what I'll do. I'm convinced—one hundred percent convinced, surer than I've ever been about anything, which I realize isn't saying much, but whatever—that someone has just tried to kill me.

Right? I mean, hadn't that been what the guy from the chess circle had said? "Good thing you moved, lady, or you'd have been the one it hit," or something like that?

And the someone who pushed that planter over could only have been Christopher Allington. Who else had access to his parents' terrace? Who else had reason to knock geranium planters onto my head? It wasn't a premeditated attempt at murder—it couldn't have been. How could he have known I'd be on my way back into the building right then?

No, he must have just looked down and decided fate was on his side and given that planter the heave-ho. If I hadn't ducked, it would have hit me, and not Jordan. And it probably would have killed me, because, you know, my head isn't anywhere near as hard as an ex-member of Easy Street's.

But why does Chris want to kill me? Just because I suspect him of being a murderer? Suspecting someone of being a murderer and actually having proof of someone being a murderer are two entirely different things. What possible proof could Chris think I have? I mean, aside from the condom—which only proves he's randy, not a killer—I have nothing on him. I don't even have proof that there've actually *been* any murders.

So why is he trying to kill me? Isn't he putting himself more at risk by trying to kill me than by just laying low? Especially since foul play isn't suspected in the deaths of Elizabeth and Roberta—

By anyone but me, anyway.

A deep, familiar voice breaks in on my meditations. I look

away from the snoring junkie I've been staring at unseeingly, and up into Cooper's calm, smiling face . . .

. . . and suddenly feel like throwing up.

"Heather," he says, with friendly nonchalance, as he folds himself into the plastic chair beside me.

"Um." That's all I can think of to say. Swift, huh? After a lot of mental turmoil, I finally add, "Hi."

Cooper gazes with mild interest at the snoring junkie. He looks, in his scruffy but form-fitting jeans and black leather jacket, good enough to eat. Better than Ho Hos, even. Cooper, I mean. Not the junkie.

"So," he says, in the same conversational tone. "What's new with you?"

I go cold all over, then hot. It's totally unfair, the hold this guy has over me. And he's never so much as asked me out! Okay, he asked me to move in with him, but, hello, that was out of pity. And I live on a whole separate floor. With a whole separate set of locks on the door. Which I've never actually used, but has he ever bothered to find that out? No!

"Nothing much," I say to him, hoping he can't see how my heart is leaping around inside my T-shirt. "Did, um, your dad call you?"

"No," Cooper says. "Your friend Patty did. When she came to your office to pick you up for lunch, Magda told her what happened. Patty had the baby with her, or she'd have come herself."

"Oh," I say. I'd forgotten all about my lunch appointment with Patty. Glancing at the waiting room clock, I see that it's after two. "Well."

"What she couldn't quite explain," Cooper says, "is what, precisely, happened."

Which is when it all comes spilling out.

I don't want for it to. I don't mean for it to. It's just . . .

well, I guess that's why Cooper's such a good detective. There's something in his deep voice that just makes you blurt out everything you know . . .

Well, okay, not *everything.* I did manage to keep the whole part about what Jordan and I had done on Cooper's hallway runner under wraps. Wild horses aren't going to drag *that* information out of me.

Oh, and the part about me wanting to, you know, peel off Cooper's clothes with my teeth, of course.

But the rest of it just comes out in this giant gush, the way the hot chocolate in the dorm cafeteria does sometimes, right after Magda's poured the mix in but before anybody's stirred it . . .

I tell him, starting with the lip-synch the night before, when I'd first begun to suspect that Christopher Allington was Elizabeth and Roberta's killer, and ending with the geraniums cracking Jordan's head open, skipping over the part in between where his brother and I made the beast with two backs in his foyer.

I've overheard Cooper in action with his clients a couple of times. The washer/dryer is on the same floor as his office, just off the kitchen, and I've been in there washing my control top underwear (I only wear it on special occasions, like customer service training seminars or cultural diversity awareness workshops) when he's met with people who've hired him. He talks to them in this totally calm, careful voice . . .

. . . a completely different voice, it turns out, than he uses on his nonpaying clientele.

"Heather, are you insane?" He looks really mad. He *sounds* really mad. "You went and *talked* to the guy?"

It would be nice to think that the reason he's so angry with me is because my near brush with death has finally made him realize his true feelings for me.

But I think all it did was reinforce his suspicions that I'm a complete and total whacko.

"Why are you yelling at *me*?" I demand. "I'm the victim here!"

"No, you're not. Jordan is. And if you'd just listened to me—"

"But if I'd listened to you, I wouldn't know that Chris Allington is the dangerous psychopath we've been looking for!"

"A fact of which you still don't have any proof." Cooper shakes his head. He has dark, thick hair that he hardly ever gets cut and that is always growing past his collar, giving him a distinctly nonconformist air, even without the whole private eye thing. "That planter could have been knocked over by anyone. How do you know the Allingtons' gardener wasn't watering the plants and accidentally knocked the thing over?"

"Directly onto me? Isn't that just a bit of a coincidence? Considering the fact that I was just questioning Chris Allington the night before?"

I swear I see the corners of Cooper's mouth twitch at this.

"I'm sorry, Heather, but I doubt your interrogation skills are such as to goad Chris Allington into a murderous frenzy."

Okay, Miss Marple I may not be. But he doesn't have to rub it in.

"I'm telling you, he tried to kill me. Why don't you believe me?" I hear myself cry, before I can shut my mouth. "Can't you see that I'm not a stupid little teen pop star anymore, and that I might just know what I'm talking about?"

Even as the words are coming out, I'm wishing them unsaid. What am I doing? *What am I doing*? This is the guy who, without my even asking, offered me a place to live when I had nowhere to go . . . well, okay, except the guest room in Patty and Frank's loft.

But, you know. Besides that. How ungrateful can I be?

"I'm so sorry," I say, feeling dry-mouthed with panic. "I didn't mean it. I don't know where that came from. I'm just—I think maybe I'm just upset. You know. From the stress."

Cooper is just sitting there, looking at me with a totally unreadable expression.

"I don't think of you as a stupid little teen pop star" is all he says, in a tone suggesting mild surprise.

"I know," I say quickly. Oh God, why can't I ever seem to keep my mouth shut? WHY?

"I just worry about you sometimes," Cooper goes on, before I can say anything else. "I mean, you get yourself into things. . . . That whole thing with my brother—"

What whole thing? Did he mean . . . my *relationship* with his brother? Or last night? Oh please, don't let him have seen the *Post*. . . .

"And it's not like you have anyone." He shakes his head again. "Any family, or anyone to look after you."

"But neither do you," I remind him.

"That's different," he says.

"I don't see how," I say. "I mean, except that I'm younger than you." But what's seven years, really? Prince Charles and Lady Diana were twelve years apart . . . and okay, that didn't turn out so well, but how likely are we to repeat their mistakes as a couple? If Cooper and I ever were to become one, I mean. Neither of us even likes polo.

"Besides," I say, remembering what I'd seen out of the ambulance window. "I do have a family. Sort of. I mean, there's Rachel and Magda and Pete and Patty and you—"

I didn't mean to add that last word. But there it is, floating in the air between us. You. You're part of my family, Cooper. My new family, now that my real family members are all incarcerated or on the lam. Congratulations!

Cooper just looks at me like I'm crazy (how unusual). So I add lamely, "And Lucy, too."

Cooper exhales slowly.

"If you really feel strongly that what happened wasn't an accident," he says at last, pointedly ignoring the We Are Family speech (don't think I don't notice), "and you really think someone is trying to kill you, then I suggest we go to the police."

"I tried that," I remind him. "Remember?"

"Yes. But this time I'm going with you, and I'm going to make sure—"

His voice trails off as a petite, attractive brunette comes rushing up to the waiting room desk, all breathless and leather-skirted, her left hand weighted down by a massive diamond ring.

Okay, so I can't actually see the ring from where I'm sitting. I still know who she is. I've seen her with her mouth around my ex's you-know-what. Her image will be forever burned onto my retina.

"Excuse me," she breathes to the stony-faced receptionist. "But I believe my fiancé is here. Jordan Cartwright. When can I see him?"

Tania Trace, the woman who'd taken my place in Jordan's heart and penthouse—not to mention my position on the music charts.

"Funny," Cooper observes. "She looks as if she's handling the pain quite well."

I glance at him curiously, then remember that he's referring to something I'd told him some time ago, after I'd first moved in.

"Oh sure," I say. "Because she's strung out on painkillers. But I'm telling you, Coop, you can't have that much plastic surgery and expect to live a pain-free life. I mean, she's been almost completely reconstructed. In reality, she's a size eighteen."

"Right," Cooper says. "Looks like my brother's in good hands now. Shall we go?"

We go.

And none too soon, if you ask me.

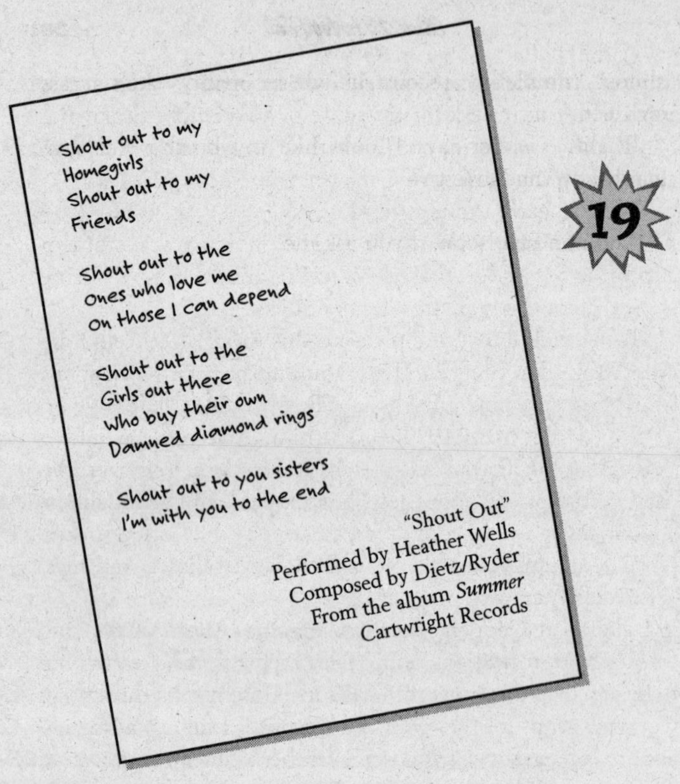
Shout out to my
Homegirls
Shout out to my
Friends

Shout out to the
Ones who love me
On those I can depend

Shout out to the
Girls out there
Who buy their own
Damned diamond rings

Shout out to you sisters
I'm with you to the end

"Shout Out"
Performed by Heather Wells
Composed by Dietz/Ryder
From the album *Summer*
Cartwright Records
19

The first person at the Sixth Precinct I tell my story to is a pretty but tired-looking woman at the front desk. She has her long black hair in a bun, which I assume is regulation hairstyle for policewomen.

I make a mental note not to major in criminal justice.

The woman directs us to a pudgy guy at a desk, to whom I repeat my story. Like the receptionist, he looks bored . . .

. . . until I get to the part about Jordan. Everybody perks up at the mention of Easy Street.

The pudgy guy has us wait a few minutes, and then we're

ushered into someone's extremely tidy office. We sit across from a very neat desk for a minute or two before the owner of the office walks in, and I see that he is none other than cigar-chomping Detective Canavan.

"You!" I nearly shout at him.

"You!" he nearly shouts back. He's holding a Styrofoam cup of coffee and—what else?—a doughnut. Krispy Kreme glazed, from the look of it. Lucky duck.

"To what do I owe the pleasure this time, Miss Wells?" he asks. "Wait, don't tell me. This wouldn't happen to be about somebody crowning a Backstreet Boy, would it?"

"Easy Street member," I correct him. "And yes, it would."

Detective Canavan sits down at his desk, removes the unlit cigar from his mouth, tears off a piece of his doughnut, and dunks it in his coffee. He then puts the coffee-soaked piece of doughnut in his mouth, chews, swallows, and says, "Pray enlighten me."

I glance at Cooper, who had remained silent at my side through two recitations of my tale. Seeing that he isn't going to be any help this time, either, I launch into it for a third time, wondering, not for the first time, what it is I find so attractive about Cooper anyway, since he can be so uncommunicative sometimes. Then I remember the whole being-so-hot-and-kind-and-generous-to-me-without-asking-anything-in-return thing, and I know why.

Detective Canavan clasps his hands behind his head as he listens, tipping his chair back as far as it will go. Either he has forgotten his Mitchum for Men or he is just a very profuse sweater, because he has large perspiration stains underneath his arms. Not that this seems to bother him.

"So," Detective Canavan says, to the water-stained ceiling panels, when I'm through talking. "Now you think the president of New York College's kid is a murderer."

"Well," I say, hesitantly. Because when he puts it that way, it sounds so . . . dumb. "Yes. I guess I do."

"But you got no proof. Sure, this guy here's got a condom. A condom we could probably prove is his. But which wouldn't be admissible in court. But you got no proof any crime has actually been committed, with the exception of this planter over the side of the terrace, which could have been accidental—"

"But those planters have been up there for years," I interrupt. "And none of them ever fell down until today—"

"Coroner's report on both dead girls states cause of death was accidental." Detective Canavan quits gazing at the ceiling and looks at me. "Listen, miss—is it still miss?"

Unaccountably, I feel myself blushing. Maybe because if it hadn't been for Tania Trace, by now it would have been Mrs. Although I sort of doubt it would have remained that way for long.

"It's Ms.," I say firmly.

Detective Canavan nods. "My wife's a Ms. now, too. Anyway, listen, Ms. Wells. Kids that age? They're dopes. Accidents are the leading cause of death for people ages seventeen to twenty-five. Kids are trying to find themselves, taking stupid risks—"

"Not those girls," I say, firmly.

"Maybe not. The point is, Ms. Wells, you got nothing on this guy. You don't even have a definite murder to pin on him. If the Backstreet Boy dies, then maybe we'll have something. Maybe. But the coroner could just as easily rule that one as accidental as well."

"Well," I say. I have to admit, I feel very let down. Detective Canavan hadn't laughed outright in my face this time, I'll admit, but he hadn't taken a single note, either. I pick up my backpack.

"Sorry to have wasted your time. Again." I get up, and Detective Canavan looks at me like I was nuts.

"Where do you think you're going?" he demands. "Sit down. I'm not through with you yet."

I sit back down, perplexed.

"What's the point?" I ask Detective Canavan, with more asperity than is, perhaps, necessary. "You obviously think I'm some kind of nutcase. What do I need to stick around here for? I can get laughed at by my own friends"—I keep my gaze averted from Cooper's face. "I don't need to go to the police for that."

Detective Canavan finishes the rest of his doughnut, then picks up his cigar. He looks at Cooper.

"She's a fiery one," he comments, nodding at me.

"Oh, she's that," Cooper agrees, gravely.

"Wait." I glance from one man to the other, suspicion dawning. "You two know each other?"

Cooper shrugs. "I've seen him around the neighborhood," he says, referring to Detective Canavan.

"Can't swing a dead cat without running into this guy behind a parked car or mailbox, shooting film of some poor schmuck whose wife is leaving him," says Detective Canavan, referring to Cooper.

"Great," I say, feeling more inadequate than ever. "That's just great. Well, I hope you two are enjoying your little laugh at my expense—"

"Do I look like I'm laughing?" Detective Canavan demands. "Do you see so much as a smile upon my face? Your boyfriend over there, I don't see him laughing, either."

"I see absolutely nothing amusing about the situation," Cooper says.

I look at him. He isn't smiling. And he hasn't, I noticed, objected to being called my boyfriend. I look back at Detective Canavan.

"He's not my boyfriend," I point out loudly—to what purpose, I cannot imagine. But I'm sure my cheeks are crimson.

Detective Canavan nods at me as if I'd said something along the lines of *The sky is blue.*

"Now, Ms. Wells," he says. "We do have a very high number of nutcases, as you call them, who come in here to report various crimes that may or may not actually have occurred. Some of these so-called nutcases are honest citizens who want to help the police to do their job. I would put you in this category. You have done your duty by relating your beliefs in this matter to me, and I, in due course, will investigate them."

"Really?" I perk right up. "You really will? You're gonna question Chris?"

"I will do so." Detective Canavan sticks his cigar back in his mouth. "Discreetly. That is my job. It is not, however, *your* job. I strongly advise you, Ms. Wells, not to involve yourself any further in this matter."

"Because you think Christopher Allington might try to kill me, too?" I ask, breathlessly.

"Because I think Christopher Allington might try to sue you for making false accusations, and he'd have a pretty good case, too." Detective Canavan ignores my crestfallen expression. "What you're suggesting, Ms. Wells, is that Christopher Allington is not only a serial killer, but a killer of such intelligence and skill that he not only leaves no evidence linking him to his crimes—save for an alleged condom—but leaves no trace that a crime has even been committed. I hate to disappoint you, but in my experience, killers aren't that smart. They are, in fact, remarkably stupid people. That is why they have killed: They are so limited intellectually, they saw no other way out."

Detective Canavan's dark gray eyebrows furrow together in thought as he goes on. "And despite all the media hoopla around them, I have yet to meet an actual serial killer myself, and I have investigated over seven hundred homicides. So I suggest you keep a low profile as far as Christopher Allington is concerned, Ms. Wells. I'd hate for you to lose your job over something like this."

I'm so disappointed that I don't think there's anything I can do to hide it. My shoulders slump, and my head sinks down between them as I murmur, "Thank you, Detective."

Detective Canavan hands me his card, tells me to call him if I think of anything else that might be helpful to his investigation, and, after asking Cooper a question or two about some case or other he's seen him snooping around the neighborhood over, sends us on our way.

Cooper hails us a cab, and maintains an air of extreme seriousness all the way back to the house. He seems to have taken my accusation—that he thinks of me as a teen pop star—to heart, and is doing everything in his power to prove it isn't true. He even tells me, in the cab, that he considers Detective Canavan a good man and a fine investigator, and says if there's something to get to the bottom of at Fischer Hall, Detective Canavan is the man to do it.

Which makes me feel better. A little.

Once back at the brownstone—I know I really ought to head back to the office, but seeing as how I'm home now anyway, I decide I'll just give Lucy a quick walk—I pause briefly in front of the antique, gilt-framed mirror in the front hallway to reapply my lip gloss, while Cooper goes back to his office to replay his messages. I've already glanced around to make sure that there are no signs of the love tussle Jordan and I shared on the runner the night before.

Still, when Cooper comes out of his office a second later and asks, "What exactly is going on with you and Jordan?" I nearly have a heart attack.

"Wh-what do you mean?" I stammer.

"Well, what was he doing outside Fischer Hall today, anyway?"

"Oh," I say, relaxing. "That. Nothing. Just talking."

"I see." Cooper leans against the doorframe, his blue eyes brighter than normal. "So you wouldn't happen to know anything about that blond he was photographed by the *Post* kissing on my doorstep?"

I almost swallow my tongue.

I can't believe he's seen it! Are things *ever* going to go my way? Or had I used up all my luck already? You know, those ten years of good luck I once read that everybody gets—one magical decade where nothing goes wrong . . . or at least, nothing major.

Had my decade of luck already gone by? And if so, can I have a do-over? Because if someone had asked me, "Hey, Heather, do you want your decade of luck between ages fourteen and twenty-four or twenty-four and thirty-four?" I'd have chosen the latter. I really would have.

Because who wants the best years of their life to be the ones they spent in *high school*?

I guess my extreme consternation must show on my face, since a second later Cooper has straightened and is going, "What's the matter?" in a voice that—almost—sounds like he actually cares.

Which just makes me want to start sobbing, right then and there.

"It's nothing," I say. "Really."

It isn't nothing, though. I mean, everyone else can deny it, but I know—I *know*—someone is trying to *kill* me. I had sex with my ex, who is engaged to someone with a way better career—and much smaller butt—than mine. And, worst of all, Cooper's seen the photographic evidence of my indiscretion . . . or at least, of what led up to it.

"Something's wrong," Cooper says, coming to stand beside me in front of the mirror. "Don't deny it. I'm a trained observer, remember? There's this little line you get between your eyebrows when you're upset—" He points at my reflection. "See it?"

God. He's right. I have a little worry line between my eyebrows. My God, if I keep this up, I'll have wrinkles by the time I'm thirty.

With an effort, I force my face to relax.

"It's nothing," I say, quickly, averting my gaze from my reflection. "Really. That thing with Jordan last night—it was just a good-bye kiss."

Cooper looks at me. Skeptically.

"A good-bye kiss," he says.

"Yeah. Because it's, you know, really over between us. Jordan and me." I clear my throat. "You know. Really, *really* over."

Cooper nods, though he still looks dubious.

"Right," he says. "Well, if you say—"

"We're both ready to move on," I interrupt, warming to my story, "at last. You know, we needed to have some closure, because the way things ended—with me storming out like that, and all—well, it wasn't healthy. Things are good now between us. We both know it's really . . . over."

"So if things are really, really over between the two of you," Cooper asks, "what was Jordan doing in front of Fischer Hall this morning when that planter fell on him?"

Dang! I forgot about that!

But it's okay. I have the situation under control.

"Oh, that?" I say, with a breezy laugh. Yes! I even manage a breezy laugh. Maybe I, like Britney and Mandy, have a film career in my future. Maybe I should be a theater major, like Marnie. Maybe someday I'll have an Oscar to put on the shelf next to my Nobel Prize. Wait. Is a Nobel Prize a statue or a medal? I can't remember.

"Yeah," I say. Still breezy. "He was just returning a, um, CD that I'd left at our place. You know, when I moved out."

"A CD," Cooper says.

"Uh-huh," I say. "My, um, *Tank Girl* soundtrack. You can't find it anymore. It's very rare."

"I see," Cooper says. I try not to notice how, now that he's taken off his leather jacket, his biceps—barely visible beneath the short sleeves of his plain gray T-shirt—are just as defined as his brother's. . . .

Only from actual work, not working *out*, I know. It's not all sneaking around with a camera when you're a PI. I imagine Cooper has to . . . you know. Lift things. And stuff. I wonder if maybe he ever gets sweaty doing it and has to take his shirt off completely, you know, because he's so hot . . .

Whoa. I so need to go back to work.

But all this detective stuff has reminded me of something.

"Yeah," I say. Now that the danger of tears has been averted, I'm feeling a little more daring. "In fact, now that Jordan and I have everything settled, I feel, you know, like celebrating."

"Celebrating," Cooper echoes tonelessly.

"Yeah. You know. I never go out anymore. So I thought, Hey, why not go to the, um, Pansy Ball tonight."

"The *Pansy* Ball?" Cooper's gaze doesn't stray from my face. I hope he isn't checking to see if I'm lying. I really *do* want to go to the Pansy Ball. Just not, you know, for the reasons I'm telling him.

"Yeah," I say. "It's a ball to honor the trustees and people who've been given Pansys. You know, for service to the college. Rachel's getting one."

It isn't my imagination. At the sound of my boss's name,

Cooper abruptly loses interest in the conversation. In fact, he walks over to the mail that has just slid through the drop slot—to Lucy's intent interest—and, after wrestling it from her, starts sorting through it.

"Rachel, huh?" he says.

"Yeah," I say. "The tickets are like two hundred bucks, though. To the ball. And God knows I can't afford one. But I was thinking, your grandfather was an alumnus, right? So I bet you have access to some free ones. Tickets, I mean."

"Probably," Cooper says, giving Lucy, who is whining piteously, a J. Crew catalog to chew on.

"So could I, maybe, have one?" I ask. Subtle. That's me. Miss Subtle.

"So you can spy on Christopher Allington?" Cooper doesn't even look up from the mail. "Not a chance."

My jaw drops.

"But—"

"Heather, didn't you hear a word that detective said? He's going to look into it. Subtly. In the meantime, stay out of it. At best, the only thing you're going to get for your efforts is sued."

"I swear I'm not gonna talk to him," I insist, raising my right hand and making the Girl Scout's honor symbol with three fingers. Except, of course, I never was a Girl Scout, so it doesn't count. "I won't go near him."

"Correct me if I'm mistaken," Cooper says, "but aren't you convinced he tried to kill you today?"

"Well, that's what I'm trying to find out," I say. "C'mon, Cooper, what could possibly happen at the *Pansy Ball*, for God's sake? He's not going to try to do anything to me there, in front of everybody . . ."

"No, he isn't," Cooper says. "Because I'm not letting you out of my sight."

I blink. Wait. What did he just say?

"You—you want to go with me?"

"Only because if I don't keep an eye on you, who knows what'll fall on your head next time." Cooper puts down the mail. His blue-eyed gaze bores into me like a pair of headlights. "And because I can see by the look in your eyes that you're going to get your hands on a ticket somehow, even if it means seducing some unsuspecting rube in the geology department."

I'm stunned. Cooper is taking me to the Pansy Ball! Cooper Cartwright is taking me out! It was almost like a . . .

Well, a *date.*

"Oh, Cooper!" I breathe. "Thank you so much! You don't know how much this means to me—"

Cooper is already moving back toward his office, shaking his head. He keeps his thoughts to himself, but I have a pretty good idea that he isn't, as I am, frantically trying to figure out what he's going to wear.

Guys have it so easy.

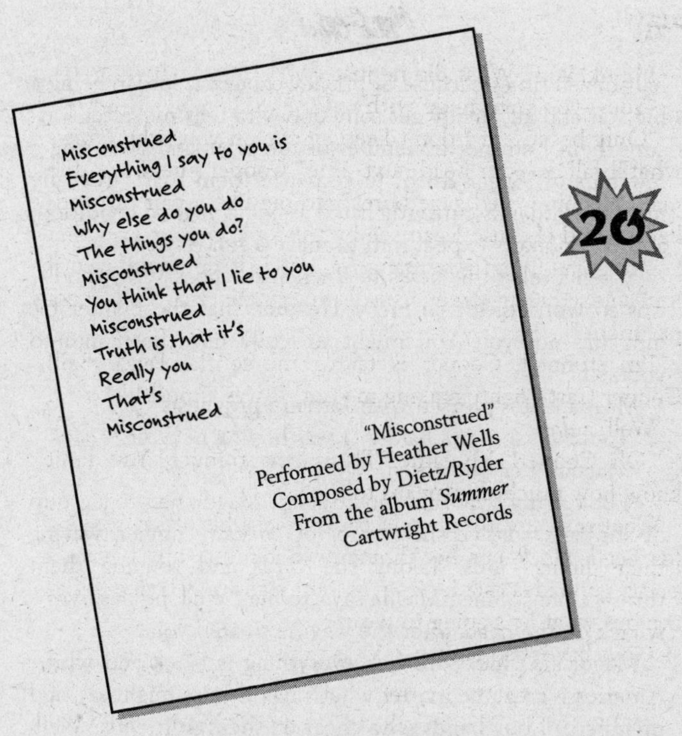
Misconstrued
Everything I say to you is
Misconstrued
Why else do you do
The things you do?
Misconstrued
You think that I lie to you
Misconstrued
Truth is that it's
Really you
That's
Misconstrued

"Misconstrued"
Performed by Heather Wells
Composed by Dietz/Ryder
From the album *Summer*
Cartwright Records

20

I can't get through the remainder of the workday fast enough.

Everyone asks after Jordan's health, causing me to realize guiltily that I don't even know how he's doing, since I've been slightly distracted since leaving the hospital, what with meeting with detectives and getting asked out (sort of) by the man of my dreams, and having to figure out what I'm going to wear on our date to the Pansy Ball, and all.

So I call St. Vincent's and after being transferred about a

half-dozen times because of privacy concerns, Jordan being a big star and all, finally get someone who tells me, after I assure them I am not a member of the press and even sing a few bars of "Sugar Rush" to convince them that I'm really me, that Jordan is currently listed as being in good condition, and that doctors expect him to make a full recovery.

When I relay this news to Rachel, she goes, "Oh, good! I was so worried. It's so lucky, Heather, that the planter hit him and not you. You might so easily have been injured yourself."

Magda is less pleased with Jordan's prognosis.

"Too bad," she says baldly. "I was hoping he'd die."

"Magda!" I cry, horrified.

"Look at my byootiful movie stars," Magda says to a group of students who've shown up for an early dinner, waving their dining cards. Taking the cards and running them through the scanner, Magda says, to me, "Well, he deserves a whack on the head, after the way he treated you."

Magda's so lucky. To her, everything is black and white. America is great, no matter what anybody else might say, and members of boy bands who cheat on their girlfriends? Well, they deserve to have planters dropped on their heads. No questions asked.

Patty is relieved to hear from me when I call her. I guess when she'd crossed the park and seen all the blood on the sidewalk in front of Fischer Hall, she'd gotten really freaked out. She'd been convinced something had happened to me. She'd had to sit down in the cafeteria with her head between her knees for twenty minutes—and eat two DoveBars Magda pressed on her—before she finally felt well enough to flag down a cab and go home.

"Are you really sure about this college degree thing, Heather?" she asks now, worriedly. "Because I'm sure Frank could set up an appointment for you with people from his label—"

"That'd be nice," I say. "Except, you know, I'm not sure how impressed Frank's label would really be about the fact that most of my past performances took place in malls—"

"They wouldn't care about that," Patty cries. Which is really sweet of her, and all, but that's exactly the kind of thing record labels *do* care about, I've discovered.

"Maybe we can get you a part in a musical, you know, like on Broadway," Patty says. "Debbie Gibson's doing it. Lot's of stars are—"

"Operative word being star," I point out. "Which I am not."

"I just don't think you should work in that dorm anymore, Heather," Patty says worriedly. "It's too dangerous. Girls dying. Flower pots falling down on people—"

"Oh, Patty," I say, touched by her concern. "I'll be all right."

"I'm serious, Heather. Cooper and I discussed it, and we both feel—"

"You and Cooper discussed *me*?" I hope I don't sound too eager. What had they talked about? I wonder. Had Cooper revealed to Patty that he has a deep and abiding love for me that he dares not show, since I'm his brother's ex and sort of an employee of his?

But if he had, wouldn't she have told me right away?

"Cooper and I just feel—and Frank agrees—that if—well, if it turns out this whole murder thing is true, you might be putting yourself in some kind of danger—"

This doesn't sound to me like Cooper had said anything at all about harboring a deep and abiding love for me. No wonder Patty hadn't called me right away to dish.

"Patty," I say, "I'm fine. Really. I've got the best bodyguard in the world." Then I tell her about the Pansy Ball, and Cooper's escorting me there.

Patty doesn't sound as excited about it as I expect her to, though. Oh, she says I can borrow her dress—the red Armani she'd worn to the Grammys when she'd been seven months' pregnant with Indy, and which I hope will consequently fit me—and all, but she isn't exactly shrieking, "Ooooh he asked you out!"

Because I guess he hasn't, really. Maybe it isn't a *real* date when the guy is just going out with you to make sure no one kills you.

God. When did Patty get so mature?

"Well, just promise me to be careful, okay, Heather?" Patty still sounds worried. "Cooper says he thinks the whole murder thing is kind of . . . unlikely. But I'm not so sure. And I don't want you to be next."

I do my best to reassure Patty that my safety is hardly in jeopardy—even though, of course, I'm pretty sure the exact opposite is true. Someone in Fischer Hall wants me dead.

Which means I am definitely on to something with my Elizabeth-Kellogg-and-Roberta-Pace-were-murdered theory.

It isn't until I've hung up with Patty that I feel someone's gaze on me. I look up and see that Sarah is sitting at her desk, stuffing Tootsie Rolls into little plastic bags as a surprise for each of the RAs, all of whom she feels need a pick-me-up after the rocky start their semester had gotten off to, given the dead girls and all.

Only I can't help noticing that Sarah has stopped stuffing, and is instead staring at me owlishly through her thick glasses—she only wears her contacts on special occasions, such as check-in (potential to meet cute single dads) or poetry readings at St. Mark's Church (potential to meet cute penniless poets).

"I didn't mean to listen in on your conversation," Sarah

says, "but did I just hear you say you think someone's trying to *kill* you?"

"Um," I say. How can I put this so as not to cause her undue alarm? After all, I get to go home every night, but Sarah has to live here. How comfortable is she going to feel knowing there's a dangerous psychopath stalking the floors of Fischer Hall?

Then again, Sarah lost her virginity on an Israeli kibbutz the summer of her freshman year—or so she'd told me—so it isn't like she's a potential victim.

So I shrug and say, "Yes."

Then—because Rachel is upstairs in her apartment getting ready for the ball (she'd managed to find something to wear, but wouldn't show it to us on account of "not wanting to ruin the surprise")—I tell her my theory about Chris Allington and the deaths of Elizabeth Kellogg and Roberta Pace.

"Have you told any of this to Rachel?" Sarah asks me, when I'm done.

"No," I say. "Rachel has enough to worry about, don't you think?" Besides—I don't mention this part to Sarah—if it turns out I'm wrong, it won't look so good at my six months' employment review . . . you know, my suspecting the son of the president of the college of a double homicide.

"Good," Sarah says. "Don't. Because has it occurred to you that this whole thing—you know, with your thinking that Elizabeth and Roberta were murdered—might be a manifestation of your own insecurities over having been betrayed and abandoned by your mother?"

I just blink at her. "What?"

"Well," Sarah says, pushing up her glasses. "Your mother stole all your money and fled the country with your manager.

That had to have been the most traumatic event in your life. I mean, you lost everything—all your savings, as well as the people on whom you thought you could most depend, your father having been absent most of your life to begin with due to his long-term incarceration for passing bad checks. And yet whenever anyone brings it up, you dismiss the whole thing as if it were nothing."

"No, I don't," I say. Because I don't. Or at least, I don't think I do.

"Yes, you do," Sarah says. "You even still speak to your mother. I heard you on the phone with her the other day. You were chatting with her about what to get your dad for his birthday. In *jail*. The woman who stole all your money and fled to Argentina!"

"Well," I say, a little defensively. "She's still my *mother*, no matter what she's done."

I'm never sure how to explain about my mom. Yes, when the going got tough—when I let Cartwright Records know I was only interested in singing my own lyrics, and Jordan's dad, in response, unceremoniously dropped me from the label—not that my sales had been going gangbusters anymore anyway—my mom got going.

But that's just how she is. I was mad at her for a while, of course.

But being mad at my mom is kind of like being mad because it's raining out. She can't help what she does, any more than clouds can.

But I suppose Sarah, if she heard that, would just say I'm in denial, or worse.

"Isn't it possible that you're displacing the hostility you feel about what your mother did to you onto poor Chris Allington?" Sarah wants to know.

"Excuse me," I say. I'm getting kind of tired of repeating

myself. "But that planter didn't just fall out of the sky, you know. Well, okay, it did, but not by itself."

"And could it be that you miss the attention you used to receive from your fans so much that you've latched on to any excuse to make yourself feel important by inventing this big important mystery for you to solve, where none actually exists?"

I remember, with a pang, what Cooper had said outside the service elevator. Hadn't it been something along these same lines? About me wanting to relive the thrill of my glory days back at the Mall of America?

But wanting to find out who's responsible for killing people in your place of work is totally different from singing in front of thousands of busy shoppers.

I mean, isn't it?

"Um" is what I say in response to Sarah's accusation. "Maybe. I don't know."

All I can think is, Sarah's lucky she met Yael when she did. The kibbutz guy, I mean. Otherwise, she's just the kind of girl Chris would go for next.

Well, except for that habit she has of psychoanalyzing people all the time. I could see how that might get annoying.

I haven't been to a dressy party in ages, so when I finally get off work that night, I have a lot of preparations to make. First I have to go to Patty's to get the dress—which fits, thank God, but barely.

Then I have to give myself a pedicure and manicure, since there isn't time to have my nails done by professionals. Then I have to wash and condition my hair, shave my legs (and under my arms, since Patty's dress is strapless), and, then, just to be on the safe side, I shave my bikini line as well, because, even though it's highly unlikely I'm going to get lucky twice in two days, you never know. Then I have to apply a facial mask, and moisturize all over. Then I have to shape my eyebrows, dry and style my hair, apply makeup, and layer fragrance.

Then, noticing that the heels of my red pumps have obviously met with an unfortunate accident involving a subway grate, I have to go over them with a red Magic Marker.

And of course, through all of that, I have to pause occasionally to snack on Double-Stuff Oreos so that I won't get light-headed from not having had anything to eat since this afternoon, when Magda smuggled that Reuben from the caf for me.

By the time Cooper taps on my apartment door, I'm just struggling to zip up Patty's dress and wondering why it had fit two hours ago in her loft but doesn't fit now—

"Just a second," I yell, trying to figure out what on earth I'm going to wear if I can't get Patty's dress to close properly. . . .

Finally the zipper moves, though, and I grab my wrap and bag and clatter down the stairs, thinking it's a shame there's no one who can open the door for me and say, "She'll be down in a minute," so I can make a sweeping entrance, like Rory Gilmore or whoever. As it is, I have to knee Lucy out of the way just so I can get to the door.

I regret to say I don't register Cooper's reaction to my appearance—if he even had one, which I kind of doubt—because I'm so completely taken aback by his. Cooper does own a tuxedo, it turns out . . . a very nice one, in fact.

And he looks more than a little sexy in it.

What is it about men in tuxedos? Why do they always look so *good* in them? Maybe it's the emphasis on the width of the chest and shoulders. Maybe it's the startling contrast of crisp white shirt front and elegant black lapel.

Whatever it is, I don't think I've ever seen a guy in a tux

who didn't look great. But Cooper is the exception. He doesn't look great.

He looks *fantastic.*

I'm so busy admiring him that I nearly forget I'm attending this event to catch a killer. For a second—just one—I really do delude myself into thinking Cooper and I are on a date. Especially when he says, "You look great."

Reality returns, though, when he looks at his watch and says distractedly, "Let's go, all right? I've got to meet someone later, so if we're going to do this, we need to get a move on."

I feel a pang of disappointment. Meet someone? Who? Who does he have to meet? A client? A snitch?

Or a *girlfriend*?

"Heather?" Cooper raises his eyebrows. "You okay?"

"Fine," I say, faintly.

"Good," Cooper says, taking me by the elbow. "Let's go."

I follow him down the stairs and out the door, telling myself that I'm being an idiot. Again. So what if he has to meet someone later? What do I care? This isn't a date. It *isn't*. At least, not with him. If I have any kind of date at all tonight, it's a date with the killer of Elizabeth Kellogg and Roberta Pace.

I repeat this to myself all the way through the park, past the Washington Square monument, and even as we cross the street to the library, where the event is being held and which has been transformed, by strategic placement of red carpets and colored lights and banners, into a ballroom for the occasion.

We have to dodge a few stretch limos and a bunch of uniformed campus security guards (Pete had been asked to pull a double for the occasion, but he'd said no, since his daughter Nancy had a science fair that night), all of whom wear white gloves and have whistles in their mouths, just to approach the massive, clay-colored building. There are velvet ropes to keep out the riffraff . . . only there doesn't seem to be either riff or raff expressing much interest in crashing the party, just some graduate students standing there, clutching their backpacks, looking angry that the party is preventing them from getting to their study carrels.

Cooper shows his tickets to a guy by the door, and then we're ushered inside and immediately assailed by waiters wanting to ply us with drinks and crab-stuffed mushroom caps. Which are actually quite tasty. The Oreos turn out not to be sitting very well beneath my control top panties, anyway.

Cooper snags two glasses for us—not of champagne, but of sparkling water.

"Never drink on the job," he advises me.

I think about Nora Charles, and the five martinis she'd downed in *The Thin Man*, trying to keep up with Nick. Imagine how many murders he might have solved if he'd followed Cooper's advice, and stayed sober!

"Here's to homicide," Cooper says, tapping the side of my glass with his. His blue eyes glint at me—almost taking my breath away, as always, with their brilliance.

"Cheers," I reply, and sip, glancing around the wide room for faces I recognize.

There's an orchestra playing a jazzed up version of "Moon River" over by the reference section. Banquet tables have been set up in front of the elevators, from which jumbo shrimp are disappearing at an alarming rate. People are milling around, looking unnaturally amused by each other's conversation. I see Dr. Flynn speaking rapidly to the dean of undergraduates, a woman whose eyes are glazed over with either boredom or drink—it's hard to tell which.

I spot a cluster of housing administrators bunched under a gold New York College banner, like a family of refugees at Ellis Island, huddled under the shadow of the Statue of Liberty. College administrators, I've noticed, don't seem to be hugely respected by either the student body or the academic population. For the most part, the building directors at New York College seem to be viewed as little more than camp counselors, and Dr. Jessup and his team of coordinators and associate directors aren't given much more respect than that. Which is unfair, because they—well, okay, we—work super hard—way harder than a lot of those professors, who breeze in to teach a one-hour class once a week, then spend the rest of their time backstabbing their colleagues in literary reviews.

While Cooper is being sucked into conversation with a trustee—an old Cartwright family friend—I study my supervisors over the rim of my glass. Dr. Jessup is looking uncomfortable in his tux. Standing beside him is a woman I take to be his statuesque wife, since she appears to be exchanging pleasantries with a woman who could only be Dr. Flynn's better half. Both women look lean and lovely in sparkly sheath dresses.

But neither one of them looks as good as Rachel. Rachel stands beside Dr. Jessup, her eyes sparkling as brightly as champagne winking in the glass she holds. She looks resplendent in form-fitting silk. The midnight blue of her gown contrasts startlingly with her porcelain skin, which in turn seems to glow against the darkness of her hair, piled on top of her head with jeweled pins.

For someone who'd declared she'd had "nothing to wear" to the ball, Rachel had done really well for herself.

So well, in fact, that I can't help feeling sort of self-conscious about the way I'm kind of spilling out of Patty's dress. And not in a good way, either.

It takes me a while to locate the college's illustrious leader, but I finally spot him over by one of the library check-out kiosks. President Allington has ditched the tank top for once, which might be part of the reason it takes me so long to find him. He's actually wearing a tuxedo, and looks surprisingly distinguished in it.

Too bad I can't say the same for poor Mrs. Allington, in her black velour, bell-bottomed pantsuit. Its wide sleeves fall back every time she lifts a glass to her mouth . . . which I must say she's doing with alarming alacrity.

But where, I wonder, is the Allingtons' progeny, the suave Chris/Todd/Mark? I don't see him anywhere, though I'd been positive he'd show up, being a cute guy in his twenties, and all. What cute guy in his twenties can resist an event like this one? I mean, come on. Free beer?

Cooper is talking about lipstick cameras or something with an older gentleman who called me "miss" and said he liked my dress (in so sincere a tone that I looked down to make sure the zipper is still holding) when suddenly a very slender, very attractive woman dressed all in black walks up and says Cooper's name in a very surprised voice.

"Cooper?" The woman, who manages to look glamorous and professorial at the same time, takes his arm in an unmistakably territorial manner—as if in the past, she's touched him in other, more intimate places, and has every right to grab his arm—and says, "What are *you* doing here? It seems like it's been months since I last heard from you. Where have you been keeping yourself?"

I can't say Cooper looks panic-stricken, exactly.

But he does look a little like a guy who is wishing very hard that he were somewhere else.

"Marian," he says, placing a hand on her back and leaning down to kiss her. On the cheek. "Nice to see you." Then he makes introductions, first to the old guy, then to me. "Heather, this is Professor Marian Braithwaite. Marian teaches art history. Marian, this is Heather Wells. She works here at New York College as well."

Marian reaches out and shakes my hand. Her fingers flutter like a tiny bird trapped between my own gargantuan mitts. In spite of this, I'm willing to bet she works out regularly at the college gym. Also that she's a showerer, and not a bather. She just has the look.

"Really?" Marian says, brightly, smiling her perfect Isabella Rossellini smile. "What do you teach?"

"Um," I say, wishing someone would shove a potted geranium on my head and spare me from having to reply. Sadly, no one does. "Nothing, actually. I'm the assistant director of one of the undergraduate dormitories. I mean, residence halls."

"Oh." Marian's perfect smile never wavers, but I can tell by the way she keeps looking at Cooper that all she wants to do is drag him away and rip all his clothes off, preferably with her teeth, and not stand around chatting with the assistant director of an undergraduate residence hall. I can't say I really blame her, either. "How nice. So, Cooper, have you been out of town? You haven't returned a single one of my calls. . . ."

I don't get to hear the rest of what Marian is saying because suddenly my own arm is seized. Only when I turn to see who is doing the seizing, instead of an ex—which would, of course, have been impossible, mine being in the hospital—I find Rachel.

"Hello, Heather," she cries. Twin spots of unnaturally bright color light her cheeks, and I realize that Rachel has been hitting the champagne. Hard. "I didn't know you were coming tonight. How are you? And Jordan? I've been so worried about him. How is he?"

I realize, with a guilty start, that I hadn't thought of Jordan all night. Not since I'd opened my door and laid eyes on Cooper, as a matter of fact. I stammer, "Um, he's all right. Good condition, in fact. Expected to make a full recovery."

"What a semester we've had, huh?" Rachel elbows me chummily. "You and I definitely need a few weeks' vacation after all we've been through. I can't believe it. Two deaths in two weeks!" She glances around, worried someone might have heard her, and lowers her voice. "I can't believe it."

I grin at her. Rachel is definitely drunk. Most likely, she hadn't had anything to eat, and the champagne has gone right to her head. Most of the hors d'oeuvres they're passing around, stuffed mushroom caps and shrimp in puffed pastries, don't look as if they're all that low carb, so Rachel's probably been eschewing them.

Still, it's nice to see Rachel happy for a change—although it's surprising that something like this, which seems kind of stodgy and boring to me, is all it takes to bring out the party girl in her. But then, I didn't go to Yale, so maybe that's why.

"Neither can I," I agree with her. "You look really nice, by the way. That dress suits you."

"Thanks so much!" Rachel sparkles. "I had to pay full price, but I think it was worth it." Then her gaze falls on Cooper, and her eyes light up even more. "Heather," she whispers, excitedly. "You're here with Cooper? Are you and he—"

I glance over my shoulder at my "date," who is still apparently trying to explain to the professor where he's been for the past few months (which, as far as I knew, is right on Waverly Place. I kind of wonder if maybe Cooper has been trying to give Marian the old heave-ho. Why else hadn't he called her? Although why any guy would dump a catch like her, I can't imagine. She's successful, intelligent, gorgeous, thin, a showerer . . . geez, *I*'d date her).

"Um," I say, feeling my cheeks warm up a little at the thought of Cooper and me being, you know. Together. "No. He just had a spare ticket, so I tagged along. We're just friends."

And destined to remain no more than that. Apparently.

"Like you and Jordan," Rachel says.

"Yeah," I say, managing a smile—though I don't know how. "Like me and Jordan."

It isn't her fault. I mean, she doesn't know she's just rubbing salt in the wound.

"Well, I better get going," she says. "I promised Stan I'd snag one of those crab cakes for him. . . ."

"Oh," I say. "Sure. Bye."

Rachel glides away on her very own cloud nine. I wonder if the rumor Pete heard, about Rachel getting a big fat promotion, was true. I wouldn't be surprised. Nobody else on campus had had to feel for two different pulses in as many weeks. What could the college do to show its appreciation, other than promote her? A Pansy Award isn't enough. After all, Magda said Justine had been nominated for a Pansy once because she'd let a student borrow her phone book.

"Hey, blondie!"

I ignore the voice from behind me, and stare at Cooper instead. He's still talking to Marian Braithwaite, who's looking up at him adoringly and laughing every now and then at whatever it is he's saying. How do they know each other? Maybe Marian had hired him. Maybe she'd suspected her professor husband was cheating on her, and she'd hired Cooper, and he'd proved that she had nothing to worry about, and *that's* why she's so glad to see him, and keeps reaching out to touch his arm—

"Blondie!"

Someone taps my shoulder, and I turn in surprise, expecting to see one of the president's aides, demanding to see my ticket . . .

. . . and find myself staring instead into his son's laughing gray eyes.

21

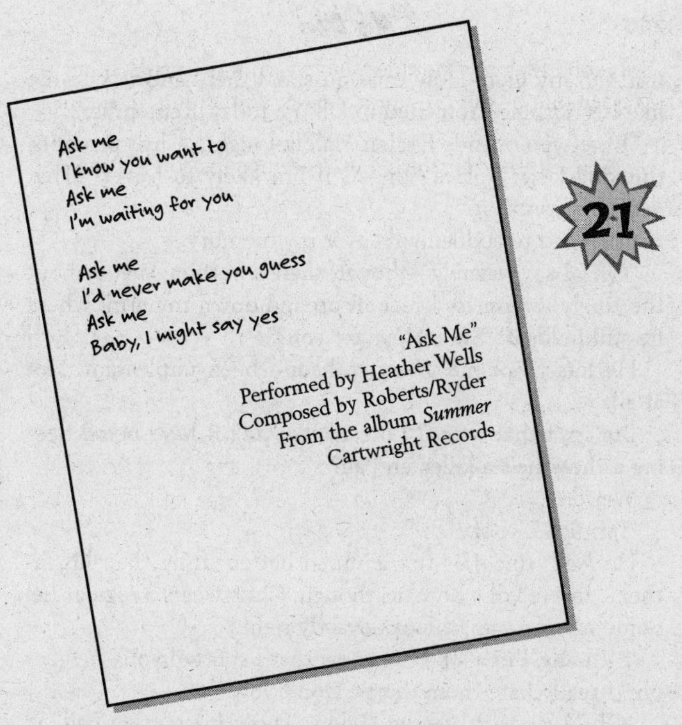

Ask me
I know you want to
Ask me
I'm waiting for you
Ask me
I'd never make you guess
Ask me
Baby, I might say yes
"Ask Me"
Performed by Heather Wells
Composed by Roberts/Ryder
From the album *Summer*
Cartwright Records

"Hey," Chris says, smilingly. "Remember me?"

I stare at him, so freaked out that I can't utter a sound.

Christopher Allington. Christopher Allington had sought me out. *Chris Allington* is holding on to my upper arm and smiling down at me like we're old friends bumping into one another at the bowling alley or whatever. He's even offering me a glass of champagne!

Well, it would be rude to say no.

I take the flute from him mutely, my heart hammering hard in my ears. Christopher Allington. Christopher Allington. Oh my God. How can you stand there and talk to me like it's nothing? You tried to kill me today. Remember?

"I met you outside Fischer Hall last night," Chris prompts, thinking I can't place him. As if I'm likely to forget! "That *was* you, wasn't it?"

I pretend to suddenly recover my memory.

"Oh," I say, vaguely—though there's nothing vague about the tingly awareness I feel all up and down my arm, where he still holds it. "Sure. How are you?"

He lets go of me. His grip hadn't been unpleasant. Not at all.

But isn't that weird? I mean, *shouldn't* it have been? Seeing as how he's a killer, and all?

Weird.

"I'm fine," he says.

He *looks* fine. His tux is much better-fitting than his father's. Instead of a bow tie, though, Chris wears a regular tie. Somehow, on him, it looks exactly right.

"Actually, I'm a lot better now that I spotted you," he goes on. "I really hate these things. Don't you?"

"Oh," I say with a shrug. "I don't know. It isn't that bad. At least there's alcohol."

I down the champagne he'd offered me in a single swallow, despite Cooper's warning about drinking on the job. After the shock Chris has given me, sneaking up on me like that, I feel like I sort of deserve it.

Chris, watching me, laughs.

"So, who're are you here with?" he wants to know. "Those tickets aren't cheap. Are you one of the student reps?"

I shrug again. Detective Canavan had said that in his experience, people who kill are excessively stupid, and I'm beginning to think that in Chris's case, this might actually be true. The fact that I'm almost ten years older than your average student government representative doesn't seem to register on him . . .

. . . which is fine by me. I mean, seeing as how I'm trying to be all sneaky and undercover to get him to slip up and confess and stuff. Not that I have any idea how I'm going to do this, of course.

And at least Chris, unlike some people, seems to appreciate how I look in my borrowed dress. I see his gaze stray toward my cleavage several times. And not because my zipper is coming apart in the back and everything is hanging loose. I know because I check.

The band starts playing a slow tune. To my surprise, some couples actually wander out onto the library's main floor and begin to dance . . . Chris's mom and dad among them. I see President Allington lead his wife out onto the dance floor with a sweeping bow that has the trustees laughing and applauding.

It's kind of sweet, actually.

At least until Mrs. Allington trips on her bell-bottoms and almost falls flat on her face. Fortunately President Allington whirls her around and makes it look like it was a fancy step he'd engineered on purpose.

Which is even sweeter. Maybe Chris isn't as unlucky as I'd originally thought. In his parentage, I mean.

"Hey," Chris says, surprising me yet again, this time by taking the champagne glass from my hand and setting it down on the tray of a passing waiter. "Wanna dance?"

My head whips around so fast to look at him, a long strand of my hair smacks me in the mouth and sticks to my lip gloss.

"What?" I ask, desperately trying to remove it. The hair, I mean. From my mouth.

"Do you wanna dance?" Chris asks. His grin is slightly mocking, to show me that he knows as well as I do that dancing at the New York College Pansy Ball is kind of . . . well, goobery. Still, he wants to let me know he's game . . .

His grin is infectious. It's the grin of the high school football captain, the handsomest boy in school, so sure of himself and his good looks that it never even occurs to him that some girl might say *No way, Jose* to his invitation. Probably because no girl ever has.

And I'm not about to be the first one.

And not just because I want to find out whether or not Chris is the one who killed Elizabeth and Roberta.

So I smile and say, "Sure," and follow Chris out onto the dance floor.

I'm not the world's greatest dancer, but it doesn't matter, because Chris is good. He's probably been to one of those prep schools where they teach all the guys the box step, or whatever. He's so good, he can talk while he dances. I have to count inside my head. One-two-three. One-two-three. Step ball change . . . oh wait, that's a different dance.

"So," Chris says, conversationally, as he presses my body to his and swings me expertly around, hardly wincing when I accidentally stomp on his toes. "What's your major?"

I'm trying to look—surreptitiously—for Cooper. I mean, he's supposed to be keeping an eye on me, right?

But I don't see him anywhere. I don't see Marian, either, for that matter. Have I been ditched for an ex-girlfriend? After that fuss Cooper made about potentially risking my life in my pursuit of the killer of Fischer Hall, has he run out on me?

Well! Nice to know how much he cares!

Although, you know, seeing as how he's letting me live in his house rent-free—well, virtually—I guess I haven't got any right to complain. I mean, how many people in Manhattan have such easy access to a washer/dryer?

In answer to Chris's question about my major, I say, "Um . . . I'm undeclared."

Well, that much is true.

"Oh, really?" Chris looks genuinely interested. "That's good. Keep your options open. I think too many people go into college with their mind already made up about what career they want to pursue when they graduate. They stick to the core curriculum for that major and don't give themselves the opportunity to try new things. You know, find out what they're really good at it. It could be something they never thought of. Like jewelry making."

Wow. I didn't know you could take jewelry making for college credit. You could actually *wear* your final. How practical.

"What are you leaning toward?" Chris asks.

I'm going to say pre-med, but changed my mind at the last second.

"Criminal justice," I lie, to see how he reacts.

But he doesn't run away to cower in fear, or anything. Instead, he says breezily, "Yeah, fascinating stuff, criminal justice. I've been thinking about heading into criminal law myself."

I bet you have. Aloud I ask, putting on a playful tone, "So what was a great big law student like yourself doing hanging around an undergraduate residence hall?"

At least Chris has the grace to look embarrassed. "Well," he says, in an aw shucks voice, "my parents do live there."

"And so do a lot of attractive coeds," I remind him. Remember? You've killed two of them?

He grins. "That, too," he says. "I don't know. The girls in my program aren't exactly—"

Over Chris's shoulder, I finally catch a glimpse of Cooper. He appears to be exchanging words with Professor Braithwaite. Really. They are having what looks like a heated conversation over by the raw bar. I see Cooper fling a glance at me.

So he hasn't forgotten. He's still keeping an eye on me.

Fighting with his ex, too, it appears.

But also keeping an eye on me.

Since I realize he doesn't know what Chris looks like, he might not know I'm dancing with my lead suspect. So I point to Chris's back, and mouth, *This is Chris* to him.

But this doesn't work out quite the way I expect it to. Oh, Cooper gets the message, and all.

But so does Marian, who, seeing that she no longer has his full attention, follows the direction of Cooper's gaze, and sees me.

Not knowing what else to do, I wave, lamely. Marian looks away from me coldly.

Whoa. Sorry.

"The girls in law school—"

I swivel my head around and realize that Chris is talking. To me.

"Well, let's just say they consider sitting in a carrel in the law library studying till midnight every night a good time," he says, with a wink.

What is he talking about?

Then I remember. Undergrad coeds versus law school students. Oh, right. The murder investigation.

"Ah," I nod, knowingly. "Law school girls. Not like those fresh-from-the-farm first years in Fischer Hall, huh?"

He laughs outright.

"You're pretty funny," he says. "What year are you?"

I just shrug and try to look like it wasn't, um, let's see, seven or so years since my first legal drink.

"At least tell me your name," he urges, in this low voice that I'm sure some former girlfriend had told him was sexy.

"You can just keep calling me Blondie," I purr. "That way you'll be able to keep me straight from all your other girlfriends."

Chris lifts his eyebrows and grins. "What other girlfriends?"

"Oh, you," I cry, giving him a little ladylike smack on the arm. "I've heard all about you. I was friends with Roberta, you know."

He looks at me like I've lost my mind. The eyebrows have furrowed. "Who?"

God, he's good. There isn't a hint of guilt in his silver gray eyes.

"Roberta," I repeat. I have to admit, my heart is pounding at my daring. I'm doing it. Detecting! I'm really doing it! "Roberta Pace."

"I don't know who you're talking about."

I seriously can't believe this guy. "Bobby," I say.

Suddenly, he laughs. "*Bobby*? You're friends with *Bobby*?"

I didn't miss both the strange emphasis on the *you're* and the use of the present tense. I am, after all, a trained investigator. Well, at least, I do the data entry for one.

"I *was* friends with Roberta," I say, and I'm not smiling or pretending to be less than twenty-one anymore. Because I can't believe the guy can be so cold. Even for a killer. "Until she fell off the top of that elevator last week."

Chris stops dancing. "Wait," he says. "What?"

"You heard me," I say. "Bobby Pace and Beth Kellogg. Both of them are dead, allegedly from elevator surfing. And you slept with both of them right before they did it."

I hadn't meant to just blurt it out like that. I'm pretty sure Cooper would have been more subtle. But I just . . . well, I got kind of mad, I guess. About him being so flippant about it. Roberta's and Elizabeth's deaths, I mean.

I guess a real investigator doesn't get mad. I guess a real investigator keeps a level head.

I guess I'm not destined for that partnership in Cooper's business after all.

Chris seems to have frozen, his feet rooted onto one black and one white tile.

But his grip on my waist doesn't loosen. If anything, it tightens until suddenly, we're standing hip to hip.

"What?" he asks, and his eyes are so wide that the blue-gray irises look like marbles floating in twin pools of milk. "What?" he asks, again. Even his lips have drained of color.

My face is only inches beneath his. I see the incredulity in his eyes, coupled with—and, shoddy investigator that I might have been, even I can see this—a slowly dawning horror.

That's when it hits me:

He doesn't know. Really. Chris had no idea—not right up until I'd told him just then—that the two dead girls in Fischer Hall were the ones with whom he'd, um, dallied just days before.

Is he really such a man-slut that he'd known only the first names—the nicknames—of the women he'd seduced?

It certainly looks that way.

The effect my announcement has on Chris is really pretty profound. His fingers dig convulsively into my waist, and he begins to shake his head back and forth, like Lucy after a good shampoo.

"No," he says. "That's not true. It can't be."

And suddenly I know that I've made a horrible mistake.

Don't ask me how. I mean, it's not like I have any experience in this kind of thing.

But I know anyway. Know it the way I know the fat content in a Milky Way bar.

Christopher Allington didn't kill those girls.

Oh, he'd slept with them, all right. But he hadn't killed them. That was done by someone else. Someone far, far more dangerous . . .

"Okay," says a deep voice behind me. A heavy hand falls on my bare shoulder.

"Sorry, Heather," Cooper says. "But we have to go now."

Where'd he come from? I can't go. Not *now*.

"Um," I say. "Yeah, just a sec, okay?"

But Cooper doesn't look too ready to wait. In fact, he looks like a man who's getting ready to run for his life.

"We have to go," he says, again. "*Now*."

And he slips a hand around my arm, and pulls.

"Cooper," I say, wriggling to get free. I can see that Chris is still in shock. It's totally likely that if I stick around awhile longer, I'll get something more out of him. Can't Cooper see that I'm conducting a very important interview here?

"Why don't you go get something to eat?" I suggest to Cooper. "I'll meet you over at the buffet in a minute—"

"No," Cooper says. "Let's go. Now."

I can understand why Cooper is so anxious to leave. Really, I can. After all, not everybody deals with their exes by, you know, sleeping with them on the foyer floor.

Still, I feel like I can't leave yet. Not after I've made this total breakthrough. Chris is really upset—so upset that he doesn't even seem to notice that there's a private eye looming over his dance partner. He's turned away, and is sort of stumbling off the dance floor, in the general direction of the elevators.

Where's he going? Up to the twelfth floor, to his father's office, to hit the real liquor—or just to use the phone? Or up to the roof, to jump off? I feel like I have to follow him, if only to make sure he doesn't do anything stupid.

Except when I start to go after him, Cooper won't let me.

"Cooper, I can't go yet," I say, struggling to free myself from his grip. "I got him to admit he knew them! Roberta and Elizabeth! And you know what? I don't think he killed them. I don't think he even knew they were dead!"

"That's nice," Cooper says. "Now let's go. I told you I have an appointment. Well, I'm late for it as it is."

"An appointment? An *appointment*?" I can hardly believe what I'm hearing. "Cooper, don't you understand? Chris said—"

"I heard you," Cooper says. "Congratulations. Now let's go. I said I'd bring you here. I didn't say I could stay all night. I do have actual paying clients, you know."

I realize it's futile. Even if Cooper did change his mind and let me go, I don't have any idea where Chris has disappeared to. And how smart would it have been, really, for me to follow him? I mean, considering what happened to the last couple of girls with whom he'd—how had I put it? Oh yeah, dallied. Hey, maybe I should be an English major. Yeah. A novelist, AND a doctor. AND a detective. AND a jewelry designer . . .

Cooper and I slip outside. I don't even have a chance to say good-bye to anyone, or congratulate Rachel on her Pansy. I've never seen a guy so eager to get out of one place.

"Slow down," I say, as Cooper hustles me to the curb. "I got heels on, you know."

"Sorry," Cooper says, and drops my arm. Then he put his fingers to his mouth and whistles for a cab that's cruising along West Fourth.

"Where are we going?" I ask curiously, as the cab pulls to the corner with a squeal of its brakes.

"You're going home," Cooper says. He opens the rear passenger door and gestures for me to get inside, then gives the driver the address of his grandfather's brownstone.

"Hey," I say, leaning forward in the seat. "It's just right across the block. I could've walked—"

"Not alone," Cooper says. "And I have to head in the other direction."

"Why?" I don't miss the fact that Marian the Art Historian has just slipped out the library doors behind us.

But instead of walking over and joining Cooper on the curb, she shoots him an extremely unfriendly look, then hurries off on foot toward Broadway.

Cooper, whose back is to the library, doesn't see the professor, or the dirty look.

"I've got to see a man," is all Cooper will say to me, "about a dog. Here." He shoves a five-dollar bill at me. "Don't wait up."

"What dog?" The cab starts to move. "Cooper, what dog? Are you getting another dog? What about Lucy? What's wrong with Lucy?"

But we're already gliding out into traffic. Cooper has turned and strode off towards West Third Street. Soon I can't see him at all.

What had all that been about? I mean, really. I know Cooper's clients are important to him, and stuff. And I know he thinks this whole thing with me and the deaths in my building is like a figment of my imagination, or whatever.

But still. He could at least have listened to me.

That's when the cab driver, who appears to be Indian—like from India, not Native American—says, helpfully, "I believe that's an expression."

I look at his reflection in the rearview mirror. "What is?"

"See a man about a dog," the cab driver says. "It's an American expression. Like rolling stone gathers no moss. You know?"

I slump back into my seat. No, I didn't know. I don't know anything, apparently.

Well, I guess I knew that. I mean, isn't that why I'm working at New York College? To get an education?

Well, I'm getting one, all right. And I haven't even started classes yet.

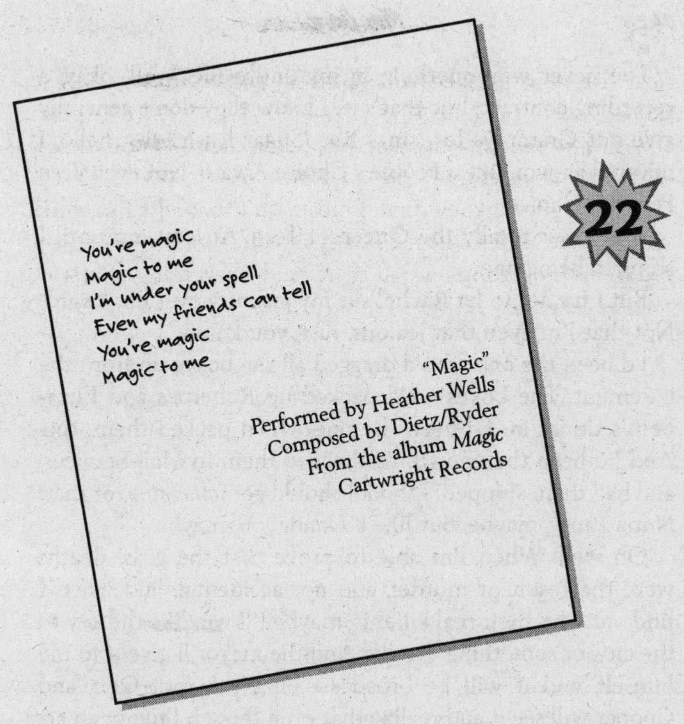
22
You're magic
Magic to me
I'm under your spell
Even my friends can tell
You're magic
Magic to me
"Magic"
Performed by Heather Wells
Composed by Dietz/Ryder
From the album Magic
Cartwright Records

After Cooper and I—and Chris Allington—left the Pansy Ball, Rachel Walcott was awarded a Pansy for exemplary service to the college.

She shows me the little flower-shaped pin the next morning, pride gleaming in her pretty brown eyes. She wears it on the lapel of her black linen suit jacket as if it were a medal of valor or something.

I guess maybe to her it kind of is. I mean, in a single semester, she's had to deal with way more tragedy than most administrators have to face in their entire careers.

I've never won anything in my entire life. Well, okay, a recording contract, but that's it. I know they don't generally give out Grammys for songs like "Sugar Rush." But hello, I never even won like a People's Choice Award. Not even *Teen* People's Choice.

And I was totally the Queen of Teen. At least, up until I stopped being one.

But I try not to let Rachel see my jealousy over her award. Not that I'm even that jealous. Just, you know.

I'd been the one who'd dragged all the boxes up from the basement. The boxes we'd packed up Roberta's and Elizabeth's things in. I'd been the one who'd packed them, too. And I'd been the one who'd dragged them to Mail Services, and had them shipped. I think I should get *something* for that. Not a Pansy, maybe, but like a Dandelion, maybe.

Oh well. When I'm able to prove that the girls' deaths were the result of murder, and not accidental, and when I find out who their real killer is, maybe I'll win like the key to the city, or something. Really! And the mayor'll give it to me himself, and it will be broadcast on New York One, and Cooper will see it and realize that even though I'm not an art history professor or a size zero, I'm still totally smart and cute, and he'll ask me out and we'll get married and have Jack, Emily, and Charlotte Wells-Cartwright . . .

Well, a girl can dream, right?

And I *am* happy for Rachel. I congratulate her and sip my coffee as she describes what it had been like, winning this prestigious award in front of all her peers. She tells me how Dr. Jessup had hugged her and how President Allington had personally thanked her for services above and beyond the call of duty. She chatters excitedly about how she's the first administrator in the history of New York College to receive seven separate nominations for the award, the most any one person has ever garnered—and she'd gotten them all in just her first four months of employment! She says how glad she is that she'd gone into higher education instead of business or law, like so many of her fellow Yale grads.

"Doesn't it feel good," she asks me, "to know you're making such a difference in people's lives, Heather?"

"Um," I say. "Sure."

Although I'm pretty sure the people whose lives I'm making the biggest difference in—the student workers—just wish Justine would come back.

While Rachel winds down from her Pansy-induced high, I get on the phone and take care of a few things that I feel I've been neglecting.

First I call Amber in her room. When her sleepy voice croaks, "Yeah?" into the phone, I gently put the receiver back into the cradle. Okay, Amber's still alive. Check.

Then I call St. Vincent's to see how Jordan is doing. He is, I learn, doing better, but they still want to hold him for observation for another night. I don't really want to, but I figure I should speak to him—you know, seeing as how it's my fault he got hurt in the first place.

But when the switchboard puts my call through to his room, a woman answers. Tania. I can't deal with fiancées early in the morning, so I hang up. I feel guilty about it though, and order a half-dozen get well balloons from a local florist, instructing them to be delivered to St. Vincent's with the highly personal message, *Get Well Soon, Jordan. From Heather*. Likely they will get lost in all of the other gifts his fans are no doubt sending him—an overnight candlelight vigil also took place outside St. Vincent's ambulance bay, apparently—but at least I can say I tried.

Thinking about Jordan and his cracked skull reminds me

of Christopher Allington. A real detective would, of course, follow up on the conversation we'd had the night before.

So I decide to take another crack at him. I tell Rachel I'm going to the bathroom. But really I go to the elevator and take it up to the twentieth floor.

No one's supposed to go up to the twentieth floor but the Allingtons and their guests, which is why the carpet in the hallway outside the penthouse is really one big motion detector that goes off whenever somebody steps on it, including the Allingtons. This alarm causes a camera to be switched on, which then conveys an image of the interloper on a viewing screen at the guard's desk in the lobby.

But since the guard on duty that day is Pete, I'm not too worried about being busted. We've caught any number of freshmen on the twentieth floor, most of whom have been sent there by conniving upper classmen in search of the "Fischer Hall pool." The elusive Fischer Hall pool did once exist, but in the basement, not the penthouse, and it's a favorite senior prank to send unsuspecting first-years to the twentieth floor in search of it, knowing they'll trigger the motion detectors and get busted for being outside the president's apartment.

I step boldly onto the nondescript carpeting and lift a finger to poke at the doorbell to the Allingtons' apartment. I can hear a strange whistling sound beyond the door, and realize that this must be Mrs. Allington's birds, the cockatoos about whom she worries so incessantly when she's had too much to drink. When I press on the doorbell, the whistling turns into maniacal shrieking, and for a minute, I panic. Really. I forget all about being a detective slash novelist slash physician slash jewelry designer, and want to run back to the elevator . . .

But before I have a chance to ding and ditch, the door

swings open, and Mrs. Allington, bleary-eyed and dressed in a green velour caftan, blinks at me.

"Yes?" she demands, in a remarkably unfriendly manner, considering the fact that just two weeks or so ago, I'd held her hand while she barfed into one of the lobby planters. Behind her, I catch a glimpse of a six-foot-tall wicker cage, within which two large white birds scream at me.

"Uh, hi," I say brightly. "Is Christopher here?"

Mrs. Allington's puffy eyelids widen a little, then go back to normal. "What?"

"Chris," I repeat. "Your son, Christopher. Is he here?"

Mrs. Allington looks truly pissed off. At first I think it's because I've woken her up, but it turns out that's only part of it.

No, what I've really done is outrage Mrs. Allington's sense of propriety.

I know! Who even knew she had one? But it turns out she does.

She says, enunciating as carefully as if I were a foreigner, "No, Chris is not here, Justine. And if you had been raised properly, you'd know that it is considered highly inappropriate for young women to pursue boys so avidly."

Then she slams the door very hard, causing her birds to shriek even more loudly in surprise.

I stand staring at the closed door for a minute or so. I have to admit, my feelings are kind of hurt. I mean, I'd thought Mrs. Allington and I were close.

And yet she's *still* calling me Justine.

I probably should have just gone away. But, you know. I still needed to know where Chris was.

So I reach out and ring the bell again. The birds' screaming rises to fever-pitch, and when Mrs. Allington pulls open the door this time, she looks not only pissed off, but practically homicidal.

"*What*?" she demands.

"Sorry," I say, as politely as I can. "I really don't mean to bother you. But could you just tell me where I might find Chris?"

Mrs. Allington has a lot of loose skin on her face. A lift here and there might have done the trick, but she really isn't the nip-and-tuck type. She's more the never-move-your-mouth-when-you-speak old money New England type. Kind of like Mrs. Cartwright. Only scarier.

Anyway, some of that loose skin beneath her chin trembles a little as she glares at me.

Finally she says, "Can't you girls just leave him alone? You're always chasing after him, causing him trouble. Can't you just go after some other boy? Aren't there plenty in this dorm?"

"Residence hall," I correct her.

"*What*?"

"It's a residence hall," I remind her. "You said dorm. But it's actually a—"

"Go to hell," Mrs. Allington says, and she slams the door in my face again.

Wow. Talk about hostile. Instead of psychoanalyzing *me* all day, Sarah should maybe turn her attention to the Allingtons. They have *way* more problems.

Sighing, I turn around and press the down button for the elevator. I can't be sure, but I think Mrs. Allington has maybe already been at the bottle . . . and it isn't even ten o'clock in the morning yet! I wonder if she's always soused this early, or if this is a special occasion. Like to celebrate Rachel's Pansy Award, maybe.

When I get back downstairs, I nearly ram into this skinny girl in the hallway. She's headed into Rachel's office, so I start to ask if I can help her, but when she turns around, I see that it's Amber.

That's right.

Chris Allington's Amber, from Idaho. The one I just woke up.

"Oh," she says, recognizing me. "Hi." Her *hi* is less than enthusiastic. That's on account of her still being half asleep. She's even in her pajamas. "You're not—you're not the hall director, are you?"

"No," I say. "I'm her assistant. Why?"

" 'Cause I just got a call saying I have to come down here this mornin' for a mandatory meeting with Rachel Walcott—"

At that moment, Rachel comes click-clacking out of our office, clutching a file folder to her chest.

"Oh, Heather, there you are," she says, brightly. "Cooper's here."

I think I must have made some sort of disbelieving noise, because Rachel peers at me curiously and says, "Yes, he is." Then her attention turns to the girl next to me. "Amber?" Rachel asks.

"Yes, ma'am." Amber sounds subdued. Well, and what eighteen-year-old freshman who'd been forced to wake up at ten o'clock in the morning for a meeting with the residence hall director wouldn't sound subdued?

"This way, Amber," Rachel says, laying hold of Amber's elbow. "Heather, if you could just hold all my calls for a few minutes—"

"Sure," I say, and go into our office. Where, sure enough, I find Cooper shaking his head at the jar of condoms on my desk.

"Hi, Cooper," I say, a little warily. Which I think is understandable, given, you know, that the last time he'd shown up in my office, it had been to tell me that my ex-boyfriend was engaged to someone else. What could have happened now?

Then I feel a stab of panic, remembering Marian Braithwaite. Oh God. She and Cooper have made up. They've made up, and are getting married, and Cooper is here to tell me he needs the apartment back because they're going to put the nanny in there—

"Hi, Heather," Cooper says, looking much more like his normal self in jeans and his leather jacket than he had in that tux. "Got a minute?"

Hi, Heather, got a minute? Hi, Heather, got a minute? What kind of way is THAT to start a conversation? Could there be three other words in the English language more effective at striking terror deep within the heart than *Got a minute?* No. No, I do NOT have a minute! Not if you're going to tell me what I think you're going to tell me. Why her? WHY? Just because she's smart and accomplished and pretty and thin—

"Sure," I say, in what I hope sounds like a cool, assured voice, but which I'm pretty sure comes out sounding more like a bleat. I gesture for Cooper to sit down, and curl up in my desk chair, wishing I could have a bottle of whatever it was Mrs. Allington had been nipping at all morning.

"Listen, Heather," Cooper says. "About last night . . ."

No! Because if there are three words in the English language worse than *Got a minute?* they can only be *About last night . . .*

And now I've had all six of them, one right after the other. It isn't fair!

And what had even happened last night? Nothing! I'd gotten out of the cab Cooper had put me in and gone straight inside to bed.

Okay, maybe I'd stayed up for an hour or so working on a new song.

And maybe that song had been about him.

But he couldn't have heard it. I played super softly. And I never even heard him come in.

Oh, why me? WHY ME???

"I think I owe you an explanation" is the next unexpected thing out of his mouth.

But wait. *I owe you an explanation*? That doesn't sound like a prelude to asking me to move out. In fact, it almost sounds like an apology. But what on earth does Cooper have to apologize for?

"I met with a friend from the coroner's office last night after we left the ball," he begins. "And she said—"

Wait a minute. *She* said? Cooper ditched me for another girl?

"*That*'s where you went?" I blurt out, before I can stop myself. "To meet a *girl*?"

Oh . . . my . . . God. What's wrong with me? Why can't I be cool and self-assured like . . . well, like Rachel? Why do I have to be such a complete spaz all the time?

Fortunately Cooper, being completely ignorant of my plans for him (you know, the fact that he's going to marry me and be the father of my three as yet unborn children and the inspiration for my Nobel Prize–winning medical career), doesn't catch on that I'm jealous. He seems to think I'm still angry because he made me leave the party early.

"I didn't want to say anything to you before," he says. "You know, in case she didn't have anything to tell me. But the fact is, there *was* something a little strange about those girls' bodies."

I just stare at him. Because I can't believe it. Not that his "friend" in the coroner's office had found something strange about Elizabeth's and Roberta's bodies. But that he'd bothered to consult with her on my behalf in the first place.

"B-but," I stammer. "But I thought . . . you thought . . . I was just making the whole thing up. Because of missing the thrill of performing . . ."

"I do," Cooper says, with a shrug. "I mean, I did. But I figured it wouldn't hurt to ask."

"And?" I lean forward eagerly. "What is it? Drugs? Were they drugged? Because I thought Detective Canavan said no drugs were detected in their systems."

"None were," Cooper says. "It wasn't drugs. It's burns."

I stare at him. "Burns? What kind of burns? Like . . . cigarette burns?"

"No," Cooper says. "Angie isn't sure." Angie? Cooper knows someone in the coroner's office named *Angie*? Just how had he and Angie met, anyway? Angie didn't sound like the kind of name a medical examiner would have. An exotic dancer, maybe. But not a doctor . . .

"And you have to take into account that those bodies," Cooper goes on. "Well, they're kind of a mess. But Angie says they did find burn marks on both girls's backs, marks they can't explain. It's not enough for them to change the coroner's ruling—you know, that the deaths weren't accidental. But it is . . . strange."

"Strange," I repeat.

"Yeah," Cooper says. "Strange."

"So . . ." I can't look him in the eye. Because I can't believe he's actually taking me seriously. *Me*, Heather Wells, of "Sugar Rush" fame!

And all it had taken were a couple of murders . . .

"So maybe I'm not just making it all up out of displaced aggression toward my mother?" I ask.

Cooped looks taken aback. "I never said you were."

Oh, right. That had been Sarah.

"But you believe me now?" I prod him. "I'm not just your little brother's crazy ex-girlfriend? But maybe, like, a rational human being?"

"I've never thought of you as anything but," Cooper says, a flash of annoyance in his blue eyes. Then, seeing my expression, he says, "Well, crazy, maybe. But I never thought of you as irrational. Honest, Heather, I don't know where you get this stuff. I've always thought of you as one of the—"

Most beautiful, ravishing creatures you've ever met? Most intelligent, stunningly gorgeous women of your acquaintance?

Sadly, before he gets a chance to tell me what he's always thought of me—or to fall to one knee and ask me to be his bride (I know. Still, a girl can dream), the phone rings.

"Hold that thought," I say to Cooper, and pick up the receiver. "Fischer Hall, this is Heather."

"Heather?" It's Tina, the desk worker on duty. "Hold on, Julio wants to talk to you."

Julio gets on the line. "Oh, Haythar, I sorry," he says. "But he's doing it again."

"Who's doing what again?" I ask.

"That boy, Gavin. Ms. Walcott told me—"

"Okay, Julio," I say, careful not to let Cooper catch on, considering what happened last time. "I'll meet you at the usual place." Then I hang up.

Talk about bad timing! Right when Cooper had been about to tell me what he really thinks about me!

Although, come to think of it, I'm not sure I want to know. Because most likely it's going to be something like "one of the best data-entry typists I've ever known."

"Stay right here," I say to Cooper.

"Is something wrong?" Cooper asks, looking concerned.

"Nothing I can't handle in a jiffy," I say. Oh my God, did I just say jiffy? Well, whatever. "I'll be right back."

Before he can say another word, I hightail it from the office, running for the service elevator, where I tell Julio, who meets me there, to take the control lever, and *Go, go, go!*

Because the sooner we get back, the sooner I can find out if, you know, there's a chance for me where Cooper is concerned, or if I should just give up on men already. Maybe

New York College offers a major in being a nun. You know, giving up guys completely, and embracing celibacy. Because that's seriously starting to look like it might be the way to go for me.

As Julio takes me up to the tenth floor, I climb the elevator walls and slide through the open ceiling panel. Up in the elevator shaft, it's warm and quiet, as usual.

Except that I can't actually hear Gavin laughing, though, which is *not* usual. Maybe he's finally gotten his head cut off by a snapping cable, as Rachel has so often warned him he might. Or maybe he's fallen. Oh, God please don't tell me he's at the bottom of the shaft . . .

I'm reflecting upon this—what I'm going to do if all I find on top of Elevator 1 is Gavin's headless corpse—as the service elevator approaches the two other cars, which are both sitting in front of the tenth floor.

As we rise above them, I see no sign of Gavin—not even his headless corpse. No empty beer bottles, no chortling laughter, nothing. It's almost as if Gavin had never been there . . .

The next thing I know, a thunderclap shakes the shaft, leaving a roaring in my ears, like the sound of ocean waves, only magnified a thousand times.

I've stood up—a little unsteadily—to get a better look at the roofs of the cabs below, and when I feel the explosion rip beneath my feet, I grab instinctively—but blindly—for something—anything—to hold on to.

Something that feels like a thousand razor blades slices my hands, and I realize I'm holding a metal rope that's vibrating crazily from the force of the explosion. Still, I hold on to the bucking steel cable, because it's the only thing that separates me from the oblivion of the dark shaft below. Because there's nothing else beneath my feet. One minute I'm standing on the roof of the service cab, and the next, the roof has caved in beneath my feet, crumpling like a can of Pringles.

Hmmm. Pringles.

It's funny what you end up thinking about right before you die.

I avoid getting hit by the rain of steel from above by sheer luck alone. The cable I've grabbed hold of continues to buck wildly, but I cling to it with both my hands and legs, wrapping one foot around the other.

Something strikes me hard enough on the shoulder as it plunges past to make me loosen my grip on the cable, stunned breathless by the impact.

That's when I look down, wild-eyed, and see that the service car is gone.

Well, not gone, exactly. It's free-falling below me like a soda can someone has thrown down a trash chute, the loosened cables—all but the one I'm holding—trailing behind it like ribbons on a bridal veil.

It can't crash, is all I could think to myself. I'd asked the elevator repairmen once if what had happened in the movie *Speed* could ever happen in real life. And they'd said no. Because even if all the cables connected to an elevator car snap at the same time (something they asserted could never, ever happen. But, um, hello), there's a counterweight built into the wall that would never let the car crash to the ground below.

I feel the deafening impact of that counterweight as it slams into place, saving the elevator car from colliding with the basement floor.

But when the broken cables rain down onto the cab's roof, the noise is unbelievable. Impact after impact shakes the shaft. I struggle to retain my grip on the one remaining cable, thinking only that with all that noise, I haven't heard a peep out of Julio. Not a single sound. I know he's still inside that car. While he'd been saved by the counterweight from being crushed, accordion style, against the cement floor of the basement, those cables have literally flattened the cab's roof. He's under that tangle of steel . . .

But God only knows if he's still alive.

The silence that follows the crash of the falling elevator cab is even more frightening than the shuddering impact of the split cables. I've always loved the elevator shafts because they're the only parts of the dorm—I mean, residence hall—that are ever totally quiet. Now, that quiet is like an impenetrable canopy between me and the ground. The quieter it gets, the higher this little bubble of hysteria rises in my throat. I hadn't had a chance to be frightened before.

But now, hanging more than ten stories with my feet dangling above nothing, I'm seized with terror.

That's when the bubble turns into a fountain, and I start to scream.

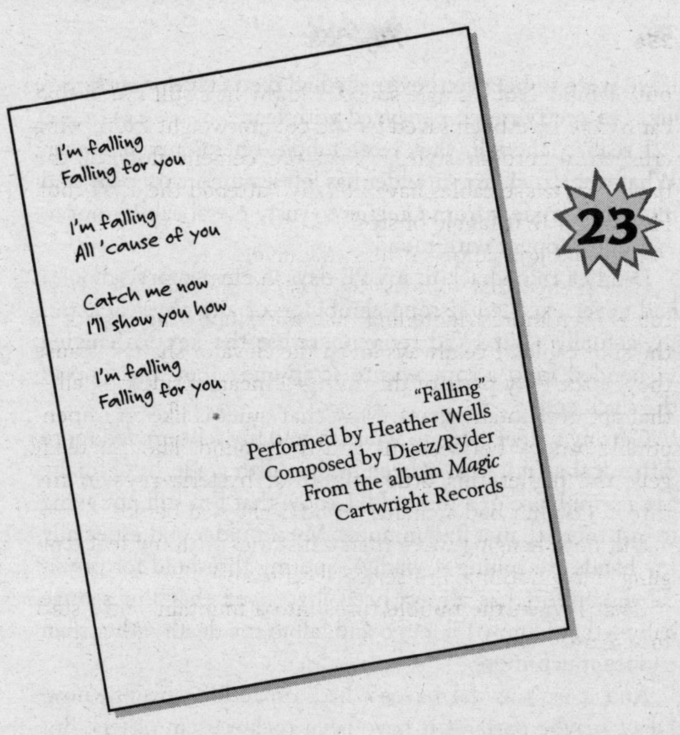
I'm falling
Falling for you

I'm falling
All 'cause of you

Catch me now
I'll show you how

I'm falling
Falling for you

"Falling"
Performed by Heather Wells
Composed by Dietz/Ryder
From the album *Magic*
Cartwright Records

23

Though it seems like hours, I think I'm only screaming for like a minute or so before I hear a distant, masculine voice shouting my name from far below.

"Here!" I shriek. "I'm up here! Tenth floor!"

The voice says something, and then, below me to my left, the two remaining elevator cabs both start moving down.

If I'd had any presence of mind, I'd have jumped for it, leaping to the roof of the nearest cab.

But it's a distance of more than five feet—the same distance Elizabeth and Roberta would have jumped, and missed, if we were to believe they really had died elevator surfing—and I'm pretty much paralyzed with fear.

I realize, though, that I can't hold on for much longer. Whatever struck my shoulder has left it numb with pain, and my palms are raw from clinging to rusty metal cable—not to mention slippery with blood.

Dimly, I think back to my PE days in elementary school. I had never excelled at rope climbing—or any physical activity, actually—but I did remember that the key to hanging suspended from a rope was to wrap one's foot in a loop in the slack end.

Getting a steel cable to wrap around my foot proved more difficult than it had ever been back in fifth grade, but I finally get a semblance of a foothold. I know that I'm still not going to last more than a few minutes. My shoulder and especially my hands are aching so badly—and my threshold for physical discomfort has always been low, given that I'm a huge baby—that I know I'll let go and fall to my death rather than endure much more.

And it isn't as if I haven't had a nice life up until now. Okay, maybe parts of it have been rockier than others. But hey, I had an okay childhood; at least my parents had seen to it that I'd never gone to bed hungry.

And I was never abused or molested. I had had a successful career—granted, it had peaked at age eighteen or so.

But still, I've gotten to eat in a lot of awfully good restaurants.

And I know that Lucy will be well taken care of. Cooper will look after her if anything happens to me.

But thinking of Cooper reminds me that I don't really want to die, not now, when things were just getting interesting. I'm never going to know what it is he really thinks of me! He'd been about to tell me, and now I'm going to die, and miss it!

Unless, of course, when you die you attain all the knowledge in the universe.

But what if you don't? What if you just die?

Well, then I guess it won't matter.

But what about those repairmen? They'd assured me elevator cables don't just snap. Okay, maybe one of them snaps, but not all of them, all at once. Those cables hadn't broken accidentally. Someone had deliberately booby-trapped them. Judging from the ball of flame that had erupted beneath my feet, I'm thinking bomb.

That's right, bomb.

Someone's trying to kill me.

Again.

Reflecting on who could possibly want to kill me takes my mind off my aching shoulder and throbbing hands—and even Cooper and the what-he-thinks-of-me thing—for a minute or so. Well, of course there's Christopher Allington, who may or may not have already tried to shove a geranium planter on my head because I suspect him of murder. He'd better have a really good alibi for this one.

But how would Christopher Allington have known that I'd be on that elevator? I rarely ride the service elevator. In fact, the only time I ever ride it is when I'm chasing elevator surfers.

Could Gavin McGoren somehow be involved in the deaths of Beth Kellogg and Bobby Pace? This seems far-fetched, but what other explanation could there be? Julio can't be the murderer. For all I know, he's dead down there. Why would he want to kill himself *and* me?

Suddenly, the elevator closest to me returns, and this time, there's somebody on the roof. But it isn't Gavin McGoren. Blinking—the shaft is filled with smoke—I see through the mist that a grim-faced Cooper is coming to my rescue.

Which must mean he likes me. At least a little. I mean, if he's willing to risk his own life to save mine . . .

"Heather," Cooper says. He sounds as cool and authoritative as ever. "Don't move, all right?"

"Like I'm going anywhere," I say. Or that's what I try I say. What I hear is actually a string of hysterical blubbering. But surely it isn't coming from me.

"Listen to me, Heather," Cooper says. He's climbed onto the roof of Elevator 1, and is hanging on to one of its cables. His face, I can see through the smoke, is pale beneath his tan. Now why is that? I wonder. "I want you to do something for me."

"Okay," I say. Or I try to, anyway.

"I want you to swing over here. It's okay, I'll catch you."

"Um," I say. And make the mistake of looking down. "No."

Well, that came out definitively enough.

"Don't look down," Cooper says. "Come on, Heather. You can do it. It's just a few feet—"

"I'm not swinging anywhere," I say, clinging more tightly to my cable. "I'm waiting right here until the NYFD arrives."

"Heather," Cooper says, and some of the old familiar impatience with me is back in his voice. "Push off from the wall and swing over here. Let go of the cable when I say so. I swear I will catch you."

"Boy, you have really lost it." I shake my head. My voice sounds funny. It's kind of high-pitched. "No wonder your family cut you off without a cent."

"Heather," Cooper says. "The janitor told me that that cable you're holding on to probably isn't stable. It could break at any minute, like all the others—"

"Oh," I say. Well, that's different.

"Now do what I say." Cooper has leaned out as far from his elevator car as he can, and still have something to hold on to.

"Push off the wall with your foot and swing over here. I'll catch you, don't worry."

From the top of the service shaft comes a groaning sound. I'm almost sure it didn't come from me. More likely from the cable I'm holding on to.

Great.

Closing my eyes, I heave on the cable, forcing it to swing toward the wall on the far side of the shaft. I unwrap my foot from the dangling end and shove, as hard as I can, at the crumbling brick. Like a stone from a slingshot, I'm propelled in the direction of Cooper's waiting arms . . .

. . . but not close enough for my liking.

Still, he shouts, "Let go! Heather, let go now!"

That's it, I think. I'm dead. Maybe they'll do a *Behind the Music* on me *now* . . .

I let go.

And know, for a second, how Elizabeth and Roberta must have felt—the sheer terror of careening through the air with no net or body of water below me to break my fall . . .

Only instead of plummeting to my death, as they had, I feel hard fingers close around both my wrists. My arms are practically yanked out of their sockets as the rest of my body slams against the side of the elevator cab. I have my eyes screwed shut, but I feel myself being lifted, slowly . . .

I don't stop scrambling for a foothold until the seat of my jeans finally rest on something solid.

It's only then that I open my eyes and see that Cooper has managed to pull me to safety. We're both panting from mingled exertion and fear. Well, me from fear, anyway.

But we're alive. *I'm* alive.

Above our heads comes the groaning sound again. Next thing I know, the cable I'd been holding on to—along with the pulley it had been connected to—rips loose from its supports and plummets down the shaft, to crash into the roof of the cab below.

When I'm able to lift my gaze from the wreckage at the bottom of the shaft, I see that I'm clinging to Cooper's shirtfront, and that his arms are around me protectively. His face has gone the color of the smoke around us. There are streaks of blood and rust all over his shirt from where I'd grabbed at him with my cut hands.

"Oh," I say, releasing the now crumpled and greasy cotton. "Sorry."

Cooper's arms drop away from me at once.

"No problem," he says.

His voice, like my own, is steady enough. But there's something in his blue eyes I've never seen before . . .

But before I have a chance to put my finger on just what, exactly, it is, a familiar voice from inside the cab we're sitting on demands, "So is she okay or what?"

I look down through the open panel in the cab's ceiling and see relief wash over Pete's face.

"You had us shittin' our pants back there, Heather," he says. And indeed, his burly Brooklynese has a tremor in it. "You okay?"

"I'm fine," I say, and prove it by climbing shakily down from the roof of the cab virtually unaided. My shoulder twinges a painful warning at one point, but Pete's steadying hand on one elbow, and Cooper's careful grip on my belt, keep me from losing my balance. I find, once I'm safely inside the elevator car, that it's difficult to stand without leaning against something since my knees are shaking pretty badly.

But I manage all right, by sagging against the wall.

"What about Julio?" I ask.

Cooper and Pete exchange looks.

"He's alive," Cooper says, but his jaw is strangely clenched.

"Leastways, he was a minute ago." Pete yanks around the key he'd inserted in the override switch. "But as to whether he'll still be alive by the time they get him out—"

I feel dizzy. "Get him out?"

"They're gonna hafta to use cutters."

I look to Cooper for a more detailed explanation, but he isn't forthcoming with one.

Suddenly, I'm not so sure I want to know.

For the second time in two days, I end up in St. Vincent's emergency room.

Only this time, I'm the patient.

I'm lying on a gurney, waiting to get my shoulder X-rayed. Cooper has gone in search of a tuna salad sandwich for me, since fear has made me famished.

While I wait, I gaze mournfully at my ragged fingers and palms, wrapped in gauze and smarting from numerous stitches. It will be weeks, an irritatingly young attending physician has informed me, before I have normal use of them again. Forget guitar playing. I can barely hold a pencil.

I'm glumly considering how I'm going to do my job properly when I have little or no use of my hands—undoubtedly Justine would have found a way—when Detective Canavan shows up, the unlit cigar still clenched between his teeth. I'm not sure it's the same cigar. But it sure looks like it.

"Hey there, Ms. Wells," he says, as casually as if we'd just bumped into one another at Macy's or something. "Heard you had quite an eventful morning."

"Oh," I say. "You mean the part where somebody tried to kill me? Again?"

"That'd be the one," Detective Canavan says, removing the cigar. "So. You sore at me?"

I am, a little. But then again, it hadn't been his fault, really. I mean, that planter could have fallen over accidentally. And Elizabeth and Roberta really could have died while elevator surfing.

Except that it hadn't. And they hadn't, either.

"Can't say as I blame you," Detective Canavan says, before I have a chance to reply. "Now we got a Backstreet Boy with a busted head and a janitor in intensive care."

"And two dead girls," I remind him. "Don't forget the two dead girls."

Detective Canavan sits down on an orange plastic chair that's bolted to the wall outside the X-ray lab.

"Oh, yeah," he says. "And two dead girls. Not to mention a certain administrative assistant who should, by rights, be dead as well." He puts the cigar back in his mouth. "We think it was a pipe bomb."

"What?" I yell.

"A pipe bomb. Not particularly sophisticated, but effective. In an enclosed space, like the brick elevator shaft, it did a lot more harm than it would have if it had been in a suitcase or a car or something." Detective Canavan chews on the cigar. "Somebody seems to want you dead in a big way, honey."

I stare at him, feeling cold again. Cooper had thrown his leather jacket over my shoulders as soon as we'd gotten down into the lobby, because I'd started shivering for some reason. And then when the paramedics had arrived, they'd added a blanket.

But I'd been freezing ever since seeing the wreckage that had once been the service elevator, crumpled at the bottom of that shaft. Firefighters had tried to pry the doors open with massive pliers—the jaws of life, they called them—but the twisted metal just shrieked in protest. Lying in that wreckage was Julio, who I later learned had suffered multiple broken bones, but was expected to survive. I had started shivering just looking at the mangled cab, and my hands have felt like ice ever since.

"A pipe bomb?" I echo. "How would somebody—"

"Slipped it on top of the elevator car. Easy to make, if you have the know-how. All you need is a steel pipe, threaded on both ends so you can cap it. Drill a couple holes in the side for twin fuses, slip a couple firecrackers through the holes, epoxy them in place, tack on some cigarettes, then fill the thing with gunpowder. Easy as pie."

Easy as pie? That sounds worse than the SATs!

Noting my raised eyebrows, Canavan removes the cigar and says, "Excuse me. Easy as pie if you know how to do it. Anyway, somebody lit that thing a few minutes before you and—what's his name?" He refers to his notebook. "Oh yeah, Mr. Guzman—went for the ride. Now, if you don't mind my asking, what the hell were you doing on top of that thing?"

Confused, I think back. A pipe bomb, with twin cigarette fuses? I have no idea what such a thing would look like, but I certainly hadn't noticed anything like it when I'd been up on the elevator car's roof.

Then again, with all the gears and machinery up there, a small bomb would be easy to hide.

But a pipe bomb? A pipe bomb, in Fischer Hall?

Behind the double doors to the waiting room, a nurse is calling, "Sir, you can't go in there! Sir, wait—"

Cooper bursts through the swinging doors, his arms full of paper bags. A pretty nurse trails after him, looking mad.

"Sir, you can't be barging back here," she insists. "I don't want to have to call security—"

"It's all right, nurse," Detective Canavan says, flipping open his wallet and showing her his badge. "He's with me."

"I don't care if he's with the Royal Academy of Medicine," the nurse snaps. "He can't be barging back here."

"Have a cannoli," Cooper says, producing one from a bag. The nurse stares at him like he's insane.

"No, really," Cooper says. "Have one. On me."

Disgusted, the nurse takes the cannoli, chomps off a large bite, then leaves, still chewing. Cooper shrugs, then eyes the detective with undisguised hostility.

"Well, if it isn't the NYPD's biggest dick," he says.

"Cooper!" I'm surprised. "Detective Canavan was just telling me—"

"What, that it's all in your head?" Cooper laughs bitterly, then stabs an index finger at the wide-eyed detective. "Well, let me tell you something, Canavan. There is no way all six cables to an elevator cab could snap at the same time unless someone deliberately—"

"Cooper!" I cry, but Detective Canavan is chuckling.

"Simmer down, Romeo," he says, waving his cigar at us. "We already established that a second attempt was made on the life of your girlfriend here. Nobody's sayin' what happened with the elevator was an accident. Keep your shirt on. I'm on your side."

Cooper blinks a few times, then looks at me. I expect him to say something like, "She's not my girlfriend." Only he doesn't. Instead he says, "The tuna salad didn't look fresh. I got you salami instead."

"Wow," I say. Cooper hands me a sandwich that has to be a foot long, at least. Not that there's anything wrong with that.

Detective Canavan peers at the many bags Cooper has scattered about. "Got any chips in there?" he wants to know.

"Sorry." Cooper unwraps my sandwich and begins breaking it up into bite-sized pieces, since I can't hold anything real well. "Olive?"

Detective Canavan looks disappointed.

"No, thanks. So," he says, as if there'd been no interruption. "Who told you to get on that elevator?"

I say, speaking with my mouth full because I'm too hungry to wait, "All I know is, I got a call from the reception desk that Gavin—he's this kid that lives in the hall—was elevator surfing again, and so I went with Julio to try and chase the kid down."

"Yeah? And when you got up there, what?"

I describe the explosion, which had occurred almost simultaneously with my realization that Gavin wasn't up there after all.

"So," Detective Canavan says. "Who told the kid at the desk to call you?"

"We all know who did this," Cooper says. The barely suppressed fury is back in his voice. "Why are you just sitting there, Canavan, instead of arresting him?"

"Arresting who?" Canavan wants to know.

"Allington. He's the killer. It's obvious Heather's got him running scared."

"I'll say," Canavan shakes his head. "The kid left town last night. He's parked himself out at his folks' place in the Hamptons. No way he could have planted that bomb, not without some help. Kid's three hours away by LIE. Somebody wants your girlfriend dead, all right. But it ain't Chris Allington."

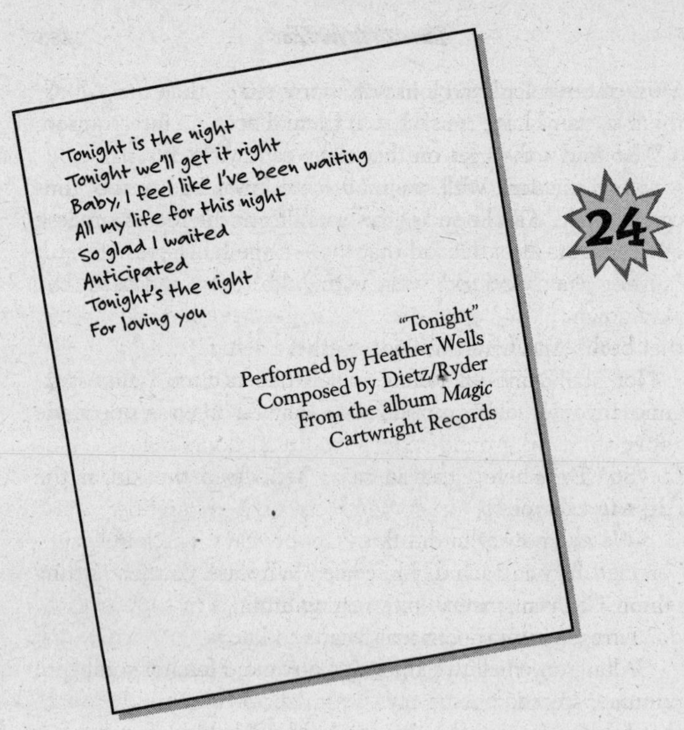
Tonight is the night
Tonight we'll get it right
Baby, I feel like I've been waiting
All my life for this night
So glad I waited
Anticipated
Tonight's the night
For loving you
"Tonight"
Performed by Heather Wells
Composed by Dietz/Ryder
From the album *Magic*
Cartwright Records
24

Getting X-rayed is way painful, since the technician has to twist my body into several unnatural positions in order to get the angle he wants to photograph. But aside from some Motrin, I'm not offered a single thing for the pain.

Hello. You can buy Motrin over the counter. Where's the Vicodin? Where's the morphine? What kind of hospitals do they run these days, anyway?

After they X-ray me, they wheel me into this waiting room with a lot of other patients who are lying on gurneys.

Most of them look to be in way worse shape than me. All of them seem to have much better painkillers.

Thankfully they let me keep my sandwich. It's my only source of comfort. Well, that and some Fritos I get out of the candy machine at the end of the ward. It's no joke getting those quarters in the slot with my bandaged fingers, believe me.

Still, even Fritos don't make me feel better. I mean, by rights, I should be dead. I really should have been killed by that bomb. But I hadn't died.

Not like Elizabeth Kellogg and Roberta Pace. What had gone through their minds when they'd been suspended above the hard ground sixteen, fourteen floors below? Had they struggled before they were pushed? There were no signs that they'd done so, just some burn marks, apparently.

But what *kind* of burn marks?

And why had *I* lived, while they had died? Is there some reason I'd been spared? Is there something I'm supposed to do? Find their murderer, maybe?

Or had I been allowed to live for some other, even higher purpose? Like to pursue my own medical career, and ensure that future pipe bomb victims would get better drugs when brought to local area hospitals?

A doctor who couldn't have been any older than me finally shows up just as I'm finishing off the last of the Fritos, holding my X-rays and smiling. At least until he gets a good look at me.

"Aren't you—" He breaks off, looking panicky.

I'm too tired to play games.

"Yes," I say. "I'm Heather Wells. Yes, I sang 'Sugar Rush.' "

"Oh," he says, looking disappointed. "I thought you were Jessica Simpson."

Jessica Simpson! I'm so appalled that I can't utter another

word, even when he blithely informs me that there isn't anything seriously wrong with my shoulder, other than some deep tissue bruising. I need bed rest, and no, he can't prescribe anything for the pain.

I swear I hear him humming the chorus from "With You" as he leaves.

Jessica Simpson? I don't look anything like Jessica Simpson! Okay, we both have long blond hair. But there the resemblance ends.

Doesn't it?

I find a ladies' room and go inside. Peering at my reflection in the mirror above the sink, I'm relieved to find that I do not in the least resemble Jessica Simpson.

But nor do I resemble a human being. Much. My jeans are torn and covered with grease and my own blood. I'm clutching Cooper's leather jacket as well as a bright orange blanket around my shoulders. There's blood and dirt all over my face, and my hair hangs in greasy tangles. There isn't a trace of lipstick anywhere in the vicinity of my mouth.

In short, I look hideous.

I try to rectify the situation as best I can. Still, the results aren't anything to write home about.

But it's a good thing I'd elected to freshen up a little, because when I wander out into the waiting room, my hospital bill—all seventeen hundred dollars of it, to be paid by New York College—in my back pocket, I'm almost blinded by the number of flashbulbs that go off. More than a dozen people I don't know are calling out, "Miss Wells! Miss Wells, over here! Just one question, Miss Wells—" and the hospital security guard is trying desperately to keep more reporters from spilling into the lobby from the street.

"Heather!" A familiar voice sounds from somewhere in the throng, but not before a woman with a lot of pancake makeup and very big hair shoves a microphone in my face and demands, "Miss Wells, is it true that you and former flame ex–Easy Street member Jordan Cartwright are back together?"

Before I can open my mouth to reply, another reporter pounces.

"Miss Wells, is it true that this is the second time in two days that someone has tried to kill you?"

"Miss Wells," a third reporter asks. "Is there any truth to the rumor that this bomb was part of an elaborate terrorist plot to eradicate America's most beloved former teen pop sensations?"

"Heather!"

Above the microphone props and shoulder-held cameras towers Cooper. He gestures to me, indicating a side door that says *Hospital Personnel Only* on it.

But before I can duck toward it, someone grabs me by my sore shoulder and shouts, "Heather, is it true that you'll be making your singing comeback representing Calvin Klein's new fragrance for his fashion company's fall line?"

Thankfully, a cop shows up, breaking through the wall of reporters and taking hold of my good arm. He physically propels me from the middle of the throng, using his nightstick as a prod to hasten our progress.

"All right, all right," he says over and over again, in the flat Brooklyn accent I've come to know and trust since moving to New York City. "Let the lady through now. Show a little compassion for the patient, folks, and get out of her way."

The anonymous officer steers me through the *Hospital Personnel Only* door, then posts himself in front of it like a Marvel comic book superhero, guarding Fort Knox.

Once inside what turns out to be the very same hallway where I'd left Cooper and Detective Canavan when I'd gone to get X-rayed, I see that they'd been joined by a number of people, including Patty and Frank, Magda and Pete, and, for some reason, Dr. Jessup.

Both Patty and Magda let out wails of dismay when they see me. I don't know why. I thought I'd cleaned myself up pretty good.

Nevertheless, Patty springs out of her plastic chair and grabs me in a hug I'm sure she means to be friendly, but which actually hurts quite a bit. She's crying and saying things like, "I told you to find a different job! This job is no good for you, it's too dangerous!"

Meanwhile, Magda's staring at my hands, her jaw moving in a weird way. I've never seen her eyes so big.

"Oh my God," she keeps saying, throwing accusing looks in Pete's direction. "You said it was bad, but you didn't say how bad."

"I'm okay," I insist, trying to extricate myself from Patty's impossibly long arms. "Really, Patty, I'm okay—"

"Jesus, Pats, you're hurting her." Frank tries to pry his wife off me. He peers down at me anxiously as he untangles Patty's arms from mine. "You really okay, kid? You look like hell."

"I'm okay," I lie. I'm still shaken up, not so much from my ordeal in the elevator shaft as from my ordeal at the hands of those reporters. Where had they come from? And how had they found out about the bomb so fast? New York College appeared in the press rarely, and positively, if at all. How was this going to reflect upon my six months' performance review? Would it be held against me?

Then Dr. Jessup coughs, and everyone looks at him. In his arms is an enormous bouquet of sunflowers. For me. Dr. Jessup has brought *me* flowers.

"Wells," he says, in his gravelly voice. "Always hafta be in the spotlight, dontcha?"

I smile, moved beyond speech. After all, Dr. Jessup is very busy, being assistant vice president and all. I couldn't believe he'd taken time out to come down to the hospital to give me flowers.

But Dr. Jessup isn't done. He leans down and kisses my cheek, saying, "Glad you're all in one piece, Wells. These are from the department." He thrusts the flowers at me, and when I helplessly raise my bandaged hands, Magda steps in, taking the bouquet for me. Dr. Jessup doesn't see her scowl, or if he does, he ignores it. He also doesn't hear her mutter, "He gives her flowers, when what he should be giving her is a big fat raise . . ."

"Rachel said to tell you she's sorry she couldn't come, but somebody has to hold down the fort." Dr. Jessup grins, showing all of his teeth. " 'Course, she didn't know about all the paparazzi. Bet she'll be sorry she missed that when she hears about it. So, who you gonna sell the story to, *Entertainment Tonight* or *Access Hollywood*?"

"The *Post*'ll offer you top dollar," Magda informs me, not aware that Dr. Jessup is kidding. "Or the *Enquirer*."

"Don't worry," I say with a smile. "I won't be talking to the press."

Dr. Jessup doesn't look convinced. His expression has gone from one of friendly concern to one of worried suspicion. I realize suddenly that the only reason he even showed up at the hospital was to see if I intended to go public with my story.

I should have known, I guess. I mean that Dr. Jessup wasn't there out of concern for me. Dr. Jessup was there for one reason, and one reason only:

Damage control.

I think he suspected it was going to be bad—why else would he have braved the traffic this far into the West Village?—but

I don't think he ever thought it was going to be *this* bad. A bomb going off in a New York College dormitory—I mean, residence hall—is news with a capital N. Something similar had happened at Yale, and it had made CNN, and been a lead story on all the local networks, even though it had turned out to have nothing to do with terrorism.

And the fact that one of the victims of this bomb is a former teen pop sensation? Well, that just makes the story that much juicier. My disappearance from the world of music had not gone unnoticed, and the reason behind it—including my mother's new Argentinian cattle ranch—had been made graphically public. I could just see the cover of the *Post*:

BLOND BOMBSHELL

Former Pop Star Heather Wells
Nearly Blown to Bits

at low-paying job she was forced to take at New York College in order to support herself after her music career tanked and she was thrown out by former fiancé, Easy Street member Jordan Cartwright.

Still, I can understand Dr. Jessup's concern. Having two of his employees injured in an elevator accident is one thing.

But a bomb in one of his dormitories—I mean, residence halls? Worse, a bomb in the building in which the president of the college lives? What's he going to tell the trustees? The poor guy probably thinks he's watching his vice presidency slip away.

I don't blame him for being more worried about his own skin than mine. After all, he's got kids. All I've got is a dog.

"Heather," Dr. Jessup begins again. "I'm sure you understand. This thing is a PR nightmare. We can't have the public thinking our residence halls are out of control—"

To my surprise, it's Detective Canavan who interrupts the assistant vice president. Noisily clearing his throat, then looking around unsuccessfully for a place to spit, Detective Canavan sighs, then swallows.

Then he says, "Hey. Hate to break this up, but the longer Ms. Wells here sticks around, the harder it's gonna be for my boys to maintain crowd control out there."

I feel an arm slip around my shoulders. Looking up, I'm surprised to see that the arm belongs to Cooper. He isn't looking at me, though. He's looking at the door.

"Come on, Heather," he says. "Frank and Patty brought their car. They parked it down below, in the garage. They'll give us a lift home."

"Oh yes, let's go," Patty urges. Her beautiful face is filled with distaste. "I hate hospitals, and I hate reporters even more." Her dark, almond-shaped eyes slide toward Dr. Jessup, and she looks as if she's about to add, *And I hate uptight bureaucrats most of all*, but she refrains, entirely for my sake, I'm sure, since I choose that moment to step on her foot sort of hard, causing her to let out a little yelp of pain.

After I say good-bye to Pete and Magda—who promise to stick around the hospital until they get to see Julio—a hospital administrator gladly shows us the way down to the parking garage, as if any sacrifice she can make to get rid of us—and ergo, all the reporters—will be well worth it.

All I can think the whole way to the car is, *Oh God. I am so fired.* When I'm not thinking, *Oh God, what's with the arm?* about Cooper, that is.

Except that once we're safely in the car, Cooper removes his arm. So then I just have the one thing to worry about.

"Oh God," I can't help saying miserably, a catch in my

throat, from the backseat. "I think Dr. Jessup is going to fire me."

"Nobody's going to fire you, Heather," Cooper says. "The guy's just looking out for his own interests."

"That man even crosses his eyes at you, baby, he's gonna hafta deal with me," Patty growls, from behind the wheel. Patty is an assertive—one might almost say aggressive—driver, which is why she, instead of Frank, does all the driving when they're in the city. She leans on the horn as a yellow cab cuts her off. "Nobody messes with my best girlfriend."

Frank, looking back at me from the front passenger seat, says, "Cooper give you his jacket?"

I look down at the leather coat still wrapped around my shoulders. It smells of Cooper, like leather and soap. I never want to take it off, not ever again. But I know I'm going to have to, when we get home.

"No," I say. "I mean, just to borrow."

"Oh," Frank say. "Because, you know, you've got your blood all over it."

"Frank," Patty says. "Shut up."

"It's all right," Cooper says, as he studies the many weirdos out his window who make up the street life of the West Village.

It's all right! My heart swells. Cooper had said it's all right that I got my blood all over his leather jacket! Probably because, you know, we'll be dating after this, and he's just going to give the coat to me anyway. And I'll have it—and Cooper—always, to keep me warm.

But then Cooper adds, "I know of a dry cleaner who's good at getting bloodstains out."

You know, it just isn't my day.

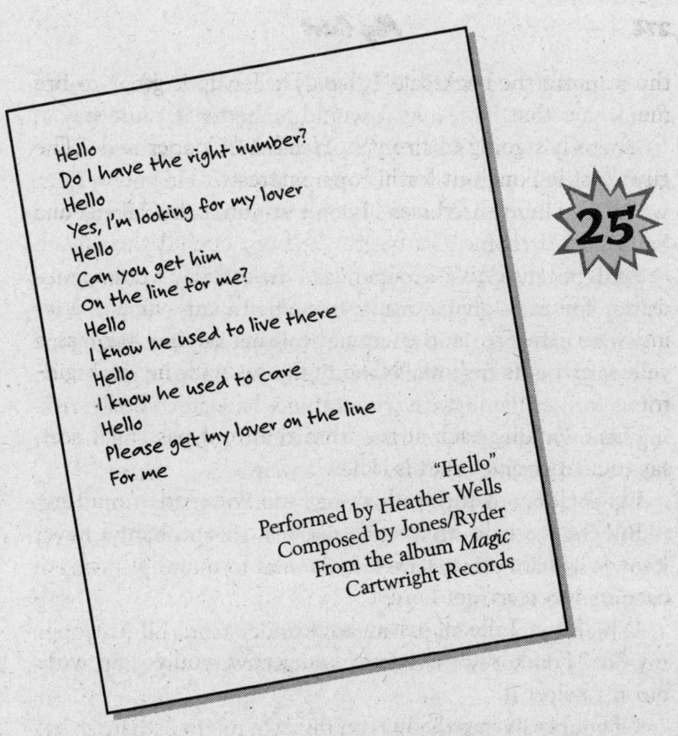

25

Hello
Do I have the right number?
Hello
Yes, I'm looking for my lover
Hello
Can you get him
On the line for me?
Hello
I know he used to live there
Hello
I know he used to care
Hello
Please get my lover on the line
For me

"Hello"
Performed by Heather Wells
Composed by Jones/Ryder
From the album *Magic*
Cartwright Records

Patty drops us off at the brownstone, even though Frank insists it isn't safe there, what with somebody wanting to kill me and all.

All I want to do is take a bath and crawl into my own bed and sleep for a thousand years. I don't want to have a big long discussion about whether whoever is trying to kill me knows where I live. Frank wants me to go stay with him and Patty.

Until Cooper points out that that might put Indy at risk.

At first I'm kind of shocked, you know, that Cooper would

say something so horrible. It's only when I see how swiftly Frank says that he thinks it would be better if I just stay at Cooper's, after all, what with Cooper being a trained crime fighter, that I realize what Cooper was up to. He knows I just want to go home. He knows I don't want to stay in Frank and Patty's guest room.

And because he's Cooper, and he's always doing nice things for me—giving me a free apartment when I have nowhere else to go, and no money for rent anyway; taking me to a party he doesn't really want to go to, since he might run into a former flame, with whom things had ended badly; risking his own life to save mine; that kind of thing—he'd done his best to get me what he knew I wanted.

Except, of course, the one thing I want more than anything.

But apparently that, for reasons I'll probably never know—and am pretty sure I don't want to, anyway—he's not prepared to give me.

Which is totally fine. I mean, I understand. I'll just open my OWN doctor's office/detective agency/jewelry shop, without his help.

Of course, having the kids on my own might be harder, but I'm sure I'll manage somehow.

Fortunately, I have an unlisted number, so there aren't any reporters lurking on my front stoop when we pull up. Just the usual drug dealers.

Lucy is wild with joy to see me—though I have to ask Cooper to walk her for the time being, since there's no way I can hold a leash with my torn-up hands. Once the two of them are gone, I slip upstairs to my apartment, where I peel off my grimy clothes and slide, at long last, into the tub.

Although it turns out that bathing with stitches in your hands is no joke. I have to get out of the tub and go into the kitchen, pull out some rubber gloves, and put those on before

I can wash my hair, because the doctor warned me that if I got the stitches wet, my hands might fall off, or something.

Once I get all the elevator grime and blood off me, let the bath refill, and I just lay there, soaking my sore shoulder for a while, wondering what I'm going to do now.

I mean, things aren't exactly looking good. Someone is trying to kill me . . . probably the same someone who'd already killed two people, at least. The only common denominator between the dead girls appears to be the president of the college's son.

But, at least according to the police, it's unlikely that Chris Allington was the one who'd tried to blow me up, because he'd been out of town at the time.

Which means that someone besides Chris is trying to kill me. And maybe that someone, and not Chris, killed the two girls.

But who? And why? Why would someone have killed Elizabeth Kellogg and Roberta Pace in the first place? What could they have possibly done to deserve to die? I mean, besides move into Fischer Hall. Oh, and date—albeit briefly—Chris Allington.

Is *that* it? Is *that* what had caused their deaths? The fact that they'd dated Chris? Had Magda been right? Not about the girls having killed themselves because, after waiting so long to have sex, they'd found out it really isn't the earth-shattering thing they'd been led to believe. But about the girls dying *because* of the sex—not at their own hand, but the hand of someone who didn't approve of what they'd just done.

Someone like Mrs. Allington, maybe? What was it that Chris's mother had said to me, just before the elevator incident? Something about "you girls."

"You girls are forever bothering him," she'd said. Or something like that.

You girls. There'd been something deeply antagonistic in Mrs. Allington's manner, an emotion far stronger than simple annoyance over my waking her up. Is Mrs. Allington one of those jealous mothers, who thinks no other woman is good enough for her precious son? Did *Mrs. Allington* kill Elizabeth and Roberta? And did she then try to kill me when I got too close to discovering her secret?

Oh my God! That's it! Mrs. Allington is the killer! Mrs. Allington! I'm brilliant! Perhaps the most brilliant detective mind since Sherlock Holmes! Wait. Is he even real? Or fictional? He's fictional, right?

Well, okay, then. I am the most brilliant detective mind since . . . since . . . Eliot Ness! He's real, right?

"Heather?"

I start, sloshing hot water and soap suds over the side of the tub.

But it's just Cooper.

"Just checking you're okay," he says, through the closed door. "You need anything?"

Um, yes. You. In here with me, naked. Now.

"No, I'm fine," I call. Should I tell him that I'd figured out who'd done this to me? Or wait until I'm out of the tub?

"Well, when you're through, I thought I'd order something to eat. Indian okay with you?"

Hmmmm. Vegetable samosas.

"Fine," I call.

"Okay, well, come out soon. There's something I need to talk to you about."

Something he needs to talk to me about? Like what? Like his true feelings for me? *I've always thought of you as one of the—* He never had finished telling me what he's always thought of me as.

Is he going to tell me now? Am I sure I want to know?

Two minutes later I slide into my usual seat at my kitchen table, bundled in my terry-cloth robe, with a towel wrapped around my wet hair. Oh, I want to know. I want to know all right.

Across the table from me, Cooper says, "That was fast."

Then he opens up his laptop.

Wait a minute. His *laptop*? What kind of guy uses audiovisual aids to tell a girl what he thinks of her?

"How much do you know," Cooper asks, "about Christopher Allington?"

"Christopher Allington?" My voice cracks. Maybe because it was hoarse from all the screaming I'd done earlier in the day. Or maybe because I'm in shock over the fact that what Cooper wants to talk to me about isn't his true feelings for me, but his suspicions about Chris. Hello. Annoying.

"But it couldn't have been Chris," I say, to get Cooper off that subject, and back onto, you know, me. "Detective Canavan said he—"

"When I investigate a case," Cooper interrupts calmly, "I investigate it from all angles. Right now, Christopher appears to be the common link between all the victims. What I'm asking is, what do you know about him?"

"Well," I say. Maybe Vulcan mind control would work again. WHAT HAVE YOU ALWAYS THOUGHT ABOUT ME? "Not much."

"Do you know where he went for undergrad?"

"No," I say. WHAT HAVE YOU ALWAYS THOUGHT ABOUT ME? Then, glancing at his face, I ask, "Why? Do you know where Chris went as an undergrad?"

"Yes," Cooper says. "Earlcrest."

"Earl what?" I ask. Vulcan mind control does not appear to

be working! Instead of telling me what he's always thought about me, he's blathering about Chris Allington. Who cares about Chris? What about how you feel about ME?

"Earlcrest College," Cooper says. "Chris went there for undergrad."

"What are you talking about, Cooper?" I wish the Indian food would hurry up and come. My stomach is growling. "And how do you even know where Chris went?"

Cooper shrugs his broad shoulders. "SIS." he says.

"S.O.S?" I echo, confused.

"No, SIS. Student Information System." When I continue to look blank, he sighs. "Ah, yes. How could I forget? You're computer illiterate."

"I am not! I surf the Net all the time. I do all your bills—"

"But your office is still antiquated. SIS hasn't been extended to the dormitory director's offices yet."

"Residence hall," I correct him, automatically.

"Residence hall," he says. Cooper is a flurry of activity. He's striking keys on the computer way faster than I can change chords on my guitar. "Here, look. I'm accessing SIS now to show you what I mean about Christopher Allington. Okay." Cooper turns the screen to face me. "Allington, Christopher Phillip. Take a look."

I peer at the tiny monitor. Christopher Allington's entire academic record is there, along with a lot of other personal information, like his LSAT scores and his course schedule and stuff. Chris, it turns out, has been through a lot of prep schools. He'd been thrown out of one in Switzerland for cheating, and another one in Connecticut, reason for expulsion unspecified. But he had still managed to get into the University of Chicago, which I've heard is quite selective. I wonder what strings his dad had pulled to help him out there.

But Chris's sojourn in the Windy City didn't last long. He'd dropped out after only a single semester. Then he'd seemed to take some time off . . . a good four years, as a matter of fact.

Then suddenly he'd shown up at Earlcrest College, from which he'd graduated last year somewhat older than the rest of his class, but with a B.A., just the same.

"Earlcrest College," I say. "That's where his dad used to be president. Before he got hired at New York College."

"Ah, nepotism," Cooper says, with a grin. "As alive and well in the halls of academia as ever."

"Okay," I say, still confused. "So he got kicked out of a few places as a kid, and could only get into a college his dad's president of. What does that prove? Not that he's a psychopathic murderer." I can't believe *I'm* the one arguing for Chris's innocence now. Is his mom really that much more appealing as a murderer? "And how did you access his file, anyway? Isn't it supposed to be private?"

"I have my ways," Cooper says, turning the computer screen back in his own direction.

"Oh my God." Is there no end to this man's fabulousness? "You hacked into the student system!"

"You were always curious about what I do all day," he says with a shrug. "Now you know. Part of it, anyway."

"I can't believe it," I say. "You're a computer nerd!" This changes everything. Now we're going to have to open a doctor's office slash detective agency slash jewelry shop slash computer hacking service. Oh, wait, what about my songs?

Cooper ignores me. "I think there's got to be something here," he says, tapping the laptop. "Something we're missing. The only connection between the girls seems to be Allington. He's the only one we know about, but, given what I see here, there must be something else. I mean, besides the fact that both girls were virgins with residence hall records before Chris got his hands on them . . ."

Mrs. Allington. It's on the tip of my tongue to say *What about Mrs. Allington?* I mean, she had the motive. She obviously had—what was it that Sarah would call it? An Oedipus complex? Only the opposite, because she had it for her son, not her dad . . .

Well, okay, Mrs. Allington has that thing where she thinks her son is hot, and she resents the girls who pursue him. Resents them enough to kill them, though? And could Mrs. Allington really have made that bomb? The one on top of the elevator? I mean, if you could just go out and buy a bomb at Saks, I totally think Mrs. Allington would.

But you can't. You have to make a bomb. And to make a bomb, you have to be sober. I'm pretty sure, anyway.

And Mrs. Allington has never once been sober—that I could tell—since she'd moved in to Fischer Hall.

I sigh and glance out the window. I can see the lights on in the president's penthouse. What are the Allingtons doing up there? I wonder. It's close to seven o'clock. Probably watching the news.

Or, perhaps, plotting to kill more innocent virgins?

The front door buzzer goes off, making me jump.

"That's dinner," Cooper says, and gets up. "I'll be right back."

He goes downstairs to get the Indian food. I keep on looking out the window while I wait for him to get back. Below the penthouse, lights appear in windows on other floors of Fischer Hall as the residents got home from class or dinner or their workouts or rehearsals. I wonder if any of the tiny figures I can see in any of the windows is Amber, the little redhead from Idaho. Is she sitting in her room, waiting for a call from Chris? Does she know he's hiding out in the

Hamptons? Poor little Amber. I wonder what she did to get in trouble with Rachel this morning.

That's when it hits me.

My lips part, but for a minute, no sound comes out from between them. Amber. I had forgotten all about Amber, and her meeting with Rachel this morning. What had Rachel needed to see Amber about? Amber herself hadn't known why she'd been scheduled for a mandatory meeting with the dorm director. What had Amber done?

Amber hadn't done anything. Anything except talk to Chris Allington.

That's all Amber had done.

And Rachel knew it, because she'd seen me with the two of them in front of the building after the lip-synch contest.

Just like she'd seen Roberta and Chris at the dance. And Elizabeth and Chris—where? Where had she seen them together? At orientation, maybe? A movie night?

Except that it didn't matter. Like it didn't matter that it was Rachel who'd told Julio to get me because Gavin was elevator surfing again.

Like it didn't matter that it was Rachel who'd snuck onto the penthouse roof and tried to push that planter onto my head.

Like it didn't matter that when the second girl died, Rachel hadn't been in the cafeteria, like she was supposed to have been. No, I'd met her coming from the ladies' room . . . around the corner from the stairs she'd been hurrying down, after pushing Roberta Pace to her death.

And the reason the elevator key had been missing, and then reappeared in such a short space of time that day? Rachel had had it. Rachel, the one person in Fischer Hall no desk attendant would ask to sign out a key, or even question the presence of behind the desk. Because she's the hall director.

And the girls who'd died—they hadn't died because they had files in Rachel's office.

They had files in Rachel's office because she'd singled them out to die.

"Hope you're hungry," Cooper says, returning to my apartment holding a big plastic *I ♥ NY* bag. "They messed up and gave us chicken *and* shrimp dansak . . ." His voice trails off. "Heather?" Cooper is peering at me strangely, his blue eyes concerned. "Are you okay?"

"Earlcrest," I manage to grunt.

Cooper puts the bag on the kitchen table and stares down at me.

"Yeah," he says. "That's what I thought you said. What about it?"

"Where is it?"

Cooper bends over to refer to his computer screen. "Uh, I don't—oh, Indiana. Richmond, Indiana."

I shake my head, so hard the towel slips from it, and my damp hair falls down over my shoulders. No. NO WAY.

"Oh my God," I breathe. "Oh my *God*."

Cooper is staring at me like I've lost my mind. And you know what? I think I *have*. Lost my mind, I mean. Because how could I not have seen it before now, even though it had been staring me right in the face. . . .

"Rachel worked there," I manage to rasp. "Rachel worked at a dorm in Richmond, Indiana, before she moved here."

Cooper, who'd been pulling white paper containers from the *I ♥ NY* bag, pauses. "What are you talking about?"

"Richmond, Indiana," I repeat. My heart is thumping so hard that I can see the lapel of my terry-cloth robe leaping over my breast with every beat. "The last place Rachel worked was in Richmond, Indiana . . ."

Comprehension dawns across Cooper's face.

"Rachel worked at Earlcrest? You think . . . you think *Rachel's* the one who killed those girls?" He shakes his head. "Why? You think she was that desperate to win a Pansy Award?"

"No." No way is Rachel going around pushing people down the elevator shafts of Fischer Hall in order to get herself a Pansy, or even a promotion.

Because it isn't a promotion Rachel is after.

It's a man.

A heterosexual man, worth more than a hundred thousand dollars a year, if you count the trust fund he's supposed to have.

Christopher Allington. Christopher Allington is that man.

"Heather," Cooper says. "Heather? Look. I'm sorry. But there's no way. Rachel Walcott is not a killer."

I suck in my breath.

"How do you know?" I ask. "I mean, why not? Why not her, as opposed to someone else? Because she's a woman? Because she's pretty?"

"Because it's crazy," Cooper says. "Come on, it's been a long day. Maybe you should get some rest."

"I am not tired," I say. "Think about it, Cooper. I mean, *really* think about it. Elizabeth and Roberta met with Rachel before they died—I bet the stuff in their files, the stuff about their moms calling, isn't even true. I bet their mothers never called. And now Amber . . ."

"There are seven hundred residents of Fischer Hall," Cooper points out. "Are all the ones who had meetings with Rachel Walcott dead?"

"No, just the ones who also had relationships with Christopher Allington."

Cooper shakes his head.

"Heather, try to look at this logically. How could Rachel

Walcott have the physical strength to throw a full-grown, struggling young woman down an elevator shaft? Rachel can't weigh more than a hundred and twenty pounds herself. It's just not possible, Heather."

"I don't know how she's doing it, Cooper. But I do know that it's a bit of a coincidence that both Rachel and Chris were at Earlcrest last year, and now they're both here at New York College. I would bet cash money that Rachel followed Christopher Allington—and his parents—here."

When he continues to look hesitant, I stand up, push back my chair, and say, "There's only one way we'll ever know for sure."

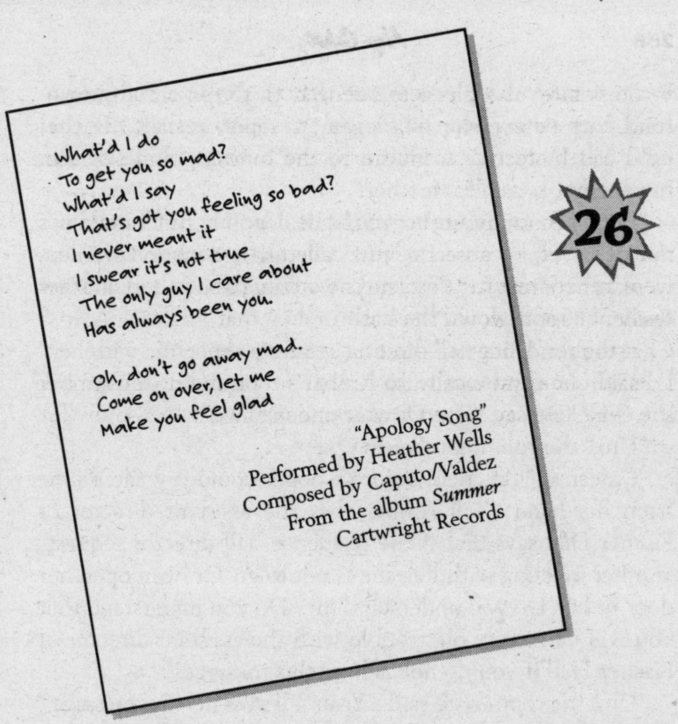

What'd I do
To get you so mad?
What'd I say
That's got you feeling so bad?
I never meant it
I swear it's not true
The only guy I care about
Has always been you.

Oh, don't go away mad.
Come on over, let me
Make you feel glad

"Apology Song"
Performed by Heather Wells
Composed by Caputo/Valdez
From the album *Summer*
Cartwright Records
26

Not surprisingly, Cooper balks at the idea of driving all the way to the Hamptons at seven o'clock on a weeknight just to have a word with a man the police themselves won't even haul in for questioning.

When I remind him that Chris is more likely to talk to either of us than the police, Cooper is still not convinced. He insists that after the injuries I'd sustained that morning, what I need is a good night's sleep, not a six-hour drive to East Hampton and back.

When I remind him that it is our duty as good citizens

to do whatever we can to see that this woman is put behind bars before she kills again, Cooper assures me that he'll call Detective Canavan in the morning and tell him my theory.

"But by morning Amber might be dead!" I cry. I know she's not dead yet, because I've just called her room and learned, from her roommate, that she is watching a movie in another resident's room down the hall.

"If the residence hall director requests a meeting with her," I'd said, semihysterically, to Amber's roommate, "tell Amber she is NOT to go to it. Do you understand?"

"Um," the roommate said. "Okay."

"I mean it," I'd cried, before Cooper could pry the phone from my hand. "Tell Amber that the assistant director of Fischer Hall says that if the residence hall director requests another meeting with her, she is not to go. Or even open her door to her. Do you understand me? Do you understand that you will be in very big trouble with the assistant director of Fischer Hall if you do not deliver this message?"

"Uh," the roommate said. "Yeah. I'll give her the message."

Which is probably not the most subtle way to have gotten my point across. But at least I know Amber is safe.

For the time being.

"We've got to go, Cooper!" I urge him, as soon as I've put the phone down. "I've got to know, now!"

"Heather," Cooper says, looking frustrated. "I swear to God, of all the people I've ever met, you have got to be the most—"

I suck in my breath. He's going to say it! Whatever it was he'd been about to say in my office! He's going to say it now!

Except that back then—in my office, I mean—it had sounded like what he'd been about to say was complimentary. Judging from the way his jaw is clenched now, though,

I don't think he's about to say something nice about me. In fact, I'm pretty sure I don't *want* to hear his next words.

Because, truthfully, the thing with Rachel is more important.

Which is why I say, "This is stupid. You know, there are trains to the Hamptons. I'll just go look up the schedule online and—"

I don't know if he gave in because he realized it was the only way to shut me up, or if he was genuinely concerned that I might do myself harm on the LIRR. Maybe he was just trying to placate the crazy injured girl.

In any case, in the time it takes me to get dressed, Cooper has retrieved his car—a '74 BMW 2002, a vehicle that invariably causes the drug dealers on my street to hoot tauntingly, because, in their opinion, the only good BMW is a new one—from its parking garage. He isn't happy about it, or anything. In fact, I'm pretty sure he was cursing whatever impulse had prompted him to ask me to move in with him in the first place.

And I feel bad about it. I really do.

But not enough to tell him to forget the whole thing. Because, you know, a girl's life is at stake.

It's easy to find the Allingtons' weekend place. I mean, they're in the East Hampton phone book. If they didn't want people to drop in, they'd have had an unlisted number, right?

And okay, there's this big wrought-iron gate at the end of their driveway, with a built-in intercom and everything, that might lead the average person to believe visitors were unwelcome.

But I for one didn't fall for it. I hop out of the car and go to press on the buzzer. And even when no one answers, I'm not discouraged. Well, very much.

"Heather," Cooper says, from the driver's window of his car, which he's rolled down. "I don't think anybody's going to—"

But then the intercom crackles, and a voice that is unmistakably Chris's says, *"What?"*

I can understand why he's so testy. I'd sort of been leaning on the buzzer, knowing that eventually the person inside would be driven insane and have to answer. It's a trick I'd picked up from the reporters who used to stake out the place Jordan and I had shared.

"Um, hi, Chris," I say into the intercom. "It's me."

"Me who?" Chris demands, still sounding annoyed.

"You know," I say, trying to sound girlishly flirtatious. "Let me in."

Then I add the three little words I'd learned from Justine's files that few students—and that's what Chris is, after all—can resist: "I brought pizza."

There's a pause. Then the gate slowly starts to open.

I hurry back to the car, where Cooper is sitting, looking—even if I do say so myself—vaguely impressed.

"Pizza," he echoes. "I'll have to remember that one."

"Works every time," I say. I don't mention how I knew. I'm kind of sick of Justine, to tell the truth.

We pull into the circular driveway, and Villa d'Allington, in all its white stucco glory, looms ahead of us.

I've been to the Hamptons before, of course. The Cartwrights have a house there, right on the water, surrounded on three sides by a federally protected bird sanctuary, so no else can build there, and ruin the view.

I've been to other people's homes there as well—houses that were considered architectural marvels and once even a chateau that had been transported, brick by brick, from the south of France. Seriously.

But I've never seen anything quite like the Allingtons' house. Not in the Hamptons, anyway. Stark white and massive, filled with airy, Mediterranean archways and bright, flowering plants, the place is lit up as brightly as Rockefeller Center.

Only instead of a great big gold guy looming over a skating rink, there's a great big white house looming over a swimming pool.

"How about," Cooper says, as we get out of the car, "you let me do the talking for a change."

I narrow my eyes at him. "You aren't going to hit him, are you?"

"Why would I do that?" Cooper asks, sounding surprised.

"Don't you hit people? I mean, in your line of work?"

"Can't remember the last time I did," Cooper says, mildly.

A little bit disappointed, I say, "Well, I think Christopher Allington's the type of guy you'd like to hit. If you hit people."

"He is," Cooper agrees, with a faint smile. "But I won't. At least, not right away."

We hear them first, and see them as soon as we part the morning glories that hang like a curtain over one of the archways. Ducking through the sweet-smelling vines, we end up in the backyard. To the left of the shimmering pool is a hot tub, steaming in the cool night air.

In the hot tub are two people, neither of whom, I'm thankful to see, is President Allington or his wife. I think that might have killed me, the sight of President Allington in a Speedo.

They don't notice us right away, probably because of all the steam and the bright floodlights that light the deck around the pool, but cast the hot tub area in shadow. Scattered here and there along the wide wooden planks of the patio are lounge chairs with pale pink cushions. Off to one side of the pool is a bar, a real bar with stools in front of it and a back-lit area that's filled with bottles.

I approach the hot tub and clear my throat noisily.

Chris lifts his face from the girl whose breasts he was nuzzling and blinks at us. He is clearly drunk.

The girl is, too. She says, "Hey, she hasn't got any pizza." She sounds disappointed about it, even though the two of them seemed to have been doing just fine for themselves in the extra cheese department.

"Hi, Chris," I say, and I sit down on the end of one of the lounge chairs. The cushion beneath me is damp. It has rained recently in the Hamptons.

It seems to take a few seconds for Chris to recognize me. And when he does, he isn't too happy.

"Blondie?" He reaches up to slick some of his wet hair back from his eyes. "Is that you? What are *you* doing here?"

"We just dropped by to ask you a few questions," I say. Lucy has come with us—I couldn't leave her cooped up in the brownstone all night—and now she butts her head against my knees and sits down, panting happily. "How are you, anyway?"

"I'm okay, I guess," Chris replies. He looks up at Cooper. "Who's he?"

"A friend," Cooper says. Then adds, "Of hers," I guess so there won't be any confusion.

"Huh," Chris says. Then, in an apparent attempt to make the best out of a bad situation, he goes, "Well. Care for a drink?"

"No, thank you," Cooper says. "What we'd really like is to talk to you about Elizabeth Kellogg and Roberta Pace."

Chris doesn't look alarmed. In fact, he doesn't even look surprised. Instead he says graciously, "Oh, sure. Sure. Oh, hey, where are my manners? Faith, honey, go inside and rustle up some grub for us, will you? And grab another bottle of wine while you're in there, why don't you?"

The girl in the hot tub pouts. "But, Chris—"

"Go on, honey."

"But my name's Hope, not Faith."

"Whatever." Chris slaps her on the backside as she climbs, dripping like a mermaid, from the hot tub. She has on a bathing suit, but it's a bikini, and the top is so skimpy and her boobs so large that the tiny Lycra triangles seem like mere suggestions.

Cooper notices the bikini phenomenon right away. I can tell by his raised eyebrows. It so pays to be a trained investigator.

Her rear proves as impressive as her front. Not an ounce of cellulite. I wonder if she, like Rachel, had StairMastered it all away.

"So, Chris," Cooper says, as soon as the girl is gone. "What's the deal with you and Rachel Walcott?"

Chris chokes on the sip of Chardonnay he'd been taking.

"Wh-what?" he coughs, when he can speak again.

But Cooper's just looking down at Chris the way he might have looked down at a really interesting but kind of gross bug that he'd found in his salad.

"Rachel Walcott," he says. "She was the director of the dorm—I mean, residence hall—you lived in your senior year at Earlcrest. Now she's running Fischer Hall, where your parents live, and where Heather here works."

Fumbling for a pack of cigarettes and a lighter he had left by the side of the Jacuzzi, Chris pulls one out with trembling fingers and lights it. He inhales, and in the semidarkness, the tip of the cigarette glows redly.

"Shit" is all he says.

I'm not a trained detective and all, but even I think this answer is kind of . . . suspicious.

"So what gives between the two of you?" Cooper asks. "You and Rachel. I mean, you might not have noticed, but people are dying—"

"I've noticed," Chris says sharply. "Okay? I've noticed. What the fuck do you think?"

Cooper apparently doesn't think this last part is all that necessary. You know, the bad language.

Because he says to Chris, in a much harsher voice than he's spoken in before, "You *knew*? How long?"

Chris blinks up at him through the steam from the bubbling jets. "What?" he asks, like someone who isn't sure he was hearing things right.

"*How long*?" Cooper demands again, in a voice that makes me glad it's Chris he's talking to, and not me. It also makes me doubt his story. You know, about not hitting people in his line of work. "How long have you known that Rachel was the one killing those girls?"

I can see that Chris has gone as pale as the watery lights beneath the surface of the pool, and it isn't from the cigarette smoke.

I don't blame him. Cooper's scaring me a little, too.

"I didn't know," Chris says, in a choked voice that is quite different from the cocky one he'd used previously. "I didn't put it together until last night, when you"—he looks at me "when you and I danced, and you told me Beth and Bobby were . . . were the ones who—"

"Oh, c'mon, Chris," Cooper says. "You expect us to believe that with all the publicity on campus after those supposed accidents—"

"I didn't know!" Chris splashes one hand into the water to emphasize his words, and gets Lucy's paws wet. She looks down at them quizzically, then goes to work with her tongue. "I swear to God, I didn't know. I don't exactly have a lot of free time, and what I do have I'm not going to waste reading the newspapers. I mean, of course I heard two girls in Fischer Hall had died, but I didn't know they were *my* two girls."

"And you didn't notice that neither of the girls was returning your calls?"

Chris ducks his head. Shamefacedly, I think.

"Because you never called them again." Cooper's voice is cold as ice.

Chris looks defensive. "Do *you*?" he demands, of Cooper. "Do you always call the next day?"

"If I want there to be a next time," Cooper replies, without missing a beat.

"Exactly." Chris's voice drips with meaning. At first I don't get what he means.

Then I do.

Oh.

Cooper shakes his head, looking as disgusted as I feel. Well, almost, anyway. "You expect me to believe that you never knew those girls were dead until you heard it from Heather the other night?"

"That's right," Chris says, and suddenly he flicks his cigarette into the rhododendrons and hauls himself out of the Jacuzzi. All he has on is a pair of baggy swim trunks. His frame is lean but muscular, his skin tanned to a light gold. There isn't a single patch of body hair on him, unless you count what curls out from beneath his arms.

"And when I heard about it, the first thing I did was, I came here." Chris stands up, wrapping himself in a wide, pale pink towel. "I needed to get away, I needed to think, I needed to—"

"You needed to avoid being hauled in for questioning by the cops," Cooper finishes for him.

"That, too. Look, so I slept with 'em—"

I can stand it no longer. Really. I feel sick—and not just because of all the Indian food we'd eaten in the car on the way over, either.

No, this isn't just indigestion. It's disgust.

"Don't act like it's no big deal, Chris," I say. "Your sleeping with those girls, then not calling them again. Not even telling them your real name in order to keep them from knowing who your father is. Because it *is* a big deal. Or it was, to them. You used them. You used them because you know you . . . you know you've got . . . well, performance inadequacies."

"What?" Chris looks shocked. "I do not!"

"Of course you do," I say, knowing I sound like Sarah, and not caring. "Why else were you looking for girls who don't have any sexual experience—until Hope here—so they don't have anything to measure your performance by?"

Chris looks as stunned as if I'd hit him.

And maybe, in a way, I have.

Cooper tugs on my sleeve and whispers, "Whoa, tiger. Simmer down. Let's not get our roles here confused. I'm the bad cop. You're the good one."

Then, patting me gently on the back—the way I pat Indy when I want him to calm down—Cooper says to a red-faced Chris, "Listen, nobody's accusing you of murdering anybody. What we want to know about is your relationship with Rachel Walcott."

"Why?" Chris is over being scared, and back to being surly. My remark about performance inadequacies has upset him. Undoubtedly because it's true.

Chris strides past Cooper, heading for the pool. "What about it?"

"Was there one?" Cooper wants to know.

"A relationship?" Dropping the towel, Chris climbs onto the diving board. A second later, he's sprung into the pool, hardly making a splash as his long, lean body arcs through the water. He swims up to the side of the pool we're standing on, then surfaces, seeming to have had a change of heart under water.

"All right," he says. "I'll tell you everything I know."

27

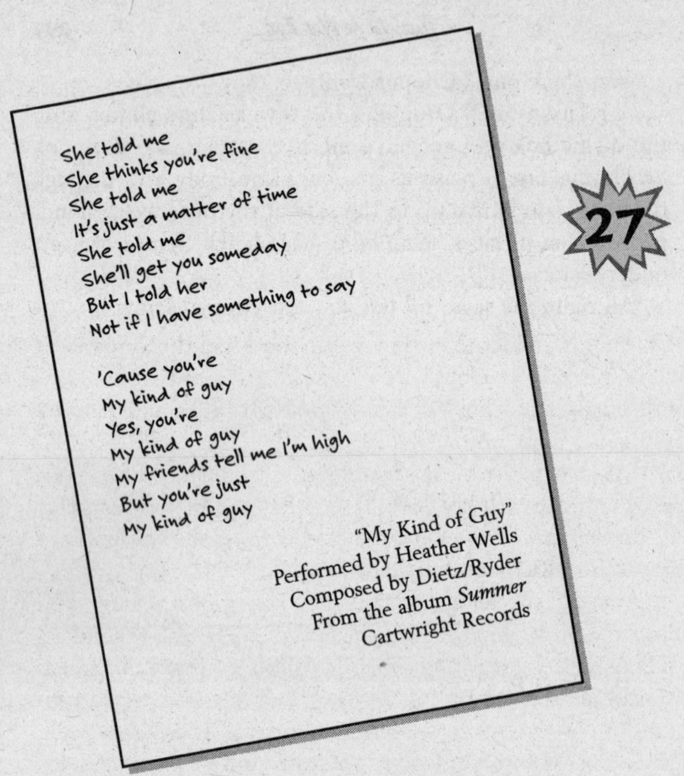
She told me
She thinks you're fine
She told me
It's just a matter of time
She told me
She'll get you someday
But I told her
Not if I have something to say

'Cause you're
My kind of guy
Yes, you're
My kind of guy
My friends tell me I'm high
But you're just
My kind of guy

"My Kind of Guy"
Performed by Heather Wells
Composed by Dietz/Ryder
From the album *Summer*
Cartwright Records

"Okay," Chris says, through chattering teeth. "Okay. So I slept with her for a few months. It's not like I asked her to marry me, or anything. But she went fucking psycho on me, okay? I thought she was going to cut my balls off."

I scoop up Chris's towel and drape it over his shivering shoulders. He doesn't seem to notice. He's on a roll. He's climbed from the pool and has started walking toward the house, Cooper and Lucy and I following behind, like an entourage after . . .

Well, some famous rock star.

"It started my junior year," Chris says. Now that he's started talking, it's like he can't stop. Or even slow down. You have to admire Cooper's technique. Not hitting the guy had done the trick. "A bunch of guys and I got in trouble for smoking pot in the dorm, you know, and we had to go see the dorm director—Rachel—for sanctioning. We all thought we were gonna get kicked outta school. So some of the guys, they were like, 'Chris, put the moves on her,' 'cause, I dunno, I was a little older than they were, and I had this reputation with the girls, you know?"

I envision Rachel—in her Manolo Blahniks and tailored Armani—being hit on by this smooth-talking, golden-haired Adonis. No, he isn't the suave businessman she'd been hoping to attract with her rock-hard glutes and blown-out hair.

But he has to have been the closest thing she was likely to get to it in Richmond, Indiana.

"Anyway, she let us off. For the pot-smoking thing, you know? Said it would be our little secret." There's a smirk in Chris's voice. But it isn't a happy smirk. "At first I thought it was because of whom my father is. But then we started running into each other in the cafeteria and stuff. More like—well, she'd run into me, you know? And the guys were like, 'Go for it, man. You start going with the dorm director, we can get away with anything we want.' And I had nothing else going on, you know, lady-wise, so I figured, 'Why not?' And one thing led to another, and then, well, we were an item, I guess."

He ducks under an archway, and we follow, through an open sliding glass door and into a dimly lit, sunken living room, where the primary decorating theme appears to be black leather. The couches are black leather. The ottomans are black leather. Even the mantel appears to be encased in black leather.

But surely not. I mean, wouldn't that catch on fire?

"Turns out, I was her first," Chris explains, going to the mantel and twisting a dial. Suddenly the room is bathed in an unearthly pink light. If I hadn't known better, I'd have thought we'd walked into a bordello. Or maybe one of those oxygen bars in SoHo. "She wasn't always as . . . put together as she looks now. She was actually kinda . . . well, when I knew her, back in Richmond, Rachel was kinda fat."

I blink at him. "What?"

Cooper throws me a warning glance. Chris is on a roll, and Cooper doesn't want me interrupting.

"You know." He shrugs. "She was fat. Well, not fat, really. But like . . . chubby. And she wore sweats all the time. I don't know what happened to her, you know, between now and then, but she slimmed down, majorly, and got, I don't know, like a makeover, or something. Because back then . . . I don't know."

"Wait." I am having trouble processing this. "Rachel was *fat?*"

"Yeah." He shrugs. "Maybe you're right. Maybe there is less . . . pressure being with someone who doesn't have anyone else to measure you by. There was definitely something—I dunno—exciting about being with this older chick who was so smart in some ways, and so dumb in others . . ."

"She was *fat?*" I am seriously stunned. "She runs like four miles a day! She eats nothing but lettuce. With no dressing!"

"Well," Chris says, with another shrug. "Maybe now. Not back then. She told me she'd been heavy her whole life, and that's why she'd never . . . you know. Had a guy before."

Whoa. Rachel had still been a virgin post–grad school? Hadn't she met *anyone* in high school? In college, even?

Apparently not.

"So how long did this go on? This affair," Cooper asks, apparently in an effort to get me off the *Rachel was fat?* thing.

Chris sinks down onto one of the black leather couches, not seeming to care whether he got the cushions wet. When you're as rich as he is, I guess things like that don't matter.

"Till midway through my senior year. That's when I realized I had to start really studying, you know, to get decent scores on my LSATs. After letting me goof off through most of my twenties, my parents were riding me, you know, to get into law school. I told her—Rachel—that I was going to hafta play it cool for a while. It seemed like a good time to break it off. I mean, it wasn't like it could go anywhere, her and me, after I graduated. No way was I sticking around Richmond."

"Did you tell her that?" Cooper asks.

"Tell her what?"

I see a muscle in Cooper's jaw twitch. "Did you tell Rachel that it couldn't go anywhere?" he elaborates, with forced patience.

"Oh." Chris doesn't meet either of our gazes. "Yeah."

"And?"

"And she flipped on me, man. I mean, really flipped. Started screaming, tearing stuff up. She picked up my computer monitor and threw it across the quad, no joke. I was so scared, I moved in with some buddies of mine off-campus for the rest of the year."

"And you never saw her again?" A part of me can't believe Chris's story. Another part of me believes it all too well. Not that I can picture Rachel throwing a computer monitor across the room.

But I can't picture her killing two girls—and almost killing three other people—either.

"No," Chris says. "Not till a couple weeks ago, when I got back from Richmond. I spent the summer there, doing volunteer stuff, as part of the deal I had with my dad about law school. Then I walked into Fischer Hall, and the first thing I see is Rachel, up at the reception desk, bawling some kid out for something or other. Only, you know, she's all . . . skinny. I nearly passed out, let me tell you. But she just smiled, cool as can be, and asked how I'd been. No hard feelings, and all that."

"And you believed her." Cooper's voice is toneless.

"Yeah." Chris sighs. "She seemed cool with it. I thought—you know, the weight loss, her new hairstyle, the clothes . . . I thought it was a good sign, you know. That she was moving on."

"And the fact that she had purposefully set out to get a job managing the building your parents live in," Cooper says. "That didn't raise a red flag that she might not be as 'cool with it' as you thought?"

"Obviously not," Chris says. "Until . . . well, what I found out last night."

A bell-like voice cries out, "Oh, there you are! I looked all over outside. I didn't know you'd come in."

Hope comes traipsing down the stairs, holding a tray of what looks—and smells—like spinach pastry puffs in one hand, and the hem of a floor-length, leopard print robe in the other.

"The canapés are ready," she says. "Do you want them in here, or out by the pool?"

"Out by the pool, okay, honey?" Chris smiles weakly at her. "We'll join you in a minute."

Hope smiles good-naturedly and detours toward the sliding glass doors.

"Don't be long," she warns us. "They'll get cold."

As soon as she's gone, Chris says, "I've gone over it and over it—since talking to you the other night, I mean—trying to figure out if Rachel could have done it. Killed those girls, I mean. Because I'm good, you know . . . but not exactly anybody worth killing over."

He smiles weakly at his own little joke. Cooper doesn't

smile back. I guess we are still playing good cop/bad cop. Since I'm apparently the good cop, I smile back. It isn't even hard. I mean, in spite of everything, I still sort of like Chris. I can't help it. He's just . . . Chris.

"I mean, when she and I broke up," Chris goes on, as if there'd been no interruption, "I told you she was—well, violent. She threw my computer across the quad. That's like a hundred and fifty feet. She's pretty strong. A girl—a small girl, like Beth or Bobby. Well, that'd be nothing for Rachel. If she was mad enough."

"And you believe that's what happened to those girls?" Cooper seems to be making sure. "Not that they died accidentally, but that Rachel killed them?"

Chris is sinking deeper and deeper into his parents' leather couch. You can tell he totally wants to disappear.

"Yes," he says, in a small voice. "I mean . . . that's the only explanation, isn't it? Because that whole elevator surfing thing . . . Girls don't elevator surf."

I throw Cooper an *I told you so* look. But he doesn't see it. He is too busy staring stonily at Chris.

In the silence that falls after this, I can hear a cricket start to chirp loudly outside. I have to admit, I'm kind of . . . well, moved by Chris's speech. Oh, I still think he's a pig and all of that. But at least he freely admits it. That's something, anyway.

Cooper doesn't look nearly as impressed as I am, however.

"Chris," he says. "You're coming back to the city with us now, and tomorrow morning, we're going to the police."

It isn't a request. It's a command.

Chris grimaces. "Why? What good will it do? They'll just arrest me. They'll never believe it was Rachel. Never."

"Not if you've got alibis for the times of the murders," Cooper says.

"I do," Chris says, brightening suddenly. "I was in class when the second girl—Bobby, I mean—died. I know, 'cause we all heard the sirens and looked out the windows. Fischer Hall is right down the street from the law building . . ."

Then Chris shakes his head. His hair is drying like a golden helmet on top of his head. "But they aren't seriously going to believe that Rachel Walcott is killing the girls I've slept with. I mean, c'mon. Rachel just won a fucking Pansy Award for Good Samaritanism, or whatever."

Cooper just stares at him. "Are there any girls you've slept with this year who *aren't* dead?"

Chris looks uneasy. "Well, no, but—"

I look over my shoulder, at the archways that lead out to the pool. "What about Hope?"

"What about her?"

"Do you want her to end up dead, too?"

"No!" Chris looks appalled. "But . . . I mean, she's the au pair from next door. How's Rachel even going to—"

"Chris," Cooper says. "Have you ever thought about taking a sabbatical from dating?"

Chris swallows.

"To tell you the truth," he says. "I'm starting to think that might not be such a bad idea."

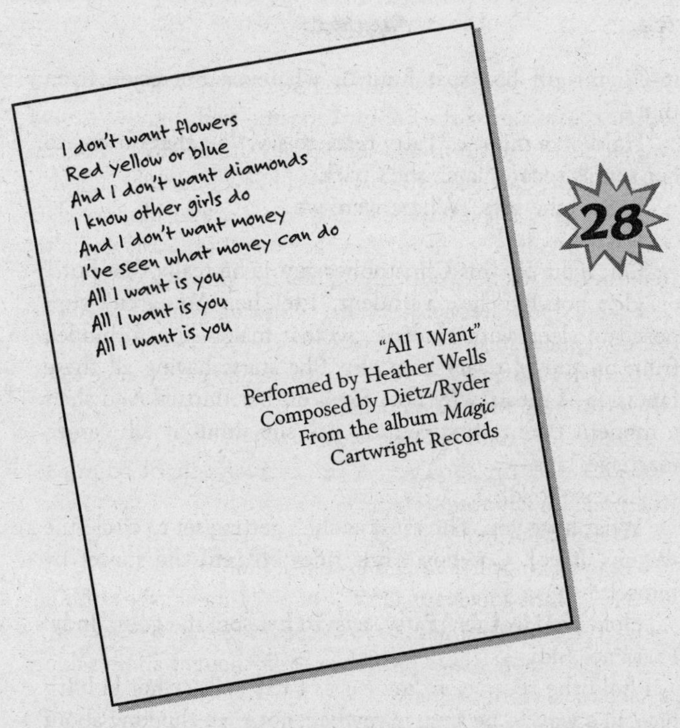

28
I don't want flowers
Red yellow or blue
And I don't want diamonds
I know other girls do
And I don't want money
I've seen what money can do
All I want is you
All I want is you
All I want is you
"All I Want"
Performed by Heather Wells
Composed by Dietz/Ryder
From the album *Magic*
Cartwright Records

"Think about it," I say to Patty. "Rachel meets this guy, this really handsome guy, who acts like he genuinely likes her, and maybe there's a part of him that really does . . ."

"Yeah," Patty agrees sarcastically. "The part he keeps in his briefs."

"Whatever. This guy, he's the first guy she's ever come across who is interested in her, let alone meets all of her qualifications for a boyfriend. You know, he's hot, he's rich, he's hetero. Okay, maybe he's a bit of a ne'er-do-well"—I lift up the glass of orange juice that's sitting by my bed and sip it—"living off his trust fund or whatever. But aside from that—"

"Hold on a minute." Patty turns to say, "Put that down," to her son. A second later, she's back.

"Right," she says. "Where were we?"

"Rachel," I say.

"Oh, right. So this Christopher guy. Is he really that hot?"

"He's hot. Plus he's a student," I tell her. "You aren't supposed to sleep with students, so that makes him forbidden fruit, on top of everything else. She starts having all these fantasies—I mean, why not? She's hit her thirties. And she's a modern twenty-first-century gal, she wants it all: career, marriage, kids—"

"License to kill."

"What have you. Then just as she's getting set to circle the wagons, li'l ol' Cowboy Chris rides off into the sunset by himself."

"Hold on, Heather," Patty says. To her son, she goes, "Indy! I said no! Indy—"

I hold the receiver to my ear as Patty yells at her kid. It's nice, in a way, to be snug in my bed, not even thinking about murderers for a change, while everyone else is out running around, actually doing something about them. I'd wanted to go with Cooper and Chris to see Detective Canavan. Really. I'd told him last night, as I'd stumbled up to bed in my apartment, to wake me up before he left in the morning.

But I guess the shock from all the excitement of the day before—the explosion, the trip to the hospital, the drive to Long Island and back—had finally taken its toll, because when Cooper had tapped on my bedroom door to see if I was up, I'd yelled at him to go away.

Not that I remember doing this. I mean, I would never have been so rude if I'd actually been conscious. Cooper left a note explaining the situation, and ending with the words, *Do* not *go to work today. Stay home and rest. I'll call you.*

And okay, he didn't sign it *Love, Cooper*. Just *Cooper*.

But still. He has to at least, you know, respect me more now. Now that it turns out I wasn't making it all up. About how someone had been trying to kill me, and all. I mean, he has to be thinking what a fantastic partner I'd make, to detect things with.

And who knows where that might lead? I mean, wouldn't the next rational step be for him to fall madly in love with me?

So yeah. I'm in a good mood. It's pouring rain outside, but I don't care. I'm snug in my bed, watching morning cartoons with Lucy by my side. Maybe it's only because I'd come so close to losing it, but life is seeming really, really good.

Or so I'm excitedly telling Patty. She seems very impressed by my theory—the one I'm hoping will send Detective Canavan, when he hears what Chris has to say, directly to Fischer Hall with an arrest warrant.

"I'm back," Patty says. "Where were we?"

"Rachel. Suddenly she's left holding the reins to the chuck wagon all by her lonesome," I say. "So what does a modern twenty-first-century gal like Rachel do?"

"Oh, wait, wait, let me try," Patty says, excitedly. "Rounds up a—what do they call it? Oh yes. A posse?"

"Gets rid of the competition," I correct her. "Because in Rachel's twisted mind, she thinks if she kills all Chris's girlfriends, she'll get him back through default. You know, if there aren't any other girls left, he'll have no choice but to return to her."

"Wow." Patty sounds impressed. "So how's she doing it?"

"What do you mean, how's she doing it? She's pushing them down the elevator shaft."

"Yeah, but how, Heather? How is a skinny bitch like Rachel pushing full-grown women—who surely don't want to die—down the elevator shaft? I mean, I can't even get my sister's damn chihuahua into his carrier, and he's just a tiny dog. Do you have any idea how hard it must be to push someone who doesn't want to die down an elevator shaft? You have to open the doors first. What are these girls doing while she's doing that? Why aren't they fighting back? Why doesn't Rachel have scratches on her face or on her arms? My sister's damned dog scratches me *hard* when I try to put him in his Sherpa."

I think back to my formative years of television viewing. "Chloroform," I say, simply. "She must be using chloroform."

"Wouldn't the coroner be able to find traces of this?"

Wow. Patty is good. Especially for someone who claims not to have time to watch *CSI*.

"Okay, okay," I said. "Maybe she conks them on the head with a baseball bat and slings 'em down the shaft while they're unconscious."

"The coroner wouldn't have noticed this?"

"They've just fallen sixteen stories," I say. "What's another bump?"

Beep.

My call waiting is going off.

"Oh, that's gotta be Cooper, Pats," I say. "Listen, I'll call you later. Want to go out for a celebratory brunch tomorrow? I mean, after they've incarcerated my boss?"

"Sure. Be there with bells on." Patty hangs up. I push down on the receiver, then say, "Hello?" after I hear the line click.

But the voice I hear isn't Cooper's. It's a woman's voice.

And it sounds like whoever it belongs to is crying.

"Heather?"

It takes me a second, but then I realize who it is.

"Sarah?" I say. "Is that you?"

"Y-yes." Sarah sniffles.

"Are you okay?" I sit up in bed. "Sarah, what's the matter?"

"It's . . . it's Rachel," Sarah say.

Whoa. Had the cops gotten there and arrested her already? It's going to be a blow, I know, for the building staff, what with Justine turning out to be a ceramic heater thief, and now Rachel turning out to be a homicidal maniac.

But they'll get over it. Maybe I'll bring in Krispy Kremes for everyone tomorrow.

"Yeah?" I say. Because I don't want to let on that I'd had anything to do with the arrest. Yet, anyway. "What about Rachel?"

"She . . . she's *dead.*"

I nearly drop the phone.

"*What?*" I cry. "Rachel? Dead? What—"

I can't believe it. It isn't possible. Rachel? Dead? How on earth . . .

"I think she killed herself," Sarah says with a sob. "Heather, I just came into the office, and she's . . . she's *hanging* here. From that grate between our office and hers."

Oh my God.

Rachel's hanged herself. Rachel realized that the jig was up, but instead of going quietly, she killed herself. Oh my God.

I have to remain calm. For the building's sake, I realize. I have to be the one in charge now. The director is gone. That leaves me, the assistant director. I'm going to have to be the strong one. I'm going to have to be everybody's beacon of light in the dark times ahead.

And it's okay, because I'm totally prepared. It won't be any different, really, than if Rachel had been hauled off to jail. She's really just going to a different place. But she's gone, just the same.

"I don't know what to do," Sarah says, her voice rising to a hysterical pitch. "If anyone walks in and sees this—"

"Don't let anyone in," I cry. Oh God. The RAs. This is the last thing they need. "Sarah, don't let anyone come in. And don't touch anything." Isn't that right? Isn't that what they always say on *Law & Order*? "Call an ambulance. Call the police. Right away. Don't let anyone into the office but the police. Okay, Sarah?"

"Okay," Sarah says, with another sniffle. "But, Heather?"

"Yeah?"

"Can you come over? I'm . . . I'm so scared."

But I've already sprung from my bed and am reaching for my jeans.

"I'll be right there," I tell her. "Hold on, Sarah. I'll be right there."

There's a place called home
Or so I'm told
I've never been there
So I wouldn't know.

There's a place called home
Where they're always glad to see you
Where they want you just to be you
This place called home

But I wouldn't know
'Cause I've never had one
I wouldn't know

Heather Wells, "Place Called Home"
29

It's my fault.

Rachel's death, I mean.

I should have known. I should have known this would happen. I mean, clearly she wasn't mentally stable. Of course at the slightest provocation, she was going to snap. I don't know how she figured it out—that we suspected her—but she had.

And she'd taken the only way out she felt she could.

Well, there's nothing I can do about it now. Nothing except be there for the people Rachel's death is likely to affect the most—the building staff.

I call Cooper on his cell. He doesn't pick up, so I leave a message, telling him what Sarah has told me. I ask him to let Detective Canavan know. And then I tell him to come to Fischer Hall as soon as he gets my message.

I can't find an umbrella, of course. I can never find an umbrella when I really need one. Ducking my head against the steady drizzle, I hurry over to Washington Square West, marveling at how quickly the drug dealers disappear in inclement weather, and wondering where they all go. The Washington Square Diner? I'd have to check it out one day. Supposedly they have a killer chicken-fried steak.

I reach Fischer Hall and hurry inside, flicking rainwater from my hair, and smiling a little queasily at Pete. Does he know yet? Does he have any idea?

"Heather," he cries. "What're you doin' here? After what you went through yesterday, I thought they'd give you a month off. You're not working, are you?"

"No," I say. He doesn't know. Oh my God, he doesn't know.

And I can't tell him. Because the desk attendant is sitting right there, watching us.

"Oh," Pete says. "And hey, Julio's doing good, by the way. They're letting him out in a few days."

"Great," I say, with as much enthusiasm as I can. "Well, see you later."

"See you."

I hurry down the hallway to the director's office door. To my surprise, it's partly open, even though I'd specifically told Sarah to close it. Anyone can walk in and see Rachel hanging there . . . unless maybe she's done it on her side of the grate. Yes, that would make more sense, actually. Her desk is pushed up against the wall beneath the grate, so it would have been easy for her to climb up there, then jump . . .

"Sarah?" I say. I push the door open all the way. No sign of Rachel. The exterior office is empty. Sarah—and the body—have to be in Rachel's office. "Sarah? Are you there?"

"In here," I hear Sarah's voice warble.

I glance at the grate. There's nothing tied around it. Sarah must have cut her down. Horrific as it had to have been to find her like that, she still shouldn't have messed with the body. That's tampering with evidence. Or something.

"Sarah," I say, hurrying through to Rachel's office, "I told you not to . . ."

My voice trails off. That's because I'm not greeted by the sight of a weeping Sarah cradling Rachel's lifeless form. Instead, I'm greeted by the sight of a perfectly healthy Rachel—wearing a new, very attractive cashmere sweater set and charcoal trousers—leaning against her desk, one booted foot balanced on her office chair . . .

. . . onto which she's tied Sarah with the phone cord and some computer cables.

"Oh, hi, Heather," Rachel says brightly. "You got here fast."

"Heather." Sarah is sobbing so hard now that her glasses have steamed up. "I'm so sorry. She made me call you—"

"Shut up." Rachel, annoyed, slaps Sarah, hard, across the face. The sound of the smack makes me jump.

It also wakes me up.

Trap. I've just walked into a trap. Automatically I turn towards the door—

"Stop or I'll kill her." Rachel's voice rings coldly through the room. Even Monet's water lilies couldn't soften it.

I freeze where I am. Rachel brushes past me and goes to the outer office door, pulling it all the way closed.

"There," she says, when the lock clicks into place. "That's more like it. Now we can have some privacy."

I stare at her, my grip tightening on the strap of my backpack, despite my stitches. Maybe, I think, I can hit her with it. My backpack, I mean. Although there isn't anything heavy in it. Just a hairbrush, my wallet, and some lipstick. Oh, and a Kit Kat bar, in case I get hungry later.

How had she known? How had she known we were on to her?

"Rachel," I say. My voice sounds funny. I realize it's because my throat has gone dry. I'm not feeling very good, all of a sudden. My fingers have gone ice cold, and the cuts on them ache.

Then I remember.

There's a canister of pepper spray in my backpack. It's several years old and the nozzle is all gunked up with sand from a trip to the beach. Will it still work?

Play it cool, I tell myself. What would Cooper do if he was faced with a killer? He'd play it cool.

"Wow," I say, hoping I sound cool, like Cooper. "What's this all about, Rachel? Is this some kind of trust game, or something? Because, if you don't mind me saying so, Sarah doesn't look like she's having a very good time."

"Cut the crap, Heather." Rachel speaks in a hard voice I've never heard her use before, not even with the basketball players. The sound of it makes me feel colder than ever. I've never heard her swear before, either. "That dumb blond act might work with everyone else you know, but it's never worked with me. I know exactly what you are, and believe me, the four-letter word I'd use to describe you is not dumb." Her eyes flick over me disparagingly. "At least until recently it wasn't."

Is she ever right. I can't believe I'd fallen for that phone call. Still, Sarah's tears *had* been real . . . just not for the reason she'd said they were.

"You might as well know," Rachel says calmly. "I know all about last night."

I try pretending like I don't know what she's talking about, even though I do.

"Last night? Rachel, I—"

"Last night," she says pleasantly. "Your little jaunt to the Hamptons. Don't try to deny it. I was there. I saw you."

"You . . . you were there?"

I'm at a total loss as to how to proceed. Every nerve in my body is screaming, *Turn around and run!*

But somehow I'm rooted to the spot, my fingers clenched around my backpack strap. I keep thinking about Sarah. What if I run? What will Rachel do to poor Sarah?

"Of course I was," Rachel says, her voice dripping with scorn. "You think I don't keep an eye on my property? Why do you think I held on to my Jetta? Nobody needs a car in this city . . . unless they're going to be following people to the Hamptons."

God. I'd forgotten all about her stupid car, which she parks in a garage on the West Side Highway.

I say, keeping my voice low-pitched so Rachel can't hear how badly it's shaking, "Okay. So I was there. So I know about you and Chris. So what? Rachel, I'm on your side. I totally understand where you're coming from. I've been dicked over by guys before, too. Why don't we talk about this—"

Rachel is shaking her head. Her expression is incredulous, as if I, not she, am the one cracking up.

"There'll be no *talking* about this," she says, with a bark of laughter. "The time for *talking* is over. And let's get one thing straight here, Heather." Rachel uncrosses her arms, her right hand going to a lump I hadn't noticed before beneath her cardigan.

"I am the director," she goes on. "*I* am the one in charge. I decide whether or not we're going to *talk* about it, because I am the one who schedules the meeting. Like I scheduled the meetings for Elizabeth and Roberta. Like I'll schedule yet another meeting for Amber, later. Like I've scheduled this meeting, now, between you and me. I am the one in charge. Do you want to know what qualifies me to be in charge, Heather?"

I nod mutely, my eyes on the lump under her sweater. A gun, I think. A gun definitely qualifies Rachel to be in charge.

But it isn't a gun at all. When Rachel draws it out, all I see is a black plastic thing that fits snugly in her hand. There are two evil-looking metal pieces sticking out of the top, giving it an appearance not unlike the head of a cockroach. I have no idea what it is until Rachel flicks a switch with her thumb, and suddenly a thin blue electric line buzzes between the twin metal prongs.

Then I know, even before she says it.

"Heather, meet the Thunder Gun." Rachel speaks proudly, like some of the parents had on the first day of check-in, when they'd been introducing their kid to me. "A second of contact with the one hundred and twenty thousand volts the head of the Thunder Gun delivers can cause confusion, weakness, disorientation, and loss of balance and muscle control for several minutes. And the wonderful thing is, if blasted through clothing, the Thunder Gun leaves only a very small burn mark upon the skin. It's a fabulously effective repellent weapon, and you can order it from any number of catalogs here in the U.S. Why, mine only cost forty-nine ninety-five, nine-volt battery not included. Of course, it's not legal to own one here in New York City, but then, who cares?"

I stare at the crackling blue fire strip.

So this is how she'd done it. No chloroform, no bashing over the head with a baseball bat. She'd simply shown up at Beth's door, and then later, at Bobby's, stunned them, then shoved their limp bodies down the elevator shaft. What could be simpler?

And Detective Canavan had said killers were dumb. Rachel isn't dumb. What kind of doofus would have the savvy to pull off this kind of crime? Because so many young people kill themselves doing stupid stunts like elevator surfing, no one would ever think that the girls had actually been murdered, not when there was no hint of suspiciousness to their deaths.

No one except a freak like me.

No, Rachel isn't dumb.

And she isn't crazy, either. She'd thought up the perfect way to get rid of her romantic rivals. No one would have suspected a thing if it hadn't been for me and my big mouth.

If it hadn't been for me and my big mouth, Sarah and I wouldn't be about to become Rachel's third and fourth victims.

"But this isn't the only thing that qualifies me to be in charge around here, you know," Rachel assures me, casually gesturing with the stun gun to emphasize her point. "I have a bachelor's degree in chemical engineering. Did you know that, Heather?"

I shake my head. Maybe one of the RAs will key in to the office to pick up his mail. Yeah. Or maybe Cooper will have gotten that message I'd left on his cell phone. . . .

"It's amazing what one can do with a bachelor's in chemical engineering. One can, for instance, learn to build small incendiary devices—so simple, yet so effective. Do you know what an incendiary device is, Heather? No, I would imagine that you don't. After all, you were far too busy twitching your ass at the local mall to finish high school, weren't you? Let me see if you know this one. What do you get when you stand a bunch of blonds next to each other, shoulder to shoulder?"

I look at Sarah. She's still sobbing, but she's trying to do it quietly, so Rachel won't slap her again.

I shake my head.

Rachel laughs humorlessly and says, "A wind tunnel, Heather! A wind tunnel!"

"Oh, wow, Rachel," I say, amending my previous thought. She's definitely crazy. Nuts, even. "That's really funny. But you know what? I have to go now. Cooper's waiting by the guard's desk. If I'm gone too long, he's bound to come back here, looking for me."

"He can look all he wants," Rachel says with a shrug. "He doesn't have a key. And we aren't going to let him in. We're *working*, Heather. We have a lot of important work to do."

"Well, you know what, Rachel?" I say. "If we don't open the door, Cooper'll just have Pete call one of the RAs to let him in—"

"But the RAs don't have keys to the office anymore. I had the lock changed." Rachel's cheeks have twin spots of color in them now, and her eyes sparkle every bit as brightly as the thin volt of electricity that leaps from the prongs of the weapon clenched in her hand.

"That's right," she says happily. "I had the lock changed yesterday, while you were in the hospital, and I'm the only one with a key." Then she turns those too-bright eyes on me and says, "You understand, don't you, Heather? I mean, this isn't a career for you. This is just a job. Assistant director to Fischer Hall. It's just a rest stop between gigs, isn't it? A steady paycheck until you get the guts to go on the road again after your little dispute with your record company. That's all this position is to you. Not like me. Higher education is my life. My life, Heather. Or at least it was. Until—"

She stops speaking suddenly, her gaze, which had become a little unfocused, fastening on me like a vise. "Until him," she says, simply.

I want to sit down. My knees shake every time I glance at the weapon in Rachel's hand.

But I don't dare. Seated, I'm an even easier target. No, somehow I have to distract her from whatever it is she intends to do to Sarah and me—and I have a pretty good idea what that is.

"Him, Rachel?" I ask, trying to sound friendly, like we're just chatting over cups of coffee in the cafeteria, something we'd actually done, once or twice, before the killing had begun. "You mean Christopher, don't you?"

She laughs bitterly, and that laugh makes me more afraid than anything so far, even the stun gun.

"Christopher," she says, rolling the word on her tongue like it's a piece of chocolate—something Rachel never allowed herself to enjoy. Too fattening. "Yes. Chris. You wouldn't understand about Christopher, Heather. You see, I love him. You've never loved anyone before, Heather, except yourself, so you can't know what it's like. No, you can't know what it's like to feel that all your happiness in life is dependent on one single individual, and then—and then to have that individual turn around and reject you—"

The look she gives me could have frozen a hot buttered bagel. I think about mentioning that I know *exactly* what she's talking about . . . that this is how I'd felt about Jordan, who is at this very moment probably playing Mad Libs with Tania Trace in his hospital bed.

But somehow I don't think she'd listen.

"No, you wouldn't understand that," Rachel says. "You've always had everything you've ever wanted, haven't you, Heather? Handed to you on a silver platter. Some of us have had to work for what we want, you know. Take me, for example. You think I always looked this good?" Rachel runs a hand up and down her lean, hard, thousand-crunches-a-day abs. "Hell, no. I used to be fat. A real lard ass. Kind of like you are now, actually. A size twelve." She laughs. "I drowned my sorrows in candy bars, never worked out, like you. Do you know I never got asked out—never, not once, until I turned thirty? While you were strutting around like a little slut for Cartwright Records, I had my nose buried in my books, studying as hard as I could, because I knew no one was going to swoop down and offer *me* a recording contract. I knew if I wanted out of my hellhole of a life, I was going to have to use my head."

I glance at Sarah. She's looking out the window, desperately hoping, I can tell, that someone will walk by and notice what's going on inside.

But it's raining so hard, no one is on the street. And the few people who are out hurry past with their heads tucked beneath umbrellas.

"It was the same with *him*," Rachel says. "I wanted him, so I did what I had to in order to get him. I knew I wasn't his type. I figured that out after he . . . left me. Which is when I knew. I knew I had to make myself over to *be* his type. You wouldn't understand that, of course. You and Sarah, you think men should want you because of your *personality*, don't you? But men couldn't care less about your personality. Believe me. If you hadn't let yourself go the way you did, Heather, you'd still have Jordan Cartwright, you know. All that fuss about wanting to sing your own songs. My God, you think he *cared* about that? Men don't care about smarts.

After all, what's the difference between a blond and a mosquito?"

I shake my head. "Honest to God, Rachel, I don't—"

"A blond keeps on sucking, even after you slap her." Rachel throws back her head and laughs some more.

Oh yeah. I'm a dead woman. No doubt about it.

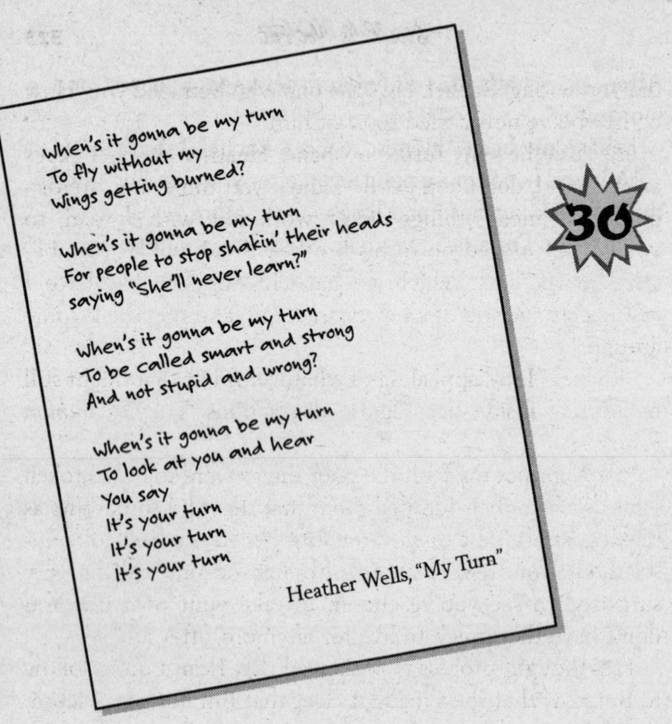

When's it gonna be my turn
To fly without my
Wings getting burned?

When's it gonna be my turn
For people to stop shakin' their heads
saying "She'll never learn?"

When's it gonna be my turn
To be called smart and strong
And not stupid and wrong?

When's it gonna be my turn
To look at you and hear
You say
It's your turn
It's your turn
It's your turn

Heather Wells, "My Turn"
30

She's crazy. I mean, only a lunatic would stand there, telling me dumb blond jokes, while threatening me with a stun gun.

I've dealt with lunatics before. I worked in the music industry all those years. Nine out of every ten people I'd met back then had probably been clinically insane, including my own mother.

Can I talk Rachel out of trying to kill me?

Well, I can try.

"Seems to me," I say carefully, "that the person you ought to be angry with is Christopher Allington. He's the one who did you wrong, Rachel. He's the one who betrayed you. How come you've never tried to toast him?"

"Because he's my future husband, Heather." Rachel glares at me. "God, don't you get it? I know you think men are disposable. I mean, things didn't work out with Jordan, so you've just moved on to his brother. But I, unlike you, believe in true love. Which is what Christopher and I have. I just need to get rid of a few distractions, and then he'll come around."

"Rachel," I say, appealing to whatever is left that might still be normal inside her. "Those distractions. They're *human beings*."

"Well, it's not my fault the poor things were so heartbroken when Christopher dumped them that they did something as reckless as attempt to elevator surf. I tried my best to counsel them. You, too, Heather. Although no one will be very surprised to see you've chosen to take your own life. You don't have that much to live for anymore, after all."

Her thought process is so skewed that I can't quite follow it. But now that she's made it clear that I'm her next victim, I'm doing some pretty fast talking, let me tell you.

"But, Rachel, it will never work. I already went to the cops—"

"And did they believe you?" Rachel asks calmly. "When they find your broken, bleeding body, they'll know you just did the whole thing to get attention—planted that bomb, then killed yourself when you realized you'd been discovered. And it won't even be so hard to understand, since your life's been in such a downward spiral lately. Jordan getting engaged to that other girl. His brother—well, his brother just doesn't seem interested, does he, Heather? And you and I both know how much you're in love with him. It's written all over your face every time he walks into the room."

Is that true? Does everyone know I love Cooper? Does *Cooper* know I love Cooper? God, how embarrassing.

Wait a minute. What am I listening to this lunatic for, anyway?

"Fine, Rachel," I say, playing along because it seems like the only way out. "Fine. Kill me. But what about Sarah? I mean, what's poor Sarah ever done to you? Why don't you let Sarah go."

"Sarah?" Rachel glances at her graduate assistant as if she's only just remembered she's in the room. "Oh, right. Sarah. You know, I think Sarah's going to just . . . disappear."

Sarah lets out a frightened hiccup, but a stony look from Rachel silences her.

"Yes," Rachel say. "I think Sarah is going to go home for a few weeks to recover from the horror of your death, Heather. Only she's not going to make it. She's going to disappear somewhere along the way. Hey. It happens."

"Oh no, Rachel, please," Sarah chokes. "Please don't make me disappear. Please—"

"Shut up," Rachel screams. She raises a hand to hit Sarah again, but freezes when the phone on my desk rings, jangling so loudly that Rachel jumps, and the blue streak of lightning between the blades of the gun sways dangerously close to me. I leap back, falling against the door, and spin around to grasp the knob.

In a split second, Rachel is on me, a spindly arm going around my neck, choking me. She's surprisingly strong for such a slight woman. But even so, I could have shaken her off . . .

. . . could have if it hadn't been for the sputtering stun gun, which she shoves beneath my nose, hissing, "Don't try it. Don't even think about it. I'll blast you, Heather, I swear it. And then I'll kill you both."

I freeze, breathing hard. Rachel is plastered to my back like a cape. The phone keeps on ringing, three times, four. I can tell by the ring that it's an on-campus call. I whisper, my voice rough with fear, "Rachel, that's probably the reception desk calling. You know I told Cooper to wait outside for me. He's at the guard's station."

"In that case," Rachel says, releasing her stranglehold on my neck but keeping the stun gun within inches of my throat, "we'll be on our way. I'll deal with you"—she flings a warning look in Sarah's direction—"later."

Then she opens the office door and, glancing furtively left and right, shoves me out into the empty hallway . . .

. . . but not far enough that she isn't within blasting range. She directs me to the elevators across from our office door—the elevators that were, unfortunately for me, unscathed by yesterday's explosion in the service shaft—and pounds on the up button. I pray that the doors will open and the entire basketball team will emerge and tackle Rachel for me.

But no such luck. The cab has been sitting empty on the first floor, and when the doors slide apart, there's no one inside.

"Get in," Rachel orders, and I do as she says. Rachel follows, then inserts her pass key and presses twenty.

We're going to the penthouse. And there won't be any other stops along the way.

"Girls like you, Heather," Rachel says, not looking at me. "I've been dealing with girls like you my whole life. The pretty ones are all alike. You go through life thinking everybody owes you something. You get the record contracts and the promotions and the cute guys, while people like me? We're the ones who do all the work. Do you know that Pansy is the first award I've received in my field?"

I glare at her. This woman is going to kill me. I don't see any reason to be polite to her anymore.

"Yeah," I say. "And you got it for cleaning up after your own murders. That stuff in those girls' files—about Elizabeth's mom wanting her sign-in privileges revoked, and Mrs. Pace not liking Lakeisha—that stuff never even happened, did it? Those women never called you. You made all that stuff up, as a way to justify your meetings with those girls. What did you talk about when you were meeting with them, anyway? What kind of twisted, sick stuff were you terrorizing them with?"

"Heather." Rachel looks at me critically. "You'll never understand, will you? I've worked hard all my life for what I have. I never got anything easily, like you. Not anything, men, jobs, friends. What I do get, I keep. Like Christopher, for instance. And this job. Do you have any idea how hard it was to get myself a position at this school, in the same *building* as him? So you understand why you have to die. You're jeopardizing too much for me. If you hadn't started snooping around, I'd have let you live. We made a nice team, you and I, I always thought. I mean, when I stand next to you, I look extra thin. That's a real bonus in an assistant."

The elevator pings, and the doors slide open. We're on the twentieth floor, in the hallway outside the president's penthouse. I know the minute we step onto the gray carpeting that the motion detector will be set off downstairs at the guard's desk. Would Pete glance at the monitor and see Rachel and her stun gun?

Please look, Pete. I try to use Vulcan mind control on Pete, even though he's twenty floors down. *Look, Pete, look. Look, Pete, look . . .*

Rachel pushes me out into the hallway.

"Come on," she says, pulling out the building's master key. "I bet you always wanted to see where the president lives. Well, now's your chance. Too bad you won't live long enough to enjoy it."

Rachel unlocks the front door to the Allingtons' apartment and steers me into the foyer. Tiled in black and white, this is where Mrs. Allington had stood and accused me of chasing after her son like a harlot. The foyer opens into a spacious living room, walled on two sides by French doors leading out onto the penthouse terrace. Like the Villa d'Allington, the predominant decorating theme appears to be black leather, and lots of it. Martha Stewart, Mrs. Allington apparently is not. Well, I kind of already guessed that.

"Nice, isn't it?" Rachel says conversationally. "Except for those hideous birds."

Just off the foyer, in that six-foot-high wicker cage, the cockatoos whistle and dance, eyeing us suspiciously. Rachel aims the stun gun at them and laughs as they shriek at the sight of the leaping blue flame.

"Idiot birds," she says. Then she grabs hold of my arm and starts pulling me toward a set of French doors. "Come on," she says. "It's time for your big finale. I figure a star like you would make a really dramatic exit. So you're not going the elevator surfing route. You're going to plunge off the roof of Fischer Hall . . . kind of like that turtle, in that movie your psychotic friend in the cafeteria is always talking about. Only you, unfortunately, won't be saved by a rope shot from inside your shell."

Before I have a chance to react, a door on the far side of the living room is thrown open, and Mrs. Allington, in a pink jogging suit, stares at us.

"What the hell," she demands, "are you two doing here?"

Rachel smiles pleasantly. "Don't mind us, Eleanor," she sings. "We'll be out of your way in no time."

"How did you get in here?" Mrs. Allington begins striding toward us, looking furious. "Get out, this instant, before I call the police."

"I wish we could, Eleanor," Rachel says, to the woman who, in a different world, might have been her mother-in-law. "But we're here on official residence hall business."

"I don't give a damn why you're here." Mrs. Allington has reached a wall phone. Now she's lifting up the receiver. "Don't you know who my husband is?"

"Look out, Mrs. Allington," I yell.

But it's too late. Like a striking cobra, Rachel lashes out with the stun gun.

Mrs. Allington stiffens, her eyes going wide, like someone who'd just gotten some very bad news . . . maybe about her son's LSAT scores, or something.

Then she seems to fling herself over the back of one of the leather couches, twitching until she lies in a heap on the parquet floor, her eyes still wide open, her jaw slack and shiny with saliva.

"Oh my God," I cry. Because it is, without a doubt, the most horrible thing I've ever seen . . . worse even than what I'd seen Tania Trace doing to my then boyfriend. "Rachel, you killed her!"

"She's not dead," Rachel says, the disgust in her voice obvious. "When she comes to, she'll have no idea what hit her. She won't remember her last name, let alone me. But that won't be unusual, for her. Come on," she says, and grabs my arm again.

Now that I've seen firsthand what that gun could do, I'm in no hurry to experience it. I realize I'd been stupid not to try to get away from Rachel downstairs. Sure, she might have zapped me, then hauled me into the elevator. But I'd have been dead weight, and it would have been difficult for her. This way, it's too easy for her, and more difficult for me. The only place I have to go is down.

This thought is enough to cause me to make a break for it.

I yank my arm from Rachel's grasp and run. I don't know why, but I head for the door through which Mrs. Allington had come. I can't run fast, being so stiff from what had happened in the elevator that day before, and all. But I know I've surprised her when Rachel lets out a furious scream. Surprising her feels good, because it means she doesn't have the upper hand anymore.

I have only fleeting glimpses of the rooms I tear through. A dining room that looks as if it hadn't seen any diners in a long time, the long mahogany table highly polished, seating for twelve, a sideboard with fake fruit on it. Fake! Then a kitchen, spotlessly clean, blue and white tiles. A kind of den, again with French doors on two sides, and a wide-screen TV in front of another leather couch, this one in avocado green. On the TV is a Debbie Reynolds movie. *Tammy and the Bachelor*, I think. On the couch is a basket of yarn and a bottle of Absolut. Mrs. Allington doesn't mess around with her leisure time.

I bang through the only door in the den that doesn't lead to the terrace and find myself in a bedroom, a dark bedroom, all the curtains pulled shut over the French doors. The bed is king-sized and unmade, the gray silk sheets in a tangle at one end. Another wide-screen TV, this one tuned to a talk show, the sound off. There're a pair of black briefs on the floor. Chris's room? But Chris lives in the law school dorm. Which can only mean the Allingtons sleep in separate rooms. Scandal!

There are no more doors, except one to President Allington's bathroom. I'm trapped.

I can hear Rachel coming, slamming doors and screaming like a banshee. I look frantically around the room for a weapon, and come up empty-handed. Because of the track lighting in the mirrored ceiling—I'll think about that one later—there isn't even a lamp I can unplug and swing at her head. I think of sliding under the bed, hiding behind a set of those damask curtains, but I know she'll find me. Can I talk my way out of this? I've talked my way out of worse jams than this. I can't quite think of any right now, but I'm almost sure I have.

Rachel comes careening into the room, stumbling over the threshold and blinking as her eyes adjust to the sudden darkness. I stand on the opposite side of the room, behind the massive bed, trying not to be distracted by my reflection on the ceiling.

"Look, Rachel," I pant, talking low and fast. "You don't have to kill me. Or Sarah, either. I swear we won't tell anyone about this. It'll just be our secret, between us girls. I totally understand where you're coming from. I've had guys jerk me around, too. I mean, Chris definitely isn't worth going to jail for—"

"I won't be going to jail, Heather," Rachel says. "I'll be organizing your memorial service. And my wedding. I'll be sure to play all of your greatest hits at both. That is, if there's more than one. Weren't you kind of a one-hit wonder, anyway? Such a shame. I wonder if anyone will even show up at your funeral. After all, you're already a has-been at—how old are you, anyway? Twenty-five? Twenty-six? Just an ex-pop star who's let herself go."

"Twenty-eight," I say. "And fine. Kill me. But not Sarah. Come on, Rachel. She's just a kid."

"Aw." Rachel smiles and shakes her head at me. "Isn't that sweet? You begging for Sarah's life like that. When in real life, I know how much she annoys you. See, that's the problem with girls like you, Heather. You're too *nice*. You have no killer instinct. When the going gets tough, you cave. You're born with all the advantages, and you just throw them away.

You let your body go, your man slip away, your career go down the toilet. Jesus, you even let your own *mother* rob you blind. And yet you're still so . . . *nice* about it. I mean, you and Jordan? Still friends. You can't stand Sarah, and here you are, pleading with me not to kill her. I bet you still send your mom Mother's Day cards, don't you?"

I gulp. And nod.

Well, what else am I going to say?

"See," Rachel says. "Now that's just sad. Because nice girls, they always finish last. I'll actually be doing the world a favor by killing you. It's natural selection, really. One less blond to watch go to waste."

With that, Rachel comes at me, diving across the bed, stun gun first.

I whirl around and throw back the curtains. I unlatch the first set of French doors I reach and hurl myself out onto the terrace.

31
Wake up, look around
Everybody's got their feet
On the ground
No way I'll do the same
I'm over you,
No one to blame

Get out, out of my life
I'm not your mother
Won't be your wife
Go on, go out that door
Don't you mess
with me no more
It's all over
Just leave it be
I'm over you
Get away from me
Heather Wells, "Get Out"

It's still raining—harder than ever, actually. The sky is a leaden gray all around me.

I've never realized it before, but Fischer Hall is the tallest building on the west side of the park, and the penthouse terrace affords spectacular views of Manhattan on four sides, of the Empire State Building to the north, just visible through the mist, the fog-shrouded void where the World Trade Center had once stood to the south, the sodden East and West Villages.

An excellent place, I realize, to shoot a scene from a movie. *Teenage Mutant Ninja Turtles*, perhaps.

Except that this is no movie. This is real life. *My* life. For however much longer it lasts.

The wind up on the twentieth floor is strong, and drizzle spits in my face. I have a hard time figuring out just where I'm headed, since everywhere I look, I see only geranium planters precariously perched on low stone balustrades over which I can picture my body very easily tumbling.

Not knowing where else to go, I duck my head and start running around the sides of the Allingtons' apartment, to the opposite side of the terrace. With no sign of Rachel following, I have a minute to pause and open my backpack, still hanging from its strap across my shoulders, and fumble inside it for that canister of pepper spray I could swear was still in it. I have no idea if the thing will still work, but at this point, anything that will keep me from meeting the volts from that stun gun is worth a try.

I find it. I release the safety catch when a deafening crash occurs just behind me, and in a shower of splintering wood and flying glass, Rachel leaps through a set of French doors—like Cujo, or a teenage mutant ninja turtle—not even bothering to unlatch them first. She hits me with the full force of her body, and we both go down onto the wet flagstones.

I land solidly on my sore shoulder, effectively knocking all the breath from my chest. But I try to keep rolling, over shards of wood and glass, to get away from her.

She's on her feet before I am, and coming toward me at full charge. Through it all, she's managed to hang on to the Thunder Gun.

But I still clutch the pepper spray, hidden in my fist. When she bends over me, her dark hair already becoming plastered to her face by the rain, her lips are curled back in a snarl not unlike Lucy's when she's riled by a tennis ball or a Victoria's Secret catalog.

"You're so weak," Rachel sneers at me, and she waves the stun gun under my nose. "How can you tell a brunette?"

I try to maneuver myself into a position from which I can spray her directly in the face. I don't want the wind whipping the stuff back at me.

"I don't know what you're talking about," I wheeze, still breathless from the impact of my fall. God. I can't believe I once bought this woman *flowers.*

And okay, they were only from the deli. But still.

"You know how you can tell a brunette?" Rachel grins, her face just inches from mine. "Turn a blond upside down!"

As she lunges to blast 120,000 volts into my right hip, I lift my hand and launch a stream of pepper spray into her face. Rachel shrieks and backs up, throwing an arm up to protect her face . . .

Only the nozzle won't push all the way down. So instead of a jet of chemical poison hitting her in the eye, the stuff just foams down the side of the canister, soaking into my stitches and burning me badly enough to make me go, "Ow!"

Rachel, realizing she hasn't been hit after all, starts to laugh.

"Oh God," she brays. "Could you *be* more pathetic, Heather?"

But this time, when she lunges at me, I've rolled to my feet, and I'm ready for her.

"Rachel," I say, as she comes at me. "There's something I've been wanting to tell you for a long time. Size twelve"—wrapping my stinging fingers around the hard canister, I slam my fist as hard as I can into Rachel's face—"is not *fat.*"

My knuckles explode in pain. Rachel screams and staggers back, both her hands going to her nose, from which an astonishing amount of blood is spurting.

"My nose!" she shrieks. "You broke my nose! You fucking bitch!"

I'm barely able to stand, my shoulder is throbbing so badly, my hands feeling as if they're on fire from the pepper spray. I have shards of glass stuck to my back, the knuckles on my right hand are numb, and blood is coming from a cut somewhere in the vicinity of my forehead: I'm blinking both rainwater and my own blood from my eyes. All I want to do is go inside and lie down for a while and maybe watch the Food Network, or something.

But I can't. Because I have my psycho boss to deal with.

She's standing there, holding her nose with one hand, and the stun gun in the other, when I tackle her, flinging my arms around her narrow waist and bringing her down like a hundred and twenty pounds of Manolo Blahniks. She falls, writhing in my grasp, while I desperately try to snatch the stun gun from her hands.

And all the time, she's sobbing. Not with fear, like she should have been—because, make no mistake about it, I have every intention of killing her—but with anger, her dark eyes glittering with such intense hatred of me that I wonder how I missed seeing it there before.

"Nice girls finish last, huh?" I say, as I kick her as hard as I can in the knee. "How's this, then? Is this *nice* enough for you?"

Except that it's like I'm kicking one of those crash test dummies. Rachel seems impervious to pain . . . unless it's something to do with her face. Her precious nose, for example.

And she's strong—so much stronger than I am, despite my killing rage, and my advantage in height and weight. I can't budge the gun from her hands. I've read about people who, in moments of desperation, develop the strength of someone twice their size—mothers who lift cars off their injured infants, mounted cops who pull their beloved horses out of sinkholes, that kind of thing. Rachel has the strength of a man . . . a man who sees his life disintegrating before him.

And she's not going to give up until someone's dead.

And I'm starting to get a very bad feeling that that someone is going to be me.

It's all I can do to keep my hands fastened over hers on the grip of the stun gun. My fingers are slick with rain and blood, and sore from the stitches and the pepper foam. It's hard to hold on. Rachel has managed to climb to her feet in spite of my attempt to kick her legs out from under her, and now the two of us struggle in the pouring rain for mastery of the weapon. The force of our struggle has sent us staggering dangerously close to the terrace wall.

Somehow, Rachel manages to twist herself so that it's *my* back that's pressed up against a overflowing geranium planter not unlike the one that nearly killed Jordan. My face toward the sky, I can't see with all the rain streaming down. I close my eyes and concentrate on the nearly impossible task of keeping Rachel's arms high above me, not letting those buzzing prongs anywhere near my body. I feel the planter wobble, and then I feel it give, and though I don't open my eyes, I hear the enormous crash it makes seconds later as it hits the sidewalk below.

The most frightening part, however, is the length of time that elapses between the moment the planter careens off the terrace and the sound of the impact as it strikes the earth. I count to nearly ten.

Ten seconds of freefall. Ten seconds to contemplate death.

My arms are weakening. I know I'm crying, because the salt from my tears stings the cuts on my face.

And above me, Rachel laughs, sensing my weakening.

"See," she's saying. "I told you, Heather. You're too nice to win. Too weak. Not in good enough shape. Because size twelve *is* fat. Oh, I know what you're going to say. It's the size of the average American woman. But guess what? The average American woman is fat, Heather."

"Oh my God." I spit rainwater and blood from my mouth. "Rachel, you're sick. There's something really wrong with you! Let me get you some help—"

"What have you got to live for, anyway?" Rachel asks, as if she hasn't heard me. Because she probably hasn't. "Your music career's in the toilet. Your boyfriend dumped you. Your own mother stabbed you in the back. You should have died yesterday, in the elevator. And you should have died the day before, only my aim was off. Just give it up, Heather. Nice girls never win—"

On the word *win*, Rachel begins slowly bending my arms. I can't fight her superior strength much longer. I'm weeping openly now, struggling against her, trying not to listen to her singsong voice as it coos, "Think about it. Your death'll make MTV News. Maybe not the *Times*, but the *Post* for sure. Who knows? They might even do an *E! True Hollywood Story* about you . . . one-hit wonders who didn't live to see thirty . . ."

I open my eyes and glare at her, unable to speak, since every bit of strength I have is concentrated on keeping her from electrocuting me.

And it's when I feel the tremble in my arms, the shaking of muscles weakened from overuse, that I hear Rachel's triumphant laugh, and her final taunt.

"Heather," she calls gleefully, her voice sounding far away, though she's still looming above me. "How many blonds does it take to screw in a light bulb?"

And then her head explodes in front of me.

Seriously. One minute it's there, laughing in my face, and the next it's gone, whipped back by the force of an object that strikes it so hard, blood sprays from the wound and blinds me. The stun gun goes dead in her hands, and her body falls away from me, landing with a sickening thud on the wet flagstones.

I cling to the terrace wall, wiping my face with the backs of my hands—the only uninjured parts of my body—and sobbing. The only sound is the hiss of the rain and someone's ragged breathing.

It takes me a while to realize that the breathing isn't my own. When I'm finally able to see, I look up, and see Rachel laying at my feet, blood pouring out of an indentation on the side of her head and tingeing the rain puddles all around her pink.

And standing before me, a bloodied bottle of Absolut in her hand, is Mrs. Allington, her pink jogging suit drenched, her chest heaving, her eyes filled with contempt as she stares down at Rachel's prone body.

Mrs. Allington shakes her head.

"*I'm* a size twelve," she says.

So go ahead and
Make your way

Back from the edge
of yesterday

No one knows what
Can't be known

'Cause when you start
You're all alone

But take enough steps
Take enough steps
Take enough steps

And someday
Someday you'll be home
Heather Wells, Untitled
32

I only end up spending one night in the hospital—on account of all my stitches tearing open and the multiple contusions and glass shards embedded in me.

And even that is one night too many, if you ask me. Do you know what their idea of dessert is in the hospital? Yeah, that'd be Jell-O. With fruit in it. Not even mini marshmallows. Everyone knows Jell-O is a *salad*, not dessert.

Plus they don't even have bathtubs in the hospital. If you want to get clean, it's a shower or sponge bath only.

Whatever. I try to use my time there wisely. My time in

the hospital, I mean. I sneak off my floor to visit Julio, whom I'm happy to find is recovering nicely from his injuries sustained during the explosion. He's supposed to be back at work next month, no worse for the wear.

I also stop by Jordan's room while I'm there. In the hospital, I mean.

He's plenty embarrassed to see me, and his bride-to-be, Tania? She's downright hostile. If I didn't know better, I'd think she was feeling threatened by me or something.

But I don't know why she would be. Her latest single, "Slut," hit number ten on *Total Request Live* the other day.

I wish them well, anyway. I tell them I think they make the perfect couple.

I'm not lying, either.

I only have to spend one night in the hospital, but I get two weeks off—with pay—from my position as assistant director at Fischer Hall. I guess that's how they reward you at New York College if you happen to bust your boss for a double homicide. Even if you haven't accrued that many sick days, or whatever.

By the time I'm back to my desk, it's starting to get cold out. The leaves on the trees in Washington Square Park are changing, turning shades of red and gold that pale in comparison with the colors the freshmen in Fischer Hall have dyed their hair in preparation for Parents' Day.

Seriously. It's like working in a clown college, or something.

Things at Fischer Hall have changed in other ways as well since I've been gone. For one thing, with Rachel in jail awaiting trial, I'm getting a new boss. I don't know who yet. They're still interviewing people.

But Dr. Jessup is giving me first pick.

I'm thinking it might be nice to work for a man for a

change. Don't get me wrong, female bosses are great and all. But I could do with a break from all that estrogen in the office.

Sarah agrees. She and all the student workers are a lot nicer to me now that, you know, I risked my life in order to catch the person who was killing their fellow residents. I hardly ever hear about Justine anymore. Except for the other day, when Tina turned to me and said, "You know, Justine used to never wear jeans to work like you do. She told me it was because she could never find any small enough to fit her. I sort of always hated her for that."

Even Gavin is finally listening to me, and has completely given up elevator surfing. He's taken up exploring the city's sewers instead.

I figure he'll be giving that up soon enough, too, though. I mean, the smell isn't exactly making him the most popular guy on his floor.

Oh, and the Allingtons moved. Just to the building next door—the one Donatello or whichever teenage mutant ninja turtle it was jumped onto in the movie. But still, it's far enough away that Mrs. Allington feels that she and the birds will be more comfortable . . . especially since they're now living in a building that they don't have to share with seven hundred undergraduates and a residence hall staff.

Those undergraduates weren't sorry to see the Allingtons go, but the same can't be said about their son. Chris's turned into something of a celebrity himself, using the notoriety he gained from Rachel's obsession with him—which made all the headlines—as leverage for his plan to open his own nightclub in SoHo. Law school, apparently, had been his father's dream for him, and now that offers for his story have come pouring in from the Lifetime Channel and *Playboy*, Chris has broken free from the filial yoke and is pursuing his own devices.

I'm betting those devices will get him arrested fairly soon.

The Fischer Hall residents, student government, and staff came up with what we consider a fitting tribute to Elizabeth Kellogg and Roberta Pace: We planted two trees—twin dogwoods—in a pretty section of the park, with a plaque under them that reads *In Memory Of* and lists their names, the dates of their births and deaths, and the words *They Will Be Missed*. Millions of people will see it—both the plaque and the trees, which the guys from the horticulture department tell me will flower in the spring—just as hundreds of students will benefit from the scholarship, also started by us, in Beth's and Bobby's names.

I'm excited to see the trees in full bloom. It's about the only thing I have to look forward to these days, since I already found out—at last—what Cooper thinks about me.

Not that he knows I know. He probably has no idea I remember. It was when he came bursting out onto the penthouse terrace, just seconds after Mrs. Allington knocked Rachel senseless with her Absolut bottle. He'd gotten the message I'd left on his cell, and had come rushing over to the hall with Detective Canavan, only to learn from Pete—who'd seen Rachel and me going into the penthouse on his monitor—that not only was Rachel alive, but that the two of us had apparently gone upstairs to pay a call on Mrs. Allington (the film quality on the security monitor wasn't fine enough for Pete to see that Rachel was actually holding a stun gun to my throat at the time, something we're working on correcting, campus-wide).

While Detective Canavan dealt with the unconscious Rachel and wobbly Mrs. Allington, Cooper knelt beside me in the rain, asking if I was all right.

I remember blinking up at him, wondering if what I was seeing was just some weird hallucination, like the one of

Rachel getting her head bashed in. I'd been pretty sure, at the time, that I was dying, on account of the sting of the pepper spray in my stitches, and the glass shards piercing my back, and my sore shoulder and stuff.

Which might be why I kept saying—the way I remember it—over and over, "Promise you'll take care of Lucy. When I'm dead, promise you'll take care of Lucy."

Cooper had taken his leather jacket off—the one with my bloodstains all over it—and draped it over me. It was still warm from his body. I remember that. And that it smelled like him.

"Of course I will," Cooper had said to me. "But you're not going to die. Look, I know you're hurting. But the paramedics are their way. You're going to be fine, I promise."

"No, I'm not," I'd said. Because I'd been sure I was going to die. Later, the paramedic told me I was in shock, on account of the pain and the cold and the rain and all.

But I'd had no way of knowing that at the time.

"I'm going to be dead at twenty-eight," I'd informed what I'd taken to be a hallucination of Cooper. "A one-hit wonder. That's all I am. Make sure that's what they put on my headstone. *Here lies a one-hit wonder*."

"Heather," Cooper had said. He'd been smiling. I'm sure of that. That he'd been smiling. "You're not going to die. And you're not a one-hit wonder."

"Oh, right." I'd started laughing. Then I'd started to cry. And I hadn't been able to stop.

It turns out this is a pretty common symptom of shock, too. But again, I hadn't known that at the time.

"Rachel was right," I remember saying, bitterly. "She's right! I had it all, and I blew it. I'm the biggest loser in the world."

That's when Cooper forced me to sit up, took me into his

arms, and said, very firmly, "Heather, you're not a loser. You're one of the bravest people I've ever met. Anyone else, if they'd been through what you have, what with your mother and my brother and your career and all of that, they'd have given up. But you kept going. You started over. I've always admired the way, no matter what happens, you just keep going."

I'm sorry to say that at this point, I responded, "You mean like that little pink rabbit with the drum?"

I like to think that was the shock, too.

Cooper played along. He'd said, "Exactly like that little pink rabbit with the drum. Heather, you're not a loser. And you're not going to die. You're a nice girl, and you're going to be just fine."

"But . . ." To my shock-clouded brain, this assertion sounded troubling, given my earlier conversation with the woman who'd been trying to kill me. "Nice girls finish last."

"I happen to like nice girls," Cooper had said.

And then he kissed me.

Just once. And on the forehead. The way, you know, your ex-boyfriend's big brother would kiss you if, say, you'd been attacked by a homicidal maniac and were suffering from shock and he didn't think you'd remember it anyway.

But I did. And I do.

He thinks I'm brave. No, wait: He thinks I'm one of the bravest people he's ever met.

And he likes me. Because he happens to like nice girls.

Look, I know it's not much. But you know what?

It's enough. For now.

Oh, and one last thing:

I never did go back to that store and buy those size 8 jeans. There's nothing wrong with being a size 12, for one thing.

And for another, I've been too busy. I passed my six months' probation. I start my freshman year at New York College in January. My first class?

Intro to criminal justice.

Well, you have to start somewhere, right?

Size 14 is not Fat Either

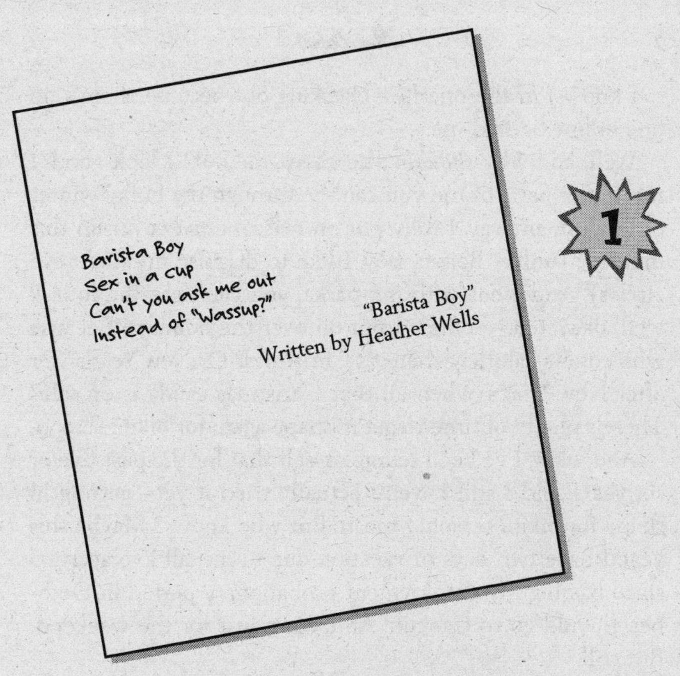

Barista Boy
Sex in a cup
Can't you ask me out
Instead of "Wassup?"
"Barista Boy"
Written by Heather Wells
1

The guy behind the counter is checking me out. No, really.

He's hot, too. Well, in a twenty-year-old barista kind of way. I bet he plays the guitar. I bet he stays up way too late at night, strumming, the way I do. I can tell by the slight shadows under his long-lashed green eyes, and the way his curly blond hair is sticking up in spikes all over his head. Bed head. No time to shower before work, because he was up so late practicing. Just like me.

"What'll it be?" he asks me. But with a look. A look that definitely says, *I'm checking you out.*

I know I'm the one he's checking out because there's no one in line behind me.

Well, and why *shouldn't* he check me out? I look good. I mean, the parts of me you can see through my bulky winter outerwear, anyway. I fully put on mascara *and* cover-up this morning (unlike Barista Boy, I like to disguise my undereye circles). And what with my parka, you can't see the four—well, okay, ten—pounds I put on over the holidays. Because who counts calories when it's Christmas? Or New Year's? Or after New Year's, when all that Christmas candy is on sale? There's plenty of time to get in shape again for bikini season.

And, okay, I've been telling myself that for the past five or six years, and I still haven't actually tried it yet—getting in shape for bikini season, I mean. But who knows? Maybe this year. I have two days of vacation due to me, all I've accrued since passing my employment probationary period in October. I could go to Cancún. And, okay, just for the weekend. But still.

So what if I'm five—well, maybe eight—years older than Barista Boy? I've still got it. Obviously.

"Grande café mocha, please," I say. I'm totally not into foamy drinks with whipped cream on top of them, but it's the first official day of spring semester (spring! Right!), and it's really cold out and supposed to blizzard later, and Cooper left this morning (for destinations unknown, as usual) without turning on the coffeemaker, and my dog Lucy wouldn't go out because it was so cold, so I'll probably find a nice surprise from her when I get home, and I REALLY need a little pick-me-up to help me quit feeling so sorry for myself.

Plus, you know, as long as I'm blowing five bucks on a cup of coffee, I might as well go for the gold.

"One grande café mocha, coming up," Barista Boy says,

doing one of those flippy things with my cup. You know, twirling it, like it's a gun and he's an outlaw in a western.

Oh, yeah. He *definitely* plays guitar. I wonder if he sits around writing songs he can never work up the guts actually to perform, like me? I wonder if he's constantly second-guessing his songwriting talent, like I am?

No. He's got the guts to get up in front of a crowd with a guitar and his own lyrics. I mean, just look at him.

"Soy or nonfat?" he asks.

Oh, God. I can't face my first day back to work after break on nonfat milk. And soy? *Soy*?

"Whole milk, please," I say. I'll be good later. At lunch I'll just have a chicken parm and a salad, and maybe just a BITE of lo-cal frozen yogurt. . . .

Mmmm, unless Magda got in more Dove Bars. . . .

"You know," Barista Boy says, as he rings me up, "you look really familiar."

"Oh," I say. I'm blushing with pleasure. He remembers me! He must see hundreds, maybe THOUSANDS of caffeine-starved New Yorkers a day, but he remembers ME! Fortunately it's so cold outside, and so warm in here, my red cheeks could easily be taken for the fact that I'm overheating in my coat, and not that I'm kvelling over his remembering me.

"Well, I live and work in the neighborhood," I say. "I'm in here all the time." Which isn't strictly true, since I'm keeping to a pretty tight budget (due to my pitiful salary), which foamy coffee drinks are definitely not part of, since I can get free coffee anytime I want from the cafeteria.

They just don't have mocha syrup in them. Or whipped cream. We tried to keep whipped cream canisters in the caf, but people kept swiping them in order to do whip-its.

"No," Barista Boy says, shaking his lusciously shaggy head. "That's not it. Actually, has anybody ever told you that you look a lot like Heather Wells?"

I take my drink from him. This, of course, is always the tricky part. What do I say? *Yes, actually . . . because I* am *Heather Wells,* and then run the risk of him asking me out simply because he thinks I still have connections in the music industry (so not. See above, re: fear of being booed off the stage)?

Or do I just laugh and say, *Why, no?* Because then what happens later, after we start dating, and he finds out I *am* Heather Wells? I mean, I could probably keep it a secret for a little while, but eventually he's going to find out my real name. Like when we're in Customs coming back from Cancún. Or when we're signing the marriage certificate. . . .

So I settle for saying, "Really?"

"Sure. Well, if you were thinner," Barista Boy says, with a smile. "Here's your change. Have a good one!"

What I can't believe is how the entire city can be gearing up for a predicted snowstorm—I mean, trucks filled with salt and sand can be lumbering down Tenth Street, breaking off tree limbs as they go by; the grocery stores can have already sold out of bread and milk; the television can show nothing but Storm Watch updates—and still, the drug dealers are out in full force in and around Washington Square Park.

I guess it just goes to show that we Americans still have a lot to learn from our hardworking immigrant population.

But there they are, standing on the sidewalk in their Perry Ellis parkas, enjoying some fresh mochaccinos of their own. Since it's the morning a significant—for New York City, anyway—amount of snow is being predicted to come down at any moment, very few people are walking by, but those who do are greeted with cheerful offers of sensimilla.

And okay, those offers are unanimously declined. But when the drug dealers notice me shuffling dejectedly toward them, they kindly shout a list of their wares in my direction.

I would laugh if I didn't still feel so grumpy about Barista Boy. Plus the fact that, every single time I step out of my house, I am accosted by these guys. It doesn't seem to matter to them that I have never once made a purchase. They only shrug as if I'm lying or something when I tell them that the strongest artificial stimulant I've consumed lately is caffeine. Sadly.

I'm not lying, though. A beer now and then is about as adventurous as I get.

Light beer, of course. Hey, a girl's gotta watch her figure.

"How you feelin' about all this white stuff that's supposed to fall from the sky soon, Heather?" one of the drug dealers, an affable guy named Reggie, steps away from his compatriots to ask me, with courtly solicitude.

"Better'n the white stuff you and your scum posse are peddling, Reggie," I am shocked to hear myself growl. God, what is *wrong* with me? Ordinarily, I'm super-polite to Reggie and his colleagues. It doesn't pay to antagonize your local dealer.

But ordinarily, I have not just been called fat by my favorite Barista Boy.

"Hey, baby," Reggie says, looking hurt. "There is no call to be offensive."

He's so right. It's wrong to call Reggie and his friends scum, while referring to those middle-aged men who toil away for the tobacco industry as senators.

"I'm sorry, Reggie," I say, meaning it. "You're right. It's just that for nine months now, you've been trying to hustle me right outside my front door, and for nine months now, I've been telling you no. What do you think is going to happen? I'm gonna turn into a raging cokehead overnight? Gimme a break."

"Heather." Reggie sighs, looking toward the thick gray clouds overhead. "I am a businessman. What kind of businessman would I be if I let a young woman like yourself, who is going through a very trying period in her life and could probably use a little pick-me-up, walk by without makin' an attempt to engage her business?"

And, to illustrate his meaning, Reggie takes a copy of the *New York Post* he's kept tucked under his arm, and opens it to the front page. There, in two-inch letters, screams the headline, *It's On Again*, over a black-and-white photo of my ex-fiancé hand in hand with his on-again, off-again bride-to-be, pop princess Tania Trace.

"Reggie," I say, after taking a restorative sip of my café mocha. But only because I'm so cold. I don't actually want it anymore, because it's covered with the taint of Barista Boy. Well, maybe I still want the whipped cream. Which is sort of good for you. I mean, it's dairy. And dairy's an important part of a well-balanced breakfast. "Do you really think I sit around all day fantasizing about getting back together with my ex? Because nothing could be further from the truth."

The fact is, I sit around all day fantasizing about getting together with my ex's brother, who continues to remain stubbornly immune to my charms.

But there's no reason my local drug dealer needs to know this.

"My apologies, Heather," Reggie says, refolding the paper. "I just thought you'd want to know. This morning on New

York One, they said the wedding is still scheduled to go on in St. Patrick's Cathedral, with the reception at the Plaza this Saturday."

I goggle at him. "Reggie," I say, stunned. "You watch New York One?"

Reggie looks mildly affronted. "I check the weather, like any New Yorker, before I leave for work."

Wow. That is so cute. He watches the weather before leaving for work to deal drugs on my street corner!

"Reggie," I say, impressed, "my apologies. I admire your dedication. Not only do you refuse to let the elements keep you from your work, but you're up on your local gossip. Please go right ahead and keep on trying to sell me drugs."

Reggie smiles, showing all of his teeth, many of which are capped—festively—in gold. "Thank you, baby," he says, as if I have just bestowed on him some very great honor.

I smile back at him, then continue my slog to my office. I shouldn't really call it a slog, though. I actually have a very short commute, which is good, since I have a problem getting up on time in the morning. If I lived in Park Slope or the Upper West Side or something, and had to take the subway to work every day, forget it (although, if I lived in Park Slope or the UWS, I'd be required by law to have a child, so it's just as well). I guess I'm really lucky, in a way. I mean, sure, I can barely afford a café mocha, and thanks to all of the holiday parties I attended, I can't fit into my size 12 stretch cords unless I'm wearing a pair of Spanx.

And okay, my ex is about to marry one of *People* magazine's 50 Most Beautiful People, and I don't even own my own car, let alone my own home.

But at least I get to live rent-free in a kick-ass apartment on the top floor of a brownstone two blocks from where I work in the coolest city in the entire world.

And okay, I only took my job, as the assistant director of a New York College dormitory, in order to get tuition remission benefits and actually attain the BA I lied about already having on my résumé.

And yeah, all right, so I'm having a little trouble getting into the School of Arts and Sciences due to my SAT score, which was so low that the dean won't admit me until I take—and pass—a remedial math course, despite my explaining to her that, in lieu of paying rent, I do all the billing for a very cute private detective, and have never once made an accounting error, that I know of.

But it is useless to expect a coldhearted bureaucracy—even the one you work for—to treat you as an individual.

So here I am, at nearly twenty-nine, about to learn the FOIL method for the first time (and let me tell you, I'm having a pretty hard time imagining a situation in which I might actually have to employ it).

And yeah, I write songs until late into the night, even though I can't, for the life of me, find the guts to actually sing them in front of anyone.

But still. My commute only takes two minutes, and I get to see my boss/landlord, on whom I have a major crush, wearing nothing but a towel from time to time as he darts from the bathroom to the laundry room to look for a clean pair of jeans.

So life's not *too* bad. In spite of Barista Boy.

Still, living super-close to my place of work has its drawbacks, too. For instance, people seem to have no compunction about calling me at home about inconsequential matters, like backed-up toilets or noise complaints. Like just because I live two blocks away, I should be able to come over at any hour to rectify matters my boss, the live-in building director, is supposed to handle.

But all in all, I like my job. I even like my new boss, Tom Snelling.

Which is why when I walk into Fischer Hall that arctic morning and find that Tom isn't there yet, I'm kinda bummed—and not just because that means there's no one to appreciate the fact that I'd made it in to the office before nine-thirty. No one except Pete, the security guard, who's on the phone, trying to get through to one of his many children's principals to find out about a detention one of them has been assigned for.

And I guess there's the work-study student manning the reception desk. But she doesn't even look up as I go by, she's so engrossed in a copy of *Us Weekly* she's stolen from the mail-forwarding bin (Jessica Simpson's on the cover. Again. She and Tania Trace are neck and neck for Tabloid Skank of the Year).

It's not until I turn the corner and pass the elevators that I see the line of undergrads outside the hall director's office. And I remember, belatedly, that the first day of spring semester is also the first day a lot of kids come back from Winter Break—the ones who didn't stay in the dorm (I mean, residence hall) to party until classes started again today, the day after Martin Luther King Day.

And when Cheryl Haebig—a New York College sophomore desperate for a room change because she's a bubbly cheerleader and her current roommate is a Goth who despises school spirit in all its guises, plus has a pet boa constrictor—leaps up from the institutional blue couch outside my office door and cries, "Heather!" I know I'm in for a morning of headaches.

Good thing I have my grande café mocha to keep me going.

The other students—each and every one of whom I recognize, since they've been in the office before due to roommate conflicts—scramble up from the cold marble floor on which they've been waiting, the couch being only a two-seater. I know what they've been waiting for. I know what they want.

And it's not going to be pretty.

"Look, you guys," I say, wrestling my office keys out of my coat pocket. "I told you. No room changes until all the transfer students are moved in. Then we'll see what's left."

"That's not fair," exclaims a skinny guy with large plastic disks in his earlobes. "Why should some stupid transfer student get dibs on all the open spaces? We got here first."

"I'm sorry," I say. I really am, because if I could just move them all, I wouldn't have to listen to their whining anymore. "But you're going to have to wait until they've all checked in. Then, if there are any spaces left, we can move you guys into them. If you can just hang on until next Monday, when we know who's checked in and who hasn't shown up—"

I am interrupted by general moaning. "By next Monday I'll be dead," one resident assures another.

"Or my roommate will," his friend says. "Because I'll have killed him by then."

"No killing your roommate," I say, having gotten the office door open and flicked on the lights. "Or yourself. Come on, guys. It's just another week."

Most of them go away, grumbling. Only Cheryl continues to hang around, looking excited as she follows me into my office. I see that she has a mousy-looking girl in tow.

"Heather," she says again. "Hi. Listen, remember when you

said if I found someone who would swap spaces with me, I could move? Well, I found someone. This is my friend Lindsay's roommate, Ann, and she said she'd swap with me."

I've peeled off my coat and hung it on a nearby hook. Now I sink into my desk chair and look at Ann, who appears to have a cold, from the way she's sniffling into a wadded-up Kleenex. I hand her the box I keep handy in case of Diet Coke spills.

"You want to trade spaces with Cheryl, Ann?" I ask her, just to make sure. I can't imagine why anyone would want to live with a person who painted the walls of her side of the room black.

Then again, it was probably annoying to Cheryl's roommate that Cheryl's side of the room was decorated with so many pansies, the New York College mascot.

"I guess," Ann says, looking wan.

"She does," Cheryl assures me brightly. "Don't you, Ann?"

Ann shrugs. "I guess," she says again.

I begin to sense Ann might have been coerced into agreeing to this room change.

"Ann," I say. "Have you *met* Cheryl's roommate, Karly? You know she, er . . . likes the color black?"

"Oh," Ann says. "Yeah. The Goth thing. I know. It's okay."

"And . . ." I hesitate to bring it up, because, ew. "The snake?"

"Whatever. I mean"—she looks at Cheryl—"no offense, or anything. But I'd rather live with a snake than a cheerleader."

Cheryl, far from being offended, beams at me.

"See?" she says. "So can we do the paperwork for our swap now? Because my dad is here to help me move, and he wants to get back to New Jersey before this big blizzard hits."

I pull out the forms, finding myself shrugging, just like Ann—it's sort of catching.

"Okay," I say, and hand them the papers they have to fill out to make the switch. When the girls—Cheryl giddy with excitement, Ann decidedly more calm—finish filling out their forms and leave, I look over last night's briefing forms. Fischer Hall is staffed round-the-clock by a security guard, student front desk receptionists, and resident assistants, students who, in exchange for free room and board, act as sort of house mothers on each of the hall's twenty floors. They all have to fill out reports at the end of their shifts, and my job is to read and follow up on these briefings. This always makes for an interesting morning.

The reports range from the ludicrous to the banal. Last night, for instance, six forty-ounce bottles of beer were hurled from an upper-story window onto the roof of a cab passing on the street below. Ten cops from the Sixth Precinct arrived and ran up and down the stairs a few times, unsuccessfully trying to figure out who the pitcher had been.

On the other end of the spectrum, the front desk apparently lost someone's Columbia House CD of the Month, causing much consternation. One of the RAs somberly reports that a resident slammed her door several times, crying, "I hate it here." The RA wishes to refer the student to Counseling Services.

Another report states that a small riot occurred when a cafeteria worker chastised a student for attempting to make an English muffin pizza in the toaster oven.

When my phone jangles, I pounce on it, grateful for something to do. I do love my job—really. But I have to admit it doesn't tax my intellect overly much.

"Fischer Hall, this is Heather, how may I help you?" My last boss, Rachel, had been very strict about how I answered the phone. Even though Rachel's not around anymore, old habits die hard.

"Heather?" I can hear an ambulance in the background. "Heather, it's Tom."

"Oh, hi, Tom." I glance at the clock. Nine-twenty. Yes! I was in when he'd called! If not on time, then at least before ten! "Where are you?"

"St. Vincent's." Tom sounds exhausted. Being the residence hall director of a New York College dormitory is a very demanding job. You have to look out for about seven hundred undergraduates, most of whom, with the exception of summer camp or maybe a stint in boarding school, have never been away from home for an extended period of time before in their lives—let alone have ever shared a bathroom with another human being. Residents come to Tom with all of their problems—roommate conflicts, academic issues, financial concerns, sexual identity crises—you name it, Tom has heard it.

And if a resident gets hurt or sick, it's the residence hall director's job to make sure he or she is okay. Needless to say, Tom spends a lot of time in emergency rooms, particularly on weekends, which is when most of the underage drinking goes on. And he does all this—is on duty twenty-four hours a day, three hundred and forty-three days a year (all New York College administrators get twenty-two vacation days)—for not much more than I make, plus free room and board.

Hey, is it any wonder my last boss only lasted a few months?

Tom seems pretty stable, though. I mean, as stable as a six-foot-three, two-hundred-pound former Texas A&M linebacker whose favorite movie is *Little Women* and who moved to New York City so he could finally come out of the closet can be.

"Look, Heather," Tom says tiredly. "I'm gonna be stuck here for a few more hours at least. We had a twenty-first birthday last night."

"Uh-oh." Twenty-first birthday celebrations are the *worst*. Inevitably, the hapless birthday boy or girl is urged to slam back twenty-one shots by his or her party guests. Since the human body cannot process that much alcohol in such a short period of time, most of the time the resident ends up celebrating his or her big day in one of our local emergency rooms. Nice, huh?

"Yeah," Tom says. "I hate to ask, but would you mind going through my appointment books and rescheduling all my judicial hearings this morning? I don't know if they're gonna admit this kid or not, and he won't let us call his parents—"

"No problem," I say. "How long you been there?"

Tom exhales gustily. "He only got up to seven before he passed out. So since midnight, or thereabouts. I've lost all track of time."

"I'll come spell you if you want." When a student is in the emergency room but hasn't been admitted, it's policy that a New York College representative stay with him or her at all times. You can't even go home to take a lousy shower unless there's someone there to take your place. New York College does not leave its students alone in the ER. Even though the students themselves will frequently check out without even bothering to tell you, so you're sitting there watching Spanish soaps for an hour before you find out the kid isn't even there anymore. "Then at least you can get some breakfast."

"You know, Heather," Tom says, "I think I'll take you up on that offer, if you really don't mind."

I say I don't and am taking money out of petty cash for cab fare before I've even hung up. I love petty cash. It's like having your own bank, right in the office. Unfortunately, Justine, the girl who'd had my position before me, had felt the same way, and had spent all of Fischer Hall's petty cash on ceramic heaters for her friends and family. The Budget Office still scrutinizes our petty cash vouchers with an eagle eye every time I take them over for reimbursement, even though each and every one of them is completely legit.

And I still haven't figured out what a ceramic heater is.

I finish rescheduling all of Tom's appointments, then polish off my café mocha in a gulp. *If you were thinner.* You know what, Barista Boy? With those long nails you won't trim because you're too poor to afford a new guitar pick, you look like a girl. Yeah, that's right. A girl. How do you like *that*, Barista Boy?

Quick stop at the cafeteria to grab a bagel to eat on the way to the hospital, and I'll be ready to go. I mean, café mochas are all well and good, but they don't supply lasting energy . . . not like a bagel does. Particularly a bagel smothered in cream cheese (dairy) over which several layers of bacon (protein) have been added.

I've grabbed my coat and am getting up to get my bagel when I notice Magda, my best work bud and the cafeteria's head cashier, standing in my office doorway, looking very unlike her usual self.

"Morning, Magda," I say to her. "You will never believe what Barista Boy said to me."

But Magda, normally a very inquisitive person, and a big fan of Barista Boy, doesn't look interested.

"Heather," she says. "I have something I have to show you."

"If it's the front page of the *Post*," I say, "Reggie already beat you to it. And really, Mags, it's okay. *I'm* okay. I can't believe she took him back after that whole thing at the Pussycat Dolls with Paris. But, hey, his dad owns her record label. What else is she going to do?"

Magda shakes her head.

"No," she says. "Not the *Post*. Just come, Heather. Come."

Curious—more because she still hasn't cracked a smile than because I actually think she has something so earth-shattering to show me—I follow Magda down the hall, past the student government office—closed this early in the morning—and Magda's boss's office, which, oddly, is empty. Normally, the dining office is filled with kvetching cafeteria workers and cigarette smoke, Gerald Eckhardt, the dining hall director, being an unapologetic smoker. He's only supposed to light up outside, but invariably I catch him puffing away at his desk, then blowing the smoke out the open window, like he doesn't think anyone is going to catch on.

But not today. Today the office is empty—and smoke-free.

"Magda," I say, as her pink smock disappears through the swinging doors to the cafeteria's loud, steaming kitchen, "what is going on?"

But Magda doesn't say anything until she's standing beside the massive industrial stove, on which a single pot has been set to boil. Gerald is standing there as well, looking out of place in his business suit among his pink-smocked employees, dwarfing everyone else with his massive frame—a result of sampling his own recipe for chicken parm a little too often.

Gerald looks—well, there's only one word for it: frightened. So does Saundra, the salad bar attendant, and Jimmy, the hot-line server. Magda is pale beneath her bright makeup. And Pete—what's *Pete* doing here?—looks like he wants to hurl.

"Okay, you guys," I say. I am convinced whatever is going on has to be a joke. Because Gerald, being in food services, is a prankster from way back, a master of the rubber rat in the desk drawer, and plastic spider in the soup. "What gives? April Fool's isn't for another three months. Pete, what are you doing back here?"

Which is when Pete—who's wearing, for some reason, an oven mitt—reaches out and lifts the lid from the merrily boiling pot, and I get a good look at what's inside.

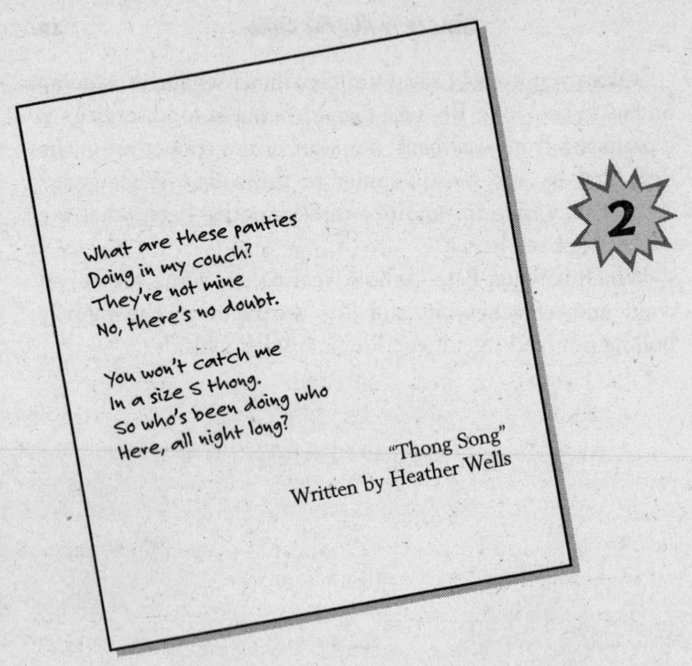
What are these panties
Doing in my couch?
They're not mine
No, there's no doubt.

You won't catch me
In a size 5 thong.
So who's been doing who
Here, all night long?

"Thong Song"
Written by Heather Wells
2

The Fischer Hall cafeteria is crowded, but not with students. We told the residents there was a gas leak—not one big enough to evacuate the whole building, but one that necessitated closing down the caf.

The sad thing is, they were all so bleary-eyed from partying the night before, the residents actually seemed to believe us. At least, no one protested—once I started handing out the free-meal voucher cards, so they could go eat in the student union.

Now the dining hall is still packed—but with college presidents, administrators, cafeteria workers, police officers, and homicide detectives, instead of hungry eighteen-year-olds.

Even so, the room is strangely hushed, so that the energy-saving bulbs in the chandeliers above our heads—casting reflections in the stained-glass windows near the edges of the high ceiling—seem to be humming more noisily than usual. Above the humming, I can hear Magda sniffling. She's sitting on one side of the cafeteria with the rest of her fellow workers, in their hairnets and pink uniforms and French manicures. A city police officer is speaking to them in a gentle tone.

"We'll let you go home soon as we get your fingerprints," he says.

"What do you need our fingerprints for?" Magda's chin is trembling with fear—or maybe indignation. "We didn't do anything. None of us killed that girl!"

The other cafeteria workers murmur in agreement. None of them killed that girl, either.

The police officer's tone stays gentle. "We need all your fingerprints so we can ascertain which prints in the kitchen are yours, ma'am, and which are the killer's. If he left any."

"Ascertain away," Gerald says, coming to the defense of his employees. "But I'm tellin' you right now, none of my folks is a murderer. Am I right, people?"

Everyone in a pink smock nods solemnly. Their eyes, however, are shining with something a little more than just tears. I suspect it might be excitement: Not only had they found a murder victim in their kitchen, right there amid the corn dogs and peanut-butter-and-jelly bars, but now they are valuable witnesses to a crime, and as such are being treated not as cafeteria workers—untouchables, as far as the students they serve are concerned—but as actual thinking human beings.

For a few of them, this might actually be a first.

I spot the head of the Housing Department, Dr. Jessup, at a table with several other administrators, all looking dazed. The discovery of a corpse's head on campus has worked as an expedient in getting the administrative staff to work before ten, despite the impending blizzard. Even the college president, Phillip Allington, is there, seated next to Steven Andrews, the new head basketball coach, who looks worried. He has good reason to: The entire New York College varsity basketball team—not to mention the varsity cheerleading squad—is housed in Fischer Hall, thanks to the building's close proximity to Winer Complex, the college sports center.

After the two student deaths in this building during the first semester—winning Fischer Hall the nickname Death Dorm—all the university employees (including sport coaches) seem to be feeling a little jumpy. And who can blame them? Especially President Allington. His tenure hasn't been an easy one. No one knows that better than me, assistant director of Death Dorm.

And now it looks as if things have just gotten immeasurably worse, not just for the president, but for my boss's boss, the head of Housing . . . and he knows it. The show-hanky tucked into his breast pocket is crumpled, as if someone—exercising my superlative investigative skills, I surmise that someone was Dr. Jessup himself—has actually been using it. Sitting slumped in a chair at a sticky cafeteria table for the past half hour hasn't done much for the creases in Dr. Jessup's suit, either.

"Heather," Dr. Jessup says to me, a little too heartily, as I come toward his table, having been summoned away from my desk—where I went directly after Pete's revelation to begin calling everyone I could think of, including Dr. Jessup and my boss, Tom—by one of the police officers. "Detective Canavan wants to talk to you. You remember Detective Canavan from the Sixth Precinct, don't you?"

Like I could forget.

"Detective," I say, extending my right hand toward the slightly rumpled-looking middle-aged man with the graying mustache, who stands with one foot resting on the seat of an empty cafeteria chair.

Detective Canavan looks up from the cup of coffee he's holding. His eyes are the color of slate, and the skin around them is wrinkled from overexposure to the elements. It's no joke, being a New York City homicide detective. Sadly, not all of them look like Chris Noth. In fact, none of them do, that I've noticed.

"Nice to see you again, Heather," the detective says. His grasp is as formidable as ever. "I understand you've seen it. So. Any ideas?"

I look from the detective to the head honcho of my department and back again.

"Um," I say, not sure what's going on. Wait—do Dr. Jessup and Detective Canavan actually want my help in solving this heinous crime? Because this is so the opposite of how they were about my helping them out last time. . . . "Where's the rest of her?"

"That isn't what Detective Canavan meant, Heather," Dr. Jessup says, with a forced smile. "He meant, do you recognize . . . it?"

Carol Ann Evans, dean of students—yeah, the same one who won't admit me into her college until I show her I can multiply fractions—happens to be seated nearby, and makes a kind of gagging noise and covers her mouth with a wadded-up tissue when she hears the word *it*.

And, to my certain knowledge, she hasn't even taken a peek at what's inside that pot.

Oh. They don't really want my help. Not THAT way.

I say, "Well, it's kinda hard to tell." No way am I going to announce, in front of all these people, that Lindsay Combs, homecoming queen and (now no longer) future roommate of her best friend Cheryl Haebig, had apparently been decapitated by person or persons unknown, and her head left in a pot on the stove in the Fischer Hall cafeteria.

I know. Ew.

"Come, now, Heather," Dr. Jessup says, with a smile that doesn't quite reach his eyes. To Detective Canavan he says, loudly enough for everyone in the caf to hear, apparently in an effort to impress President Allington, who wouldn't know me from Adam—though his wife and I were once nearly murdered by the same person—"Heather here knows every single one of Fischer Hall's seven hundred residents by name. Don't you, Heather?"

"Well, generally speaking," I say uncomfortably. "When they haven't been set on simmer for a few hours."

Did that sound flip? I guess it did. Dean Evans is gagging again. I didn't mean to be flip. It's just that . . . come *on*.

I hope the dean isn't going to hold this against me. You know, admission-to-the-College-of-Arts-and-Sciences-wise.

"So who is she? The girl." The detective seems unconscious of the fact that nearly everyone in the cafeteria is eavesdropping on our conversation. "A name would be nice."

I feel my stomach roll a little, like it had back in the kitchen when Pete had lifted the lid and I'd found myself staring into those unseeing eyes.

I take a deep breath. The air in the cafeteria is pungent

with ordinary breakfast smells . . . eggs and sausage and maple syrup. You can't smell *her.*

At least, I don't think so.

Still, I'm thankful that I haven't had time this morning for my customary cream-cheese-and-bacon bagel breakfast. The café mocha has—so far—been more than enough. The parquet of the dining hall floor is swimming a little before my eyes.

I clear my throat. There. That feels a little better.

"Lindsay Combs," I say. "She dates—dated—the Pansies' point guard." The Pansies is the (sad) name of the New York College Division III basketball team. They lost their real name, the Cougars, in a cheating scandal in the fifties, and have been stuck with being Pansies ever since—to the amusement of the teams they play, and their own everlasting chagrin.

Everyone in the room sucks in their breath. President Allington—dressed, as usual, in his interpretation of what one of his college's students might wear (if it were 1955), a New York College letter jacket and gray cords—actually cries, "No!" Beside the president, Coach Andrews—as I'd known he would—goes pale.

"Oh, God," he says. He's a big guy—around my own age—with spiky dark hair and disarmingly blue eyes . . . what they call Black Irish. He'd be cute if he wasn't so muscle-bound. Oh, and if he ever actually noticed I was alive.

Not that, if he did, anything would ever come of it, since my heart belongs to another.

"Not Lindsay," he says, with a groan.

I feel for him. I really do. Cheryl Haebig isn't the only one who liked Lindsay . . . we all did. Well, everyone except our office graduate student assistant, Sarah. Lindsay was an immensely popular girl, the captain of the New York College cheerleading squad, with waist-length honey-colored hair and grapefruit-sized breasts that Sarah maintained were the result of plastic surgery. While Lindsay's excessive school spirit could be annoyingly perky (to me, anyway) at times, it was at least a pleasant change from the usual type of New York College students we saw in our office—spoiled, dissatisfied, and threatening to call their lawyer father if we didn't get them a single or an extra-long bed.

"Jesus Christ." Dr. Jessup hadn't believed it when I'd called to say that he needed to get to Fischer Hall as soon as possible, due to the fact that one of our residents had lost her head . . . literally. Now he looks as though it's finally sinking in. "Are you *sure,* Heather?"

"Yeah," I say. "I'm sure. It's Lindsay Combs. Head cheerleader." I swallow again. "Sorry. No pun intended."

Detective Canavan has removed a notepad from his belt, but he doesn't write anything in it. Instead, he flips slowly through the pages, not looking up. "How could you tell?"

I'm trying hard not to remember those unseeing eyes looking up at me—only not. "Lindsay wore contact lenses. Tinted. Green." Such an unnatural shade of green that Sarah, back in the office, always asked, whenever Lindsay left, "Who the hell does she think she's fooling? That color does *not* occur in nature."

"That's all?" Detective Canavan asks. "Tinted contact lenses?"

"And the earrings. She's got three on one side, two on the other. She came down to my office a lot," I say, by way of explaining how I was so familiar with her piercings.

"Troublemaker?" Detective Canavan asks.

"No," I say. Most students who end up in the office of the

residence hall director are either there because they're in trouble, or they've got a problem with their roommate. Or, as in Lindsay's case, because they want the free birth control I keep in a jar on my desk instead of Hershey's kisses (lower in calories). "Condoms."

Detective Canavan raises his gray eyebrows. "I beg your pardon?"

"Lindsay stopped by a lot for free condoms," I say. "She and her boyfriend were pretty hot and heavy."

"Name?"

I realize, belatedly, that I've just managed to incriminate one of my residents. Coach Andrews realizes it, too.

"Aw, come on, Detective," he says. "Mark isn't capable of—"

"Mark what?" Detective Canavan demands.

Coach Andrews, I see, is looking panicky. Dr. Allington rushes in to his favorite employee's rescue. Well, sort of.

"The Pansies do have a very important ball game tomorrow night," the president begins worriedly, "against the Jersey College East Devils. We're eight-and-oh, you know."

To which Coach Andrews adds defensively, "And none of my boys had anything to do with what happened to Lindsay. I don't want them dragged into it."

Detective Canavan—not even sounding like he's lying, which I know he is—says, "I sympathize with your dilemma, Coach. You, too, Dr. Allington. But the fact is, I have a job to do. Now—"

"I don't think *you* understand, Detective," Dr. Allington interrupts. "Tomorrow night's game is being televised on New York One. Millions of dollars of commercial advertising is at stake here."

I stare at the president, openmouthed in astonishment. I

notice Dean Evans is doing the same thing. She meets my gaze, and it's clear we're both thinking: *Whoa. He did* not *just say that.*

You would think, considering we're both on the same cognitive wavelength, she'd be a little more sympathetic about the remedial math thing. But I guess not.

"*You're* the one who doesn't understand, Doctor." Detective Canavan's voice is hard, and loud enough to make Magda and her fellow cafeteria workers stop crying and lift up their heads. "Either your people give me the name of the girl's boyfriend now, or you'll be sending more girls home later this semester in body bags. Because I can guarantee, whatever sick bastard did this to Miss Combs, he will do it again, to someone else."

Dr. Allington stares hard at the detective, who stares even harder back.

"Mark Shepelsky," I say quickly. "Her boyfriend's name is Mark Shepelsky. He's in Room Two-twelve."

Coach Andrews slumps across the tabletop, burying his head in his arms. Dr. Allington groans, pinching the bridge of his nose between his thumb and index finger as if stricken by a sudden sinus headache. Dr. Jessup just looks at the ceiling, while Dr. Flynn, the Housing Department's on-staff psychologist, smiles sadly at me from the table where he sits with the other school administrators.

Detective Canavan looks a bit calmer as he flips his notepad back open and jots down the name.

"There," he says. "That didn't hurt, now, did it?"

"But," I say. Detective Canavan sighs audibly at my *But*. I ignore him. "Lindsay's boyfriend couldn't have had anything to do with this."

Detective Canavan turns his rock-hard stare on me. "And just how would you know that?"

"Well," I say, "whoever killed her had to have access to a key to the cafeteria. Because he'd need one to sneak in before the caf was open in order to hack up his girlfriend, clean the place up, and get out by the time the staff arrived. But how would Mark get hold of a key? I mean, if you think about it, Fischer Hall employees ought to really be your primary suspects—"

"Heather." Detective Canavan's already squinty eyes narrow even further. "Do not—I repeat, do not—be getting any ideas that you're going to be launching your own personal investigation into this girl's murder. This is the work of a sick and unbalanced mind, and it'd be in the best interest of everyone, yourself most particularly, if this time you left the investigating to the professionals. Believe me, we have things under control."

I blink at him. Detective Canavan can be scary when he wants to be. I can tell that even the deans are scared. Coach Andrews looks terrified. And he's about a foot taller than the detective, and about fifty pounds heavier . . . all of it muscle.

I long to point out to the detective that I would not have had to launch my own personal investigation into last semester's murders if he had actually listened to me from the beginning that they *were*, in fact, murders.

But it's pretty obvious he seems to get it this time around.

I should probably tell him that I have absolutely no desire at all to get involved with *this* particular criminal case. I mean, throwing girls down an elevator shaft is one thing. Chopping their heads off? So not something I want to involve myself in. My knees are still shaking from what I saw inside that pot. Detective Canavan so doesn't need to worry about me doing any investigating this time. The professionals are *welcome* to this one.

"Are you listening to me, Wells?" the detective demands. "I said I do not want a repeat performance—"

"I got it," I interrupt quickly. I'd elaborate—like how about no way do I want anything to do with headless cheerleaders—but decide it would be wiser simply to retreat.

"Can I go now?" I ask—I direct the question more at Dr. Jessup, since he is, in fact, my boss—well, Tom's my direct boss, but since Tom's busy trying to figure out if there are any cafeteria keys missing (a task he seems to relish, since it keeps him well away from what they found on the stove—and the fact that he's been asked to look is also proof that Detective Canavan is right . . . the NYPD *does* have things under control), Stan's the closest thing I've got nearby.

But Stan is staring at *his* boss, President Allington, who is trying to get Detective Canavan's attention. Which is sort of a relief, since I've had all of Detective Canavan's attention I can take for the moment. That dude can be *scary*.

"So what I hear you telling me, Detective . . ." Dr. Allington is saying, his careful phrasing illustrative of the training that had earned him his PhD. "What I hear you saying is that this unfortunate matter will most likely not be cleared up by lunch today? Because my office was planning on hosting a special function this afternoon to honor our hardworking student athletes, and it would be a shame to have to postpone it. . . ."

The look the detective levels at the college president might have frozen lava. "Dr. Allington, we're not talking about some kid barfing up his breakfast in the locker room after gym class."

"I realize that, Detective," Dr. Allington says. "However, I had hoped—"

"For Christ's sake, Phil," Dr. Jessup interrupts. He's had enough. Finally. "Someone tried to fricassee a kid, and you wanna open up the salad bar?"

"All I'm saying," Dr. Allington says, looking indignant, "is that, in my professional opinion, it would be best not to allow this incident to interfere with the residents' normal routine. You'll recall that a few years ago, when the school had that rash of suicides, it was the publicity about them that generated so many of the copycat attempts—"

Detective Canavan apparently can't help raising an incredulous gray eyebrow at that one. "You think half a dozen coeds are gonna rush home and whack off their own heads?"

"What I'm trying to say," Dr. Allington continues haughtily, "is that if the luncheon is canceled—not to mention tomorrow night's game—the truth about what's happened here is going to be impossible to keep from leaking. We're not going to be able to keep something like this quiet for long. I'm not talking about the *Post*, either, or even 1010 WINS. I'm talking about the *New York Times*, maybe even CNN. If your people don't find that girl's body soon, Detective, we may even attract the networks. And that could be very damaging to the school's reputation—"

"Corpseless head found in dorm cafeteria," Carol Ann Evans, to everyone's surprise, says. When we all turn our heads to blink at her, she adds, in a choked voice, "Tonight on *Inside Edition*."

Detective Canavan shifts his weight and removes his foot from the chair seat.

"President Allington," he says. "In about five minutes, my people are going to seal this entire wing off from the public.

And by public, I am including your employees. We are launching a full-scale investigation into this crime. We ask that you cooperate.

"You can do so, firstly, by removing yourself and your employees from the immediate vicinity as soon as my men are through with them. Secondly, I'll have to ask that this cafeteria remain closed until such time as I deem it safe to reopen. Unless I'm mistaken"—the detective's tone implies that this is hardly likely—"you've had a student murdered on school grounds this morning, and her killer is still at large, possibly right here on campus. Possibly even here in this very room. If there's anything that could be more damaging to your school's reputation than that, I can't think of it. I really don't think postponing a luncheon—or a basketball game—is comparable, do you?"

I guess I can't really blame Dean Evans for bursting into a fit of nervous giggles just then. The suggestion that there might be a killer on the New York College student life administrative staff is enough to send even the most staid individual into hysterical laughter. A more boring group of people could hardly be found anywhere on the planet. Gerald Eckhardt, with his surreptitious smoking and cross-shaped tie tack, wielding a meat cleaver? Coach Andrews, in his jogging pants and letter jacket, hacking a young girl to death? Dr. Flynn, all hundred and forty pounds of him, using a circular saw to dismember a cheerleader?

It just isn't within the realm of the possible.

And yet.

And yet even Carol Ann Evans must have figured out by now that whoever killed Lindsay had complete access to the cafeteria. Only someone who works at Fischer Hall—

or in the Student Life Department—would have access to the key.

Which means someone on the Housing staff could be a killer.

The sad part is, this doesn't even surprise me.

Wow. I guess I really *am* a jaded New Yorker.

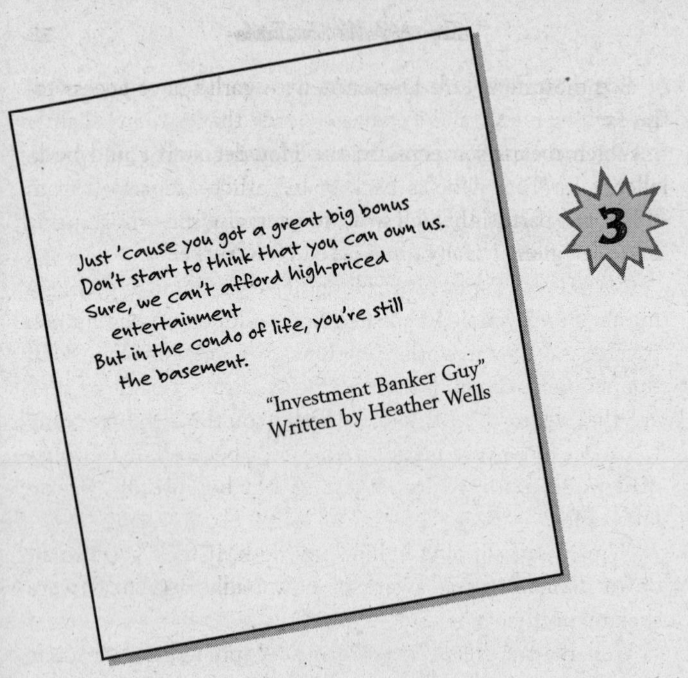

3
Just 'cause you got a great big bonus
Don't start to think that you can own us.
Sure, we can't afford high-priced
entertainment
But in the condo of life, you're still
the basement.
"Investment Banker Guy"
Written by Heather Wells

"You have a bunch of messages," Sarah, our office's graduate student assistant—every residence hall is assigned a GA, who, in exchange for free room and board, helps run the administrative aspects of the hall office—informs me tersely as I come in. "The phones are ringing off the hook. Everyone wants to know why the caf is closed. I've been using the gas leak excuse, but I don't know how long people are going to believe us, with all these cops traipsing in and out. Have they found the rest of her yet?"

"Shhh," I say, looking around the office, in case there's a resident lurking.

But the office (still festooned with garlands of fake evergreen, a menorah, and Kwanzaa gourds, thanks to my slightly manic and clearly overzealous holiday decorating) is empty, except for Tom, who is back in his office—separated from the outer office, in which I sit, by a metal grate—murmuring into the phone.

"Whatever," Sarah says, rolling her eyes. Sarah is getting a master's in psychology, so she knows a lot about the human psyche and how it works. Or thinks she does, anyway. "Half the people in the building aren't even awake yet. Or, if they are, they've hurried off to class. So do you think they're going to cancel tomorrow night's game? Not because of this blizzard we're supposed to be getting, but because of . . . you know. Her?"

"Um," I say, slipping behind my desk. It feels good to sit down. I hadn't been aware of how badly my knees were shaking until now.

Well, it's not every day you see a decapitated cheerleader's head in a pot. Especially a cheerleader you knew. It's no wonder I'm a little shaky. Plus, except for the café mocha, I still haven't had breakfast.

Not that I feel like eating. Well, very much.

"I don't know," I say. "They want to question Mark."

Sarah looks annoyed. "He didn't do it," she says scornfully. "He's not smart enough. Unless he had help."

It's true. The admission standards for New York College are some of the highest in the country . . . except when it comes to athletes. Basically any semi-decent ballplayer who wants to come to New York College is accepted, since, as a Division III school, all the best athletes tend to go to colleges in Division I or II. Still, President Allington is determined to have his legacy at New York College be that he turned it into an actual contender in the world of college ball—his ultimate goal, it's rumored, is to have the school's Division I rating reinstated.

Though the likelihood of this happening—especially in light of today's events—seems slim.

"I still can't get over it," Sarah is saying. "Where could her body be?"

"Where all bodies in New York City turn up," I say, looking at my phone messages. "In the river somewhere. No one'll find it till spring, when the temperature rises enough to cause the body to bob."

I'm no forensic expert, of course, and I haven't even been able to enroll in any criminal justice courses yet, thanks to the remedial math I need to get through first.

But I've watched a lot of *Law and Order* and *CSI*.

Plus, you know, I live with a private detective. Or "share a domicile with," I should say, since "live with" sounds like we share more than that, which we don't. Sadly.

Sarah shudders elaborately, even though it's warm in the office and she's wearing one of the thick striped sweaters woven for her by a fellow member of the kibbutz upon which she spent the summer of her freshman year. It looks quite fetching over her overalls.

"It just doesn't make any sense," she says. "How can there be another murder in this building? We really ARE turning into Death Dorm."

I'm looking at my messages. My best friend Patty—she's no doubt seen the cover of today's *Post*, and is as worried as Reggie was about how it's affected me. Someone who wouldn't give his name and said he'd call back later—creditor, no doubt. I'd maxed out the cards a little in my preholiday gift-buying frenzy. If I can hold them off until March, I'll pay it all back when I get my tax refund. And—

I wave the slip at Sarah. "Is this for real? Did he really call? Or are you yanking my chain?"

Sarah looks surprised. "Honestly, Heather," she says. "Do you think I'd joke around on a day like today? Jordan Cartwright really did call. Or, at least, someone who *claimed* to be Jordan Cartwright called. He wants you to call him back right away. He said it was vitally important. Emphasis on the vitally."

Well, that sounds like Jordan, all right. Everything is vitally important to Jordan. Especially if it involves humiliating me in some way.

"What if," Sarah says, "Lindsay's body isn't in the river? Supposing it's still in the building. Supposing . . . my God, supposing it's still in Lindsay's room!"

"Then we'd have heard from Cheryl already," I say. "Since she and Lindsay's roommate swapped spaces first thing this morning."

"Oh." Sarah looks disappointed. Then she brightens. "Maybe it's somewhere else in the building! Like in someone else's room. Could you imagine coming home from class and finding a headless body in your swivel chair, like in front of your computer?"

My stomach twists. The café mocha is not resting well.

"Sarah," I say. "Seriously. Shut up."

"Oh, my God, or what if like we find it in the game room, propped up against the foosball table?"

"Sarah." I glare at her.

"Oh, lighten up, Heather, " she says, with a laugh. "Can't you tell I'm resorting to gallows humor in an effort to break the connection between such a horrifying stimulus and an unwanted emotional response, such as revulsion or fear, which in this case wouldn't be helpful or professional?"

"I'd prefer revulsion," I say. "I don't think anyone has to be professional when there's a headless cheerleader involved."

It's at this moment that Tom chooses to appear in the doorway to his office.

"Can we not say that word?" he asks queasily, grasping the doorframe for support.

"What?" Sarah flicks some of her curly hair off her shoulder. *"Cheerleader?"*

"No," Tom says. *"Headless.* We *have* her head. Just not the rest of her. Oh, God. I can't believe I just said that." He looks at me miserably. There are purple shadows under his bloodshot eyes from his night spent at the hospital, and his blond hair is plastered unattractively to his forehead from lack of product. Under ordinary circumstances, Tom wouldn't be caught dead looking so unkempt. He's actually fussier about his hair than I am.

"You should go to bed," I say to him. "We've got things covered in here, Sarah and I."

"I can't go to bed." Now Tom looks shocked. "A girl's been found dead in my building. Can you imagine how that would look to Jessup and everybody? If I just . . . went to bed? I'm still on employment probation, you know. They'd just decide I can't hack it and—" He swallows. "Oh, my God, did I just say the word *hack?*"

"Go back in your office, shut the door, and close your eyes for a while," I say to him. "I'll cover for you."

"I can't," Tom says. "Every time I close my eyes, I see . . . her."

I don't have to ask what he means. I know, only too well. Since the same thing keeps happening to me.

"Hey." A kid in a hoodie, with a tiny silver pair of barbells pierced through the bottom of his nose, leans his head into the office. "Why's the caf closed?"

"Gas leak," Sarah, Tom, and I all say at the same time.

"Jesus," the kid says, making a face. "So I gotta walk across campus to get breakfast?"

"Go to the student union," Sarah says quickly, holding out a meal pass. "On us."

The kid looks down at the voucher. "*Sweet*," he says, because with the voucher, the meal won't be subtracted from his daily quota. Now he can have TWO dinners, if he wants to. He shuffles happily away.

"I don't see why we can't just tell them the truth," Sarah declares, as soon as he's gone. "They're gonna find out anyway."

"Right," Tom says. "But we don't want to cause a panic. You know, that there's a psychopathic killer loose in the building."

"And," I add carefully, "we don't want people finding out who it was before they've gotten hold of Lindsay's parents."

"Yeah," Tom says. "What she said." It's weird having a boss who doesn't actually know what he's doing. I mean, Tom's great, don't get me wrong.

But he's no Rachel Walcott.

Which, on balance, is something to be grateful for. . . .

"Hey, you guys," Sarah says. "What am I? Ha, ha, ha, thump."

Tom and I look at one another blankly.

"I don't know," I say.

"Someone laughing his head off. Get it? Ha, ha, ha,

thump." Sarah looks at us reprovingly when we don't laugh. "Gallows humor, people. To help us COPE."

I glance at Tom. "Who's with the birthday kid?" I ask him. "The one at the hospital? If you and I are here, I mean?"

"Oh, crap," Tom says, looking ashen-faced. "I forgot about him. I got the call, and—"

"You just *left* him?" Sarah rolls her eyes. Her contempt for our new boss isn't something she tries to hide. She thinks Dr. Jessup should have hired *her* to take over, even though she's a full-time student. A full-time student whose part-time hobby is analyzing the problems of everyone she meets. I, for instance, allegedly have abandonment issues, due to my mother running off to Argentina with my manager . . . and all of my money.

And because I have not pursued the issue as aggressively as Sarah thinks I should via the courts, I allegedly suffer from low self-esteem and passivity, as well. At least according to Sarah.

But I feel like I have a choice (well, not really, because it's not like I've got the money to pursue it in the courts, anyway): I can sit around and be bitter and resentful over what Mom did. Or I can put it behind me and just get on with my life.

Is it wrong I choose the latter?

Sarah seems to think so. Although this is only the stuff she tells me when she's not busy accusing me of having some kind of Superman complex, for wanting to save all the residents in Fischer Hall from ever coming to harm.

It really isn't any mystery to me why Sarah didn't get the job and Tom did. All Tom ever says to me is stuff like he likes my shoes, and did I see *American Idol* last night. It's much easier to get along with Tom than it is with Sarah.

"Well, I think murder trumps alcohol poisoning," I say, coming to Tom's defense. "But we still need to have someone there with the resident, especially if he doesn't end up getting admitted. . . ." If Stan finds out we have a resident in the ER with no one there to supervise his care, he will flip out. I don't want to lose my new boss just when I'm starting to like him. "Sarah—"

"I have a lab," she says, not even looking up from the sign-in sheets she's gathering to photocopy, ostensibly so the police can check to see if Lindsay had any guests the night before who might have decided to repay her hospitality by cutting her head off.

Except, of course, Lindsay hadn't. We'd been over the logs twice. Nothing.

"But—"

"I can't miss it," Sarah says. "It's the first one of the new semester!"

"I'll go, then," I say.

"Heather, no." Tom looks panicky. I can't tell if it's because he genuinely doesn't want to put me through a New York City ER waiting room after what I've already been through this morning, or if it's just that he doesn't want to be left alone in the office, considering the fact that he's so new to his job. "I'll get one of the RAs. . . ."

"They'll all have classes, too, just like Sarah," I say. I'm already on my feet and reaching for my coat. The truth is, I'm not trying to be a martyr. I'm actually seriously welcoming the chance to get out of there. Though I try not to act like it. "Really, it's fine. They'll have to admit him soon, right? Or let him go. So I'll be back soon. It *is* a he, right?"

"What girl would be stupid enough to try to drink twenty-one shots in one night?" Sarah asks, rolling her eyes.

"It's a guy," Tom says, and hands me a slip of paper with a name and student ID number on it, which I shove into my pocket. "Not the most scintillating conversationalist, but then, he was still unconscious when I was there. Maybe he's awake by now. Need petty cash for cab fare?"

I assure him I still have what I'd grabbed from the metal box earlier, when I'd been on my way to spell him . . . before we'd found out about Lindsay.

"So," Tom says to me in a quiet voice, as I'm about to head out the door. "You've dealt with this before." We both know what he means by *this*. "What, um, should I *do?*"

He looks really worried. That and the bed head make him seem younger than he really is . . . which, at twenty-six, is still younger than me. Almost as young as Barista Boy.

"Be strong," I say, laying a hand on his massive, Izod-sweater-clad shoulder. "And whatever you do . . . don't try to solve the crime yourself. *Believe* me."

He swallows. "Whatever. Like I want to end up with *my* head in a pot? No, thanks."

I give him a reassuring pat. "I'll be on my cell if you need to reach me," I say.

Then I beat a hasty retreat into the hallway, where I run into Julio, the head housekeeper, and his newly hired nephew—nepotism is as alive and well at New York College as it is anywhere else—Manuel, laying rubber-backed mats along the floor in order to protect the marble from salt the residents will track in when it finally starts snowing.

"Heather," Julio says to me worriedly as I breeze past, "is it really true, what they say? About . . ." His dark eyes glance toward the lobby, in which police officers and college administrators are still swarming like fashionistas at a sample sale.

"It's true, Julio," I stop to tell him, in a low voice. "They found a . . ." I'm about to say *dead body*, but that isn't strictly true. "Dead girl in the cafeteria," I settle for finishing.

"Who?" Manuel Juarez, an outrageously handsome guy I'd heard some of the female—and even some of the male—student workers sighing over (I don't bother, because of course I don't believe in romance in the workplace. Also because he's never looked twice at me, and isn't likely to, with so many nubile nineteen-year-olds in belly-baring tees around. I haven't bared my belly since, um, it started jutting over the waistband of my jeans), appears concerned. "Who was it?"

"I can't really say yet," I tell them, because we're supposed to wait until the deceased's family has been informed before giving out their name to others.

The truth, of course, is that if it had been anyone but Lindsay, I'd have told them in a heartbeat. But everyone—even the staff, whose tolerance for the people whose parents provide our paychecks is minimal, at best—liked Lindsay.

And I'm not going to be the one to tell them what happened to her.

Which is one of the reasons I'm so grateful to have this chance to be getting out of here.

Julio shoots his nephew an annoyed look—I guess because he knows as well as I do that I'm not allowed to give out the name—and mutters something in Spanish. Manuel flushes darkly, but doesn't reply. I know Manuel, like Tom, is still so new that he's on employment probation. Also that Julio is the strictest of supervisors. I wouldn't want to have him as *my* boss. I've seen the way he gets when he catches the residents Rollerblading across his newly waxed floors.

"I have to go to the hospital about a different kid," I tell

Julio. "Hopefully I'll be back soon. Keep an eye on Tom for me, will you? He's not used to any of this stuff."

Julio nods somberly, and I know my request will be carried out to the letter . . . even if it means Julio has to fake a spilled can of soda outside the hall director's door, so he can spend half an hour cleaning it up.

I manage to make it past all the people in the lobby and out into the cold without being stopped again. But even though—miraculously—there's a cab pulling up in front of Fischer Hall just as I walk out, I don't hail it. Instead, I hurry on foot around the corner, back toward the brownstone I left just a couple of hours before. If I'm going to be sitting in the hospital all day, there are a couple of things I need—like my remedial math textbook so I can be ready for my first class, if it isn't canceled due to snow, and maybe my Game Boy, loaded with Tetris (oh, who am I kidding? Between studying and Tetris, it's a solid bet I'll be spending my morning trying to beat my high score). Still, maybe I can convince Lucy to come outside and get her business done, so I don't have to worry about finding any surprises later.

The clouds above are still dark and heavy with unshed moisture, but that isn't, I know, why Reggie and his friends are nowhere to be seen. They've scattered thanks to the heavy police presence around the corner, at Fischer Hall. They're probably in the Washington Square Diner, taking a coffee break. Murder's as tough on the drug business as it is on everything else.

Lucy is so puzzled to see me home this early that she forgets to protest about being let outside into Cooper's grandfather's cold back garden. By the time I've retrieved my textbook and Game Boy and come back downstairs, she's sitting by the back door, her business steaming a few yards away. I let her back in and hastily clean up her mess, and am about to tear from the house when I notice the message light blinking on the machine in the hall—our house phone, as opposed to Cooper's business line. I press PLAY, and Cooper's brother's voice fills the foyer.

"Um, hi," my ex-fiancé says. "This message is for Heather. Heather, I've been trying to reach you on your cell as well as your work phone. I guess I keep missing you. Could you call me back as soon as you get this message? I have something really important I need to talk to you about."

Wow. It really must be important, if he's calling me on Cooper's house line. Cooper's family haven't spoken to him for years—since they learned the family patriarch, Cartwright Records founder Arthur Cartwright, had left his black sheep grandson his West Village brownstone, a prime piece of New York City real estate (valued at eight million dollars). Relations hadn't exactly been warm before that, though, thanks to Cooper's refusal to enter the family business (specifically, Cooper refused to sing bass in Easy Street, the boy band his father was putting together).

In fact, if it wasn't for me—and my best friend Patty and her husband Frank—Cooper would have spent Christmas and New Year's by himself (not that the prospect of this seemed to have bothered him very much), instead of basking in the warm glow of family . . . well, Patty's family, anyway, my own family being either incarcerated (Dad) or on the lam with my money (Mom. It's actually probably good I'm an only child).

Still, I'd found during the years I'd dated Cooper's brother that what was important to Jordan was rarely important to me. So I don't exactly scoop up the phone and call him right back. Instead, I listen to the rest of the messages—a series of hang-ups: telemarketers, no doubt—and then head back out into the cold toward St. Vincent's.

Now that I want one, of course I can't find a cab, so I have to hoof it the five or six blocks (avenue blocks, not short street blocks) to the hospital. But that's okay. We're supposed to get a half hour of exercise a day, according to the government. Or is it an hour? Well, whatever it is, five blocks in bitter cold seem more than enough. By the time I get to the hospital, my nose and cheeks feel numb.

But it is warm in the waiting room—if chaotic . . . though not as much as it normally is: the weather forecast has apparently frightened most of the hypochondriacs into staying home—and I'm able to find a seat with ease. Some kindly nurse has turned the channel on the waiting room television set from Spanish soaps to New York One, so everyone can keep abreast of the coming storm. All I need to get comfy is a little hot cocoa—and I come by that easily enough, by slipping some coins into the coffee vending machine—and some breakfast.

Food, however, is less easy to come by in the St. Vincent's ER waiting room, unless I'm willing to settle for Funyuns and Milk Duds from the candy machine. Which, under ordinary circumstances, I would be.

But in light of this morning's events, my stomach is feeling a little queasy, and I'm not sure it can handle a sudden influx of salt and caramel with its usual ease.

Plus, it's five of the hour . . . the time when the security guards open the ER doors and allow each patient inside to have visitors. In the case of my student, that visitor would be me.

Of course, when I need it, I can't find the slip of paper Tom had handed to me, the one with the student's name and ID number on it. So I know I'll have to wing it when I get into the ER. Hopefully there won't be that many twenty-one-year-olds in there, sleeping off way too many birthday shots from the night before. I figure the nurses might be able to help me out. . . .

But in the end, I don't need any help. I recognize my student the minute I lay eyes on him, stretched out on a gurney beneath a white sheet.

"Gavin!"

He groans and buries his face in his pillow.

"Gavin." I stand beside the gurney, glaring down at him. I should have known. Gavin McGoren, junior, filmmaking student, and the biggest pain-in-the-butt resident in Fischer Hall: Who else would keep my boss up all night?

"I know you're not asleep, Gavin," I say severely. "Open your eyes."

Gavin's lids fly open. "Jesus Christ, woman!" he cries. "Can't you see I'm sick?" He points at the IV sticking out of his arm.

"Oh, please," I say disgustedly. "You're not sick. You're just stupid. Twenty-one shots, Gavin?"

"Whatever," he mutters, folding his IV-free arm over his eyes, to block out the light from the fluorescents overhead. "I had my boys with me. I knew I'd be all right."

"Your boys," I say disparagingly. "Oh, yeah, your boys took great care of you."

"Hey." Gavin winces as if the sound of his own voice hurts. It probably does. "They brought me here, didn't they?"

"*Dumped* you here," I correct him. "And left. I don't see any of them around anymore, do you?"

"They had to go to class," Gavin says blearily. "Anyway, how would you know? You weren't here. It was that other tool from the hall office—where'd he go?"

"If you mean Tom, the hall director," I say, "he had to go deal with another emergency. You're not our only resident, you know, Gavin."

"What are you riding on me for?" Gavin wants to know. "It's my birthday."

"What a way to celebrate," I say.

"Whatevs. Not for nothing, but I was filming it for a class project."

"You're always filming yourself doing something stupid for a class project," I say. "Remember the reenactment you did of the scene from *Hannibal*? The one with the cow brain?"

He lifts his arm to glare at me. "How was I supposed to know I'm allergic to fava beans?"

"It might surprise you to know, Gavin," I say, as my cell phone vibrates in my coat pocket, "that Tom and I actually have better things to do than hold your hand every time you pull some stunt that ends up with you in the emergency room."

"Like what?" Gavin asks, with a snort. "Let those ass-kissing RAs suck up to you some more?"

It is very hard for me not to tell Gavin about Lindsay. How can he lie there, feeling so sorry for himself—especially after having done something so incredibly stupid to get himself into this position in the first place—when back in the building a girl is dead, and we can't even find her body?

"Look, can you just find out when I can get out of here?" Gavin asks, with a moan. "And spare me the lectures, for once?"

"I can," I say, only too happy to leave him to himself. Among other things, he doesn't smell too good. "Do you want me to call your parents?"

"God, no," he groans. "Why would I want you to do *that*?"

"Maybe to let them know how you celebrated your birthday? I'm sure they'll be very proud. . . ."

Gavin pulls the pillow over his head. I smile and go over to one of the nurses to discuss the possibility of his being released. She tells me she'll see what the doctor says. I thank her and go back out into the waiting room, pulling out my cell phone to see who called me . . .

. . . and am thrilled to see the words *Cartwright, Cooper* on my cell phone's screen.

I'm even more thrilled when, a second later, a voice says, "Heather."

And I look up and find myself staring into the eyes of the man himself.

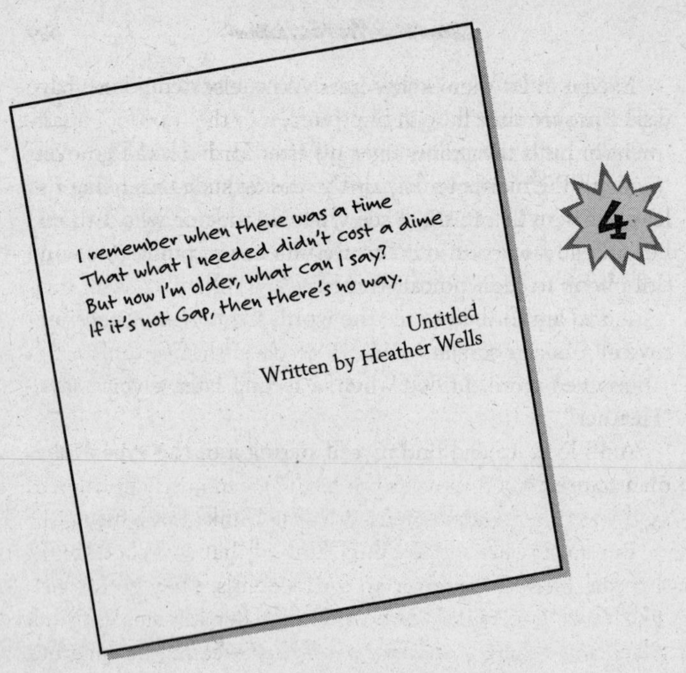

4
I remember when there was a time
That what I needed didn't cost a dime
But now I'm older, what can I say?
If it's not Gap, then there's no way.
Untitled
Written by Heather Wells

Oh, whatever. So I'm in love with him, and he has shown absolutely zero interest in reciprocating my feelings. So what? A girl can dream, right?

And at least I'm dreaming about someone age-appropriate, since Cooper's over thirty—a decade older than Barista Boy.

And it's not like Cooper's earning minimum wage in some coffee shop. He owns his own business.

And, okay, he won't actually TELL me what it is he does all day, because he seems to think it's not fitting for someone of my tender sensibilities to know. . . .

But that just means he cares, right?

Except that I know he cares. Why else would he have asked me to move in with him (well, into the top-floor apartment of his brownstone, anyway) after Jordan kicked me out (even though Jordan maintains he did no such thing, that I'm the one who left. But, I'm sorry, he was the one who let Tania Trace fall face first into his crotch—in our own apartment, no less. Who wouldn't interpret something like that as an invitation to leave)?

But Cooper's made it VASTLY clear that he only cares about me as a friend. Well, insofar as he has never hit on me, anyway.

And, okay, Cooper *did* sort of mention once—when I was in a state of severe shock from having been nearly murdered, and was only semiconscious—that he thinks I'm a nice girl.

But am I really supposed to think of that as a good thing? I mean, *nice*? Guys never go for nice girls. They go for girls like Tania Trace, who, in the video for her last single, "Bitch Slap," was rolling around in an oil slick wearing nothing but leather panties and a wife-beater.

They don't MAKE leather panties in my size. I'm pretty sure.

Still, there's always a chance Cooper isn't the leather panties type. I mean, he's already proved he's nothing like the rest of the family by being so nice to me. Maybe there's hope. Maybe that's why he's here at the hospital right now, to tell me that he can't stand to be without me a second more, and that his car is waiting outside to whisk us to the airport for a Vegas wedding and a Hawaiian honeymoon—

"Hey," Cooper says, holding up a paper bag. "I figured you hadn't eaten. I brought you a sandwich from Joe's."

Oh. Well, okay. It's not a Vegas wedding and a Hawaiian honeymoon.

But it's a sandwich from Joe's Dairy, my favorite cheese

shop! And if you've ever tried Joe's smoked mozzarella, you know it's just as good as a Hawaiian honeymoon. Possibly better.

"How'd you know I was here?" I ask dazedly, taking the bag.

"Sarah told me," Cooper says. "I called your office when I heard what happened. It was on the police scanner."

"Oh." Of course. Cooper listens to a police scanner while he's on stakeouts. That or jazz. He's a nut for Ella Fitzgerald. If Ella wasn't dead, I'd be jealous.

"Aren't your clients going to wonder where you are?" I ask. I can't believe he's blowing off a case for me.

"It's okay," Cooper says with a shrug. "My client's husband is occupied for the moment." I don't even bother asking what he means, since I know he won't tell me. "I was going for lunch, anyway, and I figured you hadn't eaten," he says.

My stomach rumbles hungrily at the word *lunch*. "I'm famished," I confess. "You're a lifesaver."

"So." Cooper leads me to an empty set of orange plastic seats in the waiting room. "What's the kid in for?"

I glance at the emergency room doors. "Who, Gavin? Chronic stupidity."

"Gavin again, huh?" Cooper produces two Yoo-Hoos from his parka pockets and hands me one. My heart lurches. YOO-HOOS! God, I love this man. Who wouldn't? "If that kid lives to graduation, I'll be surprised. So. How you hanging in there? I mean, with the dead girl."

I've sunk my teeth into the crunchy baguette—filled with freshly made smoked mozzarella, garlicky roasted peppers, and sun-dried tomatoes. It is impossible to speak after that, of course, because the inside of my mouth is having an orgasm.

"I actually put in a call," Cooper goes on, seeing that my

mouth is full (though ignorant, hopefully, of all the fireworks going on inside of it), "to a friend at the coroner's office. They got over there pretty quickly, you know, on account of business being slow, thanks to this storm we're supposed to get. Anyway, they're pretty sure she was dead well before she was . . . well, you know."

Decapitated. I nod, still chewing.

"I just thought you'd want to know," Cooper goes on. He's unwrapping a sandwich of his own. Prosciutto, I think. "I mean, that she didn't . . . suffer. They're pretty sure she was strangled."

I swallow. "How can they tell?" I ask. "Considering . . . well, there's no neck?"

Cooper has just taken a bite of his own sandwich as I ask this. He chokes a little, but manages to get it down.

"Discoloration," he says, between coughs. "Around the eyes. It means she quit breathing before death occurred, due to strangulation. They call it vagal inhibition."

"Oh," I say. "Sorry." I mean about making him choke.

He swills some Yoo-Hoo. As he does, I have a chance to observe him without his noticing. He hasn't shaved this morning . . . not that it matters. He's still one of the hottest-looking guys I've ever seen. His five o'clock—more like noon—shadow just makes the angular planes of his face more defined, bringing into even more definition his lean jaw and high cheekbones. Some people—like his father, Grant Cartwright—might think Cooper needs a haircut.

But I like a guy with hair you can run your fingers through.

You know, if he'd let you.

Still, though to me that slightly overlong dark hair gives him the appearance of a friendly sheepdog, Cooper must strike an imposing figure to others. This becomes obvious when a homeless guy carrying a bottle in a paper bag, coming into the hospital to get out of the cold for a little while, spies an empty chair next to me and wanders toward it . . .

. . . only to change his mind when he gets a look at Cooper's wide shoulders—made even more intimidating-looking by the puffiness of his anorak—and massive Timberlands.

Cooper doesn't even notice.

"They think she'd been there awhile," he says, having successfully forced down whatever it was he'd been choking on. "On the, er, stove. Since before dawn, at least."

"God," I say.

But though back in the dorm—I mean, residence hall—I couldn't think about what had happened to Lindsay without feeling a wave of nausea, I have no trouble finishing my sandwich. Maybe it's because I really *was* starving.

Or maybe it's because of Cooper's soothing presence. Love does funny things to you, I guess.

Speaking of love . . .

My cell phone chirps, and when I take it out of my pocket, I see that Jordan is calling me. Again. I hastily shove the phone back into the recesses of my coat.

Not quickly enough, though.

"He must really need to talk to you about something," Cooper says mildly. "He left a message at home, too."

"I know," I say sheepishly. "I heard it."

"I see." Cooper looks amused about something . . . at least by the way the corners of his mouth curl up beneath the quarter inch of dark fuzz growing around them. "And you aren't calling him back because . . . ?"

"Whatever," I say, annoyed. But not with Cooper. I'm annoyed with his brother, who refuses to realize that a breakup is just that: a breakup. You don't keep on calling your ex, especially when you're engaged to someone else, after you've broken up. I mean, it's common courtesy.

I guess it doesn't help that I keep sleeping with him. Jordan, I mean.

But seriously, it was just that one time on Cooper's hallway runner, and in a moment of total weakness. It's not like it's ever going to happen again.

I don't think.

I guess you could also say I'm a little annoyed with myself.

"So did you know her?" Cooper asks, artfully changing the subject, most likely because he can tell it's not one I'm relishing.

"Who? The dead girl?" I take a slug of Yoo-Hoo. "Yeah. Everyone did. She was popular. A cheerleader."

Cooper looks shocked. "They have cheerleaders in college?"

"Sure," I say. "New York College's team made it to the finals last year."

"The finals of what?"

"I don't know," I admit. "But they're proud of it. Lindsay—that's the dead girl—was especially proud of it. She was studying to be an accountant. But she had tons of school spirit. She—" I break off. Even Yoo-Hoo doesn't help this time. "Cooper. Who would *do* something like that to someone? And *why*?"

"Well, what do you know about this girl?" he asks. "I mean, besides that she was a cheerleader studying to be an accountant?"

I think about it. "She was dating one of the basketball players," I say, after a while. "In fact, I think he might be a suspect. Detective Canavan seems to think so, anyway. But he didn't do it. I *know* he didn't. Mark's a nice kid. He'd never kill anyone. And certainly not his girlfriend. And not that *way*."

"It's the *way* that strikes me as . . ." Cooper shrugs beneath his anorak. "Well, the word *overkill* comes to mind. It's almost as if the killer left her that way as a warning."

"A warning to who?" I ask. "Jimmy the line cook?"

"Well, if we knew that," Cooper says, "we'd have a good idea who did it, wouldn't we? And why. Canavan's right to start with the boyfriend. He any good? As a ballplayer, I mean?"

I look at him blankly. "Coop. We're Division Three. How good can he be?"

"But the Pansies have been playing a lot better since they got that new coach, this Andrews guy," Cooper says, with a slight smile . . . I guess at my sports ignorance. "They've even started broadcasting the games. Locally only, I know. But still. I take it tomorrow night's game will be canceled, in light of all this?"

I snort. "Are you kidding? We're playing the New Jersey East Devils at home. Don't you know we're eight-and-oh?"

Cooper's smile broadens, but his voice is tinged with frost. "The head of one of the cheerleaders was found in her dorm cafeteria, but they aren't canceling tomorrow night's ball game?"

"Residence hall," I correct him.

"Heather Wells?" A doctor has come out of the ER, holding a clipboard.

"Excuse me," I say to Cooper, and hurry over to the ER doc, who informs me that Gavin is recovering nicely and that she's releasing him. He'll be out as soon as he's signed the appropriate forms. I thank the doctor and return to Cooper's side, only to find he's already on his feet, scooping up the debris from our picnic and stuffing it into a nearby trash can.

"Gavin's ready to go," I say to him.

"So I gathered." Cooper pulls his gloves back on, readying himself for the plunge back into the arctic weather. "You guys need a lift back?"

"I doubt Gavin's up to walking," I say. "But we'll grab a cab. I'm not running the risk of him barfing in your car."

"For which I thank you," Cooper says gravely. "Well, see you at home, then. And, Heather . . . about Lindsay—"

"Don't worry," I interrupt. "In no way am I going to interfere with the investigation into her death. I totally learned my lesson last time. The NYPD is on their own with this one."

Cooper looks serious. "That wasn't what I was going to say," he informs me. "It never occurred to me that you would even consider getting involved in what happened at Fischer Hall today. Especially not after what happened last time."

It's ridiculous. And yet, I feel stung.

"You mean last time, when I figured out who the killer was before anybody else did?" I demand. "Before anyone else even realized those girls were *being* killed, and not dying of their own recklessness?"

"Whoa," Cooper says. "Slow down, slugger. I just meant—"

"Because you do realize that whoever did this to Lindsay had to have access to the keys to the caf, right?" I don't care that the homeless guy with the bottle-in-the-bag is now giving ME the wary eye he'd given Cooper just minutes before. What I lack in shoulder breadth, I make up for with hip girth. Oh, and pure shrillness.

"Because there was no sign of forced entry," I go on. "Whoever put Lindsay's head in there had to have had access to a master key. We're talking about three or four individual locks. No one could've picked three or four different locks, not in one night, not without somebody noticing. So it *had* to be somebody who works for the school. Somebody with access to the keys. Somebody I KNOW."

"Okay," Cooper says, in a soothing voice . . . probably the same voice he uses on his clients, hysterical wives who are convinced their husbands are cheating on them, and need to hire him to prove it in order to get custody of the Hamptons beach house. "Calm down. Detective Canavan is on it, right?"

"Right," I say. I don't add that my faith in Detective Canavan's investigative skills is not high. I mean, I *did* almost die once because of them.

"So don't worry about it," Cooper says. He's laid a hand on my shoulder. Too bad I'm wearing so much—coat, sweater, turtleneck, undershirt, bra—I can barely even feel it. "Whoever it was, Canavan'll catch him. This isn't like last time, Heather. Last time, no one but you was even sure there'd been a crime. This time . . . well, it's pretty obvious. The police will take care of it, Heather." His fingers tighten on my shoulder. His gaze is intent on mine. I feel like I could dive into those blue eyes of his and just start swimming, and go on and on and never reach the horizon.

"Yo, Wells."

Trust Gavin McGoren to pick *that* moment to come limping out of the ER.

"This guy bothering you, Wells?" Gavin wants to know, thrusting his wispily goateed chin in Cooper's direction.

I restrain myself—barely—from hitting him. College staff is forbidden from striking students, no matter how sorely tempted we might be. Interestingly, we aren't allowed to kiss them, either. Not that I've ever wanted to, at least where Gavin is concerned.

"No, he isn't *bothering* me," I say. "This is my friend Cooper. Cooper, this is Gavin."

"Hey," Cooper says, holding out his right hand.

But Gavin just ignores the hand.

"This guy your *boyfriend*?" he demands of me, rudely.

"Gavin," I say, mortified. I can't look anywhere in the vicinity of Cooper's face. "No. You know perfectly well he's not my boyfriend."

Gavin seems to relax a little. "Oh, that's right," he said. "You like those pretty-boy types. Jordan Cartwright. Mr. Easy Street."

Cooper has dropped his hand. He is staring at Gavin with an expression of mingled amusement and derision. "Well, Heather," he says. "Delightful as it's been meeting one of your infant charges, I think I'll be going now."

"Hey!" Gavin looks insulted. "Who you calling an infant?"

Cooper barely acknowledges Gavin's presence, saying only, "I'll see you at home," to me, with a wink, then turning to leave.

" 'See you at home'?" Gavin is staring daggers at Cooper's departing back. "You guys live together? I thought you said he wasn't your boyfriend!"

"He's my landlord," I say. "And he's right. You *are* an infant. Ready to go? Or do you want to stop by the liquor store on the way back to the hall so you can buy a bottle of Jägermeister and finish off the job?"

"Woman," Gavin says, shaking his head, "why you gots to be that way? Always up in my business?"

"Gavin." I'm rolling my eyes. "Seriously. I'll call your parents. . . ."

He drops the gangbanger act at once.

"Don't," he says, the goatee drooping. "My mom'll kill me."

I sigh and take his arm. "Come on, then. Let's get you home, before it starts snowing. Did you get a note from the doctor, to excuse you from class?"

He scowls. "They won't give notes for alcohol poisoning."

"Poor baby," I say cheerfully. "Maybe this will teach you a lesson."

"Woman," Gavin explodes again, "I don't need you to tell me how to act!"

And we walk out into the cold together, bickering like a brother and sister. At least, *I* think that's how we sound.

Little do I know Gavin thinks something entirely different.

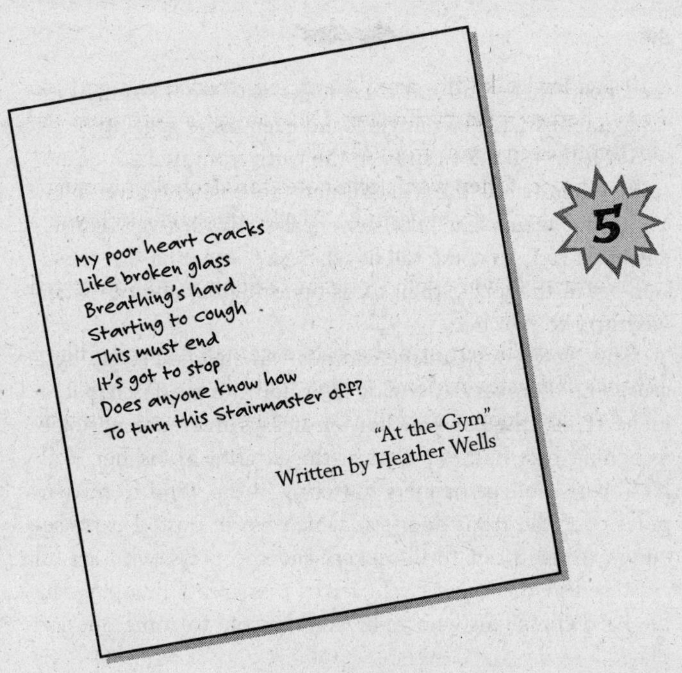
5
My poor heart cracks
Like broken glass
Breathing's hard
Starting to cough
This must end
It's got to stop
Does anyone know how
To turn this Stairmaster off?
"At the Gym"
Written by Heather Wells

The rest of the day does not exactly fly by. It's amazing, in fact, how slowly time can pass when all you want to do is go home.

At least, when I get back to Fischer Hall from the hospital, the deed has been done—Lindsay's family has been notified of her death . . . which means it's okay for us to start telling the building staff and residents about what happened to her.

But this, as I'd suspected, does not exactly make things any better. Reactions upon being told the truth—that the cafeteria is closed because of the discovery of a cheerleader's severed head there, and not a gas leak—vary from stunned astonishment to giggling, crying, and even some gagging.

But it isn't like we can keep the truth from them . . . especially when it hits the local all-news television station, New York One, which Tina, the student desk worker, very conscientiously runs to come tell us when she sees it on the television set in the lobby, then turns up as high as she can when we hurry to join her:

"The New York College campus was shocked today by a gruesome discovery at one of their dormitories, Fischer Residence Hall," the news anchorperson says, in an urgent voice, as behind him flashes a shot of the exterior of Fischer Hall, New York College banners fluttering in the wind from twin poles over the front door—at which we've posted extra security, to keep out thrill-seekers and the press, who are all clustered in the chess circle across the street, annoying the die-hard chess fans who've braved the cold to come out and play.

"Some may recall last fall's slayings of two young women in this very same dormitory," the reporter intones, "a tragedy that has led some on campus to refer to the building as Death Dorm."

I glance at Tom when the announcer says this. He presses his lips together, but otherwise says nothing. Poor guy. His first professional gig out of grad school, and it has to be at Death Dorm. I mean, residence hall.

"This morning, Fischer Hall cafeteria workers arrived at work to make another grisly discovery: a human head in a pot on the school stove."

This is met by a collective "EW!" by Tina and most of the rest of the students—not to mention a few administrators—gathered in the lobby to watch the broadcast. Tom actually groans and drops his face in his hands in anguish. Pete, the security officer, doesn't look too happy, either.

"The head has been positively identified by grieving family members as belonging to New York College sophomore and varsity cheerleader Lindsay Combs," the reporter goes on, as a photo of Lindsay fills the screen. It's the photo that was taken the night she was crowned Homecoming Queen. Her smile is as dazzling as the tiara in her honey-colored hair. She's dressed in white satin and holding a dozen red roses in her arms. Someone outside the frame of the photo had flung an arm around her shoulders and the tiara had tipped rakishly over one of Lindsay's unnaturally green eyes. I seriously don't understand why she thought this was a good look.

"According to witnesses, Lindsay was last seen yesterday evening. She left her room at approximately seven o'clock in the evening, telling her roommate she was going to a party. She never returned."

This much we already knew. Cheryl had come by the office in tears earlier, heartbroken over what had befallen her friend—and roommate . . . a roommate she'd never even gotten a chance to swap midnight giggles or shots of Southern Comfort with, since Lindsay had been dead before Cheryl ever even moved in.

Lindsay's original roommate, Ann, had taken the news a little less hysterically, and had been able to give the police their only lead . . . the one about the party. Of course, relations between Ann and Lindsay apparently not having been the best, the girl hadn't been able to tell Detective Canavan WHICH party Lindsay had been going to . . . and Cheryl, incoherent with sobs, hadn't been much help in that department, either. In fact, Tom had had one of the RAs escort Cheryl to Counseling Services, where she's hopefully getting the help she needs to cope with her grief . . . and the fact that she's pretty much guaranteed a single room for the rest of the year.

Of course, Cheryl is the one person on campus who didn't want one.

"How Lindsay ended up in the Fischer Hall cafeteria kitchen is a mystery that has authorities here baffled," the reporter goes on. The shot shifts to one of New York College President Phillip Allington standing at a podium in the library lobby, Detective Canavan looking rumpled and cranky at his side. Coach Andrews, for some reason, is standing on the president's other side, managing to look calm, but at the same time somewhat confused. But then, that's how a lot of athletic coaches look, I've noticed, as I've flipped past ESPN.

The anchorman's voice goes on, "A spokesperson from the New York City Police Department insists that even though no arrests have been made, the police have several suspects and are following more than a dozen leads. There is, college President Phillip Allington assured the academic community at a press conference earlier this afternoon, no need for alarm."

Footage from the press conference begins to run.

"We would like to take this opportunity," President Allington says woodenly, obviously reading from something that he'd had someone else write for him earlier in the day, "to reassure our students, and the public in general, that the law enforcement officials in this city are using every measure available to us to track down this vicious criminal. At the same time, we'd like to urge our students to take extra safety precautions until Lindsay's killer is apprehended. Although it is the goal of our residence halls to foster a feeling of community—which is why we call them residence halls and not dormitories—it's important for students to keep their doors locked. Do not allow strangers into your room or into any campus building. While the police believe this senseless crime to be, at this time, an isolated act of random violence, we cannot stress enough the necessity of exercising caution until the individual responsible is brought to justice. . . ."

No sooner were the words "keep their doors locked" out of President Allington's mouth than half the students in the lobby abruptly disappeared, heading toward the elevators with anxious looks on their faces. It's the habit of a lot of kids in buildings like Fischer Hall to leave the door to their room propped open to welcome drop-by visitors.

This is apparently about to change.

Of course, the fact that Lindsay hadn't been killed in her room didn't appear to occur to any of them. Any more than the fact that there hadn't been anything "random" about the act of violence that had ended Lindsay's life. Her killer had obviously known her—and also the Fischer Hall cafeteria—at least passably well.

But if this fact hadn't sunk in to the student population, it had been driven home to the cafeteria staff, who were only just now being allowed to go home after a day's worth of grueling questioning. I'm shocked to see them come streaming out of the cafeteria shortly after the end of President Allington's press conference, at quarter to five o'clock . . . well after those who were assigned to the breakfast shift usually got off work. Detective Canavan and his colleagues had really grilled them . . . no pun intended.

Still, tired as she must have been, Magda manages a smile as she comes toward me. She's slathered her fingers with Purel, and is wiping them with a Kleenex. As she gets closer, I see why: her fingertips are black with ink.

Magda's been printed.

"Oh, Magda," I say, when she's close enough. I put an arm around her shoulder, leading her out of the lobby and back toward my office, where it's quieter. "I'm so sorry."

"It's all right," Magda says, with a sniffle. The whites of her eyes are pink, her eyeliner and mascara smudged. "I mean, they are only doing their jobs. It isn't their fault one of my little movie stars—"

Magda breaks off with a sob. I hustle her into the hall office, where at least she'll be hidden from the inquiring gazes of the residents gathered in front of the elevator bank, home after their first day of classes—only to discover that they'll have to seek their evening meal elsewhere.

Magda sinks into the institutional orange couch in front of my desk and buries her head in her hands, sobbing. I hasten to shut the outer office door, which locks automatically when closed. Tom, having heard the disturbance, comes out of his own office and stands, looking at Magda uncomfortably as the words "Little movie star," and "Byootiful little baby" drift up incoherently from her knees, which is where she's sunk her face.

Tom looks at me. "What's the deal again with the movie star thing?" he whispers.

"I told you," I whisper back. For a gay guy, Tom can be surprisingly clueless sometimes. "They filmed a scene from *Teenage Mutant Ninja Turtles* here at Fischer Hall. Magda was working here at the time."

"Well." Tom stares at her some more as she cries. "It certainly seems to have made an impression. Considering it's a movie no one ever saw."

"People saw it," I say to him crossly. "Don't you have something you should be doing?"

He sighs. "I'm waiting for someone from Counseling Services. We're going to be holding grief counseling here in the office from five to seven, to help residents cope with what happened to Lindsay."

I don't say anything. I don't have to. He already knows.

"I told them no one was going to show up," he says beleagueredly. "Except maybe Cheryl Haebig and the RAs. But it came down from the president's office. The administration wants to look like we care."

"Well." I nod at a sobbing Magda. "Here's someone who needs some grief counseling."

Tom pales at my suggestion. "She's your friend," he says accusingly.

I glare at him. "You're the one with the master's degree."

"In college student personnel! I have to tell you, Heather." He looks frightened. "I don't know about this. I mean, any of this. Things were a lot simpler back in Texas."

I glare at him even harder. "Oh, no," I say. "You are *not* quitting on me, Tom. Not because of one little murder."

"Little!" Tom's face is still ashen. "Heather, nobody back home ever got their head whacked off and left in a pot on a stove. Sure, couple kids got crushed to death every year under the bonfire structure. But murdered? Honestly, Heather. Home's looking pretty good right now."

"Oh, right," I say sarcastically. "If it was so much better back there, how come you waited until you got here to come out of the closet?"

Tom swallows. "Well . . ."

"Let's talk about your quitting later, okay?" I flop down on the couch beside Magda. "I've got other things to worry about right now."

Tom throws Magda one last panicky look, then mutters,

"Okay, I'll just, um, finish up this paperwork," and disappears back into his office.

I sit beside Magda, resting a hand on her back as she cries. I know this is the right thing to do as a friend . . . but as someone who works in a helping field, I'm not sure this is what I'm supposed to do. *How could Dr. Jessup have hired someone like me?* I wonder. I mean, I know I'm the only who applied, and all. But I am thoroughly unfit for this job. I don't have the slightest idea what to do in the face of sorrow like Magda's. Where *is* that grief counselor, anyway?

"Magda," I say, patting her back through her pink cafeteria smock. "Um. Look, I'm sure they don't really suspect you. I mean, anyone who knows you knows you couldn't have had anything to do with . . . what happened. Really, don't worry about it. No one thinks you did it. The police are just doing their job."

Magda raises her tear-stained face to peer at me astonishedly.

"That's . . . that's not why I'm upset," she says, shaking her head until her—tiger-striped blond, this week—curls swing. "I *know* they're just doing their job. That's all right. None of us did it—none of us *could* do that."

"I know," I say hastily, still rubbing her back. "It's horrible of them to suspect you. But, you see—"

"It's just," Magda goes on, as if I hadn't spoken, "I heard . . . I heard it was *Lindsay*. But that couldn't be. Not little Lindsay, with the eyes, and the hair? The cheerleader?"

I stare at her. I can't believe she didn't recognize Lindsay back when she'd been looking into the pot. It's true I probably saw Lindsay more often than Magda did, on account of her affection for my condom jar. So it isn't any wonder I had no problem recognizing her. Is it?

Or is *this* the job I'm suited for? Recognizing the faces of dead people who've been boiled for a while? What kind of position would this even qualify me for? I mean, there can't be any demand for someone with a skill like this, except maybe in the few societies that are left that still practice cannibalism. *Are* there even any of these?

"Yes," I say, in answer to Magda's question. "Yes, I'm sorry. But it was Lindsay."

Magda's face crumples again. "Oh, no!" she says, with a wail. "Heather, no!"

"Magda," I say, alarmed by her reaction. Which, really, if you think about it, is way more natural than mine—which had been to flee the area for the warmth of the St. Vincent's ER. Or Sarah's, which had been to make bad jokes. "I'm so sorry. But if it's any consolation, Cooper told me the coroner thinks she was strangled first. I mean, she didn't die from . . . from having her head chopped off. That didn't happen until later."

Not surprisingly, Magda seems to find little comfort in this piece of information. I really do suck at grief counseling. Maybe I should go into accounting.

"It's just . . ." Magda sobs, "it's just that Lindsay—she was so sweet! She loved it here so much! She always wore her uniform on game days. She never did anything to anybody. She didn't deserve to die like that, Heather. Not Lindsay."

"Oh, Magda." I pat her arm. What else can I do? I notice that each of Magda's nails has been painted in the New York College school colors of gold and white. A major college basketball fan, Magda never misses a game, if she can help it. "You're right. Lindsay never did anything to deserve what happened to her." That we know of.

Oh, see? There it is again! Where does that kind of jaded cynicism even come from? It can't be because I'm a washed-up former pop star trying to put my life together, only to be told I have to take remedial math.

Can it?

"People are gonna try to make things up." Magda's gaze on mine is intense. "You know how people are, Heather. They're gonna try to say, *Well, she shouldn't have been seeing so many boys,* or something like that. But it wasn't Lindsay's fault she was so pretty and popular. It wasn't her fault boys buzzed around her like bees to honey."

Or flies around horse manure.

God, what is *wrong* with me? Why am I blaming the victim? I'm sure Sarah, if she were here, could tell me. Is it out of some desire to distance myself from what happened to Lindsay, so I can be, like, *Well, that could never happen to me, because the boys aren't exactly buzzing around* me *like bees to honey. So no one will ever strangle me and then chop* my *head off?*

Or is there some other reason I can't help thinking there might be something more to Lindsay's death than a "random act of violence"? Was she really all sunshine and school spirit? Or was she actually hiding something behind those iridescently green contact lenses?

Magda reaches out and grasps my hand in a grip so tight that it hurts a little. Her eyes—still swimming with tears—are bright as the rhinestones she sometimes has implanted in her nail tips.

"Listen to me, Heather." Magda's carefully lined lips tremble. "You've got to find the person who did this to her. You've got to find him, and bring him to justice."

I'm on my feet at once. But I can't go far due to Magda's death grip on my hand.

"Mags," I say. "Look, I appreciate your faith in my investigative abilities, but you've got to remember, I'm just the assistant hall director. . . ."

"But you're the only one who believed those other two girls, last semester, were murdered! And you were right! Smart as he is, that Detective Canavan, he couldn't've caught their killer—because he didn't even think they'd been killed. But you, Heather . . . you knew. You've just got this way with people. . . ."

"Oh," I say, rolling my eyes. "Yeah. Right."

"You may not think so, but you do. That's why you're so good at it. Because you don't *know* you can do it. I'm tellin' you, Heather, you're the only one who can catch the person who did this to Lindsay—who can prove she really was a nice girl. I'm begging you to at least *try*. . . ."

"Magda," I say. My hand is starting to sweat from her grip on it. "I'm not a cop. I can't involve myself in their investigation. I promised I wouldn't. . . ."

What is Magda even thinking? Doesn't she know that this guy, whoever it is, isn't shoving people down elevator shafts? He's strangling them, and chopping their heads off, then hiding their bodies. Hello, that is a lot different. It's a lot more deadly, somehow.

"That little pom-pom girl has the right to a good and proper rest," Magda insists. "And she can't have it until her murderer is found and brought to justice."

"Magda," I say uncomfortably. How would a grief counselor respond, I wonder, if one of his patients demanded that he solve the brutal slaying of the individual the patient was grieving over? "I think you've been watching a few too many episodes of *Unsolved Mysteries*."

Apparently this was not the proper way to respond, since Magda just clutches my hand harder and says, "Will you just think on it, Heather? Just think on it for a while?"

Magda had once told me that, in her youth, she had been a beauty queen, runner-up for Miss Dominican Republic two years in a row. It isn't actually that hard to believe now, as she gazes up at me with all the intensity of a pair of headlights set on high. Beneath all that makeup, the drawn-on eyebrows, and the six-inch-high hair, there's a dainty loveliness that the entire contents of the Duane Reade cosmetics aisle couldn't hide.

I sigh. I've always been a sucker for a pretty face. I mean, that's how I ended up saddled with Lucy, for God's sake.

"I'll think about it," I say, and am relieved when Magda loosens her grip on my hand. "But I'm not promising anything. I mean, Magda . . . I don't want to get *my* head chopped off, either."

"Thank you, Heather," Magda says, her smile beatific despite the fact that her lipstick is smeared. "Thank you. I'm sure Lindsay's spirit will rest easier knowing that Heather Wells is looking out for her."

I give Magda a final pat on the shoulder and with a little smile she gets up to go, wandering down the hallway to the dining office, where the staff hangs their coats. I look after her, feeling . . . well, a little strange.

Maybe that's because all I've had to eat today is a smoked mozzarella sandwich—with roasted peppers and sun-dried tomatoes, which are sort of vegetables, I guess—and a grande café mocha.

Then again, maybe it's because I've made her feel so much better, and I don't even know how. Or, actually, because I *do* know how. I just can't believe it. Does she honestly think I'm going to launch my own private investigation into Lindsay's death? If so, she's been inhaling way too much nail-gel dust.

I mean, what am I supposed to do, go around looking for

a guy with a cleaver and a girl's body in a fresh grave in his backyard? Yeah, right. And get my head chopped off, too. The whole thing is ridiculous. Detective Canavan isn't stupid. He'll find the killer soon enough. How can anyone hide a headless corpse? It's going to have to turn up sometime.

And when it does, I just hope I'm somewhere far, far away.

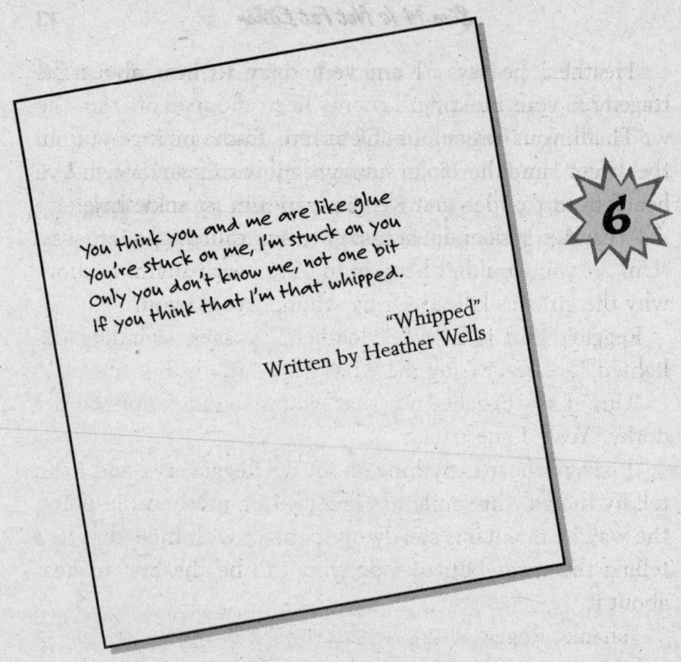

You think you and me are like glue
You're stuck on me, I'm stuck on you
Only you don't know me, not one bit
If you think that I'm that whipped.
"Whipped"
Written by Heather Wells
6

It still isn't snowing by the time I leave work, but it *is* pitch-black outside, even though it's just a little past five o'clock. The news crews are still parked along Washington Square Park, across the street from Fischer Hall—in fact, there are more of them than ever, including vans from all the major networks, and even CNN . . . just as President Allington had predicted.

The presence of the news vans isn't doing much to deter the drug trafficking in the park, though. In fact, I run into Reggie as I turn the corner to Cooper's brownstone. Although at first he hisses, "Sens, sens," to me, when he recognizes me, his expression turns grave.

"Heather," he says. "I am very sorry to hear about the tragedy in your building."

"Thank you, Reggie." I blink at him. In the pink glow from the street lamp, he looks surprisingly harmless, though I've heard from Cooper that Reggie carries in an ankle holster a .22 that he has, upon occasion, been called upon to use. "Um . . . you wouldn't happen to have heard anything about why the girl was killed? Or by whom? Would you?"

Reggie's grin is broad. "Heather," he says, sounding delighted, "are you asking me what the word on the street is?"

"Um," I say. Because put that way, it sounds so terrifically dorky. "Yeah. I guess I am."

"I haven't heard anything about it," Reggie says, and I can tell by the way his smile has faded—but, more to the point, the way he maintains steady eye contact with me—that he's telling the truth. "But if I do, you will be the first to hear about it."

"Thanks, Reggie," I say, and start back down the street . . . only to pause when I hear Reggie call my name.

"I hope you are not thinking about getting involved in whatever this young lady was messing with, Heather," he says to me. He's not smiling at all now. "Because you can bet she was messing with something . . . and that is what got her killed. I would not like to see that happen to a nice lady like yourself."

"Thanks, Reggie," I say. Which is not what I want to say. What I want to say is, *I wish people would have a little faith in me. I'm not* that *stupid*. But I know everyone is only trying to be nice. So instead I say, "Don't worry, I'm leaving the investigating to the professionals this time. Anything you tell me that you hear, I'm taking straight to them."

"That's good," Reggie says. And then, seeing a group of

typical West Village dot commers, he hastens away from me, murmuring, "Smoke, smoke. Sens, sens," at them.

I smile after him. It's always nice to see someone so dedicated to his calling.

When I finally finish undoing all the locks to the front door of Cooper's brownstone, I can barely get it open because of all the mail that's piled up beneath the slot. Turning on the lights—Cooper must still be away on his little stakeout—I scoop up the enormous pile, grumbling at all the coupon packs and AOL trial disks. I'm asking myself why we don't ever get any *real* mail—just bills and savings offers—when Lucy comes careening down the stairs, having heard me come in. In her jaws is a Victoria's Secret catalog that she's apparently spent the afternoon savaging into a droolly mess.

Lucy is truly a remarkable animal, given this special ability she has of singling out the sole catalog most likely to make me feel inadequate, and destroying it before I ever even get a chance to open it.

It's as I'm trying to wrestle it away from Lucy—to keep her from leaving chunks of Heidi Klum's torso all over the place—that the hallway phone rings, and I pick it up without even checking the caller ID.

"Hello?" I say distractedly. There is dog spit all over my fingers.

"Heather?" The voice of my ex-fiancé—sounding worried—fills my ear. "Heather, it's me. God, where have you been? I've been trying to reach you all day. There's something . . . there's something I really need to talk to you about—"

"What is it, Jordan?" I ask impatiently. "I'm kind of busy." I don't say what I'm busy doing. He doesn't need to know I'm busy trying to get my dog to stop eating a lingerie catalog. Let him think I'm busy being made love to by his brother.

Ha. I wish.

"It's just," Jordan says, "Tania told me the other day that you RSVP'd no to the wedding."

"That's right," I say. I'm starting to piece together what all this might be about. "I have plans on Saturday."

"Heather." Jordan sounds wounded.

"Seriously, I do," I insist. "I have to work. It's check-in day for the transfer students."

This isn't a complete lie. Check-in day for the transfer students is on a Saturday. It's just that it was last Saturday, not this coming Saturday. Still, Jordan will never know that.

"Heather," he says, "my wedding is at five o'clock. Are you telling me you will still be working at five o'clock?"

Damn!

"Heather, I don't understand why you don't want to come to my wedding," he goes on. "I mean, I know things were rocky between us for a while—"

"Jordan, I walked in on you getting head from the bride-to-be," I remind him. "Which, at the time, I mistakenly thought *I* was. So I think my indignation was pretty understandable."

"I realize that," Jordan says. "And that's why I thought you might feel . . . awkward about coming. To the wedding, I mean. That's why I'm calling, Heather. I want to make sure you know how important you are to me, and how important your coming to the wedding is to me, and to Tania, too. She still feels terrible about what happened, and we'd really like to show you how truly—"

"Jordan." By this time, I've made it into the kitchen with the cordless phone clutched in one hand, Lucy trailing behind me with her tongue lolling excitedly. After throwing away the damp Victoria's Secret catalog, I flip on the light and reach for the handle to the fridge. "I'm not going to your wedding."

"See," Jordan says, sounding frustrated, "I knew that's what you were going to say. That's why I called. Heather, don't be this way. I really thought we'd managed to put all that behind us. My wedding is a very important event in my life, Heather, and it's important to me that the people I care about are there with me when it happens. *All* the people I care about."

"Jordan." There, behind the milk (I went grocery shopping yesterday, when I heard about the impending blizzard, so the milk carton is full and actually well before the expiration date, for once), it sits: a white cardboard box of leftover bodega fried chicken. In other words, a box of heaven. "I'm not going to your wedding."

"Is it because I'm not inviting Cooper?" Jordan wants to know. "Because if it is—if it means that much to you—I'll invite him, too. Heck, you can bring him as your escort. I don't understand what it is you see in him, but I mean, the two of you *are* living together. If you really want to bring him—"

"I'm not bringing your brother to your wedding, Jordan," I say. I've removed the white cardboard box from the fridge, along with a hunk of goat's milk gouda from Murray's Cheese Shop, a hard red apple, and the milk. I'm holding the phone to my face with my shoulder, and have to kick the fridge door to get it to close. Lucy is not helping by sticking to my side like glue. She loves bodega fried chicken (peeled from the bone) as much as the next person. "Because I'm not going to your wedding. And quit acting like you want me there because you care, Jordan. I know perfectly well your publicist suggested I come, to make it look like I've forgiven you for cheating on me, and that we're pals again."

"That's not—" Jordan sounds affronted. "Heather, how can you imply such a thing? That is totally ridiculous."

"Is it?" I plonk everything I've gathered from the fridge onto the butcher-block kitchen table, then grab a plate and a glass and sit down. "Didn't your solo album tank? And wasn't it partially because your boy-next-door image got slightly tarnished by all the headlines when it got out that you'd been cheating on me, the Mall Princess, with your dad's latest discovery?"

"Heather," Jordan cuts me off tersely. "No offense, but the American public's memory is not quite that sharp. By the time you and I split, you hadn't had an album out in years. It's true you were once beloved by a certain segment of the population, but that segment has long since moved on—"

"Yeah," I say, stung in spite of myself. "They've moved on to wanting nothing to do with either of us. Good thing you're attaching yourself to Tania's shiny star. Just don't ask me to watch you do it."

"Heather." Now Jordan sounds long-suffering. "Why do you have to be this way? I thought you'd forgiven me for what happened with Tania. It certainly seemed as if you'd forgiven me that night in Cooper's hallway—"

I feel myself blanch. I can't believe he has the nerve to bring that up.

"Jordan." My lips feel numb. "I thought we agreed we were never going to speak about that night again." Never speak of it, and never, ever allow it to happen again.

"Of course," Jordan says soothingly. "But you can't ask me to act like it didn't happen. I know you still have feelings for me, Heather, just like I still have feelings for you. That's why I really want you there—"

"I'm hanging up now, Jordan."

"No, Heather, wait. That thing I saw on the news just now, about some girl's head. Was that your dorm? What the hell kind of place do you work in, anyway? Some kind of death dorm?"

" 'Bye, Jordan," I say, and press OFF.

I put down the phone and reach for the chicken. Lucy takes up position at my side, alert for any food that might not make it from my plate to my lips, and instead fall haphazardly onto my lap or the floor. We work as a team that way.

I know there are some people out there who prefer their fried chicken hot. But they've probably never had the fried chicken from the bodega around the corner from Cooper's brownstone—or, as Cooper and I call it, bodega fried chicken. Bodega fried chicken isn't just for everyday consumption. It's definitely comfort food on a different scale than your ordinary fried chicken, your KFC or Chicken McNuggets. I'd bought a nine-piece the day before, knowing today would be hellish, on account of it being the first day of the new semester.

I just hadn't anticipated it would be *this* hellish. I might have to eat all nine pieces myself. Cooper was just going to have to suffer. A little salt, and . . .

Oh. Oh, yes. No mouth orgasm, but close enough.

I'm plowing through my second bodega fried chicken leg—Lucy starting to whimper because I haven't dropped anything yet—when the phone rings again. This time—after I've wiped my hands on a paper towel—I check the caller ID before answering. I'm relieved to see that it's my best friend, Patty. I answer on the second ring.

"I'm eating bodega fried chicken," I tell her.

"Well, I certainly would if I were you, too"—Patty's voice, as always, is as warm and comforting as cashmere—"considering the day you've had."

"You saw the news?" I ask.

"Girl, I've seen the news *and* the newspapers from this morning. And you will not believe who called me a little while ago."

"Oh, my God, he called you, too?" I'm stunned.

"What do you mean, me, too? He called *you*?"

"To make sure I was coming. Even though I RSVP'd no."

"No!"

"Yes! Then he even said I could bring Cooper as my date."

"Holy Christ." That's what I love about Patty. She knows all the appropriate responses. "His publicist must have put him up to it."

"Or Tania's," I say, finishing off the chicken leg and reaching into the box for a thigh. I know I should probably eat the apple instead. But I'm sorry, an apple just isn't going to cut it. Not after the day I've had. "It would make her look like less of a skank if I showed up. Like I don't blame her for breaking Jordan and me up."

"Which you don't."

"Well, we were destined for Splitsville, USA, anyway. Tania just hastened our arrival. Still, I'm not going. How gross would that be? It's all well and good to invite the ex, to show there's no hard feelings and all. But the ex isn't supposed to actually *go*."

"I don't know," Patty says. "It's the in thing to go now. According to the Styles section in the *Times*."

"Whatever," I say. "I haven't been stylish since the nineties. Why should I start now? You're not going, are you?"

"Are you insane? Of course not. But, Heather, can we

please talk about what happened in your dorm today? I mean, residence hall. Did you know that poor girl?"

"Yeah," I say, picking a stringy chicken piece from between my teeth. Fortunately we're not on video phone. "Sort of. She was nice."

"God! Who would do such a thing? And why?"

"I don't know," I say. I break off a chunk of thigh meat for Lucy, after making sure it contains no cartilage or bone, and give it to her. She inhales it, then looks at me sadly, like, *Where'd it go?* "That's for the police to figure out."

"Wait." Patty sounds incredulous. "What did you just say?"

"You heard me. I'm not getting involved in this one."

"Good for you!" Patty takes the phone from her mouth and says to someone in the background, "It's all right. She isn't getting involved in this one."

"Say hi to Frank for me," I say.

"She says hi," Patty says to her husband.

"How's the new nanny working out?" I ask, since the two of them have just hired a real British nanny—a middle-aged one, because Patty swore what happened to Sienna Miller was never going to happen to her.

"Oh," Patty says. "Nanny is fine. We're both terrified of her, but Indy seems to adore her. Oh, Frank says to tell you that he's very proud of you. Leaving the murder investigation to the police . . . this shows real growth on your part."

"Thanks," I say. "Magda doesn't agree, though."

"What do you mean?"

"She thinks the cops are going to blame the victim. Which is probably true. I mean, even Reggie said something about what happened to Lindsay looking as if it might be retribution for something she did."

"Reggie . . . the drug dealer on *your street corner*?" Patty asks, in an incredulous voice.

"Yeah. He's going to ask around. You know, find out the word on the street for me."

"Heather," Patty says, "I'm sorry, I'm confused. But when you say things like that, it makes it sound like you really do plan on getting involved in the investigation."

"Well," I say, "I'm not."

There is a masculine mumble in the background. Then Patty says to Frank, "Fine, I'll ask her. But you know what she's going to say."

"Ask me what?" I want to know.

"Frank has a gig at Joe's Pub next week," Patty says, in a tense voice. "He wants to know if you'd like to join him."

"Of course I'll come," I say, surprised she feels like she has to ask. "I love that place."

"Um, not come to the performance," Patty says, still sounding tense. "He wants to know if you'll join him onstage."

I practically choke on the piece of chicken I'm swallowing. "You mean . . . *sing*?"

"No, perform a strip tease," Patty says. "Of course sing." Suddenly Frank's voice fills the phone.

"Before you say no, Heather," he says, "think about it. I know you've been working on your own stuff—"

"How do you know that?" I demand hotly, although I know perfectly well. Patty's mouth is even bigger than mine. She just doesn't tend to stuff hers with as many Dove Bars as I do mine, which is why she's a size 6 and I'm a 12. And growing.

"Never mind how I know," Frank says, ever the loyal husband. "You haven't been up on a stage in years, Heather. You've got to get back up there."

"Frank," I say, "I love you. You know I do. That's why I'm saying no. I don't want to ruin your gig."

"Heather, don't be like that. You got burned by that asshole Cartwright. Senior, not junior. But don't listen to him. I'm sure your stuff is great. And I'm dying to hear it. And the guy's'd get a kick out of playing it. Come on. It'll be a fun crowd."

"No, thank you," I say. I am trying to keep my tone light, so he won't hear the panic in my voice. "I think my songs are a little too angry-rocker-chick for a Frank Robillard crowd."

"What?" Frank sounds incredulous. "No way. They'll love you. Come on, Heather. When else are you going to get a chance to play the pub? It's a perfect venue for angry-rocker-chick stuff. Just you, a stool, and a microphone—"

Fortunately, at that moment, the call waiting goes off.

"Oops," I say. "That's the other line. I have to grab it. It could be Cooper."

"Heather. Listen to me. Don't—"

"I'll call you back." I click over to the other line, my relief over my narrow escape palpable. "Hello?"

"Heather?" a semi-familiar male voice asks hesitantly.

"This is she," I say, with equal hesitance. Because not that many guys I don't know call me. On account of I don't give out my home number. To anyone. Because no one ever asks for it. "Who is this?"

"It's me," the voice says, sounding surprised. "Your dad."

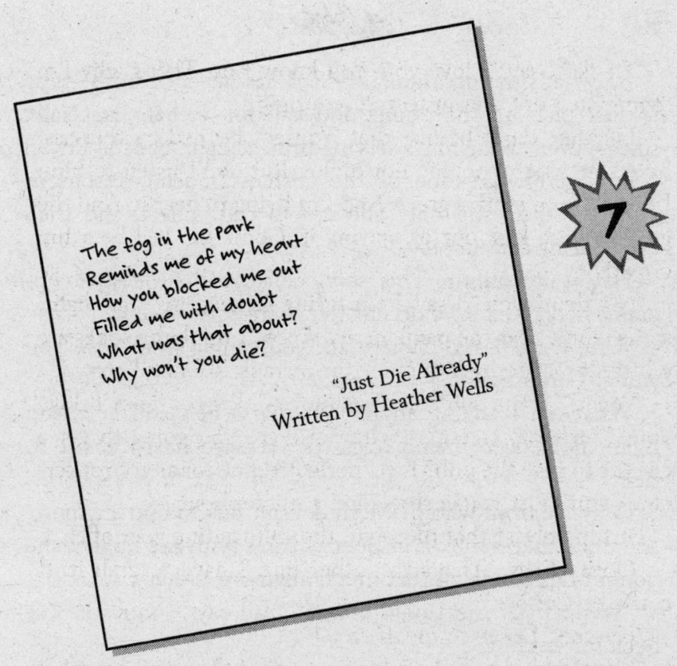
7
The fog in the park
Reminds me of my heart
How you blocked me out
Filled me with doubt
What was that about?
Why won't you die?
"Just Die Already"
Written by Heather Wells

I sit there in stunned silence for maybe three seconds.

Then I go, "Oh! Dad! Hi! Sorry, I didn't recognize your voice right away. It's—it's been a really long day."

"So I heard," Dad says. He sounds tired. Well, you would, too, if you were serving ten to twenty in a federal prison for tax evasion. "That's the dorm where you work, right? The one where they found the girl's head?"

"Residence hall," I correct him automatically. "And yeah. It was pretty upsetting." I'm frantically trying to figure out why he's calling. It's not my birthday. It's not a holiday. It's not *his* birthday, is it? No, that's in December.

So what's the occasion? My dad has never been the type to just pick up the phone and call for a chat. Especially since—even though he's serving time at Eglin Federal Prison Camp in Florida, one of the cushiest federal prisons in America—he's still only allowed to call collect, and then only during certain set—

Hey, wait a minute. This isn't a collect call. At least, no operator had asked if I'd accept the charges.

"Um, Dad," I say. "Where are you calling from? Are you still at Camp Eglin?"

What am I talking about? Of *course* he's still at Camp Eglin. If he were being released, I'd have heard about it, right?

Only . . . from whom? Mom doesn't talk to him anymore, and, now that she lives in Buenos Aires with my money, she doesn't talk to me all that much anymore, either. . . .

"Well, that's the thing, honey," Dad says. "You see, I've been released."

"Really?" I check to see how I feel about that. I am surprised to find that I feel . . . nothing. I mean, I love my dad, and all. But the truth is, I haven't seen him in so long—Mom would never take me to visit him, of course, since she hated his guts for losing all his money and forcing her to have to work (as my agent and promoter).

And once I got old enough to go by myself, I was too broke ever to make it to Florida. Dad and I were never that close, anyway . . . more like polite acquaintances, really, than parent and child. Thanks to Mom.

"Wow," I say, looking in the cardboard box to see how much dark meat is left. I am determined to save the breasts for Cooper, since they're his favorite. "That's great, Dad. So, where are you now?"

"Funny you should ask. I'm actually calling you from down the street—the Washington Square Diner. I was wondering if you wanted to get together for coffee."

Seriously. I just don't get it. I go for months—literally—where nothing at all unusual happens to me. My days are a blur of dog-walking, work, and *Golden Girl* reruns. And then WHAM! In one day, I find a head in a pot on a stove; get asked to play my songs at Joe's Pub with none other than super-mega-rock-star Frank Robillard; and my dad gets out of jail, shows up in my local coffee shop, and asks to see me.

Why can't things happen a little at a time? Like one day I find the head; another day Frank asks me to jam with him onstage; and another day my dad calls to let me know he's out of jail and in my hometown.

But I guess we don't get to choose how things transpire.

Because if we did, I definitely wouldn't have eaten all that chicken before going to see my dad. Because the sight of him sitting there in that booth—before he notices me, so I have a chance to study him before he knows he's being observed—causes my gut to twist. Not in the same way it twisted when I saw Lindsay's head in that pot—that was horror. The sight of my dad just saddens me.

Maybe because *he* looks sad. Sad and thin. He's not the robust golf player I knew from two decades ago—the last time I saw him outside of Camp Eglin's visitors' center—but a sort of shell of that man, reed-thin, with graying hair and the even whiter beginnings of a beard and mustache.

Still, that face transforms when he glances my way and finally notices me in the doorway. Not that he is overcome with joy or anything. He just plasters a grin on his face—a grin that doesn't reach his sad, tired eyes—every bit as blue as my own.

And every bit as cautiously guarded.

What do you say to the father you haven't seen for so long, with whom your relationship has always been . . . well, nonexistent, even when you lived together?

I say, "Hey, Dad," and slide into the booth across the table from him. Because what else am I *supposed* to say?

"Heather," he says, and reaches across the table to squeeze my hand, once I've stripped off my gloves. His fingers feel warm against mine. I squeeze back, with a smile.

"So this is a surprise," I say. "When did you get out?"

"Last week," he says. "I thought about calling you then, but . . . well, I wasn't sure you'd be too happy to see me."

"Of course I'm happy to see you, Dad." Dad's not the one I have a beef with. Well, not really. I mean, it wasn't exactly cool of him not to pay taxes all those years. But it wasn't MY money he wasn't paying taxes on. Or, in the case of Mom, stole. "When did you get here? To the city, I mean?"

"This morning. I took the bus. Lovely way to see the country." The waitress comes up as he's saying this, and he looks at me questioningly. "Have you had dinner?"

"Oh, yes," I say. "I'm good. Just hot chocolate would be nice"—I say this last to the waitress—"with whipped cream."

Dad orders chicken noodle soup to go with his coffee. The waitress nods and goes away. She looks distracted. She's probably worrying about the impending snowstorm, which a weatherman on New York One, playing on the TV hanging over the counter, assures us is due at any moment.

"So," I say. "The bus." For some reason I can't stop thinking about Morgan Freeman's ride to freedom on that bus in the movie *The Shawshank Redemption*. Well, I guess it isn't too surprising. Morgan Freeman had been a prisoner, too. "Isn't that like a parole violation? I mean, for you to leave the state of Florida?"

"Don't worry about me, kiddo," Dad had said, patting my hand. "I've got things under control. For a change."

"Great," I say. "That's great, Dad."

"So what do you hear from your mother?" he wants to know. I notice that he doesn't make eye contact when he asks this. He busies himself adding more half and half to his coffee.

"Well," I say, "you mean since she took off for Buenos Aires with the contents of my bank account? Not a whole heck of a lot."

Dad purses his lips and shakes his head. Now he makes eye contact. "I'm sorry about that, Heather," he says. "You can't know how much. Your mother isn't like that. I don't know what could have come over her."

"Really? Because I have a pretty good idea," I say, as the waitress comes back with his soup and my hot chocolate.

"Oh?" Dad digs into his soup like it's his first food of the day. For such a skinny guy, he has a pretty good appetite. "What's that?"

"Her meal ticket lost her recording contract," I say.

"Oh, now, Heather," Dad says, looking up from his soup. "Don't say that. Your mother loves you very much. She's just never been a strong woman. I'm sure it wasn't her idea—taking your money, I mean. I'm positive that Ricardo character put her up to it."

And I'm positive it was the other way around, actually, but I don't say so, because I don't feel like getting into an argument about it.

"How about you?" I ask instead. "Have you heard from her?"

"Not in quite some time," Dad says. He opens one of the

packs of crackers that came with his soup. "Of course, given the way I let her down, I don't suppose I deserve to."

"I wouldn't beat yourself up over that one, Dad," I say, feeling that twinge in my stomach again. Only this time, I realize the twinge is actually north of my stomach. It's more in the vicinity of my heart. And it appears to be pity. "She hasn't exactly been Miss Parent of the Year herself."

Dad shakes his head over his soup. "Poor Heather," he says, with a sigh. "When they were handing out parents up in heaven, you certainly got the short end of the stick."

"I don't know," I say, surprised to find myself prickling a little. "I think I've done all right for myself. I mean, I've got a job, and a nice place to live, and . . . well, I'm getting my BA."

Dad looks surprised . . . but pleasantly so. "Good for you!" he says. "At New York College?"

I nod. "I get tuition remission through my job," I explain. "I have to take this remedial math course before I can start taking real courses, but—"

"And what are you going to study?" Dad wants to know. His enthusiasm about the subject takes me aback, a little. "Music? I hope you're studying music. You've always been so very talented."

"Uh," I say. "Actually, I was thinking more of criminal justice."

Dad looks startled. "Good heavens," he says. "Why? Do you want to be a policewoman?"

"I don't know," I say. I'm too embarrassed to tell him the truth . . . that I'd hoped, with a BA in criminal justice, Cooper might take me on as a partner in his business, and the two of us could detect crimes together. Like *Remington Steele*. Or *Hart to Hart*.

It's a little sad that all my fantasies are rooted in eighties television shows.

"You should study music theory," Dad says firmly. "To help with your songwriting."

I flush. I forgot that I sent Dad a tape of myself singing some of my own stuff for Christmas one year. What had I been thinking?

"I'm too old for a singing-songwriting career," I tell him. "I mean, have you seen those girls on MTV? I can't wear short skirts anymore. Too much cellulite."

"Don't be silly," Dad says dismissively. "You look fine. Besides, if you're self-conscious, you can just wear slacks."

Slacks. Dad kills me sometimes. He really does.

"It would be a shame," Dad says. "No, not just a shame—a sin—to let God-given talent like yours go to waste."

"Well," I say, "I don't think I have. I did the singing thing already. I think maybe now it's time to try a different talent."

"Criminal justice?" Dad looks confused. "That's a talent?"

"Well, at least one where no one's going to boo me off a stage," I point out.

"No one would dare!" Dad cries, laying down his spoon. "You sing like an angel! And those songs of yours—they're much better than some of that garbage I hear on the radio. That girl, going on about her lumps, or her humps, or whatever she's talking about. And that other one—that Tracy Trace, the one that old boyfriend of yours is marrying this weekend. Why, she's half naked in that video!"

I have to repress a smile. "Tania Trace," I correct him. "And that's the number one video on *TRL* right now."

"Well," Dad says firmly, "regardless. It's trash."

"What about you, Dad?" I ask, thinking I'd better change the subject before he gets too overexcited. "I mean, you were at Camp Eglin for . . . gosh. Almost twenty years. What are you going to do now that you're out?"

"I have a few irons in the fire," Dad says. "Some of which look quite promising."

"Yeah?" I say. "Well, that sounds good. Here in New York?"

"Yes," Dad says. But I notice he's gotten more hesitant in his replies. And he's not making eye contact with me anymore.

Uh-oh.

"Dad," I say. Because suddenly I have a new feeling in my stomach. And it isn't horror or pity. It's dread. "Did you really call me because you wanted to see me and catch up on old times? Or was there something else?"

"Of course I wanted to see you," Dad says, with some asperity. "You're my old daughter, for goodness' sake."

"Right," I say. "*But* . . ."

"What makes you think there's a *but*?" Dad wants to know.

"Because," I say, "I'm not nine anymore. I know there's always a *but*."

He lays down his spoon. Then he takes a deep breath.

"All right," he says. "There's a but."

Then he tells me what it is.

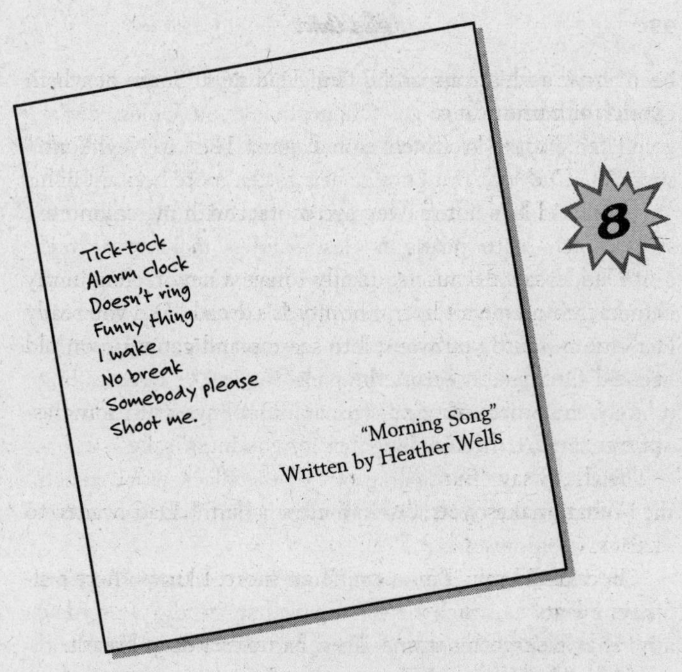

Tick-tock
Alarm clock
Doesn't ring
Funny thing
I wake
No break
Somebody please
Shoot me.
"Morning Song"
Written by Heather Wells
8

I'm fifteen minutes late to work the next day. Personally, I don't think fifteen minutes is all that long. Fifteen minutes shouldn't even count as tardy . . . especially when you take into account what happened to me the night before—you know, the whole return of the prodigal dad thing.

But fifteen minutes can be quite a long time in the life cycle of a residence hall. Fifteen minutes is long enough, in fact, for a representative from Counseling Services to find my desk and station herself at it.

And when I run breathlessly into the office and see her there, and go, "May I help you?" those fifteen minutes she's been at my desk are apparently long enough to make her feel enough at home at it to go, "Oh, no, thank you. Unless you're going for coffee, in which case I could use one, light, no sugar."

I blink at her. She's wearing a tasteful gray cashmere sweater set—with pearls, no less—and is making me feel quite underdressed in my professional wear of jeans and chunky cable-knit sweater. She doesn't even have hat hair. Her chestnut curls are swept into a perfect chignon. How the hell did she make it across the park—or, as I've been calling it lately, the Frozen Tundra—from Counseling Services without freezing her head off?

Then I spy them, sticking out of the black wool trench she's hung on the coat rack—on *my* peg. Earmuffs. Of course.

Tricky fashionista.

"Oh, Heather, there you are," Tom says, coming out of his office. He looks much better today than he did yesterday, now that he's gotten some sleep and actually washed and styled his blond hair. He is even wearing a tie.

And okay, he's wearing it with a bright pink oxford and jeans. But it's an improvement.

"This is Dr. Gillian Kilgore from Counseling Services," he goes on. "She's here to offer grief counseling to any residents who feel they might need it, in light of yesterday's events."

I smile briefly at Dr. Kilgore. Well, what else am I supposed to do? Spit at her?

"Hi," I say. "You're in my seat."

"Oh." Tom seems to notice for the first time where Gillian Kilgore has stationed herself. "That's right. That's Heather's desk, Dr. Kilgore. I meant for you to take the GA's desk—"

"I like this desk better," Dr. Kilgore stuns us both (I can tell Tom is stunned because his face goes as pink as his shirt) by saying evenly. "And of course, when students do come by for their appointments, Mr. Snelling, I'll be meeting with them in your office. For more privacy."

This is clearly news to Tom. He is standing there kind of bleating, like a lost sheep—*Baaah . . . baaah . . . but*—when Gillian Kilgore's first victim, I mean appointment, comes loping into the office. Mark Shepelsky is the Pansies' six-foot-seven power forward, and current resident of Room 212, one of the most sought-after doubles in the entire building due to its view of the park and the fact that, being on the second floor, its occupants can take the stairs instead of depending on the elevators, which are crowded at best, broken most of the rest of the time.

"Someone needed to see me?" Mark says. More like grunts, really. A skinny, pasty-skinned kid, he's good-looking in a crew-cutted ballplayer way.

But he can't hold a candle to Barista Boy, if you ask me.

Not that I like Barista Boy. Anymore.

"You must be . . ." Dr. Kilgore glances down at the appointment book open on her desk. Excuse me, I mean, *my* desk. "Mark?"

Mark shuffles his size-fourteen feet. "Yeah. What's this about?"

"Well, Mark," Dr. Kilgore says, slipping a pair of reading glasses over her nose, I guess in an attempt to look empathetic (it doesn't work), "I'm Dr. Kilgore. I'm here from Student Counseling Services. I understand that you were close with Lindsay. Lindsay Combs?"

Mark does not exactly break down in tears at the mention of his beloved's name. In fact, he looks indignant.

"Do we gotta do this?" he demands. "I already talked to the cops all day yesterday. I got a game tonight. I gotta practice."

Gillian Kilgore says soothingly, "I understand, Mark. But we're concerned about you. We want to make sure you're all right. Lindsay was, after all, important to you."

"Well, I mean, she was hot and everything," Mark says, looking confused. "But we weren't even dating. We were just playing. You know what I mean?"

"You two weren't exclusive?" I hear myself asking.

Both Tom and Gillian Kilgore turn to look at me, Dr. Kilgore with seeming annoyance, Tom with a wide-eyed, *Are you trying to get yourself in trouble?* look, which I ignore.

Mark says, "Exclusive? No way. I mean, we fooled around a little. I already told that detective dude, lately the only time I've seen her is at games, and over break I hardly saw her at all. . . ."

"Well, let's talk about that," Dr. Kilgore says, taking hold of Mark's arm and attempting to steer him toward Tom's office for some privacy (which, good luck, with that grate between his office and the outer one where I sit).

"Was Lindsay seeing anybody else?" I ask, before Mark can be pulled away.

He shrugs. "Yeah, I guess. I don't know. I heard she was doing—I mean, seeing—some frat guy."

"Really." I plunk down onto my desktop. "What frat?"

Mark looks blank. "I don't know."

"Well." It's hot in my office. I begin peeling off my coat. "Did you tell Detective Canavan about this?"

"He didn't ask."

"Mark." Gillian Kilgore's voice has gotten almost as cold as it is outside. "Why don't you step in here and we'll—"

"Detective Canavan didn't ask if you and your girlfriend were exclusive?" I demand incredulously. "And you didn't mention that you weren't?"

"No." Mark shrugs again. He's big with the shrugging, I see. "I didn't think it was important."

"Mark." Dr. Kilgore's voice is sharp now. "*Come with me, please.*"

Mark, looking startled, follows Dr. Kilgore into Tom's office. She practically slams the door behind them—but not before giving me a withering stare. Then, through the grate, we hear her say, "Now, Mark. Tell me. How are you feeling about all this?"

Has she not noticed the grate? Does she really think we can't hear her?

Tom looks at me, his expression noticeably miserable. "Heather," he says. We don't have to worry about Dr. Kilgore overhearing us, because she's chattering away so loud behind the grate. "What are you doing?"

"Nothing," I say. I get up from my desk and hang up my coat on the peg next to the one where Dr. Kilgore has hung hers. "Is it hot in here? Or is it just me?"

"It's hot," Tom says. "I turned the radiator off, but it's still . . . radiating. Seriously, though. What was all that about?"

"Nothing," I say, with a shrug. It's catching, I guess. "I was just curious. Have they reopened the caf?"

"Yes. For breakfast. Heather, are you—"

"Great. Have you had coffee yet?"

Tom sends a scowl in the direction of his office door. "No. I came in and *she* was already here. . . ."

"How'd she get in?" I ask in surprise.

"Pete let her in, with the master." Tom sighs. "Would you really bring me back a cup of coffee? With milk and sugar?"

"You got it," I say, with a smile.

"Have I told you today that you're my favorite assistant dorm director? Seriously?"

"Tom, Tom, Tom," I say. "Don't you mean I'm your favorite assistant RESIDENCE HALL director?"

Not surprisingly, when I get to the caf, it's practically empty. I guess the discovery of a severed head in the kitchen has a way of putting off your pickier eaters. Except for a few lone diners, I'm the only person in there. I stop by the register to say hi to Magda on my way in. She does not look good. Her eyeliner has already faded, and her lip liner is on crooked.

"Hey," I say to her, in my warmest voice. "How are you, Mags?"

She doesn't even crack a smile. "None of my little movie stars will come in," she says mournfully. "They're all eating at *Wasser Hall*." She says the words like they contain poison.

Wasser Hall, a residence hall across the park that was recently renovated to include its own pool in the basement, is our bitterest rival. After the press—and students—started calling Fischer Hall Death Dorm, I got a lot of calls from parents demanding their kids be moved to Wasser Hall. Can I just say that the assistant hall director there thinks she's all that because of it?

I got her back, though, during a trust exercise we were all required to do at in-staff training over Winter Break, when we each had to fall back into each other's arms and I accidentally-on-purpose dropped her.

"Well," I say soothingly, "it's only natural. They're scared. They'll come back after the police figure out who the killer is."

"*If* the police figure out who the killer is," Magda says gloomily.

"They will," I assure her. Then, to cheer her up, I add, "Guess who I had dinner with last night."

Magda brightens. "Cooper? He finally asked you for a date?"

It's my turn to look gloomy. "Um, no. My dad. He got out of jail. He's here, in the city."

"Your dad's out of the pen?" Pete is walking by, an empty coffee mug in his hand. He's on his way in for a refill. "No kidding?"

"No kidding," I say.

"So." Pete has forgotten about his coffee. He looks intrigued. "What'd you two talk about?"

I shrug. Damn that Mark and his contagious shrugging. "I don't know," I say. "Him. Me. Mom. A little of everything."

Magda is equally fascinated. She leans forward and says, "I read a book once where the man, he goes to prison, and when he gets out, he's . . . you know. Like your boss, Tom. On account of not having been with a woman in so long."

I raise my eyebrows. "I'm pretty sure my dad's not gay now, Magda," I say. "If that's what you mean."

Magda looks disappointed and leans back into her seat. "Oh."

"What's he want?" Pete asks.

"Want?" I stare at him. "He doesn't want anything."

"The man comes to see you first thing out of jail," Pete says, looking incredulous. "Says that he doesn't want anything from you . . . and you *believe* him? What's wrong with you?"

"Well," I say hesitantly. "He did say he just needed a place to stay for a few days while he gets on his feet."

Pete lets out a bark of *I told you so* laughter.

"What?" I cry. "He's my *father*. He raised me for my first ten years or so."

"Right," Pete says cynically. "And now he wants to mooch off your fame and fortune."

"What fortune?" I demand. "He knows perfectly well his ex-wife stole all my money."

Pete, chuckling, heads for the coffee machine.

"Why can't he just want to rebuild his relationship with the daughter he barely knows?" I shout after him. Which just makes him laugh harder.

"That's all right, honey," Magda says, patting my hand. "Ignore him. I think it's nice your daddy came back."

"Thank you," I say indignantly. "Because it is."

"Of course it is. And what did Cooper say when you asked him if your daddy could move in?"

"Well," I say, unable to meet Magda's gaze all of a sudden. "Cooper hasn't said anything about it yet. Because I haven't asked him."

"Oh," Magda says.

"Not," I say quickly, "because I don't believe my dad is totally on the up and up. I just haven't actually *seen* Cooper yet. He's busy with a case. But when I do see him, I'll ask. And I'm sure he'll say it's all right. Because my dad really wants to turn his life around."

"Of course," Magda says.

"No, Magda. I really mean it."

"I know you do, honey," Magda says. But her smile doesn't reach her eyes. Kind of like Dad's, as a matter of fact.

But that, I tell myself, has nothing to do with anything I've just said to her. It has to do with what happened yesterday, with Lindsay.

And as for Pete . . . well, let him laugh. What does *he* know?

Although considering he's a widower with five kids to support on his own, he might actually know quite a lot.

Dang.

Scowling, I head for the bagel bar and pop a plain in the toaster. Then I hit the coffee dispenser. I make one for Tom—

with cream and sugar—and one for me, half coffee, half hot cocoa, lots of whipped cream—then return to the bagel bar as mine pops up from the toaster, slather each side in cream cheese, slap on some bacon, then meld. Voilà, the perfect breakfast treat.

I put it on a plate, the plate on a tray with the coffees, and am heading out of the caf when I happen to spy, out of the corner of my eye, a flash of gold and white. I turn my head, and see Kimberly Watkins, one of the Pansies' varsity cheerleaders—in uniform because it's a game day—sitting by herself at a table, a large textbook open in front of her, alongside a plate appearing to contain an egg-white omelet and half a grapefruit.

And before I think about what I'm doing, I find myself plonking my tray across the table from hers and going, "Hey, Kimberly."

9
Touching me
Something always touching me
When I ride the subway.
"Subway Song"
Written by Heather Wells

"Um," Kimberly says, looking up at me suspiciously, clearly uncertain who I was, and why I was suddenly sitting across from her. "Hi?"

"I'm Heather," I say. "Assistant hall director?"

"Oh!" Kimberly's suspicious expression changes to one of recognition, even casual welcome. Now that she knows I'm not there to try to—well, whatever it was she thought I was there to do . . . hit on her? proselytize?—she seems to relax. "Hi!"

"Listen," I say. "I just wanted to see how you were doing. I mean, about this whole thing with Lindsay. I know you two were friends. . . ."

Actually, I don't know this. But I just assume two girls who were on the same cheerleading team would be friends. Right?

"Oh," Kimberly says, in a different tone, and the bright, Crest-Whitestrip smile she'd flashed me vanishes. "I know. It's so awful. Poor Lindsay. I . . . I can't even think about it. I cried myself to sleep last night."

For a girl who'd cried herself to sleep the night before, Kimberly looks pretty good. She apparently spent her break somewhere warm, because even though it's winter, Kimberly's bare legs are tanned. Apparently she isn't too concerned about the cold outside, or the blizzard New York One still insists we're supposed to be getting at any moment, but which has currently stalled over Washington, DC.

She doesn't seem too concerned about eating breakfast in the place where, twenty-four hours ago, her good friend's severed head was found, either.

"Wow," I say. "You must be devastated."

She crosses her long, coltish legs beneath the table and begins to twist a strand of her long black hair—straightened, naturally—around and around one finger.

"Totally," she says, her doe eyes wide. "Lindsay was, like, my best friend. Well, after Cheryl Haebig. But Cheryl doesn't really like to hang out anymore, 'cause, you know, she spends most of her free time with Jeff. Jeff Turner." Kimberly blinks at me. "You know Jeff, right? He's one of Mark's roommates, in Two-twelve."

"Sure, I know Jeff," I say. I know all the basketball players, they've been down to the office so many times for disciplinary hearings, primarily of the keg-smuggling variety. Fischer Hall is supposed to be dry.

"Well, the two of them, they're, like, practically married. They hardly ever want to party anymore."

And now that Cheryl's moved into Lindsay's room and will most likely not receive a new roommate, she and Jeff will be able to canoodle uninterrupted. . . .

But wait. That's no reason so kill someone.

"So, after Cheryl, Lindsay was your best friend," I say. "Gosh, that must be awful, to lose someone that close. I'm surprised you can—no offense—even eat in here."

Reminded of her food, Kimberly takes a big bite of her egg-white omelet. Inspired by this, I take a bite of my bacon-and-cream-cheese bagel. Mmm. *Heaven.*

"Yeah, well," Kimberly says, "I don't go in for ghosts, and all of that. When you're dead, you're dead."

"That's very practical of you," I say, after taking a sip of my cocoa-coffee.

"Well," Kimberly says, with a shrug, "I'm in fashion merchandising." And indicates the intimidating-looking textbook in front of her. *Introduction to Managerial Accounting.*

"Oh," I say. "So since you knew Lindsay so well, would you know of anyone who maybe had a grudge against her? Maybe wanted her out of the way? Enough to kill her, I mean?"

Kimberly twists the long strand of dark hair around her other finger for a while. "Well," she says slowly. "A lot of people hated Lindsay. I mean, they were jealous of her, and stuff. I did tell that policeman, the one who came by last night, about her roommate, Ann."

"Ann hated Lindsay?"

"Well, maybe not hate. But they didn't get along. That's why Lindsay was so psyched when Ann finally agreed to swap rooms with Cheryl. Even though Cheryl doesn't hang out with us much anymore, at least Lindsay didn't have to worry about all the stupid shit Ann was doing to annoy her."

"Stupid shit like what?" I ask, taking another bite of my bagel.

"Oh, just dumb stuff. Erasing messages people left for Lindsay on her dry-erase board on the door. Drawing devil horns on all of Lindsay's photos in the school paper before handing it to her. Using all of Lindsay's tampons and not replacing the box. Stuff like that."

"Well, Kimberly," I say, "it sounds like Ann and Lindsay didn't exactly get along. But you don't really think Ann actually killed her, do you? I mean, why would she? She knew she was moving out, right?"

Kimberly looks thoughtful. "Well, yeah, I guess. But anyway, I told that detective guy to make sure she's got a, whadduya call it? Oh, yeah, an alibi. 'Cause you never know. It could be one of the *Single White Female*–type thingies."

I'm sure Detective Canavan jumped on the "*Single White Female*–type thingie" lead. Not.

"What about boyfriends?" I ask.

This cognitive leap is too much for Kimberly's tender young brain to process. She knits her slender eyebrows in confusion. "What?"

"Was Lindsay seeing anybody? I mean, I know she was dating Mark Shepelsky. . . ."

"Oh." Kimberly rolls her eyes. "Mark. But Lindsay and Mark, I mean, they were pretty much over, you know. Mark's so . . . immature. Him and Jeff—you know, Cheryl's boyfriend—all they're into is drinking beer and watching sports. They never took Lindsay and Cheryl out clubbing, or whatever. Which I guess is fine for Cheryl, but Lindsay . . . she wanted more excitement. More sophistication, I guess you could say."

"So is that why she started seeing someone else?" I ask.

When Kimberly's eyes widen, I explain, "Mark stopped by the office this morning and mentioned something about a frat guy?"

Kimberly looks contemptuous. "Is that what Mark called him? A frat guy? He didn't mention he's a *Winer*?"

"A what?" For a minute, I think she's saying Lindsay's new boyfriend complains a lot.

"A Winer. W-I-N-E-R. You know." When I continue to regard her blankly, she shakes all her long hair in disbelief. "Gawd, don't you know? *Doug Winer*. The *Winer* family. Winer *Construction*. The Winer Sports Complex, here at New York College?"

Oh. Now I know what she's talking about. You can't pass by a building under construction in this city—and, despite the fact that Manhattan is an island and you'd think every piece of usable land on it has been developed already, there are quite a few buildings under construction—without noticing the word WINER written on the side of every bulldozer, spool of wire, and piece of scaffolding connected with the job site. No building in New York City goes up unless Winer Construction puts it up.

And apparently the Winers have earned a bit of money because of that fact. They may not be Kennedys or Rockefellers, but apparently, to a New York College cheerleader, they come close. Well, they did donate a big chunk of cash to the college. Enough to build the sports complex, and everything.

"Doug Winer," I repeat. "So . . . Doug's well off?"

"Um, if you call being filthy rich well off," Kimberly says, with a snort.

"I see. And were Doug and Lindsay . . . close?"

"Not engaged or anything," Kimberly says. "Yet. But Lindsay thought Doug was getting her a tennis bracelet for her birthday. A diamond one. She saw it in his dresser." Momentarily, the pathos of Lindsay's death strikes, and Kimberly looks a little less bubbly. "I guess he'll have to take it back now," she adds mournfully. "Her birthday was next week. God, that's so sad."

I agree that the fact Lindsay did not live to receive a diamond tennis bracelet for her birthday is a shame, then ask her if Lindsay and Doug had had any disagreements that she knew of (no), where Doug lives (the Tau Phi Epsilon House), and when Doug and Lindsay had last seen each other (sometime over the weekend).

It soon becomes clear that though Kimberly claims to have been Lindsay's best friend, either the two of them hadn't been all that close, or Lindsay had led a remarkably dull life, because Kimberly is unable to reveal anything more about Lindsay's last week on earth. Anything more that could help me to figure out who killed her, anyway.

Except, of course, that's not what I'm doing. I'm not getting involved in the investigation into Lindsay's death. Far from it. I'm just asking a few questions about it, is all. I mean, a person can ask questions about a crime without actually launching a private investigation into said crime. Right?

I'm telling myself this as I walk back into the hall director's office, holding Tom's coffee (I got him a new one, after the original went cold while I was talking to Kimberly) in one hand, and a new coffee-cocoa-whipped-cream concoction for myself in the other. I'm not too surprised to see that Sarah, our grad assistant, has shown up to work wearing an unhappy expression. Sarah's unhappy most days.

Today, her bad mood appears to be catching. Both she and Tom are slumped at their desks. Well, technically, Tom is slumping at *my* desk. But he looks plenty unhappy, until he sees me.

"You," Tom says, as I plop his coffee in front of him, "are a lifesaver. What took you so long?"

"Oh, you know," I say, sinking onto the couch next to my desk. "I had to comfort Magda." I nod at Tom's office door, which is still closed. Behind it, and through the grate, I hear the low murmur of voices. "She still in there with Mark?"

"No," Sarah says disgustedly. "Now she's in there with Cheryl Haebig."

"What's with you?" I ask Sarah, because of the scowl.

"Apparently," Tom replies in a long-suffering voice, since Sarah just sinks more deeply into her chair, refusing to speak, "Dr. Kilgore is one of Sarah's professors. And not one she likes very much."

"She's a Freudian!" Sarah bursts out, not even attempting to lower her voice. "She actually believes that sexist crap about how all women are in love with their fathers and secretly want a penis!"

"Dr. Kilgore gave Sarah a D on one of her papers last semester," Tom informs me, with only the tiniest of smirks.

"She's anti-feminist!" Sarah asserts. "I went to the dean to complain. But it was no use, because she's one of *them*, too." *Them*, apparently, referred to Freudians. "It's a conspiracy. I'm seriously considering writing a letter to the *Chronicle of Higher Education* about it."

"I've suggested," Tom says, still with that very slight smirk, "that if Dr. Kilgore's presence is such an aggrievance to Sarah, she take the petty cash vouchers over to Budget for disbursement. . . ."

"It's like five degrees outside!" Sarah yells.

"I'll go," I volunteer sweetly.

Both Sarah and Tom stare at me incredulously.

"Seriously," I say, setting down my coffee-cocoa and getting up to grab my coat. "I mean, it's not like I'll be able to get any work done, with you at my desk, Tom. And I could use some fresh air."

"It's like five degrees out!" Sarah shouts again.

"It's no big deal," I say. I wind my scarf around my neck. "I'll be back in a jiff."

I scoop up the petty cash vouchers sitting on Sarah's desk, and sail from the office. Out in the lobby, Pete starts laughing when he sees me. Not because I look comical in all my outside layers, but because he's remembering what I'd said about my dad.

Well? Why *can't* he just want to rebuild his relationship with the daughter he barely knows?

Seriously, with friends like Pete, who needs enemies?

Ignoring Pete, I go outside—and almost turn back, it's so cold. The temperature seems to have plummeted since my walk to work an hour ago. The cold sucks the breath from my chest.

But I've made up my mind. There's no turning back now.

Lowering my head against the wind, I start across the park, ignoring the offers of "smoke, smoke," from Reggie's compatriots as I make my way toward the other side of campus—the opposite direction from the Budget Office. Which also happens to be the direction from which the wind is blowing in subarctic blasts.

Which is why, when I hear my name being called out from behind me, I don't turn around right away. My ears are so numb beneath my knit cap, I think I must be hearing things. Then I feel a hand on my arm and whip around, expecting to see Reggie with his gold-toothed grin.

I don't think it's necessarily the wind that sucks away my breath when I see that it's Cooper Cartwright.

"Oh," I say, goggling at him. He's as bundled up as I am. Except for the squirrels (and the drug dealers) we're the only two living beings stupid—or desperate—enough to be in the park on this frosty morning.

"Cooper," I say, through wind-chapped lips. "What are you doing here?"

"I stopped by to see you," Cooper says. He's breathing slightly heavily. Apparently he's been running to catch up with me. Running. In this weather. In all those clothes. If it were me, I'd have collapsed into a gelatinous heap. But since it's Cooper, he's just breathing slightly harder than usual. "And Sarah and Tom said you were on your way to the Budget Office." He jerks a gloved thumb over his shoulder. "But isn't the Budget Office that way?"

"Oh," I say, thinking fast. "Yeah. It is. But, uh, I thought I'd kill two birds with one stone and just stop by to see this one guy about this thing. Was there something important you needed to see me about?" *Please*, I'm praying. *Please don't let him have spoken to my dad before I've gotten a chance to speak to him about my dad. . . .*

"Yeah," Cooper says. He hasn't shaved again this morning. His dark razor stubble looks delectably prickly. "My brother. And why he might have left a message asking to speak to me about you. Any idea what that might be about?"

"Oh," I say, feeling slightly sick with relief. Although possibly that's from all the whipped cream. "Yeah. He wants me to come to his wedding. You know, to show there's no hard feelings—"

"In front of the photographers from *People*," Cooper finishes for me. "I got it. I should have known it wasn't anything important. So." His icy blue gaze focuses on me like a laser. "You're stopping by to see this one guy about *what* thing?"

Damn! How does he always know? *Always*?

"Well," I say slowly. "See, it turns out Lindsay was seeing a new guy before she died. A Winer."

"A what?"

"You know." I spell it. "As in Winer Construction."

His dark-lashed eyelids narrow. "Heather. Why does this sound to me like you're investigating that dead girl's murder?"

"Because I am," I say, then hold up both gloved hands in protest when he inhales to begin his tirade. "Cooper, think about it! Winer Construction? The Winer Sports Complex? They're bound to have skeleton keys to locks all over the city. Doug could totally have had access to the caf—"

"Did anyone sign him in that night?" Cooper demands.

Damn. He knows the workings of Fischer Hall almost as well as I do.

"Well, no," I say. "But there's a thousand ways he could have snuck in. Chinese food deliverymen do it all the time, to slip menus under the kids' doors—"

"No." That's all Cooper says. He accompanies the word with a single head shake.

"Cooper, listen to me," I say, even though I know it's pointless. "Detective Canavan isn't asking any of the right questions. He doesn't know how to get information out of these kids. I do. I swear that's all I'm doing. Gathering information. Which I will fully turn over to him."

"Do you honestly believe I'm that gullible, Heather?" Cooper demands.

He is glaring down at me. The wind is biting into my face and making my eyes sting, but it doesn't appear to be bothering him at all. Possibly because he's got all that razor stubble to protect him.

"You know, it's very stressful to work in a place people are calling Death Dorm," I say. "Tom only just started working there, and he already wants to quit. Sarah's being impossible. I'm just trying to make Fischer Hall a fun place to work again. I'm just trying to do my job."

"Counseling some kid because she put Nair in her roommate's shampoo bottle," Cooper says, mentioning an all-too-frequent form of roommate torture around New York College, "and finding the person responsible for boiling a cheerleader's head on a cooking range are two entirely different things. One of them is your job. One is not."

"I just want to talk to the Winer kid," I say. "What harm can TALKING do?"

Cooper continues to stare down at me, as the wind goes on whistling. "Please don't do this," he says, so quietly I'm not entirely sure he's said it at all. Except that I saw his lips move. Those oddly lush (for a guy) lips that sometimes remind me of pillows, against which I'd like to press my—

"You can come with me," I offer brightly. "Come with me and you'll see. All I'm doing is talking. Not investigating. Not at all."

"You've lost it," Cooper says. Not without some disgust. "I mean it, Heather. Sarah is right. You *do* have some kind of Superman complex."

"Up, up, and away," I say. And take his arm. "So. Coming?"

"Do I have a choice?" Cooper wants to know.

I think about it.

"No," I say.

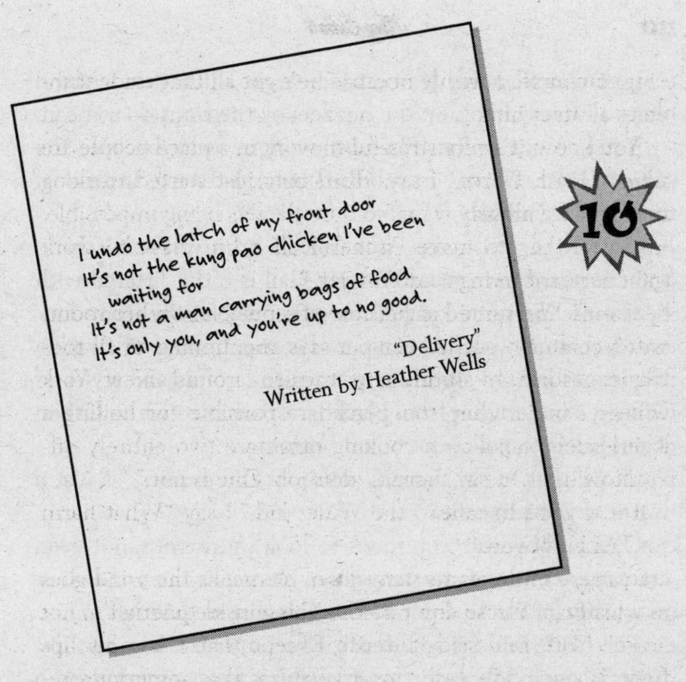

16
I undo the latch of my front door
It's not the kung pao chicken I've been
waiting for
It's not a man carrying bags of food
It's only you, and you're up to no good.
"Delivery"
Written by Heather Wells

Fraternity Row, otherwise known as Waverly Hall, is a huge building on the opposite side of Washington Square Park from Fischer Hall. Set back from the street by a stone wall around a courtyard, and entered beneath an archway, it's more Parisian in style than other buildings around the square, and for that reason, more distinctive. Maybe that's why it was determined by the trustees that this building would house the college's Greek fraternities (the sororities, of which there are fewer, are housed in a more modern building on Third Avenue), one frat per floor.

I, of course, never learned Greek, so I don't understand what all the symbols on the buzzers by the front door mean.

But I recognize Tau Phi Epsilon right away, because the sign TAU PHI EPSILON, in subdued black lettering, instead of the Greek symbols.

Unlike the well-swept sidewalk in front of Fischer Hall, the courtyard in front of Waverly Hall is filthy, littered with beer cans. The potted shrubs on either side of the front door are decorated with women's underwear instead of twinkly Christmas lights—all different sizes and colors and styles of women's underwear, from black lacy thongs to white Calvin Klein briefs to polka-dot bikini bottoms.

"Now, that," I say, looking down at the panties, "is just a waste of good lingerie."

Cooper, however, continues to look murderous, not even cracking a smile at my semi-joke. He yanks open the door and waits for me to enter before going inside himself.

The heat inside is so intense, I feel my nose begin to defrost at once. We enter a fairly clean foyer guarded by a gray-haired New York College security officer, whose face is crisscrossed by so many broken capillaries that his off-duty (one can only hope) predilection for whiskey is plainly obvious. When I show him my staff ID and tell him we're there to see Doug Winer of Tau Phi Epsilon, he doesn't even bother buzzing up to see if Doug's there. He just waves us toward the elevator. As we pass, I realize why: he's busy watching soap operas on one of his desk monitors.

Joining Cooper in the tiny, three-person elevator, I'm silent during the bouncy ride . . . until the cab lurches to a stop on the fifth floor, and the door opens to reveal a long, somewhat dingy hallway, along which someone has spray-painted in three-foot-high flourescent pink letters: FAT CHICKS GO HOME.

I blink at the letters, which reach nearly to my hip, and are scrawled across doors and walls indiscriminately. The Tau Phi Epsilons are going to have some pretty hefty floor damage charges come the end of the school year.

"*Well,*" I say, staring at the wall.

"This," Cooper bursts out, "is *exactly* why I don't think you ought to be getting involved in this investigation."

"Because I'm a fat chick, and I ought to go home?" I ask, struck to the quick.

Cooper's expression darkens even further . . . a feat I hadn't thought possible.

"No," he says. "Because . . . because . . . guys like this . . . they're *animals*."

"The kind of animals who would chop off a cheerleader's head and cook it on a stove in a dorm cafeteria?" I ask him pointedly.

But he's apparently speechless with indignation. So I knock on the door closest to the elevator, the one with TAU PHI EPSILON written over the frame.

The door swings open, and a dark-haired woman in an honest-to-God maid's uniform—not one of those sexy ones they sell on Bleecker Street, but a real one, with long sleeves and a skirt below the knees—blinks at us. She's fairly young, probably early forties, and has a dust rag in one hand. She's not wearing a lace cap, though. Thank God.

"Yes?" she says. She has a heavy Spanish accent. Heavier than Salma Hayek's, even.

I show her my staff ID. "Hi," I say. "I'm Heather Wells, and this is my friend Cooper Cartwright. I'm with the Housing Department. I just wanted to—"

"Come in," the woman says disinterestedly. She steps out of the way so that we can enter, then closes the door behind us. We find ourselves in a spacious, well-lit loft—the old-fashioned kind, with high ceilings, crown molding, and parquet floors—in a foyer surrounded by doors on all four sides.

"They're in there." She nods her head toward a set of closed French doors off to the right.

"Um, well, we're actually looking for someone in particular," I say. "Doug Winer. Do you know which room is—"

"Look," the woman says, not unpleasantly. "I just clean here. I don't actually know any of them by name."

"Thank you for your time," Cooper says politely, and, taking me by the arm, steers me toward the closed French doors. He's muttering something beneath his breath that I don't quite catch . . . possibly because the minute his hand closed over my arm, my heart began to drum so loudly in my ears, it drowned out all other sound. Even through seven layers of material, Cooper's touch excites me no end.

I know. I really *am* pathetic.

Rapping sharply on the glass panes of the double doors, Cooper calls out, "Hello, in there."

A voice from within hollers something indistinguishable. Cooper looks down at me, and I shrug. He throws open the French doors. Through the thick gray fog of marijuana smoke, I'm able to make out the green felt of a billiard table, and, in the background, a wide-screen TV transmitting the flickering images of a football game. The room is lit by a bank of windows that let in the uneasy gray of outdoors, and by the warm glow of a brass and stained-glass lamp that hangs over the pool table. In a far corner, a spirited game of air hockey is taking place, and to my immediate left, someone opens a mini-fridge and pulls out a beer.

That's when I realize Cooper and I must have just died—possibly on that rickety old elevator—and I'd somehow ended up in Guy Heaven by mistake.

"Hey," says a blond kid leaning over the pool table to make a difficult shot. He has a joint pressed between his lips, the tip of which glows red. Incredibly, he's dressed in a red satin smoking jacket and a pair of Levi's. "Hang on."

He draws back the cue and shoots, and the click of balls is drowned out by the sudden thunder of the football fans as they cheer on a favorite player. Straightening, the kid removes the joint from his mouth and studies Cooper and me from behind a hank of blond hair. "What can I do you for?" he inquires.

I look longingly at the beer the kid reaches for and sucks back while he waits for our response. A glance at Cooper tells me that he, too, is fondly recalling a time in his life when it was okay—even encouraged—to drink beer before lunchtime. Although I never actually lived through a time like that, never having gone to college.

"Um," I say, "we're looking for Doug Winer. Is he here?"

The kid laughs. "Hey, Brett," he calls over his red satin shoulder. "This babe wants to know if Doug's here."

Brett, at the air hockey table, snorts. "Would we be enjoying this excellent ganja if the Dougster wasn't here?" he inquires, raising his beer bottle in the air like that guy in that play who held up the skull and said he knew him well. "Of course the Dougster is here. The Dougster is, in fact, everywhere."

Cooper is staring longingly at the wide-screen TV, apparently unaware that I've just been called a babe—which, while still sexist, is a nicer welcome than I'd have expected, based on the signage outside.

Still, with my partner apparently in a trance, I feel it's up to me to steer the conversation in a more profitable direction.

"Well," I say. "Could you tell me where, specifically, I might find Mr. Winer?"

One of the guys in front of the TV suddenly swivels around and barks, "Christ, Scott, it's a cop!"

Every joint in the room, and a surprising amount of beer, disappears in a split second, crushed under Docksiders or stashed behind sofa cushions.

"Cops!" Scott, the kid at the pool table, throws down his joint disgustedly. "Aren't you guys supposed to announce yourselves? You can't peg me for nothing, man, 'cause you didn't announce yourself."

"We're not cops," I say, holding up both gloved hands. "Relax. We're just looking for Doug."

Scott sneers. "Yeah? Well, you gotta be buyin', 'cause in threads like those, you sure ain't sellin'." A number of snickers sound in agreement.

I look down at my jeans, then glance surreptitiously at Cooper's anorak, which he has unzipped to reveal a Shetland sweater featuring a green reindeer leaping over a geometric design in which the color pink figures prominently, a sweater I happen to know he received for Christmas from a doting great-aunt. Cooper is quite popular with the more elderly of his relatives.

"Um," I say, thinking fast, "yeah. What you said."

Scott rolls his eyes and pulls his beer out from the ball socket in which he'd stashed it. "Outside and down the hall, first door on your left. And be sure to knock, okay? The Winer usually has company."

I nod, and Cooper and I retrace our steps back to the FAT CHICKS GO HOME hallway. The maid is nowhere to be seen. Cooper looks as if someone has hit him.

"Did you," he breathes, "smell that?"

"Yeah," I say. "Why am I thinking they've got a slightly better source for their weed than Reggie?"

"Isn't this part of the Housing Department?" Cooper wants to know. "Don't they have an RA?"

"A GA," I say. "Like Sarah. But in charge of the whole building, not one for each floor. He can't be everywhere at once."

"Especially," Cooper says, under his breath, "when Tau Phis are obviously paying him not to be."

I don't know what makes him think that . . . but I'm willing to bet he's right. Hey, grad assistants are students, too, and more often than not, financially insolvent ones.

The first door on the left is covered with a life-sized poster of Brooke Burke in a bikini. I knock politely on Brooke's left breast, and hear a muffled "What?" in response. So I turn the knob and go in.

Doug Winer's room is dark, but enough gray light spills from around the shade to reveal a very large water bed, on which two figures recline, amid a plethora of beer cans. The predominant decorating theme, in fact, seems to be beer, as there are piles of beer cans, bottles, and cases strewn about the room. On the walls are posters of beer, and on the shelves creative stacks of it. I, who like beer just as much as the next person, if not slightly more, feel a little embarrassed for Doug.

After all, drinking beer is one thing. Decorating with it is quite another.

"Uh, Doug?" I say. "Sorry to wake you up, but we need to talk to you a minute."

One of the figures on the bed stirs, and a sleepy male voice asks, "What time is it?"

I consult Cooper's watch—since I don't own one—after he presses the button on it that lights up the face. "Eleven," I say.

"Shit." Doug stretches, then seems to become aware of the other presence in his bed. "Shit," he says, in a different tone, and pokes the figure—rather sharply, in my opinion.

"Hey," Doug says. "You. Get up."

Mewling fitfully, the girl tries to roll away from him, but Doug keeps poking, and finally she sits up, blinking heavily mascaraed eyes and clutching the maroon sheets to her chest. "Where am I?" she wants to know.

"Xanadu," Doug says. "Now get the hell out."

The girl blinks at him. "Who are you?" she wants to know.

"Count Chocula," Doug says. "Get your clothes and get out. Bathroom's over there. Don't flush any feminine hygiene products down the john or you'll clog it."

The girl blinks at Cooper and me in the doorway. "Who're they?" she asks.

"How the hell should I know?" Doug says crankily. "Now get out. I got stuff to do."

"All right, Mr. Cranky Pants." The girl swings herself out of bed, awarding Cooper and me with a generous view of her heart-shaped backside as she struggles into a pair of panties that didn't make it to the shrubs outside. Clutching a spangly-looking dress to her chest, she simpers as she wriggles past

Cooper on her way to the bathroom, but gives me a narrow-eyed glare as she passes.

Well, same to you, sister.

"Who the hell are you?" Doug demands, leaning over and lifting the blind just enough to allow me to see that he's built like a lightweight wrestler, small, but muscular and compact. In the odd New York College campus fashion of the day, his head is shaved on all sides, but rises in a spiky blond flattop at the crown. He appears to be wearing a St. Christopher medallion and little else.

"Hello, Doug," I say, and I'm surprised when my voice comes out dripping with animosity. I hadn't liked the way Doug had treated the girl, but I'd hoped I'd be able to hide it better. Oh, well. "I'm Heather Wells and this is Cooper Cartwright. We're here to ask you a few questions."

Doug is fumbling along his bedside table for a pack of cigarettes. His square, stubby fingers close around a pack of Marlboros.

That's when Cooper takes two long strides forward, seizes the kid's wrist, and squeezes very hard. The kid yelps and turns a pair of angry pale blue eyes up at the larger man.

"What the fuck do you think you're doing?" he brays.

"Smoking stunts your growth," Cooper says, reaching down and pocketing the cigarette pack. He doesn't let go of Doug's wrist, but subtly begins applying pressure to it, in response to the kid's trying to pull it away. "And have you ever seen a photograph of a smoker's lungs?"

"Who the fuck do you guys think you are?" demands Doug Winer.

I think about saying something smart like, *Your worst nightmare*, but I glance over at Cooper and realize that what we are, really, is an assistant hall director whose BMI is in the overweight range, and a Shetland-sweater-wearing private detective, neither of whom has ever belonged to a fraternity.

Still, Cooper could intimidate by his sheer size alone, and apparently chooses to do so, looming over the kid's bed like a six-foot-three headboard.

"Who we think we are doesn't much matter," Cooper says, in his scariest voice. And that's when I realize Cooper hadn't liked the way Doug had treated the girl, either. "I happen to be a detective, and I have few questions I'd like to ask you concerning the nature of your relationship with Lindsay Combs."

Doug Winer's eyes widen perceptibly, and he says, in a high voice, "I don't have to tell the cops shit. My dad's lawyer said so!"

"Well," Cooper says, lowering himself onto the pitching water mattress, "that's not strictly true, Douglas. If you don't tell the cops shit, they'll have you arrested for obstruction of justice. And I don't think either your dad or his lawyer is going to like that."

I have to hand it to Cooper. He's scared the living daylights out of the boy, and without even lying to him. He *is* a detective . . . and the cops *could* arrest Doug for obstruction of justice. It's just that Cooper isn't a *police* detective, and wouldn't be able to do any arresting himself.

Seeing the kid's truculent expression go suddenly soft with fear, Cooper lets go of his wrist and stands back, folding his arms across his chest and looming quite menacingly. He manages to look as if he feels like breaking Doug Winer's arm—and might still do it, if provoked.

Doug massages his wrist where Cooper grasped it, and

looks up at him resentfully. "You didn't have to do that, man," he says. "It's my room, I can smoke if I want to."

"Actually," Cooper says, with the same amiableness that, I'm sure, always misleads his less savory clients into thinking he was secretly on their side, "this room belongs to the Tau Phi Epsilon Association, Douglas, not you. And I think the Tau Phi Epsilon Association might be interested to learn that one of their pledges is conducting a lucrative business in dealing controlled substances from their property."

"What?" Doug's jaw drops. In the gray light, I can see now that the kid's chin is peppered with acne. "What are you talking about, man?"

Cooper chuckles. "Well, let's leave that aside for a while, shall we? How old are you, Douglas? Tell the truth, now, son."

To my surprise, the kid doesn't say, *I'm not your son*, the way I would have, if I'd been him. Instead, he sticks out his pimpled chin and says, "Twenty."

"Twenty," Cooper echoes, looking pointedly about the room. "And are all these beer cans yours, Douglas?"

Doug isn't quite as stupid as he looks. His face grows dark with suspicion as he lies sullenly, "No."

"No?" Cooper looks mildly surprised. "Oh, I beg your pardon. I suppose your fraternity brothers, the ones who are over twenty-one, I mean, which is the legal drinking age in this state, drank all these beers and left them in your room as a little joke. Forgive me if I'm wrong, but isn't the New York College campus a dry one, Heather?" Cooper asks me, though he knows the answer very well.

"Why, yes, I believe it is, Cooper," I reply, seeing his game and playing along. "And yet, in this young man's room, there are many, many empty beer containers. You know what, Cooper?"

Cooper looks interested. "No, what, Heather?"

"I think that Tau Phi Epsilon is perhaps in violation of that dry campus ordinance. I think the Greek Association will be very interested to hear about your room, Mr. Winer."

Doug props himself up on his elbows, his bare, hairless chest heaving suddenly. "Look, I didn't kill her, all right? That's all I'll tell you. And you guys had better stop harassing me!"

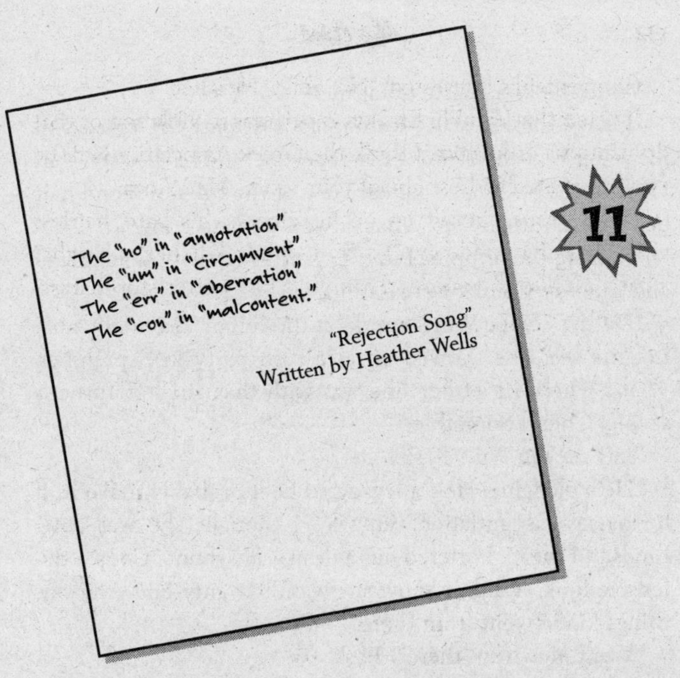
11
The "no" in "annotation"
The "um" in "circumvent"
The "err" in "aberration"
The "con" in "malcontent."
"Rejection Song"
Written by Heather Wells

Cooper and I exchange astonished glances. The astonishment, anyway, isn't feigned.

"Did anyone here accuse you of killing anyone, Douglas?" Cooper spreads out his hands innocently.

"Yeah, really." I shake my head. "We were only accusing your fraternity of supplying alcohol to their underaged brother."

Doug scowls. "You leave my fraternity out of this, okay?"

"We might be able to do that," Cooper says, stroking his whiskered jaw thoughtfully. "If you could be a little more forthcoming with the information my friend here requested."

Winer flicks a glance up at me.

"Okay," the kid sighs, leaning back against the pillows of his water bed and twining his fingers behind his head so that Coop and I both have a great view of the tufts of blond hair beneath his arms. Ew. "What do you want to know?"

Ignoring the armpits, I say, "I want to know how long you and Lindsay Combs were dating."

"Dating." Doug Winer smirks at the ceiling. "Right. Dating. Let me see. She showed up at a rush party in September. That's where I met her. She was with that girl Jeff Turner's seeing. Cheryl Something."

"Jeff's a Tau Phi?" I ask.

"He's pledging. He's a legacy, so he'll probably make it, if he passes his initiation. Anyway, I thought she was cute. Lindsay, I mean. I offered her a drink." He shoots Coop a defensive look. "I didn't know she wasn't twenty-one. Anyway, things kinda went from there."

"Went *how* from there?" I ask.

"You know." Doug Winer shrugs, then shoots Cooper such a smugly superior smile that I feel hard-pressed not to launch myself at the guy, tear a hole in the water mattress, and hold the kid's head in it until he drowns.

Not, of course, that I would ever do something like that. Because then I'd probably get fired.

"No, I don't know," I say, through gritted teeth. "Please explain it to me."

"She gave me head, okay?" Winer snickers. "Fucking homecoming queen, my ass. And she was a pro, let me tell you. I never had it like that from any girl—"

"Okay," Cooper interrupts. "We get the picture."

I feel my cheeks burning and curse myself. Why do I have to respond like such a Goody Two-shoes to words like *head*?

Especially around Cooper, who is already convinced I'm "a nice girl." By going around blushing all the time, I'm just reinforcing the image.

I try to make out as if I'm not blushing, just flushed. It *is* warm in Doug's room—especially since, judging from the sound of water coming from his bathroom, his girlfriend (or whatever she is) appears to be showering. I start unwinding my scarf.

"Never mind," I say to Cooper, to show him I'm all right with the gritty language. To Doug I say, "Go on."

Douglas, still looking smug, shrugs. "So I thought it'd be a good idea to keep her around, you know? For emergencies."

I'm so surprised by the coldness of this that I can't think of anything to say. Cooper's the one who inquires, calmly examining his own cuticles, "What do you mean, keep her around?"

"You know. Put her number in the little black book. For a rainy day. Whenever I was feelin' down, I'd give ol' Lindsay a call, and she would come over and make me feel better."

I really can't remember the last time I'd felt so much like killing someone—then recall that only an hour or so ago I'd wanted to pummel Gillian Kilgore with almost the same intensity as I now longed to throttle Doug Winer.

Maybe Sarah is right. Maybe I *do* have a Superman complex.

Cooper glances at me, and seems to sense that I'm having a difficult time restraining myself. He looks back down at his fingernails and asks Doug casually, "And Lindsay didn't have any complaints about this kind of relationship?"

"Shit, no," Doug says with a laugh. "And if she had complained, she'd've regretted it."

Cooper's head turns so fast in Winer's direction that it's nothing but a blur. "Regretted it how?"

The kid seems to realize his mistake and takes his hands away from his head, sitting up a little straighter. I notice that his abdomen is perfectly flat, except where it's ridged with muscles. I had abs that tight once. When I was eleven.

"Hey, not like that, man." Winer's blue eyes are wide. "Not like that. I mean, I'd've stopped calling her. That's all."

"Are you trying to tell us"—I've found my voice at last—"that Lindsay Combs was perfectly willing to come up here any old time you called and give you—ahem—oral sex?"

Doug Winer blinks at me, hearing the hostility in my voice, but apparently not understanding where it's coming from. "Well. Yeah."

"And she did this because?"

The kid stares at me. "What do you mean?"

"I mean that girls do not generally perform oral sex for no reason." At least, no girl with whom I was acquainted. "What did she get out of it?"

"What do you mean, what did she get out of it? She got *me* out of it."

It was finally *my* turn to smirk. "*You*?"

"Yeah." The kid sets his jaw defensively. "Don't you know who I am?"

Cooper and I, as if on cue, exchange blank stares. The kid says insistently, "I'm a Winer."

When we both continue to look uncomprehending, Doug prompts, as if he thinks we're slow, "Winer *Construction*. Winer Sports Complex? You guys haven't heard of it? We fucking own this city, man. We practically built this fucking college. At least the new buildings. I'm a Winer, man. A *Winer*."

He certainly sounds like one.

And if this was the reason Lindsay Combs had been bestowing blow jobs so liberally upon this kid, I for one didn't believe it. Lindsay hadn't been that type of girl.

I don't think.

"Plus, I gave her shit," Doug admits grudgingly.

Now we were getting somewhere.

Cooper raised his eyebrows. "You what?"

"I gave her shit." Then, seeing Cooper's expression, Doug glances nervously in my direction, and says, "I mean, stuff. I gave her stuff. You know, the kind of stuff girls like. Jewelry and flowers and stuff."

Now, Lindsay was *that* kind of girl. At least, from what I knew of her.

"I was even gonna give her this bracelet for her birthday—" Suddenly the kid slings himself out of bed, affording us a view I'd have preferred not to have of his snug black Calvin Klein briefs. He goes to a dresser and draws a small black velvet box from a drawer. Turning, he casually tosses the box to me. I fumble, but manage to catch it. "I don't know what I'm gonna do with it now."

I open the black velvet lid and—I will admit it—my eyes widen at the slender strand of diamonds lying inside the box on a bed of royal blue silk. If this is the kind of payback Lindsay was routinely receiving for her services, I guess I could understand it a little better.

Stifling a desire to whistle at the costliness of such a gift, I tilt the box at Cooper, who raises his dark eyebrows. "That's quite a trinket," he comments mildly. "You must have some allowance."

"Yeah." Doug shrugs. "Well, it's just money."

"Is it Dad's money?" Cooper wants to know. "Or your own?"

The kid had been rooting around, looking for something

on top of the dresser. When his fingers close around a bottle of aspirin, Doug Winer sighs.

"What difference does it make?" he wants to know. "My money, my dad's money, my grandfather's money. It's all the same."

"Is it, Doug? Your father and grandfather's money comes from construction. I understand that you traffic an entirely different substance."

The kid stares. "What are you talkin' about, man?"

Cooper smiles affably. "The boys down the hall intimated that you know your way around certain hydroponics."

"I don't give a shit what they intimidated," Doug declares. "I do not deal drugs, and if you accuse me of selling so much as one of these to someone"—He shakes the bottle of aspirin at us—"my dad'll have your ass in a sling. He's friends with the president, you know. Of this college."

"That's it," I say, feigning terror. "I'm scared now."

"You know what? You better be. . . ." Doug starts toward me. But he gets no farther than a step before Cooper blocks his path, a hulking mass of muscle, anorak, and razor stubble.

"Just where do you think you're going?" Cooper asks lightly.

As Cooper had evidently hoped he would—guys are so predictable—the kid takes a swing at him. Cooper ducks, his grin growing wider. Now he has license to beat the crap out of Winer, as he'd no doubt been longing to do.

"Coop," I say. Because suddenly I realize things are not going at all the way I'd hoped. "Don't."

It's useless. Cooper takes a step toward the kid just as Doug is taking a second swing, catches the kid's fist in his hand, and, by applying steady pressure with his fingers alone, sends Winer to his knees.

"Where were you," Cooper growls, his face inches from the kid's, "the night before last?"

"What?" Doug Winer gasps. "Man, you're hurtin' me!"

"Where were you the night before last?" Cooper demands, evidently increasing the pressure on the kid's hand.

"Here, man! I was here all night, you can ask the guys! We had a bong party. Jesus, you're gonna break my hand!"

"Cooper," I say, my heart beginning to drum. Hard. I mean, if I let Cooper hurt a student, I'll be in serious trouble. Fired, even. Also . . . well, much as I dislike him, I find I can't stand by and see Doug Winer get tortured. Even if he deserves it. "Let the kid go."

"All night?" Cooper demands, ignoring me. "You were at a bong party all night? What time did it start?"

"Nine o'clock, man! Lemme go!"

"Cooper!" I can't believe what I'm seeing. This is a side of Cooper I've never witnessed before.

And am pretty sure I never want to see again. Maybe this is why he won't tell me what he does all day. Because what he does all day is stuff like this.

Cooper finally releases the kid, and Winer slumps to the floor, clutching his hand and curling into a fetal position.

"You're gonna regret this, man," the kid wimpers, fighting back tears. "You're gonna be real sorry!"

Cooper blinks like someone coming out of a daze. He looks at me and, seeing my expression, says sheepishly, "I only used one hand."

I am so stunned by this explanation—if that's even what it is—that I can only stare at him.

A tousled blond head peeks in from the bathroom doorway. The girl from the water bed has managed to pour herself back into a bright orange party dress, but she's barefoot, her wide eyes focused on Doug's prone form.

But she doesn't ask what happened. Instead, she asks, "Are my shoes in there?"

I lean down and lift up two orange high-heeled pumps. "These them?"

"Oh, yes," the girl says gratefully. She takes a few hesitant steps around her host and seizes the shoes. "Thank you very much." Slipping the pumps onto her feet, she says to Doug, "It was very nice meeting you, Joe."

Doug just moans, still clutching his injured hand. The girl scoops some of her blond hair from her eyes and leans down, displaying an admirable amount of cleavage.

"You can reach me at the Kappa Alpha Theta House anytime. It's Dana. Okay?"

When Doug nods wordlessly, Dana straightens, grabs her coat and purse from a pile on the floor, then wiggles her fingers at us.

" 'Bye, now!" she says, and jiggles away, her backside swaying enticingly.

"You get out, too," Doug says to Cooper and me. "Get out or I'll . . . I'll call the cops."

Cooper looks interested in this threat.

"Really?" he says. "Actually, I think there are a few things the cops need to know about you. So why don't you go right ahead and do that?"

Doug just whimpers some more, clutching his hand. I say to Cooper, "Let's just go."

He nods, and we step from the room, closing Doug's door behind us. Standing once again in the Tau Phi House's hallway, inhaling the rich odor of marijuana and listening to the sounds of the football game drifting out from the game room, I study the spray paint on the wall, which the maid who'd answered the door is trying to wipe off with paint remover and a rag. She's barely started on the F in FAT CHICKS. She has a long way to go.

She has a Walkman on, and smiles when she sees us. I smile automatically back.

"I don't believe a word that kid said," Cooper says, as he zips up his anorak. "How 'bout you?"

"Nope," I say. "We should check his alibi."

The maid, who apparently hadn't had the volume on her Walkman turned up very high, looks at us and says, "You know those guys are gonna back him up whatever he says. They're his fraternity brothers. They have to."

Cooper and I exchange glances.

"She has a point," I say. "I mean, if he didn't talk when you had him in that hand lock, or whatever it was . . ."

Cooper nods. "The Greek Association really is a marvelous institution," he remarks.

"Yes, it is," the maid says, just as gravely. Then she bursts out laughing and goes back to scrubbing the F.

"About what happened back there," Cooper says to me, in a different tone of voice, as we stand waiting for the elevator. "That kid . . . he just . . . the way he treated that girl . . . I just . . ."

"Now who's got the Superman complex?" I want to know.

Cooper smiles down at me.

And I realize I love him more than ever. I should probably just tell him that, and get it out in the open so we can stop playing these games (well, okay, maybe he's not playing games, but Lord knows I am). At least that way I'll know, once and for all, if I have a chance.

I'm opening my mouth to do just that—tell him how I

really feel about him—when I notice he's opening his mouth, too. My heart begins to thump—what if he's about to tell me that *he* loves *me*? Stranger things have happened.

And he *did* ask me to move in with him, pretty much out of the blue. And okay, maybe it was because he felt bad about the fact that I'd just walked in on my fiancé, who happens to be his brother, getting a blow job from another woman.

But still. He *could* have done it because he's secretly always been in love with me. . . .

His smile has vanished. This is it! He's going to tell me!

"You'd better call your office and tell them you're going to be late getting back," he says.

"Why?" I ask breathlessly, hoping against hope that he's going to say, *Because I plan on taking you back to my place and ravishing you for the rest of the day.*

"Because I'm taking you over to the Sixth Precinct, where you're going to tell Detective Canavan everything you know about this case." The elevator doors slide open, and Cooper unceremoniously propels me into the car. "And then you're going to keep out of it, like I told you."

"Oh," I say.

Well, okay. It isn't a declaration of love, exactly. But at least it proves he cares.

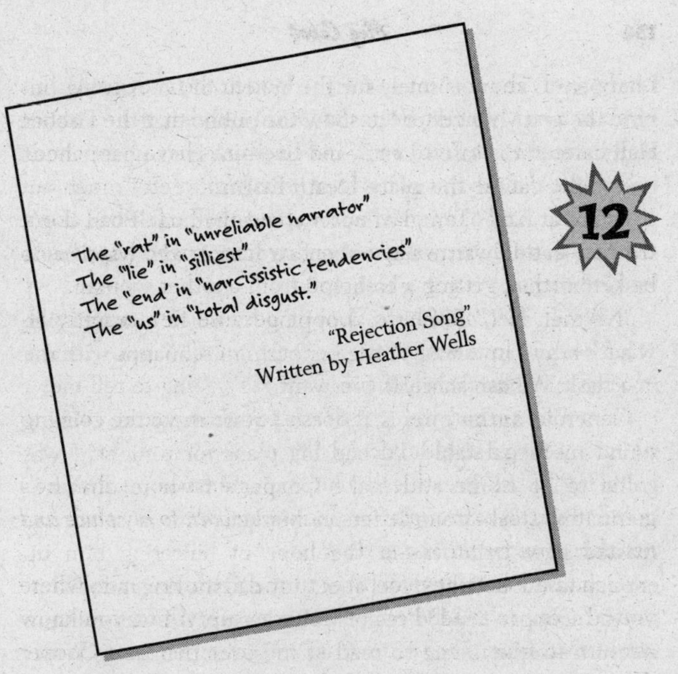
12
The "rat" in "unreliable narrator"
The "lie" in "silliest"
The "end" in "narcissistic tendencies"
The "us" in "total disgust."
"Rejection Song"
Written by Heather Wells

"What do you mean, we *have* to go to tonight's game?"

"Departmental memo," Tom says, flicking it onto my desk. Or should I say his desk, since he's apparently taking it over for the duration of Gillian Kilgore's stay? "Mandatory attendance. To show our Pansy Spirit."

"I don't have any Pansy Spirit," I say.

"Well, you better get some," Tom says. "Especially since we're having dinner beforehand with President Allington and Coach Andrews here in the caf."

My jaw drops. "WHAT?"

"He thinks it's just the ticket," Tom says, in a pleasant voice

I happen to know is solely for the benefit of Dr. Kilgore, behind the grate next door, "to show the public that the Fischer Hall cafeteria is safe to eat—and live—in. He's upset about everybody calling this place Death Dorm."

I stare at him. "Tom, I'm upset about that, too. But I don't see how eating warmed-over beef stroganoff and watching a basketball game is going to help."

"Neither do I," Tom says, dropping his voice to a whisper. "That's why I'm taking a little peppermint schnapps with me in a flask. We can share, if you want."

Generous as this offer is, it doesn't quite make the evening sound more palatable. I'd had big plans for tonight: I was going to go home and make Cooper's favorite dinner—marinated steak from Jefferson Market, with a salad and roasted new potatoes—in the hope of buttering him up enough to ask how he'd feel about my dad moving in for a bit.

And Cooper needed major buttering up, if I was going to get him to quit being so mad at me over the Doug Winer thing. After his initial chagrin over the way he'd manhandled the kid (or over me *witnessing* the way he'd manhandled the kid) had worn off—about midway through our meeting with Detective Canavan—Cooper had been quite vocal in his disapproval over my involving myself in the investigation into Lindsay's death at all. I believe the words "damned stupid" were mentioned.

Which did not bode well for my plan of bearing Cooper's children, much less asking him if my dad could move in.

Sadly, Detective Canavan was not in the least bit interested in any of the information I was able to impart pertaining to Lindsay's complicated love life. Or at least, if he was, he didn't act like it. He sat at his desk with a bored expression on his face through my entire recitation, then, when I was done, all he said was, "Ms. Wells, leave the Winer boy alone. Do you have any idea what his father could do to you?"

"Chop me up into little pieces and bury them in cement beneath the concrete foundation of one of the buildings he's constructing?" I asked.

Detective Canavan rolled his eyes. "No. Sue you for harassment. That guy's got more lawyers than Trump."

"Oh," I said, deflated.

"Was the Winer boy signed in the night Lindsay was killed?" the detective asked, though he clearly already knew the answer. He just wanted me to say it. "Not just by Lindsay, but by anyone else? Anyone at all?"

"No," I was forced to admit. "But like I was telling Cooper, there are tons of ways people can sneak into the building if they really want—"

"You think whoever killed that girl acted alone?" the detective wanted to know. "You think the murderer and his accomplices all snuck in past a guard who is paid to keep people from sneaking in?"

"Some of his accomplices could live in the building," I pointed out. "That could be how they got the key. . . ."

Detective Canavan gave me a sour look. Then he went on to inform me that he and his fellow investigators were already aware of Doug Winer's relationship with the victim, and that I should—in fancy detective-speak—butt out, a sentiment that was echoed by a still-steaming Cooper on our way home.

I tried to explain to him about Magda and her request—that Lindsay's character need not be assassinated during the investigation into her death—but this only resulted in Cooper's pointing out that beautiful girls who love too much, as Lindsay appeared to have done, often meet unpleasant ends.

Which really only served to illustrate Magda's point.

Cooper, however, was of the opinion that if the shoe fit, Lindsay was going to have to wear it. To which I replied, "Sure. If anyone could find her foot."

Our parting, at the front door of Fischer Hall, was not what anyone would reasonably call amicable. Thus the need for steak before I introduced the topic of my father.

"I have to go home and walk my dog," I say to my boss, making one last effort to get out of what I just know is going to be an evening filled with hilarity. Not.

"Fine," Tom says. "But be back here by six. Hey, don't give me that look. You were at the 'Budget Office' "—He makes air quotes with his fingers—"for two hours this morning, and I didn't say anything about it, did I?"

I make a face at him but don't protest further, because he's got a point. He could have busted me for my disappearing act earlier in the day, but he didn't. Possibly he's the coolest boss in the world. Except for the part where he wants to quit and go back to Texas, where girls apparently don't get decapitated in their residence hall cafeteria.

Having to attend this mandatory dinner and game is putting a serious crimp in my groveling plans. But when I get home to let Lucy out, I see that Cooper's not around, anyway. The message light on the machine is blinking, and when I press PLAY, I realize why Coop might be avoiding home. I hear Jordan's voice, saying irritably, "Don't think you can just hang up on me like that, Cooper, and that it's all over. Because it's not. You have a real opportunity here to show the family that you can be a stand-up fellow. Don't blow it."

Wow. *Stand-up fellow*. No wonder Cooper hung up on him.

Poor Cooper. Having me around has put a real crimp in his resolve never to speak to his family again. I mean, considering that my living with him basically drives Jordan crazy. So instead of ignoring his black sheep brother, as he might have were I not around, Jordan instead focuses inordinate amounts of attention on trying to figure out what's going on between us.

Which, sadly, is nothing.

But I don't have a problem with Jordan thinking otherwise. The only problem, of course, is that it's highly unlikely Cooper is ever going to fall in love with me if he's constantly being harangued about me by his brother. That, and my annoying tendency nearly to get myself killed all the time, has to be extremely off-putting. Not to mention the fact that he's seen me in sweats.

There are no other messages on the machine—not even, weirdly, from my dad, though he'd said he was going to call. A quick scan of New York One shows the meteorologist still talking about this blizzard we're supposed to get—now it's hovering somewhere over Pennsylvania. I lace on my Timberlands, fully expecting that I'll just be taking them off later that night without having encountered a flake of snow. On the plus side, at least my feet will get gross and sweaty from wearing snow boots inside a hot, crowded gymnasium.

Back outside, I'm hurrying around the corner to Fischer Hall when I spy Reggie conducting a transaction with someone in a Subaru. I wait politely for him to finish, then smile as he approaches.

"Business is picking up," I observe.

"Because this storm they predicted is holding off," Reggie agrees. "If we're lucky, it will pass us by completely."

"From your lips to the weather god's ears," I say. Then,

pushing aside my—only slightly—guilty conscience, since I knew I was about to do something both Cooper and Detective Canavan wouldn't like (but really, if either of them would show just a modicum of respect for the deceased, I wouldn't feel obligated. I mean, how come guys who have a lot of sex are considered players, while girls who have a lot of sex are considered sluts?), I continue, "Listen, Reggie. What do you know about a kid named Doug Winer?"

Reggie looks blank. "Never heard of him. Should I have?"

"I don't know," I say. "He appears to be Big Man on Campus. He lives over at one of the fraternities."

"Ah," Reggie says knowingly. "A party kid."

"Is that what they're calling them these days?"

"That's what *I* call them," Reggie says, looking mildly amused. "Anyway, I haven't heard of him. But then, party kids and me? We travel in vastly different social circles."

"Probably not as different as you might think," I say, thinking about the marijuana haze hanging over the Tau Phi Epsilon pool table. "But will you ask around about him, anyway?"

"For you, Heather?" Reggie gives a courtly bow. "Anything. You think this boy has something to do with the young lady who lost her head?"

"Possibly," I say carefully, conscious of Detective Canavan's threat about the litigiousness of Doug's father.

"I'll see what I can do," Reggie says. Then he knits his brow. "Where are you going? Back to work? They're making you keep very long hours this week."

"Please," I say, rolling my eyes. "Don't even get me started."

"Well," Reggie says, "if you need a little pick-me-up . . ."

I glare at him. "*Reggie.*"

"Never mind," Reggie says, and drifts away.

Back at Fischer Hall, the excitement about the staff's Dinner and B-Ball Game With the President is palpable. Not. In fact, entirely the opposite is true. Most of the staff are milling around the lobby looking disgruntled. The cafeteria staff—day shift—are being particularly vocal in their protest that, as this is a mandatory function, they should be receiving overtime pay for it. Gerald, their boss, is maintaining that they're getting a free meal out of it, so they should just shut up. Understandably, his employees seem to feel that eating the food they helped prepare in the cafeteria they help maintain and which was, just the day before, the sight of a grisly murder is not as great a treat as he seems to feel it is.

It's odd to see the maintenance staff out of uniform. I barely recognize Carl, the chief engineer, in his leather jacket and jeans (and multiple gold neck chains). Head housekeeper Julio and his nephew Manuel are almost unrecognizable in sports coats and ties. Apparently they went home to change before coming back.

And Pete, out of his security uniform, looks like any other father of five . . . harried, rumpled, and anxious about what the kids are up to back home. His cell phone is glued to his ear, and he's saying, "No, you have to take them out of the can first. You can't microwave SpaghettiOs still in the can. No, you can't. No, you— See? What did I tell you? Why don't you listen to Daddy?"

"This," I say, coming up to Magda, who is resplendent as usual in tight white jeans and a gold lamé sweater (the school colors), "sucks."

But there are bright spots of color in each of Magda's cheeks . . . and not the painted-on kind, either.

"I'm seeing so many more of my little movie stars, though," she says excitedly, "than come in during the day!"

It's true that the dinner hour is the most highly attended meal of the day at Fischer Hall. And it looks as if the president's decision to set an example, by boldly taking a tray to the hot food line and choosing the turkey with gravy, has had an impact: the residents are trickling in, getting over their skittishness about eating in Death Dorm.

Or maybe they just want to see the president's expression when he takes a bite of the caf's (in)famous potatoes au gratin.

Tom sidles up to me, looking grim-faced. A second later, I notice why. Gillian Kilgore is following him, looking unnaturally perky.

"See, wasn't this a good idea?" she asks, looking at everyone milling around the tray cart, trying to grab forks and knives. "This shows that you all have some real bonding in the workplace. Now the healing can begin."

"Apparently nobody told her attendance is mandatory," Tom whispers to me as he slips into line behind me.

"Are you kidding me?" I whisper back. "This had to have been all her idea. You think the president came up with this one on his own?"

Tom glances over his shoulder back at Dr. Kilgore. She's at the salad bar, checking out her lettuce options (iceberg and . . . iceberg). "*Evil,*" Tom says, with a shudder.

We're joined, a second later, by a panting Sarah. "Thanks for telling me," she says sarcastically to Tom, as she slides her empty tray next to his.

"Sarah," Tom says, "this is just for full-time staff, not students."

"Oh, right," Sarah says. "Because we're second-class citizens? We don't get to share in the therapeutic benefits of bonding together over shared pain? Was that Kilgore's idea?

Excluding the student workers? God, that is so typical of a Freudian—"

"Shut up," Tom says, "and eat."

We find a table at what we consider a safe distance from the president's and start to sit down, but President Allington catches us.

"Over here," he says, waving to Tom. "Come sit over here by us, Scott."

"Tom," Tom corrects him nervously. "It's, um, Tom Snelling, sir."

"Right, right," the president says, and beside him, Dr. Jessup—who clearly felt it important to show support for Dr. Allington's plan and was attending both the dinner and game with the Fischer Hall staff—points out, "Tom's the director of Fischer Hall, Phillip."

But it's futile. President Allington isn't listening.

"And you're Mary, right?" he says to me.

"Heather," I say, wishing there was a hole nearby I could crawl into. "Remember me? From that time in the penthouse, when you used to live here in Fischer Hall?"

His eyes glaze over. President Allington doesn't like being reminded of that day, nor does his wife, who rarely, if ever, comes into the city from their summer home in the Hamptons anymore because of it.

"Right, right," President Allington says, as Dr. Kilgore joins us with her tray, apparently not noticing she is being followed by an angry-faced Sarah. "Well, I think we all know each other—"

"Excuse us, President Allington?"

Five cheerleaders are lined up in front of our table, all staring at the president.

"Uh," he says, looking anxiously at Dr. Kilgore, as if for assistance. Then, remembering he's supposed to have a reputation for being accessible to the students, Dr. Allington attempts a smile and says, "Hello, girls. What can I do for you?"

Beside the president, Coach Andrews heaves a sigh and lays down his fork.

"Look, girls," he says to them slowly, clearly continuing a conversation that had started elsewhere, "we already discussed this. And the answer is—"

"We aren't talking to you," Cheryl Haebig says, a slight flush rising on her cheeks. Still, she holds her ground. "We're talking to President Allington."

The president glances from the girls to the coach and back again.

"What's this all about, Steve?" he wants to know.

"They want to retire Lindsay's cheerleading sweater," Coach Andrews says, beneath his breath.

"They want to *what*?" President Allington looks confused.

"Let me handle this," Coach Andrews says. To the girls in front of the table, he says, "Ladies, I feel as bad as all of you do about Lindsay. Really, I do. But the thing is, I think a formal memorial service, with input from Lindsay's family—"

"Her family's all here tonight," Megan McGarretty—Room 1410—informs him tersely. For such a tiny thing, she looks pretty intimidating, with her arms folded across the big letter P on her chest, and one hip jutting out like a warning. "And they don't want a memorial service. They're expecting somebody to say something tonight at the game."

"Oh." President Allington's eyes widen. "I'm not sure that would be appropriate."

"You can't just pretend like it didn't happen," Hailey Nichols—Room 1714—declares.

"Yeah," Cheryl Haebig says, her luminous brown eyes swimming with tears. " 'Cause we won't let Lindsay be forgotten. She was as much a part of your team as any of the boys."

"I believe we all recognize that," Dr. Kilgore says, trying to come to the president's rescue. "But—"

"If any of the boys on the team died," Tiffany Parmenter—Megan's roommate—interrupts, "you'd retire his number. You'd hang his jersey from the rafters, along with the championship banners."

"Er." Dr. Kilgore appears flummoxed by this. "That is certainly true, girls. But basketball players are athletes, and—"

"Are you saying cheerleaders aren't athletes, Dr. Kilgore?" Sarah's voice is icy.

"C-certainly not," Dr. Kilgore stutters. "Only that—"

"So why can't you retire Lindsay's sweater?" Hailey wants to know, her blond ponytail swinging in emphasis of her words. "Why can't you?"

I glance at Kimberly Watkins to see if she's going to chime in, but she remains uncharacteristically silent. All five girls are in their cheerleading uniforms, white sweaters with gold letter P's on the fronts, and very short, pleated gold and white skirts. They have on flesh-colored hose beneath their skirts, and white footies with fuzzy gold balls on the back of them. Their white sneakers are by Reebok and their hair color almost unanimously by Sun-In. Except Kimberly's, which is dark as midnight.

"Look." Coach Andrews looks tired. There are dark circles under his eyes. "It's not the jerseys themselves we retire when a player dies. It's the player's number. And Lindsay didn't have a number. We can't retire an article of clothing."

"Why not?"

All eyes turn toward Manuel, who, from the table he's sharing with his uncle and various other members of the custodial staff, blinks back.

"Why not?" he asks again, as his uncle Julio, beside him, looks mortified with embarrassment.

I glance around the table and happen to see Magda at the far end of it, watching the cheerleaders with a troubled gaze. I know what she's thinking without even having to ask. Because I'm thinking the same thing.

"I agree with Manuel," I hear myself say.

Of course, everyone turns to look at me. Which must be a relief to Manuel. But which causes me a certain amount of discomfort.

But I hold my ground.

"I think it could be a lovely gesture," I say. "If done tastefully."

"Oh, it will be," Cheryl assures us. "We already asked if the band can play the school song real slow. And we all chipped in and bought a wreath made out of gold and white roses. And I've got Lindsay's sweater, all nice and pressed."

I notice that everyone—including Dr. Jessup, the head of Housing—is staring at me.

But what's the big deal? It's just a stupid basketball game. Who cares if they—what is it again? Oh, yeah—retire a girl's sweater during it?

"I think it would be a touching tribute to a girl who had more Pansy spirit than just about anybody else in this school," I say to President Allington, who is still looking confused.

"But"—he looks worried—"the game is going to be televised. Live. The entire tri-state area will see Lindsay Combs's cheerleading sweater being retired."

"We'll be the laughingstock of college basketball," Coach Andrews mutters.

"And you're not already," I say, genuinely curious, "with a name like the Pansies?"

Coach Andrews looks sad. "True," he says. I'm sure when he was applying for coaching positions, he never dreamed he'd end up at a Division III school with a flower for a mascot.

He sighs, looking heavenward, and says, "It's all right with me if it's all right with President Allington."

The president looks startled—mostly because he's just taken a big bite of potatoes au gratin, and, from his expression, it's clear the bite included a big clump of flour.

After chugging half a glass of water, the president says, "Whatever. Do whatever you want." He's been beaten, by five cheerleaders and a lump of flour.

Cheryl Haebig immediately stops crying. "Rilly?" she asks brightly. "Rilly, Mr. President? You mean it?"

"I mean it."

Then, as Cheryl and her friends scream—shrilly enough to cause Dr. Kilgore to put her hands over her ears reflexively—Coach Andrews, raising his voice to be heard above the ruckus, says, "They won't broadcast the halftime show, anyway."

President Allington looks relieved. "Well," he says. And brings a forkful of turkey to his mouth. Then, relief turning quickly to disgust, he says, "Well," in a different tone of voice.

And reaches hastily for his water glass again, signifying to all that this will probably be the last meal the president will choose to enjoy in the Fischer Hall cafeteria.

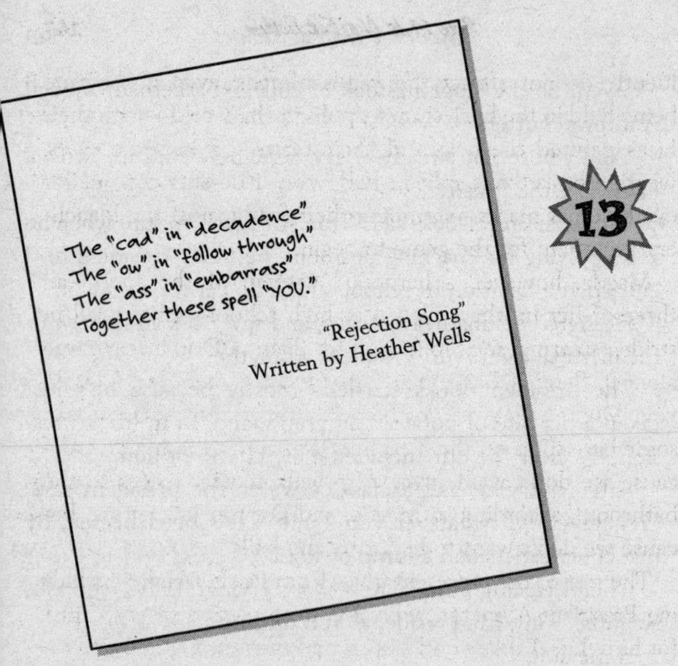

13
The "cad" in "decadence"
The "ow" in "follow through"
The "ass" in "embarrass"
Together these spell "YOU."
"Rejection Song"
Written by Heather Wells

Okay, so I'll admit it. I've never been to a basketball game before. Not a professional one (although Jordan used to beg me to accompany him to Knicks games all the time. Fortunately, I was usually able to come up with a good excuse . . . such as needing to wash my hair), not a high school game (I dropped out of high school after my first album took off), and certainly not a college game (I have generally been able to find other ways to occupy my time).

I can't really say what I'd been expecting, except . . . not what greeted me as I came through the gymnasium doors, which was hundreds of fans—because Division III games evidently do not attract thousands of fans, even if they are being held in the busiest metropolis in the world—with their faces painted the colors of their team—or, in some cases, wearing basketballs split in half, with little slits cut out for eye holes, as masks—stomping their feet against the bleachers, impatient for the game to begin.

Magda, however, a hardened veteran of the sport—all three of her brothers played in high school—takes it all in stride, steering me, followed by Tom ("Don't leave me alone"), Sarah ("Basketball is so sexist"), and Pete ("I told you. Don't put your brother's hamster in there"), toward some bare spots on the bleachers that aren't too high up, because we don't want to have to walk too far to get to the bathroom, according to Magda, and not too low, either, because we don't want to be hit by any balls.

The rest of the representatives from Fischer Hall—including President Allington, who goes to a section reserved just for him, Drs. Kilgore and Jessup, and the trustees, looking relieved to finally be brushing off the residue from Death Dorm—stream into the bleachers, and, since the impulse is contagious, begin stomping their feet as well, until the steel rafters a hundred feet overhead seem to reverberate.

It's only after the band starts the first few notes of "The Star Spangled Banner" that the crowd quiets down, then sings happily along with a pretty blond musical theater major who seems to give the tune her all. Probably she thinks there's a representative from a major record label in the audience, who's going to sign her then and there to a contract. Or maybe a Broadway producer who is going to come up to her when she's done singing and be all, "You were brilliant! Won't you star in the revival of *South Pacific* that I'm planning?"

Yeah. Good luck with that, honey.

Then, when the last echo of "brave . . . brave . . . brave . . ." dies away, the band rips into the school song, and Cheryl and her sister cheerleaders appear, flipping and cartwheeling their way across the court. They really are very impressive. I've never seen such flexibility—outside of a Tania Trace video, I mean.

The cheerleaders are followed by the gangly-legged Pansies team, in their gold and white jerseys. I hardly recognize Jeff and Mark and the other residents of Fischer Hall. On the court, in their uniforms, they look less like hapless sophomores and juniors, and more like . . . well, athletes. I guess because that's what they are, really. They high-five each of the New Jersey East Devils, in their red and gold jerseys, as they stream by. I'm impressed by this good sportsmanship, even though I know they've been told they *have* to do it. The television cameras swirl around Coach Andrews as he and several other men—assistant coaches, no doubt—walk to their seats on the sideline, and shake hands with the opposing team's coach before something happens that Magda explains is called the tip-off.

Despite the subzero temperatures outside, it's overly warm in the gym, what with all the people and their winter coats and the screaming and all. Tempers are short. Sarah, in particular, seems to feel the need to complain. She expresses strong opinions on multiple subjects, including but not limited to the fact that the money spent on athletics at New York College would be better spent helping to fund the psychology labs, and that the popcorn tastes stale. Beside her, Tom placidly sips from his flask, which he informs Sarah he needs for medicinal purposes.

"Yeah," Sarah replies sarcastically. "Right."

"I could use some of that medicine," Pete observes, after finally hanging up his cell phone. The hamster crisis has been averted.

"Be my guest," Tom says, and passes the flask to Pete. Pete takes a sip, makes a face, and passes it back.

"It tastes like toothpaste," he rasps.

"I told you it's medicinal," Tom says happily, and swills some more.

Meanwhile, Sarah has started paying attention to the game.

"Now, why'd that kid get a foul?" she wants to know.

"Because that boy was charging," Magda explains patiently. "When you have the ball, you can't knock people out of the way if they've established defensive position—"

"Oh!" Sarah cries, seizing Magda's wrist with enough force to cause her to slosh some of her soda. "Look! Coach Andrews is yelling at one of the umpires! Why's he doing that?"

"Ref," Magda mutters. She dabs at her white pants with a napkin. "They're referees, not umpires."

"Oh, what's that man saying?" Sarah bounces up and down excitedly on the bleacher bench. "Why's he look so mad?"

"I don't know," Magda says, flashing her a look of annoyance. Her endless patience isn't so endless, it turns out. "How should I know? Would you stop that bouncing? You made me spill my soda."

"Why is that boy getting a free throw? Why does he get to do that?"

"Because Coach Andrews called the ref a blind son of a—" Magda breaks off, her eyes getting wide. "Holy Mary, mother of God."

"What?" Sarah frantically scans the court. "What, what is it? A steal?"

"No. Heather, is that *Cooper*?"

I feel my insides seize up at the sound of the word. "Cooper? It can't be. What would *he* be doing here?"

"I don't know," Magda says. "But I could swear that's him down there, with some older man. . . ."

At the words *some older man*, my heart grows cold. Because there's only one older man Cooper could be with—with the exception of Detective Canavan, of course.

Then I spot them both, down by the Pansies bench. Cooper is scanning the crowd, obviously looking for me, while Dad is . . . well, Dad seems to be enjoying the game.

"Oh, my God," I say, dropping my head to my knees.

"What?" Magda lays a hand on my back. "Honey, who is it?"

"My father," I say to my knees.

"Your *what*?"

"My father." I lift up my head.

It didn't work. He's still there. I'd been hoping, by closing my eyes, I'd make him disappear. No such luck, apparently.

"That's your dad?" Pete is craning his neck to see. "The jailbird?"

"Your dad was in jail?" Tom wasn't out of the closet back when I was a household name, and so knows nothing about my past life. He wasn't even a secret Heather Wells fan back then, which is odd, because most of my most diehard supporters were gay boys. "What for?"

"Would you guys lean back?" Sarah complains irritably. "I can't see the game."

"I'll be right back," I say, because Cooper has finally spotted me in the crowd and is making his way determinedly toward me, my dad following, but slowly, his gaze on the game. The last thing I need is my friends witnessing what I'm sure is going to be a fairly unpleasant scene.

My heart pounding, I hurry to meet Cooper before he can join us in our room. His expression is inscrutable. But I can see that he's taken the time to shave. So maybe the news isn't all bad. . . .

"Heather," he says coolly.

Well, okay. It's pretty much all bad.

"Look who I found ringing our doorbell a little while ago," he goes on. And although my heart thrills at his use of the word *our*, I know he doesn't mean it in the domestic bliss kind of way I'd like to hear it. "When were you going to tell me your dad was in town?"

"Oh," I say, glancing behind me to see if anyone from my gang is eavesdropping. Not surprisingly, they *all* are . . . with the exception of Sarah, who seems to have been hypnotized by the game.

"I was just waiting for the right moment," I say, realizing even as the words are coming out of my mouth how lame they sound. "I mean . . . what I meant to say was. . . ."

"Never mind," Cooper says. He seems to be as hyper-aware as I am that everyone is listening to our conversation—well, what they can hear of it above the screaming and the band. "We'll talk about it at home."

Hideously relieved, I say, "Fine. Just leave him here with me. I'll look after him."

"He's not bad company, actually," Cooper says, gazing down at my dad, who is standing stock-still in the middle of the bleachers—unconscious that all the people behind him are trying to see around him—staring at the game. I guess it's been a while since he's been at a live sporting event. And the game *is* pretty exciting, I guess, if you're into that kind of thing. We're tied at twenty-one. "Hey. Is that popcorn?"

Sarah surprises everyone—well, okay, me, anyway—by

showing she was paying attention to us all along when she shakes her head and says, not taking her gaze from the court, "It's almost gone. Make Heather go get more."

"Get me a soda," Pete says.

"I could use some nachos," Tom adds.

"No!" Magda shrieks, apparently at a call down below. "He really *is* blind!"

Cooper says, "What?" and slides down into the seat I've vacated. "What was the call?"

"Offensive foul," Magda spits. "But he barely touched the kid!"

Shaking my head in disgust, I turn and make my way down the bleachers toward my father. He is still staring, enraptured, at the ball court.

"Dad," I say, when I reach him.

He doesn't take his eyes off the game. Nor does he say anything. The scoreboard over the middle of the court is counting down the time left in the game. There appear to be nine seconds left, and the Pansies have the ball.

"Dad," I say again. I mean, it really isn't any wonder he doesn't realize I'm talking to him. No one has called him dad in years.

Mark Shepelsky has the ball. He's taking it down the court, dribbling hard. He has a look of concentration on his face I've never seen him wear before . . . not even when he's filling out a vending machine lost-change report.

"Dad," I say for a third and final time, this time much louder.

And my dad jumps and looks down at me—

Just as Mark stops, turns, and throws the ball across the court, sinking it into the basket right before the halftime buzzer goes off, and the crowd goes wild.

"What?" Dad asks. But not me. He's asking the fans around him. "What happened?"

"Shepelsky made a three-pointer," some helpful soul shrieks.

"I missed it!" Dad looks genuinely upset. "Damn!"

"Dad," I say. I can't believe this. I really can't. "Why'd you come to the house? You said you were going to call first. Why didn't you call?"

"I did call," he says, watching as the Pansies run from the court, high-fiving one another, their expressions ecstatic. "No one answered. I thought you might be trying to avoid me."

"Did it ever occur to you I might not be avoiding you?" I ask. "That I just might not have gotten home yet?"

Dad realizes, I guess from the stress in my voice, that I'm not happy. Plus, all the action on the court is over for the moment, so he actually spares a second to look down at me.

"What's the matter, honey?" he asks. "Did I screw up?"

"It's just," I say, feeling idiotic for getting so upset, but unable to help myself, "things with Cooper, my landlord . . . I mean, they're *delicate*. And you showing up like that, out of the blue—"

"He seems like a nice guy," Dad says, glancing over at where Cooper is sitting. "Smart. Funny." He grins down at me. "You certainly have your old man's approval."

Something inside me bursts. I think maybe it's an aneurism.

"I don't need your approval, Dad," I practically shout. "I've been getting along fine for the past twenty years without it."

Dad looks taken aback. I guess I shouldn't blame him. It's not his fault what he seems to think is going on between Cooper and me isn't.

"What I mean is," I say, softening my tone guiltily, "it's not like that. With Cooper and me, I mean. We're just friends. I do his billing."

"I know," Dad says. He looks confused. "He told me."

Now *I'm* confused. "Then why'd you say you approve? Like you thought we're dating?"

"Well, you're in love with him, aren't you?" Dad asks simply. "I mean, it's written all over your face. You might be able to fool him, but you aren't fooling your old dad. You used to get that same look on your face back when you were nine years old and that Scott Baio fellow would come on TV."

I gape at him, then realize my mouth is hanging open. I close it with a snapping sound probably only I can hear over the din of the gymnasium. Then I say, "Dad. Why don't you go sit down with Cooper? I'll be back in a minute."

"Where are you going?" Dad wants to know.

"To get the nachos," I say.

And stagger away to do so.

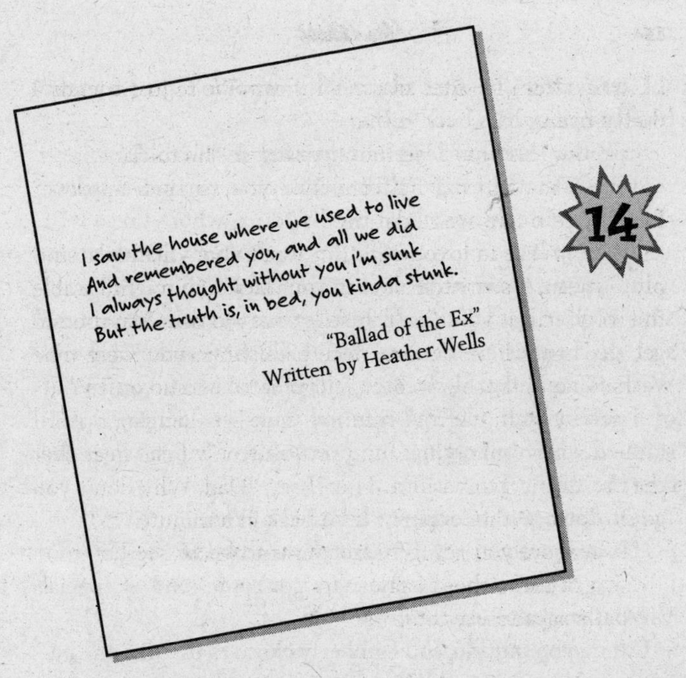

14
I saw the house where we used to live
And remembered you, and all we did
I always thought without you I'm sunk
But the truth is, in bed, you kinda stunk.
"Ballad of the Ex"
Written by Heather Wells

I'm not totally unfamiliar with the layout of the Winer Sports Complex. I'd signed up for a twenty-five-dollar-a-semester aerobics class there last semester, after passing my employment probation, and had even shown up for one session.

Unfortunately, I'd soon learned that only skinny girls take aerobics at New York College, and that larger young ladies like myself—if the waifish young things were to be able to see the instructor around me—had to stand in the back, where we, in turn, couldn't see anything, except tiny arms flailing around.

I quit after the first class. They wouldn't give me my twenty-five dollars back, either.

Still, the lesson at least familiarized me with the sports center, so that during halftime I'm able to find a ladies' room deep in the bowels of the building, where there isn't a mile-long line to use a stall. I'm washing my hands afterward, gazing at my reflection in the mirror above the sinks and wondering if I should just let nature take its course and go brunette, when a toilet flushes and Kimberly Watkins, in her gold sweater and pleated skirt, comes out of a nearby stall. Her red-rimmed eyes—yes, definitely red-rimmed, and from crying, I'm pretty sure—widen when she sees me.

"Oh," she says, freezing in her tracks. "You."

"Hi, Kimberly," I say. I'm pretty surprised to see her, too. I'd have thought the cheerleaders got some kind of special VIP bathroom to use.

But maybe they do, and Kimberly chose to use this one because in here, she could cry in private.

She seems to recover herself pretty quickly, though, and starts washing her hands at the sink next to mine.

"Enjoying the game?" she wants to know. She apparently thinks I can't see that her mascara is smudged where she's wiped away her tears.

"Sure," I say.

"I didn't know you were a fan," she says.

"I'm not, really," I admit. "They're making us attend. To show everyone that Fischer Hall isn't really a Death Dorm."

"Oh," Kimberly says. She turns off the water and reaches for the paper towels at the same time I do.

"Go ahead," she says to me.

I do.

"Listen, Kimberly," I say, as I dry. "I paid a little call on Doug Winer today."

Kimberly's eyes go very wide. She seems to forget her hands are dripping wet. "You *did*?"

"I did."

"*Why*?" Kimberly's voice breaks. "I *told* you, it was her freaky roommate who killed her. Her roommate, not Doug."

"Yeah," I say, tossing the wadded-up paper towels I'd used into the trash. "You said that. But it just doesn't make sense. Ann's no killer. Why would you say she was? Except maybe to throw the police off the scent of the person who *really* did it."

This gets to her. She averts her gaze, and seems to remember her hands. She pulls out a wad of paper towels from the dispenser on the wall. "I don't know what you're talking about," she says.

"Oh," I say. "So you're saying you didn't know Doug deals?"

Kimberly purses her perfectly made-up lips and stares at her reflection. "I guess. I mean, I know he's always got coke, I guess. And E."

"Oh," I say sarcastically. "Is that all? Why didn't you say something about this before, Kimberly? Why were you trying to make me think Ann was the guilty party, when you knew all this about Doug?"

"Geez," Kimberly cries, tearing her gaze away from her reflection and glaring at me. "Just 'cause a guy deals drugs doesn't mean he's a murderer! I mean, heck, a lot of people deal. A *lot* of people."

"Distribution of controlled substances is illegal, you know, Kimberly," I say. "So's possession. He could go to jail. He could get *expelled*."

Kimberly's laugh is like a hiccup, it's so brief. "But Doug Winer'll never go to jail or get expelled."

"Oh? And why is that?"

"He's a *Winer*," Kimberly says, as if I were supremely stupid.

I ignore that. "Did Lindsay do drugs, Kimberly?"

She rolls her eyes. "Geez. What's *wrong* with you? Why do you care so much? I mean, I realize you're, like, a frustrated ex-rock star or something. But nobody listens to your music anymore. Now you're just a desk jockey at a Division III school. I mean, a monkey could do your job. Why are you *trying* so hard?"

"*Did Lindsay do drugs*?" My voice is so loud and so cold that Kimberly jumps, her eyes wide.

"I don't know," she shouts back at me. "Lindsay did a lot of things . . . and a lot of people."

"What do you mean?" I narrow my eyes at her. "What do you mean, a lot of people?"

Kimberly gives me a very sarcastic look. "What do you think? Everyone's trying to make out like Lindsay was some kind of saint. Cheryl and those guys, with that stupid sweater thing. She wasn't, you know. A saint, I mean. She was just . . . Lindsay."

"What people was she doing, Kimberly?" I demand. "Mark and Doug and . . . who else?"

Kimberly turns back to her reflection with a shrug and dabs at her lip gloss. "Ask Coach Andrews," she says, "if you want to know so badly."

I stare at her reflection. "Coach *Andrews*? How would *he* know?"

Kimberly just smirks.

And my mouth falls open.

I can't believe it. "No, come on," I say. Lindsay and *Coach Andrews*? "Are you serious?"

It's right then that the ladies' room door opens and Megan McGarretty pokes her head in.

"Gawd," she says to Kimberly. "There you are. We've been looking all over. Come on, it's time to do Lindsay's sweater."

Kimberly flashes me a knowing glance, then turns and heads for the door, her pleated skirt swishing behind her.

"Kimberly, wait," I say. I want to ask her what she means about Lindsay and Coach Andrews. She can't possibly mean what I think she means. Can she? I mean, Coach Andrews? He seems like such a . . . well . . . putz.

But Kimberly just sashays out of the room. Not surprisingly, she doesn't even say goodbye.

I stand there, staring at the door the girls have just disappeared through. Lindsay and *Coach Andrews*?

But even if it were true, and he's a potential suspect, I can't think of a reason why Coach Andrews might kill Lindsay. Lindsay's over eighteen. Yeah, okay, the college disapproves of faculty sleeping with their students. But it isn't like Coach Andrews would ever get fired over it. He's Phillip Allington's golden boy, the man who is going to lead New York College back to Division I glory . . . somehow. Or something. Coach Andrews could sleep his way through the entire Women's Studies Department and the trustees wouldn't blink an eye, so long as the Pansies keep winning games.

So why would he kill Lindsay?

And what had that little brat called me? Desk jockey? I'm *way* more than just a desk jockey. Fischer Hall would fall apart if it weren't for me. Why does she think I'm asking so many questions about Lindsay, anyway? Because I *care* about that place, and the people who live in it. If it weren't for me, how many more girls would have died last semester? If it weren't for me, nobody would get their vending machine refunds. How would Kimberly Watkins like living in Fischer Hall *then*?

Fuming, I leave the ladies' room. The hallway outside is dead silent. That's because, I realize, the girls have started their tribute to Lindsay back in the gym, and everyone has hurried back to their seats to watch it. I can hear the faint strains of the school song, played real slow, just like they'd said they'd have the band do it. I sort of want to be in there watching, too.

But I haven't gotten Tom's nachos yet, or Pete's soda. Not to mention Cooper's popcorn. Now is actually a good time to do so, with everyone inside watching Lindsay's sweater ascend to the rafters. Maybe there won't be a line at the concession stand.

I turn the corner, hurrying past empty squash court after empty squash court—if Sarah ever took a serious look around the sports center, she'd come up with a lot more reasons to complain about how the Psychology Department is treated. There must be twenty or thirty million of the Winer family's dollars poured into this building alone. It's almost brand-new, with special ID card scanner gates you have to pass through to get in. Even the soda machines have built-in scanners so you can buy a can of Coke using your dining card. . . .

Except, for such fancy, new-fangled soda machines, they sure seem to be making a funny noise. Not the usual electronic—and, let's admit it, to a soda-lover, comforting—hum, but a sort of thud—thud—thud.

But soda machines don't thud.

Then I see, suddenly, that I'm not the only person in the

hallway. When I come around the side of the bank of soda machines, I see that the thudding noises are coming from the hilt of a long kitchen knife as it repeatedly strikes the ribs of a man in a sports coat and tie. The man lies slumped against the wall to one side of the soda machines, and above him crouch three other men, each wearing half a basketball over his face, with small slits cut out in the rubber so that they can see.

When all three men hear my scream—because if you come across a scene like this when you are just walking along minding your own business, thinking about nachos, you're going to scream—they turn their heads toward me—three half basketballs, with eye slits cut in them, swiveling my way.

Of course, I scream again. Because, excuse me, but, creepy.

Then one of the men pulls the knife out of the man on the floor. It makes a sickening sucking sound. The blade that has just come out of the man is dark and slick with blood. My stomach lurches at the sight of it.

It's only when the man with the knife says, "Run," to his companions that I realize what I've just done—stumbled across the scene of a crime.

But they don't seem interested in killing me. In fact, they seem interested in getting away from me as quickly as possible, at least if the squeaking of their sneaker soles on the polished floor is any indication as they flee.

Then, the New York College fight song (*Hail to thee New York College / Colors gold and white / We will honor you forever / Bite them, Cougars, bite!*—the words to the song not having been changed after New York College lost its Division I standing and mascot) playing dimly in the background, I sink to my knees at the side of the injured man, trying to remember what I'd learned in the emergency first-aid seminar Dr. Jessup had over Winter Break. It was only what information they could cram into an hour, but I do recall that first and foremost, it's important to call for help—a feat I accomplish by whipping out my cell phone and dialing Cooper's cell number, the first one that pops into my head.

It takes him three rings to answer. I guess Lindsay's tribute must be especially moving.

"Somebody's been stabbed by the squash courts," I say into the phone. It's important to stay calm in an emergency. I learned that during my assistant hall director training. "Call for an ambulance and the cops. The guys who did it are wearing basketball masks. Don't let anyone in basketball masks leave. And get a first-aid kit. And get down here!"

"Heather?" Cooper asks. "Heather—what? *Where* are you?"

I repeat everything I've just said. As I do, I look down at the stabbed man, and realize, with sudden horror, that I know him.

It's Manuel, Julio's nephew.

"Hurry!" I shriek into the phone. Then I hang up. Because the blood from Manuel's body is starting to pool around my knees.

Whipping off my sweater, I stuff it into the gaping hole in Manuel's stomach. I don't know what else to do. The emergency first-aid course we took didn't cover multiple stab wounds to the gut.

"You're going to be all right," I tell Manuel. He's looking up at me with half-lidded eyes. The blood around him is gelatinous and almost black as it seeps into my jeans. I stuff my sweater more deeply into the biggest hole I can find, keeping my fingers pressed over it. "Manuel, you're going to be fine. Just hang on, okay? Help will be here in a minute."

"H-Heather," Manuel rasps. Blood bubbles up out of his mouth. I know this is not a good sign.

"You're going to be fine," I say, trying to sound like I believe it. "You hear me, Manuel? You're going to be just fine."

"Heather," Manuel says. His voice is nothing more than a wheeze. "It was me. I gave it to her."

Pressing hard against the wound—blood has soaked through my sweater and is gathering under my fingernails—I say, "Don't talk, Manuel. Help is on its way."

"She asked me for it," Manuel says. He's obviously delirious with blood loss and pain. "She asked me for it, and I gave it to her. I knew I shouldn't've, but she was crying. I couldn't say no. She was . . . she was so . . ."

"Would you shut up, Manuel?" I say, alarmed by the amount of blood coming out from between his lips. "Please? Please don't talk."

"She was crying," Manuel keeps saying, over and over again. *Where is Cooper?* "How could I say no to her when she was crying? I didn't know, though. I didn't know what they were going to do to her."

"Manuel," I say, hoping he can't hear that my voice is shaking. "You have to stop talking. You're losing too much blood. . . ."

"But they knew," he goes on, clearly off in his own world. A world of pain. "They knew where she got it—"

At that moment, Cooper turns the corner, Pete and Tom right behind him. Pete, seeing me, pulls out his security walkie-talkie, and begins squawking into it about how they've found me, and to get a stretcher down to the squash courts ASAP.

Cooper falls to his knees beside me and, miraculously, reveals a first-aid kit he's snagged from somewhere.

"Ambulance is on the way," he says, while Manuel, beneath my blood-soaked fingers, rambles feebly on.

"I gave it to her, don't you see, Heather? It was me. And they knew it was me."

"Who did this to him?" Cooper demands, pulling a huge roll of Ace bandages from the first-aid kit. "Did you get a look at him?

"They all had basketballs on their heads," I say.

"What?"

"They had basketballs on their heads." I grab the roll of bandages from him, pull away my sweater, and ram the roll of bandages into the biggest wound. "Half a basketball, over their faces, with little eye holes cut out—"

"My God." Tom, looking pale, blinks down at us. "Is that . . . is that *Manuel*?"

"Yes," I say, as Cooper leans forward and pulls down one of Manuel's eyelids.

"He's going into shock," Cooper says, pretty calmly, in my opinion. "You know him?"

"He works at Fischer Hall. His name is Manuel." Julio, I know, is going to flip out when he sees this. I pray that he doesn't come looking for his nephew.

"They did this as a warning," Manuel says. "A warning to me not to tell that I gave it to her."

"Gave what to who, Manuel?" Cooper asks him, even as I'm shushing him, telling him to save his breath.

"The key," Manuel says. "I know I shouldn't have, but I gave her my key."

"Who?" Cooper wants to know.

"Cooper," I say. I can't believe this. I can't believe he's interrogating a dying man.

But he ignores me.

"Manuel, who'd you give your key to?"

"Lindsay," Manuel says. Manuel shakes his head. "I gave Lindsay my key. She was crying . . . she said she'd left something in the cafeteria, something she needed to get. At night, after it was closed—"

His eyelids drift shut.

Cooper says, "Damn."

But then the EMTs are there, shoving us both out of the way. And I'm actually relieved, thinking everything is going to be okay.

Which just goes to show how much I know.

Which is nothing.

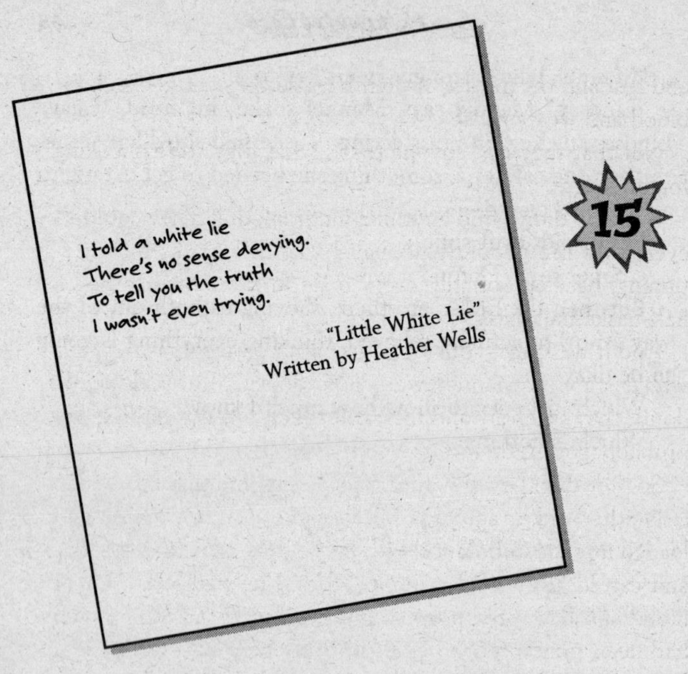
I told a white lie
There's no sense denying.
To tell you the truth
I wasn't even trying.
"Little White Lie"
Written by Heather Wells
15

You know what happens when someone nearly gets murdered during a Division III college basketball game that is being televised live on New York One?

Everyone keeps right on playing.

That's right.

Oh, they posted cops at all the exits, and after the game—which the Pansies lost, twenty-four to forty. They just never came back after the second half. And not even because they heard about what happened to Manuel. Because no one told them. No, basically, the Pansies just suck—the cops made everybody stop on their way out and show them their hands and feet and the insides of their bags, so they could check for blood and weapons.

Not that they *told* anyone that's what they were checking for, of course.

But they didn't find anything incriminating. They couldn't even hold the people with half-basketball masks for questioning, because roughly every male in the audience had a half-basketball mask.

And it was pretty obvious—to me, anyway—that the guys who'd stabbed Manuel were long gone. I mean, I highly doubt they stuck around to watch the rest of the game. They probably got out before the cops even arrived.

So they didn't even witness the Pansies' humiliating defeat.

Neither did I, actually. Because no sooner was Manuel loaded into an ambulance with his heartsick uncle at his side and carted away—the paramedics said he had lost a lot of blood and had some internal injuries, but that nothing vital had been punctured, so he'd probably be okay—than I was whisked off to the Sixth Precinct to look at mug shots with Detective Canavan, even though I EXPLAINED to him I hadn't seen their faces, due to the masks.

"What about their clothes?" he wants to know.

"I told you," I say, for the thirtieth time at least. "They were wearing regular, everyday clothes. Jeans. Flannel shirts. Nothing special."

"And you didn't hear them say anything to the victim?"

It's kind of irritating to me that Detective Canavan keeps referring to Manuel as "the victim" when he knows perfectly well that he has a name, and what that name is.

But maybe, like Sarah's gallows humor, saying "the victim" is a way of distancing himself from the horror of acts of such violence.

I wouldn't mind distancing myself from it, either. Every time I close my eyes, I see the blood. It wasn't red like blood on TV. It was dark brown. The same color the knees of my jeans are now.

"They didn't say anything," I say. "They were just stabbing him."

"What was he doing there?" Detective Canavan wants to know. "By the soda machines?"

"How should I know?" I ask with a shrug. "Maybe he was thirsty. The line at the concession stand was really long."

"What were *you* doing there?"

"I told you. I had to go to the bathroom, and the line at the other ladies' room was too long."

When Detective Canavan arrived at the sports complex—because of course we called him, to tell him what Manuel had said, about giving a key to Lindsay—I had suggested that he stop the game and question every single person present—particularly Coach Andrews, whom I now had reason to believe was more deeply involved than previously thought.

But President Allington—who unfortunately had to be informed of what was going on, given how many cops were lurking in the building—balked, saying that New York One would be on the story in a red-hot minute, and that the college had had enough bad publicity for one week. The last thing the school needed was reporters going around asking questions about a crime that, for all we knew, might in no way be connected to Lindsay—despite what I told everyone Manuel had said.

Then President Allington went on to assure us that, bad publicity aside, New York One would also be within their rights to sue if the game were stopped, claiming they stood to lose a million dollars in advertising if the game didn't continue.

I honestly never suspected those Bowflex commercials brought in so much revenue, but apparently Division III college basketball is considered must-see TV by those folks most likely to be interested in purchasing exercise equipment for the home.

"One thing I want to be sure everyone understands," President Allington also said to Detective Canavan, unfortunately (for him) within my earshot, though he was speaking softly so that no lurking reporters might overhear, "is that New York College is in no way responsible for either the death of that girl or the injuries sustained by Mr. Juarez this evening. And if he did give her a key with which she might have accessed the cafeteria, we are in no way responsible for that, either. Legally, that's still trespassing."

Which caused Detective Canavan to remark, "So what you're saying, Mr. Allington, is that if Lindsay used Manuel's key to gain access to the cafeteria, she damn well deserved to get her head chopped off?"

President Allington looked understandably flustered by this statement, and one of his flunkies stepped in to say, "That is not what the president meant at all. What he meant was, the college cannot be held responsible for the fact that someone in our employ gave his keys to a student who later got herself killed on college property. . . ."

Detective Canavan didn't stick around to hear more. And, to my everlasting relief, he took me away with him.

Or at least it was a relief at first. Because it meant I could put off having to talk to Cooper about my dad for that much longer.

Unfortunately, it meant I had to talk to Detective Canavan instead.

"And that's it? That's all you can remember? Jeans, flannel shirts, basketballs on their heads. What about their shoes? Were they wearing tennis shoes? Loafers?"

"Sneakers," I say, remembering the squeaking on the floor.

"Well." He blinks at me. It's late, and he's probably been at the precinct all day. The number of Styrofoam cups littering the floor by his desk indicates how he's managed to sustain his energy level for so long. "That narrows it down."

"I'm sorry. What do you want me to say? They were—"

"Wearing basketballs on their heads. Yes. You mentioned that."

"Are we done here?" I want to know.

"We're done," Detective Canavan says. "Except for the usual warning."

"Warning?"

"Not to involve yourself in the investigation into Lindsay Combs's murder."

"Right," I say. I can be just as sarcastic as he can. "Because I so stumbled across poor Manuel getting stabbed by her killers on purpose."

"We don't know the attack on Mr. Juarez and Lindsay's murder are connected," Detective Canavan points out. Seeing my raised eyebrows, he adds, "Yet."

"Whatever," I say. "Can I go?"

He nods, and I'm out of there like a shot. I'm tired. All I want to do is go home. And change my pants, which are stiff with Manuel's blood.

I go out into the lobby of the Sixth Precinct, expecting to see Cooper there, sitting in the same seat he always takes when he's waiting for me to come out of one of my many visits with Detective Canavan (today is a new record, twice in less than twelve hours).

But the seat is empty. In fact, the lobby is empty.

That's when I notice it's snowing really hard outside. I mean, *really* hard. I can barely make out the shape of the Range Rover parked in front of the station. But when I go outside and peer through the driver's-side window, I recognize Patty's husband Frank. He starts when I tap on the window, and puts it down.

"Heather!" Patty leans over from the passenger seat. "There you are! Sorry, we didn't see you, we're listening to a book on tape. One about parenting that the new nanny recommended."

"The nanny who terrifies you?" I ask.

"Yes, that's the one. God, you should have seen her face when we told her we were coming here. She nearly . . . Well, never mind. Get in, you must be freezing!"

I hop into the backseat. The interior is warm and smells faintly of Indian food. That's because Frank and Patty had been enjoying some samosas as they waited for me.

"How'd you know where I was?" I ask, as they pass me one, loaded with tamarind sauce. Yum.

"Cooper called," Frank explains. "Said he had to run and could we pick you up. Off on one of his cases, I guess. What's he working on, anyway?"

"How should I know?" I ask, with my mouth full. "Like he's going to tell me."

"Did you really see someone get stabbed?" Patty asks, turning around in her seat. "Weren't you scared? What is that all over your jeans?"

"I didn't have time to be scared," I say, chewing. "And that's blood."

"Oh, God!" Patty turns quickly around to face the windshield again. "Heather!"

"It's okay," I say. "I can just get new ones." Although, with my luck, I'll have gone up a size, thanks to all the holiday cheer in which I imbibed.

Size 14 is still average for an American woman. Still, you don't want to have to buy all new jeans to accommodate your new size. That can be hard on the wallet. What you want to do instead is maybe reduce intake on the bodega fried chicken. Maybe.

Although it depends on how you look in the new jeans.

"It's really coming down hard," Frank observes, as he pulls out of his primo parking space. In ordinary circumstances, that space would be instantly taken by some waiting vehicle. But it's a blizzard, and no one is out on the streets. The flakes are falling thick and fast, already coating the street and sidewalks with an inch of fluffy white stuff. "I can't imagine Cooper's going to be able to do any real detecting in this weather."

Frank is just slightly obsessed with the fact that Cooper is a private detective. Most people fantasize about being rock stars. Well, it turns out rock stars fantasize about being private detectives. Or, in my case, being a nonvanity size 8 and still able to eat anything I want again.

Although I'm not actually a rock star. Anymore.

"Heather, I hope you're being careful this time," Patty frets, from the front seat. "I mean, about this dead girl. You aren't getting involved in the investigation, are you? Not like last time?"

"Oh, heck, no," I say. Patty doesn't need to know about my trip to the Tau Phi House. She has enough to worry about, being a former model and rocker's wife, not to mention the mother of a toddler who, at last reportage, ate an entire H & H everything bagel—almost as big as his own head—in one sitting.

The nanny hadn't been too happy about that one.

"Good," Patty says. "Because they don't pay you enough to get yourself nearly killed, like last time."

When Frank pulls up in front of Cooper's house, I see that a few of the lights are on . . . which surprises me, since it means Cooper must be home.

But before I can get out of the car, Frank says, "Oh, Heather, about the gig at Joe's—"

I freeze with my hand on the door handle. I can't believe—what with all the blood and everything—I'd forgotten about Frank's invitation to jam with him and his band.

"Oh," I say, frantically trying to think up an excuse. "Yeah. About that. Can I get back to you? 'Cause I'm really tired right now, and can't really think straight—"

"Nothing to think about," Frank says cheerfully. "It's just gonna be me and the guys and a hundred and sixty or so of our friends and family. Come on. It'll be fun."

"Frank," Patty says, apparently having caught a glimpse of my face. "Maybe now's not the best time to ask about that."

"Come on, Heather," Frank says, ignoring his wife. "You're never gonna get over your stage fright if you don't get back up there. Why not do it among friends?"

Stage fright? Is that my problem? Funny, I thought it was just fear of having people boo and throw things at me. Or, worse . . . snicker, the way Jordan and Cooper's dad did, when I played them my own songs that fateful day in the Cartwright Records offices. . . .

"I'll think about it," I say to Frank. "Thanks for the ride. See ya."

I plunge from the car before either Patty or her husband can say anything, then run to the front door, ducking my head against the onslaught of flakes.

Phew. Talk about narrow escapes.

Inside, Lucy meets me in the foyer, excited to see me, but not in an *I gotta go out right this minute* kind of way. Someone's already let her out.

"Hello?" I call, shedding my coat and scarf.

No one answers. But I smell something unusual. It takes me a minute to place the scent. Then I realize why: it's a candle. Cooper and I are not candle people—Cooper because, well, he's a guy, and me because I've seen them cause so many fires in Fischer Hall that I'm paranoid I, too, will forget and leave one burning unattended.

So why is someone burning a candle in the house?

The smell is coming from upstairs . . . not the living room or kitchen, and not Cooper's office. It's coming from upstairs, where Cooper sleeps.

Then it hits me. Cooper must be home, and entertaining.

In his room.

With candles.

Which can only mean one thing: He's got a date.

Of course. That's why he couldn't wait for me down at the precinct, and had to call Frank and Patty! He's got a date.

I pause at the bottom of the stairs, trying to sort out why this realization has made me suddenly so upset. I mean, it's not like Cooper KNOWS about the enormous crush I have on him. Why SHOULDN'T he see other people? Just because he HASN'T seen anyone (that I know of . . . he certainly hasn't brought anybody back to the house) since I moved in doesn't mean he SHOULDN'T or CAN'T. Now that I think of it, we never really did discuss the issue of overnight guests. It's just not something that ever came up.

Until now.

Well, so what? He's having a sleepover. It doesn't have anything to do with me. I'll just creep up to the third floor and go to bed. No reason to stop and knock and ask him how he's doing. Even though I'm dying to see what she looks like. Cooper has a reputation in his family for always dating super-intelligent, incredibly beautiful, even exotic women. Like brain surgeons who are also former models. That kind of thing.

Even if I thought I ever had a chance with Cooper romantically, one look at his many exes would cure me. I mean, what guy would want a washed-up ex-pop star who now works as an assistant residence hall director and wears vanity size 8 jeans (or possibly 10s) when he could have a physicist who was once Miss Delaware?

Yeah. Right. No one. I mean, unless the physicist happens to be really boring. And maybe doesn't like Ella Fitzgerald (I've got all her songs memorized, including the scat). And maybe isn't the warm, funny human being I just happen to believe I am. . . .

Stop. STOP IT.

I'm creeping up the stairs to the second floor as quietly as I can—Lucy panting at my side—when I notice something strange. The door to Cooper's bedroom is open . . . but there's no light on. Whereas the door to the guest room down the hall from Cooper's bedroom is open, *and* there's a light on, *and* the light is flickering. Like a candle flame.

Who on earth would be in our guest room with a candle?

"Hello?" I say again. Because if Cooper's entertaining lady friends in our guest room, well, that's just his tough luck if I come busting in. His room is his inner sanctum—I've never dared venture into it . . . if only because he's so rarely to be found in it. Also because thousand-dollar sheets scare me.

But the guest room?

The door is really only slightly ajar. Still, it's technically open. Which is why I push on it to open it a little farther, and say, "Hello?" for a third time. . . .

. . . then shriek at the sight of my father doing the downward-facing dog.

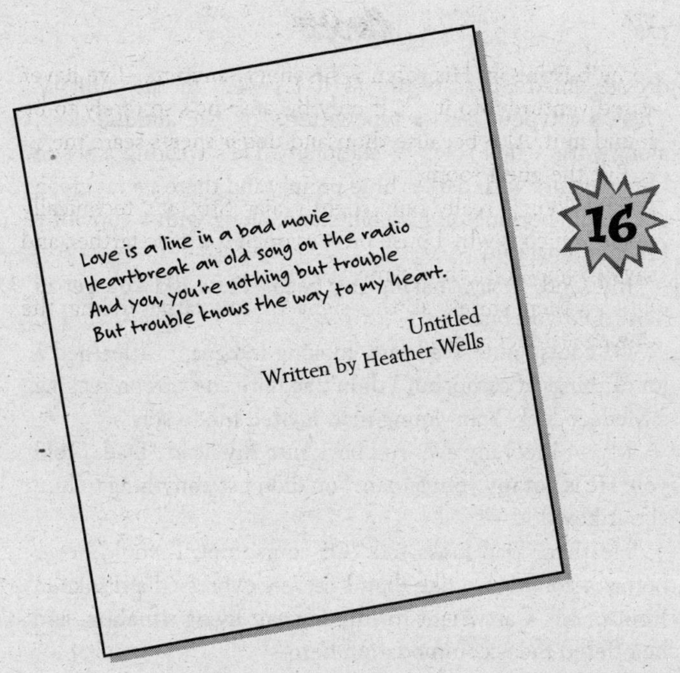

16
Love is a line in a bad movie
Heartbreak an old song on the radio
And you, you're nothing but trouble
But trouble knows the way to my heart.
Untitled
Written by Heather Wells

"I find yoga extremely relaxing," Dad explains. "Back at camp, I did it every morning and every night. It's really rejuvenated me."

I stare at him from across the room. It's strange to hear your father call jail camp. Especially while he's doing yoga.

"Dad," I say. "Could you quit that for a minute and talk to me?"

"Of course, sweetheart," Dad says. And comes back to his feet.

I can't believe this. He's clearly moved in. His suitcase is open—and empty—on the window seat. His shoes sit by the dresser, lined up as neatly as if he were in the military. There's a typewriter—a typewriter!—on the antique desk, along with a tidy stack of stationery. He's wearing a set of blue pajamas with darker blue piping, and there's a fat green tea candle burning on his nightstand, along with a copy of a Lincoln biography.

"My God," I say, shaking my head. "How did you get in here? Did you *break* in?"

"Of course not," Dad says, looking indignant. "I learned a lot of things at camp, but I didn't acquire any tips on picking a Medeco lock. Your young man invited me to stay."

"My—" I feel my eyes roll back into my head. "Dad. I told you. He is not my young man. You didn't say anything to him about how I lo—"

"Heather." Dad looks sad. "Of course not. I would never betray a confidence like that. I merely expressed a dislike in front of Mr. Cartwright for my current living situation, and he offered me accommodation here—"

"Dad!" I groan. "You didn't!"

"Well, the Chelsea Hotel was hardly a suitable place for a man in my position," he says patiently. "I don't know if you're aware of this, Heather, but many people with criminal records have resided in the Chelsea Hotel. Actual murderers. That's not the kind of environment a person who is trying to rehabilitate himself should be in. Besides which, it was quite noisy. All that loud music and honking horns. No, this"—he looks around the pleasant white bedroom happily—"is much more *me*."

"Dad." I can't help it. I can't stand up anymore. I sink down onto the side of the queen-sized bed. "Did Cooper say how long you could stay?"

"In fact," Dad says, reaching out to ruffle Lucy's ears, since she's followed me inside, "he did. He said I could stay as long as it took in order for me to get back on my feet."

"Dad." I want to scream. "Seriously. You can't do that. It's not that I don't want to work on our relationship—yours and mine, I mean. It's just that . . . you can't take advantage of Cooper's generosity this way."

"I'm not," Dad says matter-of-factly. "I'm going to be working for him, in exchange for rent."

I blink. "You're . . . what?"

"He's taking me on as an employee of Cartwright Investigations," Dad says . . . a little proudly, I think. "Just like you, I'm working for him. I'm going to help him tail people. He says I've got just the right looks for it . . . sort of unnoticeable. He says I blend."

I blink some more. "You *blend*?"

"That's right." Dad opens up the drawer to his nightstand and takes out a small wooden flute. "I'm trying to take it as a compliment. The fact that I'm so unnoticeable, I mean. I know your mother often felt that way, but I wasn't aware it was true of the world in general. Oh, well. Listen to this little tune I learned at camp. It's quite restful. And after the night you've had, I'm sure you could use a little relaxation." He proceeds to lift the flute to his lips and begins to play it.

I sit there for a minute more as the notes—plaintive and, as he'd mentioned, oddly restful—wash over me. Then I shake myself and say, "Dad."

He immediately stops playing. "Yes, dear?"

It's the endearments that are killing me. Or possibly making me want to kill HIM.

"I'm going to bed now. We'll talk about this again in the morning."

"Well, all right," he says. "But I don't see what there is to talk about. Cooper is obviously a man of good sense. If he wants to hire me, I don't see why you should object."

I can't see why I should object, either. Except . . . how am I going to get Cooper to realize I'm the woman of his dreams if my DAD's around? How am I ever going to make him that romantic steak dinner for two I'd been planning? There's nothing romantic about steak for *three.*

"I realize I haven't been the best father to you, Heather," Dad goes on. "Neither your mother nor I provided you with very good role models growing up. But I hope the damage isn't so serious that you are incapable of forming loving relationships now. Because it's my sincerest wish that that is what you and I can have with one another. Because everyone needs a family, Heather."

Family? Is that what I need? Is that what's wrong with me? I don't have a family?

"You look tired," Dad says. "Which is understandable, after the day you've had. Here, maybe this will help soothe you." Then he starts playing the flute again.

Okay. *This* I don't need.

I lean down, blow out Dad's green tea candle, and snatch it from the nightstand.

"These are a fire hazard," I snap, in my most assistant residence hall directory voice.

Then I stalk from the room and upstairs to my own apartment.

The snow doesn't stop. When I wake up in the morning, I look out the window and see that it's still coming down—slower now, and less of it. But still in big fluffy flakes.

And when I get out of bed—which isn't easy, considering how snug it is in there, with Lucy sprawled half across me—

and go to the window, I find myself looking out at a winter wonderland.

New York City looks different after a snowfall. Even an inch can make a difference—it covers all the dirt and graffiti, and makes everything look sparkly and new.

And twenty inches—which is what it appears we got overnight—can make the city look like another planet. Everything is quiet . . . no honking horns, no car alarms . . . every sound is muffled, every branch straining under the weight of so much fluffy white stuff, every windowsill coated in it. Gazing out at it, I realize, with a sudden zing to my heartstrings, what's going on:

It's a Snow Day.

I realize it even before I pounce on the phone and call the college's weather hotline. Oh, yes. Classes are canceled for the day. The school is closed. The city, in fact, is shut down. Only necessary emergency personnel should be on the streets. *Yes.*

Except, of course, when you live two blocks away from where you work, you can't exactly plead that you couldn't get in.

But still. You can be late.

I take my time bathing—because why stand up if you don't have to?—and getting dressed. I have to resort to the backup jeans because of the bloodstains on my primary pair, and I am dismayed to find they are slightly snug. Okay, more than slightly. I have to pull my old trick of stuffing wadded-up socks along the waistband of my jeans to stretch them out, while doing deep knee bends. I tell myself it's because they just came out of the dryer. Two weeks ago.

And when I remove the socks before going downstairs, they are a little less tight. At least I can breathe.

It's as I'm breathing that I realize I'm smelling something unfamiliar. At least, unfamiliar in this house.

Bacon. And, if I'm not mistaken, eggs.

I hurry down the stairs—Lucy at my heels—and am horrified when I walk into the kitchen and find Cooper there, reading the paper, while my dad stands at the stove in a pair of brown cords and a woolly sweater. Cooking breakfast.

"This," I say loudly, "has to stop."

Dad turns around and smiles at me. "Good morning, honey. Juice?"

Cooper flicks down one side of the paper. "Why are you up?" he wants to know. "They just said on the news New York College is closed."

I ignore him. But I can't ignore Lucy, who is at the back door, scratching to be let out. I open the door, letting in an arctic blast. Lucy looks disappointed by what she sees out there, but bravely soldiers ahead. I close the door behind her and turn to face my father. Because I've come to a decision. And it has nothing to do with the wooden flute.

"Dad," I say. "You cannot live here. I'm sorry, Cooper. It was nice of you to offer. But it's too weird."

"Relax," Cooper says, from behind his newspaper.

I feel my blood pressure shoot up another ten points. Why does this always happen whenever anyone says the word *relax*?

"Seriously," I say. "I mean, I live here, too. I'm also an employee of Cartwright Investigations. Don't I get a say in this?"

"No," Cooper says, from behind his newspaper.

"Honey," Dad says, turning around and handing me a steaming mug of coffee. "Drink this. You never were a morning person. Just like your mother."

"I am not like Mom," I say. Though I take the coffee. Because it smells delicious. "Okay? I am *nothing* like her. Do you see, Cooper? Do you see what you've done? You've invited this man to live here, and he's already telling me I'm like my mother. And I am nothing like her."

"Then let him stay here," Cooper says, still not looking out from behind his paper, "and find that out for himself."

"Your mother is a lovely person, Heather," Dad says, as he puts two sunny-side-up eggs and some bacon on a plate. "Just not in the mornings. Rather like you. Here." He hands the plate to me. "This is how you used to like them as a little girl. I hope you still do."

I look down at the plate. He has arranged the eggs so that they are like eyes, and the bacon is a smiling mouth, just like he used to do when I was a kid.

Suddenly I am overwhelmed by an urge to cry.

Damn him. How can he *do* this to me?

"They're fine, thanks," I mutter, and sit down at the kitchen table.

"Well," Cooper says, finally lowering the paper, "now that that's settled, Heather, your dad is going to be staying with us for a while, until he figures out what his next move is going to be. Which is good, because I can use the help. I have more work than I can handle on my own, and your dad has just the kind of qualities I need in an assistant."

"The ability to *blend*," I say, chomping on a strip of bacon. Which is, by the way, delicious. And I'm not the only one who thinks so. Lucy, whom Dad lets back in after she scratched on the door, is enjoying a strip I snuck her, as well.

"Correct," Cooper says. "An ability which should never be

underestimated when you are in the private investigative field."

The phone rings. Dad says, "I'll get that," and leaves the kitchen to do so.

The second he's gone, Cooper says, in a different tone, "Look, if it's really a problem, I'll get him a room somewhere. I didn't realize things were so . . . unsettled . . . between you two. I thought it might be good for you."

I stare at him. "*Good* for me? How is having my ex-con dad live with me *good* for me?"

"Well, I don't know," Cooper says, looking uncomfortable. "It's just that . . . you don't have anyone."

"As I believe we have discussed before," I say acidly, "neither do you."

"But I don't need anyone," he points out.

"Neither do I," I say.

"Heather," he says, flatly. "You do. No one died, left you their townhouse, and made you independently wealthy. And, no offense, twenty-three thousand dollars a year, in Manhattan, is a joke. You need all the friends and family you can get."

"Including jailbirds?" I demand.

"Look," Cooper says. "Your dad's an extremely intelligent man. I'm sure he's going to land on his feet. And I think you're going to want to be around when that happens, if only to inflict enough guilt on him to get him to throw some money your way. He owes you college tuition, at least."

"I don't need tuition money," I say. "I get to go free because I work there, remember?"

"Yes," Cooper says, with obviously forced patience. "But you wouldn't have to work there if your dad would agree to pay your tuition."

I blink at him. "You mean . . . quit my job?"

"To go to school full-time, if getting a degree is really your goal?" He sips his coffee. "Yes."

It's funny, but though what he's saying makes sense, I can't imagine what it would be like not to work at Fischer Hall. I've only been doing it for a little over half a year, but it feels like I've been doing it all my life. The idea of *not* going there every day seems strange.

Is this how everybody who works in an office feels? Or is it just that I actually *like* my job?

"Well," I say, miserably, staring at my plate. My empty plate. "I guess you're right. I just . . . I feel like I take enough advantage of your hospitality. I don't want my family sponging off you now, too."

"Why don't you let me worry about protecting myself from spongers," Cooper says wryly. "I can take care of myself. And besides, you don't take advantage. My accounts have never been so well organized. The bills actually go out on time for a change, *and* they're all accurate. That's why I can't believe they're making you take remedial math, you do such a great job—"

I gasp at the words *remedial math*, suddenly remembering something. "Oh, no!"

Cooper looks startled. "What?"

"Last night was my first class," I say, dropping my head into my hands. "And I spaced it! My first class . . . my first course for college credit . . . and I missed it!"

"I'm sure your professor will understand, Heather," Cooper says. "Especially if he's been reading the paper lately."

Dad comes back into the kitchen, holding the cordless phone from the front hallway. "It's for you, Heather," he says.

"Your boss, Tom. What a charming young man he is. We had a nice chat about last night's game. Really, for a Division Three team, your boys put on quite a show."

I take the phone from him, rolling my eyes. If I have to hear one more thing about basketball, I'm going to scream.

And what am I going to do about what Kimberly said last night? Was there something going on between Coach Andrews and Lindsay Combs? And if so . . . why would he *kill* her over it?

"I know the school's closed," I say to Tom. "But I'm still coming in." Because, considering my newest housemate, a monsoon couldn't keep me away, let alone a little old nor'easter.

"Of course you are," Tom says. Clearly, the idea that I might do what all the other New Yorkers are doing today—staying in—never even occurred to him. "That's why I'm glad I caught you before you left. Dr. Jessup called—"

I groan. This is not a good sign.

"Yeah," Tom says. "He called from his house in Westchester, or wherever it is he lives. He wants to make sure a representative from Housing shows up at the hospital to visit Manuel today. To show we care. Also to bring flowers, since there are no florist shops open, thanks to the storm. He says if you buy something from the hospital gift shop, I can reimburse you from petty cash. . . ."

"Oh," I say. I'm confused. This is a sort of a high-profile assignment. I mean, Dr. Jessup doesn't usually ask his assistant hall directors to step in as representatives of the department. Not that he doesn't trust us. Just that . . . well, I personally haven't been the most popular person on staff since I dropped the Wasser Hall assistant hall director during that trust game. "Are you sure *I'm* the one he wants to go?"

"Well," Tom says, "he really didn't specify. But he wants someone from the Housing Department to go, to make it look like we care—"

"We *do* care," I remind him.

"Well, of course *we* care," Tom says. "But I think he meant *we* as in the Housing Department, not *we* as in the people who actually know Manuel. I just figured since you and Manuel have a previously existing relationship, and you're the one who, in effect, saved his life, and—"

"And I'm two blocks closer to St. Vincent's than anyone else at Fischer Hall right now," I finish for him. It's all becoming clear now.

"Something like that," Tom says. "So. Will you do it? Swing over there before coming here? You can take a cab there and back—if you can find one—and Dr. Jessup says he'll reimburse you if you bring back the receipt. . . ."

"You know I'm happy to do it," I say. Anytime I get to spend money and charge it to the department is a happy day for me. "How are *you* doing, though?" I ask, trying to sound nonchalant, even though the answer is vitally important to my future happiness. There's no telling what kind of heinous boss I might get assigned if Tom left. Possibly someone like Dr. Kilgore. . . . "Are you still thinking . . . I mean, the other day you mentioned wanting to go back to Texas—"

"I'm just trying to take this one day at a time, Heather," Tom says, with a sigh. "Murder and assault were never covered in any of my student personnel classes, you know."

"Right," I say. "But, you know, in Texas they don't have fun blizzards. At least, not very often."

"That's true," he says. Still, Tom doesn't sound convinced of New York's superiority over Texas. "Anyway, I'll see you in a bit. Stay warm."

"Thanks," I say. And I hang up . . .

. . . to find Cooper looking at me strangely over his coffee.

"Going to St. Vincent's to visit Manuel?" he asks lightly. Too lightly.

"Yes," I say, averting my gaze. I know what he's thinking. And nothing could be further from the truth. Well, maybe not *nothing*. . . . "I doubt I'll find a cab, so I better go bundle up—"

"You're just going to give Manuel get-well wishes," Cooper says, "and then head back to work, right? You wouldn't, say, hang around and try to question him about who attacked him last night and why, would you?"

I laugh heartily at that. "Cooper!" I cry. "God, you're so funny! Of *course* I wouldn't do that. I mean, the poor guy was brutally stabbed. He was in surgery all night. He probably won't even be awake. I'll just sneak in, leave the flowers—and balloons—and go."

"Right," Cooper says. "Because Detective Canavan told you to stay out of the investigation into Lindsay's murder."

"Totally," I say.

Dad, who has been watching our exchange with the same kind of intensity he watched the basketball game the night before, looks confused. "Why would Heather interfere with the investigation into that poor girl's death?"

"Oh," Cooper says, "let's just say that your daughter has a tendency to get a little overinvolved in the lives of her residents. And their deaths."

Dad looks at me gravely. "Now, honey," he says, "you really

ought to leave that sort of thing to the police. You don't want to be getting hurt, now, do you?"

I look from Dad to Cooper and then back again. Suddenly it hits me: I'm outnumbered. There's two of them now, and only one of me.

I let out a frustrated scream and stomp out of the room.

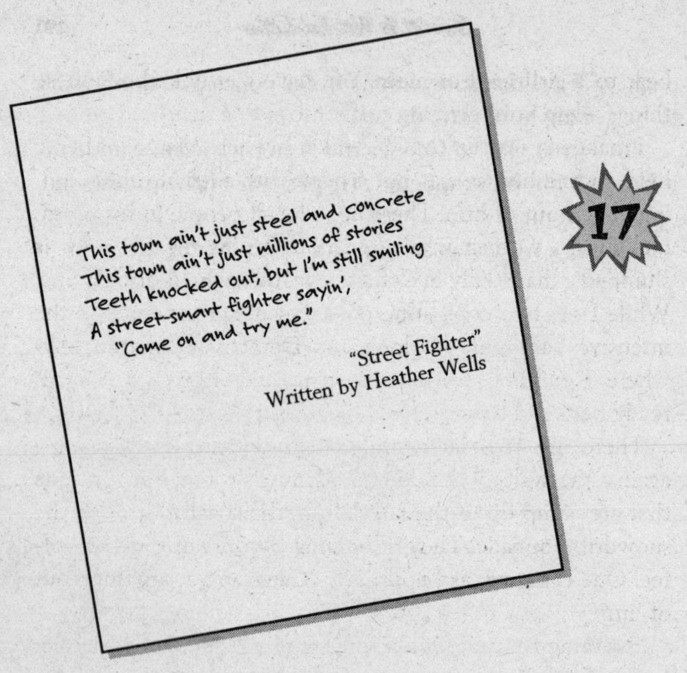

17
This town ain't just steel and concrete
This town ain't just millions of stories
Teeth knocked out, but I'm still smiling
A street-smart fighter sayin',
"Come on and try me."
"Street Fighter"
Written by Heather Wells

The gift shop is open, thank God. The flowers aren't exactly very fresh-looking, though—no delivery that morning, on account of the road conditions, which are so bad I not only couldn't get a cab, but had to walk in pretty much the center of the street in order to avoid drifts up to my knees.

Still, they have balloons of every size and description, and the helium tank is working, so I have fun making an enormous balloon bouquet. Then I have them throw in a GET WELL SOON bear for good measure, after first making sure the GET WELL SOON banner comes off, so Manuel can regift the bear to a girlfriend or niece. You have to think about these things when you're giving stuffed toys to a man.

I make my way up to ICU, which is where Manuel is being held, to find him awake, but groggy, with a lot of tubes coming in and out of him. There are a lot of people in his room, including a woman who appears to be his mother, who is slumped exhaustedly in a chair near Julio, who is also dozing. While I see two cops—one posted at either entrance to the intensive care unit—I don't see Detective Canavan anywhere. He either hasn't made it into the city yet, or was already here and left.

There are two law enforcementy-looking guys leaning against the wall by the door to Manuel's room, both in suits that are damp up to the knees from their walks through the snowdrifts outside. They're holding Styrofoam cups of coffee. One is saying, as I approach, "Canavan get anything out of 'im?"

"Nothing he could make any sense of." The younger man is wearing a tie in a festive tropical print. "Asked him if he knew why he'd been stabbed. All he did was groan."

"Canavan ask him about the key?"

"Yep. Got about the same response. Nothing."

"What about the girl?"

"Nothing."

"Maybe we should get the kid's uncle to ask him," the older one says, nodding at a dozing Julio. "Might be he'll respond better to a face he recognizes."

"The kid's completely out of it," his colleague says with a shrug. "We're not getting shit out of him."

Both men notice me at the same time. I'm kind of hard to miss, with my enormous balloon bouquet. Also, I'm clearly eavesdropping.

"Can we help you, miss?" the younger one asks, sounding bored.

"Oh, hi," I say. "I didn't mean to interrupt. I'm here to see Manuel Juarez? I'm from the Housing Department, over at New York College, where Manuel works. They sent me to see how he's doing."

"You got ID?" the older detective, or whatever he is, asks, in as bored a voice as his colleague has used.

I fumble for my staff ID. I have to have the younger one hold the balloons while I do so.

"Nice bear," he comments dryly.

"Thanks," I say. "I thought so."

They check the ID. Then the older one hands it back and says, "Knock yourself out," while nodding toward Manuel's room.

I take back my balloons and, with some difficulty, maneuver them through the door, then quietly approach Manuel's side. He watches me the whole time, without making a sound. The only noise I can hear, as a matter of fact, is the steady breathing of his uncle and a woman I assume is his mother. And the clicking of all the machines next to his bed, doing whatever they're doing to him.

"Well, hey, there, Manuel," I say with a smile, showing him the balloons. "These are for you, from all of us over at Fischer Hall. We hope you feel better soon. Sorry about the bear, I know it's a bit, you know. But they were out of flowers."

Manuel manages a slight smile. Encouraged, I go on, "You aren't feeling so hot, are you? I'm so sorry those guys did this to you, Manuel. It really stinks."

Manuel opens his mouth to say something, but the only thing that comes out is a grunting noise. I see his gaze go to the brown pitcher on the table by his bed. There are some paper cups next to it.

"You want some water?" I ask. "Did anybody tell you that you weren't supposed to have any? Because sometimes they don't want you to drink, if you're going to have more surgery or something."

Manuel shakes his head. So, after letting the balloons drift to the ceiling so I don't have to hang on to them anymore, I pour some of the water into a paper cup.

"Here you go," I say, and hold the cup out to him.

He's too weak to lift his hands, though—they're weighted down by all the tubes going into them anyway—so I put the cup to his lips. He drinks thirstily.

When he finishes the first cup, he looks pointedly at the pitcher, so, figuring he wants a refill, I pour him another one. He drinks that one, too, only slower. When he's done with that one, I ask if he wants more. Manuel shakes his head, and is finally able to speak.

"I was so thirsty," Manuel said. "I tried to tell those guys—" He nods at the two detectives in the hallway. "But they didn't understand me. I couldn't talk, my throat was so dry. Thank you."

"Oh," I say. "No problem."

"And thank you for what you did last night," Manuel says. He can't seem to speak very loudly—though Manuel, even in the peak of health, was never a loud talker—so it's hard to hear what he's saying. But I lean forward and am able to catch most of it. "Uncle Julio says you saved my life."

I shake my head. "Oh, no," I say. "Really, that was the paramedics. I was just in the right place at the right time, is all."

"Well," Manuel says, managing a smile, "lucky for me, then. But no one will tell me . . . did we win?"

"The basketball game?" I can't help laughing. "No. We got creamed in the second half."

"It was my fault," Manuel says, looking pained.

"It wasn't your fault." I'm still laughing. "The Pansies suck, is all."

"My fault," Manuel says again. His voice cracks.

That's when I stop laughing. Because I realize he's crying. Fat tears are beading up under his eyelids, threatening to come spilling out any minute. He seems to want to lift his hands up to wipe them away, but he can't.

"It's *not* your fault, Manuel," I say. "How can you even think such a thing? The guys on the team didn't even know what happened to you until later. Coach Andrews didn't tell them—"

"No," Manuel says. The tears are sliding out from beneath his eyelids and streaming down his face. "I meant it's my fault about Lindsay. My fault that she died."

Whoa. "Manuel," I say. "It isn't your fault that someone killed Lindsay. It isn't your fault at all."

"I gave her the key," Manuel insists. And he does manage to move one of his hands then. He curls his fingers into a fist and thumps the mattress, pathetically softly.

"That doesn't mean you killed her," I assure him.

"She wouldn't be dead if I hadn't given it to her. I should have said no when she asked. I should have said no. Only . . . she was crying."

"Right," I say. I glance at the two detectives outside the room. They've disappeared. Where did they go? I want to run out after them, tell them to get in here . . . but I don't want Manuel to stop talking. "You said that last night. When did she come to you crying, Manuel? When did she ask you for the key?"

"It was right before I went home," he says. "Monday night. After the cafeteria was closed at seven. I was pulling a double, because Fernando had to go to his grandmother's birthday party. The holiday. You know. And she came up to me, as I was putting on my coat to go home, and said she needed to borrow the key to the cafeteria, because she'd left something in there."

"Did she say what?" I ask, glancing at the door. Where were those guys? "What it was she left, I mean?"

Manuel shakes his head. He's still crying.

"I should have gone with her. I should have gone and opened the door for her and waited until she got whatever it was. But I was supposed to meet someone"—from the way he says the word *someone,* it's clear he means a girlfriend—"and I was running late, and she's . . . well, she was Lindsay."

"Right," I say encouragingly. "We all knew Lindsay. We all trusted her." Though I'm starting to think maybe we shouldn't have.

"Yeah. I know I shouldn't have given it to her," Manuel goes on. "But she was so pretty and nice. Everybody liked her. I couldn't imagine she wanted the key for anything bad. She said it was really important—something she had to give back to . . . the people she borrowed it from. Or they'd be angry, she said."

My blood has run cold. That's the only way I can think of to explain why I suddenly feel so chilly. "She didn't say who *they* were?"

Manuel shakes his head.

"And she definitely said *they*, plural, like it was more than one person?"

He nods.

Well, that was weird. Unless Lindsay had said *they* instead of *him* or *her* to hide the sex of whoever it was she was talking about.

"So you gave her the key," I say.

He nods miserably. "She told me she'd give it back. She said she'd meet me by the front desk the next morning at ten o'clock and give the key back. And I waited. I was out there waiting when the police came in. Nobody told me what was going on. They just walked right past me. I was waiting for her, and the whole time, she was inside, dead!"

Manuel breaks off. He's choking a little, he's crying so hard. One of the machines that's hooked up to him by a tube starts beeping. The woman I assume is his mother stirs sleepily.

"If . . ." Manuel says. "If—"

"Manuel, don't talk," I say. To the woman who has just woken up, I say, "Get a nurse." Her eyes widen, and she runs from the room.

"If . . ." Manuel keeps saying.

"Manuel, don't talk," I say. By now Julio is up, as well, murmuring something in Spanish to his nephew.

But Manuel won't calm down.

"If it wasn't my fault," he finally manages to get out, "then why did they try to kill me?"

"Because they think you know who they are," I say. "The people who killed Lindsay think you can identify them. Which means Lindsay must have said something to you to make them think that. Did she, Manuel? Try to remember."

"She said . . . she said something about someone named—"

"Doug?" I cry. "Did she say something about someone named Doug? Or maybe Mark?"

But the beeping is getting louder, and now a doctor and two nurses come rushing in, followed by Manuel's mother . . . and the two detectives.

"No," Manuel says. His voice is getting fainter. "I think it was . . . Steve. She said Steve was going to be so mad. . . ."

Steve? Who's *Steve*?

Manuel's eyelids drift closed. The doctor barks, "Get out of the way," and I jump aside, while she messes around with Manuel's tubes. The beeping, mercifully, goes back to its normal, much quieter rate. The doctor looks relieved. Manuel, it's clear, has drifted off to sleep.

"Everyone out," says one of the nurses, waving us toward the door. "He needs to rest now."

"But I'm his mother," the older woman insists.

"You can stay," the nurse relents. "The rest of you, out."

I feel horrible. I shuffle out, along with the two detectives, while Julio and Mrs. Juarez stay with Manuel.

"What happened to him?" the younger detective asks me, when we hit the hallway.

And so I tell him. I tell him everything Manuel said. Especially the part about Steve.

They look bored.

"We knew all that," the older one says—sort of accusingly, like I'd been wasting their time on purpose.

"No, you didn't," I say, shocked.

"Yeah, we did," the younger one agrees with his partner. "It was all in the report. He said all that stuff last night, about the key."

"Not the stuff about Steve," I say.

"I'm pretty sure there was a Steve in the report," the older detective says.

"Steve," the younger one says. "Or a John, maybe."

"There's no John," I say. "Only a Doug. Or maybe a Mark. Mark was the dead girl's boyfriend. Well, except she was seeing a guy named Doug on the side. And now there's Steve. Only there's no Steve that I know of—"

"We already got all that," the younger detective says again, looking annoyed.

I glare at them. "Where's Detective Canavan?"

"He couldn't get into the city this morning," the older one says. "On account of the road conditions where he lives."

"Well," I say, "are you going to call him and tell him about this Steve guy? Or do I have to do it?"

The younger detective says, "We already told you, miss. We know about—"

"Sure, we'll call him," the older one interrupts.

The younger one looks startled. "But Marty—"

"We'll call him," the older one says again, with a wink at the younger one. The younger one goes, "Oh, yeah. Yeah. We'll call him."

I just stand there and stare at them. It's clear Detective Canavan already told them about me. It's also clear he didn't say anything good.

"You know," I say truculently, "I have his cell number. I could just call him myself."

"Why don't you do that?" Marty, the older detective says. "I'm sure he'd love to hear from you."

The younger one cracks up.

I feel myself blush. Am I really that big a pain in Detective Canavan's ass? I mean, I know I am. But I never thought he went around complaining about me to the rest of the detectives. Am I the joke of the Sixth Precinct?

Probably.

"Fine," I say. "I'll just be going now." And I turn to leave.

"Wait. Ms. Wells?"

I turn back to face them. The younger detective is holding out a pen and a notepad.

"Sorry, Ms. Wells, I almost forgot." He looks totally serious. "Can I have your autograph?"

I narrow my eyes at him. What kind of joke is this?

"Seriously," he says. "I told my kid sister you hang around the station a lot, and she asked me to get your autograph for her, if I could."

He *looks* sincere. I take the pen and notepad, feeling a rush of embarrassment for having been so huffy to him.

"Sure," I say. "What's your sister's name?"

"Oh, she just wants your signature," the detective says. "She says autographs don't sell as well on eBay when they're personalized."

I glare at him. "She wants my autograph just so she can sell it?"

"Well, yeah," the detective says, looking as if he can't believe I'd think anything else. "What else is she going to do with all those old CDs of yours? She says she has a better chance of selling hers if she can throw in an autograph. She says it'll make her stand out from all the millions of other people selling their Heather Wells collection."

I hand the pad and pen back to him. "Goodbye, Detectives," I say, and turn to go.

"Aw, come on," the detective calls after me. "Heather! Don't be that way!"

"Can't we all just get along?" Marty wants to know. He's laughing so hard, he can barely get the words out.

When I get to the elevator, I turn and tell them what I think of them. With my middle finger.

But this just makes them laugh harder.

They're wrong, what they say about a crisis bringing out the best in New Yorkers. It so doesn't.

Don't let love pass you like a headlight
Carrying your heart on through the night
No use in waiting for things to happen
Pull on over, put up a fight.
"Don't Let Love"
Written by Heather Wells
18

I make it back to Fischer Hall in one piece . . . more or less. I can't find a cab—there just aren't any. The few cars I see on the road are cop cars. One of them bottoms out on Sixth Avenue, then sits there, its rear wheels spinning, while a bunch of people come out of the nearby coffee shop and Gap to help them get unstuck.

Not me, though. I've had my fill of cops for the day.

I'm still grumpy about the autograph thing when I finally step into my office . . . only to find Tom in my seat, and the door to his office closed. Behind it, I hear the murmur of Dr. Kilgore's voice.

"Oh, come *on,*" I say, yanking off my knit hat. I can feel my hair floating in the air because of all the static, but I don't care. "You're telling me she's here again?"

"For the rest of the week, I'm afraid," Tom says glumly. "But cheer up. Tomorrow's Friday."

"Still." I pull off my coat and slump into Sarah's chair. "I feel violated. Who's in there?"

"Cheryl Haebig," he says.

"Again?"

He shrugs. "Her roommate got killed. She's all broken up about it."

I glower at the Monet print on the wall. "Lindsay wasn't as great as everyone thinks she was," I hear myself say.

Tom raises his eyebrows. "Hello?"

"Well, she wasn't," I say. "You know she totally sweet-talked Manuel into giving her his key to the caf. What did she need it for? She told him she left something in there that she had to get. But why didn't she go to one of the RAs if that was the case? They'd have been able to let her in just as easily as Manuel, if all she needed to do was grab something. No, she went to him because he was on his way out to a date and she knew he didn't have time to wait for her to get whatever it was, and would just hand over the key if she asked for it. So then she'd have it all night. She was working him. The way she worked all the boys. And the girls, even. I mean, Magda was gaga for her."

"You seem to have a lot of issues with Lindsay," Tom says. "Maybe you need to talk to Dr. Kilgore next."

"Shut up," I advise him.

He grins wickedly. "You got some messages." And hands them to me.

Jordan Cartwright. Jordan Cartwright. Jordan Cartwright. Tad Tocco.

Wait. Who's Tad Tocco?

"I'm getting coffee," Tom says, getting up with his mug. "You want any?

"Yeah," I say, barely paying attention. "Coffee'd be good." Who is Tad Tocco, and why is his name so familiar?

Then, after Tom's left the office, I yell, "Put some hot cocoa in it!"

"Okay," Tom yells back.

Tom's office door is tugged open, and Dr. Kilgore sticks her head out to look at me.

"Could you," she says testily, "keep your voice down, please? I have a very distraught student in here."

"Oh, sure," I say guiltily. "Sorry."

She glares at me and slams the door.

I slump more deeply into my seat. Sarah has left a copy of the school paper on her desk, open to the sports page. There's a photo of Coach Andrews on it, clapping his hands and yelling at a blur on the court in front of him. The caption reads, *Steven Andrews shouts encouragement to his players.*

And my blood goes cold in my veins.

Steven. Steven *Andrews*.

And the next thing I know, I'm on the phone to the Athletic Department.

"Uh, hi," I say, when someone finally answers the phone. "Is Coach Andrews in today?"

Whoever answers sounds cranky . . . possibly because he, like me, was forced to come in to work on a Snow Day.

"Where else would he be?" the cranky person asks. "He's got another game this weekend, you know."

The guy hangs up on me. But I don't care. Because I've found out what I need to know. Coach Andrews is around. Which means I can go over to the Winer Complex and question him about his relationship with Lindsay. . . .

No, wait. I can't do that. I promised. I promised everyone I wouldn't get involved this time. . . .

But I promised Magda I wouldn't let Lindsay's name be dragged through the mud. And if Coach Andrews was sleeping with her, as Kimberly suggested, then that meant Lindsay was being taken advantage of by a person in a position of power. Well, as much power as a basketball coach can have over a cheerleader. At the very least, the relationship was completely inappropriate. . . .

But what could Lindsay possibly have left in the cafeteria that she'd needed to give back to Coach Andrews so desperately?

There's really only one way to find out. Which is why I get up from Sarah's desk and, after stopping by the recycling pile at the bottom of the basement stairwell and snagging a good-sized box, I hurry out into the lobby, winding my scarf back around my neck and nearly colliding with my boss, who is carrying two mugs of coffee out of the cafeteria.

"Where are you going?" Tom wants to know, eyeing the box.

"Lindsay's parents called," I lie. It is seriously scary how easily these things trip off my tongue. It's no wonder I can't seem to find the guts to sing in front of anyone. It's becoming more and more clear my true talent lies in a completely different direction than vocal performance. "They want somebody to clean out her locker over at the Winer Complex."

Tom looks confused. "Wait . . . I thought Cheryl and her friends did that already. When they got the sweater."

"I guess not," I say, shrugging. "I'll be back in a bit. 'Bye!"

Before he can say another word, I throw myself out into the wind and cold, using the box to shield my face from the snow. It's slow going—no one has had a chance to shovel the sidewalks yet, due to the fact that the snow has only slowed down a bit, not stopped. But I have my Timberlands on, so my feet stay dry and relatively warm. And anyway, I like the snow. It covers the empty marijuana baggies and nitrous oxide canisters that litter the sidewalks, and muffles the sounds of sirens and honking car horns. True, car owners won't be able to dig out their vehicles for a week, since the snowplows—their lights blinking orange and white, orange and white, as they go by, reflecting against high drifts piled on either side of the street—will just cover them again.

But it sure is pretty. Especially in Washington Square Park, where snow now completely fills the basin of the fountain, and has capped the statues of George Washington with wigs of winter white. Icicles glisten on the twisted black branches of trees from which, in another age, criminals were hanged. Only squirrels disturb the white expanse of snow beneath those trees, where once paupers' graves, not green benches, rested. The dog run is empty, as are the play areas, swings dangling forlornly back and forth in the wind. The only signs of life come from the chess circle, which is, as always, occupied, by homeless people who eschew the dubious safety of the local homeless shelter, and diehard players who are willing to brave the elements in order to get in a good game.

This is how I like my city: all but empty.

God, I really *am* a jaded New Yorker.

Still, pretty as the town looks, I'm relieved when I pull open the door to the sports complex and am able to stomp the snow off my boots and onto the rubber-backed mats inside. My face slowly defrosts as I pull out my ID and show it to the security guard, who waves me through the hand scanner. The building, as always, smells of sweat and chlorine, from the pool. It's pretty empty—most students don't seem to feel the need to brave the elements in order to get in their daily workout.

Not so with the Pansies basketball team, though. I spot them as I look over the atrium railing, down on the parquet court below, practicing the slam dunks they aren't allowed to try during a game, hanging on the rim, that sort of thing. The court looks bigger with all the bleachers pushed back. As I watch, someone passes Mark—I recognize his flattop—the ball.

"Shepelsky," his teammate says. "Go for a layup."

Mark expertly catches the ball, dribbles, then shoots. I swear there are three feet of air at least between the soles of his sneakers and the court. When he lands, I hear the same squeak of rubber on a smooth, shiny surface that I heard last night, when Manuel's masked assailants fled the scene.

Not that that means anything. I mean, all sneakers sound like that. Besides, Mark and his friends were probably in the locker room while Manuel was being stabbed, getting reamed out by their coach. They couldn't have had anything to do with what happened to him.

Unless.

Unless Coach Andrews was the one who sent them to do it.

I'm letting my imagination run away with me. Best to take myself and my box to Coach Andrews's office and see if there's actually anything to this crazy idea of mine before I start making up scenarios in which Steven Andrews is a Svengali with the ability to convince late-adolescent boys to do his smallest bidding. . . .

Maybe in Division I schools, where the basketball coach is second only to God—even more important than the university president—would someone like Coach Andrews have his own personal assistant to guard his privacy. As it is, there's just a snarky student worker sitting in the outer part of the Athletic Office, reading a battered copy of *The Fountainhead*.

"Hey," I say to him. "Coach Andrews around?"

The kid doesn't even look up from his book, just jerks a thumb in the direction of an open door.

"In there," he says.

I thank him and approach the doorway, through which I see Steven Andrews sitting at a desk covered with what looks like playbooks. He's got his head in his hands, and is staring dejectedly down at a piece of paper with a number of *X*'s and O's on it. He looks, for all the world, like Napoleon planning a battle.

Or maybe me, making room assignments, since I still haven't figured out how to work the Housing Department computer system.

"Um, Coach Andrews?" I say.

He looks up. "Yes?" Then, as I pull my hat off and all of my hair tumbles down in a staticky mess around my face, he seems to recognize me. "Oh, hi. You're . . . Mary?"

"Heather," I say, lowering myself into the chair across from his desk. I don't mind pointing out that the office furniture in the Winer Sports Complex is way nicer than the furniture in my office. No orange vinyl couches here, no sirree. Everything is black leather and chrome.

I'm betting Coach Andrews makes more than twenty-three thousand five hundred a year, too.

Although he doesn't get all the free Dove Bars he can eat. Probably.

"Right," he says. "Sorry. Heather. You work over in Fischer Hall."

"Right," I say. "Where Lindsay lived."

I watch his reaction to the name *Lindsay* carefully.

But there is no reaction. He doesn't flinch or go pale. He just looks questioning. "Uh-huh?"

Man. This is one tough nut to crack.

"Yes," I say. "I was just wondering . . . did anybody clean out her locker?"

Now Coach Andrews looks confused. "Her locker?"

"Right," I say. "Her locker here at the sports complex. I mean, I assume she had one."

"I'm sure she did," Coach Andrews says. "But that's something you'd probably be better off asking the cheerleading coach, Vivian Chambers? She'd be the one who'd be able to tell you which locker was Lindsay's, and what the combination is. She's got an office down the hall. Only I don't think she made it in today. On account of the snow."

"Oh," I say. "The cheerleading coach. Right. Only . . . well, I'm here now. And I've got this box."

"Well." Coach Andrews looks like he really wants to help me. Seriously. I mean, the guy has a big game coming up, and he's actually willing to take the time to help out a fellow New York College employee. One who makes way less money than he does. "I think I could probably get the number and combination from Facilities. Let me give them a call."

"Wow," I say. Is he being so super-helpful because he's actually a nice guy? Or because he feels guilty over what he did to Lindsay? "That is so nice of you. Thanks."

"No problem," Coach Andrews says, as he picks up his

phone and dials. "I mean, as long as the guys made it into work today . . ." Someone on the other end picks up, and Steven Andrews says, "Oh, Jonas, great, you made it in. Look, I got a woman from the Housing Department who needs to clean out Lindsay Combs's locker. I was wondering if you guys had access to the combination. Oh, and also which locker it was, since Viv didn't make it to work this morning. . . . You do? Great? Yeah, that'd be great. Okay, yeah, call me back."

He hangs up and beams at me. "You're in luck," he says. "They're gonna look it up and call back with it."

I'm stunned. Seriously. "That's . . . thanks. That was really nice of you."

"Oh, no problem," Coach Andrews says again. "Anything I can do to help. I mean, what happened to Lindsay was so terrible."

"Wasn't it?" I say. "I mean, especially since Lindsay—well, she was so popular. It's hard to believe she had any enemies."

"I know." Coach Andrews leans back in his chair. "That's the part that gets me. She was, like, universally liked. By everyone."

"Almost everyone," I say, thinking of Kimberly, who honestly doesn't seem to have been all that fond of her.

"Well, right," Coach Andrews says. "I mean, besides whoever it was who did that to her."

Hmmm. He doesn't seem to be aware of the animosity between Kimberly and Lindsay.

"Yeah," I say. "Clearly someone didn't like her. Or was trying to shut her up about something."

Steven Andrews's blue eyes are wide and guileless as they gaze into mine. "About what? I mean, Lindsay was a good kid. That's what's been so hard about all this. For me, I mean. For you guys, I'm sure it's worse. I mean, you and your boss . . . what's his name again? Tom Something?"

I blink. "Snelling. Tom Snelling."

"Yeah," the coach says. "I mean . . . he's new, right?"

"He started last month," I say. Wait. How did we get off the subject of Lindsay, and on to Tom?

"Where'd he come from?" Coach Andrews wants to know.

"Texas A & M," I say. "The thing about Lindsay is—"

"Wow," the coach says. "That must be a big change for him. I mean, going from College Station to the Big Apple. I mean, it's been rough for me, and I just came down from Burlington."

"Yeah," I say. "I imagine that was tough. But Tom's handling it." I don't mention the part about how he wants to quit. "About Lindsay, what I was wondering was—"

"He's not married, is he?" Coach Andrews asks. Casually.

Too casually.

I stare at him. "Who? *Tom?*"

"Yeah," he says. Suddenly I notice his cheeks are turning sort of . . . well, pinkish. "I mean, I didn't see a ring."

"Tom's *gay,*" I say. I realize he's a Division III college basketball coach and all. But really, how dense can this guy be?

"I *know,*" Coach Andrews says. Now his cheeks are red. "I was wondering if he's in a relationship with anyone."

I find myself shaking my head at him, blinking. "N-no. . . ."

"Oh." The coach looks visibly relieved—even happy—to hear this news. "Because I was thinking, you know, it's hard moving to a new city and starting a new job and all. Maybe he'd want to grab a beer sometime, or something. I don't—"

His phone rings. Coach Andrews answers it. "Andrews," he says. "Oh, great. Here, let me grab a pen."

I sit there while Steven Andrews jots down Lindsay's locker number and combination, trying to understand what I think I've just learned. Because unless I'm mistaken, Coach Andrews is *gay*.

And seems to want to date my boss.

"Great, thanks so much," the coach says, and hangs up the phone.

"Here you go," he says, sliding the piece of paper he's written toward me. "Just go on down to the women's locker room, and you'll find it. Number six twenty-five."

I take the paper, fold it, and slip it into my pocket in a sort of daze. "Thanks," I say.

"No problem," Coach Andrews says. "Where were we, again?"

"I . . . I . . ." I feel my shoulders sag. "I don't know."

"Oh, right, Tom," he says. "Tell him to call me sometime. You know. If he ever wants to hang out."

"Hang out," I echo. "With you."

"Yeah." Coach Andrews must see something in my face that alarms him, since he asks, looking suddenly anxious, "Wait, was that totally inappropriate? Maybe I should just call him myself."

"Maybe," I say faintly, "you should."

"Right." The coach nods. "You're right. I should. I just felt like—well, you know. You seem cool, and maybe you'd . . . but never mind."

This was, I decided, either the most elaborate attempt ever to draw suspicion away from a murder suspect, or Coach Steven Andrews was, in fact, gay.

Had Kimberly lied to me? It's starting to look like it. Especially when Steven Andrews leans forward and whispers, "Not to sound like a girl or anything, but . . . I *totally* have all your albums."

I blink at him one last time. Then I say, "Great. I'll just be going now."

" 'Bye," he says happily.

And I take my box and leave. Fast.

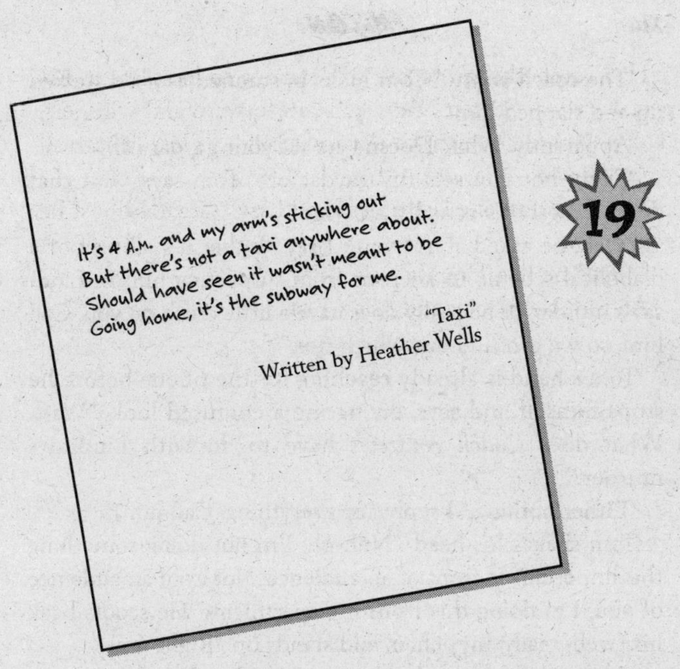

19
It's 4 A.M. and my arm's sticking out
But there's not a taxi anywhere about.
Should have seen it wasn't meant to be
Going home, it's the subway for me.
"Taxi"
Written by Heather Wells

"Call Coach Andrews," I say to Tom, when I get back to the office.

He looks up from his computer—or I should say, *my* computer. "What?"

"Call Steve Andrews," I say, collapsing into Sarah's chair and tossing my box—empty; someone had already cleaned out Lindsay's locker, just like Tom had said—onto the floor. "I think he has a crush on you."

Tom's hazel eyes goggle. "You are fucking shitting me."

"Call him," I say, unwinding my scarf, "and see."

"The coach is *gay*?" Tom looks as stunned as if I'd walked up and slapped him.

"Apparently. Why? Doesn't he set your gaydar off?"

"Every hot guy sets my gaydar off," Tom says. "But that doesn't mean it's actually *accurate*."

"Well, he asked about you," I say. "Either it's all part of a diabolical scheme to keep us from suspecting him in Lindsay's murder, or he really does have a little crush on you. Call him, so we can find out which it is."

Tom's hand is already reaching for the phone before he stops himself and says, giving me a confused look, "Wait. What does *Coach Andrews* have to do with Lindsay's murder?"

"Either nothing," I reply, "or everything. Call him."

Tom shakes his head. "Nuh-uh. I'm not doing something this important in front of an audience. Not even an audience of you. I'm doing this from my apartment." He scoots back his (well, really, my) chair, and stands up. "Right now."

"Just let me know what he says," I call, as Tom hurries out the door and toward the elevator. When he's gone, I sit there and wonder just how far Andrews will be willing to take this thing, in the event he isn't actually gay. Would he put out for Tom? All in an effort to throw off investigators? Could a straight guy even do that? Well, probably, if he's bi. But Coach Andrews didn't seem bi.

Of course, he hadn't seemed gay to me, either, until today. He did an excellent job of hiding it. But then, maybe if you're a gay basketball coach, you *have* to be good at hiding it. I mean, if you want to keep your job.

I'm wondering if President Allington has any idea that his golden boy is a gay boy, just as Gavin McGoren strolls into the office.

"Wassup?" he says, and throws himself onto the couch across from my—I mean, Tom's—desk.

I stare at him.

"How should I know what's up?" I say. "It's a Snow Day. No one has class. Why are you here? Shouldn't you be off in a bar somewhere in SoHo, drinking yourself blind?"

"I would be," Gavin says, "except that boss of yours says I have to see him for"—he digs a much-folded, very grimy disciplinary letter from his back pocket—"follow-up counseling pertaining to an incident involving alcohol."

"Ha," I say happily. "You loser."

"Has anyone ever told you that you don't have a very professional attitude towards your job?" Gavin wants to know.

"Has anyone ever told you that trying to drink twenty-one shots in one night is extremely dangerous, not to mention stupid?"

He gives me a *no-duh* look. "So how come they haven't caught the guy that iced Lindsay?" he asks.

"Because no one knows who did it." And some of us are driving ourselves crazy trying to figure it out.

"Wow," Gavin says. "That makes me feel so safe and secure in my living environment. My mom wants me to move to Wasser Hall, where people don't get their heads chopped off."

I stare at him, genuinely shocked. "You're not going to, are you?"

"I don't know," Gavin says, not making eye contact. "It's closer to the film school."

"Oh, my God." I can't believe this. "You're thinking about it."

"Well, whatevs." Gavin looks uncomfortable. "It's not cool, living in Death Dorm."

"I would imagine it would be very cool," I say. "To a guy who aspires to be the next Quentin Tarantino."

"Eli Roth," he corrects me.

"Whatever," I say. "But by all means, move to Wasser Hall if you're scared. Here." I lean down and pick up the empty box I'd lugged to the Winer Sports Complex and back again. "Start packing."

"I'm not scared," Gavin says, shoving the box away and sticking his chin out. I notice that the straggly growth on it is getting less straggly and more bushy. "I mean . . . aren't you?"

"No, I'm not scared," I say. "I'm angry. I want to know who did that to Lindsay, and why. And I want them caught."

"Well," Gavin says, finally looking me in the eye, "do they have any leads?"

"I don't know," I say. "If they do, they aren't telling me. Let me ask you something. Do you think Coach Andrews is gay?"

"Gay?" Gavin lets out a big horse laugh. "No!"

I shake my head. "Why not?"

"Well, because he's a big jock."

"Historically, there have been a few gay athletes, you know," I say.

Gavin snorts. "Sure. Lady golfers."

"No," I say. "Greg Louganis."

He stares at me blankly. "Who's that?"

"Never mind." I sigh. "He could be gay and just not want everyone to know. Because it might freak out the players."

"Gee, ya think?" Gavin asks me sarcastically.

"But you don't think he's gay," I say.

"How would I know?" Gavin asks. "I never met the guy. I just know he's a basketball coach, and they aren't gay. Most of the time."

"Well, have you ever heard anything about Coach Andrews and Lindsay?"

"What, like, romantically?" Gavin wants to know.

"Yeah."

"No," he says. "And, might I add, gross. He's, like, thirty."

I narrow my eyes at him. "Yeah. That's ancient."

Gavin smirks, and says, "Whatever. Besides, I thought Lindsay was all hot-and-heavy with Mark Shepelsky."

"They've cooled off, apparently," I say. "Lately she's been hooking up with a kid named Doug Winer. Do you know him?"

"Not really." He shrugs. "I know his brother, Steve, better."

And the earth suddenly seemed to tilt on its axis.

"What?" I can't believe what I've just heard.

Gavin, startled by my response, stammers, "St-Steve. Yeah. Steve Winer. What, you didn't know—"

"*Steve?*" I stare at him. "Doug Winer has a brother named *Steve*? Are you *serious*?"

"Yeah." Gavin looks at me strangely. "He was in one of my film classes last semester. We worked together on a project. It was kind of lame—which makes sense, since Steve's kind of lame. But we hung out some. He's a senior. He lives over at the Tau Phi House."

"He's a Tau Phi, too?" I can't seem to digest any of this.

"Yeah. He's, like, president of the house, or something. Well, he should be, 'cause he's the oldest guy there. The dude's twenty-five, and he's still taking classes like Intro to Social Work and shit. Steve wants to be a big-time breadwinner, like Daddy. But he's too stupid and lazy to think of any way to do it except through dealing. So . . ." Gavin shrugs. "He deals coke and shit to college party kids, while

Dad—and New York College, as far as I can tell—turns a blind eye. I mean, it makes sense the school won't do anything about it, because old man Winer donated the sports complex." He chuckles. "Too bad his own kids are too fucked up most of the time to use it."

"So the Winer boys are big-time dealers?" I ask. Suddenly Coach Andrews isn't interesting me half as much as he was earlier.

"I don't know about big-time," Gavin says, with a shrug. "I mean, they both deal, and all, which is fine. But you aren't supposed to sample your own wares. But back when I had class with him, Steve was using, all the time. And so he was always asleep—crashing, you know—when we were supposed to be working on the project. I had to do the whole thing myself, practically. We got an A, of course. But no thanks to Winer."

"So what's he deal?" I ask.

"You name it, the Winer can get it. Though he's got principles. He only sells to people who are ready to experience the alternative planes of reality that drugs can help them achieve. It's like this thing." Gavin rolls his eyes. "Some principles. You know what that guy's hobby used to be when he was a kid? Burying cats up to their necks in dirt in the backyard, then runnin' over their heads with the lawn mower."

"That," I say, wide-eyed, "is disgusting."

"That's not all. Steve'd tie a brick to their tails and throw 'em in the pool. That guy is a maniac. Plus, he's got this thing about money. See, their old man made a pile of money in construction. And he wants his boys to do the same. You know, find their own entrepreneurial fortunes, and shit? So soon as they graduate from college, they're cut off. That's why Steve's trying to keep the gravy train go as long as he can."

I eye him. "Gavin," I say. "How do you know all this stuff?"

"What stuff?"

"All this stuff about the Winers."

Gavin looks blank. "I dunno. I've partied with them."

"You've *partied* with them?"

"Yeah," Gavin says. "You know. I think Steve's a loser, but the guy's got connections. That is one bridge I'm not burning, even if he did totally fuck up our project. But, you know, when I get my own production company going, I'll need investors. And drug money is better than no money. I don't have to ask where it came from. Plus, some great-looking chicks show up at those Tau Phi parties. There's one tonight. . . ." His voice trails off, and he looks at me warily. "I mean, women. Not chicks. Women."

"There's a party at the Tau Phi House tonight?" I ask.

"Um," Gavin says. "Yes?"

And suddenly I know where I need to be tonight.

"Can you get me in?"

Gavin looks confused. "What?"

"Into the party. To meet Steve Winer."

Gavin's perpetually sleepy brown eyes actually widen. "*You* wanna score some coke? Oh, man! And I always thought you were straight! All those anti-drug ads you did when you were a star—"

"I don't want any *coke,*" I say.

" 'Cause coke's no good for you. Reefer's the way to go. I can get you some excellent reefer, mellow you right out. 'Cause you can be a real tight-ass sometimes, you know that, Heather? I always noticed that about you."

"I don't want any reefer," I say, through gritted teeth.

"What I want is to ask Steve Winer a few questions about Lindsay Combs. Because I think Steve might know something about it."

Gavin's eyelids droop back down to their normal width. "Oh. Well, shouldn't the police be doing that?"

"You would think so, wouldn't you?" I give a bitter laugh. "But the police don't really seem to care, as far as I can make out. So. What do you say? Do you think you can score me an introduction?"

"Sure," Gavin says. "I can do that. I mean, if you want me to. I can take you with me tonight to the party."

"Really?" I lean forward on Sarah's desk. "You would really do that?"

"Uh," Gavin says, looking as if he doubts my sanity, "yeah. I mean, it's no big deal."

"Wow." I stare at him. I can't tell if he's trying to get into my good graces to pull some kind of scam, or if he sincerely wants to help. "That'd be . . . great. I've never been to a frat party before. What time will it start? What should I wear?" I try not to think about the FAT CHICKS GO HOME sign. Will it still be there? What if they won't let me in because they think I'm too fat? God, how embarrassing.

I mean, for them.

"You've never been to a frat party before?" Now Gavin looks shocked. "Jesus, even when you were in college?"

I decide to let that one slide. "Slutty, right? I should dress slutty?"

Gavin isn't making eye contact anymore. "Yeah, slutty usually works out good. Things don't usually start going until eleven. Should I pick you up then?"

"Eleven?" I practically scream, then remember Dr. Kilgore,

who, I can tell from the murmuring behind the grate, is meeting with someone in Tom's office, and lower my voice. "Eleven?" By eleven o'clock, I've usually got out my guitar, for a few pre-bedtime rounds of whatever song I'm currently working on. Then it's lights out. "That's so late!"

Now Gavin looks back at me, grinning. "Gonna have to set the alarm, huh, Grandma?"

"No," I say, frowning. Who's he calling Grandma? "I mean, if that's the earliest—"

"It is."

"Well, fine. And no, you can't come pick me up. I'll meet you outside Waverly Hall at eleven."

Gavin smiles. "What's the matter? You afraid of your boyfriend seeing us?"

"I told you," I say. "He's not my—"

"Yeah, yeah, yeah," Gavin says. "He's not your boyfriend. Next thing you're gonna be saying, this isn't a date."

I stare at him. "It isn't. I thought you understood that. It's an exploratory mission, to get to the bottom of Lindsay Combs's murder. It isn't a date at all. Although I really appreciate your—"

"Jesus!" Gavin explodes. "I was just messing with you! Why you gotta be like that?"

I blink at him. "Like what?"

"All professional and shit."

"You said a minute ago I *wasn't* very professional," I point out.

"That's just it," he says. "You run all hot and cold. What's up with that?"

He says all this just before Tom walks in, beaming.

"What's up with what?" Tom wants to know, sliding into

the seat behind my desk. I can tell from his expression that his phone call with Steve Andrews had gone well.

What does this mean? Did I have the wrong Steve, after all?

But why would Kimberly lie to me?

"This thing," Gavin says, waving the disciplinary letter in Tom's face. "Man, look, I know I screwed up. But do we really have to go through all this? I don't need no alcohol education, I already got it in the St. Vinnie's ER, man."

"Well, Gavin," Tom says, leaning back in my chair. "You are a lucky man, then. Because, due to the fact that I currently have no access to my office—and happen to be in an excellent mood—you are off the hook from alcohol counseling this week."

Gavin looks shocked. "Wait . . . I *am*?

"For *this* week. I *will* reschedule. For now . . . fly," Tom says, waving his hand toward the outer door. "Be free."

"Holy shit," Gavin says happily. Then he turns and points at me. "I'll see you later, sweetcheeks."

And he runs out.

Tom looks at me. "Sweetcheeks?"

"Don't ask," I say. "Really. So, I take it you and Steve—"

"Seven o'clock tonight," Tom says, grinning ear to ear. "Dinner at Po."

"Romantic," I say.

"I hope so," Tom gushes.

So do I . . . for his sake. Because if it turns out I am wrong, and Steven Andrews isn't gay, that means there is actually something to what Kimberly told me in the ladies' room last night.

Until I know for sure, though, I'm concentrating on the

only other lead I have . . . Manuel's mysterious "Steve," which all too coincidentally turns out to be the name of Doug Winer's brother. If he knows something about Lindsay's death, I'll be able to tell . . . at least I hope so.

If I don't get thrown out for being a fat chick, first.

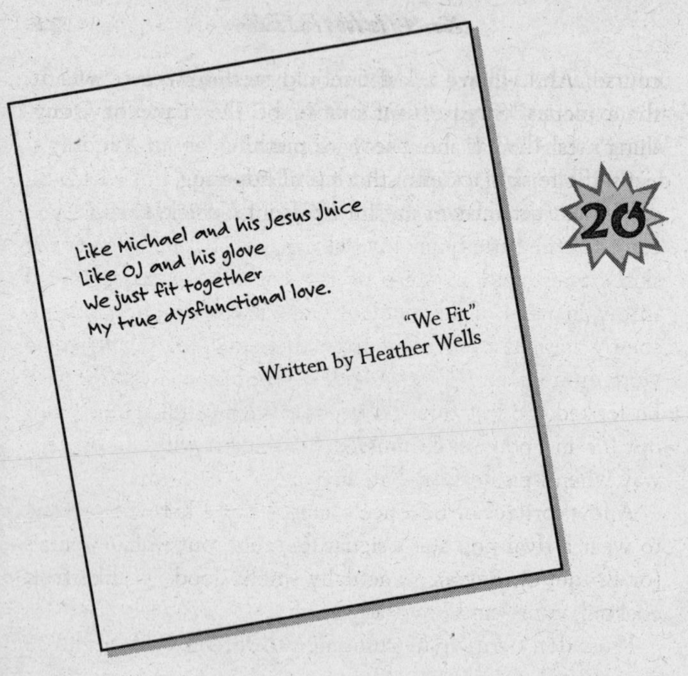
Like Michael and his Jesus Juice
Like OJ and his glove
We just fit together
My true dysfunctional love.
"We Fit"
Written by Heather Wells
20

Never having been to a frat party before, it's sort of hard to figure out what to wear to one. I understand sluttitude is in order. But to what degree? Plus, it's cold outside. So do I really want to venture out in pantyhose and a mini? Is a mini even appropriate on a woman of my age, not to mention one with as many thigh dimples as I seem to have developed recently?

And it's not like I even have anybody I can ask. I can't call Patty, because then she'll remember I never gave Frank an answer about the gig at Joe's, and Magda's no help at all. When I call and ask her if I should wear a mini, she just says, "Of course." And when I ask if I should wear a sweater with it, she explodes, "Sweater? Of course not! Don't you have anything mesh? What about leopard print?"

I settle for a black mini that fits a little snug, but with a diaphanous (though not mesh) top from Betsey Johnson, you can't see the little bulge my belly makes as it hangs over the skirt's waistband in spite of my control-top pantyhose. I throw on a pair of skinny black knee boots (which will be instantly trashed by the salt from the snowplows) and go to work on my hair. I want to look very different from the way I'd looked the last time I'd been at the Tau Phi House, so I opt for an updo, sexily mussed . . . since it will end up that way when I pull off my hat, anyway.

A few spritzes of Beyoncé's latest—hey, I know it's wrong to wear a rival pop star's signature scent, but unlike Tania's (or Britney's), Beyoncé's actually smells good . . . like fruit cocktail, yum—and I'm ready to go.

I just don't anticipate running into Jordan Cartwright on my way out.

Seriously. Why me? I mean, I sneak all the way downstairs—making it safely past the other two men in my life without either of them suspecting a thing, Dad in his room tootling his flute, and Cooper in his room doing whatever it is he does in there after dark, which God only knows what that is, but I think it must involve headphones because I don't see how he could stand doing whatever it is while listening to whatever it is Dad is playing—and out the front door, only to encounter a freakishly bundled-up Sasquatch-like figure trying to figure out how to climb the stoop with cross-country skis on.

"Heather?" Sasquatch squints up at me in the light spilling from the door I've just opened. "Oh, thank God it's you."

Even though his voice is muffled because of all the scarves he's wrapped around his neck and face, I recognize it.

"*Jordan.*" I hasten to close and lock the front door behind me, then make my way carefully down the steps—not an easy feat in three-inch spiked heels, given the ice. "What are you doing here? Are those . . . *skis*?"

"You wouldn't return my calls." Jordan lowers the scarves so I can see his mouth, then raises the ski goggles that were hiding his eyes. "I really need to talk to you. And Dad's got the limo, and none of the car services can get over the bridges, and there were no cabs. So I had to ski down Fifth Avenue to get here."

I stare at him. "Jordan," I say, "you could have taken the subway."

His eyes widen in the light streaming down from the street lamp overhead. "The *subway*? This time of night? Heather, there are *muggers*."

I shake my head. It's finally stopped snowing, but it's still bitterly cold. My legs are already frozen, with just a thin layer of nylon to protect them.

"Jordan," I say impatiently, "what do you want?"

"I . . . I'm getting married day after tomorrow," Jordan says.

"Yes," I say. "You are. I hope you didn't come all the way down here to remind me about it and to beg me to come to your wedding. Because I'm still not going."

"No," Jordan says. It's hard to tell in the streetlight, but he looks a little peaked. "Heather. I'm getting *married* day after tomorrow."

"I know," I say. Then, all at once, I realize what he's doing there.

Also that he's drunk.

"Oh, no." I show him the flat of my gloved palm. "No. You

are not doing this to me now. I don't have time for this, Jordan. I have to meet someone."

"Who?" Jordan's eyes look moist. "You do look kinda . . . dressed up. Heather . . . do you have a boyfriend?"

"God!" I can't believe this. Fortunately my voice doesn't carry very far along the street. The two feet of snow blanketing the tops of all the parked cars—not to mention the clouds, hanging so low that they're reflecting the light of the city with a pinkish hue—muffle it. "Jordan, if you changed your mind about marrying her, tell *her*, not me. I don't care what you do. We broke up, remember? *You* broke up with *me*, as a matter of fact. For *her*."

"People make mistakes," Jordan murmurs.

"No, Jordan," I say. "Our breaking up wasn't a mistake. We needed to break up. We were *right* to break up. We don't belong together."

"But I still love you," Jordan insists.

"Of course you do," I say. "The same way I love you. Like a sibling. That's why we *had* to break up, Jordan. Because siblings aren't supposed to—you know. It's gross."

"It wasn't gross that night we did it up there," he says, nodding toward Cooper's front door.

"Oh, right," I say sarcastically. "That's why you ran so fast when we were done. Because it wasn't gross."

"It wasn't," Jordan insists. "Well . . . maybe it was weird. A little."

"Exactly," I say. "Jordan, you only want to be with me because I'm familiar. It's easy. We were together so long . . . we grew up together, practically. But that's not a good reason for two people to stay together. There has to be passion. And we don't have that. Whereas I think you and Tania do."

"Yeah." Jordan looks bitter. "She's chock-full of passion, all right. I can barely keep up."

This is so not what you want to hear about your ex's new girlfriend. Even if you DO think of him as a brother. Mostly.

"Well, ski on back uptown," I say, "and take an aspirin and go to bed. You'll feel better about things in the morning, I promise."

"Where are you going?" Jordan asks mournfully.

"I have to go to a party," I say, opening my purse to make sure I've brought my lipstick and my new can of pepper spray. Check, and check.

"What do you mean, *have* to?" Jordan wants to know, skiing beside me as I carefully pick my way along the sidewalk. "What's it for, work or something?"

"Something like that," I say.

"Oh." Jordan skis with me until we reach the corner, where a traffic light blinks forlornly along a trafficless street. Not even Reggie is out in weather like this. The wind from the park whips around us, making me reconsider this entire venture, and wish I were in my tub with the latest Nora Roberts instead of out on this empty street corner with my ex.

"Well," he says finally. "Okay, then. 'Bye."

" 'Bye, Jordan," I say, relieved that he's finally going away.

As he skis slowly off toward Fifth Avenue, I start across the park, bitterly regretting my decision not to wear jeans. True, I wouldn't look as alluring. But I'd be a heck of a lot warmer.

Getting across the park is murder. I no longer admire the beauty of the new-fallen snow. The paths are plowed, but not well, and new snow has covered them. My boots aren't waterproof, being designed primarily for indoor use, preferably in front of a roaring fire on a bearskin rug. At least, that's what the girl in the catalog was doing in the picture. I knew

I should have ventured over to the gazillion shoe stores on Eighth Street instead of ordering them online. But it's so much safer to order online. There's no Krispy Kreme sign blinking HOT NOW on my computer.

I'm half hoping that when I get to Waverly Hall, Gavin won't be there and I can turn around and go home.

But he's there, all right, shivering in the arctic wind from the park. As I totter toward him in my high heels, he says, "You owe me, woman. I'm freezing my 'nads off."

"Good," I say, when I reach him. "Your 'nads get you into too much trouble, anyway."

I have to place a hand on his shoulder to steady myself as I knock snow from my boots. He looks down at my legs and whistles.

"Jesus, sweetcheeks," he says. "You clean up good."

I drop my hand from his shoulder and smack him on the back of the head with it instead.

"Eyes forward, Gavin," I say. "We're on a mission, here. There'll be no ogling. And don't call me sweetcheeks."

"I wasn't," Gavin insists. "Oggl—ogle—what you said."

"Come on," I say. I know I'm flushing. That's because I'm beginning to have strong reservations about all of this—not just the miniskirt, but enlisting Gavin's aid. Is this really the way a responsible college administrator behaves, meeting students—even ones who are twenty-one—in the dead of night outside of frat parties? Gavin's already shown a marked immaturity when it comes to handling his alcohol consumption. Isn't my agreeing to accompany him to an event like this just reinforcing his poor judgment? Am I an enabler? Oh, God, I *am*!

"Look, Gavin," I say, as we move through the courtyard of the building toward the front door. I can't see the underwear in the shrubbery anymore because it's all covered with snow, but I can hear the pounding music coming from an upper floor, so loud it seems to reverberate inside my chest. "Maybe this isn't the best idea. I don't want to get you into trouble. . . ."

"What are you talking about?" Gavin asks, as he pulls the door open for me—always a gentleman. "How am I going to get in trouble?"

"Well," I say. A blast of warm air from inside the lobby hits us. "With the drinking thing."

Gavin shudders, despite the warmth. "Woman, I am never drinking again. You think I didn't learn my lesson the other night?"

"Come in or close the door," the guard roars from the security desk. So we hurry inside.

"It's just," I whisper, as we stand there stamping our feet under the glare of the security officer, "if Steve and Doug really are behind what happened to Lindsay, they're extremely dangerous individuals. . . ."

"Right," Gavin says. "Which is why you shouldn't drink anything, either, once we get in there, that you didn't open or pour yourself. And don't leave your beer alone, even for a second."

"Really?" I raise my eyebrows. "You really think—"

"I don't think," Gavin says. "I *know*."

"Well, I—"

Behind us, the outer door opens, and Nanook of the North follows us inside.

Except it isn't Nanook. It's Jordan.

"Aha!" he says, flipping up his goggles and pointing at me. "I knew it!"

"Jordan." I can't believe this. "Did you just *follow* me?"

"Yes." Jordan is having some trouble getting his skis inside the door. "And good thing I did. I thought you said you didn't have a boyfriend."

"Close the door!" the crusty old security guard bellows.

Jordan is trying, but his skis keep getting in the way. Annoyed, I go to him to help, giving one of his ski poles a vicious tug. The door finally eases shut behind him.

"Who's *this* guy?" Gavin demands. Then, in a different tone of voice, he says, "Oh, my God. Are you *Jordan Cartwright*?"

Jordan removes the ski goggles. "Yes," he says. His gaze flicks over Gavin, taking in the goatee and Dumpster-wear. "Rob the cradle much, Heather?" he asks me bitterly.

"Gavin's one of my *residents*," I sniff. "Not my boyfriend."

"Hey." Gavin is wearing a tiny smile on his lips. I should have taken this as a sign that I wasn't going to like what he was about to say. "My *mom* really enjoyed your last album, man. So did my grandma. She's a huge fan."

Jordan, most of his scarves halfway unwound, glares at him. "Hey," he says. "Fuck you, kid."

Gavin feigns offense. "Is that any way to talk to the son of one of the only people who bought your last CD, man? Dude, that is cold."

"I'm serious," Jordan says to Gavin. "I just cross-country skied down here from the East Sixties, and I am in no mood for shenanigans."

Gavin looks surprised. Then he grins at me happily. "Jordan Cartwright said *shenanigans*," he says.

"Stop it," I say. "Both of you. Jordan, put your skis back on. We're going to a party, and you're not invited. Gavin, buzz up so we can get someone to sign us in."

Gavin blinks at me. "The frats don't have to sign anyone in."

"Don't be ridiculous," I say to him. "The sign-in policy is

campus-wide. I'd show my ID to get us in, but, you know, I don't want them knowing a housing official is on the way up." I look at my ex, who is still unwinding his various scarves. "Jordan. Seriously. Gavin and I are here on a mission, and you're not invited."

"What kind of mission?" Jordan wants to know.

"One that involves keeping a low profile," I say. "Which we aren't going to be able to do if we waltz in there with Jordan Cartwright."

"I can keep a low profile," Jordan insists.

"The sign-in policy doesn't include the Greek system," Gavin says, in a bored voice.

I glance at the security guard. "Really?"

"Anyone can go up there," the guard says, with a shrug. He looks almost as bored as Gavin. "I just don't know why they'd want to."

"Does this have something to do with that dead girl?" Jordan wants to know. "Heather, does Cooper know about this?"

"No," I say, through gritted teeth. I can't help it, I'm so annoyed. "And if you tell him, I'll . . . I'll tell Tania you cheated on her!"

"She already knows," Jordan says, looking confused. "I tell Tania everything. She said it was okay, so long as I didn't do it again. Listen, why can't I go with you guys? I think I'd make an awesome detective."

"No, you wouldn't," I say. I'm still reeling from the information that his fiancée knows he cheated on her. I wonder if she knows it was with me. If so, it's no wonder she always gives me such dirty looks whenever she sees me.

On the other hand, dirty looks are the only kind Tania ever gives anyone.

"You don't *blend*," I accuse Jordan.

Jordan looks insulted. "I do, too, blend," he insists. He looks down at the skis he's holding, then hastily leans them, and the ski poles, against the wall, along with his goggles. "Can you watch these?" he asks the security guard.

"No," the guard says. He's gone back to whatever it is he's watching on his tiny desk-drawer television.

"See?" Jordan holds his arms out. He's wearing a shearling coat, multiple scarves, jeans, ski boots, a woolly sweater with a snowflake pattern stitched into it, and a balaclava. "I blend."

"Can we go up already?" Gavin wants to know, giving a nervous look out the door. "A whole bunch of people are coming. The max capacity of the elevator is three. I don't want to wait."

Tired of arguing with Jordan, I shrug and point to the elevator. "Let's go," I say.

I'm almost positive Jordan says, "Goodie!" under his breath.

But that's not possible.

Is it?

When night ends
At breaking dawn
You know you've been partying
Way too long.
"Party Song"
Written by Heather Wells
21

I've never really liked parties. The music's always turned up too loud, and you can never hear what anyone is saying to you.

Although at a party like the one at the Tau Phi House, that might actually be a good thing. Because no one here looks like much of a scintillating conversationalist, if you know what I mean. Everyone is super-attractive—the girls with stick-straight blow-outs, the guys with product carefully layered through their rumpled locks, to give them the appearance of having bed head, when you so know they just got out of the shower.

And though it might be below freezing outside, you wouldn't know it by the way the girls are dressed—spangly halter tops and low-riders so low they'd make a stripper blush. I don't see a single pair of Uggs. New York College kids are nothing if not up on their Hot or Not lists.

I am dismayed when we come off the rickety elevator to see that the words FAT CHICKS GO HOME are still spray-painted along the hallway, though it looks as if a little progress has been made in removing them. They're not quite as fluorescent as they were last time I was here.

But they're still there.

And I certainly don't see anyone above a size 14 at the party. If I had to guess, I'd say the average size present is a 2.

Although I don't know how these girls find thongs in the children's section, which is undoubtedly where most of them have to shop in order to find anything that fits them.

But not everyone seems to find their incredibly slim waists (how do all their internal organs even *fit* in there? I mean like their liver, and everything? Isn't it all squashed? Don't you need at least a twenty-nine-inch waist in order for everything in there to have enough room to do its job?) freakish. Jordan is soon having a very nice time, since the minute he walks through the door, a size 2 runs up to him and is all, "Ohmigod, aren't you Jordan Cartwright? Weren't you in Easy Street? Ohmigod, I have all your CDs!"

Soon more size 2s are gathered around him, wriggling their narrow, nonchildbearing hips and squealing. One of them offers Jordan a plastic cup of beer from a nearby keg. I hear him say, "Well, you know, after my solo album came out, there was a bit of a backlash from the media, because people aren't comfortable with that which isn't familiar," and I know he's gone, sucked into the Size 2 Zone.

"Leave him," I say to Gavin, who is staring at Jordan in concern—as who wouldn't? Those girls look as if they haven't eaten in days. "It's too late. He's going to have to save himself. Have you seen Doug anywhere?"

Gavin looks around. The loft is so crowded with people—and the lights are turned so low—that I don't see how he could recognize anyone. But he manages to spy Doug Winer in a corner over by the wide windows, making out with some girl. I can't tell if the girl is Dana, his paramour of the other morning. But whoever she is, she is keeping Doug occupied . . . enough so that I don't have to worry about him lifting his head and spotting me for the time being.

"Great," I say. "Now, which one is Steve?"

He looks around again. This time he points in the direction of the billiards table and says, "That's him. Playing pool. The tall one, with the blond hair."

"Okay," I say. I have to shout in order for him to hear me, because the music is pulsing so loud. It's techno pop, which I actually sort of like. To dance to. Sadly, no one is dancing. Maybe it's not cool to dance at college parties? "We're going in. You're going to introduce me, right?"

"Right," Gavin says. "I'll say you're my girlfriend."

I shake my head. "He'll never believe that. I'm too old for you."

"You're not too old for me," Gavin insists.

I'm unbuttoning my coat and pulling off my hat. "You called me Grandma!"

"I was joking," Gavin says, looking sheepish. "You couldn't really be my grandma. I mean, how old are you, anyway? Twenty-five?"

"Um," I say. "Yeah." Give or take four years. "But still. Tell him I'm your sister."

Gavin's goatee quivers indignantly. "We don't look anything alike!"

"Oh, my God." The techno pop is starting to give me a headache. What am I even doing here? I should be home, in bed, like all the other late-twenty-somethings. *Letterman* is on. I'm missing *Letterman*! I fold my coat over my arm. I don't know what else to do with it. There's no coat check, and I don't dare leave it lying around. Who knows who might throw up on it? "Fine. Just say I'm a friend who's looking to alter her state of consciousness."

Gavin nods. "Okay. But don't go off with him alone. If he asks."

I can't help preening. Just a little. I finger the tendrils that have escaped from my updo. "Do you think he will?"

"Steve'll do anything that moves," is Gavin's disconcerting reply. "He's a dog."

I stop preening. "Right," I say, giving my miniskirt a tug to make it a millimeter longer. "Well, let's go."

We make our way through the crowd of writhing bodies to the pool table, where two guys are taking turns shooting, in front of an appreciative audience of size 2s. Where did all these tiny girls come from? Is there some kind of island where they're all kept, and only let out at night? Because I never see them during the daytime.

Then I remember. The island is called Manhattan, and the reason I never see them in the daytime is because they're all busy at their internships at Condé Nast.

Gavin waits politely for a tall guy to put the six ball in the corner pocket—much to the appreciative sighing of the size 2s—before going, "Steve-O."

The tall guy looks up, and I recognize Doug Winer's pale blue eyes—but that's it. Steve Winer is as lanky as his little brother is stocky, a basketball player's body to Doug's wrestling frame. Wearing a black cashmere sweater with the sleeves pushed up to reveal a set of very nicely tendoned forearms, and jeans so frayed they could only be designer, Steve sports the same carefully mussed hairdo as all the other guys at his party—with the exception of Gavin, whose hair is mussed because he really didn't comb it after he got up.

"McGoren," Steve says, a smile spreading across his good-looking face. "Long time no see, man."

Gavin saunters forward to shake the hand Steve's stretched out across the table. Which is when I notice that Steve's jeans are hanging low enough on his hips to reveal a few inches of his washboard stomach.

It's the sight of the stomach that does it—plus the fact that there are a few tawny tufts of hair sticking up from under his waistband, as well. I feel as if someone just kicked me in the gut. Steve Winer may be a student and potential murderer, and therefore off-limits.

But he's got a wicked bod.

"Hey, dude," Gavin says, in his habitually sleepy drawl. "How's it goin'?"

"Good to see you, man," Steve says, as the two of them clasp right hands. "How's school? You still a film major?"

"Aw, hells yeah," Gavin says. "Made it through Advanced Experimental last semester."

"No shit?" Steve doesn't seem surprised. "Well, if anyone could make it, it'd be you. You ever see that Mitch guy who was in our group in Tech Theory?"

"Not so much," Gavin says. "Got busted for meth."

"Shit." Steve shakes his head. "That fuckin' sucks."

"Yeah, well, they sent 'im to minimum security federal, not state."

"Well, that's lucky, anyway."

"Yeah. They let 'im take two pieces of sporting equipment, so he packed his hacky-sack and a Frisbee. He's already got a killer Frisbee team started. First one in the prison system."

"Mitch was always an overachiever," Steve observes. His gaze strays toward me. I try to adopt the same vacuous expression I see on the faces of the size 2s around me. It's not hard. I just imagine I haven't eaten in twenty-four hours, like them.

"Who's your friend?" Steve wants to know.

"Oh, this is Heather," Gavin says. "She's in my Narrative Workshop."

I panic slightly at this piece of improvisation by Gavin—I know nothing about film workshops. But I lean forward—making sure my boobs, in their black frilly demicup bra, plainly visible beneath the diaphanous shirt, strain against the material as hard as possible—and say, "Nice to meet you, Steve. I think we have a mutual friend."

Steve's gaze is hooked on my boobs. Oh, yeah. Take that, you size 2s.

"Really?" he says. "Who would that be?"

"Oh, this girl Lindsay . . . Lindsay Combs, I think her name is."

Beside me, Gavin starts choking, even though he hasn't had anything to drink. I guess he doesn't appreciate my improv any more than I'd appreciated his.

"Don't think I know anyone by that name," Steve says, tearing his gaze from my chest and looking me straight in the eye. So much for what those body language experts in *Us Weekly* are always saying, about how liars never make direct eye contact while they're telling a fib.

"Really?" I'm pretending like I don't notice how all the size

2s around us are elbowing one another and whispering. *They* know who Lindsay Combs is, all right. "God, that's so weird. She was telling me all about you just last week. . . . Oh, wait. Maybe she said *Doug* Winer."

"Yeah," Steve says. Is it my imagination, or has he relaxed a little? "Yeah, that's my brother. She must have meant him."

"Oh," I say. And giggle as brainlessly as possible. "Sorry! My bad. Wrong Winer."

"Wait." One of the size 2s, who appears to be slightly drunker—or whatever—than the others, hiccups at me. "You heard what happened to her, right? To Lindsay?"

I try to look as wide-eyed and expressionless as she does. "No. What?"

"Ohmigod," the girl says. "She got, like, totally murdered."

"Totally!" agrees the size 2's friend, who looks as if she might be pushing a size 4. "They found her head in a pot on the stove in Death Dorm!"

To which all the size 2s and 4s around the pool table respond by going, "Ewwww!"

I gasp and pretend to be shocked. "Oh, my God!" I cry. "No wonder she hasn't been in Audio Craft lately."

Gavin, beside me, has gone pale as the white ball. "Lindsay was an accounting major," he murmurs, close to my ear.

Damn! I forgot!

But it's okay, because the music is pounding loud enough, I don't think anyone heard me but him. Steve Winer, for his part, has reached for his martini glass—seriously, the guy is drinking martinis at a frat party—while his opponent lines up a shot that requires those of us around the pool table to back up a little.

I feel that I've lost the momentum to the conversation, so

when we all gather back around the table to watch Steve take his next shot after his opponent misses, I say, "Oh, my God, why would somebody do that? Kill Lindsay, I mean? She was so nice."

I see several of the size 2s exchange nervous glances. One of them actually leaves the table, muttering something about having to pee.

"I mean," I say. "I did hear something about her and the basketball coach. . . ." I figure I'll just throw this out there and see what happens.

What happens is pretty predictable. The size 2s look confused.

"Lindsay and Coach *Andrews*?" A brunette shakes her head. "I never heard anything about *that*. All I heard was that you didn't leave your stash lying around in plain sight when Lindsay was around—"

The brunette breaks off as her friend elbows her and, with a nervous glance at Steve, says, "Shhhh."

But it's too late. Steve's shot has gone crazily wild. And he's not happy about it, either. He looks at Gavin and says, "Your friend sure does talk a lot."

"Well," Gavin says, seeming abashed, "she's a screenwriting major."

Steve's pale blue gaze fastens on mine. I don't think it's my imagination that, good-looking as he is, there's something genuinely creepy about him—hot abs aside.

"Oh, yeah?" he says. "Anybody ever tell you that you look a lot like what'sername? That pop star who sang in all the malls?"

"Heather Wells!" The size 4 isn't as drunk—or whatever—as anyone else (undoubtedly due to having slightly more body fat, in order to absorb the alcohol), and so is pretty swift on the uptake. "Ohmigod, she DOES look like Heather Wells! And . . . didn't you say her name was Heather?" she asks Gavin.

"Heh," I say weakly. "Yeah. I get that a lot. Since my name is Heather. And I look like Heather Wells."

"That is so *random*." One of the size 2s, markedly unsteady on her feet, has to cling to the side of the pool table to stay upright. "Because you are not going to believe who's here. Jordan Cartwright. From Easy Street. Not just a look-alike with the same name. The *real* one."

There are excited squeals of disbelief from the other girls. A second later, they're all asking their friend where she'd seen Jordan. The girl points, and the majority of the spectators of Steve Winer's game of eight ball, have tottered off to get Jordan's autograph . . . on their breasts.

"God," I say to the guys when the girls have all gone. "You'd never guess Jordan Cartwright was that popular by the sales of his last album."

"That guy's a queer," Steve's opponent assures us. He's taken control of the table since Steve missed his last shot, and is picking off Steve's balls one by one. Steve, down at the far end of the felt, doesn't look too happy about it. "I heard this whole wedding thing with Tania Trace is to cover up the fact that he and Ricky Martin are butt buddies."

"Wow," I say, excited that there's a rumor like this going around, even though I know it's not true. "Really?"

"Oh, yeah," Steve's opponent says. "And that hair of his? Transplants. Guy's going bald as this cue ball."

"Wow," I say again. "And they do such a good job of covering it up whenever he's on *Total Request Live*."

"Well," Gavin says, taking my arm for some reason, "sorry to interrupt your game. We'll just be going now."

"Don't go," Steve says. He's been leaning on his pool cue, staring at me, for the past two minutes. "I like your friend here. Heather, you said your name was? Heather what?"

"Snelling," I say, without skipping a beat. Why my boss's last name should come so trippingly to my lips, I have no idea. But there it is. Suddenly my name's Heather Snelling. "It's Polish."

"Really. Sounds British, or something."

"Well," I say, "it's not. What's Winer?"

"German," Steve says. "So you met Lindsay in one of your screenwriting classes?"

"Audio Craft," I correct him. At least I can keep my lies straight. "So what was that girl talking about, back there? About Lindsay only being nice so long as you don't leave your stash lying around in plain sight?"

"You sure are interested in Lindsay," Steve says. By this time, his opponent has finally failed to sink a shot and is waiting impatiently for Steve to take his turn, saying, "Steve. Your turn," every few seconds.

But Steve is ignoring him. The same way I'm ignoring Gavin, who continues to tug on my arm and say, "Come on, Heather. I see some other people I know. I want to introduce you," which is a total bald-faced lie anyway.

"Well," I say, looking Steve dead in the eye, "she was a special girl."

"Oh, she was special, all right," Steve agrees tonelessly.

"I thought you didn't know her," I point out.

"Okay," Steve says, dropping his pool cue and moving swiftly toward me—and Gavin, whose grip has tightened convulsively on my arm. "Who the fuck *is* this bitch, McGoren?"

"Jesus Christ!" The voice, coming from behind us, is, unfortunately, familiar. When I turn my head, I see Doug Winer, one arm around the shoulders of a very scantily garbed non-vanity size 8 (it's nice to see the Winer boys aren't sizeist). Doug's pointing at me, his face very red. "That's the chick who was with the guy who tried to break my hand yesterday!"

All the amiability has vanished from Steve's face. "Soooo," he says, not without some satisfaction. "Friend from class, huh?" This is directed at Gavin. And not in a friendly way.

I instantly regret the whole thing. Not the fact that I'm not home on my bed, strumming my guitar, with Lucy curled at my side. But the fact that I've gotten Gavin involved. Granted, he volunteered. But I should never have taken him up on his offer. I know that the minute I see the glint in Steve's eyes. It's as cold and hard as the frozen metal statues of George Washington in the park below us.

I don't know if this is the guy who killed Lindsay. But I do know we're in trouble. Big trouble.

Gavin doesn't appear to be as convinced as I am that we're in for it. At least if the calm way he's going, "What're you talkin' about, man?" is any indication. "Heather's my friend, man. She was just hoping to score some blow."

Wait. *What? I was what?*

"Bullshit," scoffs Doug. "She was with that guy who came to my room and asked me all those questions about Lindsay. She's a fuckin' cop."

Since Gavin genuinely has no idea what Doug is talking about, his indignation is quite believable. "Hey, man," he says, turning to glare at the smaller Winer. "You been samplin' a little too much of your own wares? Crack is whack, ya know."

Steve Winer folds his arms across his chest. In contrast to

his black sweater, his forearms look darkly tanned. Steve has obviously been in a warm climate recently. "I don't deal crack, nimrod."

"It's an *expression*," Gavin says with a sneer. I watch him in admiration. He may be in film school because he wants to direct, but as an actor, he's not half bad. "Listen, if you're gonna go ape-shit on me, I'm outta here."

Steve's upper lip curls. "You know what you are, McGoren?"

Gavin doesn't look the least bit concerned. "No. What am I, man?"

"A narc." As Steve speaks, two bodies disengage themselves from a couple of black leather couches, where, previously unnoticed by me, they'd apparently been sitting for some time, staring at a basketball game on the wide-screen TV. The girls who'd run off to get Jordan's autograph are trickling back, but have stopped giggling, and now stand gaping at the drama unfolding before them, as if it were an episode of *Real World*, or something.

"We don't like narcs," one of the Tau Phis says. A little younger than Steve, this one has considerably large biceps.

"Yeah," says his twin. Well, bicep-size-wise.

I glance from one to the other. They aren't related, probably, and yet they look exactly alike, same cashmere-sweater-and-jeans combo Steve favors. And same blue eyes without a hint of warmth—or intelligence—in them.

"Jesus, Steve-O," Gavin says, scornfully enough to sound like he really does resent the implication. He jerks a thumb in my direction. He hasn't let go of my arm. "She's just a friend of mine, lookin' to score. But if you're gonna act like assholes about it, forget it. We're outta here. C'mon, Heather."

But Gavin's attempt at a retreat is cut short by Doug Winer himself, who steps directly into our path.

"Nobody threatens a Winer and gets away with it," Doug says to me. "Whoever you are . . . you're gonna be sorry."

"Yeah?" I don't know what comes over me. Gavin is trying to drag me away, but I just plant my high heels on the parquet and refuse to budge. To make matters worse, I actually hear myself ask, "The way somebody made Lindsay sorry?"

Something happens to Doug then. His face goes as red as the lights on the aerial towers I can see blinking in the dark windows behind him.

"Fuck you," he yells.

I probably shouldn't have been too surprised when, a second later, Doug Winer's head met my midriff. After all, I *had* been asking for it. Well, kind of.

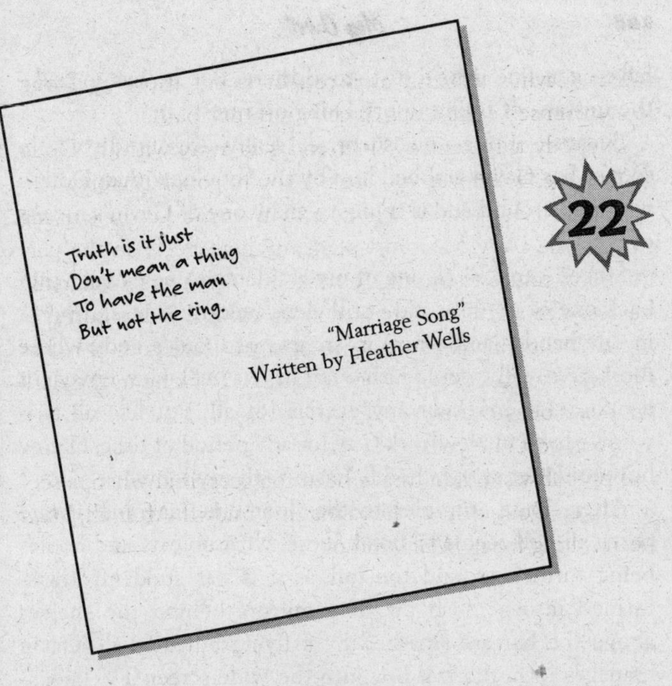
22
Truth is it just
Don't mean a thing
To have the man
But not the ring.
"Marriage Song"
Written by Heather Wells

Having two hundred pounds of frat boy hit you in the gut is a special feeling, one that's hard to describe. To tell you the truth, it's actually a good thing I'm as big a girl as I am. I might not actually have survived if I'd been a size 2.

But since (truth be known) Doug doesn't actually outweigh me by all that much—plus, I saw him coming, and so had time to reflexively clench—I just lie on the floor with the breath knocked out of me. I haven't sustained any internal injury. That I can detect, anyway.

Gavin, on the other hand, doesn't do as well. Oh, he'd

have been fine if he'd just stood there. But he has to make the mistake of trying to pry Doug off me.

Because Doug—no surprise, really—fights dirty. No sooner has Gavin grabbed him by the shoulders than Doug's whipped around and is trying to gnaw one of Gavin's fingers off.

Since I can't allow one of my residents to be eaten, I pull back one of my legs and—still clenching my coat and purse in one hand—land a heel in an area of Doug's body where most guys really would rather not have a heel. Hey, I may not do yoga—or much of any exercise at all. But like all girls who've lived in New York City for any period of time, I know how to inflict serious bodily harm with my footwear.

After Doug crumples to the floor clutching his private parts, all hell seems to break loose, with objects and bodies being thrown around the loft as if it has suddenly transformed into a mosh pit. The mirrors behind the shelves above the bar are smashed by a flying billiard ball. Gavin manages to hurl a frat boy into the wide-screen TV, knocking it over with a crash and a burst of sparks. The size 2s are squealing and fleeing out into the hallway past the FAT CHICKS GO HOME sign, just as one of the pinball machines collapses under Jordan's weight (I don't ask what he was doing on top of it . . . or why his pants are halfway around his ankles).

Fortunately there's so much chaos that I'm able to grab Gavin and shriek, "Let's go!" Then the two of us each throw one of Jordan's arms around our neck (he is in no condition to walk on his own) and drag him from the loft and down the hall . . .

. . . just as the sprinkler system goes off due to the fire started by the knocked-over television.

As the size 2s in the hallway shriek because their blowouts are starting to curl, we duck through an exit marked STAIRS, and don't stop running—and dragging a semiconscious ex–boy band member—until we burst out onto the street.

"Holy crap," Gavin yells, as the cold air sucks at our lungs. "Did you see that? Did you *see* that?"

"Yeah," I say, staggering a bit in the snow. Jordan isn't exactly dead weight, but he's not light, either. "That was not cool."

"Not cool? Not cool?" Gavin is shaking his head happily as we slip and slide along Washington Square North, trying to make our way west. "I wish I'd had my video camera! None of those girls was wearing a bra. When the water hit them—"

"Gavin," I say, cutting him off quickly, "look for a cab. We need to get Jordan back to the Upper East Side, where he lives."

"There are no cabs," Gavin says scornfully. "There's no one even out on the street. Except for us."

He's right. The park is a dead zone. The streets around it have barely been plowed at all. There isn't a car to be seen, except way over on Eighth Street. None of the cabdrivers there can see us, however, no matter how frantically I wave.

I'm flummoxed. I don't know what to do with Jordan. I believe his claim that none of the car services are able to make it over the bridges. And no way am I calling his dad—the man who told me nobody wants to listen to my "angry-rocker-chick shit"—to see if he can swing by in the family limo.

Jordan himself is happy as a clam, stumbling along between us, but he's definitely the worse for wear. I can't just leave him on someone's doorstep—tempting as the idea seems. He'll freeze to death. And it's blocks—*long* blocks, not short ones—to the subway, and in the opposite direction—we'd have to go past Waverly Hall to get to Astor Place.

And I'm not risking running into any angry frat boys. Especially since I can hear sirens in the distance. The fire department must be automatically notified when the sprinkler system goes off.

Between us, Jordan raises his head and cries happily, having heard the sirens as well, "Oh, hey! Here come the cops!"

"I can't believe you were ever engaged to this guy," Gavin says in disgust—revealing, albeit accidentally, that he's been Googling me. "He's such a tool."

"He wasn't always like this," I assure Gavin. Although the truth is, I think Jordan probably *was* always like this. I just never noticed, because I was so young and stupid. And besotted with him. "Besides, he's getting married the day after tomorrow. He's a little nervous."

"Not day after tomorrow," Gavin says. "Tomorrow. It's past midnight. It's officially Friday."

"Crap," I say. The Cartwrights have to be wondering what happened to their youngest son. Tania's probably frantic. If she's even noticed he's gone, that is. I can't send him back to her like this—with his pants half open and lipstick marks all over his face. God, why can't he be just a *little* more like his brother?

Oh, God. His brother. Cooper is going to *kill* me when he finds out where I've been. And I'm going to have to tell him. I can't drag Jordan home like this and not explain.

And I *have* to take Jordan home. It's the only place I can bring him. I don't think I can carry him much farther. Plus, I'm freezing to death. Pantyhose are definitely not suitable legwear the night after a blizzard in Manhattan in January. I don't know how those girls in the low-riders could stand it. Weren't their belly buttons cold?

"Okay," I say to Gavin, as we reach the corner of Washington Square Park North and West. "Here's the deal. We're taking him to my house."

"Are you serious? I get to see where you live?" Gavin's grin, in the pink glow of the street lamps, alarms me. *"Sweet!"*

"No, it's not sweet, Gavin," I snap. "It's the *opposite* of sweet. Jordan's brother is my landlord, and he's going to be upset—*very* upset—if he hears us come in and sees Jordan like this. So we've got to be quiet. Super-quiet."

"I can do that," Gavin says gallantly.

"Because it's not just Cooper I don't want to wake up," I tell him. "My, um, dad is staying there, too."

"I get to meet your *dad*? The one who was in *jail*?" Oh, yes. Gavin's definitely been Googling me.

"No, you don't get to meet him," I say. "Because hopefully he, like Cooper, will be asleep. And we're not waking him up. Right?"

"Right," Gavin says, with a sigh.

"Heather." Jordan is dragging his feet a bit more.

"Shut up, Jordan," I say. "We're almost there."

"Heather," Jordan says again.

"Jordan," I say. "I swear to God, if you throw up on me, I will kill you."

"Heather," Jordan says for a third time. "I think someone slipped something into my drink."

I look at him in some alarm. "You mean this isn't how you always are after a party?"

"Of course not," Jordan slurs. "I only had one beer."

"Yeah," I say. "But how many glasses of wine did you have before you got downtown?"

"Only ten," Jordan says innocently. "Hey. Speaking of which. Where are my skis?"

"Oh, I'm sure they're fine, Jordan," I say. "You can pick them up in the morning. Why would someone put something in your drink?"

"To take advantage of me, of course," Jordan says. "Everyone wants a piece of me. Everyone wants a piece of Jordan Cartwright pie."

Gavin, who gets a faceful of Jordan's beery breath as he says this, wrinkles his nose. "Not me," he says.

We've reached Cooper's house. I stop to dig my keys from my purse, and give a mini-lecture as I do so.

"Now, when we get inside," I say to Gavin, "we're just going to dump Jordan on the couch in the living room. Then I'm taking you back to Fischer Hall."

"I don't need no escort," Gavin says scornfully, his street slang coming back now that there are no Tau Phis in sight and he's feeling cocky again.

"Those frat boys are angry," I say. "And they know where you live—"

"Aw, hell, woman," Gavin says. "Steve-O don't know shit about me except my name. I was never cool enough for him 'cause I don't like putting chemicals in my body."

"Except twenty-one shots."

"I mean except for alcohol," Gavin amends.

"Fine," I say. "We'll argue about it later. First we'll put Jordan down on the couch. Then we'll worry about getting you home."

"It's two blocks away," Gavin says.

"Heather."

"Not now, Jordan," I say. "Gavin, I just don't want you—"

"Heather," Jordan says again.

"*What*, Jordan?"

"Cooper's looking at us."

I look up.

And sure enough, there's Cooper's face in the window by the door. A second later, we hear the locks being thrown back.

"Okay," I say to Gavin, my heart beginning to pound. "Change of plans. On the count of three, we ditch Jordan, then run like hell. One. Two."

"Don't even think about it," Cooper says, as he comes out onto the stoop. He's wearing cords and a wool sweater. He looks warm and calm and sensible. I long to throw myself at him, bury my head against his hard chest, breathe his Cooper-y scent, and tell him what a terrible evening I've had.

Instead, I say, "I can explain."

"I'm sure you can," Cooper says. "Well, come on. Get him inside."

We drag Jordan inside, with effort—especially since Lucy appears and begins jumping excitedly all over us. Well, me, actually. Fortunately, my thighs are so frozen I can't feel her nails as they rake my nylon stockings.

It's as Lucy leaps up in an effort to lick Jordan's hand that he suddenly becomes very vivacious, saying, as we haul him past Cooper, into the foyer, "Hi ya, bro! What's happenin'?"

"Your fiancée called," Cooper says, as he closes the door behind us and begins working all the locks. "That's what's happening. Did you just take off without telling anyone where you were going?"

"Pretty much," Jordan says, as we let him go and he flops back against his grandfather's somewhat dilapidated pink couch, where Lucy begins licking him in earnest. "Ow. Nice doggie. Make the room stop spinning, please."

"How did he even get down here?" Cooper wants to know. "There aren't any cabs. And no way Jordan took the subway."

"He skied," I explain lamely. It's mercifully warm in the house. I can feel my thighs twitching as they defrost.

"He skied?" Cooper raises both eyebrows. "Where are his skis?"

"He lost them," Gavin says.

Cooper seems to notice Gavin for the first time. "Oh," he says. "You again, eh?"

"You shouldn't be mad at Heather," Gavin begins. "It was all that guy's fault. See, she was trying to sober him up with a brisk walk around the park, but he wouldn't go for it. Fortunately I was passing by and was able to help get him here, or who knows what would have happened. Guy could have frozen. Or worse. I hear there's a doctor who jumps on any drunks he finds in the park and harvests their kidneys to donate to wealthy Bolivians on dialysis. You wake up in the morning all achy and you don't know why—and boom. Turns out someone stole your kidney."

Wow. Gavin really is the king of the improv. He lies with such ease, and so convincingly, I can't help wondering how many of the stories he's fed me over the months I've known him were fabrications like the one he just came up with.

Cooper, however, doesn't look impressed.

"Right," he says. "Well, thank you for your aid. I think we can handle it from here, though. So goodbye."

"I'll walk you back," I start to say to Gavin, but a voice from the hallway interrupts me.

"There she is!" My dad comes in, dressed in pajamas and a robe. It's clear from the way a tuft of what's left of his hair is sticking up in the back that he'd been asleep, but Tania's call had wakened him as well as Cooper. "Heather, we were so worried. When that Tania person phoned, and then we couldn't find you—don't you ever do that again, young lady! If you're going to go out, you had better darn well tell one of us where you're going."

I blink, looking from my father to Cooper and back again. "Are you serious?" I ask incredulously.

"*I'll* walk Gavin back," Cooper says, making it evident that he's anticipated my next move—avoidance. "Heather, get some blankets for Jordan. Alan, call Tania back and tell her Jordan's crashing here for the night."

Dad nods. "I'll say he was at an impromptu bachelor party," he tells us. "And came here to sleep so as not to disturb her."

I just stare—mostly because I've forgotten my dad has a first name, and that Cooper had just used it. But also at the preposterousness of what Dad's just said.

"Jordan doesn't have any friends," I say. "Who's going to throw him a bachelor party? And he'd never be that considerate, not to disturb her."

"I do so have friends," Jordan insists from the couch, where Lucy has progressed to licking his face. "You two are my friends. Or six. Or however many you are."

"I don't need anyone to walk me back," Gavin declares, as Cooper reaches for his coat.

"Maybe not," Cooper says grimly. "But I need some fresh air. Come on."

The two of them go out, leaving me alone with Jordan and my father—two men who both abandoned me when I needed them most, and then both came crawling back when I didn't need—or want—them at all.

"You owe me," I say to Jordan, after I've stalked back into the living room with a blanket—and a salad bowl to throw up in—for him. Even though I'm fairly positive he won't remember any of this in the morning, I add, "And I'm still not coming to your wedding." To my dad, I say, "Don't tell Tania I was with him when you call her."

"I may have been in prison for the past two decades, Heather," Dad says, with wounded dignity. "But I still have some idea how these things work."

"Well, good for you," I say. Then, calling for Lucy, I hurry up the stairs to my own apartment, hoping if I lock the door and get in bed fast enough, I'll miss Cooper's return. I know Sarah would accuse me of practicing avoidance techniques.

But hey, when it comes to Cooper sometimes avoidance is the only way to go.

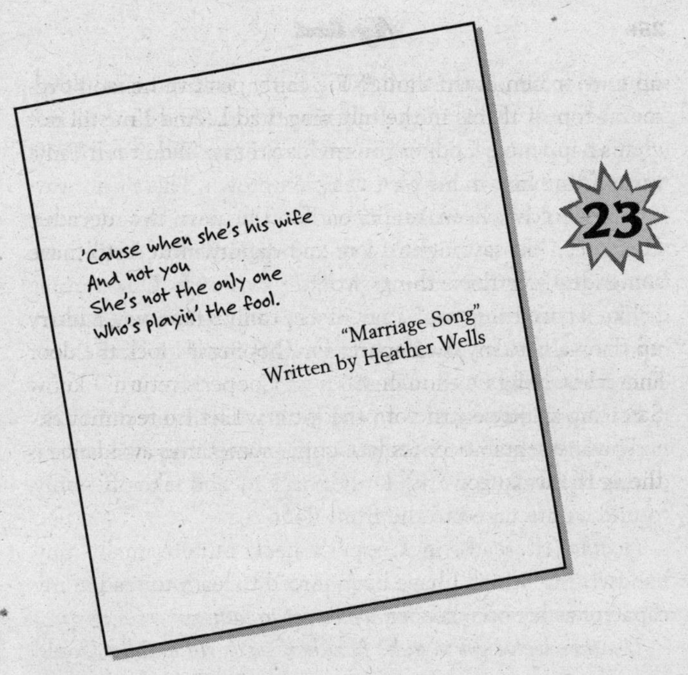

'Cause when she's his wife
And not you
She's not the only one
Who's playin' the fool.
"Marriage Song"
Written by Heather Wells
23

I sneak away the next morning to avoid Cooper. I do this by rising at the ungodly hour of eight, and manage to get bathed and dressed and out the door by eight-thirty. This is so unlike my usual schedule—of not appearing downstairs before eight fifty-five—that I avoid everyone in the house, including my dad, who is still tootling his Indian flute "tribute to the morning" song when I creep by his room, Timberlands in hand so as not to cause the floorboards to creak.

There's no sign of Cooper—a peek through his partly open bedroom door reveals a neatly made bed—or, more ominously, Jordan. The blankets beneath which Jordan had slept are folded at the end of the couch, and the salad bowl sits on top of them, mercifully empty. It seems clear to me what's happened: Cooper roused his brother and is currently transporting him in his own vehicle uptown. There's no way Jordan would have woken so early on his own the morning after a tear like last night's. I've known Jordan to sleep until four in the afternoon the night after a carouse. Our mutual dislike of morning was one of the only traits we had in common—besides an affection for Girl Scout cookies (him: Thin Mints. Me: Do-Si-Does).

Feeling as if I've just won the lottery, I let Lucy out to do her business, grab a chocolate-chip protein bar (for energy during the walk to work), let her back in, and take off—only to find a note taped to the front door.

Heather, it reads, in Cooper's neat, infinitesimally tiny handwriting, which I have been forced to learn to read in my capacity as his bookkeeper, *we've got to talk*.

Heather, we've got to talk? Heather, we've got to talk? Could there be four more ominous words in the English language than *we've got to talk*? I mean, seriously, who wants to see a note that says THAT taped to their front door?

No one, that's who.

Which is why I pull it off and crumple it into my pocket on my way out the door.

What could Cooper want to talk to me about? The fact that I dragged his brother home last night, dead drunk, to sleep it off on his couch, when Cooper's made it more than clear he wants nothing to do with his immediate family? The fact that I snuck out to investigate Lindsay Combs's murder, without telling anyone where I was going and after I'd sworn that this time I would leave the detecting up to the professionals? Or possibly the fact that I endangered the life of one of my residents while doing so?

Or maybe it didn't even have anything to do with what happened last night. Maybe Cooper's decided he's sick of putting up with the Wellses and all of their quirks—Dad's Indian flute and my tendency to drag home drunk pop stars and twenty-one-year-old baggy-panted wannabe gangstas. Maybe he's going to toss us all out on our ears. Some of us would certainly deserve that kind of treatment.

And I'm not talking about Lucy or my dad.

My walk to work is reflective and sad. Even the protein bar tastes a lot more like cardboard and a lot less like a Kit Kat bar than usual. I don't want to get kicked out of Cooper's house. It's the only home I've ever known, really, not counting the apartment Jordan and I lived in together, now forever tainted by the memory of seeing him with Tania Trace's lips locked around his—

"Heather!" Reggie, back on his usual corner, seems surprised to see me out and about so early. *I'm* surprised to see him back at work. Though the snow has stopped and the plows have made some headway, the streets are still mere narrow strips between vast mountains of piled-up snow.

"Morning, Reggie," I say, coming out from behind a six-foot drift covering some unfortunate person's car. "That was some storm, huh?"

"I wasn't too happy about it," Reggie says. He's bundled up against the cold in a gold Tommy Hilfiger parka. A paper cup of coffee steams in his gloved hands. "Sometimes I think it might be better to return to the islands."

"But what would you do there?" I ask, genuinely interested.

"My parents have a banana plantation," Reggie says. "I could help manage it. They have wanted me to come home to do so for a long time. But I make more money here."

I can't help but mentally contrast the Winer boys and their family situation with Reggie's. Doug and Steve Winer's dad wants them to make their own fortunes, and so the boys have turned to selling drugs. Reggie's parents want him to take over the family business, but he makes more money selling drugs. The whole thing is just . . . stupid.

"I think you'd be better off on the banana farm, Reggie," I say. "For what it's worth. It'd be a lot less dangerous."

Reggie seems to consider this. "Except during hurricane season," he finally concedes. "But if I were back there, I would miss seeing your happy face every morning, Heather."

"I could come visit," I say. "I've never been to a banana farm."

"You wouldn't like it," Reggie says, with a grin that shows all his gold teeth. "We get up very early there, before light. Because of the roosters."

"God," I say, horrified. "That sounds awful. No wonder you prefer it in New York."

"Plus, if you can make it here, you can make it anywhere," Reggie says, with a shrug.

"Totally," I say. "Hey, did you hear anything about that Doug Winer guy I asked you about?"

Reggie's smile fades. "I did not," he says. "Although I did hear there was a bit of a ruckus in one of the fraternities last night."

I raise my eyebrows. "Really? Wow. What kind of ruckus?"

"One that apparently involved your ex, Jordan Cartwright," Reggie says. "But that must be just a rumor, because what would the famous Jordan Cartwright be doing at a fraternity party two nights before his wedding?"

"You're right," I say. "That must be just a rumor. Well, I better go. Don't want to be late!"

"No," Reggie agrees gravely. "Not you."

"See you later! Stay warm!" I wave cheerfully, then duck around the corner onto Washington Square West. Phew! That was close. I can't believe word about what happened last night has already reached the drug dealers. I wonder if it will make Page Six. Thank God the Greeks don't have a sign-in policy. I'd be in so much trouble at work if it got out I'd been there. . . .

When I walk through the front door of Fischer Hall at twenty of nine, Pete, who is at the security desk, nearly chokes on his bagel.

"What happened?" he asks, with mock worry. "Is it the end of times?"

"Very funny," I say to him. "I've been here on time before, you know."

"Yeah," Pete says. "But never *early*."

"Maybe I'm turning over a new leaf," I say.

"And maybe I'll get a raise this year," Pete says. Then laughs heartily at his own joke.

I make a face at him, check in with the student front desk worker to collect the briefing forms from the night before, and head to my office. I see, to my relief, that the outer door is closed and locked. Yes! I'm the first one in! Won't Tom be surprised when he sees me!

I strip off my coat and hat, then head to the caf for coffee and a bagel. Magda, I'm happy to see, is back at her regular post. She looks better than she has all week. Her eye shadow is fluorescent pink, her hair standing its normal six inches off her forehead, and her eyeliner is unsmudged and black as coal. She smiles at me when I come in.

"There she is," she cries. "My little pop star. Did you miss your Magda?"

"Yes, I did," I say. "Have a good day off?"

"I did," Magda says, growing sober. "I needed it. You know what I mean? It was nice not to think about this place—and what happened here—for a change." She heaves a shudder, then, as two students come up behind me, cries, in a completely different voice, "Oh, look. Here come two of my movie stars. Good morning, little movie stars!"

The students eye her uneasily as she runs their meal cards—which double as their IDs—through her scanner. When she's handed them back and the kids are gone, Magda says, in her normal voice, "I heard you went to visit Manuel. How is he?"

"Um, when I was there yesterday, not so good," I say. "But when I left last night, I heard he'd been moved out of the ICU and was being listed as stable."

"Good," Magda says. "And the police still haven't caught the people who did it to him?"

"No," I say. I'm tempted to tell Magda *I* have a pretty good idea who they were. But I need to see how Tom's date went first. "But I'm sure they're working on it."

Magda scowls. "They aren't working to find who killed little Lindsay," she says. "Three days it's been, and no arrest. It's because she's a girl," she adds, glumly resting her chin in her hands. "If it were a man's head they found in there, they'd have someone under arrest already. The police don't care what happens to girls. Especially girls like Lindsay."

"Magda, that's not true," I assure her. "They're working as hard as they can. I'm sure they'll be making an arrest soon. I mean, they got snowed in yesterday, just like you did."

But Magda just looks skeptical. I realize it's futile to try to change her mind when she's so convinced she's right. So I get my bagel—with cream cheese and bacon, of course—and cocoa-coffee and return to my desk.

I'm sitting there wondering who Tad Tocco is and why he wants me to call him—he has a New York College office extension—when Tom stumbles sleepily into the office, looking surprised to see me.

"Whoa," he says. "Is this an illusion?"

"No," I say. "It's really me. I'm here on time."

"You're here *early*." Tom shakes his head. "Will miracles never cease?"

"So." I'm watching him carefully. "How'd it go? With Coach Andrews, I mean."

He's pulling out his keys to unlock his office door, but I see the swift, secret smile before he can hide it.

"Fine," he says tonelessly.

"Oh, right," I say. "Come on. Spill."

"I don't want to jinx it," Tom says. "Seriously, Heather, I have a tendency to rush into things. And I'm not doing that this time. I'm just not."

"So . . ." I study him. "If you're going to take things slow with him, that means things must have gone pretty well."

"They went great," Tom says. He can't hide his smile anymore. "Steve's just . . . well, he's amazing. But like I said, we're taking things slow."

We. He'd already started saying *we*.

I'm happy for him, of course. But a little bummed out for myself. Not because I'd like to be part of a *we* someday—though I would, naturally.

But because now I have to wonder just why Kimberly so obviously lied to me . . . I mean, unless Steven Andrews is as good an actor as Heath Ledger, which I sort of doubt.

Still, I can't help but feel happy for Tom.

"So if you're taking things slow," I say, "that means you must be planning on sticking around for a while after all, right?"

He shrugs, blushing. "We'll see," he says. And goes into his office.

Which reminds me of something else. "So where's Dr. Death? She coming in today?"

"No, thank God," Tom says. "Counseling Services has decided that if any more students need to work with grief counselors, they can go across the park."

"Let me guess," I say. "Cheryl Haebig stopped by to see Dr. Kilgore a few too many times."

"I think Cheryl nearly drove Dr. Kilgore to distraction," Tom says happily. "My office is mine again. All mine! I'm going to the caf to get a tray—a *tray*—and have breakfast *at my desk*."

"Enjoy," I say happily, thinking how nice it is to have a boss who thinks eating breakfast at his desk is totally appropriate in the workplace. I have really scored in the boss department with Tom. I'm glad he's not going anywhere. At least, for now.

I am going over the briefing forms when Gavin appears, looking strangely uncomfortable.

"Um, hi, Heather," he says, standing stiffly in front of my desk. "Is Tom around? I'm supposed to reschedule my alcohol counseling appointment."

"Yeah, he's here," I say. "He just went into the caf to grab something to eat. Have a seat. He should be right back."

Gavin sits down on the couch next to my desk. But instead of sinking into it, his legs splayed apart obscenely, as he's tended to do in the past, Gavin sits very straight in his seat, keeping his gaze straight ahead. He doesn't mess around with the paper clips or McDonald's *Toy Story 2* action figures on my desk, the way he usually does, either.

I stare at him. "Gavin? Are you okay?"

"What?" He blinks at the Monet print on the wall, resolutely not looking at me. "Me? Sure, I'm fine. Why?"

"I don't know," I say. "You just seem sort of . . . distant."

"I'm not being distant," Gavin says. "I'm just giving you space."

It's my turn to blink. "You're what?"

Finally, he looks at me.

"You know," he says. "I'm giving you space. Your friend Cooper told me last night that you really need your space. So I'm trying to give it to you."

Something cold passes over me. I think it's foreboding.

"Wait," I say. "Cooper told you I need space?"

"Yeah," Gavin says with a nod. "Last night. When he was walking me back here. Which I didn't need, by the way. I mean, I'm twenty-one years old. I don't need anyone to escort me back to my dorm."

"Residence hall," I say. "And what else did Cooper tell you about me?"

"Well, you know." Gavin shrugs uncomfortably and turns back to the Monet on the opposite wall. "That you were really, really hurt when his brother Jordan cheated on you, and that you were confused, and you're still getting over the loss, and aren't ready for any new romantic relationships—"

"*WHAT*?" I've risen to my feet. "He said *what*?"

"Well," Gavin says, turning his head to look at me quizzically, "you know. I mean, on account of how you're still in love with him—"

My heart seems to explode inside my chest. "*In love with WHO*?"

"Well, Jordan Cartwright, of course." Gavin looks taken aback. "Oh, shit," he adds, when he sees my expression. "I forgot. Cooper said not to tell you what he said—you won't tell him I told, will you? That guy kinda scares me. . . ."

Gavin's voice trails off as he stares at me in alarm. I can't imagine why. Maybe it's because of the way I'm hanging over my desk with my mouth wide open and my eyes spinning around in their sockets.

"Well, I mean, isn't that why you don't want to go to Jordan's wedding tomorrow?" Gavin is starting to babble. "Because you're still so in love with him, you can't stand to see him marry someone else? Because that's what your friend Cooper thinks, anyway. He thinks that's why you haven't been able to move on to someone else, because you're still mourning Jordan's loss, and that it will be a while before you get over it—"

The scream starts at the bottom of my feet and rises steadily, like steam from a kettle. I'm about to tilt my head back to let it out when Tom comes staggering into the office, his face white as the snow outside. He's not carrying a tray with breakfast on it.

"They just found the rest of her," he says, right before he collapses onto the couch beside Gavin.

The scream disappears.

"The rest of who?" Gavin wants to know.

"Lindsay," Tom says.

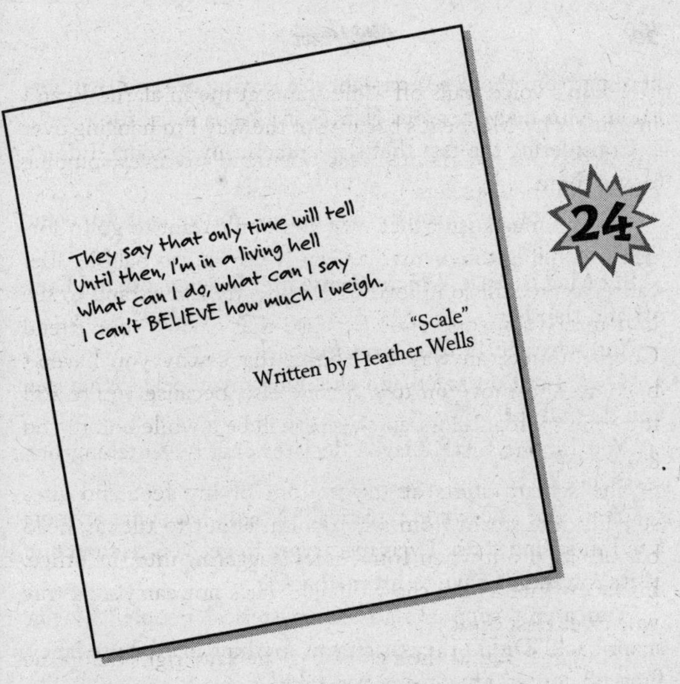

They say that only time will tell
Until then, I'm in a living hell
What can I do, what can I say
I can't BELIEVE how much I weigh.
"Scale"
Written by Heather Wells
24

Magda is at her cash register, weeping.

"Magda," I say, for what has to be the fifth time, "just tell me. Tell me what happened."

Magda shakes her head. Against all laws of physics and hairspray, her hair has collapsed. It droops sadly to one side of her face.

"Magda. Tell me what they found. Tom won't talk about it. Gerald won't let anybody into the kitchen. The cops are on their way. Just *tell* me."

Magda can't speak. She is constricted with grief. Pete doesn't have to argue with any of the residents he is busy herding from the cafeteria—they're leaving of their own volition, with many nervous glances in Magda's direction.

Considering the fact that she's practically keening, I don't blame them.

"Magda," I say. "You're hysterical. You've got to calm down."

But Magda can't. Which is why, after heaving a sigh, I haul off and slap her.

And why she, in turn, slaps me back.

"Ow!" I cry, outraged and clutching my cheek. "What did you do *that* for?"

"You hit me first!" Magda declares angrily, clutching her own cheek.

"Yeah, but you were hysterical!" Magda has some arm on her. I'm seeing stars. "I was just trying to get you to snap out of it. You didn't have to hit me back."

"You aren't supposed to slap hysterical people," Magda snaps back. "Didn't they teach you anything in all those fancy first-aid courses they made you take?"

"Magda." My eyes finally stop swimming in tears. "Tell me what they found."

"I'll show you," Magda says, and holds out the hand she hadn't used to smack me in the face. There, in her palm, is nestled a strange-looking object. Made of gold, it resembles an earring, only much larger, and curved. There's a diamond on one end of it. The gold is pretty banged up, like it's been chewed on.

"What is that?" I ask, gazing down at it.

"WHERE DID YOU GET THAT?"

Both Magda and I are startled by the reaction of Cheryl Haebig as she and her boyfriend Jeff pass us on the way out of the cafeteria. Cheryl's eyes are wide, her gaze glued to the object in Magda's hand. Pete, who is trying to herd everyone out of the place, looks frustrated.

"Cher," Jeff says, tugging on his girlfriend's arm, "come on. They want us to leave."

"No," Cheryl says, shaking her head, her gaze still fixed on what Magda is holding. "Where you did get that? Tell me."

"Do you recognize it, Cheryl?" I ask her—though it's obvious from her reaction that she does. Also that I probably don't want to know why. "What is it?"

"It's Lindsay's navel ring," Cheryl says. Her face has gone as white as the blouse she's wearing. "Oh, God. Where'd you get it?"

Magda presses her lips together. And closes her fingers. "Oh, no," she says, in the singsong voice she only uses when students are around. "Never mind. You go to class now, or you'll be late—"

But Cheryl takes a step forward and says, her eyes going hard as the marble floor beneath us, *"Tell me."*

Magda swallows, glances at me, then says, in her normal voice, "It was stuck at the bottom of the garbage disposal. The one that hasn't been working right all week. The building engineer finally got around to taking a look at it. And he found this."

She flips it over. On the other side of the gold, the word LINDSAY is engraved—hard to make out, after all the mashing. But still there.

Cheryl gasps, then seems to find it difficult to stand. Pete and Jeff help her to a nearby chair.

"Tell her to put her head between her knees," I tell Jeff. He nods, looking panicky, and makes his girlfriend lean forward until her long, honey-colored hair is sweeping the floor.

I turn back to Magda and stare down at the ring. "They put the rest of her down the disposal?" I whisper.

Magda shakes her head. "They tried. But bones won't grind up."

"Wait, so . . . *they're still down there*?"

Magda nods. We're whispering so Cheryl won't overhear. "The sink was stopped up. No one thought to wonder why— it's always stopped up. We just used the other one."

"And the police didn't look in there, either?"

Magda wrinkles her nose. "No. The water was all . . . well, you know how it can get back there. Plus they served chili Monday night. . . ."

I feel a little bit of vomit rise into my throat.

"Oh, my God," I say.

"I know." Magda looks down at the belly button ring. "Who could do such a thing to such a nice, pretty girl? Who, Heather? *Who*?"

"I'm going to find out," I say, turning away from her and striding blindly—because my eyes are filled with tears— toward Cheryl, still sitting with her head between her knees. I squat down beside her so that I can ask her, "Cheryl. Were Lindsay and Coach Andrews sleeping together?"

"WHAT?" It's Jeff who looks astonished. "Coach A and Lind—NO WAY."

Cheryl raises her head. It's very red from all the blood that's rushed into it while she was hanging upside down. There are tear tracks down her cheeks, and unshed tears still glisten on her long eyelashes.

"Coach Andrews?" she echoes, with a sniff. "N-no. No, of course not."

"Are you *sure*?" I ask her.

Cheryl nods. "Yeah," she says. "I mean, Coach A, he . . ." She looks up at Jeff. "Um."

"What?" Jeff looks frightened. "Coach A *what,* Cher?"

Cheryl sighs and looks back at me. "Well, none of us are sure," she says. "But we always just assumed Coach A is gay."

"WHAT?" Now Jeff looks as if *he's* the one who's about to cry. "Coach Andrews? No way. *NO WAY.*"

Cheryl blinks up at me tearfully. "You can see why we kept that suspicion to ourselves," Cheryl says.

"I can," I say. I give Cheryl a pat on the wrist. "Thank you."

And then I'm gone, brushing past Pete to head out of the caf and toward the elevator.

"Heather?" Magda trots after me in her stilettos. "Where are you going?"

I jab at the UP button, and the elevator door slides open.

"Heather." Pete follows me out into the lobby, gazing after me in concern. "What's going on?"

I ignore them both. I get in the elevator and stab the button for the twelfth floor. As the doors close, I see Magda tottering toward me, trying to stop me from going alone.

But it's just as well she doesn't come with me. She isn't going to like what I'm about to do. *I* don't like what I'm about to do.

But someone has to do it.

When the doors open on the twelfth floor, I get off the elevator and stalk toward Room 1218. The hallway—which the RA has decorated in a Tigger the Tiger motif, being a Pooh fan . . . only an ironic Tigger, since she's given him dreadlocks—is silent. It's just past nine in the morning, and the kids who aren't in class are asleep.

But one of them I fully intend to wake up.

"Director's Office," I yell, thumping on the door once with my fist. We are not allowed to enter any room unannounced. But that doesn't mean we have to wait for the resident to answer the door. And I don't. I insert my master key into the lock and turn the knob.

Kimberly, as I hoped, is curled up in her bed. Her roommate's matching twin—they've even got the same bedspreads, in New York College gold and white—is empty. Kimberly is sitting up, looking groggy.

"Wh-what's going on?" she asks sleepily. "Omigod. What are *you* doing in here?"

"Get out of bed," I say to her.

"What? Why?" Even when just waking from a dead sleep, Kimberly Watkins looks pretty. Her face—unlike my own, when I'm just waking up—isn't smeared with various anti-zit-and-wrinkle creams, and her hair, instead of standing comically on end, falls into perfectly straight planes along either side of her face.

"Is there a fire?" Kimberly wants to know.

"There's no fire," I say. "Come on."

Kimberly has clambered from her bed and is standing there in an oversized New York College T-shirt and a pair of boxers. On her feet are a pair of baggy gray socks.

"Wait," she says, tucking a lock of hair behind one ear. "Where are we going? I have to get dressed. I have to brush my—"

But I've already got her by the arm and am dragging her out the door. She tries to resist, but let's face it: I'm a lot bigger than she is. Plus, I'm fully awake, and she isn't.

"W-where are you taking me?" Kim stammers, as she trots to keep up with me as I haul her toward the elevator. Her alternative is to let me drag her, which she apparently realizes I am totally willing to do.

"I've got something to show you," I tell her in reply.

Kimberly blinks nervously. "I—I don't want to see it."

For a minute, I consider throwing her up against the nearest wall as if she were a handball. Instead, I say, "Well, you're going to see it. You're going to see it, and then you and I are going to have a talk. Understand?"

The elevator cab is still waiting at the twelfth floor. I pull her into the car and jab the button for the lobby.

"You're crazy," Kimberly says, in a shaky voice, as we glide down. She's starting to wake up now. "Do you know that? You're going to get fired for this."

"Oh, yeah?" I laugh. That's the best one I've heard all day.

"I mean it. You can't treat me like this. President Allington's gonna be mad at you when he finds out."

"President Allington," I say, as we reach the lobby and the elevator doors open, "can kiss my ass."

I drag her past the door to my office, and down the hall toward the front desk, where the student worker actually looks up from the copy of *Cosmo* she's snagged from somebody's mailbox to stare at me in shock. Pete, who is waving firemen into the building—why, no matter what we call 911 for, from a resident freaking out on meth to human bones in a garbage disposal, does the New York City Fire Department always manage to show up first?—pauses in his coordination efforts to stare at me.

"I hope you know what you're doing," he says, as I drag Kimberly past him.

"Don't just stand there," Kimberly shouts at him. "Stop her! Don't you see what she's doing? She's holding me against my will! *She's hurting my arm!*"

Pete's walkie-talkie crackles. He lifts it to his lips and says, "No, it's all clear here in the lobby."

"Stupid rent-a-cop!" Kimberly sneers at him, as I thrust her through the cafeteria doors.

Magda, who is standing at the entrance next to her boss, Gerald, and several firemen, looks startled. Her hand is open to show the firemen her discovery. Cheryl, I see, is still sitting nearby, a very white-faced—but solemn—Jeff Turner at her side. I grab Kimberly by the back of her neck and shove her face toward Magda's open palm.

"See that?" I demand. "Do you know what that is?"

Kimberly is squirming to escape my grasp. "No," she says sullenly. "What are you talking about? You better let me go."

"Show her," I say to Magda, and Magda very nicely holds the belly button ring right up to Kimberly's face.

"Recognize it?" I ask her.

Kimberly's eyes are as wide as quarters. Her gaze is riveted on the object Magda is holding.

"Yeah," she says faintly. "I recognize it."

"What is it?" I ask, letting go of her neck. I don't need to hold on to her anymore to make her look. The truth is, she can't look away.

"It's a navel ring."

"Whose navel ring is it?"

"Lindsay's."

"That's right," I say. "It's Lindsay's. Do you know where we found it?"

"No." Kimberly is starting to sound congested. I wonder if she's starting to cry or merely coming down with something.

"In the garbage disposal," I say. "They tried to grind your friend's body up, Kimberly. *Like she was garbage*."

"No," Kimberly says. Her voice is growing even fainter. Which is unusual, for a cheerleader.

"And you know what the person who killed Lindsay did to

Manuel Juarez at the game the other night," I say. "Just because they were afraid Lindsay might have said something to him about them. What do you think about that, huh, Kimberly?"

Kimberly, her voice still faint, her face now swollen with tears, mumbles, "I don't see what that has to do with me."

"Don't mess with me, Kimberly," I say. "First you tried to tell me Lindsay's roommate might have killed her out of jealousy. Then you tried to make me think Coach Andrews and Lindsay were romantically involved, when you know perfectly well Coach Andrews is same-sex oriented—"

I hear, from behind me, a little gasp. I know it's come from Cheryl Haebig.

"Face it, Kimberly," I say, not turning around. "You know who killed Lindsay."

Kimberly is shaking her head, hard enough that her hair has fallen into her eyes. "No, I—"

"Do you want to see it, Kimberly?" I demand. "The disposal they tried to stick Lindsay down? It's all clogged up. With her blood and bones. But I'll show it to you, if you want."

Kimberly lets out a little moan. The firemen are staring down at me like I'm some kind of sick freak. I guess they're right. I *am* a sick freak. I don't feel bad at all about what I'm doing to Kimberly. Not even a tiny bit.

"You want to know what they did to Lindsay, Kim? Do you want to know?" She shakes her head some more, but I go on anyway. "First, someone strangled her—so hard and for so long, the capillaries around her eyes burst. She was probably gasping for air, but whoever had hold of her didn't care, and didn't let go. So she died. But that wasn't enough. Because then they chopped her up. Chopped her up and put the different parts of her body down the disposal. . . ."

"No." Kimberly is sobbing now. "No, that isn't true!"

"It is so true. You know it's true. And you know what else, Kimberly? You're next. They're coming after you next."

The tear-filled eyes widen. "No! You're just saying that to scare me!"

"First Lindsay. Then Manuel. Then you."

"No!" Kimberly jerks away from me—but unfortunately ends up in front of Cheryl Haebig, who has risen to her feet and is standing there, eyes blazing, glaring at Kimberly.

Only Kimberly doesn't seem to notice the glare. She cries, "Oh, thank God," when she sees Cheryl. "Cheryl, tell her—tell this bitch I don't know anything."

But Cheryl just shakes her head.

"You told her Lindsay and Coach A were involved?" she snaps. "Why would you do that? Why? You know it wasn't true."

Kimberly, seeing she's not going to get any support from Cheryl, backs away from her, still shaking her head. "You . . . you don't understand," she hiccups.

"Oh, I understand, all right," Cheryl says. For every step she takes forward, Kimberly takes another step back, until Kimberly's back is up against Magda's desk, where she freezes, looking fearfully up into Cheryl's face. "I understand you were always jealous of Lindsay. I understand you always wanted to be as well liked and popular as Lindsay. But it was never going to happen. Because you're such a fucking—"

Only Cheryl doesn't get to finish. Because Kimberly has collapsed against the cashier's desk, sliding slowly down it until she's on the floor, a puddle in New York College white and gold.

"No," she sobs. "No, I didn't do it. I didn't do anything. I didn't kill her!"

"But you know who did," I step forward to say. "Don't you, Kimberly?"

She's shaking her head. "I don't! I swear I don't! I just—I know what Lindsay did."

Cheryl and I exchange puzzled glances.

"What did Lindsay do, Kimberly?" I ask.

Kimberly, her knees curled up to her chest, murmurs softly, "She stole his stash."

"She *what*?"

"She stole his stash! God, what are you, dense?" Kimberly glares up at us through her tears. "She stole his entire stash, about a gram of coke. She was mad at him, 'cause he was so stingy with it. Like, she'd blow him and he'd just give her a line or two. Plus he was seeing other girls, too, on the side. It was pissing her off."

Cheryl takes what seems like an involuntary step backward when she hears this. "You're lying," she says to Kimberly.

"Wait," I say, confused. "Whose stash? Doug Winer's? Are you talking about Doug Winer?"

"Yes." Kimberly nods miserably. "She didn't think he'd miss it. Or if he did, he'd think one of his frat brothers took it. Oh, don't look at me like that, Cheryl!" Kimberly is glaring at her fellow squad member. "Lindsay wasn't a fucking saint, you know. No matter what you and the other girls want to think. God, I don't know why you guys could never see her for what she was . . . a coke whore. Who got what she fucking deserved!"

Kimberly's sobbing has risen to hyperventilation level. She's clutching her arms to her stomach as if she were suffering from appendicitis, her knees to her chest, her forehead to her knees.

But while Cheryl has backed off, looking horrified, I'm still not about to let Kimberly off the hook.

"But Doug did miss the coke," I say. "He missed it, and he came looking for it, didn't he?"

Kimberly nods again.

"That was why Lindsay needed to get into the caf. To give him his coke back. Because she hid it in here, didn't she? Because she didn't think it would be safe to leave in her room, where Ann might find it." Nod. "So she got the key from Manuel, let herself in here, smuggled Doug into the building somehow, and . . . Then what? If she gave it back . . . why'd he kill her?"

"How should I know?" Kimberly lifts her head slowly, as if it were very heavy. "All I know is that Lindsay ended up getting what she deserved after all."

"You . . ." Cheryl is glaring down at the other girl, her chest rising and falling rapidly with emotion, her eyes bright with unshed tears. "You . . . you . . . *bitch*!"

Which is when Cheryl draws her arm back to slap Kimberly, who cowers—

But Cheryl's hand is seized before she can bring it down across Kimberly's face.

"That," Detective Canavan, who has come up behind us, says calmly, "is enough of that, *ladies*."

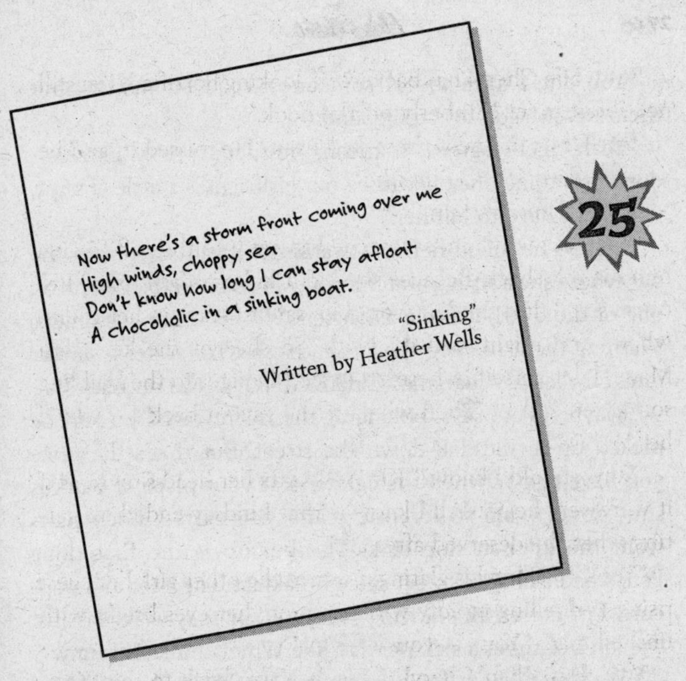

25
Now there's a storm front coming over me
High winds, choppy sea
Don't know how long I can stay afloat
A chocoholic in a sinking boat.
"Sinking"
Written by Heather Wells

"So there you go," I say to Pete, as we sit at the sticky table in the back of the Stoned Crow after work. "There's your motive, plain as day."

A glance at the security guard's face reveals that he's at least as confused as Magda. "*What?*" they both say at the same time.

"That's why he killed her," I explain patiently. "Lindsay was going around, shooting her mouth off to her friends about his drug dealing. He had to silence her, or risk getting caught eventually."

"You don't have to cut someone's head off just to shut them up," Magda says indignantly.

"Yeah," Pete agrees. "I mean, murder's pretty extreme, don't you think? Just because your girlfriend's a little gossipy, you don't have to kill her."

"Maybe he killed her as a warning," Sarah says, from the bar where she's sitting watching a college basketball game on one of the overhead television sets. "To his other customers. Warning them to keep their mouths shut, or suffer a similar fate. Oh, Jesus! Charging! CHARGING! Is the ref blind?"

"Maybe," Pete says, poking at the microwaved burrito he picked up in the deli down the street. But that's the price you have to pay when the cafeteria at your place of work is shut down again so forensic teams can extract body parts from the kitchen slop sink. The burrito is the first thing Pete's had a chance to eat since breakfast. The beer and popcorn I'm currently enjoying is mine. "Or maybe it was just the kind of thing a sick pervert like Winer thinks is funny."

"We don't know for sure it was the Winer boy," Magda points out.

Both Pete and I stare at her.

"Well," she says, "you don't. Just because that girl said he was the one Lindsay was supposed to meet doesn't mean he was the one who *did* meet her. You heard what the detective said."

"He said we should mind our own business," I remind her. "He didn't say anything about whether or not he thought Doug—or his brother—did it." Even though I'd taken him aside and, after telling him what I'd observed at last night's frat party, had added, "It's obvious that Doug—and Steve, remember what Manuel said, that Steve was the name Lindsay mentioned—killed her for shooting off her mouth about their drug dealing, then left her head as a warning for the rest of their clients. You have to arrest them. You HAVE to!"

Detective Canavan, however, hadn't appreciated being told that he "had" to do anything. He'd just frowned down at me and said, "I should have known that was you at that party last night. Can't you go *anywhere* without causing bedlam?"

At which I took umbrage. Because I've been lots of places where fights didn't break out. Lots of them. Look at me here at the bar across from Fischer Hall.

And okay, it's only, like, four minutes after five, so hardly anyone else has gotten off work yet and the place is pretty much empty except for us.

But no bedlam has broken out. Yet.

"So when are they going to do it?" Magda wants to know. "Arrest those boys?"

"*If* they're going to arrest them," Pete corrects her.

"But they have to," Magda says, blinking rapidly over her alcoholic beverage of choice—a White Russian. Pete and I can't even look at it without gagging a little. "I mean, they took that Kimberly away with them to interview her after she said all those things in front of us . . . even if she lied to them later, they heard what she told us in the cafeteria."

"But is that evidence?" Pete asks. "Isn't that—what do they call it on *Law and Order*? Hearsay?"

"Are you telling me they didn't get one fingerprint from that kitchen?" Magda demands. "Not one stray hair they can get DNA from, to find out who did it?"

"Who knows what they found?" I say, mournfully shoving a handful of stale barroom popcorn in my mouth. Why is stale barroom popcorn so delicious, anyway? Especially with a cold beer. "We'll probably be the last to find out."

"At least Manuel's going to be all right," Pete says. "Julio says he's getting better every day. Although they still have policemen posted outside his hospital room."

"What's he going to do when they discharge him?" Magda wants to know. "They aren't going to post a policeman by his house, are they?"

"They'll *have* to have arrested Doug by then," Sarah says, from the bar. "I mean, Doug has to be the one who strangled her. The only question is, did he do it accidentally? Like did he asphyxiate her during sexual play, then panic? From what you told me, he doesn't seem like the type who has much control over his temper—"

"Yeah. Did I mention he totally head-butted me in the gut?" I ask.

"But putting her limbs down a disposal to get rid of the evidence?" Sarah shakes her head. "Doug doesn't have the brains for something like that—even if it did turn out not to work thanks to the disposal breaking. Oh, my God, foul! FOUL!"

I look up from the empty popcorn basket and notice that Pete and Magda aren't the only ones staring at Sarah in disbelief. The bartender, Belinda, a punk rock waif with a shaved head and overalls, is blinking at her with astonishment as well.

Sarah notices, looks around, and says defensively, "Excuse me, a person can have multiple interests, you know. I mean, I can be interested in psychology and sports, too. It's called being well-rounded, people."

"More popcorn?" Belinda asks her, looking pretty scared for someone with so many nose rings.

"Uh, no," Sarah says. "That stuff is stale."

"Um," I say, "I'll take some. Thanks."

"On that note," Pete says, rising from his chair, "I have to get home before my kids tear the place apart. Magda, you want a ride to the subway?"

"Oh, yes," Magda says, getting up as well.

"Wait," I protest. "I just got more popcorn!"

"Sorry, honey," Magda says, struggling into her faux-rabbit fur coat. "But it's about twelve degrees out there. I'm not walking to the subway. See you on Monday."

"See you guys," I say mournfully, watching them leave. I'd leave, too, but I still have half a beer left. You can't just leave a beer like that. It's un-American.

Except a minute later I'm regretting not having made my escape when I had the chance, since the door opens, and who should walk in but . . .

Jordan.

"Oh, there you are," he says, spotting me at once. Which isn't hard, since I'm the only one in the bar, with the exception of Sarah and a couple of Math Department types, who are playing pool. Jordan slides into the chair Pete just vacated, and explains, as he peels off his jacket, "Cooper told me you sometimes come here after work."

I glare at him over my beer. I don't know why. I guess it's just that he mentioned Cooper's name. Cooper's not high on my list of favorite people right now.

Actually, neither is his brother.

"Nice place," Jordan says, looking around. It's clear he's being sarcastic. Jordan's idea of a nice place is the bar at the Four Seasons. Which isn't exactly in my price range. Anymore.

"Well, you know me," I say, more lightly than I feel. "Only the best."

"Yeah." Jordan stops looking around and looks at me instead. This is somehow worse. I know I'm not exactly ravishing at the moment. Last night's wild ride didn't do much for the bags under my eyes, and I didn't actually wash my hair this morning. Instead, I washed it the night before, to get the smell of Tau Phi House cigarette smoke out of it. Sleeping on my hair while wet has a way of making it look . . . well, sort of matted the next day. Add that to the fact that I'm wearing my second-best pair of jeans—I still haven't managed to replace the ones with the blood-stained knees—which aren't exactly loose, to the point where I have to constantly worry about camel toe, and you have the picture.

But Jordan's no prize today, either. He's got dark circles where I've got bags, and his case of hat head is even worse than mine. His blond hair is sticking up in tufts all over his head.

"You want a beer?" I ask him, since Belinda is looking over at us questioningly.

"Oh, God, no," Jordan says, and shudders. "I'm never drinking again after last night. I seriously think someone slipped something in my drink. I only had that one—"

"You told me you had ten glasses of wine before you even got downtown," I remind him.

"Yeah," Jordan says, with a *So what?* look on his face. "That's what I have most nights. I've never been as blotto as I was last night."

"Why would someone roofie you?" I ask. "It's not exactly like you're unwilling to have sex with strangers."

He glares at me. "Hey, now," he says. "That's not fair. And I don't know why someone would do it. Maybe it was, like, an ugly girl, or someone I wouldn't ordinarily go with."

"I didn't see any ugly girls at that party." Then I brighten. "Maybe it was one of the guys! Frats are known hotbeds of latent homosexuality."

Jordan makes a face. "Please, Heather . . . let's just drop it, okay? Suffice it to say, I'm never drinking again."

"Well, that will make the champagne toasts tomorrow a bit of a letdown," I say.

Jordan fingers the initials someone has carved into the tabletop, not meeting my gaze. "Look, Heather," he says. "About last night—"

"I don't know where your skis went, Jordan," I say. "I called Waverly Hall and the guard said no one left any skis there, so obviously someone stole them. I'm really sorry, but you know—"

He flinches. I think it's because I've spoken so loudly.

"I don't care about the stupid skis," he says. "I'm talking about us."

I blink at him. Then I remember that Cooper must have driven him home this morning.

Oh, no.

"Jordan," I say quickly. "I am *not* still in love with you. I don't care what Cooper told you, okay? I mean, sure, I used to be in love with you. But that was a long time ago. I've moved on—"

He blinks at me. "Cooper? What are you talking about?"

"Didn't he give you a ride home this morning?"

"Yeah. But we didn't talk about you. We talked about Mom and Dad. It was nice. I haven't talked to Cooper—just one-on-one—like that in a long time. I think we worked out some things. Our differences, I mean. We both agreed that we're nothing alike—but that that's all right. Whatever his relationship with Mom and Dad . . . well, it's no reason he and I can't get along."

I stare at him. I can't quite believe what I'm hearing.

Cooper can't stand Jordan. I mean, to the point of refusing to take his calls or open the door when he comes over.

"Wow," I say. "That's . . . that's . . . well, progress. Good for you."

"Yeah," Jordan says. He continues to finger the graffiti. "I think I talked him into coming to the wedding tomorrow. I mean, he didn't agree to be my best man, like I asked, but he said he'd come."

I'm genuinely shocked. Cooper can't stand his family, and now he's planning on attending a big blowout wedding at St. Patrick's Cathedral, with a reception at the Plaza, in their company? Those are so not his type of events. . . .

"Well," I say. Because I really don't know what else to say. "That's . . . that's amazing, Jordan. Really. I'm so happy for you."

"It really means a lot to me," Jordan says. "The only thing better would have been if . . . well, if you would have agreed to come tomorrow, Heather."

I clutch my beer. "Oh, Jordan," I say. "That's so sweet. But—"

"That's why it's so hard for me to say what I'm about to say," Jordan goes on, as if I hadn't spoken. "And that's this. Heather." He reaches across the table to grip the hand that isn't curled around my pint glass, then looks earnestly into my eyes. "It really hurts me to say this, but . . . I can't let you come to my wedding tomorrow."

I blink at him. "Jordan," I say. "I—"

"Please let me finish," Jordan says, squeezing my hand. "It isn't that I don't want you there, Heather. More than anyone in the world, I want you there. You're the person I've been closest to for the longest in my life. If there's anyone I want to be by my side for the most important event of my life, it's you."

"Um, Jordan," I say. "I'm flattered. I really am. But shouldn't the person you most want at your side for this be—"

"It's Tania," Jordan interrupts.

"Right," I say. "That's what I mean. Shouldn't Tania be the person you most want at your side? Considering she's the one you're—"

"No, I mean Tania is the one who doesn't want you there," Jordan says. "Not after last night. See, she wasn't too happy when she found out I spent the night with you—"

"Oh, my God, Jordan!" I burst out, yanking my hand away from him, and glancing quickly toward Sarah and Belinda to make sure they haven't overheard. "You didn't spend the night with me! You spent it on your brother's living room couch!"

"I know that," Jordan says, having the dignity to flush. "But Tania doesn't believe it. See, Tania thinks you're still in love with me, and—"

"Oh, my God!" I cry again. "What is it with everybody thinking I'm still in love with you? I'm so not! I fell out of love with you way before I ever walked in and saw Tania with your—"

"Hey, now," Jordan says, ducking his head as the two math geeks look over at us interestedly. "No need for that kind of language."

"Seriously, though, Jordan," I say. "I fell out of love with you that time we were touring in Japan, remember, and you kept going to visit all those temples. Only they weren't really temples, were they?"

Jordan's flush deepens. "No. I didn't know you knew. You never said anything."

I shrug. "What was there to say? Besides, I thought maybe you'd work it out of your system. But you didn't."

"I just never knew any woman could do that with a ping-pong ball," Jordan says, in a dreamy voice.

"Yes," I say briskly. "Well, fortunately for you, Tania is a girl of many talents."

His fiancée's name snaps him out of his reverie, as I'd known it would.

"So you're really all right with it?" he asks me, with a worried expression. "Not coming to the wedding?"

"Jordan, I never had any intention of coming your wedding tomorrow. Remember? I *told* you that. Like five times."

He reaches out to grasp my hand again. "Heather," he says, gazing into my bloodshot eyes with his own. "I can't tell you what this means to me. It proves that, no matter what you say, you do care about me . . . at least a little. And I hope you'll believe me when I say I'm sorry things turned out this way. But it's time for me to start my new life, with my new partner. If it's any comfort to you at all, I hope that someday you, too, will find someone to share your life with. . . ."

"Jordan," I say, leaning forward to pat his hand. "I *have* found that someone. Her name is Lucy."

Jordan makes a face and lets go of my hand. "I mean a man, Heather, not a dog. Why do you always have to make a joke out of everything?"

"I don't know," I say, with a sigh. "That's just the kind of girl I am, I guess. You're lucky you escaped when you did."

Jordan looks at me sadly, shaking his head. "You'll never go back to the way you used to be when we first met, will you? You were so sweet back then. Never cynical."

"That's because back then my boyfriend didn't feel like he was missing out on the fact that I never did vaginal tricks with a ping-pong ball," I tell him.

"That's it," Jordan says, putting his jacket back on and standing up. "I'm leaving. I'll see you . . . well. Later."

"After you get back from the honeymoon," I say. "Where are you going, anyway?"

Jordan can't seem to make eye contact. "Japan. Tania's touring."

"Well," I say. "*Ja mata.*"

Scowling, Jordan storms from the bar. Only when he's gone does Sarah turn her attention from the game (there's a commercial), and says "Jesus Christ. What did you say to him, anyway?"

I shrug. "Goodbye."

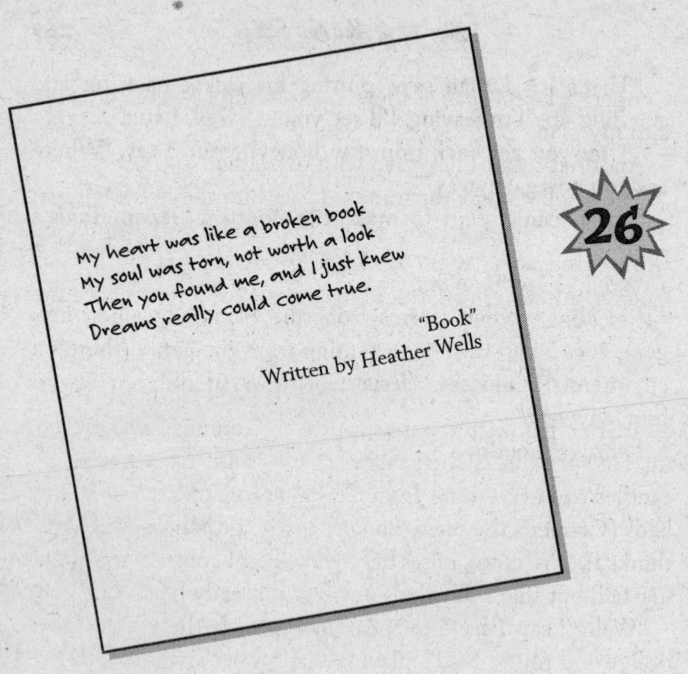

26
My heart was like a broken book
My soul was torn, not worth a look
Then you found me, and I just knew
Dreams really could come true.
"Book"
Written by Heather Wells

After the day I've had, I'm looking forward to an evening alone. I plan on taking out the old guitar and giving it a thorough workout, then lighting a fire and curling up on the couch to watch all the TV shows I've DVR'd through the week. I think there's some leftover Indian takeout in the fridge. I'm going to chow down on samosas and nan and *America's Next Top Model* reruns. Could there be a better plan for a Friday night? Especially a Friday night coming after a week of dealing with bodyless corpses and frat boys.

Except that when I walk through the front door of

Cooper's place, I realize there's something I forgot to factor into my plan.

And that's that I now live with my father.

The smell hits me the minute I step into the foyer. It's unmistakable. Someone is cooking the steaks I snuck out of work to buy at Jefferson Market. The steaks I got for me and Cooper, but never got around to cooking for him, on account of . . . well, everything that was going on.

Wrenching off my coat, I stalk into the kitchen. Dad is there in an apron in front of the stove, cooking my steaks in a cast-iron pan with the mushrooms and onions I also picked up. He's set the kitchen table for two, with napkins and lit candles and everything. Lucy, curled in one of her many dog beds (Cooper's the one who keeps buying them, not me. He thinks they're cute), raises her head when I come in and wags her tail, but that's all. She's obviously already been out.

"Well," I say. I have to speak loudly to be heard over the Bollywood music Dad's playing on Cooper's stereo system. "Expecting company?"

Dad jumps and turns around. He's drinking one of my Diet Cokes. Some of it slops out of the can because he turns so abruptly.

"Heather!" he cries. "There you are! I didn't hear you come in."

I'm glaring at the steaks. I can't help it. Those were in *my* fridge in my apartment upstairs. Which it's true I never lock, but that doesn't mean I welcome strange men prowling around up there, poking through my stuff.

Because Dad *is* a strange man. To me. I mean, relatively speaking.

"I hope you don't mind," Dad says, apparently noticing the direction of my gaze. "I figured somebody better fry these up, or they were going to spoil. I was in your apartment, looking for your mother's number."

"In the *refrigerator*?" I ask.

"I was just wondering what you eat," he says affably. "I feel like I barely know you. I'm sorry, were you keeping these steaks for some special occasion? Because if so, you really ought to have stuck them in the freezer. They'll last longer that way."

The smell of sizzling meat and onions is delicious, it's making me a little dizzy.

"I was kind of saving them . . . but it doesn't matter," I say, a little mournfully. It doesn't matter because, at least according to Gavin, Cooper thinks I'm still head over heels for his brother, anyway. Making him dinner isn't going to change that. I'm probably going to have to resort to shooting ping-pong balls from my ying yang onstage before anyone ever believes I'm over Jordan. Including Jordan.

"Well, that's good," Dad says. "Because they're almost done. You like your steak a little rare, right?"

I raise my eyebrows, genuinely surprised. "Wait . . . you cooked them for *me*?"

"Who else?" Dad looks a little surprised.

"Well." I chew my lower lip. "A lady friend, maybe?"

"Heather, I've only been out of prison a week," Dad says. "That's hardly enough time to make a lady friend."

"Well, then, Cooper," I say.

"Cooper is busy with his latest case," Dad says. "So I'm afraid it's just you and me. I wasn't sure when you'd be home, of course, but I took a chance. Have a seat. There's a bottle of wine there. I hope you don't mind drinking alone. I'm sticking with soda these days."

Shocked, I pull out a chair and sink down into it, as much

because I'm not sure I can stand up anymore as because he asked me to.

"Dad," I say, looking at the carefully set table, "you don't have to cook dinner for me. Or breakfast, either, for that matter."

"It's the least I can do," Dad says. He takes the steaks out of the pan and sets them on two plates, along with the mushrooms and onions. "I'll just let these sit a minute," he explains. "They're better that way. Juicier. So." He pulls out the chair across from mine and sits down in it. "How was your day?"

I stare at him for a minute. I'm tempted actually to tell him, *Well, Dad, not so good, actually. We found out what they did with the rest of Lindsay Combs, and it wasn't pretty. Then I manhandled a student and when the higher-ups find out about it, I'll probably be fired.*

But instead I say, "It was fine, I guess. How was your day?" Because I really don't want to get into it.

"Fine, fine," Dad says. "Cooper had me follow a man from his office to his lunch appointment, then back to his office."

My eyebrows go up. Way up. I can't believe I'm finally learning something about what Cooper does all day.

"Really? Who hired him to follow the guy? What's the guy supposed to have done?"

"Oh, I can't tell you any of that," Dad says pleasantly. "Here." Dad pours me a glass of red wine and hands it to me.

"But I work for the company," I say. "Client-detective privilege should extend to me."

"Oh, I don't think so," Dad says, shaking his head. "Cooper was quite explicit about me not telling you anything."

"But that's not fair!" I cry.

"He said you'd say that. I'm sorry, honey. But he seems really to prefer that you don't know. I think it's due to your tendency to get yourself involved in situations you really ought to stay out of. Like this murder at your dorm. I think the steaks are ready now."

Dad pops up to get them. I sip my wine, scowling into the candle flames.

"Residence hall," I say, as he plops a plate filled with perfectly cooked steak down in front of me.

"I beg your pardon?"

"It's a residence hall," I say. "Not a dorm. Saying *dorm* does not foster a warm sense of community, which is what we're aiming for. Well, aside from all the senseless killing." I cut off a piece of meat and chew. Heaven. Marinated to perfection.

"I see," Dad says. "That's very like how we called Eglin a camp and not what it was—prison."

"Right," I say, taking a sip of wine. "Made you forget about the shivs, and concentrate on all the lavalieres."

"Oh, no one had a shiv," Dad says, with a chuckle. "How do you like your steak?"

"It's great," I say, swallowing another bite. "Okay, so as long as we're exchanging pleasantries about our places of work—or incarceration—what's the deal? Why are you here, Dad? It's not really because you have nowhere else to go, because I know you've got plenty of rich friends you could be shacking up with instead of me. And this getting-to-know-your-daughter-better thing—sorry, I'm not buying it. So level with me. What's the scam? And please keep in mind that I'm pretty sure I outweigh you."

Dad puts down his fork and lets out a sigh. Then he takes a sip of Diet Coke and says, "You're so like your mother, it's uncanny."

I feel the usual bubble of animosity that pops up every time he says this. But this time, I tamp it down.

"Yeah, I think we've established that you believe that," I say. "So let's move on. Why were you looking for Mom's number in my apartment today?"

"Because," Dad says, "for some years now, I've been working a sort of . . . program. It has certain steps that its practitioners must follow if, by the end, they hope to achieve spiritual enlightenment. And one of the steps is that they must make amends with those they have harmed. That is why I wanted to phone your mother. To try to make amends."

"Dad," I say. "Mom *left* you. Don't you think *she*'s the one who needs to be making amends? With both of us?"

Dad shakes his head. "I promised your mother when I married her that I would love and support her. That didn't just mean emotionally. I promised to support her financially, as well, especially while she stayed home and raised you. When I went to prison, I was forced to renege on my part of that bargain. It's my fault, really, that your mother had to take you out on the road in order to support you both."

"Right," I say sarcastically. "She couldn't just get a job as a receptionist in a doctor's office somewhere. She had to parade her freakishly musical kid around in front of the masses at various malls."

Dad makes a *tsk-tsking* sound.

"Now, Heather," he says. "Don't try to rewrite history. You loved performing. We couldn't keep you *off* the stage. Believe me, I tried. Your mother only did what she felt she had to . . . and you certainly never complained."

I lay down my fork. "Dad. I was eleven. Do you really think that was the kind of decision that should have been left to me?"

Dad looks down at his food. "Well, that's an issue you're

going to have to work out with your mother. I'm afraid by that time, I was no longer in a position to be actively involved in your parenting."

"True," I say. And fat chance of me ever having an opportunity to "work out" my issues with Mom. That's something that's a little hard to do over the phone. Though Dad seemed perfectly willing to try. "So. Did you find the number?"

"Yes," Dad says. "It was in your address book. Some of the addresses in there are quite old, you know. You should think about getting a new book. If you want, I could do that for you tomorrow."

I ignore this offer.

"Did you call her?"

"I did," Dad says.

"And did you make amends?"

"I tried to," Dad says. "But your mother can, as you know, be very difficult. She refused to admit that I had hurt her in any way. In fact, she reminded me—as you did, just now—that it was she who left *me*, and that if anyone should be making amends, it's her. But that she doesn't care to, because, according to her, I deserve everything I got."

I nod. "Yeah, that sounds like Mom, all right. It really sucks when you say I'm like her, by the way. If you tried to make amends with me, I'd be much more receptive."

"Well," Dad says. "That's good, because you're next on my list."

I shrug. "Amends accepted."

"I haven't even made them yet."

"Yeah, you have," I say. "This dinner is enough. It's totally delicious."

"This dinner is hardly enough," Dad says. "You were basically deprived of a father figure during your formative teen years. That's the kind of hurt that can't be cured with a single steak dinner."

"Well," I say, "now that you're living here, maybe you can cure it with multiple steak dinners. Like every Friday night, or something. Although you might want to vary the menu a little. I like pork chops, too. Oh, and fried chicken."

"Heather," Dad says, sounding sad. "Food can't serve as a balm for all the harm I've caused you. I understand that, of all the people I hurt when I broke the law, you are the one who suffered the most. Leaving you alone with your mother, who then put you on that mall tour. Even if you did enjoy it, that's no way for anyone to spend her childhood, living in a trailer and traveling from mall to mall, being exploited by the one person who should have been looking out for your best interests."

"It *was* more fun than going to school," I point out. "And, like you said—it was hard to get me off the stage back then."

"But you were deprived of the normal joys of childhood. And I can't help but feel that that deprivation is partially responsible for the way you are today."

I stare at him. "What's wrong with the way I am today?" I ask.

"Well, for one thing, you're nearly thirty and you don't have a husband or children. You don't seem to realize that family is the most important thing in the world—not that guitar I hear you plinking late into the night, and not your job. *Family*, Heather. Take it from someone whose lost his—family is what matters."

I lay my fork down again and say gently, "There are lots of different types of families nowadays, Dad. They don't all consist of a husband and wife and kids. Some of them consist of a girl, her dog, a PI, her dad, her best friend, and the various people she works with. Not to mention the drug dealer down the street. My feeling about it is, if you care about someone, doesn't that person automatically become your family?"

"But don't you worry," Dad says, after he spends a moment digesting this information, "that if you don't have children, there'll be no one to care for you in your old age?"

"No," I say. "Because I could have children, and they could turn out to hate me. The way I see it, I have friends who care about me now, so I'll probably have friends who'll care about me when I'm old, too. We'll take care of each other. And in the meantime, I'm putting the max into my 401(K), and setting aside as much as I can into a SEP IRA as well."

Dad gazes at me over his steak. I'm disturbed to note that there are tears in his eyes.

"That's very profound, Heather," he says. "Especially since I sense that, in many ways, these so-called family members of yours have been kinder to you than your actual blood relations."

"Well," I admit, "at least none of them has stolen all my money and fled the country. Yet."

Dad raises his Diet Coke can. "I'll drink to that," he says. I clink his can with my wine glass. "So you really don't mind," he says, when we're done clinking, "if I stick around and try to make amends—even though you say I don't have to?"

"I don't care," I say. "Just so long as you aren't expecting me to take care of you in your old age. Because I've only been contributing to my 401(K) for a couple of months. I don't have enough money in it to support myself, let alone an aged parent."

"I'll tell you what," Dad says. "Why don't we agree to support each other emotionally only?"

"Sounds good to me," I say, spearing the last of my steak.

"Looks like you're ready for salad," Dad says, getting up and going to the fridge, from which he takes the salad bowl into which Jordan did not, thankfully, barf. In it is what appear to be various types of lettuce, some cherry tomatoes, and—much to my delight—croutons.

"I'll toss," Dad says, proceeding to do so. "I hope you like blue cheese dressing." Without waiting for an answer (because, really, why would he need one? Who doesn't like blue cheese dressing?), he goes on, "Now. About you and Cooper."

I nearly choke on the sip of wine I've taken.

"This is just my opinion," Dad says, "and I've been out of the dating scene for a long time, I'll admit. But if you really want things to progress to a romantic level with him, I'd suggest not spending quite so much time with his younger brother. I realize you and Jordan were together for a terribly long time, and that it's hard to let go. But I sense a certain amount of friction from Cooper concerning his family, and if I were you, I'd limit my interactions with them. Especially Jordan."

I stab at some of the lettuce he's spooned onto my plate.

"Gee, Dad," I say, "thanks for the tip." Because what else can I say? I'm not going to get into my love life—or lack thereof—with my *dad*.

But he apparently doesn't realize this, since he goes on.

"I think that once Jordan is married, and Cooper realizes you're finally over him, you'll have a much better chance with him." Dad sits back down and starts on his own salad. "Though it wouldn't hurt if you'd make a little more effort to be pleasant in the mornings."

I eat more salad. "Good to know," I say. "I'll take it under advisement."

"Although you did seem to make quite a positive impression last night," Dad comments.

I stop chewing. "Last night? You mean when Cooper caught me hauling his dead-drunk brother in the door?"

"No," Dad says amiably. "I meant the fact that you were wearing a skirt. You should do that more often. Young men appreciate a girl in a skirt. I saw Cooper staring."

I don't bother telling my dad that the reason Cooper was staring wasn't because I was in a skirt and he appreciated it, but because I was in *such a short skirt* that I looked like a hooker. Probably Cooper was trying not to laugh.

Still, these aren't the kinds of things you can say to your father.

"I never even asked you," Dad says, a little while later, over dessert (Dove Bars, of course). "Did you have plans for tonight? Am I keeping you from something?"

"Just *America's Next Top Model,*" I say.

"What's that?" Dad asks innocently.

"Oh, Dad," I say. And show him. I mean, if he really wants to make amends, watching *ANTM* with me is an excellent way to start.

27

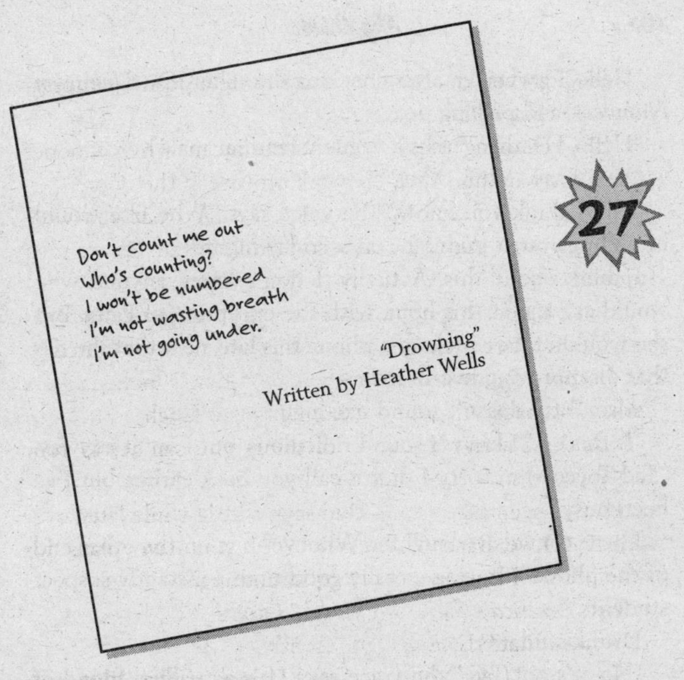

Don't count me out
Who's counting?
I won't be numbered
I'm not wasting breath
I'm not going under.
"Drowning"
Written by Heather Wells

Dad is asleep after our fourth episode of *ANTM* in a row. I guess I can't really blame him. While women find watching pretty girls play complicated mind games with one another endlessly fascinating—like today in the caf, with Cheryl and Kimberly—your average heterosexual man can only take so many hours of it before he—like Dad, and Patty's husband, Frank—passes out from sheer boredom.

He's sleeping hard enough that when the phone rings, it doesn't even wake him. There might be something to this yoga stuff after all, if it makes you sleep so hard even a ringing phone can't wake you.

"Hello?" I whisper, after checking the caller ID—*Unknown Number*—and picking up.

"Hello, Heather?" asks a vaguely familiar male voice.

"Yes," I say. "Who's this?"

"Oh, I think you know," the voice says. "Who else would be calling you at midnight on a Friday night?"

I think about this. Actually, I don't know anyone who would call me at this hour, with the exception of Patty. But she wouldn't dare pick up a phone this late, now that she has that disapproving live-in nanny.

Also, Patty doesn't sound like a guy.

"Is this . . ." I know I sound ridiculous, but I say it anyway. "Tad Tocco? I'm sorry I didn't call you back earlier, but I've been busy."

I hear convulsive laughter. Whoever it is on the other end of the phone is having a really good time. I instantly suspect students.

Drunk students.

"No, it's not Tad," the voice says. "It's actually a friend of yours from last night. Don't tell me you don't remember."

And suddenly the memory of those ice-blue eyes on mine comes flooding back.

And all the blood seems to leave my extremities. I'm sitting there, frozen to the spot, holding the phone with my dad asleep on one side of me, and Lucy asleep on the other.

"Hello, Steve," I manage to say, through lips that have gone cold. "How did you get my number?"

"How'd I figure out your last name and look it up, you mean?" Steve asks, with a laugh. "A little bird told me. Do you want to speak to him? He's right here."

The next thing I know, a voice that is unmistakably Gavin McGoren's is swearing—steadily, and with much imagination—

into the phone. I'd recognize those "motherfuckin's" anywhere. They are the same ones Gavin regularly uttered back when I used to catch him elevator-surfing.

Then I hear a smacking sound—like skin on skin—and a second later, Steve is saying, "Tell her, goddamn you. Tell her what we told you to say."

"FUCK . . . YOU," is Gavin's response. This is followed by a scuffling sound, and more smacking. When I hear Steve's voice again, it's out of breath.

"Well, I think you get the idea, anyway," he says. "We're having another party. And this time, you're actually invited. And to make sure you show, we have your friend Gavin here. Unless you do exactly what I tell you, he's going to suffer some bodily injury. And you wouldn't want that, now, would you?"

I'm so horrified I can barely breathe. I say, "No."

"I didn't think so. So here's the dealio. You come here. Alone. If you call the cops, he will get hurt. If you don't show, he—"

"HEATHER, DON'T—" I hear Gavin start to bellow, but his voice is quickly smothered.

"—could get very, very hurt," Steve finishes. "Got it?"

"I got it," I say. "I'll be there. But where's here? The Tau Phi House?"

"Please," Steve says, sounding bored. "We're *here*, Heather. I think you know where."

"Fischer Hall," I say, my gaze going toward my living room windows, which look out at the back of the twenty-story building that is my place of work. It's still early, by New York College residence hall standards, which means that most of the lights in the windows are blazing as the building's occupants prepare to go out, apparently completely unaware that down on the first floor, in the closed and locked cafeteria, something unspeakable is about to take place.

Which is when I stop feeling cold, and start feeling angry. How dare they? Seriously. How dare they think they can get away with this *again*? Do they really believe I'm going to sit idly back and *let* them turn Fischer Hall into Death Dorm?

And okay, maybe it already *is* Death Dorm. But I'm not going to let it stay that way.

"Heather?" Steve's voice is warm in my ear. It's amazing how charming psychopathic killers can be, when they put their minds to it. "Are you still there?"

"Oh, I'm here," I tell him. "And I'll be right over."

"Good," Steve says, sounding pleased. "We'll be looking forward to seeing you. Alone, like I said."

"Don't worry," I assure him. "I'll be alone." Like I need any help kicking his skinny ass. Steve Winer is making an extremely bad decision, challenging me to a confrontation on my own turf. He might have been able to off a girl as tiny as Lindsay without getting caught, but if he thinks a girl like me is going to go down without a fight—a fight loud enough to bring the entire building banging on the cafeteria doors—he's got another think coming.

But then again, he, like his brother, doesn't strike me as the sharpest knife in the drawer.

"Good," Steve says. "And remember. No cops. Or your boyfriend's a dead man."

I hear a thump, and then a scream. The scream comes from Gavin.

And I know that, stupid though he might be, Steve Winer isn't someone to underestimate.

I slam down the receiver and spin around to see my dad sitting up, blinking groggily.

"Heather?" he says. "What's the matter?"

"Something's going down at the dorm," I say, grabbing a piece of paper and writing a number on it. "I mean, residence hall. Something bad. I need you to call this person and tell him he needs to get over there as fast as possible. Tell him I'll meet him in the caf. Tell him to bring backup."

Dad squints down at the number. "Where are you going?"

"I'm going to Fischer Hall," I say, grabbing my coat. "I'll be back as soon as I can."

Dad looks confused. "I don't like this, Heather," he says. "They don't pay you enough for you to be hurrying over there in the dead of night like this."

"Tell me about it," I say, and I'm out the door.

The walk to Fischer Hall has never seemed so long. Even though I'm half running, it seems to take forever to get there. Partly because of the slick sidewalks I have to navigate, but also, I'm convinced, because of how hard my heart is hammering inside my chest. If they did anything to hurt Gavin . . . if they so much as bruised him—

I'm so intent on getting where I'm going that I don't even see Reggie until I crash into him.

"Whoa, little lady," he cries, as we collide. "Where would you be off to in such a hurry so late at night?"

"Geez, Reggie," I say, struggling to catch my breath. "Don't you ever go home?"

"Fridays are my best nights," Reggie says. "Heather, what's the matter? You're white as—well, a white girl."

"It's those guys," I pant. "The ones I told you about. They have one of my residents. In the caf. They're going to hurt him if I don't get there, fast—"

"Whoa, whoa, whoa." Reggie has hold of both my arms

and doesn't seem eager to let go. "Are you serious? Heather, don't you think you should call the police?"

"I did!" I have to windmill both my arms before I manage to break free of his grip. "My dad's calling them. But someone has to get in there in the meantime—"

"Why does that someone have to be you?" Reggie wants to know.

But it's too late. I'm already off and running again, my Timberlands pounding on the newly shoveled sidewalk, my heart pounding in my throat.

When I throw open the door to Fischer Hall, the mystery of how Doug and his fellow frat brothers—not to mention his real brother—got into the building to kill Lindsay without actually being signed in is cleared up the minute I walk through the door and see the security guard.

"You!" I cry. It's the crusty old guard from the security desk in Waverly Hall.

"ID," he says. *He doesn't even recognize me*.

"You were at Waverly Hall last night," I pant, pointing at him accusingly.

"Yeah," Crusty Old Guard says, with a shrug. "That's my regular spot. I fill in other places when there's an opening. Like here, tonight. I need to see your ID before I can let you in."

I'm flipping open my wallet to show him my staff identification. "I'm the assistant director of this building," I say to him. "I know you let a bunch of Tau Phis in here tonight without making them sign in. Just like you did Monday night, when they killed someone."

Crusty Old Guard—his name tag says Curtiss—grunts. "I don't know what you're talking about," he says grumpily.

"Yeah," I say. "Well, you'll find out in a minute, believe me.

In the meantime, I want you to phone up to the building director and tell him to head to the caf. And when the cops show up, send them there, too."

"Cops?" Crusty Curtiss looks startled. "What—"

But I'm already running past him.

I don't head for the main doors to the caf, though. I'm not about to go walking blindly into their trap—lame as it might be. Instead, I dash down the hall, past my office, then the student government's office—closed and locked, as always—and finally past the dining manager's office, to the back entrance to the kitchen. The door, as I'd known it would be, is locked.

But I have my master key. I slip it from my pocket and—cradling a can of pepper spray in my free hand—unlock the door as quietly as I can and let myself into the kitchen.

It's dark. As I'd expected, they're in the dining hall itself. They don't have anyone stationed in the kitchen. They haven't even bothered turning the lights on in here. Amateurs.

I creep along the galley, straining my ears. I can hear the murmur of male voices out in the dining area. There's a light on there, as well . . . but not the lights in the chandeliers. They haven't turned on the overheads. Instead, they've got some kind of flickering lamp on . . . flashlights?

Or flames?

If they're burning candles in there, they are in so much trouble. Burning candles isn't allowed in any of the residence halls.

I'm not really sure what my plan is. I figure I'll creep as close as I can behind the service counters, then peer out over them to see what the boys are up to. Then I'll creep back and report what I've seen to Detective Canavan when he arrives with backup. That way they'll have a good idea how many people they're dealing with.

I crawl along behind the steam tables, thinking that I'm really going to have to have words with Gerald, because it is just disgusting back there. Seriously, the knees of my jeans are getting filthy, and my hand lands on something squishy that I sincerely hope is a furry Tater Tot.

Except that Tater Tots don't make squeaking noises and jump away.

It's all I can do to restrain a scream.

Good thing I go to the trouble, though. Because when I peek up over the top of the steam tables, I see something that both horrifies and stuns me.

And that's a dozen figures in deeply hooded robes—like monks wear—only blood red, standing around one of the dining tables, which has been dragged from its normal place and put in a position of prominence in the center of the room, and covered with a blood-red cloth. On top of it are various items I'm too far away to identify. One of them, though, has to be a candelabra or something. The flickering light I'm seeing really is candlelight.

I'm not too far away to identify the figure that's sitting off to one side, his wrists tied to the arms of one of the dining chairs. It's Gavin. With duct tape over his mouth.

That is totally going to hurt when I pull it off. I mean, when it catches on his goatee.

Of course, I know right away what I'm looking at. I subscribe to all the premium cable channels, after all. It's some kind of fraternity initiation ritual, like in that movie *The Skulls*.

And I want no part of it. Gavin appears to be all right—at least, he doesn't seem to be in any imminent danger. I decide the best thing to do might be to retreat and wait for reinforcements.

Which is why I'm crawling back toward the kitchen when my coat pocket catches on a steel mixing bowl stashed way too low on a shelf. It falls to the (grimy) floor with a clatter, and the next thing I know, there are a pair of Adidas in front of me, peeping out from the hem of a red robe.

"Look what we have here," a deep male voice says. And a second later, hard hands slip beneath my armpits and pull me to my feet.

Not that I go quietly, of course. I lift my hand to direct a stream of pepper spray inside the hood, only to have the canister knocked from my hand. I am, however, wearing Timberlands, the footwear of choice for the intrepid Manhattan assistant dorm director. I level one of my steel-encased toes at the shins of my captor, causing him to swear colorfully.

Sadly, however, he doesn't release me, and the only result is that another robed guy comes up and grabs me, too. Plus a lot more mixing bowls fall down, making a horrendous racket.

But a racket is what I *want* to make now. I want everyone in the building to come running. Which is why I start screaming my head off as I'm dragged over to the ceremonial table the Tau Phis have set up.

At least until Steve Winer—or a guy I assume is him; he's the tallest and has fancy gold trim around the cowl of his robe, as befitting the president of a frat house—walks over to where Gavin is sitting and smacks him, hard, across the face with some kind of scepter he's holding.

I stop screaming. Gavin's head has snapped back at the blow. For a minute it stays that way. Then, slowly, he turns his neck, and I see the gash that's opened up on his cheek . . . and the fury blazing in his eyes.

Along with the tears.

"No more screaming," Steve says, pointing at me.

"She kicked me, too," says Adidas, beside me.

"No more kicking," Steve adds. "You kick and scream, the kid gets whacked again. Understand?"

I say, in what I consider a relatively calm voice, "The cops are going to be here any minute. I know you said not to call them, but . . . too late."

Steve pushes back his hood so he can see me better. The only light source—it really is a candelabra, sitting on the middle of the altar he's created—isn't exactly bright, but I can see his expression well enough. He doesn't, however, look alarmed.

And this alarms *me*.

Especially when, a second later, the double doors to the caf are thrown open, and Crusty Curtiss comes shuffling in, looking annoyed. He's got a half-eaten sandwich in his hand. It appears to be a Blimpie Best.

Which just happens to be one of my favorites, especially with sweet and hot pickles.

"Can't you keep her quiet?" he asks Steve, in an irritated voice. "People are wondering what the hell is going on in here."

I stare at him in horror. Seeing my expression, Steve chuckles.

"Oh, yes," he says. "There are loyal Tau Phis all over the world, Heather. Even working as security guards at major urban colleges."

"Some cops showed up," Curtiss says to me, taking another bite from his sandwich and speaking with his mouth full. "I told 'em I didn't know what they was talkin' about, that I'd been here all night and hadn't see you. So they left. They looked kinda pissed off. I don't think they'll be back."

I glare at him. "You," I say, "are so fired."

Curtiss laughs at that. He seems to genuinely be enjoying himself.

"Fired," he says, chuckling. "Right."

He turns around and shuffles back the way he'd come.

I look at Steve. "Okay," I say. "Let's get this over with. But let Gavin go. Your problem's with me, not him."

"We don't have a *problem*," Steve explains politely, "with either of you."

"Well." I look around the room at the assorted Tau Phis, wondering which one is Doug. "What am I doing here, then?"

"Oh, did I not explain over the phone?" Steve wants to know. "I guess I forgot." He steps forward and lifts a long, ornamental knife from the altar he's made. Ornamental in that the handle is gold and covered with semiprecious stones.

The blade, however, looks plenty real. And sharp.

"Pledges," Steve says, "it's time."

And from out of the shadows step another half dozen robed figures, who'd apparently been lurking in the back, over by Magda's register.

"Time for what?" I ask curiously.

"Initiation," Steve informs me.

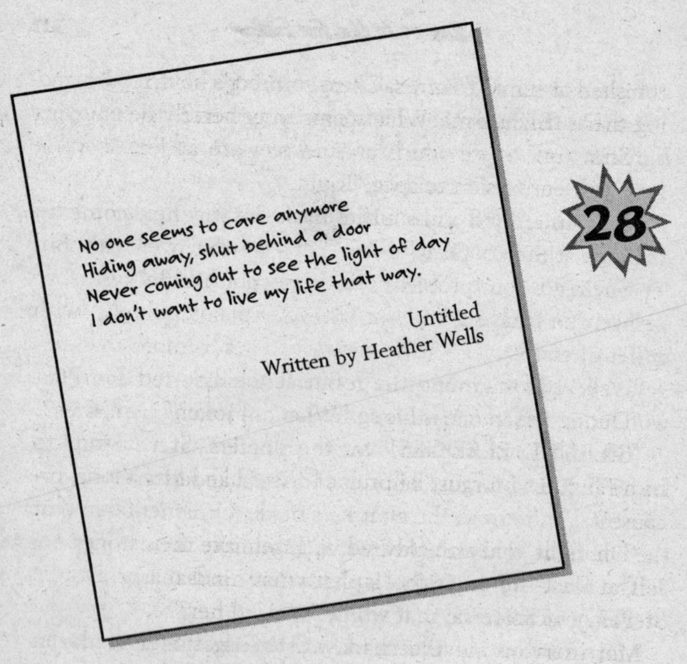

No one seems to care anymore
Hiding away, shut behind a door
Never coming out to see the light of day
I don't want to live my life that way.
Untitled
Written by Heather Wells
28

"Oh, you have got to be kidding me with this" I say disgustedly.

"Pledges," Steve says, ignoring me, "now is the time when you will be given the opportunity to prove your dedication to the house of Tau Phi Epsilon."

"Seriously," I say. "This is freaking stupid."

Steve finally looks over at me. "If you don't shut up," he says, "we'll off your boyfriend first, then you."

I blink at him. I want to be quiet. I really do. But . . .

"Gavin's not my boyfriend," I say. "And seriously. Don't you think there's been enough killing?"

"Um." One of the pledges throws back his hood. I'm astonished to see Jeff Turner, Cheryl Haebig's boyfriend, standing there. "Excuse me. What's she doing here?"

"Shut up!" Steve whirls around to glare at Jeff. "No one gave you permission to speak!"

"But, dude," Jeff says. "She's the assistant director of the building. She's gonna tell—"

"She isn't going to tell," Steve interrupts. "Because she's going to be dead."

This news appears to come as a shock to more than just Jeff. A few of the other pledges stir uneasily.

"Dude," Jeff says, "is this some kind of joke?"

"SILENCE, PLEDGES!" Steve thunders. "If you want to be a Tau Phi, you must be prepared to make sacrifices for the cause!"

"Oh, right," I say quickly, while I still have the pledges—or Jeff, at least—on my side. "Is that what Lindsay Combs was, Steve? A sacrifice? Is that why you killed her?"

More nervous movement from the pledges. Steve turns his head to glare at me.

"That bitch betrayed a member of our order," he snaps. "She had to be punished!"

"Right," I say. "By chopping off her head and grinding her body up in a garbage disposal?"

Jeff throws a shocked look in Steve's direction. "Dude. That was *you?*"

"Oh, it was Steve, all right," I say. "Just because Lindsay stole—"

"Something that didn't rightfully belong to her," Steve barks. "Something she wouldn't give back—"

"She tried," I insist. "She let your brother in here—"

"And it was gone!" Steve shouts over me. "She claims someone must have stolen it. Like we were supposed to believe that! She was a liar as well as a thief. She deserved to be put to death for her betrayal!"

"Dude." There's hurt as well as disbelief in Jeff's face. "Lindsay was my girlfriend's *best friend*."

"Then you ought to be thanking me," Steve says imperiously. "For if your girlfriend had continued to consort with the likes of that woman, she'd have eventually learned her ways and betrayed you, too, the way she betrayed one of our brothers."

It seems to take a minute for this to sink in for Jeff. But when it finally does, he doesn't hesitate a second longer.

"That's it." Jeff Turner shakes his head. "I'm out. I only joined this stupid frat 'cause my dad was in it. I did not sign on to go around killing people. You want to hit my butt with a paddle? Fine. You want to force me to chug a twenty-four-pack? No problem. But kill chicks? No way. You guys are fucking nuts—"

As he's saying this, he's reached down to pull off his robe. Steve, watching, shakes his head sadly. Then he nods at two of the robed figures in the circle around his altar, and they cross the room to deliver several blows to Jeff's midriff—while he's still floundering around in his robe, no less—until he finally falls to the ground, where they begin kicking him, heedless of his screams of pain. The other pledges, seeing this brutal treatment of one of their peers, stand frozen in place, watching.

They're not the only ones who feel frozen. I cannot believe what I am seeing. Where are the cops? They couldn't really have believed that idiot Curtiss, could they?

Knowing there's only one person who's going to be able to put a stop to this—or die trying, anyway—I say loudly to the other pledges, who are just standing there watching their friend get the snot kicked out of him, "Just so you guys know, the thing Lindsay stole? It was Doug Winer's stash of coke."

It's impossible to tell what the boys' reaction to this information is, since their faces are still hidden beneath their hoods. But I see them stir even more uneasily.

"Don't listen to her," Steve instructs them. "She's lying. It's what all of them do—try to demonize the order by spreading malicious lies about us."

"Um, we don't have to demonize you guys," I say. "You do a good enough job of that on your own. Or are you saying your brother Doug didn't strangle his girlfriend to death because she stole his nose candy?"

One of the people kicking Jeff Turner stops, and a second later Doug Winer is striding toward me, his hood down.

"You take that back!" he cries, eyes blazing. "I didn't! I didn't kill her!"

Steve reaches out to grab his little brother's arm. "Doug—"

"I didn't!" Doug cries. "You have no proof!" To Steve he says, "She has no proof!"

"Oh, we have plenty of proof," I say. I'm stalling for time. Steve has to know that. But he seems to have forgotten about Gavin and using him as a means to keep me silent. And that's all I want. "We found her body today, you know. What was left of it, anyway."

The look Steve throws me is one of total incredulity. "What the fuck are you talking about?"

"The body. Lindsay's body. See, the thing you didn't take into account was the fact that disposals don't grind up bones . . . or navel rings. We found Lindsay's this morning."

Doug makes the kind of noise girls sometimes make when I tell them they can't have a single next year. It's a sound between a sigh and a protest, and comes out like, "Nuh-uh!"

Steve's grip on the knife tightens. The blade flashes in the candlelight. "She's bluffing. And even if she's not . . . so what? There couldn't have been anything to lead them to us. Not after the way we cleaned up."

"Yeah." I'm sweating now, I'm so hot in my winter coat. Or maybe it isn't heat. Maybe it's nerves. My stomach is in knots. I probably shouldn't have had that second Dove Bar. Jeff is lying totally still now. I don't know if it's because he's unconscious, or just pretending to be so the kicking will stop. "You guys may be good at partying and putting on fancy initiation rites, but at cleaning, you really suck. They totally found hairs."

Doug throws a startled look at his brother. "Steve!"

"Shut up, Doug," Steve snaps. "She's bluffing."

"She's not!" Doug has gone white as a ghost in his robe. "She knew! She knew about the stash!"

"Leaving the head was your first mistake," I go on conversationally. "You might have gotten away with it, if you hadn't left the head on the stove like that. They'd have noticed the bones and belly button ring and all, but chances are they wouldn't have known what they were. It would have been like Lindsay had just disappeared. No one would have known you guys had been there, so no one would have wondered about how you got in. That was your second mistake, trying to off Manuel. He wouldn't have told anybody about the key if you hadn't scared him like that. And if he had, what difference would it have made? He's just a janitor. Nobody listens to the janitor." I shake my head. "But no. You had to get cocky."

"Steve," Doug whines. "You said no one would know it was us. You said no one would know! If Dad finds out what we did—"

"Shut up," Steve yells. I jump a little at the volume of his tone. So do the guys who still have hold of my arms. "For once in your life, shut the fuck up, you little shit!"

But Doug's not about to do as his brother says. "Christ, Stevie!" he cries, his voice breaking. "You told me Dad'd never know. You told me you'd take care of it!"

"I *did* take care of it, you little shit," Steve snaps. "Just like I take care of all your stupid fuckups."

"Don't worry about it, you said. Leave everything to me, you said." Doug's practically crying. "You son of a bitch! You didn't take care of *shit*! Now Lindsay's dead, we're gonna get busted—and I *still* don't know what happened to my stash."

Apparently oblivious to the fact that his sibling has just incriminated them all, Steve shouts, "Yeah, well, who's the asshole who fucking killed the bitch in the first place? Did I tell you to kill her? Did I tell you to fucking kill her? No, I did not!"

"It wasn't my fault she died!" Suddenly Doug is stumbling forward and, to my abject horror, clamps both his hands on the front of my coat. A second later, he's sobbing into my face. "I didn't mean to kill her, lady. Honest I didn't. She just made me so goddamned mad, stealing my coke like that. And then she wouldn't give it back! That whole thing, telling me someone musta stole it out of here—it was such bullshit. If she'd just given it back when I asked . . . but no. I thought Lindsay was different, you know. I thought Lindsay really liked me, not like those other girls, who only hang out with me because of my last name. I didn't mean to choke her so hard—"

"Shut up, Doug." Steve's voice is hard again. "I mean it. Shut the fuck up."

Doug lets go of me and spins around to appeal to his older

brother, tears streaming down his face. "You told me you'd take care of it, Steve! You told me not to worry. Why'd you hafta do that with her head, huh? I told you not to—"

"Shut up!" Steve, I can tell from the way his hands are shaking, is losing it. The knife he's holding points one minute at me, and the next at Doug. A detached part of my brain wonders if Steve Winer would really stab his own brother.

The same part kind of hopes he will.

"What did you expect me to do, huh, you little shit?" Steve is so mad, his voice is now no louder than a hiss. "You call me in the middle of the fucking night, crying like a baby, and say you killed your fucking girlfriend. I have to get up, come all the way over here, and clean it up for you. And you have the nerve to criticize *me*? You have the goddamned *audacity* to question *my* methods?"

Doug gestures helplessly at me. "Jesus Christ, Steve! This fucking DORM MANAGER figured it out. How long do you think it's gonna be before the police catch on?"

Steve blinks at me, then licks his lips nervously, his tongue darting out like a snake's. "I know. That's why we have to get rid of her."

Which is when one of the red-robed figures beside me stirs and says, "Uh, dude. You said we were just gonna scare 'em, like we did the janitor guy—"

"Scare him? He nearly bled to death!" I cry.

"If you say one more word," Steve says, pointing the knife blade at me, "I'll kill you now, where you stand, instead of letting you out the easy way." The tip of the knife travels away from me, and ends up pointing at the glass on the altar. It appears to be filled with water. "Drink that," Steve commands.

I look at the glass. I have no idea what's in it. But I can guess, judging by what happened to Jordan the other night.

Rohypnol, otherwise known as roofies, a popular sedative on the college circuit. One dose, already dissolved in water, ought to make me much more malleable, when it comes time for cutting.

It's right about then that I decide I've had about enough. I'm hot, my stomach hurts, and I'm pretty worried about Gavin and Jeff. I wish I had let Cooper kill Doug Winer when he'd had the chance. I wish I myself had taken one of Doug's pillows and stuffed it over his head and held on until the kid stopped struggling.

No. That's too kind. I wish I had wrapped my own hands around that thick neck and squeezed, squeezed the life out of him the way Doug had squeezed the life out of Lindsay. . . .

"Come on, Heather," Steve says, beckoning impatiently with the knife. "We don't have all night."

"Uh, Steve," the other guy next to me says. "Seriously, man. This is getting weird."

"Shut up," Steve says to his fellow Tau Phi. He grabs the glass, brings it over to me, and shoves it under my nose. "DRINK IT."

I turn my face away. "No."

Steve Winer gapes at me. *"What?"*

"No," I say. I can feel that I have the support of the room. The Tau Phis are starting to realize their leader has lost it. They won't let him hurt me. I'm pretty sure. "I am not going to drink it."

"What do you mean, you aren't going to drink it?" The shadow of a smile returns to Steve's face. "Are you blind? I'm holding a knife to your throat."

"So?" I shrug. "What's the difference to me? I'm gonna get killed anyway."

This is not what Steve wants to hear. The smile fades from his lips, and there isn't a hint of humor in his face when he hands the glass to the guy on my right, turns around, walks over to Gavin, grabs him by the hair, yanks his head back, and raises the knife toward his exposed throat—

"Steve, man, don't!" one of my guards yells, just as I say, "Whoa, I'll drink it, I'll drink it," grab the glass, and down its contents.

"That's it," the guy who'd been holding the glass says. "I'm out of here. Jeff's right, you guys are fucking crazy."

And he begins striding from the cafeteria—along with several other Tau Phis—including all the pledges but Jeff Turner, who is still lying on the floor, still as death.

"Don't let them go," Steve barks at the Tau Phis who'd kicked Jeff into unconsciousness. But even they hesitate.

"Did you hear me?" Steve lets go of Gavin's hair and stands there, staring confusedly as his frat brothers begin to leave him, one by one. "You guys. You can't do this. You took a pledge. A pledge of total loyalty. Where are you . . . you can't—"

Doug is starting to look scared. "Jesus, Steve," he says. "Let 'em go. Just—"

Doug breaks off midsentence, though. That's because Steve has dropped the knife, and, from somewhere deep inside his robe, he's managed to bring out a small handgun, which he is now holding level with his brother's chest.

"Douglas," Steve says. "I am getting fed up with you and your whining."

"Jesus, Steve!" Doug cries again. But this time the fear and tears in his voice cause his fellow Tau Phis to turn around to look.

Which is when I do what I know I have to. After all, no

one's paying the least bit of attention to me. Everyone's gaze is on Steve, whose back is to me.

Which is why, as soon as I see his index finger tighten on the trigger, I dive, my arms spread wide, at the floor. Because I know something about the floor of the caf of Fischer Hall that Steve Winer will never know: it is squeaky clean. Julio may not be in charge of the floors behind the steam tables, but he's in charge of the cafeteria floor, and he's waxed it until it's slick as ice. Which means I slide across it like an Olympic skater doing a belly flop, until I've collided with the elder Winer's legs, which I then throw my arms around, pulling him down.

Then I reach up, seize Steve's wrist, and sink my teeth into it, forcing him to drop the gun. Also to scream and writhe in pain and terror.

Doug seems to get over his astonishment at what I've just done first—perhaps because he's the only one who didn't have the sense to duck when Steve was waving that gun around, and so is the only person in the room still standing. He stumbles forward until his hand closes over the butt of the gun his brother has dropped. His fingers trembling, he raises the pistol and aims it—

Well, at me.

"No," cries Steve hoarsely. "Don't shoot, you little fuck! You might hit me!"

"I *want* to hit you!" Doug screams. Really. He screams it. Tears are streaming down his face. "I am so sick of you always telling me what a fuckup I am! And okay, I may be a fuckup . . . but at least I'm not a freak! Yeah, I killed Lindsay—but I didn't mean to. You're the sick fuck who thought it would be a good idea to leave her head on the stove. Who even fucking does shit like that, Steve? *Who*? And then you made us stab that poor janitor . . . and now you want us to kill this lady here . . . and why? To make yourself look like a badass in front of your frat buddies. Because *Dad* was a badass when *he* was a Tau Phi."

The mouth of the gun Doug is pointing at us keeps straying from me to Steve in a very unnerving manner. Steve, beneath me, is beginning to sweat. Copiously.

"Doug," he says. "Dougie. Please. Give me the—"

"But Dad didn't kill people, Steve!" Doug goes on, as if he hadn't heard. "He didn't cut people up! He was a badass without doing shit like that! Why can't you see that? Why can't you see that no matter what you do, *you're never going to be like Dad*?"

"Fine," Steve says. "I'm never going to be like Dad. Now put the gun down—"

"No!" Doug screams. "Because I know what's going to happen! You're going to turn this all around and blame it on me somehow. Like you always do! Like you've always done! And I'm not putting up with it anymore! Not this time!"

Which is when he points the gun in the dead center of Steve's forehead.

And also when a calm, slightly familiar voice says from the cafeteria's doorway, "Drop it, son."

Doug looks up, his expression one of mingled astonishment and indignation. I turn my head as well, and am quite confused to see Reggie—yes, drug dealer Reggie—leveling a very large and shiny Glock 9mm at Doug Winer's chest.

"Drop the weapon," Reggie says. Strangely, his Jamaican accent is completely gone. "I don't want to have to hurt you, but if I have to, I will. I think we both know that."

Steve, still pinned beneath my body, cries, "Oh, Officer,

thank God you're here! This guy went berserk and was trying to kill me!"

"Uh-huh," Reggie says tonelessly. "Give me the gun, son."

Doug glances down at his brother, who nods encouragingly beneath me. "Go on, Dougie. Give the gun to the nice policeman."

By this time, Doug is crying too hard to shoot anyway. "You're such a fuck, Steve," he says, as he hands the gun to Reggie, who passes it to Detective Canavan, who is looming in the doorway behind him, his gun drawn as well.

"You may not know it, Officer, but you just saved all our lives," blathers Steve Winer. "My brother was trying to kill me. . . ."

"Right," Reggie says, reaching to his belt for his handcuffs. "Heather, please get off Mr. Winer."

Obligingly, I roll off Steve Winer. As I do, I notice that the room kind of spins around. But in a pleasant manner.

"Reggie!" I cry, from where I'm splayed on the floor. "You're an undercover cop? Why didn't you *tell* me?"

"Because he's a Fed." Detective Canavan is standing over me, directing about twenty uniformed officers to handcuff everyone in a red robe. "With your usual aplomb, Wells, you managed to stumble into the middle of a sting operation the DEA's been working on for months. Congratulations on that, by the way."

"Detective!" I cry happily, staring up at Detective Canavan. "What took you so long?"

"We had a little trouble getting in," he explains. "The security guard was being . . . resistant. And no one could find a key." He rolls his eyes. "Typical of this place, by the way. Why are your pupils so big?"

"'Cause I'm so happy to see you!" I cry, sitting up to fling my arms around his neck as he leans down to help me to my feet. "I just love you so much!"

"Uh," Detective Canavan says, as I cling to him—because the room is spinning around quite a bit by now. "Wells? Are you on something?"

"They made her drink something." This comes from Gavin, who has been untied by the maid/undercover DEA agent, and whose facial gash is being examined by a pair of EMTs who've come in, apparently from nowhere. As I'd expected, the duct tape has left an angry red mark across his mouth, and taken away some of his soft, wispy mustache, making it even wispier-looking.

"Gavin!" I cry, letting go of Detective Canavan and throwing my arms instead around him—much to the annoyance of the paramedics trying to clean him up. "I love you, too! But only as a friend."

Gavin doesn't look as happy to hear this as I think he should be. "I think it's roofies," he says, attempting to extricate himself from my embrace. Which I find rude, to say the least.

"Okay," Detective Canavan says, taking me by the arm. "Come on."

"Where are we going?" I want to know.

"Oh," Detective Canavan says, "I think the hospital will be a good place to start. Get some fluids into you."

"But I'm not a bit thirsty," I assure him. "I could use some ice cream, though. Hey, want a Dove Bar? They're right in the freezer over there. Hey, everyone should have a Dove Bar. Hey, everybody," I turn to yell. "Have a Dove Bar! On me!"

"Come on, Wells," Detective Canavan says, keeping a firm grip on my arm. "That's enough."

And then, as he's leading me out of the cafeteria and into

the lobby, I see a sight that makes me forget all about the Dove Bars. And it's not Crusty Curtiss in handcuffs—although that's very pleasant to see. And it's not half the residents standing there, trying to see what's going on, and Tom and the RAs, along with Sarah, trying to talk them into going about their Friday night business.

No. It's my father.

"Dad!" I cry, breaking free from Detective Canavan's grasp and throwing myself into my waiting father's arms.

"Heather!" he says, seeming very surprised by my greeting, but not unhappy about it. "Thank God you're all right!"

"I love you *so much*," I tell him.

"She loves everyone quite a bit at the moment," I hear Detective Canavan explain. "She's on Rohypnol."

"That's not why I love you," I assure my father, worried his feelings will be hurt otherwise. "And it's not just because you called the cops and kept me from getting decapitated, either."

"Well," Dad says, with a chuckle, "that's good to know. Her mouth is bloody. Why is her mouth bloody?"

And that's when I notice Dad's not standing there alone. Cooper is by his side! He's reaching for one of his ubiquitous handkerchiefs. Handkerchiefs are apparently a very important tool in the private investigations field.

"Oh," Detective Canavan says. "She bit a guy. That's all."

"Cooper!" I cry, throwing my arms around his neck next, as Cooper reaches to dab Steve Winer's blood from my mouth. "I'm so glad to see you!"

"I can tell," Cooper says. He's laughing, for some reason. "Hold still, you've got some—"

"I love you *so much*," I tell him. "Even though you told Gavin I'm still in love with your brother. Why did you do that, Cooper? I'm not in love with Jordan anymore. I'm *not*."

"Okay," Cooper says. "We'll take your word for it. Here, hold still."

"I'm not, though," I assure him. "I don't love Jordan. I love *you*. I really, really do."

Then Reggie steps into my line of vision one more time, just as Cooper is finishing washing me up, and I shout, "Reggie! I love you! I love you so much! I want to come visit you on your banana plantation!"

"I don't actually have a banana plantation, Heather," Reggie says. He's laughing, too. Why is everyone laughing? Seriously, maybe I should give up the songwriting thing and go into stand-up comedy, since I'm apparently so hilarious. "I'm from Iowa."

"That's okay," I say, as some EMTs gently pry my arms from around Cooper's neck. "I still love you anyway. I love *all* of you! You, Tom—and Sarah—and even Dr. Kilgore. Where *is* Dr. Kilgore, anyway?"

And then the room starts spinning fast—I mean, *really* fast—and my sleepiness becomes too much to resist anymore.

And I don't remember anything more after that.

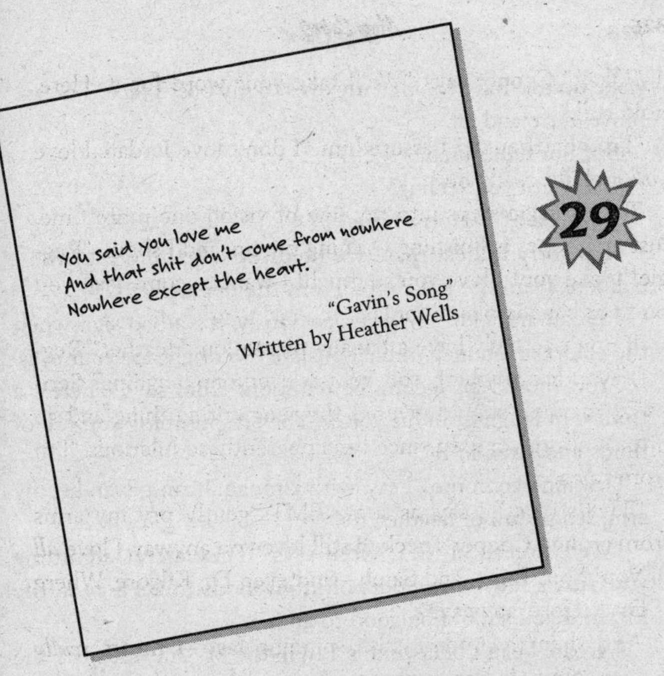
29
You said you love me
And that shit don't come from nowhere
Nowhere except the heart.
"Gavin's Song"
Written by Heather Wells

My head is POUNDING.

Seriously.

It isn't funny.

I can't believe people do this drug recreationally. If this is how Jordan felt yesterday—was it only yesterday?—at the Stoned Crow, well, it's no wonder he turned down a beer. I never want to drink again. Anything. Not even water. Not even—

"Heather."

I open one eye. I can't believe who I see standing there beside my gurney. My boss. Of all the people in the world to wake up to, I have to open my eyes to my boss's face? I mean, I love Tom, and all.

But not *that* much.

"How are you feeling?"

"Like crap," I inform him.

"I'm sorry to hear that." He holds up a fistful of GET WELL balloons from the gift shop. "From the department."

I groan and close my eyes. Seriously, it's a bad sign when the colors of a bunch of balloons are too bright for your eyes.

"You should be feeling better soon," Tom says. There's a tremor of laughter in his voice. "They're pumping you full of fluids and vitamin B."

"I wanna go home," I say, with a moan. I can't even lift my arm, it's so full of needles.

"Well, you're in luck," Tom says. "They aren't admitting you. Just a few more hours of intravenous fluids here in the ER, and you should be good to go."

I groan. I can't believe this. I'm in the St. Vincent's ER, the same ER where I've visited so many students in exactly my current condition.

But I never realized they felt this crappy.

"Listen," Tom says, in a voice that's got no laughter left in it. "I wanted you to be the first to know."

I open one eye. "You really are quitting?" I ask.

"Not at all," Tom says, with a chuckle. "I'm getting promoted. To area coordinator."

I open my other eye. "*WHAT?*"

"Stan was so impressed by how I handled the whole Lindsay situation," Tom explains excitedly, "that he promoted me. I'll still be in Housing, but now I'll be assigned to Waverly Hall. The frats, Heather. Stan says he realizes now that the building needs an on-site adult presence . . . it's a ten-thousand-dollar-a-year raise. Of course, I'll have to be working with pills like the Tau Phis . . . but they shouldn't be so hard to handle, now that Steve and Doug are under arrest. And Steven—Coach Andrews—says he'll be happy to help. . . ."

I close my eyes. I can't believe this. I finally get a boss I like, and they take him away.

And excuse me, but Tom didn't handle the Lindsay situation. *I* did. I'm the one who nearly got killed getting her killers to fess up. Where's *my* promotion?

In a way, I kind of wish they *had* killed me. At least my head wouldn't hurt so much.

"Wow," I say. "That's great, Tom."

"Don't worry," Tom says. I feel him pat my hand. "I'll make sure we get you a really kick-ass new boss. Okay?"

"Yeah," I say. "Okay."

I must have fallen back asleep, because when I open my eyes again, Tom is gone. In his place are Magda, Sarah, and Pete.

"Go away," I say to them.

"Oh, thank God," Magda says, looking relieved. "She's all right."

"I'm serious," I say. "My head is killing me."

"That's the benzodiazepine wearing off," Sarah says chipperly. "It's a central nervous system depressant. You're going to feel like crap for a while."

I glare at her. "Thanks."

"We just wanted to see how you were doing," Pete says. "And to tell you not to worry."

"Yes," Magda says, grabbing the side of my gurney and bouncing excitedly. "They found the cocaine!"

"Right," Pete says. "They found the cocaine. Doug Winer's stash. The one Lindsay stole."

This makes me open my eyes more fully. "Really? Where was it?"

"Where do you think?" Sarah asks. "In Kimberly Watkins's room."

"But . . ." I know I'm out of it. But I can't believe I'm *that* out of it. "Kimberly and Lindsay were in on it together?"

Sarah shakes her head. "No. Lindsay taped the bag under her favorite cafeteria table—which is why it wasn't there when she went looking for it, to give it back to Doug when he figured out she was the one who had it. Because someone else had already found it. Someone who regularly shares that table with Lindsay. Or used to, anyway."

I stare at her. "*Kimberly Watkins*? Kimberly had Doug's coke the whole time?" When Sarah nods, I ask, "How did you find out?"

"Cheryl," Magda explains. "She was so angry—over what Kimberly said about Lindsay and Coach Andrews, and then, later, over what happened to her poor Jeff—who is going to be all right, just a few broken ribs—that she went to confront Kimberly, and . . . well . . . let's just say they didn't act like a couple of movie stars."

"Well, unless you mean Paris Hilton and Nicole Richie," Sarah says.

"Cheryl beat the crap out of Kimberly," Pete says. "And Kimberly confessed. She was going to start her own little drug-dealing operation, it seems. She saw Lindsay hide the coke, and stole it next chance she got. Only after what happened to Lindsay, she was too scared to do anything. She was terrified the Winer boys would find out she was the one who had the stuff, and do to her what they did to Lindsay."

"That's why she kept trying to throw me off their scent," I murmur.

"Exactly," Sarah says. "Anyway, Cheryl went straight to the cops with what she found out, and now Kimberly's under arrest, as well. I guess the DEA'd been working for months to bust what they considered the biggest student drug ring on campus. Only, until Lindsay's murder, they really didn't have any idea where the kids were getting the stuff. That's why they had Reggie working undercover in the park. They were hoping he'd pick up some clues . . . which he finally did, when you asked him about the Winer boys. But even then, they still didn't have proof. . . ."

Sarah shrugs. "Now, in addition to possession and dealing, the Winer boys have murder and attempted murder charges against them . . . along with a couple of the other guys from their frat. Daddy Winer has already hired the top criminal lawyer in town. But I don't see how they're gonna beat the rap with you around to testify. Oh, and Kimberly, who's turned state witness in exchange for them dropping the possession charges against her. . . ."

"So Kimberly's kicked out of school?" I murmur.

"Uh," Magda says, "yeah. They all are. Even the Winers."

"Good," I say faintly, as my eyelids drift closed again. "That's more spaces for me to make room changes into next week, when the housing freeze lifts."

Everything goes mercifully black for a while—that must be my central nervous system depressing again. When I open my eyes again, I find myself looking up at Detective Canavan and Reggie.

"You," I say to Reggie. "You lied to me."

He smiles. I am heart-struck to note the gold teeth are gone.

"Sorry," he says. "It was in the line of duty."

"Brian's a special agent with the Drug Enforcement

Agency, Heather," Detective Canavan explains. "He's been working undercover for nearly a year in the park, trying to figure out where the influx of party drugs on campus was coming from. Thanks to your tip about the Winers, Brian was able to direct his people to send in a fellow agent disguised as a maid"—the maid I'd seen in the hallway at the Tau Phi House scrubbing the FAT CHICKS GO HOME sign—"and get all the evidence they needed to bust the Winers not just for drug trafficking, but eventually for murder and assault as well."

I look at Reggie. "Brian?"

He shrugs. "Reggie sounds more street, you know?"

"Have you ever even been to Jamaica?" I ask him.

"Oh, God, no," he says. "I get any vacation time, I head straight for the mountains. I'm a skier."

I look back at Detective Canavan. "Do I get a medal or something?"

"Um," Detective Canavan says. "No. But I got you this." He holds up a dark chocolate Dove candy bar. "The ice-cream kind would have melted," he explains.

I lift my hand—the one with all the IVs in it—and snatch the candy bar away from him.

"This city," I say, "is getting pretty cheap with the rewards for valor."

They go away, and I eat my candy bar. It's delicious. So delicious that I fall back asleep. When I wake up again, Gavin McGoren is leering down at me.

"Well, well, well," he says, with a grin. "Isn't this a fine turn of events? For once *you're* the one on the gurney, instead of me. I have to say, I like it a lot better like this."

"Who let you in here?" I want to know.

Gavin shrugs. "I'm a fellow patient, not a visitor," he says.

He turns to show me his cheek where Steve hit him. "Seven stitches. What do you think? That'll leave a pretty sweet scar, huh?"

I close my eyes. "Your mother is going to *kill* me."

"What are you talkin' about, woman?" Gavin scoffs. "You saved my life."

"I caused you to be kidnapped and beaten," I say, opening my eyes again. "Gavin, I—I can't tell you how sorry I am. Really. I never should have involved you in any of this."

The red marks are gone from around Gavin's mouth. So is the goatee. He apparently took the time to shave before coming in to see me. Which I should have taken as a sign of what was about to come, but my faculties are still slightly befuddled from the drug.

"There's a way you can make it up to me, if you want," he says.

"Yeah? How?" I genuinely think he's going to ask for a single with a view of the park.

Instead, he asks me out.

"You know," he says. "Just sometime. We could kick it together. Play pool or something. When you're feeling better. It doesn't have to be a date," he adds hastily. "I know you're still all in love with Jordan Cartwright, and shit. But, you know. Just to try it out. Just to see."

"Gavin." I'm not positive, but I'm fairly sure I'm the first assistant director of a New York College residence hall to be asked out while lying on a gurney in the St. Vincent's ER recovering from being roofied. "I can't date you. You're a resident. I'm not allowed to date residents."

Gavin considers this. Then he shrugs. "I'll get an apartment."

I open my eyes wider. "Gavin. Do you have any idea how much rents are in Manhattan? Besides, you're still a student.

New York College administrators are forbidden from dating students."

Gavin thinks about this for a minute. Then he says evenly, "Okay, well, then, after I graduate. Next year. Will you go out with me then?"

I'm too tired to resist. "Yes, Gavin," I say, closing my eyes again. "Next year, after you graduate, I will go out with you."

Gavin looks pleased. "Cool. You said you loved me, you know."

My eyes fly open. "Gavin, I was under the influence."

"I know," he says, still looking pleased. "But that shit don't come from nowhere. Nowhere except the heart."

When I open my eyes next, I see Patty and Frank.

"Hi," I croak.

"You could have just told me you aren't ready to play in front of anyone yet," Frank says, "instead of going to all this trouble to get out of doing the gig."

"Frank!" Patty sounds exasperated. "Don't listen to him, Heather. We just heard. How are you doing?"

"Oh," I say. My voice still sounds awful. "Great."

"Seriously," Frank says. "We'll be playing the pub all week. So if you aren't feeling up to it tonight, there's tomorrow night. And the night after that, too."

"Frank," Patty says, looking annoyed. "Leave her alone. Can't you see that singing is the last thing she's got on her mind?"

"No," I surprise myself by saying.

Frank and Patty both look at me strangely. "No, what, honey?" Patty asks.

"No, I want to," I say. It is only as the words are coming out of my mouth that I realize I mean it. "I want to play with you guys. Just one song, though."

Patty shakes her head. "Oh, Heather. You're still on drugs."

"No, she's not," Frank says, grinning. "She means it. You mean it, Heather, don't you?"

I nod. "Not tonight, though, okay? Because I've got a headache."

Frank grins some more. "Totally fine," he says. "So whatcha gonna sing? Something you wrote? Something new?"

"No," I say. "Something Ella."

Frank's grin fades. "You're right," he murmurs to Patty. "She *is* still on drugs."

"She means Ella Fitzgerald," Patty hisses at him. "Just smile and nod."

Frank smiles and nods. "Okay, Heather. Night-night, Heather."

I close my eyes, and they go away. When I wake up, later, my dad is peering down at me.

"Honey?" He looks worried. "It's me, Dad."

"I know." Every word is like a stab wound to my head. I close my eyes again. "How are you, Dad?"

"I'm good," Dad says. "I'm so glad you're all right. I called your mother, to let her know."

This causes me to open one eye. "Dad. Why would you do that? She didn't even know I was—whatever."

"I think she has a right to know," Dad says. "She's still your mother. She loves you, you know. In her own way."

"Oh," I say. "Right. I guess. Well. Thanks for getting hold of Detective Canavan."

"Well, that's what family's for, honey," he says. "Listen, I was just talking to the doctor. They're going to let you go home soon."

"Are they going to give me anything for this headache first?" I ask. "I can barely see, my head's pounding so hard."

"Let me see if I can go find the doctor," Dad says. "Heather . . . what you did. I'm really proud of you, honey."

"Thanks, Dad," I say. And the tears in my eyes aren't just from the pain in my temples. "Dad. Where's Cooper?"

"Cooper?"

"Yeah. I mean, everybody else has been by to see me, except Cooper. Where is he?" He hates me. I know it. I said something to him—I can't remember what it was. But I know I did. And he hates me for it.

"Well, he's at Jordan's wedding, honey. Remember? It's Saturday. He was here for a long time while you were sleeping, though. But finally he had to leave. He promised his brother, you know."

"Oh," I say. The disappointment I feel is ridiculous. And crushing. "Sure."

"Oh, here comes your doctor," Dad says. "Let's see what he has to say."

They let me go that evening. Over twelve hours of intravenous fluids, and, while I don't feel a hundred percent by any means, at least my headache is gone and the room has stopped spinning around. A look in the ladies' room mirror tells me more than I want to know about what Rohypnol does to a girl's complexion—my face is chalky white, my lips chapped, and the circles under my eyes look like bruises.

But, hey. I'm alive.

That's more than poor Lindsay Combs can say.

I sign my discharge papers and head out, a sample packet of Tylenol my only souvenir—Tylenol, that was the best they could do—expecting to see my dad waiting for me in the lobby.

But instead of Dad, I find Cooper.

In a tux.

I almost turn around and check myself back in, considering the way my heart turns over in my chest at the sight of him. Surely that isn't normal. Surely that's a sign that my central nervous system needs more fluids, or something.

He stands up when he sees me, and smiles.

Oh, now, see. Smiles like that should be against the law. Considering what they do to a girl. Well, a girl like me.

"Surprise," he says. "I let your dad go home. He'd been here all night, you know."

"I heard you were, too," I say. I can't make eye contact, both on account of the way my heart is hammering and because I'm so embarrassed. What had I said to him earlier? I'm pretty sure I'd told him I loved him.

But Dad said I'd been saying that to everyone—including the twin planters outside Fischer Hall.

Still, surely Cooper had to know it had only been the drugs.

Even though of course in his case, it hadn't.

"Yeah," Cooper says. "Well, you do have a tendency to keep me on my toes."

"I'm sorry," I say. "You must be missing the reception."

"I said I'd go to the wedding," Cooper says. "I didn't say anything about the reception. I'm not the hugest salmon fan. And I do not do the chicken dance."

"Oh," I say. I can't really picture him doing the chicken dance, either. "Well, thank you."

"You're welcome," Cooper says.

And we head out into the cold, to where he's parked his car along Twelfth Street. Once inside, he starts the engine and lets the heater run. It's dark out—even though it's barely five o'clock—and the streetlights are on. They cast a pinkish glow over the drifts piled up alongside the street. The snow, so beautiful when it first fell, is fast turning ugly, as soot and dirt stain it gray.

"Cooper," I hear myself saying, as he finally puts the car in gear. "Why did you tell Gavin I'm still in love with your brother?"

I can't believe I've said it. I have no idea where the question came from. Maybe there's some residual Rohypnol in my central nervous system. Maybe I need to check back into the hospital to get the rest of it out.

"That again?" Cooper asks, looking amused.

The amusement sends a spurt of irritation through me.

"Yes, *that* again," I say.

"Well, what did you want me to tell him?" Cooper asks. "That he has a chance with you? Because I hate to be the one to break it to you, Heather, but that guy has a major crush on you. And the more you ask him to take you to frat parties and the like, the more you're just reinforcing it. I had to tell him something to try to nip his little infatuation in the bud. I thought you'd be grateful."

I am careful not to make eye contact with him. "So you don't believe that. About me and your brother, I mean."

Cooper is quiet for a minute. Then he says, "You tell me. I mean, it's kind of hard to believe there's nothing there when every time I turn around, you two are together."

"That's him," I say adamantly. "Not me. I do not have feelings for your brother. End of story."

"All right," Cooper says, in the soothing tone in which one might speak to the mentally disturbed. "I'm glad we got that straightened out."

"We haven't," I hear myself say. What am I doing? WHAT AM I DOING?

Cooper, who'd been about to pull out of the parking space, puts his foot on the brake. "We haven't what?"

"Got it straightened out," I say. I cannot believe the words that are coming out of my mouth. But they just keep coming. There's nothing I can do to stop them. This has to be the Rohypnol. It *has* to be. "How come you've never asked me out? Is it because you're not interested in me that way, or what?"

Cooper sounds amused when he replies, "You're my brother's ex-fiancée."

"Right," I say, beating a fist on the dashboard. "*Ex. Ex*-fiancée. Jordan's married now. To someone else. You were there, you saw it for yourself. So what's the deal? I know I'm not really your type . . ." Oh, God. This is going from bad to worse. Still, I can't go back. "But I think we get along. You know. For the most part."

"Heather." Now there's a hint of impatience creeping into Cooper's voice. "You've just come out of a really bad long-term relationship—"

"A *year* ago."

"—started a new job—"

"Almost a year ago."

"—reconnected with a father you barely know—"

"Things with Dad are cool. We had a nice talk last night."

"—are struggling to figure out who you are, and what you're going to do with your life," Cooper concludes. "I'm pretty sure the last thing you need right now is a boyfriend. In particular, your ex-fiancé's brother. With whom you live. I think your life is complicated enough."

I finally turn in my seat to look at him. "Don't you think I should be the judge of that?" I ask him.

This time, he's the one who looks away.

"Okay," he says. "*My* life is too complicated. Heather—I

don't want to be your rebound guy. That's just . . . that's not who I am. I don't chicken dance. And I don't want to be the rebound guy."

I'm flabbergasted. "Rebound guy? Rebound guy? Cooper, Jordan and I broke up a year ago—"

"And who have you dated since?" Cooper demands.

"Well, I . . . I . . ." I swallow. "No one."

"There you go," Cooper says. "You're ripe for a rebound guy. And it's not going to be me."

I stare at him. *Why?* I want to ask him. *Why don't you want to be my rebound guy? Because you don't actually want me?*

Or because you want something more from me than that?

Looking at him, I realize I'll probably never know.

At least . . . not yet.

I also realize I probably don't want to know. Because if it's the latter, I'll find out, one of these days.

And if it's the former. . . .

Well, then, I'll just want to die.

"You know what," I say, averting my gaze, "you're right. It's okay."

"Really?" Cooper asks.

I look back at him. And I smile.

It takes every last little bit of strength I've got left. But I do it.

"Really," I say. "Let's go home."

"Okay," he says.

And smiles back.

And it's enough.

For now.

Tad Tocco
Assistant Professor
Office Hours
2–3 P.M. weekdays

That's what the sign on the door says.

Which is why I don't understand what, when I open the door, a Greek god is doing there, sitting in front of me.

Seriously. The guy sitting at the computer behind the desk has long, golden hair—like as long as mine; a healthy, ruddy glow of good health about him; a placard on his desk that says KILLER FRISBEE 4-EVER; and the sleeves of his button-down shirt pushed back to reveal a set of forearms so muscular and gorgeous that I think I must have walked into some snowboard shop, or something.

"Hi," the guy behind the desk says, with a smile. A smile that reveals a set of white, even teeth. But not so even that they're, like, perfect. Just even enough for me to be able to guess that he'd probably fought with his family over not wanting to get braces.

And that he'd won.

"Wait, don't tell me," he says. "Heather Wells, right?"

He's my age. Maybe a little older than me. Thirty, thirty-one. He has to be, even though he's wearing reading glasses . . . adorable gold-rimmed ones, though. Still, there's a *Scooby Doo* lunch box on a shelf above his head. Not a new one, either. An original *Scooby Doo* lunch box, the ones kids had when I was in the first grade.

"Um," I say. "Yeah. How did you . . ." My voice trails off. Right. I forget, sometimes, that my face was once plastered all over the bedroom walls of teenage girls—and some of their brothers.

"Actually, I saw you perform the other night with Frank Robillard and his band," the guy says cheerfully. "Over at Joe's Pub?"

My stomach lurches. "Oh. You saw that?"

"Jazz isn't really my thing," the guy says. "But I liked that song you did."

"It was an Ella Fitzgerald cover," I say. I really want to throw up now. Rodgers and Hart's "I Wish I Were in Love Again" happens to be one of Cooper's favorite songs. Which isn't necessarily why I chose to sing it, but . . . well, it might have been one of the reasons.

Thank God he'd been called away at the last minute by some kind of PI emergency. I don't think, in the end, that I could have gotten up there if I'd known he was in the audience.

"Frank and I—" I stammer. "W-we were just fooling around."

Well, *Frank* had been fooling around. I'd been deadly serious . . . at least until no one booed us. Then I began to relax and have a little fun with it. Afterward, people clapped . . . but of course they were applauding for Frank (even though Patty assures me they were also clapping for me. But only for having the guts to get up there, I'm sure. I'd been rusty . . . and I hadn't missed the fact that my dad, in the audience, had been clapping the hardest of anyone. I guess it's nice to know, whatever else happens, I've got one parent watching my back).

"Well, it sounded great to me," Mr. Gorgeous says. "So, you finally got my messages?"

I blink at him. "Um, I guess so. I got a message from someone named Tad Tocco—"

"That's me," Tad says. The smile gets even bigger. So does he, as he stands up and holds out his right hand. He's taller than me. And possibly even outweighs me. He's a big, muscular guy. "Your remedial math professor." His hand swallows mine. "I was going to introduce myself after the show the other night, but you seemed to disappear right after your song."

I say something. I have no idea what. His hand is callused. From playing so much killer Frisbee, no doubt.

"Anyway, I have to say," he says, letting go of my hand, finally, and sinking back into his chair, just as my knees give out and I sort of fall back into the one on the other side of his desk, "you have a way better excuse for blowing off my class than most of my students. I mean, I've never had anyone miss the first week of school because they were busy catching a murderer."

My jaw drops. "You're my . . . you're my . . ." I've forgotten how to formulate words.

"I'm your remedial math professor," Tad says cheerfully. "I

wanted to get in touch with you about scheduling some makeup sessions. You know, for the classes you've missed? I don't want you falling behind. So I figured we could meet. At your convenience, of course. How's after work? There's a bar near that place you work—Fischer Hall? The Stoned Crow. A bunch of us plays darts down there, so it would be convenient for me if we could meet there, seeing as how we're both over twenty-one." Then he winks at me. *He winks at me*. "I find algebra goes down a lot easier with popcorn and beer. That okay with you?"

I can only stare at him. He's just so . . . hot.

Way hotter than Barista Boy.

Suddenly I think I'm going to like college.

A lot.

"That sounds *great* to me," I say.